Kingdom of Fraun

Tabatha Shipley

Internal artwork by Jonathan Shipley, 2020.
Cover art by Jonathan Shipley, 2023.

Hardcover 979-8-9880129-3-1

Tabatha Shipley Books

For information, email tabatha@tabathashipleybooks.com

Dear Reader,

This book you are holding in your hand is a special edition copy of the entire Kingdom of Fraun series. This series was originally published as four separate titles: Breaking Eselda (2018), Redeeming Jordyn (2019), Training Tutor (2020), and Empowering Sawchett (2021). Formatting has been changed in order to put them all together, a few typographical errors have been corrected, and fonts have been adjusted. Otherwise, they are exactly the same story bound together for the first time. Enjoy.

Faithfully Yours,
Tabatha Shipley

Also by Tabatha Shipley

30 Days Without Wings

Projection

A Spark of Magic

Noises From the Other Side

Kingdom of Fraun

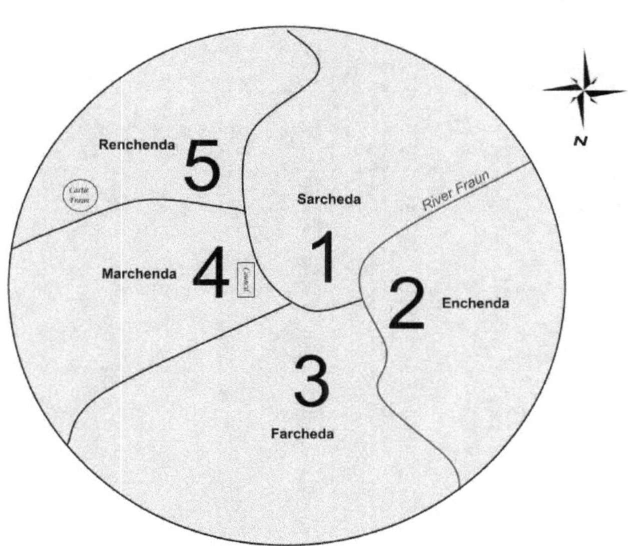

Breaking Eselda

Breaking Eselda was first published in the summer of 2018. It was Eselda's story. We were introduced to the Kingdom of Fraun and all its (many) imperfections. Our big driving questions were: What kind of ruler would Eselda be? Is she the person who will save Fraun?

But our flagship story was also threaded through with chapters from our evil King, our big bad villain. This is one BAD guy. We doubted who he was, a little. When his identity was revealed at the end of *Breaking Eselda*, it was with a whole lot of "I knew it" mixed with "Oh no, what now?"

The story had a long history, which at the time I pretty much detailed on my blog. If you weren't a fan then but you're curious, you can catch up on all that fun history by heading to the blog https://tabathashipleybooks.com and searching FRAUN. But, fair warning, there's a LOT there.

Anyway, *Breaking Eselda* was not the original title. Originally, this story was drafted in third person omniscient and was supposed to be called Royal Blood (a nod to what Eselda learns early on in the story). It's better and stronger with the changes, but it was a work of love to get it to this point.

Other major changes? It starts in a different spot. Originally the story began with the school visit. This made for a boring opening because without being interested in the world and Eselda you weren't overly interested in Fraun's history. This chapter was moved, Tutor's sharing of the information about blood was moved up, and the rest is history.

Want some fun facts? Of course you do, that's why you're here.

1. I actually didn't like Eselda when I wrote this book. After I rewrote it to be from her point of view I liked her a little more, but not much.
2. My favorite character from *Breaking Eselda* is probably Jordyn. I also love Tutor but he doesn't come into his best qualities yet in this book. He's still learning himself.
3. My favorite scene in this one is the scene where Jordyn is battling with his age marker in the throne room by himself. It was my favorite to write and it's still my favorite to read. It's also probably why Jordyn is a favorite.

Whether this is your first read or a reread … enjoy. I know I did.

Chapter 1

"But men do not live forever." My voice echoes off the stone walls and back to me, lifeless and flat. That's wrong. I missed a word again. The school visit is tomorrow. I must be ready today. One would assume, after annuals of delivering this speech, that I would have it down. But no, I keep messing up the lines.

I close my eyes and tip my head back to the ceiling. I can feel my hair swishing along the back of my dress. Hair is such a status symbol in Fraun. I was so worried that my hair would be thin, making me look like a peasant. The thick ropes with their reddish hue leave no doubt I am royalty. I can do this.

I return to the practiced stance and adopt my best speech voice. "But men, even great men, do not live forever. Oberian died, passing the rule of Fraun to his son." I stomp my foot. "Damn it. I missed another one." The angry words echo off the chamber back to me. Not very regal sounding, Princess. Deep breath. Try again.

"But men, even great men, do not live forever. Oberian died, passing the rule of Fraun to his only son." There. The one extra word my father and his council cannot live without. Apparently, this single word explains we're discussing the king who only had one son instead of the guy with many.

"Good morning, Princess."

I recognize the voice but startle at the arrival. I did not hear Tutor walking the hallways. I spin to find my ears have not deceived me. Tutor has arrived. I can only smile at the classic I-don't-care-about-my-appearance look my personal tutor has thrown together. My heart softens as his smile dances across his lips and reaches his brown eyes, hiding behind the lenses he has manufactured to improve his vision. "Tutor, I'm glad you are here. I'm having difficulty with the speech. I'm sure I'm overthinking it. Can we practice?"

"Actually, Princess, we have something we should discuss. You are approaching an age where you will no longer be in need of my services." He shifts on his feet and wrings his hands.

"You're nervous. Why are you nervous?" The question halts his shifting, telling me I'm on the right track. "We have been at this training for many annuals knowing that I am one day to take the throne of Enchenda. What more could we possibly have to discuss?"

"I was speaking with the king this morning and new information has reached me. There are things we have not yet discussed about mannerisms and royal blood. I thought—" He shakes his head. "It doesn't matter what I thought. The point is we have much to cover."

"Am I unprepared to serve the second realm?" I feel a fluttering in my chest. I change my mind, deciding I don't want to hear his answer.

"I fear you may be unprepared for the men you serve Fraun with," he answers.

What does that mean? "Tutor, you're being strange. Explain yourself."

"Let's just begin the training for the day, please."

I fold my legs under me as I flop to the cold, stone floor. Maybe if I play along, he'll give me more information.

"Let's review your basics. A queen must know the basics better than she knows her own name. Name the five virtues in order of the realms they represent," Tutor prompts.

I sit up straight. First would be Sarcheda. “Strength." Then us. “Humility." Third would be Farcheda. “Speed." Fourth is Marchenda. “Mirth." Fifth is Renchenda. What is Renchenda known for? Oh no. I can’t remember. If only I were a little smarter.

Oh. “Wisdom."

“You hesitate. A queen cannot hesitate. If you are being introduced to some underling from the third realm, you must instantly know to compliment his speed and not his humility.” Tutor leans down toward me. “You must focus. The council is going to be waiting for you to err, Eselda. Do not give them that.”

“You make the council sound positively wicked.”

Tutor throws his hands up. “Eselda, I cannot think of another way to explain it to you. The men on the council will not be trusting of you because of your age alone. You will have to be flawless.”

“I have time. Has something changed?" I try to match his frustrated pitch. I hate when he gets cross with me and treats me like a child. I contemplate teasing him again about his name—what did his parents expect him to do with his life after giving him a name like that?—but decide I’ll see where this goes instead. He is obviously sitting on something important.

“That is not my place to discuss with you.” He sighs. “Let’s just focus on getting this all right, please. Name the leaders of the realms in ascending order.”

“King Tin of Sarcheda, King Gregario of Enchenda, King Mick of Farcheda, King Larecio of Marchenda, and King Jordyn of Renchenda.”

Tutor drops to the floor in front of me, adopting my cross-legged stance. “That was better. Now think, Eselda. Tell me what you know of the ages of these kings.”

Ages? What an odd question. “I don’t know much. I know Tin and Jordyn are young, closer to my age than my father’s. The others are older. I’m not sure how many have grayed.”

“Two of the three. King Mick’s hair remains dark,” Tutor says.

“Why are we speaking of age?”

“You are royal blood. If you knew the full ramifications of that we would speak of nothing else.”

I rise, glaring down at him. "Tell me."

"I had hoped your father would tell you before you came of age."

"I have already passed fifteen annuals, Tutor. If he was going to tell me before that, he has missed his timing. I suggest you spit it out." I stretch myself tall, showing off the two marks I reach on the medicine tent display, and fix him with what I can hope is a stern look. I'm trying to remind him that I am a princess in this house and it would be unwise to defy me. In truth, he runs these tutoring sessions, but I hope he won't remember that right now.

"Tell me the age markers that affect all in Fraun."

"At five a person is capable of full speech." I know all of these markers; I would usually balk at having to deliver them. Today, I can tell Tutor is building to something, leading me to an understanding. I will not argue today. "At ten, they are full height and fully mature. At fifteen the hair becomes silken and soft but ceases to grow. Citizens are considered adults once this stage has passed. Finally, at forty, the hair will whiten or gray and the citizen will die."

"There are age markers the council keeps silent," Tutor whispers. "Markers that only affect those born of the royal blood." Tutor's voice is low and light like a summer breeze blowing through the room. I sit back down opposite him; I don't want to miss a word of this.

"At twenty annuals, citizens with the blood of Oberian in their veins will become dark and malicious. They will want power above all else and will stop at nothing to get it. This age marker will bring out the worst in the royal."

I recoil from the words, sliding back a little on the floor. "How have I never heard this before? Is it exactly twenty annuals? Tutor, I haven't been tracking how long it's been since I passed the fifteenth."

"I haven't either, but it's been at least three annuals, Princess. I was hoping he would tell you."

"This will happen to me? We are sure of it?" Fear begins to build in my belly, hot and strong.

"It will. There is more. Should I go on?"

"Well, yes. Get it all out there now. No point in delaying again."

"At twenty-five annuals, a citizen with the blood of Oberian will replace that longing for power with one for flesh. They will be consumed by their desire to procreate and satiate their lust." A blush rises in Tutor's cheeks. "This age marker helps to ensure the bloodline continues."

"Are you kidding me?" I stand up from the floor again and begin pacing. "When do these fantastic little bombs you've brought me end?"

"I'm told they each last five annuals."

"Let me summarize here. In less than two annuals, I will become mad with power. That will last five annuals and end only when I suddenly begin lusting after any warm-bodied man. That will also last five annuals. I shudder to think how many men I will chase in that time. If my math is correct, that leaves me with ten annuals to be a level-headed ruler of Enchenda before my hair grays and I die. Sound about right?" I hit him with a cold stare.

He sits silently on the floor, watching me. He continues to look like a smart child with a book, studious. It angers me further. I wish he would show emotion. "With all of this affecting everyone who has ever ruled the people of Fraun continue to believe that those of us with royal blood are better rulers. Would you care to explain that to me? It seems as though Fraun would be better off with someone who isn't affected in this way," I point out.

"Royal blood has served us for over a century, Princess."

"Yet it has also been making rulers crazy for over a century, apparently."

"It is your cross to bear, Eselda, not mine." He removes his glasses and rubs the bridge of his nose. "It is my job to prepare you to bear it. I understand the shock of this knowledge and I had anticipated your anger. You must learn to control that before you are twenty annuals. You cannot sit on the council and let that anger out. It is what they will fear the most."

"But they all went through it. They all experienced it."

"Experience," he corrects.

"What?" I stop pacing and look back down at Tutor.

He sighs. "Kings Jordyn and Tin are both inside the malicious age marker."

"Two of the five rulers at the table are driven by a desire for power? How is that best for Fraun?"

"I have never sat at that table nor been invited to that room, Eselda. All I can tell you is that it would be in your best interest to not show them anger and remind them how close you come to being a third."

I draw a deep breath. "Now I'm scared," I admit. Tutor is one of my oldest friends in the world, always at my side to help me learn. I see him daily. He is the person I can confide in. Suddenly I'm glad he was the one to tell me about the age markers. I drop back to the floor and take his hands. "Honestly I haven't been counting the annuals since my hair turned. Are you sure it's been at least three? How long do I have?"

"You father may know better than me but I think this will be the third school visit you've conducted since it turned. I kept hoping that he would tell you when you met about the visits. Twice I've been disappointed but not had the gumption to tell you myself."

"I appreciate that you told me today. I can't believe this secret was kept from me for so long."

"I should let you think on this. You're prepared for the visit tomorrow; your practice was well done. I'm going to let you have the rest of the day and I will see you tomorrow." Tutor stands. "Eselda, you handled the knowledge well. I'm proud of you."

The complement swells in my chest like a balloon. It doesn't completely lift my spirits out of the fear they've rooted themselves, but it helps. I nod.

When he leaves and I'm alone the fear overwhelms me. Craving power above all else? What will that feel like? I'm the person who will turn from something bad or dangerous, I'm a coward. This leaves me with a whole new problem. After all, I can't run from my own blood.

I will have to face this, one way or another.

Chapter 2

"Princess Eselda?"

The voice floats through the oaken door that blocks me from the rest of my house. My ancestors built this house to be of good quality, but the door doesn't quite fit into the frame. It leaves little gaps so the sound travels right to my sleeping ear. "Yes?" I bellow.

"The school visit is today. The king would like to speak with you before you depart."

Squeaky voice, slow speed. This is a common roach. "Thank you, Eee." I wait for the sound of the scurrying feet on the brick floor before throwing off the warm blankets and rising. My first stop is the reflection wall. I'm not a person who spends time standing at this wall. I'm a representative of the house of humility in Fraun, how would that look?

But today I want to see if any obvious physical signs of the fear brewing under my skin are present. Can you tell I'm afraid of what will happen to me in a few annuals? My green eyes look the same, my pale face looks the same. There are no new wrinkles or taught stretches of skin. There is no new fear anywhere on the outside.

I cross the room again, this time headed to the cabinet holding my clothing. I pull the heavy wooden door open and begin running my fingers along each garment. The clothes are all tailored to fit me, repurposed from the clothing left behind by the giants. There are so many fabrics and colors here, I don't know how to choose today.

I linger a little longer on a purple silken dress. "This will do," I say to the empty room. "After all, I'm spending the day with school children."

My feet move quickly through the empty hallways. The entrance hall with its tall ceilings is bustling today with roaches and the footmen preparing to take me to the school visit. "I need only a single roach, no carriage. That formality is not befitting of the house's humble image," I call the order as I continue my fast pace through the room.

Turning left I enter my favorite room, the dining room. Across the room from me a fire burns, warming the air and sending off a pleasant smell. Seated at the head of the table in the center of the room is the king of Enchenda, looking completely annoyed that I have arrived after him. "Good Morning father," I greet him. I bend down and kiss his forehead through the shock of white hair that is perpetually falling there.

"You are late."

I restrain the sigh that wants to escape. "Yes, sir. My apologies. I forgot this was the morning of the school visit."

"The school visit is one of the single most important acts of a princess."

I start eating my bowl of berries and grains. This speech could take a while, I have time.

"Our people should know of the greatness of our ancestry. The five brothers created Fraun, but each gave something different to our realms. The children of Enchenda cannot hope to live up to our ideals if the princess does not speak the ideals to them," his booming voice commands authority. It is impressive.

However, I could give this speech myself after the number of times I have heard it. I can feel my frustration brewing, just under my skin. This speech you repeat but you never thought to sneak in a tidbit about my blood?

"It's bad enough," father continues, "we have such a young

council. Your generation has not married and given birth to many. What will become of Fraun when there are no princes or princesses to speak this truth? I fear for our future."

I turn my head enough to hide the rolling of my eyes behind the ropes of my hair. My father and his council bring up two things more than anything else. My age, which makes sense now that I am fully informed, and my lack of children. I have had all my reproductive parts since I was ten, like everyone else around here. I have been considered an adult since I was fifteen. Why do I not have a spouse or children?

Actually, their problem goes deeper than that. Two of the five rulers, Jordyn and Tin, also have no spouses or heirs. Another two, my father and Larecio, each have only a single heir and have lost their spouse. That leaves one realm, Farcheda, who they believe is fully prepared to continue to serve Fraun in the future. Farcheda is run by both a king and a queen, they have children, and some of their children are even married with children of their own. The council of people I rarely see wishes me to be more like this realm and less like theirs.

"If some disaster strikes Tin or Jordyn, what will become of Fraun?" Father asks.

"What would be the disaster if someone not of the brother's blood were running a realm?" The look of frustration and disdain that crosses the king's eyes makes me wish I had the sense to refrain from asking the question. My hand freezes midway to my mouth from the bowl.

"The brothers personified important ideals that the people of Fraun need to emulate. It is only when all five ideals are balanced that we are our strongest as a people. The royal blood of the brothers flows in your veins. Do you not feel the power of that blood within you?"

My anger brews. I drop the spoon back into the bowl where it splats against the berries. "The power of the blood? You mean the blood that will make me a vehicle for violence in less than five annuals?" The sentence is out before I remember that, despite this comfortable setting, I am speaking to my king in that tone of voice. My hand slaps over my mouth too late to stop the anger that shows in his narrowed eyes.

There's only one way I fix this. I throw my shoulders back, toss my hair over my shoulder, and plaster a royal smile on my face. "On second thought, I know what you mean. Our blood is our lineage and our lineage has served Fraun well. I am the product of the brothers who brought Fraun to greatness."

Father's angry eyes never leave my face, but he reaches for his spoon and begins eating. I follow his lead but I know this isn't over. He is not happy.

Chapter 3

In the center of each realm, a small area is designated for the education of the young. Children attend the facility from five annuals until fifteen annuals. They learn all about Fraun. They are taught basic rules of speaking; a few exceptional ones are taught to write. They are taught numbers and gardening. Each is taught the ideal of their realm. Once each annual the children are visited by the royal family of their realm to hear the history of Fraun and have their questions answered.

The realm of Enchenda is bordered on all sides by the River Fraun, which curves around and disappears into the thick forest marking the end of Fraun territory. Enchenda houses hundreds of families, all living in homes made of materials the giants of legend abandoned. Enchenda, like all other realms of Fraun, makes no materials of their own save food.

As I disembark from the roach who has carried me to the school, whispers spread through the assembled crowd of children. There are many of them today. The teacher, who rushes over to shake my hand and welcome me to the school, is taller than I remember and stands probably two clicks above my head. I straighten my posture. Height is a big deal to us here and one I am always aware of.

The older children, the ones who have heard this speech before, are seated at the back of the crowd. Younger children, eager to hear what I have to say, are in the front. Some smile, others stare with reverence. Either way, I'm known here.

"Good morning, children," I greet as I take my place on the log at the front of the clearing.

"Good morning Princess Eselda." The line has been rehearsed. It was said as one. Equally as rehearsed, the students flop to seated positions on the floor silently. The teacher, beaming with pride, settles herself in a standing position behind me.

I take a deep breath, settle my hands in my lap, and launch into my speech. "The world we inhabit now was once a land of Giants. The giants built massive cities with all materials they could find. No material was sacred. No land was spared. The Giants created much and used more than they needed. Even their production levels, legendary as they were, could not provide enough for their endless needs.

"During the time of the giants, our people lived quiet lives. Hidden among the houses of the giants, repurposing items the giants forgot, our people survived. It was a lonely existence, never knowing if others lived on. All that changed with the war.

"The giants declared war on each other. For years blasts and fighting were the sounds that filled the world. Our people stayed holed up in their homes, hidden from the battle we didn't understand. Then came the explosions, which rocked those homes. When the silence began, we waited. After a time, our scouts went out to find the giants all dead or gone." A quick check of the faces in the crowd shows me I have their attention. "One man, Oberian, began to organize our people."

Some of the younger children in front begin excitedly twisting and whispering. "That's Fraun." The whisper floats to my ear. I can appreciate the innocent interruption, a child too excited to realize they know this story. The teacher does not share my appreciation; she slams her finger to her lips in a shushing gesture.

I continue. "Bonded together by our mutual fear of an outcome similar to the giants we organized cities from the ruins of the giant villages.

Fraun became our name, and Oberian our king. Oberian proved himself a good man and an honest ruler. He established many laws to keep us safe. We learned to use only what we needed and waste not, to rectify the wrongs of the giants who had died for this error. Under the rule of Oberian, Fraun became strong.

"But men, even great men, do not live forever. Oberian died, passing the rule of Fraun to his only son. Oberian the Second believed it was his right, and our duty, to amass his wealth and power. The people of Fraun were commissioned to build a palace for their king, which stands in Fraun to this day. The king took three wives in his time, having five boys born to him before his death. He was a greedy man, but he was not all bad.

"In the wake of the giants we were not the only race who rose up. During the time of Second, we learned of large bugs who had survived and created the society of Roach. Second ordered scouts to travel to Roach and speak with them. No treaty could be reached. Instead, Second ordered a war. Frightened by this word, our people hesitated. Second was an insistent man, and war ensued.

"Our people were triumphant, and the inhabitants of Roach became a part of Fraun. Many of them took jobs as servants in exchange for food and homes. Their people are small to the ground, many-legged, and fast. They are excellent warriors and they mind not being ridden into battle. Earning their partnership was the legacy of Second.

"After the death of this king, the sons wanted to avoid a fight over the throne. They requested two sun paths of bereavement for their father as they devised a plan for his replacement. At the end of that time, the brothers had agreed upon a plan to divide power. Absolute power, they claimed, was dangerous to Fraun. Their father had abused that power to earn a castle, they did not want to fall into similar temptations.

"Their plan was five realms. Each realm would have a royal family to rule them. In the realm, your king would be the final word. The five realms would be numbered. The royal family of the first realm would lead the council of rulers. The council would vote on all decisions affecting Fraun as a whole. No decision would be carried forth without a majority vote of the council.

"Over the next century, the numbering of the realms changed often with leaders. The council would choose to renumber in favor of a strong king, or to overthrow one corrupt or weak. Rule of a realm was passed through families, all descendants of the great brothers who named our realms. As Fraun grew in number and power we remembered our past.

"Today you have heard the tale as your parents heard before you. Someday we will tell the tale to your offspring as well. This is our legacy."

A few children clap even as one tiny hand shoots up from among the crowd. I point to the young child, who likely doesn't even reach the first mark on the measurement chart. She rises and squeaks out her question, "How were they numbered, Majesty?"

"Good question." I rise and approach the child, placing my right finger lightly on the girl's forehead. As the children watch with rapt attention, I trace a circle to the right repeatedly around the girl's face. "The realms are always numbered along this same circle. The first realm is chosen by the council and the rest fall into place." I know, even with my back turned as I return to the log, that the children will pull her excitedly back into their midst. When I seat myself again I see a few children tracing the same line along her face, like I have left something there for them to gather at their fingertips.

My eyes travel the faces of the audience as I begin to speak again. "The realms were named after the five brothers. Let us name them." I know the children will name the realms in the order they now fall, and I recite with them. "Sarcheda, Enchenda, Farcheda, Marchenda, and Renchenda."

My eyes fall upon an older student at the back. Yellow hair brushes near his eyes and his clothes look hand altered to fit him. He is handsome, he looks familiar, and yet I cannot place his face among the many in my memory. He is too old for schooling, I think. What is he doing here?

Without removing my eyes from the familiar stranger, I continue my rehearsed story. "The eldest brother being the oldest, had the first choice of realms. Not all the realms are equal in size or power, my children. But the eldest brother did not choose the most powerful or the largest for himself. Does anyone know why he didn't want the first realm?"

Hands from the back shoot skyward. Of course, the older students have heard this tale. They have heard it repeated every annual since they began their education. I nod in acknowledgment and make a gesture that forces their hands to fall back to laps as I answer my own question. "He was scared."

The younger students gasp. Immediately a small boy raises his hand and waits to be acknowledged by his princess. "Princes no have afears," he says.

"I assure you, child, they fear just as you fear." I gesture for the child to sit before continuing. "The eldest prince feared himself. You see, when his father was alive a castle was erected. The prince loved the status the castle gave him. The prince recognized that his love of the castle was truly a love of power." Was that prince perhaps twenty annuals? Has this secret been before me my entire life, waiting for me to notice?

The handsome man catches my eye again. This time it's the tilt of his head that draws my attention. The man is nodding at my statement. Who is this man who believes I crave his support?

"The prince knew," I push on through the speech, "that if he accepted the power of the first realm, and with it the castle of Fraun, he would abuse it. Can anyone tell me where the eldest son chose to reside?" I choose a girl from the middle of the room.

"Enchenda." The girl drops quickly back down after speaking her answer.

"Very good maiden. Because the eldest son chose our kingdom, farthest from the castle, for the sake of the good of Fraun we are blessed to be humble. Our humility, as your teacher has doubtless taught you, allows us to guide the council to decisions which benefit all of Fraun."

A hand from the middle precedes another question. "Enchenda was always second realm?"

"Perhaps an older student will respond to that good question in my place." I smile at the back of the room.

The handsome boy speaks without rising. "Enchenda has been every number except fifth. For Enchenda to be fifth, Farcheda would need to be first. The youngest son, Farcheda, bestowed his speed upon his people. They are quick to do many things, including react. They are quick of temper. This quality bodes negatively for a position of power." The boy's voice is strong and captivating. It fills the clearing like sunlight, warming me in the same way.

Despite my frustration at his rudeness, I am impressed. "Correct good sir, but why rise you not for your princess?" I ask.

"My apologies, Majesty. My legs are injured." The man smiles.

"Fair enough. Thank you for your intelligent and thorough answer." His eyes stay fixed on my face as his mouth turns up in a smile. I feel my face flush and move my eyes quickly to focus on something else. "What further questions have my people?"

"Why you ride roaches?" a boy asks.

I grit my teeth to hide my impatience. "As I explained, inhabitants of the land once known as Roach became part of Fraun after the second war. They hold jobs here, including transportation. They have real names. In fact, the one who brought me here is called Zee. However, many citizens of Fraun call the species Roaches, after the town they once ran."

"What really happens at a council meeting?" The question is posed by a boy near the back of the crowd and I have to choke back the groan that begs to escape. This has long been a question I want answered for myself.

Although a princess by rights, I am not ruling at this time. That means I am not allowed to attend the council meetings. Council meetings are for kings or queens alone. A princess would not be permitted attendance unless the king was absent for whatever reason. Exceptions are never made.

Still, I am familiar with the answer Tutor would expect me to give. "Council meetings are run by the king of the first realm. They are a place for the leaders of Fraun to discuss important issues and make decisions for the betterment of Fraun. At a council meeting strength, humility, speed, mirth, and wisdom are truly balanced."

A strange noise comes from the back of the room. I look around only to discover the handsome intelligent man with the face I cannot place is trying to wipe the small laugh from his face. "Excuse me, sir. Did you have a comment?" My face is burning. Did he laugh at me?

"Pardon me, your Majesty. It was a cough." The excuse is feeble, as he chuckles amidst the words.

I choose to push on, although my building irritation is making it difficult. "See the medicine tent for that cough, good sir, and for your legs as well. Are there further questions?"

Another child is recognized and rises. "Why don't we make nice things here?" The question is rehearsed, likely fed to the child by a parent eager for answers.

I stand and sweep my hand delicately down the front of the long purple dress I selected. This morning I completed the outfit with a grey overskirt, wrapping it around my backside but not fully attaching it to the front. In this way, it protects the fabric of the dress when I sit on this rough log. My feet are bare, but I wear a thin chain around my right ankle, a gift that had once belonged to my mother. I have tied the top of my hair up in a purple ribbon but left the curlier under-layer to flow down my back. "Do I not wear nice things?"

A few older children in the back snicker, laughing lightly at the corner I have backed the poor boy into. "You look nice, Princess," he answers, bowing. "But our homes have broken things. Why not we make more?"

"Enchenda follows the laws of Fraun young lad. We build not from a desire to show power, but from necessity. Why build anew when the giants left behind so many ruins we can use? We waste less time, energy, and resources this way." I return to my seat, and the small boy follows my lead and takes his as well. This time when I smile at him, the young boy returns the gesture.

I finish the question session without further incident, the school visit has gone well. I shake a few hands, mostly older students who will not be attending next annual. One such girl asks me to consider taking her on as a lady-in-waiting, which doesn't seem like a bad idea. It is during this exchange that I notice the man who laughed at me leaving on his own accord on his apparently fine set of legs, his head towering over the other students as he makes his retreat.

Chapter 4

"Welcome home, Princess." The royal attendee, my father's hire, greets me at the wall bordering my family's home. "How went the school visit?"

"Well, thank you." I let the man take the reins of Zee's harness and reach for the doorknob. Before I can even wrap my hand around the cold metal, the thin wooden door is whipped open.

"Child, we need a meeting," father barks. His expression is grim, his eyes dark.

"Is something amiss Majesty?"

"Nothing to worry you, just a thing or two to discuss. We shall meet in one hour. That leaves you enough time for eating and chores, I believe."

"It does, Majesty. Shall we meet in your study when the hour has passed?"

"That is a plan." Father turns on his heel and returns down the dim hallway he came from as I enter the house.

Across the room my eye spies a lady-in-waiting. The servants in this house see and hear all. A plan forms in my brain. "I require some lunch, good lady. I do not like to dine alone. Would you care to join me?" The lady needn't look so surprised. The servants here spread rumors around like butter. If anyone would know of the agenda for the meeting with the king, I intend to find it.

"It would be my pleasure, Princess."

"Excellent." I clap with joy. "Follow me to the garden."

The garden of the royal family of Enchenda houses bushes marked with ripe berries, tomatoes the size of my body, and cabbage that have to be picked before they are full size. My eyes land on a cucumber that I decide my mouth is craving. It is long, having been allowed to grow long into the season. Likely, it will take both of us to get it onto the table. I select the cucumber and the woman helps me hoist it up on the table in the center of the garden. The servant girl brandishes a sword and begins making cuts in the vegetable.

"I realize," I begin, "that I do not know your name." I cross the garden and start gathering leaves from a nearby tree. I bend up the fabric of my overskirt to make a basket to deposit them into.

"Linchanta is my name, Majesty."

"Well, Linchanta, you are cutting beautiful chunks of that cucumber. Would you be so kind as to chop a tomato next?"

"Yes, Majesty. Of course."

The woman is loosening up, responding to the simple tasks and reveling in the ability to complete them to my liking. I drop the leaves into a glass container and begin grinding them with a long stick. "I think, Linchanta, that we should have some tea with our lunch as well. What say you?" I am already adding water hot from the sun pitcher as I ask this.

"Majesty that is not necessary. Such a big meal for two people," Linchanta answers.

This answer is expected. The people of Enchenda have rather small appetites. This much food would fit to serve us both for quite some time. However, I notice that Linchanta doesn't hesitate in her chopping. It is possible the woman is hungrier than she plays at being.

"Well you and I shall eat our full," I declare, "then you can take the rest among the people of Enchenda while I meet with father." The line is delivered masterfully. I can tell by her smile that she is pleased with my answer.

I, on the other hand, am watching for signs that the woman knows of the meeting with the king. There. The eyes flashed quickly toward the house. The woman knows something.

I sweep the cucumbers, now chopped into tiny pieces, into a large pot and drop a tomato on the table. "I wish I knew what the king desires to speak with me about. He scares me," I whisper.

The servant's eyes steal a glance at my face. I have time to look suitably scared. It's not really an act. "The feeling is worse if I am unprepared," I admit.

"I may know something of his agenda, Princess." The voice is merely a whisper carried on the breeze.

I allow myself a smile before squealing with girlish glee. "Oh, you must tell me what you've heard."

Linchanta takes her time adding the tomatoes to the bowl. "I shouldn't, Majesty. I am sworn to silence."

"I understand." I return her smile. "Let us just enjoy our lunch." I set glasses of fresh tea on the table and serve us both portions of the cucumber and tomato salad. We eat in silence for a few minutes. How long do I have to pretend to let the matter rest before asking again? What is polite? "Please consider telling me, Linchanta. I won't speak of it to anyone." I place my right palm over my heart, a symbol of promise.

Linchanta leans conspiratorially toward me. "Repeat nothing." I notice the servant has dropped the formality of my title, this is a good sign. "I hear your father wishes to take your ideas before the council."

I could not have been more surprised if a magic fairy had risen from my tea and turned me into a giant. For a moment, my surprise is such that I forget the details of my plan. "He what?" I yell. "My father thinks my ideas are ludicrous daydreams. There is no way in Fraun that my father would care for my opinion in front of his council."

The servant jumps and immediately drops her eyes downward. "My apologies, Princess, perhaps I heard wrong," Linchanta says.

I feel horrid. The bad information doesn't warrant being yelled at by your princess. "I am sorry. My shock seems like anger, but it is with the news and not with you, maiden." I reach for the woman's hand but she moves it too quickly from the table, leaving me grasping at air. "Linchanta, would you be so kind as to distribute these leftover plates to the people?" I ask, rising.

"My pleasure, your Majesty, and your people thank you." The servant's formality has returned; her voice is controlled.

I feel a second of sadness, but only a second. For the good of my cause, I have learned the secret I came for. I will spend what is left of my allotted hour pacing the floors of my home and thinking.

I am familiar with my father's opinion of me being over fifteen annuals and not yet engaged. Perhaps he wants to discuss betrothal. It certainly wouldn't be out of character for him to bang his fists on the table and demand I marry ... who would he demand I marry? Well, someone, anyway. It is within his right to choose a mate for me.

Upon the second tumble through my nervous brain, I conclude he would never do that. Gregario prides himself on being humble, as do all from Enchenda. He will never pretend to know who is better for me than I do. If I cannot think of a suitable mate, surely he will not push one on me either.

That arrangement, of course, only works in my favor so long as my union is not a burden on the greater good. My father is many things, but selfish is not one of them. King Gregario serves Fraun above himself at all costs.

A knock at the door pulls me from my reverie. "Yes?"

"Princess, it is time for your audience with the king." Slow speech, soft clicking of feet.

"Thank you, Eee. I will be along presently." The walk to the study is torture. Each step brings with it a new worry about the topic of our conversation. We speak at breakfast, hardly any other time.

When the door opens my fears are not abated. On the contrary, they double. My father, recently grey hairs catching the firelight and reminding me of his age, is sitting straight-backed in the chair and has fixed his cold eyes on the door frame. He does not look happy to see me. I bow low. "Good afternoon, father."

"My daughter, I have something I must tell you. But first, how was the school visit?" He gestures to the seat opposite him, commanding me to sit with only a flick of his wrist.

The ease with which he orders this as well as the booming voice reminds me of the strange man from school. "It was well, father. There was, however, an odd person in attendance who didn't rise for me."

Father chuckles. "He was a child, my dear. Children can be trying, but don't let it vex you. His teacher will likely sort that out."

"I am not convinced he was a child, Majesty. He was probably three marks once he rose."

At this, the king startles. "Three marks is impressive indeed. What did he say when he spoke but didn't rise?"

"He merely answered the question asked by a younger child. But the answer was eloquent and informed."

"He was well spoken?"

"Indeed."

"Well dressed?"

"Certainly so, father."

Something in the king's expression clouds. His voice drops in sudden anger. "Talk no more of this man."

"But father —"

"No." He cuts me off with a wave of his regal hand. "We have more important issues to discuss. This man will be tabled for a later time. I have learned some news that affects your life, Princess."

"Good news, my king?" Hope sparkles in my chest, please let it be good news.

"I believe so, yes. It has become necessary for you to attend council meetings beginning in a fortnight's time." Father delivers this blow casually, not at all like one should deliver such news.

The excitement begins a slow simmer, the thought of finally seeing what happens in council meetings makes me giddy. To be seated with other kings, even for only a short time, is intoxicating. "I do not understand, Majesty. Why would I attend?"

"I have fallen ill. The medicine man confirms it. It is my age. I have not long left in this world, I am sure. Enchenda requires an educated queen."

As fast as it began, the excitement is gone. In its stead, there is only consuming sadness. I want to sit at the table, but not at the expense of my father. "Surely something can be done. You are the king. Who deserves miracles if not the king?"

Father's voice is low as he answers, an acknowledgment of the pain likely written on my face. "The lowliest of our people deserve miracles if it serves Fraun. Always remember that. I have you to follow me, miracles need not be wasted here. I must prepare you for the council, there is much you have yet to learn."

"Father, another time. I want to process this new situation."

His voice rises. "There is no more time. We talk now."

Despite my opinion, I nod at my king. I have always been taught to put my own feelings aside for the sake of my people. I will swallow this sadness.

"Things have been heating up between the first and third realms, Daughter. Mick, King of Farcheda, believes the last eight kings of Sarcheda to be corrupt."

"What reason has he?"

"They have been building much. It has been done quietly and always in the name of growth, but it makes the council nervous. Once or twice we can turn a blind eye. But when your realm nearly doubles in buildings, the council needs to ask questions. So claims Mick."

"Does this include King Tin?" I know little of Tin, King of Sarcheda. Tin is not much my senior, and he rules alone. He was crowned king of the first realm when his parents fell to their deaths down a ravine.

"Growth has continued during his reign, yes. Mick has taken these claims seriously, Daughter. He calls for a dramatic solution. Be prepared for all options to be presented in turn."

"I will think on this before council, father. You have my word." I start to push myself off the chair.

"One more thing, Eselda."

I'm not sure I can handle one more thing. Yet I know I cannot stop the king of my realm or my powerful father from explaining whatever he desires. I hesitantly nod my head.

"The council knows of my illness. That man today may have been sent to see how your education progresses. The council may well be nervous about your pending rule."

I swallow the rush of anger at hearing my father's precious council knew of his demise before his only daughter. It must have benefited Fraun if that is the decision he made. "Who could that man have been, that the council would see fit to send him?"

"That I do not know. Perhaps you should ask at your council meeting. That is all for today, Daughter. I must rest. You may go."

Outside the door, alone in the hallway, I try out the words. "I'm sitting on the council in a fortnight." I almost cannot contain the squeal of joy.

Chapter 5

Council of Kings of Fraun,
As you likely are aware my health begins to fail me. Forty annuals have come and gone, marked by the silver now atop my head. My only daughter, Eselda, will join me at our council meeting next, preparing herself to take the throne of Enchenda in my demise. Please welcome her as you would me.
Respectfully,
King Gregario
Enchenda

The parchment is rolled back up and dropped onto the heavy wooden desk. In the dark room, under the light of the small fire, the smile that stretches eerily across the face of the young king is barely visible.

The elderly king is preparing for death; this is good news. I have been waiting for the tables to turn in my favor. The council is old, weak, and useless. I cannot hope to change Fraun if I first do not change the council. I need young blood at the table if I am to make the changes. Eselda is young herself if memory serves correctly. The young queen can be swayed to my side.

The king turns his attention to the young chambermaid cleaning in the corner. "I am a nice enough looking young man, am I not?"

The young maiden blushes fiercely but looks in his direction anyway. Her eyes quickly return to her feet before she allows herself to answer. "Of course, Majesty."

The king crosses the room in two strides. He drops to a single knee in front of the chambermaid, who is scrubbing the floor on her own bruised knees. When the woman raises her eyes to him he holds her chin in his right hand to keep her eyes on his. "Look properly, maiden," he commands.

Intentionally he softens his tone to that of a potential lover, "What do you see in me?"

The blush on the young woman deepens but a coy smile touches her lips. "You are markedly handsome, Majesty. Any woman would be weak in the knees at your touch."

The king returns the smile and stands abruptly. "Thank you, that is what I hoped you would say."

Yes, if this chambermaid can be lead to believe in the touch of the king then Eselda can be just as easily swayed. After all, for a king in Fraun, anything is possible. Eselda can be brought to my side.

Fraun is about to change.

Chapter 6

It is dark, not yet dawn. The house is full of the shadows of my greatest fears. Sounds carry on echoes in every direction. I have risen early and seated myself on the study room floor. If I am to sit before the council Tutor has warned me about, I am going to need to face my fears. I close my eyes, take a deep breath, and extinguish the torch.

The room plunges into total darkness.

The darkness is briefly broken by the slice of light surrounding the door. Tutor slowly walks along the outer edge of the room, using a candle to light the torches on the wall. He turns to face the center of the room and he throws himself backward at the sight of me sitting there, my lithe legs curled underneath me in the darkness.

I hold my hand up, stopping any words Tutor had been prepared to hurl. "Before you speak I have something to say. I have accepted my fate, as have my ancestors before me. I am strong and I believe I can rise above my instincts as I mature. If Fraun desires me to rule, then rule I shall. Speak no more of it, but prepare me to accept my birthright."

"Name the five virtues in order of the realms they embody," he prompts.

"Strength, humility, speed, mirth, and wisdom." I dare you to find something amiss with that, old friend.

"Name the rulers of the realms of Fraun."

"King Tin of Sarcheda, King Gregario of Enchenda, King Mick and Queen Salicia of Farcheda, King Larecio of Marchenda, and King Jordyn of Renchenda." I do not drop my chin or hesitate.

"Soon many of our kings may approach death. Tell me, Princess, what would become of each realm if the king were to expire?"

"I will answer as best I can, good sir, although the topic brings me personal sadness. The first realm would crumble, causing other realms to absorb the land because King Tin has no heir to speak of. Second realm command would fall to Princess Eselda. The third realm would fall to the reign of Prince Hector, the eldest prince. Queen Salicia, regal though she may be, has not a drop of royal blood. The fourth realm would be run by Prince Carsen. The fifth realm would fall the way of the first, to be absorbed for lack of an heir," I answer.

Realization drags its icy fingers down my spine. This is what the council fears. Two of their realms are but one tragic death away from being absorbed and leaving Fraun with only three realms to rule.

"Why was Fraun set to be run by five realms?" Tutor leads.

Because there were five sons. No, that can't be the answer he seeks. That would be too simple, something anyone could answer. Tutor seeks the solution of a queen. Tutor seeks the thinking of one who runs a realm. "Five council members means there will never be an issue that results in a tie. There are enough people to keep balance in the kingdom, but not enough to throw us into chaos. Five is the same as the fingers on your hand." I hold up my own hand for emphasis. "When they all work together they keep your hand balanced. With five realms there is always someone to hold the kingdom together."

I take my time closing my hand into a fist, one finger at a time. "With five realms, someone is always strong enough to protect Fraun even if the others are vulnerable." I close the fist by placing the thumb gently on the other fingers.

There are no words of encouragement from Tutor, merely a nod.

The round door to the room bursts open, shattering the approving quiet and catching us off guard. A small squat man holds out a scroll, his head bowed low to the floor. "Princess, excuse me, I bring a message from King Tin of Sarcheda," he says.

I snatch the scroll away, angry at being shocked after the careful display of my readiness to rule. The man is gone, retreated out of my sight, before I can even begin to think of how best to chastise him for his interruption. Instead, I angrily slice the waxen seal of strength with my fingernail.

Dearest Princess Eselda,
News travels through Fraun faster than, perhaps, it should. I hear talk that you will join us at the council meeting in a fortnight. I should not be writing to you, as council policy dictates we keep business only in the chambers and your anticipated presence is a council secret at this time. I trust two outcast young rulers, such as we, can keep that secret. My messenger can be trusted. Besides, he cannot read.
I look forward to seeing you again, it has been too long.
Faithfully Yours,
Tin

I read the short message quickly. The last time I saw Tin I had just turned ten annuals. Tin, recently fifteen annuals, visited Enchenda. Slightly taller than I, he is a gorgeous dark-haired boy. He was on a visit, his last before the accident befell his parents, to see what lies beyond the River Fraun. Never in his life, he explained, had he visited the realm across its border. I remember the boy well. The pull of my first crush tugs warmly at my center. I allow the fantasy to spread its sunshine across my chest briefly before forcing myself to remember the reality.

Tin is now a king. A king who has lost both parents and has been thrown to rule earlier than planned. A king accused of being harsh. A king I don't really know at all.

"Princess, should I continue to wait?"

I startle a little at the voice, having forgotten Tutor was in the room. "No." I roll the scroll again and slip it beneath my green robe. "I can continue."

"What says King Tin?" Tutor inquires. Irritation and distrust are apparent in his tone.

"He merely wanted to express well wishes for the health of our king."

"I feared he may have been discussing council politics in an attempt to sway you."

"Fear not, sir." I hold my face in my most honest smile, hoping my lie is not showing through. This letter was merely an innocent letter between two young people, more like flirtation than outward disrespect of council protocol.

"Well. I am sure he breached trust with good intentions. However, a breach must be dealt with milady. I shall report it to your Father, yes?"

"Allow me to deal with the matter myself, Tutor. Put a little trust in your future queen. I will speak with both Father and Tin when the timing is right." I sweep to the door, turning my head over my shoulder just before my exit. "I must away, good Tutor. I will see you tomorrow and we can continue this lesson then."

"Yes, Majesty. Thank you."

In the hallway, I pause to read the letter through once again. This time, when the flame of the crush ignites I don't have the desire to extinguish it.

Chapter 7

The council meets in a small building toward the center of Fraun. As you are riding up to it the building almost looks like a rock, round and grey. It is not until you draw closer that you see there is a single door. This door brings you to an antechamber, lit and warmed by torches. There is another door, directly across from that one, which leads to the council room. This is the room I find myself in this morning, nervously awaiting the men who rule Fraun.

The table in the center of the room is a large circle. Around the circle are six chairs. The chairs are very close together, probably due to the fact that there are customarily only five chairs at this particular table. At my left sits father, in all his regal glory. For the meeting, Father insisted upon us both wearing Green, the color of Enchenda.

A very small, very round man enters the room. Despite his unusual shape, the man has a commanding presence. His hair is white and his eyes have a sad look about them. He is wearing yellow, identifying himself as King Larecio of Marchenda. "Gregario." Larecio's voice booms throughout the room, echoing off the bare walls. He wears the largest smile I have ever known. Father effortlessly rises and I have to scramble to get my feet underneath myself. I watch as my father's hand envelopes the smaller man's and shakes it vigorously.

"Good morning Larecio, how are things in the fourth realm?"

"Well, as usual. We are a happy lot. How are things in Enchenda?" As he asks, Larecio frees his hand from father's grip and lets it fall to his side.

"Things are well with us. Larecio this is my daughter, Princess Eselda."

Beside him, I curtsy politely and dip my head. "Pleasure to meet you, your Highness."

"I have a son about your age, and we've met before." The tone holds no negativity whatsoever. In fact, it rings with a clear sound, not unlike a bell.

They really are the embodiment of happiness over in Marchenda. I wonder if this king ever gets mad. "That's right, I had almost forgotten. How is Carsen?" I ask politely. In truth, the fact had not escaped my mind at all, I had almost hoped to meet the young prince.

Larecio smiles. "He is well; I cannot wait to tell him you joined us at the council meeting. He will hold a high interest in the beautiful princess."

Another man enters the room, this one loud and boisterous. My gaze turns to the doorway and falls upon a tall, thin man with light hair. I guess the man to be just under three clicks tall, impressive. His eyes are darting around the room, taking in all who are present and making me feel like a specimen he is examining. The man is wearing blue, the color of Farcheda. The speed at which he moves to his council seat, on the left of my father, confirms that he is indeed from the third realm.

"Gregario, Larecio, Eselda." The man nods at each of us in turn. "Welcome. I know I am not tardy, so I acknowledge your earliness. I hope I did not offend. We will begin shortly, I am sure."

I notice he even speaks quickly. I blink my eyes in surprise.

"King Mick, I have never known you to be later than I. Welcome." Father returns to his seat as he greets the king of the third realm.

Looking around I notice Larecio is already sitting as well. I need to pay more attention. I hastily plop back into my chair, embarrassed. Before I can worry about what to say to the proud group of assembled men, another enters the room. This one is even taller than the last, standing proudly at three marks. He is very thin and his blonde hair falls almost to his bright blue eyes. He is startlingly beautiful, standing in the doorway in his orange shirt. But it is not his hair or eyes that draw my breath from my body in a gasp.

This is the man who refused to rise for me at the school.

He moves calmly around the table, shaking hands with each person in turn. I can see his mouth moving, but my brain is not processing the words. What would be the reason for Renchenda, the kingdom of wisdom, to spy upon my speech?

The man reaches my seat and holds out his hand to shake. "Greetings, Princess Eselda. We are glad you could join us." There is a twinkle in his eyes.

Is he daring me to mention the school visit? I don't think I have the nerve to do so in a room full of kings. "Greetings, King Jordyn." I bow my head slightly and the man moves on.

Only once Jordyn is seated at the table do I take my eyes from him. I may have let him off the hook in front of the council, but I plan to find out what he was doing in Enchenda unannounced.

I move my eyes around the table again, cataloging the behavior of the kings. Father, Jordyn, and Larecio sit comfortably in their chairs. Mick, however, is tapping his fingers on the table unnaturally loud. My eyes fall on the empty chair to my right. Of course, he is waiting for King Tin to arrive and begin the meeting.

Since the beginning of Fraun, the numbering system has been in place. There is always one realm who is given the task of leading the council. This member is expected to run the meeting and uphold the norms at all costs. I have been studying those norms for ten moons, in preparation for this night. The king from the first realm, presently Tin of Sarcheda, ensures all meetings begin and end on time. That king can call for a vote on any issue being presented at any time, but they have no sway on its outcome. All present must vote and all votes are a simple majority. Disagreements are accepted, neigh encouraged; but words are your only weapon in Council Hall. At any time, a member of the council may call for a renumbering of realms if they feel as though the first realm royalty is not leading the council well, but again a majority vote must back that up. The council historically does not like to dishonor a current first realm without a very good reason. In fact, Sarcheda has ruled Fraun for the last twenty-five annuals without question or call to vote.

My ruminating on the rules of the council is interrupted by the entrance of a muscular man dressed in red and black. Probably half a mark taller than I, he is not the tallest in the room, but his bulk is the most impressive. Arms, legs, chest, and shoulders show muscles I have rarely seen. He is dark of hair and eyes and carries himself as a living embodiment of strength. This must be King Tin.

"Good Afternoon gentlemen …" His gaze falls upon my face. "… and lady." He winks in my direction before dropping into the seat beside me. "Let's begin without further ado. What issues have we to discuss?"

Up close I notice even more muscles than I first saw. Tin is a stark contrast to Jordyn, seated to his right. Jordyn is lanky and thin everywhere Tin is filled out and strong. Jordyn is light skinned, light haired, and bright-eyed. They are opposites in every way I can measure with my eyes.

Beside my father, King Mick raises his hand and begins speaking in a clear, loud, but rapid voice. "We need to discuss the safety of Fraun."

He gestures to the table, pulling my eyes down toward it. Painted on the table is a map of Fraun. Each king sits proudly within his territory. Father and I share the space that is Enchenda. The border lines look carved into the table, as do the names of the five realms. The borders enclosing Enchenda have been painted a blue color representative of The River Fraun. My eyes trace the beautiful painting, taking in the colors the artist has used. In addition to the faint traces of the realms colors; Red, Green, Blue, Yellow, and Orange, the artist has added touches that indicate the type of flora one may find in the realm. There are green spots that look like tree groves, brown patches that may be sand, and even a black spot which I have heard is uncharted territory toward the border of the fourth realm.

A circle in the fifth realm shows the Castle Fraun. At the beginning of our history, that castle was inside the first realm. I have been to the castle one other time in my history, for the announcement of King Mick's youngest child, Margina. Each royal baby in the history of Fraun is presented to the other royals at a ball held in Castle Fraun. In fact, any special occasion that would call for all royals of Fraun to be together would be held there. It is simply the way of the kingdom.

I jump slightly when I feel the weight of my father's hand upon my own. "Pay attention, child," he whispers.

I hope I was the only one who heard that. I force myself to focus on King Mick's rapid speech. "The kingdom of Fraun needs this for the safety of our people. We must secure the borders against what lies beyond. My son, Hector, discovered the body of a large flying bird in the outskirts of our realm. What brought about the death of such a large animal? I desire not to encounter that villain alone."

"What do you propose we do about it?" King Larecio asks. He is sitting upright, actively listening to Mick's speech. Father is equally attentive.

King Jordyn, however, looks as though he is listening, but there is a cloud to his expression. Does he not agree with the stance of the third realm?

King Tin is the only one communicating obvious disgust with his body language. I have never seen a king look so uninterested in a conversation. Certainly, my father would never sit so relaxed. Tin is turned a little in his chair, leaning toward Jordyn. His knees are drawn up to the arm nearest my chair, and he is leaning his head back. In this manner, he is now focused not on King Mick, but on the ceiling above. I turn my eyes back toward Mick, not wanting to be caught searching other faces.

"I propose that we enlist a guard of young Fraunians to patrol the borders of each realm. The guard can be trained up together, a guard of Fraun, and report to the realms after training. I am willing to conduct the training myself," says Mick.

"Now there I must stop you, sir." Tin's voice accompanies a shuffle. I turn to see he is now seated in a more proper position, leaning on the table. His eyes, dark and dangerous, are now glaring full at King Mick. Bubbles of nerves tickle up my throat. "You are asking this council to assume an awful lot, sir." Tin growls the words.

"I am doing no such thing. Jordyn can tell you that I am being logical here. I have presented only facts."

"No, you have presented a hearsay account of a dead bird. Birds are living creatures, Mick. They die."

My heartbeat quickens in fear. It is impressive to be able to call emotions from listeners simply with your speech. This is a skill I must learn, as queen.

Tin continues, "Let's assume, for a moment, that you are correct. Let's assume that something killed that bird, something large. I see no reason at all why the entire kingdom of Fraun should have to put together a patrol. It seems to me the problem lies in the third realm. Should you desire to train up a guard of your men to waste their days patrolling, I'm sure the council will see fit to allow you such." King Tin relaxes his posture again but does not pull his knee up. The gesture clearly communicates his belief that this conversation is finished.

"Now see here, Tin. I want all of Fraun to be safe. One kingdom, one goal," Mick says.

This is a mantra I have heard before. Each generation seems to let this concept become less and less spoken of, to the point where my generation doesn't hear it much at all. It's hard to stand behind such a concept when you can go most of your life never meeting someone from another realm. Even I, a royal princess, have only met these people on a few occasions.

There are nods of assent around the room, however. "I must agree with Mick," Larecio states.

"There's a surprise," mutters Tin.

I turn to him, shocked at the informal outburst. Instead of pretending to ignore me, as I would probably do after such an error, he meets my eyes and winks. I force my eyes down to the table again, even as the fiery blush fills my cheeks.

"If the people of our realms are to remain carefree and happy," Larecio continues, "then we must provide them some security. If word of this patrol in the third realm spreads, then our people will want one as well."

"Enchenda would be in favor of a patrol as well." Father's voice booms from beside me.

I jump. Would we? Father's task on this council is to put the safety of Fraun above all else. All of Fraun. It makes sense that he backs this concept. I smile in agreement.

"Well then …" Tin lets his eyes travel slowly around the room. "Far be it for me to keep you from something the majority agree on. We can have a vote on this issue at the meeting's end. I do have one more point to clear up, however. If we are in favor of a patrol, why in the name of Fraun would we have this man …" He gestures to Mick. "… train up our patrol?"

Mick slams his fist down on the table, but the sturdy wood gives nothing. Instead, I feel vibrations in the floor where my feet rest. "What are you implying, Tin?"

"I imply nothing. I accept that you would be the fittest to train them for speed, but I am the most fit to train them for strength."

"I am not giving you a personal army to raise how you would like," Mick spits.

"I am not giving that to you, either, with all due respect."Somehow Tin makes it sound as though no respect were due. His words drip with irony. The room crackles with tension.

"I have a comment," Jordyn says.

All eyes in the room turn toward Jordyn, who has been silent up to this point. I have heard, from Tutor, that in Renchenda this is often the case. People there, known for their wisdom, often do more listening than talking. Because of this, they are able to draw more logical conclusions without interjecting their own personal feelings.

"If a patrol is to be started and trained as one, which is what I am hearing …" He pauses and waits for the council to nod. I notice they all do, including Tin. "I believe the idea of training them with the king of strength makes logical sense." He gestures to Tin.

Mick rises. "Of course you believe that. These two, both of a malicious age, are ready to organize an army. What would stop them from declaring war on the rest of us with their army to back them up?" Mick's eyes are locked on Larecio's face as he speaks and gestures wildly with his arms.

I have never in my life heard someone speak like this. I'm suddenly glad my father is still beside me to bear the brunt of this anger.

"Mick, sit down," Tin says. "I would like the council to recall, before this ridiculous accusation, it was Mick's idea to begin a patrol. Neither Jordyn nor myself made that suggestion. Surely if we desired to … what did you call it … organize an army? Surely we would've suggested it ourselves."

"That is true, I hold no such desire," Jordyn says. "I was merely saying that if our goal is to have a strong patrol that can battle whatever large being may be beyond our borders then strength would be a desirable characteristic of this patrol. If I was mistaken in the goal, and we are instead desiring someone who can warn us fast enough to take action, then yes they should be trained for speed in the third realm." Jordyn's voice has a calming effect on the men. It's not hard to understand why, as I feel calm washing over myself as well.

Listening to him talk, I cannot believe I didn't realize Jordyn was royalty when he visited the school. It seems so clear to me now, he is obviously educated and confident. How did I miss this?

Mick drops back into his seat. "If this is what the council chooses to vote on, I will have no part of it," he states. His anger sounds dispersed.

"It was your idea, Mick. But I see no reason to call a vote if you are no longer in favor," Tin smiles at the room as he speaks.

"Then call it not, Tin. What else have we to discuss?" Mick drops his hands, resignedly, to his lap. The room falls silent.

I look around the room again. Everyone looks beaten. These men have been called together to make decisions for the sake of Fraun, but they accomplished nothing but arguments in their time. It is a frustrating way of conducting business. I am aware that many meetings, in the past, have been more fruitful. Many meetings have stretched endlessly, with no party willing to concede until a decision of some kind has been made. In this case, however, it appears as though they have reached an impasse. I don't really understand why. Can Mick truly fear Tin's nature that much?

It makes sense to train a patrol in strength. Why would they oppose that? I remember what Tutor told me, at twenty annuals those with royal blood can become dark. Tin is that age. Perhaps this is all about age markers. Does the council fear Tin could not control himself with an army at his command?

Wait, could he?

Cold fingers of fear enclose my heart. I swallow the building fears with an audible gulp. What is coming my way?

"If there is no further business, I call this meeting to a close," Tin states.

"I second," Larecio croons with a smile.

"Meeting adjourned. See you fine people in one lunar cycle." Around the table, everyone rises. Tin leans in toward me, "I am glad you could join us, it brought beauty and grace to the table. I look forward to the day when you can speak your mind freely here. I'd love to hear your thoughts on this issue, I'll contact you regarding a meeting if you have no objections."

This close to him, I feel flutters in my stomach. The man before me is truly remarkable in his strength. He reaches to touch my arm, and his exposed muscles flex. "I object not, your Majesty," I answer. My voice cracks, embarrassingly. I resist the urge to groan at my own youth. "Thank you."

Tin smiles warmly. "Thank you," he practically purrs. He winks at me, again, as he turns to leave.

I feel warm all over. That man has a decidedly commanding presence. I shake myself back to reality and hustle to catch up with father. In the antechamber, my father waves to me. "Daughter, I must chat with King Mick. Stay here until I am finished and call for you." He calls this over his shoulder as he disappears out the front door.

I can see daylight is waning as the exterior door slips closed behind him. I am alone in the dark antechamber. I walk to the side of the chamber, turn my back toward it, and rest my foot up against the cold wall. I prepare myself for a long wait.

I feel the presence of another person in the room before I hear anything. When I turn my head I find King Jordyn standing in the doorway to the council chambers. "Good Afternoon, Princess." He smiles but doesn't step any closer.

"Hello again Majesty."

"Again?" he asks. His eyes give away his amusement; he is enjoying this.

"Were you not witness to the school visit I conducted in Enchenda recently?" I try to mirror his mock amusement in my own expression.

"Oh that. Yes, I was there. Fine job you did, Princess." Jordyn chuckles. "Did I offend you?"

"Why was the king of Renchenda spying on my school visit?" I take one aggressive step toward him, dropping my foot from the wall.

"Spying?" His face falls. "I was not spying. I am sorry you thought that." Something in his expression tells me he is serious.

"Why, then, were you there?"

"I have no heirs, Princess. I conduct my own school visit annually. I wanted to witness another realm and see how the visit is conducted there. I was hoping to learn something, and I did. You demonstrated remarkable confidence and preparedness. I was thoroughly impressed."

"Thank you." My resulting blush is deep. I can even feel my chest redden. "I am proud to have impressed the king of wisdom."

"Can I ask you something?" Jordyn takes another step.

He is now close enough that I could reach out and lay my hand on his chest if I so desired. "You may ask me something, yes."

"What is your opinion on the issue the council discussed?" his blue eyes hold steady to my green ones.

Do I deserve this focused attention? "I am but a princess, Majesty. My opinion is not as important as that of my king."

"We are not at a council meeting; you can speak freely. I did not ask you to put your opinion on the table in front of the kings. I merely asked for you to give it to me. It will go no further."

"Very well. I believe it would be in the best interest of Fraun to have a patrol. I see no harm in it being one of strength. Your logic appears sound to me. I don't understand the problem with it."

"Rest assured, there was no problem with the logic." Jordyn's eyes flash with a sudden anger; giving a rare glimpse of what may be brewing under the surface.

"I didn't mean to offend. I only meant I agreed with you," I quickly explain.

Jordyn's gaze softens. "Of course. Thank you." He leans back on his left foot, pulling away from me.

"Does that answer not please you?"

"I fear the council would see it as though you were siding with the young kings. How many annuals are you?"

The question is fired quickly and catches me off guard. It is probably for this reason alone that I answer such a personal question. "Past fifteen."

"Not yet to twenty?"

"Not that I'm aware, Majesty." How do I admit I have not been counting my own age? Is that a normal thing? Don't most Fraunians know their own ages? A question has pounded my brain for days. A question I was too afraid to ask anyone else. Pulling together my courage I quietly ask,

"Would I be aware of it?"

"You would." Jordyn sounds so certain, almost sad.

I wish he would elaborate. Time ticks by in silence.

Finally, Jordyn speaks again. "Have you thought about what you will do when your father betroths you?"

I sigh at the sudden change in topic. I don't want to talk about this. I want to talk about what is coming my way. "What makes you think he will?" I throw my chin out in a show of regal strength I don't really feel.

"You are aware he will die soon, yes?" Jordyn's tone is not confrontational. He delivers the line like someone merely stating the scientific results of a test.

I am mildly affronted by his attitude. This is my father's death he speaks of. On the other hand, I am finding I quite like the way he seems to always speak with logic and reason on his side. How can one not trust a king backed by such high morals? "I am aware of that, yes."

"That would leave three of us ruling our realms during a malicious age without heirs to speak of. Avoiding a war between the three of us would be ..." He turns his eyes upward as he thinks of the perfect word. "… difficult."

"You think we would war with each other?" I watch Jordyn's face carefully as he thinks. It is as impressive as watching a machine move, each movement of his eyes is so controlled. He looks down again, locking eyes with me.

"I think that when you reach twenty annuals you will truly understand how much Tin and I are holding ourselves together for the sake of Fraun. It is harder than I imagined it would be." His honest answer is touching.

I have an urge to comfort him but talk myself out of it. I feel as though my arms wouldn't really move anyway. "Is it scary?"

"It can be. Sometimes I find myself in a situation where I know my instinct is not right. It is hard to fight your own instincts. If it weren't for my wisdom, I'm not sure I'd be able to stop myself."

My heart races. This is the closest I've been to another person who has experienced the feeling I have feared since I learned of it. I have so many questions to ask him.

Jordyn interrupts before I can ask another. "So that is why I think your father, one of the men on our council who have greyed, will be sure to marry you to someone who has passed this state before his death. Have you considered that?" Jordyn asks.

"I have not."

"There are a few I would see as good options, I wonder if your father has already spotted that." Jordyn's eyes focus on something over my shoulder. I turn my head and see nothing but the cold stone wall behind me. I am about to ask him what he is looking at when the outside door opens, letting in a cool breeze. Immediately, Jordyn steps back, putting respectable space between us.

"Eselda, we can away," father calls. His voice leaves no room for questions. I nod my assent and begin to follow my father, who has already turned away from the building.

"It was a pleasure meeting you, Your Majesty."

"Please, call me Jordyn." His smile makes his slim face even more handsome.

Instincts kick in and I feel my own smile tugging at my cheeks. "Goodbye, Jordyn."

"Until we meet again, Eselda."

I am aware my thoughts should be on betrothal, patrols, and policies. Instead, they fall on the two young kings who have captured my attention today. I spend the ride home childishly daydreaming about them in turn.

Chapter 8

The night brings air thick with humidity and dark clouds which threaten to bring rain. Out the window of his home, the king watches. The only noises around are related to the weather and the night. Everyone in the realm is asleep.

Asleep or dead.

At the king's back lies the body of the young chambermaid who drew her last agonizing breath tonight. The young chambermaid who helped to bring confidence to the king, the same chambermaid who occupied his bed in secret for the last twelve moons. The chambermaid who overstayed her welcome when she chose to call him by his given name, instead of calling him her king. *The chambermaid who would've surely ruined my reputation by telling someone about the affair when she had the chance.*

She won't have the chance now. The thought makes him chuckle.

In the morning he will have to have his men remove her body from the house silently. Surely people will not miss such a girl, he had never known her to take time to spend with a family. He will either have to choose men who can be trusted with a secret or men he can kill after the job is done. No one can know of this affair. Least of all the young princess.

The king has a plan now and Fraun help anyone who tries to stop the plan. "You're next, Princess," he whispers into the night.

Any Fraunian on the grass of his lawn, were any present, would only have heard the laugh that followed; high and dangerous.

It is a laugh that promises terrible changes for Fraun.

Chapter 9

I have no idea why I'm awake. The bed is warm and comfortable, it's silent in my house, and yet I find myself staring up at the ceiling with thoughts of the council meeting yesterday running through my head.

"Princess Eselda." The voice carries through the door.

I jump out of bed and close the space quickly. I send the door swinging on the hinges as I whip it open. "You are losing your touch, Eee. I woke on my own this morning," I tease, smiling down at her.

"My apologies, Majesty. I will arrive earlier in the morning."

Roaches are notoriously bad at understanding jokes. "Eee, I was only kidding. Please relax." I will have to resign myself to waking earlier now, roaches can be so difficult.

"As you wish, Majesty." Eee hurries out of sight.

I dress quickly and hustle through the hallways to the dining room, well aware that being late for breakfast with my father would cause the old man grief. Lately, my father has been acting strangely. At first, when we arrived home from council, I assumed it was because of the tensions at the meeting. Now a fortnight later I am concerned it may be another sign of his failing health. Though I put on a brave face it isn't easy to accept the fact that my father and king is not long for this world.

"Good morning your Majesty." I bend to kiss him on the cheek before taking my customary chair across the large table. "How are you feeling this morning?"

"I am well, Daughter. How are you fairing?"

"Well, thank you. Is there business to discuss this morning?" Traditionally we will talk about schedules in the morning. Lately, we have been discussing policies around Fraun, grooming me for the inevitable takeover of Enchenda.

"Not really. I have a short meeting with a few leaders from the realm this afternoon, it will be boring and is not necessary for you to attend. Two of the gentlemen are simply requesting permission to increase the amount of food grown on their land. As you know our population has been growing lately, I will grant this request when they make it. Is there anything on your schedule, daughter?" the king asks.

I think through my scant itinerary. "I believe Tutor is scheduled to come by this morning. Otherwise, I have nothing planned."

"Perhaps you can do a favor for an old man since you are free this evening."

"Anything father."

"It has been requested that I meet with King Tin this evening for dinner to discuss in further detail his idea for the patrol, which you heard suggested at the council meeting. I grow weary in the evening and although I made the arrangement I fear I will be too tired to hold up my end. Would you consider traveling by roach to the meeting in my stead? I am sure King Tin will be more than willing to hear your side of the issue."

Father's speech sounds strained, leaving me no doubt that he speaks the truth when he talks of his fatigue. The man has tired already and it is only morning. "I could do that for you, Majesty. King Tin mentioned a desire to hear my opinions on the issue after the meeting, actually."

His hand halts partway to his mouth. His eyes leave his plate and land on my face. "When was this exactly?" he asks.

"Directly after the meeting, before I even left the table in the council chambers. It was nothing serious, father." I can't even begin to fathom what the king's problem could be. He is about to send me to the king's house for dinner with him, alone in his home. Surely a quiet conversation in a room full of other kings is no concern.

After a beat, the king resumes eating with vigor. Assuming this means all is forgiven, I follow his lead and devour my meal as well. When the plates are cleared away by a lady in waiting, I rise. "I should be off to meet Tutor, your Majesty." I bow, respectfully. "I shall meet Eee as the sun begins to fall to travel across the River Fraun."

"Thank you, Daughter. Please remember to keep your discussion with the king of strength to that of policy."

I scrunch my face, "What else would we speak of, Majesty?"

"I know not, Daughter. I was speaking without thinking."

My father doesn't speak without thinking. I decide not to challenge this and, instead, head for the garden.

Chapter 10

Gregario remains in his chair, looking every minute of his forty-four annuals. Although he would prefer not to remember his age, he has always counted. Few Fraunians actually count the annuals as they pass, but Gregario has always enjoyed numbers. For example, he remembers that exact moment eighteen annuals back when Eselda was first placed into his arms. Any father can tell you that when you look at a child, regardless of age, you still see shades of the baby they were.

He can still recall little Eselda wrapping her whole hand delicately around his pointer finger and cooing gently at him. *When*, he wonders, *did that baby become the beautiful woman I just dined with?* Some days the old king worries that he is not preparing her for ruling in Fraun. Some days he worries that she is not the right queen for the job.

But what choice do I have?

A small roach enters the room. This is the new baby born to Eee. Gregario knew the baby would be a good addition to his household, Eee was irreplaceable in raising his stubborn daughter. He is pleased to be returning the favor by working with this baby. "Majesty." The voice of the roach is high-pitched, different from that of an adult roach.

"Yes, young Ekk."

"King Mick is here, sir."

"Very well, show him in." Gregario feels mildly guilty for not mentioning this meeting to Eselda. He knew Mick would likely be early to the meeting, being king of speed and all, but he neglected to mention it in hopes that Eselda would be gone when Mick arrived. The old king of Farcheda is often controversial and does not look favorably on the princess.

This way is easier for everyone.

"Gregario, how goes things?"

Mick, Gregario knows, is younger than himself. Although he knows not how many annuals the king has walked the Fraun, he knows they entered the world within five annuals of each other. By all accounts, Mick should look worn and tired like Gregario himself, but that is not the case. Perhaps because Mick has always been faster. *If you slow a race roach down, can it still not beat a common roach?* "It is well, Mick. Welcome to Enchenda."

"Thank you. Let's get down to business, shall we?"

"We shall. You called this meeting, what say you?"

"We need to talk about war." Mick's voice booms clearly in the room.

Gregario's eyebrows raise, as do the small hairs on the backs of his arms. "War?" The concept is scary to all from Fraun, certainly not in the best interest of the kingdom.

"Yes." Mick sits forward, his elbows on the table. "I believe we could declare war on Sarcheda. If we win, Sarcheda would be absorbed into the Fraun and we would need to redraw the realm lines. Each realm would increase in size, but we would be able to rebuild without the fear of Sarcheda beginning a war." Mick's voice, although he is not yelling, carries across the room.

Neither man notices the small observer hiding in the shadows of the mostly closed door, listening to every word.

Gregario pauses to give the impression that he is thinking over the ludicrous idea. When he speaks, he chooses his words carefully to avoid offending the guest. "I am not in favor of starting a war to avoid one, Mick. Besides, what chance have we against the realm of strength?" Gregario wishes for Jordyn to be at the meeting. He would even settle for any representative from the realm of wisdom. He cannot seem to think of words that will convince, but not offend, his visitor. *I cannot simply tell a king he is being an imbecile.*

"The fear of war is only effective if those in power can remember what war causes. If we bring a new war to the forefront, it will keep them in line for a lot longer. Longer than you and I will be ruling, that is for sure," Mick answers.

Gregario rubs his face, fatigue clouding his emotions. "Mick, I fear war," he answers, honestly. "I wish to avoid it at all costs. Let us discuss other options."

"Gregario, do you believe that King Tin should be allowed to lead Fraun?" Mick delivers a loaded question.

The king of Enchenda has thought of this often, as is his duty. *True, Tin harbors obvious hatred for the king of Farcheda. But is that feeling not returned? It seems unfair to punish one without punishing the other. In his time as king, Tin has stopped the vote on many things that the rest of the council would like a word on. But renumbering the realms is always controversial.* Gregario feels every moment of his age pile upon him. He rubs his hand along his face. "I don't know what I think, honestly."

"Let's think this through. If I called for a renumbering at the next meeting, what would happen? Assuming you sided with me …"

Gregario looks abashed. *Did Mick not hear me just now?*

"… which I realize is still left to be decided."

Gregario smiles. *Good, he got that message.*

"Assuming though, for just a second, that you did side with me in favor of renumbering, we are still not guaranteed for it to be approved. We know that realm five would side with Tin in voting to keep the numbers as they are, those boys agree on everything. We cannot be sure which way Larecio will fall, the man is inconsistent. So, even if you do agree with me today and we call for a renumbering at the next council meeting there is still a chance it could be ineffective," Mick says. Suddenly he adopts the deflated look that Gregario knows means he has convinced himself of the flaws in his own plan.

"What has you so convinced that King Tin cannot rule the Fraun, besides his age?" Gregario's voice is cautious, hesitant.

"What if I told you I believe the man killed his parents?" Mick asks.

Chapter 11

I have never known Tutor to be late. Today, I sit in my favorite garden and cannot enjoy the place at all. I mindlessly work my fingers through my long hair and watch the sun move up the sky slowly. "What if I had somewhere to be today?" No, that's ridiculous. Tutor would know my scheduling conflicts better than I do. In fact, having spent ten annuals as a boy living in Farcheda, Tutor is a stickler for schedules, which is why he's never tardy.

Cold fingers of worry start inching their way up my spine. What if something has happened to the man? The longer I sit with this thought in my head, the more it becomes a real fear. I rise, intending to find my father and express my concerns to him. He will know how best to proceed.

I race back to the dining room, holding my long black skirt bunched up in my hand. As I approach the door, which is unlatched and not quite flush with the frame, I slow to a walk and catch my breath. I am in the act of reaching for the door handle when a voice reaches my ears and turns me to ice. Interested, I lean my ear to the door frame.

"Then we agree on the need to remove power but it seems we cannot agree on the best solution." It is King Mick, speaking in a booming voice.

"Not war, Mick. I will not abide war. I've told you already I do not think we have a chance in a war against that realm," father answers. I know that tone of voice. It is the tone father takes with me when I am being argumentative and he is annoyed. I have never heard it taken with another, especially another king. I wince for Mick, that is a tone of voice I never like hearing. Poor guy.

"Then we shall need a renumbering," Mick says.

Renumbering? What are they talking about? Why would we need a renumbering? I really wish I had shown up at this door a little earlier. Why did I wait so long?

"It appears so," says Father.

"We will need Larecio's vote to fall with us."

"How do you propose we ensure the vote of the king of mirth?"

"There is a way—"

"No," father's voice cuts through the room like a blade. I wince again at the power. "That decision is not ours to make," he softens his tone with this new sentence. My shoulders relax, slightly.

"As you wish, Gregario."

"If we only need one vote, must it be Larecio's?"

"I suppose not, what are you proposing?"

"Perhaps we can get to Jordyn?" Father's voice rises at the end, turning it into a question.

Outside the door, I am perfectly shocked. Two kings of Fraun are behind closed doors discussing ways to sway council votes. I don't understand what is happening, but it is giving me a terrible feeling.

I shift nervously and the voices halt. I must have made noise and betrayed my position. I inhale deeply and swing the door open. On my face is a careful smile belonging to someone showing up to the conversation and not one who has overheard. For a beat, I panic because I cannot remember why I came to the room. I hope that comes across as shock at seeing a guest in the room. "Oh, King Mick, what a pleasant surprise." I bow low to the king. "Pardon my interruption, Majesties, but I wanted to inform you that my tutor is mysteriously absent. I have chosen to head to town and mingle with the people. If Tutor should happen to show up, please handle it accordingly in my stead." I am shocked at the words which leave my mouth. I had intended to ask my father's opinion on the absence. Perhaps my brain rightfully thinks overthrowing Kings of Fraun is more pressing than a missing tutor.

The door clicks softly behind my retreating back as I dash from the room before questions can be asked. I freeze just outside the room, wondering if the conversation will continue.

"What did she overhear?" King Mick asks, in a quieter tone.

"I trust my daughter, she heard nothing."

I take that as permission to run out of the building entirely, although I wait until I'm outside to allow myself to breathe deeply.

What did I just witness?

Chapter 12

I have always found the realm to be calming. Enchenda is filled with small houses, lined up neatly in rows along dirt streets for roaches and feet to travel. Many people have gardens in front of their homes. Some grow food, others grow flowers, few grow both. In this land, it is normal and expected that if you are one to grow food you will share with one who does not. The same is true for flowers.

The day is shaping up to be beautiful. The sun is radiating warmth down on Enchenda, making me glad I wore a sleeveless dress this morning. The black ensemble is one I often wear with a traveling cloak. Obviously, I left in a rush. The heat on my shoulders makes me smile. The silver lining to the secret meeting I overheard may just be this excuse to walk in the warmth.

I use my walking time to think through the overheard conversation. Why would the kings want a renumbering? I remember how they spoke to each other at the council meeting; Kings Mick and Tin are obviously not friends. Surely that is why Mick wants Tin out of the first seat. But father?

What reason would he have to want the realms renumbered? Who are they numbering in favor of?

I slow as I approach a busy area of the realm. I am out of the tree-lined area surrounding my home and fast approaching the center of town, where the school and a few shops are located. There are kids playing in the road here, kicking a mini watermelon around and running. Women are working in their gardens at two homes by the end of the road. A few men are working on a cart, one that will attach behind a roach. They look as though they are fixing broken parts underneath the cart, one is trying to hold it up high for the other. "Is there anything I can do to help?" I ask.

The man underneath the cart slides out and looks at me, not able to hide the shock on his face. "Do you know how to work on a cart, Princess?" he asks.

"Not truly. However, I do believe I have a better solution to holding that thing off the ground than using your friend here." I gesture to the smaller man, who is dripping sweat from his head onto the ground as he lowers the cart back into the dirt. I look around the street, searching for something. The men watch in disbelief as I collect a long, strong stick and three rather large rocks. I bring the items to the men one at a time.

"Now, please hoist that cart up one more time for me. Be sure it's as high as you can, please. I'm going to prop this stick underneath it," I instruct the younger man.

He nods his agreement, cracks his knuckles, and raises the cart.

I hurry, nervous as I watch the man's arms quake from the exertion. I push the stick underneath the cart, keeping it at an angle with the ground. Then, while he is still holding the cart high, I gather the rocks around the base of the stick. I test the contraption, trying to wiggle it from side to side. It holds firm.

"Okay, you can start to put the weight on the stick. Please lower it slowly, I'd like to be sure it isn't going to slide." The man begins to comply. At first, the stick holds and pride swells within my chest.

As if to remind me to practice humility, the stick begins to slip. "Wait, please."

The man halts, taking the weight of the cart again with a loud grunt.

Feeling guilty, I push the stick firmly into the soil before gathering the rocks closer. "Try again, please." This time, the stick holds the full weight of the cart.

The older man leans onto the cart, which continues to hold. "Princess, this is brilliant. Is it safe for me to crawl under?"

"It should be, although I'd advise against hitting the stick with anything. I also wouldn't stay under there for a very long time."

"What should we call this?" the young man asks, excitement showing on his face now.

"My tutor calls it a lift. You two gentlemen have a good day." When I leave the two men are hugging. It feels good to be helpful. I feel as though the day's warmth is now matched in my soul.

I continue on my path to the center of the realm, pleased to see so many people out in the main area of town this morning looking happy and alert. There have been times in the history of Fraun when people could not mingle like this; times that weren't this happy. I should be glad to be taking over the rule now, as opposed to then.

A woman nearby, arms loaded with vegetables, is calling to her children behind her. The woman silently offers me a carrot stick, which I delight in accepting. This is the beauty of Enchenda. This walk has been exactly what I needed to raise my spirits and my mood out of their funk. I close my eyes and breathe in the smells of food cooking somewhere, feeling the last of my stress leave my body.

A noise startles me. Eyes now open, I find a rock has landed on the ground a little way in front of me. A look around finds a group of sheepish-looking young boys, one of whom is holding a stick. "Sorry, Majesty. We didn't see you there when we hit it," he nervously calls.

I pick up the rock and toss it back to them, smiling.

"Thanks, Majesty. You're the best," calls the tallest boy. The boys turn their backs to me, resuming their game.

"Your Majesty?" The quiet voice comes from a woman, seated on some stairs in the shadows to my right. The woman is grey, tired looking, with wrinkles cascading down her face.

"Good morning madam."

"I thought that was you." The woman smiles, yellowing teeth filling her mouth. The grey hair of the woman falls in two even parts down her front, carefully and lovingly braided by someone. It is still beautiful and glistening, despite its coloring. Someone cares for this woman.

"What can I do for you this morning?" I ask.

"You can tell that old father of yours that his time is near," she croaks.

"Excuse me?" What a rude thing to say.

"Your father is greying. He may have doctors who help him hide his age well, but some of us remember. I know as well as he that his time draws to an end. It shall be a race which of us perishes first like it was once a race for our mothers to birth."

"You know my father?" It is the first thing out of my mouth, and yet I silently chastise myself for the stupid comment. Everyone knows my father. He is the king. "I mean; you personally have met my father?"

The woman laughs cordially. "Our mothers were childhood friends. The king, your grandfather, could've had either wife. He chose your grandmother because her baby was born first."

My shock must be evident on my face because the woman laughs again. "I take it your father never told you he was born before your parents were wed? You better come inside, Princess. I have a tale to tell you."

I turn to look at the sky. Judging by the position of the sun I have enough time for this before I am supposed to head to Sarcheda. Then again, after an introduction like that to set a match to my curiosity, I would make time even if there was none. I follow her inside.

The house is smaller than I am used to and made of wood instead of the warm stone of my family home. The pieces have been borrowed from the ruins of the Giants, so they are not even in length. Because of this, the roof tilts a little to the right. The room we have entered into must be a kitchen. There are three chairs around a wooden table, a small cooking stove made of stone, and a chimney reaching to the heavens through an opening in the wooden planks that make the roof. There is a bucket in the corner, underneath another small opening in the roof. A length of fabric is draped along the left side of the room, blocking my view of anything further. "Is that hiding your sleeping space?" I ask, pointing at the curtain.

The woman follows my gaze. "Yes, my bed is beyond there." She bustles to the small stove and sets a kettle down on the wood. She then leans in and blows softly on the wood, causing flames to stir up from the embers. She sits at the table and gestures for me to do the same.

"My name is Charlotte. My mother's name was Devon. You should remember those names; your father will confirm that he knew us well. Before your years, when King Kris and his wife Laurina ruled the realm, my mother and your grandmother lived next door to each other in matching houses. They were beautiful girls, and they did everything together. Kris and Laurina had a son, Stefan, your grandfather. Stefan was a young prince who didn't like to be cooped up in his father's home. He often ran through the village, playing with the townsfolk and hiding in plain clothes. Of course, like you, they knew who he was. But he enjoyed pretending to blend in."

Haven't I been playing the same game? The long-buried tie to my grandfather pulls me into the story, I lean across the table on my forearms.

"One day when Stefan was out in the village he came across two beautiful girls playing in the River Fraun. At first, he chastised them; the River wasn't safe for playing. Technically, he told them, the River is not part of Enchenda. The girls laughed at him and invited him to play in the river. When he refused, they pulled him in. After that, I'm told, the three got along swimmingly." The old woman chuckles at her pun. "Stefan would often leave the home of his father to seek out Angeliq and Devon."

Behind the woman, the kettle whistles. She rises and slowly pours water into two mugs. I watch the woman add mint sprigs and tea leaves, crushing them with a spoon. Angeliq and Stefan were my father's parents. The rest of this story I have never heard. I hold my doubts in my throat, where they have balled up. The woman cannot answer my questions, I will let her tell her story. The king will fill in the details. The thought of bringing this topic to my father, fuel for an epic fight, makes me impatient for the woman to finish the tale. My leg begins to bounce under the table, making a noise as my bare foot strikes the ground.

Setting the teacups on the table in front of us, Charlotte continues. "Where was I? Stefan had met the women of his dreams, yes? Well, the problem was the girls were always together. My mother, Devon, and your grandmother, Angeliq, were often mistaken for sisters. I'm told they loved this mistake. When the girls were fifteen annuals they were invited to a party at the home of King Kris. Stefan took each one away from the party, alone, and professed his love. He told each girl that she was the one he had decided to court, but that she must keep it a secret because she had no royal blood. He let each woman believe that it was not worth the heartache it would cause her friend to know the truth. He explained to each that he would personally tell the other when it came time. In this way, he was able to court both women, in secret, without the other knowing.

"It drove a wedge between them. Devon and Angeliq would no longer see each other. They were either sneaking out with Stefan or hiding in fear that their friend would ask where they were. It was no fun for anyone." Charlotte pauses and sips her tea. "Well, I suppose it was fun for Stefan." She laughs.

I don't know what to say. Instead, I wrap my hands around the mug of tea and take a sip. It is delicious and warm, comforting.

Charlotte continues, "It wasn't long before both Devon and Angeliq were with child."

"Excuse me," I interrupt. "This is all fine, except how can we be sure that he managed to impregnate both women at the same time? Are we sure there was not another man?"

Charlotte laughs again. "They were twenty annuals before they were pregnant, Princess. This means your grandfather had reached his twenty-fifth annual. Let's say that this meant they spent a lot of time in bed, not ..." she clears her throat "... sleeping." She winks at me.

Is this woman speaking of the age markers? My cheeks flush with embarrassment at what she is implying. Who wants to think of their grandparents like that?

"Anyway, they were both with child together. This is what drove the women back together. Now they were about to be unwed mothers, people who are shunned even in Enchenda. They fell to each other for comfort. In tears, the women told each other everything. In this way, they came to be angrily standing on Stefan's doorstep. Stefan would need a queen. His father had died recently. His mother was greying. The women proposed that Stefan choose one of them to be his wife. It was decided that he would save the other from banishment by claiming that child belonged to his foot soldier, a man named Shawn. Stefan would provide money to Shawn and his bride for as long as he lived. The problem was that Stefan loved both women and couldn't choose.

"It was decided that he would take the first to deliver the baby. Greg was born three suns before I was, so he became a prince and I became a commoner. Our parents were wed on the same day." Charlotte leans back a little. The smile is gone from her face. "Stefan was true to his word about providing for my family, and Greg has helped since Stefan's death, but I expect that will stop with you."

I look again around the shabby home with the leaking roof. "My father continues to provide?"

"Your father provides much. That tea you drink comes from your family gardens."

There is no sign in the small house of another being. Yet the woman appears cared for. I decide to push the issue and see if I can gain more information. "If you have never married and you claim you aren't long for this world; who do you wish I provide for?"

Charlotte swallows and drops her eyes to the teacup, turning it in her hands. "I want my story to live on. Stefan was as much my father as Greg's, you owe me that."

I swallow hard. My foot ceases its tapping as the truth of this conversation slaps me in the face. There is royal blood in Enchenda that the council knows not of. "You are my aunt."

"I am."

"It seems so strange, I have never met you. I have never heard of you."

"That is what I wish you to fix." For the first time since beginning her story, Charlotte looks tired again. Telling of her heritage had given her energy.

"I will speak to my father about this." I rise from the chair. "You have my word."

"Thank you, Princess. That is all I could ask. Please see yourself out, I feel I must rest now," Charlotte says, her voice barely a sigh.

I show myself to the door and march straight back to my father's home. Once there, I am greeted by a chambermaid of my father's. "Excuse me, ma'am. Can you please tell my father that I wish to meet with him tonight after I have met with King Tin? I will meet him in the garden upon my return, we have important issues to discuss." I deliver the speech with my chin raised high, completely at odds with the flutter under my skin.

Technically I do not have the right to summon my king, but this woman does not have the right to question her princess. The chambermaid nods and scurries from the room. I rush off to my chambers. I must push aside the thoughts of Enchenda and royal blood.

I have a king to meet with.

Chapter 13

The ride to Tin's home near the Southern border of Sarcheda is brisk. I have decided to keep the same dress, for lack of time, but dress it up for the occasion. Feeling it is appropriate to represent the colors of Enchenda, I have gone with a dark green overcoat. Around my neck, I have looped something long and silver with touches of a beautiful stone that glitters the color of blood. I hope to please the King of Sarcheda by wearing red, the color of his realm.

The roach, Gee, was chosen by the stable hand. It is the largest roach in our employ, making him able to withstand such a journey. He is pleasant, normally, but cannot talk on this ride because of the weight he is carrying and the distance he is traveling. This leaves me alone with my thoughts, again.

The news this afternoon, upon meeting my "Aunt" Charlotte for the first time, is leaving me with much to consider. I try to recall my family tree into my memory. The family lineage is painted along one wall in the dining room. On the tree, those with royal blood are circled. I can effortlessly recall my father's name, painted in the eloquent scroll, Gregario. His name appears next to that of my mother, Rubina, and is connected to her by a faint line. Underneath, and connected to both, is my own name, Eselda. Both my father's name and my name are faintly circled. Mother's is not. Those details are easy to recall.

It's recalling further up the chain, to the parts of the lineage we have never discussed, that is proving challenging. Stefan and Angeliq appear above my father, that memory is hazy but present. Obviously, Stefan's name must be the one circled; but I cannot really remember that detail. Is there a faint line trailing off from Stefan's name in an unknown direction? Is there any mention of Charlotte's existence at all? Surely my family must be aware that another with royal blood exists? Aren't there implications for that?

Beyond that, Charlotte knew of the age markers. She commented on my grandfather spending a lot of his time in bed. I have only recently learned of those age markers myself. Someone must have explained them to Charlotte. There must be another person tutoring this woman in the ways of the royal blood.

Armed with this new realization, I can hardly wait to get my conversation with father underway, I am clenched by a strong desire to turn the roach around and head back to confront him straight away.

My humble training kicks in, guilting me into continuing my ride. What would happen to the relationship between Enchenda and Sarcheda if a meeting like this were canceled with no notice? Surely it wouldn't be good. Besides, if I'm being honest, it cannot hurt to see King Tin again. I feel the flare of my crush again and I allow my mind to wander toward those muscles of his. I can picture the shape of his arms, wildly different than the tubes of everyone else. I certainly can admit to myself that I am partially traveling all this way just to see him again.

I arrive at King Tin's home just as darkness consumes it. A foot soldier is waiting to take the Roach from me and lead him to food and water. A lady-in-waiting, whom I assume was hired for the occasion since no women live in Tin's home, is ready to lead me to the dining room. Tin is seated at one end of a long table. His home, like my own, is made of rocks and stones. It is warm, owing to the fact that a large fire burns brightly behind Tin. He is illuminated completely, both by the fire at his back and the candles on his table. The table has only one other place setting, to Tin's right. I sit in it and smile at my host.

"Good Evening, your Majesty," I greet, bowing my head as much as the heavy wooden table will allow. It is hard to show regal respect to one my own age, even if he is a king. Tin's face breaks into a smile, and my crush burns full force. How can someone this handsome be talking to me?

He has dressed in all black again, although more casually than he was for the council meeting. There are touches of red in the shirt, straining against the muscles underneath. I hope the lighting is such that he cannot see the blush that I can feel taking up residence along my cheeks.

"Good Evening, Eselda." Tin reaches out his hand, and I place mine lightly in his. He bends, placing his lips upon the back of my hand. His dark eyes never leave my face. I feel my heart flutter. "You look lovely in red beads," he says, straightening in his chair.

"Thank you. I thought it fitting for a meeting in Sarcheda." The thought of pleasing this man warms me more than the fire could.

"Shall we dine? You must be hungry from your travel." Tin waves his arm and a chambermaid flees from the shadows through a door in the wall. When she returns seconds later she is leading another woman and both are carrying trays of food. Each woman steps behind a royal party and begins placing identical dishes in front of us. I lean back to allow them access to the table.

The soup sends swirls of steam into the air above the bowl, it smells faintly like zucchini, one of my favorite vegetables. A small plate of bread lands next, dark in color and shining as though butter has recently been spread. There are not many in Enchenda who make bread, I am excited to eat it again. Next is a smaller plate, this one holding slices of large strawberries. Finally, there are glasses of water placed in front of each place. When the women depart, I follow Tin's lead as he grabs a spoon and begins eating the soup.

"So, Eselda, tell me your opinion on the matter of a patrol," Tin prompts between spoonfuls of the hot stew.

My opinion. What should I tell this king? Should I mention my initial reaction, which was to agree with him and Jordyn? Perhaps that is not the best answer. My father must know more than I if he is willing to entertain the idea of a renumbering to overthrow Tin from his given position of authority. "I feel as though I am not learned enough to have a true opinion yet, Majesty. I was shocked to even learn we were in need of safety." The answer is honest but incomplete. It will have to do for tonight.

Beside me, Tin nods. His dark hair shines almost blue in the firelight, I have never seen hair that color. It looks soft and supple, as it should since he is past fifteen annuals. I am distracted by my sudden desire to reach out and touch it. Tin glances my way and finds my eyes on him. I drop my eyes to the table, where they find the basket of bread. In an attempt to cover my embarrassing stare, I reach for a slice and take a large bite. It is warm and sweet, a pleased sound escapes my lips and my eyes slip closed as I savor it.

"The bread brings you pleasure, milady?"

My eyes snap open again to find the king smirking at me. "We don't have many bakers in Enchenda."

"I expect that's because it takes some strength to form the loaves. I'll have to send you home with a few for your father. Tell me more about life in Enchenda, since you obviously intend to shy away from political conversations tonight." Tin reaches for a slice of strawberry as he leans on one elbow toward me.

"Enchenda is a beautiful land. Warm and bright, happy and delightful." I recall my walk through the town today, before meeting Charlotte. The memories flood me and I find this is exactly what I need to talk about to forget all my recent concerns. "The people are so friendly. Everyone is willing to drop what they are doing and help another person. Just today I helped someone learn a new way to get a job done efficiently. The men were so gracious and accepting of the help. They spoke kind words they must have known I needed to hear. I knew immediately the men would take what I had taught them and pass it on to more people, as I had done. It is truly a great place to live."

"An embodiment of the humility you learn."

The complement feels awkward. "We try Majesty. Thank you for noticing."

"I didn't mean your town. I meant you, Princess. You speak of your adventures today, but talk of the men you helped instead of yourself. You say 'we' as if to ensure you include all the people of your land, lest I think it is only of your house you speak. You are sure to tell me how nice everyone else is. You are a beautiful example of the humble nature your realm attempts to cultivate. If all around Enchenda were like you, there would be no worries there." As he speaks, his eyes travel my body. I can feel their warmth spread through me as though he had touched my body with his hand. My stomach flutters in a way that has nothing to do with the meal lying on the table between us. When he reaches out his hand and brushes mine, I feel a spark jump between us.

"You are too kind, Majesty." I choke on the words leaving my mouth as a whisper. "Tell me about Sarcheda," I request, out of my need to hear more of his voice.

"Sarcheda is a solid place. Everyone here is an excellent builder, so we make good use of what the Giants have left behind." I can tell this is true, the table I sit at is a much better quality than the one in my own home. "We have repurposed many tools to allow us to make bread and other foods. We have annual competitions for strength, and the people enjoy this time to show their skills. We are a tenacious people here and we have a lot of pride."

His voice washes over me like water, relaxing me. I can imagine the people he speaks of, built strong like himself. I can imagine groups of people, not unlike those I saw around Enchenda today, gathered together baking. Gathered together throwing large stones as far as they can. Cheering one another on.

The men in Tin's realm must have no need for contraptions that lift for them. They could easily heft that weight without thinking. My eyes fall to Tin's arms, thick and muscular. I feel the blush creep slowly back along my face. What is wrong with me today? I reach for a strawberry slice to hide my sudden desire to reach for Tin.

"Your soup is gone. Let us begin the next course."

Before I can object, Tin raises his hand to alert the chambermaid that the next course can be delivered. The women return with laden trays. This time they are following two women carrying empty trays. The empty trays are loaded with the plates from the soup course as the next course is laid before us. A single plate hits the table in front of me. The smell is amazing, but the food is not one I recognize.

As if reading my mind Tin explains, "Ant and rice, Princess. I hope you'll find it to your liking." He reaches for his spoon and slips it below the creamy surface in the bowl.

In Enchenda we often eat ants. Many of the scouts who patrol the land beyond Fraun bring back the bodies of ants they have killed for safety. I know our kitchen staff is well-skilled in preparing the meat, although I have never observed the process. I take the spoon and try a taste of the mixture. It slips down my throat. The taste is magnificent. "I have never had ant cooked like this, it's wonderful. What did you call this?" I pick up a single white grain, holding it in my fist.

"Rice, princess. It is harvested from along the Eastern border. The people of Renchenda have taught us how to prepare it. It's a remarkable treat." Tin gives me the impression he is amused by my naiveté. I'm not sure whether to be offended he thinks I am sheltered or happy he is broadening my horizons.

"It's delightful." I smile and return to the bowl.

Between the two of us, we probably have two ant legs steamed up and chopped. This is mixed with a few grains of rice and a creamy sauce. The kitchen staff has likely used the entire ant, hopefully parceling out the remaining meat amongst the staff.

We consume the dish without more conversation, I simply cannot get enough. When I finally finish and push the plate away, my stomach is more full than it has been in a long time. I am not one to go hungry, but I have also never eaten to excess before. I assume this spread was put together to impress me. I must ensure that he knows it has been a success. I adopt the smile I associate with tasks of the princess, one that is Regal and yet feels awkward at the corners. "This meal was simply divine, Majesty. Thank you for inviting me."

"We are not finished yet, Princess. Allow me to share my favorite dessert with you, please."

I am not sure I can fit more food into my stomach, but Tin has already gestured for it to be brought to the table. The women clear the dishes and place a single silver dish between the two of us. Inside is a brown, sweet-smelling dish. There are two spoons resting alongside. Tin smiles at me and takes one spoon, indicating I should take the other. "This is called a cookie. My chefs are amazing at preparing it, but it would not be possible without a rather large fire. Try it, please," he explains.

I am surprised to find my spoon slips effortlessly into the food and comes out gooey. I lift the spoon to my mouth and the explosion of flavor sends me leaning back in my chair. "What is this made of?" I ask once I have swallowed the delight.

Tin laughs at my reaction. "Larecio informs me it's called Chocolate. They have a supply of it in Marchenda that the giants left behind. He sent it here, especially for me to treat you with, at my request. Do you like it?"

I can only nod and reach for another spoonful. The flavor is so impressive that I have completely forgotten how full I am as I devour as much as I can.

Tin sits back in his chair and watches me eat the dessert. When I have eaten as much as I can, he leans forward again to rest on his forearms. The women clear the table and fill our cups with more water from the River Fraun.

"Can I ask you a personal question, Eselda?"

A little afraid of what kind of question may be hiding behind the dark eyes which are setting my skin on fire everywhere they land, I merely nod.

"Are you being courted by anyone in Enchenda?" This time I am sure he must notice the blush that creeps up my neck and dots my cheeks. "I don't mean to be forward, milady, but I find myself bewitched by you." He reaches for my hand, closing his own around my fingers, and swiping his thumb across my palm as he waits for my response.

"I am not being courted, Majesty." My voice trembles as I consider what he is implying and feel the electricity coursing through my hand.

"It would not be proper for me to request to court you, a princess awaiting a throne, without first speaking with your father. Allow me to ask you to wait, I will speak with him shortly. That I promise." He raises my hand to his lips and kisses it, closing his eyes as though imagining it is my lips he brushes instead.

"I have enjoyed meeting with you more than you can imagine, but I fear I must allow you to return home while it is still possible for me to let you leave. You see, I fear if I keep you here longer I would simply need you to stay forever. I grow fonder of you by the second." Tin rises. "Until we meet again, Eselda." He closes one eye, winking at me in a gesture that makes my heart race and my stomach flutter.

The lady-in-waiting reappears to lead me out of the home. This time I notice intricate details I missed on my rush in. There are decorations around the home I don't quite understand the purpose of. Paintings of Tin himself, paintings of landscapes, and a small reflective wall hung up across from the door. Unlike my own, this one has been trimmed around the edges with a wood that has been ornately carved. As I leave through the front door and mount the waiting roach, I notice that the door fits securely and latches well. In fact, I see no small defects at all in the manufacturing of this home.

I find myself, on the ride home, thinking of the promised courtship. Thinking, despite my earlier woes, that Sarcheda would be a nice place to live.

Chapter 14

The wind whips through the garden, stirring up the plants and shaking my thin frame. Just pulling up in sight of my house sent the questions I have pushed out of my mind all evening to resume their buzzing in my brain. I practically dove off Gee to race to this garden to see if father has honored my request to meet. There is so much to discuss.

The cold soil beneath my feet drops my body temperature. I wrap my arms around myself and jiggle my legs to keep warm. The empty garden speaks volumes. I'm so stupid. Who am I to demand a meeting with the king? I will have to catch him at breakfast.

The thought of breakfast gives me another idea. The family tree is painted on the far wall across from the fireplace in the breakfast hall. Perhaps I can still get answers from the tree. Glad to have a warmer destination, I bolt for the dining hall.

I pause just inside the door to listen for noises. The house is silent. My dinner with Tin was late and the ride home was long. It appears that I have stayed awake longer than even the roaches and servants who normally travel the halls at night. I creep along the corridors quietly. After being in Sarcheda I see things in my own home with new eyes. The bricks making up the walls here are scratched, damaged, and used. Were Tin's walls marked this way? Perhaps I will ask him how to clean off such imperfections.

I light the torch at the entryway to the dining hall and free it from its hanger to carry it to the family tree. The tree has been painted in gold, careful script along the stone. At the top of the wall, very near the roof where I would need a ladder to reach I see Oberian's name. The name is circled, indicating royal blood, and starred, indicating he served as King. There is a line connecting Oberian to his wife, Alicia. Underneath that is another line connecting him to his single son, Oberian II.

Oberian II had three wives. Therefore, I can see three lines connecting to him; Suzeth, Ramona, and Rebekah. I know there are descendants of all three women living in Fraun today. This tree, however, only shows those of Suzeth's single son, Enchenda.

My eyes trace downward, past the scrawls of names that have come before me. Circles and stars decorate the tree, reminding me again of the power royal blood holds over this family. Just beyond halfway down the wall, around my eye height, I see the names for which I search. Kris and Laurina, my great-grandparents. Laurina's name is circled and starred but Kris' is not. That information, for some reason, startles me. My great-grandmother was royal-born and served as queen of Enchenda. Interesting.

Underneath their names I see Stefan, as expected, circled and starred. He is connected to Angeliq, just as I recalled. Of course, my father, Gregario, was their only son. I lovingly run my fingers along my mother's name, Rubina, before tracing the line that connects to me.

Mother was always a warm woman. I remember my mother teaching me the traditional age markers. She would talk to me about the markers and my future while she sat behind me on my bed, brushing my hair. She would fantasize with me of the day when my hair would be shiny and bright. It's heartbreaking that Mother never lived to see that day.

I pull my eyes away from mother's name. This is not why I came in here. I trace the line back up to Stefan. Seeing nothing, I trail further up. There is another line jutting from Laurina's parents. Following it, my eyes take in another circled name, Tricia. Apparently, Tricia, Laurina's sister, married a man named Stu and birthed a child Tometh. This man, this

Tometh, has no further lines connecting to him. What happened to him? He has royal blood, but never served as king. Did he die as a child? Is he still alive? He would be Stefan's cousin and my great-uncle.

There is a black spot of coal dirtying the wall near Tometh's name. Absent-mindedly I begin to rub the spot as I think. Pulling my finger away to clean the soot, I notice there is none on my finger. I lean closer to the blemish and scratch it with my nail. From this angle, with my nose practically touching the surface, I can see it is actually black paint.

This odd oval is covering something.

I look around it. Sure enough, I find a very thin, very faint black paint line connecting the blemish to Stefan's name.

Did I just find proof of Charlotte?

I grab a nearby chair and stand on it, eagerly poring over every detail of the family. Up near the top of the wall, I notice a spot with only a few descendants. In fact, the ruling stars had jumped from one branch of the tree to the other. There, underneath King Charles and his wife Elena, I find two black ovals. These two are connected to each other and faintly connected to Charles and Elena. I rub my fingers over the circles, and again my finger comes away clean.

What stories are buried here? Why write the names if the children were not to be tracked? What becomes of them after their names have been erased?

If I had come here for answers tonight, I am not going to get them.

Clearly, these blemishes cannot be cleaned away so simply.

Chapter 15

"Eselda," Gregario's voice booms, echoing off the walls of the dining hall.

My eyes flutter open and take stock of my surroundings. I am curled up on the floor underneath the family tree. There is a chair beside me and the torch is in a holder beside the painting. I meet my father's angry expression and drop my eyes in shame. "Father, forgive me. I must have fallen asleep after my late meeting with King Tin."

"What were you doing in this room, then?"

"I was only looking at the tree, father. Please, I have many questions. Is this a good time for us to talk?"

"Very well, I suppose I cannot delay our conversations much longer. There is much to discuss. I will have the chambermaid prepare our breakfast. You should make yourself presentable. I will meet you back here shortly."

"Thank you, father." Despite my desire to start this conversation now, I don't wish to anger him. I dash out of the room quickly, before he can change his mind.

I rush through the tasks of scrubbing my face, rinsing out my mouth, and brushing my hair. Then I change into a simple green dress. Satisfied, I race back out of the room. I arrive in the dining room just as a chambermaid is dropping a bowl of fruit into my place. I smile in thanks at her while simultaneously bowing at father.

"Where shall we begin our talk this morning, Daughter? Or do you wish to eat first?"

"I couldn't possibly eat around all these questions in my gullet, father." I struggle to decide which issue, which question, to bring up first. "I think we should begin with your meeting with King Mick. Please, tell me what that was about."

"I suspect you overheard some of what we discussed."

"I did hear some, I didn't mean to eavesdrop." I take a bite of watermelon to stop myself from trying to further explain. Sometimes a simple answer satisfies.

"Mick has concerns about King Tin's loyalties to Fraun," Father says.

"But why?"

"Each realm has a family tree, not unlike the one you slept beneath, painted somewhere in their home. Mick claims to have seen all five trees, something I personally have never done. According to the king of speed, the trees hold evidence of some dirty secrets hiding in Fraun's past. Secrets that prove Tin, and his family, to be breaking council rules."

Rules like hiding royal blood as common folk in their realm? I take a deep breath in, wondering how bad this could truly be. On my exhale I ask, "What rules?"

"The council ruled, many annuals past, that our kings are to take only one wife. Mick claims to have evidence of this rule being broken."

I stop myself from rolling my eyes and take a bite of melon before moving the conversation forward. "How exactly would taking multiple wives prove Tin is unfit to rule? Remember, father, he has not even one wife."

"Eselda, why do you think the rule was put in place?"

I am used to ruminating over questions like this for Tutor, so I don't answer right away. Questions like these usually require answers that are different than my true opinion. For example, I'm sure Father isn't looking for me to say a man should marry only the one person they truly love and no other. I sit straighter in my chair, hold my head high, and project my answer in my strongest voice. "To ensure our kings are decent people."

Father laughs. My posture deflates and all confidence leaves me with a sigh.

"The kings can be whomever they want, so long as they uphold the quality they are asked to possess. I can murder if I so choose," he explains. My eyebrows fly up. Father picks up on the gesture effortlessly. "You doubt that? I certainly can, so long as it is in the best interest of the Fraun. So long as my doing so isn't for my own pride. So long as I remain humble.

"No, my daughter, the rule was not created to ensure we are good people. The rule was created to keep the royal blood contained. If a king takes many wives, as Second did, there are often many children born. In this day and age, if a current king were to do that, there would be many children who will never be needed to lead producing offspring with royal blood."

What a perfect opportunity to ask about Charlotte. "Father, is that not an issue that exists anyway?" I ask, attempting to flood my voice with innocence.

"I suppose it could be, I know not." Yet his eyes cast downward and he takes a bite of food.

"Then what of Charlotte?" I ask.

Now I have his attention. His eyes snap to my face. I brace myself for a scolding.

"Your curiosity never ceases to amaze me, Daughter." He surprises me with his soft tone. "Charlotte was an accident."

"How can a person be an accident, father?"

"Stefan was a fool. Any man can fall in love, a fool believes he has fallen in love with two. A fool believes that love is for him and not the one he loves. Stefan forgot to be humble, as we are taught, and it was his undoing."

I watch as the king drinks his tea and eats his fruit. Evidently, he expected this conversation to end here. I have no such desire. "Father, are you upset that I know of Charlotte?"

"No. I thought that I would be when you found out. My father disgraced our trait by bedding another woman, after all. But I find myself relieved to have someone to share this burden with. I have carried

Charlotte's weight on my soul for a long time. It is nice to share it with you." He reaches out and squeezes my hand, briefly.

"Is that her name, blacked out on the wall there?" I ask, gesturing to the first of the three ovals I found.

He doesn't even turn to look at the wall behind him. "It is. I had our tree painter add her to the wall but black her out. I felt terrible knowing that my father didn't even feel she needed to be up there. In gold paint, below the black, you'd find the name Charlotte. I also had him circle it. It remained up, drying, for a full sun before I allowed him to cover it."

"What gave you this idea?" I ask, hoping father knows of the other two similar circles.

"It is tradition to shun a woman and a baby when the baby is born out of wedlock. This is how the kingdom handles that shunning. The names are painted but covered. I knew of this tradition and felt it befit Charlotte."

I hold my new knowledge in a secret hug; the other two ovals must have been an unwed mother and her infant. "What becomes of those women, father?"

"A shunned woman is free to live a normal life among the commoners, but not to speak of her experiences."

"But what if they have families? Are those families not added to the wall?"

"For Fraun we ask them not to have children. Again, royal blood must be contained." Gregario's voice sounds sad and tired.

"That's a terrible fate."

"I agree with you, but it cannot be helped. It is something we do for Fraun," he says. "Now do you understand why it was easier for the rule to be one wife? Those kings were trying to prevent sorrow like this from reaching the offspring."

"I'm beginning to see it, yes. I'm afraid I still do not see what this has to do with King Tin, the bachelor." I emphasize the last word carefully.

"Yes, well. The problem is not exclusively with Tin himself. Mick believes that the kings before him have taken many wives in secret. He claims the evidence is written on the wall, not even blacked out. The wall, however, is hidden in a location none others have ever seen. I am not sure how Mick came to bear it witness. Mick supposes that the wives were taken to help ensure a line of strong, male rulers. Sarcheda is the one realm among us that has always birthed a king to lead and never a queen. This, combined with the fact that Tin himself often opposes issues the council is in favor of, has led Mick to believe it is time to renumber."

"That hardly seems like solid evidence to remove someone from a seat of power," Eselda answers.

"You must remember, Eselda, we are not talking about stripping him of his title. No one can do that. We all have blood rights at that table. We are merely talking about renumbering. If he were, for example, King of the fourth realm, what would really be different?"

I mentally count out the circle, curious about what would make Sarcheda fourth. I bristle as I realize it. "You're talking about making Farcheda first realm?"

"It was an example daughter, calm down."

"Farcheda is not fit to be the first realm." My voice rises of its own accord. "They are too quick of temper." Those are Jordyn's words, I recall. The king of wisdom fed me that information at the school visit.

"They have never been given a chance, Eselda. They are the one realm that has not held the seat. Besides, of the five of us, Mick's house is the most prepared for the future. Surely even you can see that."

My jaw falls open. "We are back to the idea of children, age, and marriage again."

"We are of royal blood. We are always going to be thinking about royal blood. There is never enough of it." The king punctuates each sentence with a slam of his fist on the table. The tea and plates jump.

"Apparently there is often too much of it, or should we ask Charlotte what she thinks?" I yell back. Our little show of mutual respect has completely faded. His anger is evident on his face and, I'm sure, matched by my own.

"That is enough." Father swipes his hand across the table and sends my teacup flying toward the fire. I cower back from him, shrinking into my chair. "You are not thinking clearly. I will leave you time to process this information. Perhaps you will be more insightful when you have more time." This time, it is my father who storms from the room.

I find myself sitting in the room alone with my thoughts. Tin has done nothing wrong. They have no basis to accuse him. This means that for the first time in my life my father is wrong about something important. It's like a perfect bubble wrapping around his image has finally popped. The problem is, I'm not at all sure I like the man I've found inside.

Chapter 16

Tutor is aware of how much trouble he could be in today. In the last few suns, he has missed probably a dozen appointments with the princess. Sure, it could not be helped, but the royals are not exactly known for being understanding.

People have been fired for less than this.

Gingerly, he pushes the door to the small study room open and lights the torch. He shakes his head, finding the room empty. It was foolish to think, after all his missed meetings, Eselda would still rise to sit in this room and await him. He will check the garden. It is her favorite spot.

In the garden, the wind is blowing and the sun is rising into the sky. Tutor glances up and allows himself a moment to wonder what else is out there in the world. He has recently had the pleasure of meeting a troop of scouts, who gave him a rather savage lesson in the reality beyond Fraun. They were filled with experience, only some of which Tutor himself was privy to. They certainly lead an interesting life.

Tutor snaps himself back to reality. The princess is nowhere to be found. Intending to leave a message for her with a hired hand, Tutor heads for the dining room. Typically, at this time of day, the help can be found cleaning the room in which the princess and the king have just finished consuming breakfast. He is surprised when he finds the object of his search, instead, occupying the room. "Princess Eselda?"

My attention is pulled from the wall. I squint at the man standing in the doorway. "Tutor?" The feelings churning inside me are mixed. I am happy he is alive and well, for I had feared worse when he failed to turn up for our sessions. That brings with it a brief wave of anger. Why has he missed sessions? None of that changes the fact that this is my oldest friend and he is here. I don't stop myself from running to him and pulling him into an embrace.

It takes a second before Tutor recovers from his surprise and returns the hug. The second his arms tighten around me I notice their strength. Where did a private tutor gain this strength? The hug is over quickly and I'm staring at the man who has been absent from his position in my home. "Where have you been?"

"I have been ill, Princess. I was not well enough to travel. This prevented me both from getting word to you and from tutoring you."

"Could you not send another to give me word? We worried."

"I have no others, Princess, save for some who are either too old or too young to travel Enchenda alone."

"I searched for you in town, but I know not where to look." I find myself embarrassed at this admission. Why do I know nothing of his family; has he never offered or have I never asked?

"You shouldn't have done that Princess. My home is of no consequence to you. Please forgive me for missing meetings. Can we continue today or have I been let go?"

I take a step back from Tutor, toward the chair in which I had been sitting when he arrived. I wonder if he notices that the chair has been moved to the lineage tree. I wonder if he questions my sanity. "I do not believe a new tutor could adequately prepare me for the role I am to undertake before it is too late. Please stay, but know that another missed meeting like those of late will not be tolerated." I return to the chair, turning my back to Tutor and fully refocusing on my newest obsession.

Tutor takes another chair from the table and drags it to the wall beside me, the noise of the scraping wood along the concrete giving away his progress. "What are we studying today, Princess?" he asks.

"Lineage."

"I had gathered such. What is it about lineage we are learning?" Tutor keeps his eyes on me instead of on the wall.

"Truth," I whisper.

"A noble quest, Majesty."

I turn to face him. "Do you know the truth of this wall, Tutor? Do you know of the people who have been blacked out?"

Tutor pulls his eyes from me to look at the wall. He has been in this room before; he has even seen the lineage tree before. Yet he gives it a careful look now, one you would give a puzzle or a challenge.

"I have heard rumors. Rumors that royal families in Fraun intentionally leave bloodlines off their trees. That there are women who are shunned, babies who are left off the wall, or lines that appear to stop when this is not the case at all. Of course, rumors are never specific. There is no incident in Enchenda that I am personally aware of."

I can see the moment when his eyes register the black ovals high up on the wall. He squints in frustration, trying to draw the memory out. "I know not who they are, but I am aware of the reason they have been blacked out."

"Because they were shunned?" I ask.

"Yes, that would be my assumption."

"But why? What would cause a family to shun a child?" I look back to the wall, finding the names above the black ovals. "Why would Elena and Charles shun one child and not the other?" I use my finger to gesture timidly toward the circle around Selena, evidently the sister of the shunned name. This name is circled and starred. "Whomever this shunned person was, their sister was Queen of Enchenda for a time."

Tutor sighs. "It is the belief of the ruling family that the shunned persons become nameless commoners. They are told not to have children. They are asked to live a life devoid of their past. They are asked to speak not of their beginnings. If anyone asks, they are to make something up or avoid the question altogether."

He shakes his head. "Princess, I know not of this tale. I do know people are shunned for many reasons. Royalty here does their best to be practical and humble. If someone here was shunned, causing their name to be removed, there must have been a good reason."

I sigh. He is hiding something. I can see it in the way his eyes cast downward when I ask a question. "I had hoped you were more adept at your history, friend." The final word rings with mockery.

"I fear I have let you down. I would tell you information I was privy to, Princess." He places a hand, lightly, on my arm. When I smile at him, he removes his hand quickly like one would remove it from hot coals.

"Perhaps you are better with more recent events." I rise from my chair, reach out my hand and smack it, hard, over Charlotte's covered name.

Tutor's eyes take in the area surrounding my hand. "What are you covering, Princess?" He leans toward the wall to better see. When I don't immediately move my hand, Tutor reaches out and pries my fingers off. I have drawn his interest. If I can get him interested, he will talk.

As Tutor takes stock of the wall surrounding the oval he mumbles to himself. "It appears to be connected to King Stefan, but no mother is linked. Typically, when one sees a blackened oval on a lineage chart you would expect to see an unwed mother blacked out as well, as is the case on the other spot. This, however, is a strange one. King Stefan must have had another child. But why would that child even be acknowledged on this wall?"

"Do you know what name this blemish hides?" I ask.

Tutor does not remove his eyes from the wall. "No, I honestly do not know."

"So it wasn't a scandal you had heard?" At this, Tutor turns to me. I try to flatten my hair and my disheveled dress under his gaze. Surely he notices I have been spending entirely too much time analyzing this wall.

"I have not heard anything that would make me think of this mark, no," Tutor says.

"I find that hard to believe. You have lived in this town most of your life. You have worked in this house much of your life. Yet you have heard nothing?"

"Eselda, how old do you think I am?" Tutor chuckles. "I have been alive only about five annuals longer than you. Whoever this is …" he places his finger on the spot "… would be a generation older than I. Their tale would have happened before I was born."

I sigh and sit back in my chair. Tutor follows my lead but remains sitting straight as I slump back. I pull my feet carefully underneath me and hide them beneath the folds of my dress. We sit in silence for a beat, I have resumed staring at the wall but I can feel Tutor's eyes on me, watching.

"Her name is Charlotte," I whisper.

"Whose name?"

I turn my eyes to him. "The shunned girl, the daughter of Stefan."

Tutor narrows his brown eyes at me, doubtful. "How would you know this?"

"I met her."

"When?"

"When you failed to show up I went looking for you. A woman told me her name was Charlotte and that she was my father's half-sister."

Without warning, Tutor wrenches his eyes from mine and stands. In his rush, he almost topples the chair. "What reason do you have to believe her? It's rather convenient that you wanted this information and she gave it." His arms gesture wildly as his voice raises.

His sudden anger is out of place with his previous calm. I'm not sure how to proceed. He's never been like this in front of me before. I try to speak in a low tone like one would calm an animal. "I actually talked to her first. I found the black spot afterward, confirming her story."

Tutor bristles and takes a step back from me, toward the door. "No. You have something wrong. Something is wrong." His voice is too loud. His face is darkening dangerously.

"My father confirmed it, Tutor. I don't understand why you think it is wrong." I gesture toward the empty chair. "Please, sit and explain it to me."

Tutor shakes his head. "No, I have to go. I have to research this." He turns on his heel and stomps to the door.

"Tutor, wait." From somewhere inside me I must have summoned some authority because he pauses, but does not turn. I rise and walk to him, placing my hand on his shoulder. I can feel an angry heat emanating from his slight frame. When Tutor was stomping his way to my door I noticed a slight limp. My curious nature craves an explanation for this, but my humble nature tells me it would be wrong to push Tutor now.

I am not this close to Tutor often. From here it is evident we are basically the same height. In fact, if I angle my chin skyward, I can whisper directly into his ear. "You are favoring your left leg. There is a story there, I'm sure. When you are ready to tell it, I am ready to hear it."

He nods once. When my hand leaves his shoulder, he doesn't hesitate to escape the room. Whatever that information meant to Tutor, it disturbed him. Quickly, I race out the door to follow behind him. I stay a distance behind, wanting to see where he goes. His feet carry him along the dirt path out of my home and into town. Where could he be headed?

Tutor seems startled when he reaches a doorstep. But then he slowly nods, like he knows this is where he needs to be. He disappears into a house. I hurry up to the area, turning the corner I was hiding around. Clearly, my friend and tutor knows more than he was letting on.

This is Charlotte's home.

Chapter 17

Eselda. Eselda. Eselda.

The name itself has become like a pulse for the king. The princess of Enchenda has occupied his thoughts so much lately his staff is beginning to notice his distracted nature. Well, either that or they are shying away from me because of the disappearance of the chambermaid. Likely it's the second, but it's more fun to blame Eselda for the distraction.

Eselda. Eselda. Eselda.

Shortly after he met her he realized what she could offer him. Beauty. An interesting blend of humility and pride. And the promise of the vote of the second realm. Best still her humble upbringing keeps her from the knowledge of her own attractiveness. If he can earn her favor, she will be sure to vote the way he wants her to vote on all issues.

There is a reason women usually don't do well in a position of power. They are too easy to bend. A few kind words, a little flirting, and they are eating out of the palm of some poor man's hand.

He chuckles to the empty room. A beautiful girl like Eselda might even be able to sway the votes of a few other men on the council. This could be grand.

Doubt creeps into his mind unchecked. *But I must be wary. It would not do to let my heart, or other parts below the waist, lead the march. Eselda can be allowed to occupy only my brain if I am to remain in control of the situation.*

Men are fickle as well, that much we know. Men who allow themselves to be led by the heart, or by the genitals, are often consumed. In those cases, the woman has the power, and that is simply unacceptable.

As he sits in front of the family tree in his home, he promises himself one thing. *Eselda may occupy my mind, even take time from my day as I think of her. If necessary, she may even have a time in my bed.*

But I promise all the ancestors before me, Eselda will never occupy my heart.

Chapter 18

Eselda,
I have been thinking about our conversation following the council meeting and I have more I would like to discuss with you. If you are available, I'd be willing to travel to Enchenda and see you. My messenger will stay until you have finished reading this notice, awaiting your word.
Logically,
Jordyn

I smile at the messenger who has brought me the letter. "Can you wait while I write a response?"

"Yes, Majesty." The man bows low.

I grab a parchment and quill from the table nearby, grateful I was in the study room when this man arrived. Quickly, I compose a response.

Jordyn,

No, that will never do. Jordyn, although barely my senior, is King of his realm. He may have used an informal greeting in his letter to me, but I cannot do the same. I hastily tear the top off the parchment and begin again.

King Jordyn,
I have thought about our conversation as well. It would please me a great deal if you would visit us in Enchenda. I am available any time your Majesty wishes to come this coming few suns. I look forward to your visit.
Humbly,
Princess Eselda

I read the notice over one time. Satisfied that the response is appropriate, I roll it and seal it with wax. I cross the room and hand the note over to the waiting man. "Thank you for waiting, sir. If you visit my kitchen on your way out I trust you will be well fed and watered for your journey home."

The man bows low again. "Thank you, Princess."

When he is gone I allow myself to think of the last conversation with Jordyn. So much has happened since the meeting that I plainly can't remember all the details.

Hopefully, this will not be a problem when he arrives in Enchenda. I'm sure I can count on Jordyn to explain the purpose of his visit in more detail. With any luck, he will also be able to shed a little light on the topics I have uncovered since.

I am oddly surprised to find how much I want to see Jordyn again. Rarely in my life do I have contact with young men. Although lately, it seems to be happening more and more frequently.

A girl could get used to this kind of attention.

Chapter 19

There is something satisfying about gardening. Without someone to tend the garden, the weeds would overgrow and consume the life force of the edible plants. Without proper soil and technique, one could not hope to grow such a vast variety of vegetables all in one location.

This is a skill I learned from my mother, who tended gardens in the home of my father before they were wed. According to Father, this is how they fell in love. Mother was tending the garden and he caught sight of her from his window. When he tells the tale it is love at first sight.

I have never felt that way, but the beauty of the story is that it makes things like that possible. That instant warmth you might feel when just seeing your destined lover for the first time. Will it be like lightning striking? My parents are that love story; two people entwined together in an embrace that no human can tear apart.

Of course, in reality, death broke them.

I turn my attention back to the soil in my hands, breaking up clumps as I run my fingers through it. The last of the peas have been harvested. I am turning over the soil in preparation for the next crop. The kitchen staff has saved me some garlic bulbs; I am excited to plant this delectable seasoning. I know what a flavor it can bring to the cooking, and it is an easy one to cultivate.

I dig my trowel into the soil, churning the deeper under-layer to the surface. When this rich layer, dark in color and cold to the touch, flips to the surface a small piece of earthworm comes with it. I dart my hand below the surface, in search of the rest of the creature. My hand closes around it. I dig my heels into the ground and stand. Using all of my strength I pull on the night crawler. I can feel it holding tight. Hopefully, the thing will not break further. I pull a little harder and the earth shifts around it. Before I can brace myself better for our change in momentum, the worm comes free. The sudden change sends me reeling backward onto my behind.

Laughter comes from behind me, turning my face instantly red.

"Well done, Daughter." Father pushes a bucket toward me. "Slide him in here, the kitchen will be happy to butcher him for our next stew."

I do as my king has ordered. Then I wipe my hands on the brown smock I have donned for gardening and sit back, resting my palms on the ground behind me. "Were you searching for me, father? Or perhaps just out for a walk?"

"I was searching for you. I have not had a moment to meet with you about your meeting with Tin since your return. The last time we talked you had other things on your mind. I did not want you to feel neglected, but I was a busy man. I'd like to know what you discussed with the king of strength."

Father is being coy. He has not been too busy for me; he has been in bed. The doctor has been to see him at least three times since we met about the family tree. It was a mistake to confront a dying man with something that would upset him. I will remain calm with him today. I take a breath of the garden air before smiling at him. "Honestly, Majesty, it was not much of a political conversation."

Thinking about the dinner, the way Tin's hand brushed mine, has my blush rising again. Then all at once, the memory washes over me like the cold water of the River Fraun. Tin's promise. Has he spoken with my father? Perhaps Tin has asked permission to court me. That could be what Father wishes to discuss. My heart gallops at the thought.

"You met with a king, one who was expecting me, and did not discuss politics?"

"Well he asked my opinion, but I didn't know what I should say."

"What is that supposed to mean? You are a daughter of Enchenda. Your opinion is whatever opinion befits Fraun." Father sounds tired and irritated. I fear I am failing at keeping him calm.

"We hadn't discussed which option was best for Fraun. I was unprepared."

Gregario sighs. "So the king asked your opinion. You offered none. Then you left the home?" he summarizes.

"Basically."

"Basically?" The echo is a command to explain, I can hear it in his voice.

I slam my eyes shut as though I was slapped. "We ate a delightful meal and talked of our realms." Perhaps Tin hasn't spoken to Father. What is he waiting for? Could he be losing interest? Was he merely pretending to be interested?

"What of the realms?" Father asks.

"He asked what people in Enchenda are like. He told me about strength competitions in Sarcheda. It was a nice meal, father. He treated me well." Wouldn't a father want to know his daughter was treated well by a possible suitor? Surely he notices Tin is my age and could be a suitor. Surely he does not begrudge Tin simply for his age like Kings Mick and Larecio seem to do.

"You are telling me you discussed nothing of consequence?"

"Have you spoken to King Tin, Majesty?" The question flies out of my mouth, an escaped butterfly I cannot hope to catch.

"No. Should I be expecting communications from him?" he asks, his guard clearly up.

"I know not, father. I merely wondered why you seemed to doubt my recitation of events." There is my answer. Tin has yet to speak with Father. Perhaps he overstated his feelings? Good, I don't need the hassle anyway.

"Eselda have you given any thought to betrothal?"

Wait, what? *Keep calm. Keep calm. Keep calm.* People in Fraun continue to ask about my love life. Could this be more normal questioning or was I wrong to assume father told the truth about not speaking with Tin? "No. Why do you ask?"

"Daughter, you have grown into a beautiful woman of eligible age. You are awaiting a throne. You would be a fool to think no Fraunians will be interested in you. I merely want to know if there is one who has already expressed an interest or one who you perhaps fancy."

"I have no such thoughts, father. I will fall in love, as you did, and marry one who is fit to help me rule Enchenda. Fear not." Anger builds in me. Why does no one trust me to do what is right for Fraun? It's as though everyone is waiting for me to bring our entire history crashing down. As though by merely not taking a spouse I am capable of unweaving everything that has come before me.

"Tell me what happens if you take a commoner for your beau, daughter."

"The commoner becomes Enchenda royalty. He would attend council meetings with me, as he is the king. I would still attend, as I am of royal blood. Is that what information you seek, Majesty?" The title drips with sarcasm. I am a princess, but I am also your daughter. Stop talking about my love life as policy.

"It is. What happens if you marry a prince?"

I know this answer, but what prince does he speak of? Marchenda has Carsen, although I cannot recall how many annuals he is. Farcheda has Hector. No, that's not right. Hector is married. Although, if memory serves, Hector does have a son called Patt. Technically Patt would be a prince, although one too young for me. "If I marry Carsen …" I pause to allow my father to point out another prince. He does no such thing, forcing me to continue the answer, "… then he would become King of Enchenda. He would lose all claims and rights to the realm of Marchenda and sit on the council in my stead. Although I have royal blood, his royal blood would be sufficient."

Gregario nods his agreement. "Tell me, daughter, what happens if you were to take a husband who is already a seated king?"

I small flame of hope ignites. A smile sneaks to my lips, which I cover by wiping my brow, glistening from the heat of the forgotten gardening. He could be speaking of Tin. "Our realms would unite and I would again lose my seat on the council in favor of my royal blood husband."

"I see you have considered all the options, daughter. But the repercussions are stated like one answering their tutor. You speak not like a queen who is considering her realm. Think, daughter, what happens to your people if you marry the king of strength?" Father's voice is a knife pointed at me.

I pull back from him, frightened of his sudden anger. He knows something. Otherwise, why would that example be thrown out with such ease? "Father, you are far ahead of my heart on this matter," I speak with a calm I do not feel. My own heart has galloped away like a race roach. I hope to calm my father. Certainly, this anger is not good for his condition.

"Perhaps that, daughter, is the problem," he says. "Leave this garden. Return not to this haven you have created until you have thought about what your people need of you. My time draws to a close and you must prepare to be the queen Enchenda needs. It's time to stop being so selfish, daughter, and embrace the humble nature you're able to speak of with practice."

I could not have been more insulted if my father had pierced my heart with the trowel. Selfish? The future queen of humility, selfish? I clamor to my feet, tears stinging my throat. I will not cry in front of the king. "I fear you simply do not remember what it was like to be young, father." I deliver the line like a slap and run for the house before he can see me cry.

Inside, doubt begins to creep in. What if he is right? That parting line was bold. It was probably stupid. Was it selfish? Am I selfish? I sink to the floor behind my closed bedroom door. How can a selfish princess even hope to become the queen of humility?

Chapter 20

In the garden, Gregario whispers a response to his angry daughter. It is not for her ears, but Gregario's heart. "I fear you have no idea what is coming your way. Being young can't help you in your pending heartache."

Gregario sighs as the memories of his innocent youth flood his brain. *Dancing women, beautiful women, I certainly had my pick. I remember my tutor, Den, teaching me the ways of Enchenda. How angry Den was when I dared to take out the woman he had his eye on.*

How angry I was when they had to wed.

It was this very garden I ran to that night when my father told me why the couple's wedding had been rushed. This is the garden where I crashed into the woman who would later be my wife.

What would have been different in my life had I married the other woman?

It's silly to think about it now. Stefan would never have allowed the other marriage to happen. He chuckles. *The old man would've swallowed nails if I had even asked for the other hand.*

Ancient history. It does no good to dwell on it. Rubina was a beautiful woman and a remarkable queen for Enchenda. The other woman simply was not to be. *I learned to love Rubina. When it comes time, Eselda will learn to love whomever it is best for her to be with.*

The old king rises, feeling every day of his life in the old bones. His daughter will need to wed, that much is certain.

Perhaps it is time for him to choose a spouse for her.

Chapter 21

I flop onto the bed in my room, stomach down, and bury my face in the puff of pillow. Without question, this has been the longest, most confusing three moon cycles of my life. The school visit was the last time I was anything resembling normal.

Wait, that's not right. Jordyn arrived in Enchenda unannounced for the school visit. That cannot be classified as perfectly normal, now can it?

I roll over letting my hair flare out around me on the pillow. A sigh escapes my lips. Despite my honest attempt at keeping my cool yesterday, my father lost patience with me yet again. I know my father is seeing the doctor at this moment, I saw the man arrive. I had hoped to take my mind off my father's health by meeting with Tutor, but he failed to show up again.

That's another problem altogether; what to do about Tutor.?The last time we spoke I made it clear that another missed meeting would not go unnoticed. But how much of the fault for this one lies with me? In keeping with my apparent knack for angering people, Tutor's last meeting was a total disaster.

I play the conversation again looking for the threat that worked him up. Tutor's first outburst had occurred at the mention of me wandering the town. Could this simply be a case of another man in my life feeling like I cannot handle myself? Could it be that Tutor is worried I will discover something about him in town? Could he be protecting some secret of my father's?

Tutor's anger had intensified at the mention of Charlotte's name. So that eliminates the possibility he was worried merely about my safety. Surely he knows an old woman would pose no threat? But could she have something to do with Tutor himself?

Obviously, Charlotte holds secrets of my father's in her weathered hands. Tutor obviously knew I had unraveled that secret. Is it possible this old woman is hiding something else? She knows of the age markers. Perhaps Tutor has been a tutor to more than just me. Perhaps Father's "taking care" of Charlotte includes providing her with a solid education. Is that what Tutor is hiding? It certainly fits.

I try to recall the rest of our conversation, turning the information as I turn soil looking for rich bits to bring nutrients. Tutor's body language was stiff throughout the conversation. In retrospect that was probably an indication of whatever malady he was hiding. I can easily call up a picture of his limp in my mind and replay it. As he was storming toward the door, his back muscles had first drawn my attention. Where did a private tutor work up muscles of that caliber? My eyes had then been drawn down his backside and that was when I noticed the limp. Tutor had been keeping his weight unevenly on his right leg, accommodating the left.

Standing that close to him, pointing out his limp, I noticed a pleasant smell. Something light, like sunshine. Somehow knowing his true age has me seeing him differently. I guess since he has always been in a position of authority over me, I had assumed he was much older. It shocks me to learn he is so young. Yet, as I picture him in my head now, I'm further surprised that I missed the signs.

The slight muscular build, the thick light hair, the youthful energy radiating from him. I close my eyes and try to bring the smell back to my senses. Sunshine and hard work. My entire body warms as I think of the way he trembled beneath my hand when my breath graced his ear.

Then he left here and went to see Charlotte. I'm standing before

I've fully formed the thought. Charlotte will give me the answers Tutor hides. The riding cloak is snuggly fit to my shoulders before doubt can settle there. Everyone in my life is hiding things, Charlotte is revealing. She will be able to tell me something. I will not leave until she does.

Chapter 22

Outside my home, the air is chillier than it has been. The days are shortening, meaning the cold weather is drawing closer. The sun is still shining and no clouds mar the sky, but the people of Enchenda are piling extra wood and preparing fabric for layers. Soon the cold will come, and it does not do well to be caught unprepared.

I walk with a new determination, my bare feet striking the dirt in a rapid rhythm. I march past the house where I taught the men about the lift and notice the contraption being utilized on a nearby cart. Further up the road, a young woman is struggling with something in a yard to the right. My training takes over and I feel my body slow, despite my desire to get to Charlotte quickly. The woman is yanking something in a small garden. Even as I try to talk myself out of helping, I feel my feet approaching the woman. "Is there something I can be of assistance with?"

The woman turns, surprise registering on her face as she recognizes me as her princess. Already hovering low to the ground, bent over something, the woman tries to bend lower in a bow. "Princess Eselda, I am not needing your help Majesty, but thank you."

"Would you take the help of a neighbor were it her offering?" I ask, squatting beside the woman.

"Perhaps," the woman answers hesitantly.

From this angle, I can now see the woman is pulling on the root of a weed that has taken residence in her garden. She must have pulled on the head of the plant at first, dislodging it. This makes the task of removing the root much more difficult. I crack my knuckles. "Well, you are in luck then, neighbor. I live just up the road and I came to help." I lean in and grasp the root below the woman's hands. "We shall pull on three, together. Straight up toward the heavens, lady. Ready?" I feel the woman's grip tighten.

"One …" I plant my feet securely, "… two …" I lock my elbows, "… three!" We both pull with every bit of strength we have. The weed does not release all in one movement. Instead, it shifts slowly. I give hearty tugs, grunting under the pressure.

Finally, the weed is separated from the ground. I take deep breaths to restore my lung capacity. Beside me, I hear the woman doing the same. She recovers first. "Thank you, Majesty."

"Happy to help. Good luck with your garden, maiden."

Having detoured, I now feel as though I must travel even faster. I am moving so swiftly, holding my rusty colored skirt in my hands, that I nearly run into a child as I round the corner into the town square. "Oh, excuse me," I call. The child, undeterred, continues to run at full speed up the road. I force myself to slow down and take in the entire square with my eyes.

There are fewer people out this afternoon than the last time I was here. A shopkeeper is brushing the dirt from his stoop. A few women are walking, one holding the hand of a smaller child. Someone is picking strawberries from the bush near the edge of the square, across from my chosen path of entrance. Two small boys, maybe the same ones I saw on my last visit, toss a cherry pit back and forth. The boys are taking one step back after each toss, testing how far away you can be from another person before you drop that which they are asking you to save. As I resume walking, at a slightly slower pace, my eyes fall back to the strawberry picker. He is now standing and I recognize him immediately. My desire to see Charlotte fades as I change course and head right for him.

"Jordyn!"

"Good afternoon Eselda. I trust this is a good time for my visit." He smiles, the gesture reaching his blue eyes.

In the short time since I have seen the king, I had forgotten how tall he really is. The top of my head could fit snuggly inside the king's armpit. He is wearing brown traveling pants and a white shirt, which is open slightly at the neck. He is wearing some kind of chain there, but I cannot clearly see what it is. "How did you get here?" I see no sign of a traveling animal with him.

"Ladybug, actually. I was walking through Renchenda and a nice ladybug offered me a ride to Enchenda in exchange for food when I arrived." He holds up an aphid he must have found among the bushes. "I was on my way back to the edge of town to pay the insect. Care to join me?" Jordyn hoists the bug into his right arm and offers me his left elbow.

"Gladly." I slip my arm through the offered limb and allow myself to be led around the strawberry patch outside of the Enchenda town square. A few steps past the opening the bright red of the ladybug comes into view. A few steps farther and it is clear the creature sees us as well.

"I thought you had turned your back on our deal, King of Renchenda." Unlike the roaches I have heard many times, the ladybug's voice is low-pitched and deadly. It makes me shudder.

"I would never do that. I am, after all, the king of wisdom." Jordyn bends low, placing the restitution on the ground in front of the ladybug. "What would be the wisdom in causing problems with another species?"

"It would not have been wise, King. Thank you for the food." The ladybug grasps the smaller species, turns, and hustles off out of sight.

"What a beautiful breed," I say.

Jordyn stands, wiping his hands on his pants. He turns his attention to me, looking at me properly from my messy strands of hair piled on my head past my rather orange dress and down to my naked and dirty feet. I feel insecure under his gaze, fidgeting as he watches.

"Have you been working hard this morning, Princess?" he asks. "You have a shine about you."

I blush deeply and cast my eyes on the ground. "I was walking rather quickly, I suppose."

"For what purpose? Where were you headed?"

I look back up at the king, but the sun falls into my eyes and I have to squint. "Into town. I was in search of my tutor. He failed to show up for our lesson."

"So you were worried about him?" Jordyn's face scrunches up under the confusion.

"It's no matter. I had no other business this morning, I thought I would seek him out and perhaps get some answers." I look around the little clearing we are standing in. Around us grass grows tall, keeping people out. This area is flattened, and there is a piece of wood that must have been dragged here off to the side. I gesture toward it. "We should sit. You have at least one mark on me, I have to stare up at the sun when we speak."

Jordyn laughs. "I had noticed my neck tilts at an awkward angle to inspect you as well. Let us sit."

I stand beside the wood to let the king sit first. When he does so he slumps slightly, I wonder if this is to give off a relaxed air or a further attempt to get closer to my height. He turns his upper body toward the right, leaning back on the stalk of a plant growing behind the wood. I sit beside him and allow my posture to relax as well.

"Last time we spoke, Eselda, I mentioned betrothal to you. I wonder if you've learned anything new on that topic or had any further insights." Jordyn's position continues to appear relaxed, but his eyes flash with a curiosity that interests me. Are all in his realm this interested in conversation?

"Everyone has been speaking of my love life lately. It seems to be everyone's favorite topic of conversation."

"Oh?" Jordyn questions, "Who else is asking?"

"My father, my tutor, you, and King Tin." I had not made up my mind to mention the meeting with Tin, but it slips from between my lips.

"Interesting. My apologies for bringing it up again. We can talk about something else if you would like." Jordyn turns his head and looks at the ground, the gesture makes it clear he is uncomfortable.

His offer is moving. Many others in this position would try to convince me that this conversation is important and worth having. Jordyn has faith in my decision. For this reason alone, I will talk to him openly about it. "I have done nothing but think on this topic, honestly," I whisper.

Jordyn's blue eyes return to my face. "Go on." Somehow it does not come out as the command from a king, but the reassurance of a friend. This is a safe place to talk.

"I know what happens to Fraun and Enchenda depending on whom I choose to marry. But what of love? Our ancestors filled our heads with the idea that we will one day be slaves to an emotion so great we would literally die for it. I have never felt such a pull toward another. I often think I feel something, but how will I know when I feel that?" The words gush from me, pulled toward the tide of a logical listener who will not judge. "King Tin professes to feel something as well. He desires to ask permission to court me." Although he certainly has not rushed to make good on that, I remember. "At least that's what he claimed. He has yet to speak with Father."

"When did he claim this?" Jordyn asks.

"I had dinner in Sarcheda not long ago, maybe seven suns. Toward the end of dinner, he asked if I were being courted, and said he would like to do just that." I drop my eyes from Jordyn's, embarrassed to be having such a conversation with him. I feel the blush, fast becoming a characteristic of my face, creep into my cheeks.

"What was your opinion of King Tin?"

"I'm not sure."

"Before he mentioned courting you, what had you felt about the evening?"

I think back. "I found him interesting. I felt warm when we were talking, I wanted him to continue talking. What does all that mean?" I dare myself to return my eyes to Jordyn's face. He is looking off to the right, eyes narrowed. Perhaps he is thinking.

"I do not know what that means. I know what hate feels like, it is the age marker I fight against each day."

I watch as Jordyn tenses under the chosen topic. I am afraid to move. Am I about to hear a firsthand account of what I will face when I am under the malicious age marker?

"Hate boils in your heart, quickens your breathing, and drives your adrenaline to spike. Hate fuels your body to act on every indiscretion. To think on every mistake. You feel hate in varying degrees for different people. One thing is constant, hate dominates your mind if you let it."

I could not hope to comment even if I wanted to. I am frozen in fear, my eyes locked on the king, new appreciation for what he is battling coursing through my veins. Then he turns his head, just a little, and those sharp blue eyes come into my vision again.

"Hate I understand, but of its counter, I know not."

He turns away again. I silently pray for his voice to continue, for his eyes to find mine again. Please, Jordyn, you can trust me. When I cannot wait any longer, I speak. My voice is quiet and soothing. "Perhaps love is as strong as its antagonist. Love then could warm your heart." I reach out and touch the king's chest, feeling the beat of his heart beneath his ribs. "Love could quicken your breathing and spike your adrenaline as well. Where hate may feel harsh when this happens, perhaps love will feel soft and free."

The king still keeps his gaze steady, but I feel his heartbeat quicken. He is listening. I slide my body closer to Jordyn and continue in an even softer tone. "Love will fill our hearts to act on every impulse to be with the one we love, perhaps to ignore their every mistake and flaw." My speech is rewarded. Jordyn lifts his chin and meets my gaze. Warmth spreads out over my entire body.

"Perhaps, like its reverse, love is also felt to varying degrees." I move my hand to the center of his ribcage, flattening my palm. "I feel it right here as I talk to you, compelling me to move closer to you and heal your pain. It stands to reason that love would devour you as well if you let it."

"The power of hate scares me, Eselda. What if love has the same power?"

"I am sure it does. But how can I fear something with such promise?"

Jordyn dips his head toward me until our noses are practically touching. He closes his eyes and sighs. "I feel it now. Thank you for helping me find it. This may be just what I need to fight the hate inside me."

Jordyn leans closer yet and his lips find mine. The short kiss is enough to spark bursts of flame all over my body. I have never known such a feeling.

When Jordyn sits back in his relaxed position, I have to stop myself from pulling him back toward me. Instead, I take a deep breath and fight with my body to force it back into my original position as well. "You're welcome. Just remind me of this when I am twenty annuals and struggling with my inner monster." I try to force my voice to be light, but the kiss has left my head somewhere in the clouds. It sounds forced.

Jordyn laughs. "I will do just that. I must say, Eselda, the wisdom and logic you displayed there would make a citizen of Renchenda proud."

"Truly?" Praise from their king? Am I worthy of that?

"Of course. Applying the principles of hate to love is remarkably wise. I'm surprised I did not think of it myself."

"Don't feel too bad. Had you not been consumed by your age mark, I am confident you would have discovered it as well."

"There is that humility you are so fond of here. You cannot take the praise without returning it." Jordyn chuckles. "It is a beautiful trait. I shall try to adopt it as well if we are to be friends."

"Is that what we are to be?" I ask. Instead of blushing and looking away, I keep my eyes fixed on Jordyn. He is still smiling, but somehow it is uncomfortable. Perhaps even a little sad.

"I fear it is all we can be, Eselda. What would happen to our realms if we were to be anything more?"

He speaks the truth, I know. After that moment we just shared, I do not want to chase him away by asking for too much. Friends I can do. "I want to be your friend, Jordyn. We will be the best of friends."

Jordyn said you can feel hate in varying degrees for various people. That must be true for love as well. Therefore, I must not feel guilty for having feelings for other people. I can even help this whole betrothal thing along by acknowledging my feelings as they come. I feel some love for Jordyn, but didn't I also feel a little for Tin? Maybe even for Tutor?

"I am glad you feel that way. I want to be your friend as well," Jordyn says. Again when he smiles I see sadness. Then again perhaps I am only hoping there is a small grain of sadness for the love that cannot be allowed to bloom.

"Now, friend, shall we head to my father's home and dine at his table? We can talk more about Fraun after dinner?" I ask.

"Lead the way, Eselda."

Chapter 23

My heart flutters so fast I fear it will fly right out of my chest. Jordyn and I are walking back toward my home, hands clasped between us, talking about Enchenda. He is so eager to learn everything about my realm. "That is my father's home, ahead," I point out.

"It's only slightly larger than the homes of the people nearby. Your family did well in keeping themselves humble to the people they serve."

"It is only larger because of the people who live in it. Aside from my father and myself, there is a lady in waiting, a cleaning employee, and a few who care for the roaches. They can all live in the home if they like. We also have a room alongside the kitchen where a warm bed, water, and meals can be provided for anyone in Enchenda in need of a place to stay. It's been used from time to time but is empty at the moment."

"People do not take advantage of that?" Jordyn asks.

"I'm not sure why they would. If you can find someplace else to sleep you would leave that room for someone who cannot. It's quite a simple concept."

"Interesting."

I pull the door to my home open. "I should head to my room and freshen up."

"Could you point me toward the room we were speaking of? I'd like to see it."

I point through the doorway across from us. "The dining room is through there. The kitchen door is on the right wall. The spare room is to the left once you are inside the kitchen." I think through the dress I would like to put on, what I wish I could do to my hair. I will keep things simple, it won't take me long, "On second thought, I can go with you. I should tell the staff you are here anyway."

"No, I can handle it. Trust me, after the Castle Fraun this little house should be the perfect size to navigate." Jordyn enters through the dining room doorway, ducking slightly to enter, and disappears from view.

Who am I to argue with a king? I drop my hair from its tie and run my fingers through it to untangle the curls as I walk. I brush my hands over the skirt, dislodging stray dirt. When I reach my room I grab a black overskirt and tie it around my waist. A quick turn in the reflecting wall satisfies me. Next, I use a small bowl of clean water nearby to wash my face and other exposed skin. There. Fresh enough for dinner with two seated kings, assuming the one I'm related to is well enough to join us for dinner.

Back in the dining room, I find Father and Jordyn have already been seated. "Eselda, so glad you could join us," Father greets. There are plates piled with salad before both kings and another at the empty place in front of the fire. I take my seat. "King Jordyn, it is an honor to have you at our table. To what do we owe the pleasure?" Father asks. When he reaches for his fork, I do the same. I realize how hungry I am and have to force myself to chew slowly and be presentable.

"I have been thinking about the future of Fraun. Your daughter holds the key to our kingdom remaining at five realms, I was interested in speaking to her of this," Jordyn explains between bites.

The key to the kingdom? That seems a little overzealous.

"What opinion have you on these issues?" Gregario asks.

"The same opinion as you, I am sure. The princess must have an heir, in case of accident or death —"

"Are you lecturing me on marriage and babies as well? Where are your heirs, King of wisdom?" I snap. The two kings turn their attention to me, falling silent for a beat.

"Do you approach twenty annuals, Princess?" Jordyn asks, quietly.

"No, I approach the end of my patience with people trying to plan my life." I stand up quickly, almost toppling the little chair. "If you two wish to discuss what I should or should not do, you can do so without me. Good evening." I leave the room quickly but stop just outside the door. I hope one of them will call me back into the room or perhaps follow me out.

"You were saying?" Gregario prompts.

"Oh, yes. I was saying Eselda needs an heir. I fear King Tin will win her heart, leaving us with only four realms. Four realms could vote in a tie. Four realms could change our way of life. It is not wise to have an even number of realms, sir. I merely came to see if my fears were becoming reality."

"King Tin is not the only one who could cause this, I feel as though I need to remind you of that."

"True. However, regardless of my feelings on the subject, I am wise enough to know this would be bad for Fraun. You do not need to fear my intentions, good King. I merely wish to help in any way that I can," Jordyn says.

"You strike me as a good and honest king, Jordyn."

"Thank you, Majesty."

"Have you ever met with King Mick on your own?" Gregario asks.

"I have not. Have you?"

"I have. He doubts the good of King Tin. How feels Renchenda on this topic? You are as much their neighbors as we are, perhaps you have seen or heard things. Perhaps you have even met with King Tin on your own."

"I believe Tin struggles with his age marker more than I. He allows himself to fall victim to it at times. However, I must say I have no reason or evidence to believe Tin is guilty of anything resembling rule-breaking for Fraun. Like yourself, Tin is a king in Fraun. I put my trust in that title," Jordyn answers.

It is quiet for a bit. I assume both kings are enjoying the salad I abandoned. I am tempted to return to the table and finish my meal. I could also continue what I started to do and head to my room. I should do anything but stand here in the hallway eavesdropping on yet another conversation between two seated kings of Fraun.

"On the issue with my daughter, have you spent time talking with her? I find myself in a difficult position. She often will not speak with me, losing her temper as you just witnessed. I do not wish to choose a spouse for her, but I fear for Fraun I may have to if she cannot choose one herself."

What? My father could not choose a spouse for me. That cannot possibly be what is best for Fraun. What is he thinking?

"Eselda and I are friends. I wish not to break any confidences she may have trusted me with. However, I feel as though it would be acceptable to tell you King Tin expressed a desire to court your daughter. For reasons we have previously discussed, this should not be allowed. I hope you will think about that before he approaches you for permission."

"He will not be given my permission, Jordyn," father answers.

"Thank you."

"Again, I must reiterate that you will not be given that permission either, good sir."

"And again I must remind you that I will not be asking for it, good sir."

I hear the change in the voices, they are deeper and more edged. Well good. Here they sit planning my entire life and discussing who I can and cannot marry. It's revolting. They should be ashamed.

"You demonstrate impressive control of your age marker. Are you approaching twenty-five annuals?" my father asks.

"I am barely twenty, actually. I believe my will to fight it is simply stronger than most."

"You do not wish to let your darker side take hold? I remember my own years fighting the beast within. I picked fights with everyone. The desire to give into the darkness was so strong some days that I would need to get in fights just to sleep."

"Never," Jordyn answers.

"I am impressed. You have earned my trust; I will give you this. Mick is thinking war."

In the hallway, the word makes my anger and likely my color leave. War? We cannot abide by that.

"I had feared as much. What does he want from the council,

assuming he wants something to avoid war?"

"A renumbering."

"In favor of his realm?"

"Yes. Your brain has reached that quickly. You are truly wise."

"Obviously. Gregario, a renumbering cannot happen. Farcheda is known for being too quick, which would be highly unwise. I would not vote in favor of that," Jordyn says.

"He knows he will not have your vote. He needs another to vote with us."

"You favor a renumbering?" Jordyn asks.

"I am not so sure anymore."

I hear the chair scrape along the floor, indicating someone is rising. I turn to head down the hall. My feet move slowly like the new information I've gleaned is weighing me down physically.

"I enjoyed this meal and the chance to speak with you freely Gregario. I believe it would be wise for me to speak with Eselda again before I leave. Therefore, please excuse me," Jordyn says.

That is the last I hear before I'm down the hall. I do not stop until I'm lying on my bed behind a closed door. I am braced for a knock, for my name to be called, something. It takes a remarkably long time. My body relaxes and my breathing slows. I wait.

Finally, I hear the faint knock at my door and the voice of Eee calling out my name. "What do you need, Eee?" I ask, my voice muffled by the pillow on the bed.

"King Jordyn is searching for you, Princess," the roach calls.

I sit up and run my fingers through my hair again. Then I cross the room and fling the door open. "Where is …" but there is no need to finish the question. The tall king is standing in the doorway, his blue eyes shining directly into my face. "Thank you, Eee."

"Eselda, can we talk?" Jordyn asks.

"Oh, you would like to talk to me now?" I step to the side and wave him into the room. I pull a chair out from under a table near the reflecting wall for Jordyn before dropping myself onto my bed.

"I am sorry if I offended you at dinner," Jordyn states. He sits in the offered chair.

"I am tired of everyone pushing me."

"I noticed that." He smiles. "But if your father dies and you have not wed, I fear many men will want to marry you for the title alone."

"You fear I will not be happy with these men?"

"I fear it will be bad for Fraun. Honestly, I hadn't considered your happiness on the matter. I apologize for that as well."

"What do you propose I do then, Jordyn?" I throw my hands up. "All of you want to tell me what is wrong and what I cannot do. Would you please offer some advice on what I should or can do?"

"Meet with Carsen, find a nice boy from Enchenda, or meet unwed men from the family trees still holding branches like that. You may find you have feelings for these men, but how can you learn that if you will not meet with them?"

"Why does this all fall to me?"

"You are a princess in a realm where there is no one else and your king is ill."

"There is no one besides you in your realm," I point out. "Don't people pressure you the same way?"

"Yes." He makes no further attempt to explain. Offers no advice on how to deal with it or what to do about it. He doesn't explain why he can't take his own advice to meet someone nice.

"I want you to be wrong, but I feel I cannot say you are until I have tried meeting with these people. I suppose this is the price of being royal."

"It is. The people of Fraun deserve the best from us. They deserve a future. We must do our level best to prepare Fraun for that."

"You make a good point."

"Of course I do, that is my way," Jordyn says.

I laugh at the true statement. It feels good to laugh with him.

"I am still your friend, Eselda. I want what is best for you, but it must also be wise for Fraun." Jordyn rises. "I have a long journey ahead of me. Can I trust we will remain in touch?"

I stand up in front of him. "We will keep in touch." I offer the king my hand. He shakes it, but I pull him into a hug instead. He smells of rainwater and fresh air. "Travel well, Jordyn."

"Thank you. See you soon."

The door clicks softly behind Jordyn and I flop back onto my bed. Today I learned what power love and hate can have. I have learned you can catalog your feelings of love, felt to different degrees, and perhaps I can use this to find a prince suitable for my kingdom. I have also heard a word I never wanted to hear. Can war truly be on the mind of King Mick? Is that ever best for a kingdom?

Honestly, I cannot imagine a situation where war would be an option I would condone.

Chapter 24

I woke up this morning with the desire to find Charlotte burning in my soul again. I need to ask her about Tutor. I cannot be stalled again. I dressed quickly and hurried to the town square. But when I arrived at the door, there was no answer. I dropped myself onto the stoop in front of her home to watch the morning unfold.

The sun is just now beginning to rise, sparkling off the drops of dew on the grass square. A group of hunters traipses out of one house, long swords tied to their backs. Men with cutting implements take to the grass, laying on their bellies to be sure and cut it low enough. Mostly, it is quiet and peaceful. I could easily let myself slide back into sleep, but I fight the pull of my eyelids.

"Princess Eselda?" a small voice questions.

I turn my head to find a young girl, blonde and small. She is probably approaching ten annuals, if not already there. Her brown eyes are flecked with green and she wears the most enchanting little smirk, one not yet marred by the realities of life. She is also standing on the doorstep of

Charlotte's home. "Good morning young maiden. I am actually waiting here to speak with Charlotte. Do you know the woman?"

"Charlotte is my mother," the girl answers.

My mouth drops open. "C-C-Can I speak with her?" I ask, my voice rising in pitch.

The girl spins on her heel and enters the now open front door, calling for Mother as she jogs through the little house. Beyond the girl I can see Charlotte standing in the kitchen, hunched over near the stove. She issues a small, tired laugh. It is followed by a cough that wracks her small frame. When her coughing ceases she stands tall. "I knew you'd be back, Princess. Please come in."

The young girl steps out of the way to allow me entrance. The fire has just been lit, it is sparking wildly but not yet giving off much warmth. Charlotte is holding a teapot, waiting for the flames to get themselves under control before lowering the metal into them. She is dressed in a nightgown, the bare material brushing her ankles. Her long grey hair is to her waist and slightly curled, as though the braids I last saw in her hair have caused the crimps to remain permanently. Her eyes looked clouded, but I cannot tell if it is worry, fear, or illness that causes this today.

"Have a seat, I'm just preparing tea. We can chat."

I hear the door click closed behind us, leaving us alone in the house. "I met your daughter," I challenge.

"Ah, I feared that may come up. Silly girl was told to say I was her Aunt if anyone asked. Still, I suppose that would've made you ask questions as well." Charlotte shakes her head, drops the tea kettle into the flames, and sits at the table across from me. "Let's have it then, say what you must." She reaches up and parts her hair into two long skinny halves on either side of her face.

"I am a royal member of the House of Enchenda, madam. You were shunned and told to bear no children." I try to make my voice sound authoritative and stern. Truthfully, inside my nerves are shaking and frayed.

"That much I know child, what plans have you for dealing with us?" Charlotte begins to braid one segment of hair. Her fingers work efficiently.

"I do not know. I will have to speak with the king," I answer. What other choice do I have in the matter?

"Well, then I have no fears. Gregario knows of the child."

"I would love nothing more than to tell you that cannot be true. I fear with the last tale you told me checking out …" I taper off, sure my meaning is cutting through. My father has been keeping much from me, no wonder he is worried I cannot handle Enchenda. Look how easily he spilled the talk about his own battle with royal blood to Jordyn. "That young child has royal blood?"

"Shhh." Charlotte places a finger to her lips. "She doesn't know that. Keep your voice down." She removes her finger and leans closer to me, her hands resting on the table between us. The braid she just finished begins to slowly unravel at the ends. "No one around here knows this family is anything other than ordinary, including my daughter. You'll keep that to yourself, or your father may change his mind about our situation."

I hesitantly nod. Charlotte relaxes back in her chair and finishes the braid, affixing it with a length of string from the table. The braid is sloppier than the last one I saw. Perhaps the girl braided the last. "Tell me the story of the girl," I say.

"Sawchett is her name. If I tell you the story, can we continue to have our anonymity once you are queen?"

My father has been guarding this secret for years, evidently. No further harm can come from this promise at this time. I nod. "If that is your wish, yes. I will make our tea this time, you tell the story."

"Very well."

I have remarkable recall. I find the silver mugs exactly where they were last time. I busy myself grinding some leaves I pull through the open window.

"I grew up not knowing I was any different than anyone else around here," Charlotte says. "I attended the school like everyone else, beginning at five. I don't know how it is for you, being royalty and all, but around here girls start looking for a mate around thirteen annuals. Just about the time a maiden turn fifteen and has hit all her age markers, she's usually found her spouse and they can wed. It keeps our population moving if you know what I mean."

I pour water over the leaves, not wishing to discuss the implications of that statement with an old woman. Yes, I know what you mean. Move on.

"One day I met someone in town, I was just shy of fifteen annuals myself. We spent the day together, talking about nothing. We were friends. I told myself we could be nothing more."

My sadness returns as I think of Jordyn. But Jordyn is a seated king, his reason for us to be nothing more is that it would be bad for Fraun and leave us with only four realms once my father passed. It stands to reason that there are other reasons in the world, but I can't think of any others. "Why could you only be friends, Charlotte?"

"Plainly, his job would make things difficult. Let's leave it at that. He is not the girl's father. I bring him up only because he introduced me to the father. Shall I continue?" Charlotte asks.

I nod.

"Anyway my friend and I saw each other often, we would stroll the realm and talk about all things. He was a great companion. One day, on such a walk, we came across his father. His father was known to be a strict man and I had seen him on a few occasions. He recognized me and greeted me warmly. I fear he spoke to his son about me, however. After that, the boy was different." Charlotte's eyes look sadly to the right.

Possibly because I was already thinking of him, the movement of her eyes reminds me again of Jordyn. He always looks to the right when he is deep in thought. The sadness ebbs a little when I picture him doing that. I bring a mug of tea to Charlotte and take a sip of one myself.

"When I turned fifteen annuals the boy had me over to dinner. I foolishly thought he was going to announce that he'd figured something out, we could be wed. Instead, he and his father introduced me to another man. This man, Den, worked inside the royal home. Just as now, that was a noble profession. He was a good solid man with a good solid work ethic. It was clear Den had the blessings of my friend and his father to court me."

"Why would he need their permission and not that of your own mother and father?"

Charlotte throws me a dangerous glare for the interruption. "He didn't, of course. Not technically. But this was a family I was obviously close with, as I was having dinner in their home. I think it was the honor of the thing. For me it was a way to make it obvious; I could not have the son but I could have Den."

"Weren't you sad?" I know I was. I pretend not to care that Jordyn can so easily dismiss me as a friend and ignore those feelings. It hurt to hear him tell my father he would not ask to court me.

"I was. Sometimes I still am, when I think about it. But it was for the best, Princess. Trust me on that." Charlotte takes a sip of her tea and begins braiding the other half of her hair. "Anyway, I was telling you about Den. There is no question I loved Den. Shortly after meeting him, I felt all the signs within me whenever we were together. My mother noticed I was acting differently. That is when she chose to tell me about my past, my real past. She explained to me, as I will have to explain to Sawchett, the truth of our shunning. She told me about Gregario and Stefan, the story I have already related to you."

I nod. My head is swimming with the new world I have been learning and I find myself leaning toward Charlotte's voice, eating up the story like a starving man.

"When my mother told me I was shocked, I felt betrayed. It was Den who comforted me. I poured out my feelings to him, I told him everything."

"Everything," I echo the word reverently. This one little word has so many implications here. I turn them all over in my mind.

"Everything," Charlotte repeats the word with a veneration to match my own. "I probably should have been concerned. He could've revealed it to everyone. He did not. Instead, he pulled me into a hug and he promised to keep my secret.

"He even told me that I could use him as an excuse. We could tell everyone that he was unable to bear children. That way, he told me, the shame would be his." Charlotte finishes the final braid and ties it off.

"What a humble gesture," I say. I know that coming from me, the princess of humility, this will carry much weight.

"I told you he was a good man," Charlotte says.

"That's true you did. So you married Den?" I push the story onward, eager for the next tidbit. If they had promised one another no children, where did Sawchett fit in?

"We did. Your father attended the wedding. It was a nice gesture, although one that proved rather tough to explain to a few local women." Charlotte chuckles at the memory. "Greg and I began staying in contact, he helped with food when we needed it. I think he needed the family connection as much as I did. It was a rather odd friendship. I can only describe it as strained. We were so obviously on different paths. Den and I were forced to be careful in our bedroom, we could not make children. Greg and Rubina were having the opposite problem, with all of Fraun pressuring them for an offspring."

I can relate well to that pressure.

"Den and I made a mistake, though. One I tried to hide even from Greg. I became pregnant. The thought of giving the baby to Greg to raise, since it would have royal blood, crossed my mind. He needed an heir, I needed to not have one. Perhaps it would be best. It was only thoughts of my mother's struggles, being forced to live a life she didn't ask for, that made me keep the baby away from Greg. I pushed him away, refused to see him or let him visit, and hid all signs of the pending infant from him."

This story has taken a strange turn. The math does not work out. Why would Enchenda still need an heir? Clearly, Sawchett is younger than I am. "What happened to this baby?" I ask, finding I crave the answer.

"He died at birth." The answer is clipped and curt.

I pull back from the change in tone. Perhaps talking about this is too painful? "I'm sorry."

"It's no matter. When Greg found out that I had hidden a child, he was furious. He threatened to withdraw his family's support from my life. We didn't speak for ages and my family got by just fine without his help." Defiantly, Charlotte drinks her tea.

"What changed?" I use my gentlest voice to remind Charlotte I am not my father. I am not the enemy. Give me a chance and I will do what is right.

"You were born," Charlotte answers.

"Me?"

"Yes. Your father changed a lot after your birth. He reached out to me, he began helping again. I think seeing you helped him understand what I went through. For a while, things were well. Then two things happened to change all that. Your mother died and Den lost his job. Although unrelated events, they each took their toll on someone from my tale. I handled Den's termination poorly, as did Greg handle the death of his wife."

"I remember that, my mother's death I mean. I was close to ten annuals."

"You were. Anyway, Gregario and I had a huge row. Really we haven't spoken since. I was eager to make him miserable, as he had made me with the fight. I also wanted Den to be happy, I think. Either way, I must admit Sawchett was no accident. Once she came to be I knew there was no chance Greg would ever speak to me again. If help comes now, it is often delivered by a staff member. He knows of the child, but he has never met her. He refuses to. It's all well and fine, he keeps our secret buried deep. But the other kings, they cannot know. The council would order our deaths. It is the only way."

How revolting. That cannot be true. The kings are good people. Wait, according to father, they don't have to be good people. They merely have to protect their trait. The council I have met is not like the council I imagined. They are not rational when speaking of royal blood. Perhaps what Charlotte says is true. Perhaps Sawchett is not safe if they know. "I will keep your secret, Charlotte. You have my word."

"Thank you, Eselda. I cannot tell you what that means to my little family."

"What became of Den?" I ask, glancing around the room for signs of another soul.

"He died a few annuals past. He was older than I, he greyed shortly before Sawchett was born. He never even heard her speak, she was not yet five annuals as he lay dying here on the floor." Charlotte glances to the curtain, the memory overtaking her.

I can see water building in the woman's eyes. "What will become of Sawchett when you pass?" I ask.

"I suppose I don't know."

"She will live in my home," I state. What did I just say? I don't know the first thing about children. Then again it was wrong of my family to disown this woman. I can make this right. "I can raise her. I know a good tutor who will see to her education. No one needs to know she is in my home until we are ready to tell them." As I say it, I feel the idea taking hold of me. Another girl in the house will be nice.

"But Greg ..." Charlotte lets the protest fall into the room, unfinished.

"He is not long for this world. I can keep this promise, I assure you. Let me figure out the details."

"Thank you." Tears fall down Charlotte's cheeks. "I cannot tell you what this means to me. To think one of my family will be accepted by one of yours. It's too much to take." Charlotte stands. "I must think on this. Princess, be well." She plants a kiss on my forehead and disappears behind the curtain hanging in the home.

Not sure what else to do, I rinse the teacups and set them upside down to dry. I quietly leave the house. Outside, the sun has risen in the sky and people flood the town. As I head back toward my house, I feel excited about the future.

I will set my grandfather's mistake right.

Chapter 25

My bare feet pad silently down the cold hallway. Early this morning Eee woke me with a message; my father is too ill to attend breakfast at the table but desires a meeting. My heart is beating rapidly against my chest. I am confident I know what the king wants to discuss. After all, I overheard him tell the king of wisdom that he plans to choose a spouse for me. The thought of having such a conversation, one that will surely be full of emotion, while he is sick in his bed scares me.

I reach the door to my father's bedroom and tap lightly on the wood. "Enter." His voice sounds so brave and strong. A man who sounds so powerful cannot possibly be sick. It gives me a burst of adrenaline to carry me through the doorway.

The room is dark, preventing me from seeing the king clearly at first. When my eyes adjust to the darkness and allow me to see him, I gasp. Lying in the bed, looking pale and weak, is a man I don't associate with my strong father. This man is a shadow of what I have grown to know. His hair is completely white and his skin sags around his face. His head is propped on the pillow, not being held high as I am accustomed to seeing. When he coughs, the sound is rough and wet. I sit on a chair at the foot of the bed and reach an arm out to touch the king's leg. "Father, how are you feeling?"

"Old." He chuckles, forcing another bout of coughing.

I choke on the giggle bubbling up my throat as it catches with the tears I am trying to swallow down. "What can I do?"

"Become the queen Enchenda needs. Meet with Prince Carsen, Daughter. Allow him the chance to speak to you about the future he envisions for Fraun. Decide if this is a future you can be a part of." Again, coughs rack the old man's body.

This is no longer an argument I wish to continue. "I will meet with him, father."

"This is about Fraun, daughter."

"I will talk with him about the future we can build." What can it hurt to have similar conversations with Jordyn and Tin? A future warrants looking toward.

"Another thing, there is a council meeting in two suns. Mick and Tin have agreed to revisit the issue of a patrol. You will attend alone. You will need to stay strong."

"I will, Father." I consider the confusing issue, smiling at the ease of the new decision. "I am in favor of a patrol," I tell him. Somehow this feels like a meeting of equals this morning. I already know he will not argue with me on this decision.

"That is your choice." Father closes his eyes. They are closed for longer than a normal blink. When he opens them again they are misty with tears. "It is a wise choice, Eselda."

"Father, I spoke to Charlotte again." I hope he knows I wish to discuss this openly, not argue. "She told me of Sawchett."

Sadness crosses his eyes briefly, but he recovers. "That is something the queen should be privy to. What are your thoughts on the matter?"

Any fear I had anticipated at this revelation is mysteriously absent. "Sawchett, with her royal blood, will be raised by me and my staff upon Charlotte's death."

Gregario nods. The gesture painfully slow. "So be it."

It is this show of faith in my decision, no discussion or debate, that builds my royal nucleus. I feel my chin rise regally. "It is time Charlotte and her family were accepted by the royal family who serves her."

Gregario's eyes close slowly, and a tear slips down his cheek unchecked. "Very wise," he whispers.

That is the second time my king has complimented me on wisdom instead of humility. Perhaps he tires. "You look as though rest is vital, Father. Is there anything else I should know?" I feel the weight of the question fill the room. What else is there preventing me from leading Fraun alone? I am giving my father permission to leave me, despite my heart's desire to force him to stay forever.

His eyes open slightly, as though he cannot quite see my face clearly without squinting. "You are ready, even if more secrets should fall into your path."

"I will leave you to rest then." I walk to the head of his bed and lean to kiss his forehead. "Sleep well, Father. I love you."

A second tear joins the already fallen one on Gregario's cheek. "Thank you, Majesty."

I slip out of the room quietly and close the door behind me. I rest my palm on the door at my back, smiling in acknowledgment of the Regal term used by my father and king.

I am ready.

Chapter 26

"Good sir," my voice echoes throughout the walls of the stall house, a place no royal regularly visits.

The young man who had been crouched near a stall, fixing its door, jumps at the voice. When he stands upright and faces me, he is rubbing a sore spot on his head which he'd just knocked on the stall. "Princess, good morning." He stumbles for an appropriate greeting. "How may I serve you?"

"I am in need of transportation to Renchenda."

"I had heard of no such journey, Princess. None of our roaches are —"

"You will ready them, I will away today." I turn on my heel and walk back to the entrance of the stall house. Spying a nearby rock large enough to use as a chair, I set my rump on it and cross my ankles. Seeing that I intend to wait, the man hurries off to ready a roach.

I allow my shoulders to slump a little once he is out of sight. There is no explanation for why I feel like traveling to Renchenda. I simply need a friendly face and Jordyn is just that.

Of course, I'll have to tell him I agreed to meet with Carsen. That could be uncomfortable.

Why uncomfortable? Surely Jordyn doesn't feel as I feel. I call up the memory of the strawberry field with a smile. The warmth of that kiss.

Somehow the memory makes it a more beautiful day. The sun is just beginning to rise. There is a dew covering the grass, so each blade is glistening with light. I am wearing a cloak with a hood this morning, as the weather is cold before the hour of high sun. Underneath the cloak, however, I wear a dress with minimal caps for sleeves. When the sun is at its highest point later, and bringing its heat to my body, I will be ready.

Perhaps Jordyn will have a solution other than Carsen. In the quiet of my home's backyard, alone, I can allow myself this fantasy. Perhaps Jordyn will find a way in which we can court each other. I think again of the kiss, and a smile flies to my face. Perhaps there will be more of those kisses this afternoon. A bubble of laughter floats from my mouth. The sound is quickly lost in the vast expanse of nature surrounding me.

The small man returns to my line of vision and I straighten my posture. "Princess, I have a roach who says he can make the journey if you allow him two short rests along the way. He is afraid, however, that he will not be able to make the return journey tonight."

"If I am to return tonight, I am sure that King Jordyn will see fit to provide me transportation." I recall the beautiful ladybug he brought along and smile anew. "In fact, I'm confident he will."

"Very well, Princess. I will fetch the roach." The servant turns. Once his back is to me he mutters, "I know that expression in her eyes, someone fancies that king."

Chapter 27

Castle Fraun, commissioned during the time of Oberian the Second and built by Fraunians, is the only three-story stone structure in the kingdom. Honestly, it is a beautiful building. The people of Fraun take great pride in knowing that such a masterpiece was erected by the hands and ingenuity of their people and their people alone.

Jordyn allows his gaze to trace the room, taking in the details. The inset wall torches are spaced evenly to fill the entire room with light. The brickwork has intricate details carved into the lowest layers purely for decoration. Although Jordyn understands the logic behind reusing instead of creating better than most Fraunians, even the king of wisdom in his tortured state cannot deny the beauty of the palace.

The room Jordyn occupies at this time of the afternoon was designed as a ballroom for special occasions. Other than five ornate thrones of gold on a raised platform along one wall, there is no furniture in this room.

There are many rooms in this vast expanse of a home, but this is

Jordyn's favorite. Typically, on any given day, it is empty of people and quiet. On a day like today, when the beast has taken control of the king's being, he can hide out here and not be disturbed.

Today, he is perched on the fifth and final throne, stewing in his own inner turmoil and wrestling to get it under control. It is in this chair, he knows, he would be sat for all major events in the kingdom, were any to take place. He has never rested here for anything formal in his lifetime. The young king cannot help but associate the metal with his mother, the last person to sit in the chair in front of others.

He runs his long fingers on the cold gold arm of the chair. *What would mother think of Fraun now?*

Doubtless, the council will regal one with stories of Aine, the ruler. Aine, the great queen of Renchenda. Aine, the logical. Jordyn remembers a very different woman, one isolated and cold. The mother he remembers expected nothing short of perfection from her only son. *Would Mother be ashamed of how I battle the demon within?*

Thoughts of the monster cause the hate building inside Jordyn to respond like an animal leaning into the hand of its master to be stroked. *Mother is not here. She wasn't even here when she was alive. She was content to lock herself up in rooms on the top floor and leave me to be raised by a common father and a staff of common servants. No matter how loving they were, no one could explain the curse of the royal blood that would be my future.*

The anger builds to a steady boil in the king's blood and he raises his hand level with his head, fingers curled inward like a claw. He rationalizes with himself. "You do not believe these things your brain is telling you, Jordyn." Even as his voice echoes off the stone and back to him, he feels his fist begin to curl. The monster is winning today. "You can do this," he tells himself. "One moment of outburst, then we will be in control of the beast." He closes his fist tightly and brings it crashing down on the arm of the chair.

The sound is magnified by the silence of the room, echoing for seconds after. The outburst does nothing to calm the king. In a rational state, Jordyn would understand what is causing this controlled rage is nothing more than his age marker, but he is not rational right now. The anger takes hold and rails unchecked inside him.

He stands and crosses to the opposite wall, the only one with a window, in ten long strides. He rests his palms on the thick glass and looks out over Renchenda. The sun is on its descent across the sky now and from this vantage point, two floors up, he can see much of the realm bathed in its light.

He breathes deeply. *It is the logical air of Renchenda I breathe in and the beast I breathe out.* Usually, on a day like today when the battle has raged on for hours, this is the only way Jordyn can win the upper hand. Isolate himself and focus on breathing. It is not working today.

Instead, thinking of isolation feeds the flames of anger even more. *Isolation, that's what this tower was really about. Our ancestors knew. They knew the dark pull of our blood. They were not proclaiming us better than all of Fraun by erecting this castle. They were using this brick monstrosity, this fortress, to lock us inside. We are doomed to be isolated.* He punctuates his thoughts by slamming his palm repeatedly into the glass. The thick pane does not give under his anger.

A figure emerging from the woods connecting his realm to that of Marchenda catches the king's eye. He shakes his head to clear the fog of anger, shields his eyes from the sun with his right hand, and squints at the figure. *Whoever dares to cross into my land today is riding a roach and traveling light.*

As Jordyn watches the dainty face turns upward, taking in the full view of the impressive structure. "Eselda," the name escapes Jordyn with a sigh. He closes his eyes and rests his head on the glass. In this way he allows himself to remember the feeling of her slender hand on his chest and recalls her words.

"… love would devour you as well …"

When the king lets out his breath again, the beast is under control.

"Perhaps love is stronger than hate," he sighs.

Chapter 28

The castle Fraun has always been a beautiful sight. Today, after a full day's rather uncomfortable journey across the kingdom, bathed in the setting sun, it is enough to take my breath away. I feel a moment of pride and awe. Someone of my size, or perhaps even smaller, was able to build such a large monument.

I glance upward again, taking in the full height of the building. I wonder what the view from the top floor would be like. The times I have been in the castle, I have either been on the first floor or the second. I recognize a window on the second floor that tI have gazed out of before but never have I been allowed higher. "Maybe someday I will ask Jordyn to let me up there." I practically giggle at the thought.

As if he heard his name spoken, Jordyn suddenly appears at the base of the castle. He waves his arm in greeting as the roach closes the gap between us. I dismount and pull Jordyn into a hug. "Oh we've had such a long journey," I tell the king. "I do hope you have food and water for my tired friend here." I indicate the roach I traveled on.

"Absolutely, I do. It's so nice to see you Eselda." Jordyn looks down at the traveling companion. "Good sir, thank you for bringing my friend to me. I was not expecting either of you today, although I am grateful for your timely arrival. Allow me to find someone to bring you a meal while you stay here in the shade of the castle and rest."

"Thank you, King Jordyn. That is most kind of you," the roach responds. Jordyn wordlessly offers his arm to me and leads me into the building. The roach scurries to the shade and gives in to the desire to lie down and sleep.

"Eselda, I don't know what brings you to Renchenda today but I frankly couldn't have been happier to see you just now." Jordyn positively beams down at me.

He is happy to see me. But happy as a friend or happy as one who feels something more? "Well, friend, I had a rather eventful day yesterday and I wished for someone to talk it over with," I explain. I watch carefully for reactions to the choice of label for our relationship. Did he look sad for just a beat?

"Then allow me to suggest we find a quiet place to talk," Jordyn says.

"Please, can we visit the ballroom?" I ask. "I long to look out that window again."

"We can." He leads the way to the room, pausing only once along the way to send someone to fetch the promised food for the roach. When we arrive, he opens the door to allow me to enter in front of him. I dash across the room, directly for the window.

It's thin and yet I have no doubt it is strong enough to support my wee frame. Despite the fact that it's a childish gesture in front of a man I am trying to impress, I press my entire frame flat against the window to peer out at Renchenda. "It's so beautiful, Jordyn. How do you not spend all of your life in front of this window?"

Jordyn moves across the room to stand behind me. He looks out over the scenery, taking in the view as I must be seeing it. Renchenda is a vast space, but no more people live here than in my realm. To me, the homes seem very scattered. Each person in Renchenda is asked to care for a large lot. Many of them have trees and bushes reaching as tall as their homes, they would have to stand on their houses to trim those trees.

"I do spend a lot of time here, but I also spend time out among the people." Jordyn places a hand on my back. "Now, Princess, tell me what you wish to discuss."

I turn and smile up at the king. "Shall we sit?" I ask. Jordyn nods before turning away from me. I flop down into a seated position on the floor.

Jordyn releases a hearty laugh. "I thought you meant to sit on the thrones," he says.

"I don't think I could sit there. My father is still King," I answer.

"Honestly I feel odd sitting there myself, I still feel it as my mother's seat." Something dark plays across the blue of his eyes. I turn my head, searching for a source of light that would cause that trick. I find nothing. "Surely you didn't travel here to talk of our thrones." Jordyn sits beside me on the floor, his long legs stretching toward the window.

"No, I didn't. I came to talk about promises."

"Promises?"

"My father requested to speak with me yesterday. He is not doing well, Jordyn. I fear he really may be leaving this world soon."

Jordyn reaches out and takes my hand before speaking. "We knew he was ill." This fact, simply stated, may have been taken rudely by others. Some may not be as familiar with Jordyn's way of relying on facts in difficult situations. I understand he intends to comfort me.

"It's different, somehow. Seeing a person who is sick begin to fade away right in front of your eyes is so much harder than knowing it may happen soon," I explain, my voice ringing with sadness.

"I suppose that is true."

"I cannot be a child any longer, Jordyn. It is time I became the queen that Enchenda needs."

"I understand. My mother had never made plans for me to take over. When she died, it was a surprise. It is good that you have time to process this pending change before you take the throne," he answers.

The sadness in my eyes deepens, but this time it is directed at Jordyn. I squeeze the hand I have been holding. "Oh, that's right. I had forgotten how you took the throne of Renchenda. I am so sorry to burden you with this, Jordyn. The memories must be very painful."

"No," he answers. "I have made peace with my past. If you can learn from anything I have to offer, then it was worth the lessons I learned."

"That is so wise," I gush, awed by his capability to think logically in all situations.

"If you are going to insist on telling me every time I say something wise, I fear you'll have no time to talk of much else." We both laugh at the truth behind the statement. It is Jordyn who recovers first and moves the conversation forward. "You spoke of promises?"

"I did. I didn't know what to say to father when we spoke. He was so frail and sickly. I had not the strength to argue with him again about betrothal. I made him a promise." My voice trails down to nothing.

"What promise?"

"I promised to meet with Carsen, listen to him talk of the future, and give him a chance." I cannot bring myself to ask what I want to know: does the king of wisdom have any feelings about that?

Jordyn chuckles, "You had me scared he wanted something more from you, the way you presented that information."

I look up from my lap, meeting Jordyn's eyes. "You have no opinion on this promise?" The hope I had been holding onto, the hope that he would have a different solution entirely, begins to fade.

"Of course I have an opinion."

"Let's hear it then." The hope begins to send off small sparks, enough to prove it is not dead. Will he resuscitate it?

"I told you. I believe that Carsen is an intelligent choice for you." Jordyn pours cold water over the flame of my hope.

I try not to show my disappointment. "That is true."

"You wanted a different answer?" Jordyn questions.

"I am not sure what I want. I do want to do what is best for Fraun, but how am I to know what that is?"

"That is a good question. I cannot tell you that. I can tell you that Fraun will need someone to keep the balance in our kingdom. To do that, we cannot be left with an even number of realms."

"As would happen if I were to marry a seated king." I get it. Let's skip the lecture. I cannot look Jordyn in the eye. Instead, I turn my head to the window.

"Yes," he touches my arm lightly, drawing my gaze again. "There is no one in your realm who has royal blood. There is no one to take on your role if you do not."

"Someone else could take it?" This is new information.

"Of course. A few times in the course of our history someone from an alternate bloodline has taken the throne. If your father had a brother, for example, the brother could take the throne upon the death of your father. Or that brother's child. It has happened before."

"Anyone with royal blood would do?"

"I suppose. Why do you ask?"

I drop my voice, "I have heard talk that others exist. Others who have not been tracked on our family trees."

"You would need proof. The council would need to accept the lineage of this person, once that has been done they could serve as a ruler."

Perhaps this is the answer. What if Sawchett could be groomed to take over the throne? I could leave it all in her hands and then the pressure is simply gone. I could move to Renchenda and be with Jordyn. I could …

"Eselda," Jordyn is watching me carefully, "you will be a fantastic queen. I feel the need to point that out."

"But if I didn't need to be … if someone better suited were available …" my voice trails off.

"The council would need to accept the lineage of someone else before that would even be possible. It is not a timely solution."

I rise. "I feel as though you have given me hope in a situation that felt hopeless such a short time ago. Can I see your family tree?"

"My family tree?"

"Your lineage chart. It is painted here in the castle somewhere, yes?"

"Yes." Jordyn's single-word answer still rings with hesitancy.

"I am very interested in lineage. I have studied my own at great length and found some interesting things. I'd like to have a look at yours to see if similar things exist. Perhaps while we look I can tell you about what I have found on mine."

Jordyn rises. "You have ignited my interest, Princess. Follow me."

Chapter 29

As it turns out, the lineage tree for Renchenda is painted on the wall of a windowless room on the first floor. I can decipher no use for the room, other than to display the chart. As with my own, this chart is painted in delicate gold scripting letters. The chart begins in the same way as ours; Oberian and his wife Alicia at the top, Oberian the Second below. From the second sprout his three wives, Suzeth, Ramona, and Rebekah.

It is from the branch of Rebekah that this tree, however, grows. Rebekah had two sons, Renchenda and Sarcheda. Standing on a contraption made of wooden dowels strung between two large pieces of wood, I run my finger along this line. "I never realized Renchenda and Sarcheda came from the same mother." I turn away from the wall to look at my handsome host.

"Sarcheda was his younger brother," Jordyn says.

My eyes resume their trace of the lineage. I take in the many names, starred and circled. Both women and men have served this realm. My fingers brush up against a name, Tawn. This name draws my eye for many reasons. Both Tawn and Kriep, husband and wife, are circled. Tawn has a black smudge, the kind I am quickly becoming familiar with, above her name. It is too small to hide an entire name. What have we here? "Tell me of this."

Jordyn leans down toward me so I can feel the heat of his breath on my cheek. "Oh, that is quite the tale. Tawn was a seated queen of Farcheda at the time she wed Kriep. Kriep, as you can tell, was from a line of Renchenda blood that was not serving the throne at the time." Jordyn follows the line up with his finger, leaning around me to do so. He is practically enveloping my smaller frame with his large one to reach around. His finger returns all the way back to Renchenda and his wife. Even he is not this tall, he must be standing on a lower rung of the wooden contraption.

"Renchenda and his wife had three children. The rule passed to his oldest girl, Alexa." Jordyn's hand points to the far right of the wall, away from the subject of my query. "As is the custom in most realms, this caused the other two children to live in the common areas and cease to be tracked for many years."

I review the children he speaks of. The middle child, Markin, is noted as having a wife but no children. I wonder if this is truly the case, or if there are others of royal blood in Renchenda who are not tracked by the council or this chart. Three moons ago, I would've thought such a thing to be impossible. Now I know better.

"Eventually," Jordyn continues, "the bloodline of Alexa ran out." I take notice of the end he speaks of. Two children were born to this line, Malkin and Liseth. Neither had children, although both are shown to be married. "This is what would happen to your line," he simply states.

"Or yours," I point out.

"True. In cases like these, where there are no longer direct descendants alive to be royalty the council is forced to track down the lineage of the siblings. In the case of Alexa, the council sent someone who discovered Kriep, alive and well and living in Farcheda."

I turn my cheek slightly to look back at the spot I asked about. My face comes into contact with Jordyn's. Instantly my heartbeat quickens at the touch and my breath catches in my throat.

"In the interim, while his bloodline was not being tracked, Kriep had moved to Farcheda and married a princess there. Shortly after their marriage, Tawn had become queen of Farcheda. The pair already had two children before the council approached them about their Renchenda blood." Jordyn has lowered his voice with the contact, it is merely a whisper in my ear.

I trace the small black smudge on Tawn's name, feeling the cement grind under the padding of my fingertip. "What is this then?"

"Under that black paint, you would find a gold star. Tawn was a ruler of Fraun, but never in Renchenda. She would still have her gold star in Farcheda." Jordyn points to a black oval underneath Tawn's name. "This child, the youngest of the pair, remained in Farcheda with her parents."

"Wait, I don't understand. I thought Kriep was tracked down because Renchenda needed a ruler."

"He was. He could not be married to a queen of Farcheda and serve as a king here at the same time, you know this. Their oldest child, Freth," Jordyn indicates that name, circled and starred, "became our king."

I allow my eyes to follow the rest of the chart down, noting that all further relatives come from this man. Including, a few generations removed, the man currently pressing against my back to explain the history of his realm.

"What became of their youngest?" I ask.

"I am told he became a ruler in Farcheda."

"This is a great story." I smile. Jordyn pulls slightly back from my body, leaving my cheek feeling cold. "Freth was okay with living here while his family served in Farcheda?"

"More than okay with it. In fact, during his reign, Renchenda became the first realm for the only time in history."

"That really is remarkable," I answer.

Jordyn takes a step back, putting his feet safely back on the floor. I remain on the makeshift ladder, analyzing the lineage further. "In my own realm, we see this black paint over a few things as well," I reveal.

"As you see it for Tawn?"

"More like as I see it here." I point my finger at the youngest child of Tawn again. "On our wall, the entire name has been removed."

"As I explained, this was done because that child is now tracked in Farcheda. They are no longer tracked here, they are Farcheda royalty."

"That is not the case with the names I see in Enchenda," I say, continuing to search the wall for more black spots. Finding none, I turn on the ladder so I am facing the king. At this spot, with my feet on the second rung of the ladder, I am actually taller than he.

"Why were those marks removed?" Jordyn asks.

"They represent people who have been shunned."

"Shunned? For what purpose?"

"I am told it is for dishonoring their families by having infants before they were wed."

"I was not aware that could happen." Jordyn looks genuinely confused. "Are there many people like this on your family wall?"

"Not many, no. There was one in the past that I know nothing of. But there was one more recently that I've become aware of."

"What happens to these women who are shunned?" Jordyn asks. "Does the council know of this? Do they receive any training? Do we monitor them at all? How many are we discussing?" The questions are fired rapidly, too rapidly for me to interject an answer.

This must be how Jordyn processes. I hide my smile by lightly biting the inside of my cheek.

"Why would this have been approved? What becomes of their bloodlines?" he continues.

"I can answer many of those questions. Would you like me to?" I ask, teasing him a little for his rapid-fire style.

The king stops talking and nods.

I step off the ladder. "The women are sent to live, not unlike the relatives you spoke of earlier, among the common people in Fraun. The council is often informed, although I'm not sure if it is expected. As for the bloodlines, it is my understanding that these women are asked not to have children."

I am familiar with the confusion playing across the king's face. It is the same emotion I felt myself when confronted with this very issue. I wait patiently, watching him think, something I am finding I enjoy.

Finally, he speaks. "How is it that you know of this while I do not?"

"I met a woman who was removed from my family lineage tree."

The effect of this information on Jordyn is obvious. His face melts into shock and he sits down on the ladder. "You met one." He shakes his head from left to right as if the information needs to move an inch before he can catalog it and use it. "Fascinating."

"That is not the word I would have used." I chuckle. Jordyn glances up at me, confused by my reaction. "I have reason to believe the council knows not of this woman."

Jordyn rises and begins pacing in front of the wall. "We cannot speak more of this then. The council must be informed of all matters discussed between two members of royal houses. We are not to discuss issues like this outside of council. There is a meeting in a few suns, we shall bring this before council then."

"Wait!" I exclaim, stopping Jordyn's tirade. This is not at all how this conversation was supposed to go.

He turns to me, pacing forgotten for a moment. "Why? This is a council issue."

"Jordyn, they cannot know. To know that a woman who was given direct orders from a seated king broke those orders? No, Jordyn. We cannot condemn this woman to death."

"What orders? She had a child, you said. You said this made her an outcast. You said they lived among the commoners. The council needs to know this woman exists."

"Jordyn, please. There is more to this story. Sit, I will tell you the tale." I try to calm the king with my hands, gesturing to the floor.

"I will not. I'm sorry, Eselda, but we cannot discuss this alone. If you want to tell the tale, you must tell it to the council."

"Jordyn there is more to this tale than you are hearing. It makes my family look …" I search for an adequate description, "… unclean."

I can see the anger rising on his face. I watch as his eyes darken like the sky before a storm. "Eselda, I am a king in Fraun. I will not be found to have conversations about policy outside of council. If you have become aware of an issue in Enchenda that requires a decision, you will need to discuss that before a full council."

"Okay, okay. You are right." I concede, fear of the anger forcing my hand. "I will think about bringing it to the council."

"Thank you." Jordyn takes a few deep breaths. I silently watch him as his eyes return to their clear blue and his face relaxes. "I'm sorry." He continues to look at the ground, but his voice has lost all trace of anger now.

"I lost my temper there; I fear it is partially the age marker." When he looks at me, I meet his gaze and give him a small smile which he returns.

"I feel strongly about issues of the council being brought before all representatives of Fraun equally. The process we have undertaken works only when we allow it to. When we find ourselves questioning the process or looking for shortcuts, we do not allow the system to work," he explains.

"I hadn't really thought of it that way."

"I find it is the only way to believe in the vision of the brothers. To follow it with nothing short of perfect intentions."

"Can I summarize what I have learned from your lineage tree today?" I ask. I wait for his nod before pressing forward. "Sarcheda and Renchenda were brothers, meaning their family lines are very similar. However, because we divide realms, none of Sarcheda's bloodline is traced here."

"Yes," Jordyn states, crossing his arms.

"You also have branches here that appear to end. But, as is with the tale of Kriep, we know that to not always be true."

"That is accurate." Jordyn's eyebrows rise with the unanswered question. He is wondering where I am going with this.

"Furthermore, the bloodline currently reigning here in Renchenda is a direct lineage to Farcheda as well."

"That I am."

"So how are we to know for certain that the issue I am facing, a woman who is royal blood but not tracked on my lineage tree, is not also true for other realms? Including this one? How are we to assume our lineage trees are accurate when there is so much confusion in the process?" I am tempted to squeeze my eyes shut in case his face turns angry again.

"It is not our task today to question the accuracy of these bloodlines. It is not our task to follow them to their ends. It is our task to recognize our place among them and step up to lead our realms." Jordyn keeps his voice even and controlled.

"You said yourself that other people with royal blood if they were recognized by the council, could lead."

Jordyn steps closer to me and takes my hand. "I did say that. You said this was a story you didn't want to share with the council. How could they accept the lineage of this woman if you will not tell the story?"

I sigh and my shoulders slump. Of course, he is correct. There is no obvious solution here. Charlotte's story cannot be brought to council because of the negative light it casts on the house of Enchenda. But Sawchett cannot be prepared as a princess without such recognition. The depression is a pool so deep I could drown in it. There is no way out of this.

Jordyn steps to my side and wraps his arm around my shoulder. I feel myself melting into the touch, resting my head on him. "Eselda, I am a smart man," he begins, "Your objection to ruling Enchenda, I fear, has more to do with me than with blood or self-confidence." He pulls back from the embrace enough to hook his finger under my chin and turn my face up to him. "Is that accurate?"

Leaving the ruling of Enchenda to someone like Sawchett while I move to this beautiful castle with you just feels perfect. You could attend council meetings and make decisions for us both. I'm sure Sawchett could handle the pressure. My solution would be easier. I cannot find my voice to say any of this. Instead, I nod.

"I feared as much." Jordyn sighs. "Eselda, I am not the right match for you." He drops my chin, but my gaze does not falter. "No matter how you feel —" he shakes his head. "No matter how we feel." He emphasizes the changed word, correcting himself. "We are better for Fraun as equal rulers of two realms."

Despite my sadness, I cannot help but nod. Jordyn continues. "The people of Enchenda will need you when your father passes. You are a face they trust to get them through the sadness of losing a king. The council will only benefit from two minds such as ours sharing a table. We are both smart, you are humble. You are going to make a fine queen of Enchenda." Jordyn places a kiss on my forehead and steps back, putting space between us.

"You have made your point," I state. "I fear I may have traveled here today to find an escape. My path is not going to be easy."

"It never is."

"But as usual, friend, you have helped me. I believe I am ready for that journey now."

"I see it in your face that you are ready. I will fetch you a ride home and see you at council next. Think about your issue more, decide if our fellow kings need to hear it." He turns to leave the room.

"Jordyn?" The sound of his name softly leaving my mouth turns him again in my direction before I even realize I spoke his name aloud. "I know I should not ask this. I find I cannot help myself. Humor me. If I were a commoner in Renchenda, would you have wanted to court me?" My voice is merely a whisper carrying what is left of my dreams of what might have been. Pain begins in my stomach, thick and hot. What if he laughs at the thought?

Jordyn closes the space between us and pulls me close. I close my eyes as he leans in, so by the time our lips connect I only feel it. The warmth spreads through my entire body and I lean into him, deepening the kiss.

It is Jordyn who pulls away. When he leaves the room, I know he gave me the only answer he is capable of giving.

Chapter 30

The morning of the next council meeting arrives. The sun is rising over the beautiful kingdom, but the cold has begun. The people of Fraun have kept wood-burning stoves running as they slept, and will be waking soon to feed the flames. Outside, people pull on warm cloaks to complete their daily chores and shoes adorn the feet of children, an unusual sight to be sure.

It has been a few suns since I visited with the king of wisdom and the kiss which signaled goodbye and yet my father has not risen from his bed and is resting quietly. Having been taking on much of the duties of leading the realm, I was exhausted when I reached my bed last night. I gave orders to a manservant that I not be woken today. It is this manservant you would find standing on the front lawn of the home in Enchenda, toe to toe with Tutor, anger crackling dangerously from one man to the other.

"You cannot keep me from her. Until she is crowned, I am her personal tutor," the younger man's voice rings out. This argument has been building for a few minutes, the men are close to solving it with their fists if another solution does not present itself soon.

"I have my orders. If you will not leave, I will have no choice but to make you leave," the other voice is lower, more controlled, but equally as dangerous.

"You are a traitor if you would make me leave. I am not a threat to this house," Tutor yells.

"If you try to shove your way in, that makes you a threat."

"Get out of my way!"

"Make me!"

Behind the older man, sprawling out in both directions lies my family home. An opening in the wall to the man's left is covered with curtains which part in one swift movement as I thrust my head out the open window. "HEY!" I bellow.

Both men freeze and turn their full attention in my direction. "What in the name of Fraun are you two arguing about?" I ask.

"Majesty you asked not to be disturbed and this man wanted to wake you. I could not let that happen," the manservant explains.

"Yeah, well done on that," Tutor says. He claps the man enthusiastically on the shoulder. "Princess, I need a word. Will you meet me in the garden?"

I nod once and disappear back into my room. "Never a moment of rest for me and I'm not even Queen yet," I complain to my reflecting wall. Speaking with Tutor was actually on my list of things to do today. Admittedly I had planned to wait until a decent hour of the day. It is for this reason that I allow myself to be summoned to a meeting with him.

I mentally rehearse what must be said to Tutor as I walk the halls. It is my belief that, since I will be assuming the day-to-day operations of a queen, I no longer require tutoring services. I do feel sadness at having to cut ties with my old friend. But in truth, I cannot fault myself for this. Tutor has been putting enough distance between us lately. This is for the best.

Dressed in an orange-colored long-sleeve dress that sweeps the ground and wearing black shoes on my feet, I enter the garden to find Tutor sitting on the bench by my vegetables. I sit beside him. "Good morning, Tutor." He blinks at the edge of authority in my voice.

"Good Morning, Majesty. Sorry to have woken you."

The wry smile on his face suggests otherwise. "You certainly don't sound sorry," I tease.

"Fair point. It could not be helped."

"Then I shall listen to what you came to say, out of respect for our past. Then we have business to discuss."

Tutor turns his brown eyes away from me, as though something interesting was transpiring in the garden. "Eselda I have come to tell you that I can no longer be your tutor. In light of new information I have recently received, I feel I cannot be of service to you any longer." His eyes catch the sunlight as he looks up from the garden. "I am not at liberty to say much else. It is my hope that you will let me out of my service immediately."

I recover from my shock in time to return the stony expression to my face. "What service have you been completing lately that I should let you out of? In my pressing time of urgency, you have been absent." I coat my voice with anger and authority.

"That is true. Perhaps that will make it easier to let me go."

"Perhaps. Tell me what information you have received and I will decide." No more secrets.

"I cannot do that, Majesty."

"I am your princess. You will tell me." I catch myself just shy of stomping my foot in an immature show of frustration.

"With all due respect, Princess, I cannot."

"When I am Queen, I can force you to tell me or have your head."

Tutor sighs, "If that is what you wish, we can discuss this again then."

Oh, this is not working. I must try another tactic. I soften my voice. "We were friends once Tutor, before you stopped coming around. Can you not tell your friend the truth of this decision?"

Something softens in his expression. "I have learned things that I wish I could share with a friend. Things I cannot bear alone. I wish I could do that, Eselda, but believe me when I say you don't want to hear this truth. I must refuse." He stands to his feet, sighing with the effort. "Ask me again when you are Queen if you feel like demanding it. But know that you still will not want this truth then, as I do not really want it now. Good day, Majesty."

I brush the arm of the man as he leaves, but he slips his arm from my fingers before I can gain purchase there. He never once turns around to look back. I find the sadness overwhelming, another friend lost. I allow myself a moment to reflect.

You could always make me laugh, I will miss that most. You pushed me but always knew when to let something rest. It's the end of our time together. Shouldn't someone feel that sadness?

Of course, it's also the end of the skipped lessons with no explanation. The limp he cannot explain and the secrets he refused to talk about will end now as well.

When I rise from the bench, I am no longer sad. "I am in no further need of a tutor anyway," I state for my own benefit.

Chapter 31

Tin sits alone at the head of the council table, tapping his fingers rhythmically. He has never in his reign as king been this early to a council meeting. He arrived before the shadow has even begun to reach the building, indicating it is time for the meeting of the council. The king of strength is aware such an act will not be lost on his comrade of speed. In fact, the act was carried out for this purpose.

Speed is such an undesirable trait to have alone. What good would it do one to be quick? You could run from a fight, sure, but why run when the strength of Sarcheda can guarantee you the win?

Tin is eyeing the doorway when Jordyn's lanky frame fills it. *Wisdom, now that is a quality I can use. Wise enough to know the strategies of the enemy in war. This is why I must always try to keep Jordyn on my side.*

"King Tin, you are early today," Jordyn greets. He offers his hand to the slightly older king. Tin accepts the hand and they shake.

"I thought it would do me some good to sit here and think in the room where great men before me have sat to think," Tin explains as Jordyn takes his seat.

"Great women have sat there as well," Jordyn points out.

Tin acknowledges this comment with a simple wave of his hand. "Have you been thinking any more on the patrol?" Tin asks, hoping the fact that they are in the council room will be reason enough for the rule-abiding king to discuss policy.

"I have. Let us wait for our partners in leadership and I will share my thoughts."

Having no other course of action to suggest, the pair settle in to wait. Jordyn absently stares at the table while he ponders. Tin continues to focus on the doorway. Both men are lost in thoughts of what they want for the future of Fraun. Neither King seems aware their colleague's opinion differs so much from his own.

After the passing of some time, King Mick enters the room. As is his style, he is moving fast. "Gentlemen, this is two meetings in a row when I am not the first to arrive," he points out in lieu of a greeting.

"Perhaps you are losing your touch in your old age," Tin challenges.

"I am not late, that much is certain," Mick answers, taking his seat. "Have either of you heard from—" the man is interrupted by the arrival of King Larecio and Princess Eselda, who enter the room laughing. All eyes in the room turn to the pair.

"Good afternoon everyone," Larecio heartily calls as his eyes sweep the company. He turns back to Eselda. "Apparently they were waiting for us."

Tin sits up straighter in his chair. "Well, let's begin. I have an issue from our last council meeting that I feel we should revisit. The idea of a patrol to provide safety to Fraun. Are there any further points on this topic?"

Chapter 32

I look around the room, taking in the faces of the kings of Fraun. They are a proud bunch; their faces tell me that. King Tin, to my right, is seated regally in his chair today. He is holding his gaze steady as he also stares down the men from the table. He is wearing his stubborn desire to argue like a cloak.

To my left King Mick is equally ready for a challenge. He is stiff-backed and smiling a smile one would expect after a large meal; altogether satisfied and happy. To his left, King Larecio holding up to his realm's trait looking full of mirth. In my own eyes, the man looks like he doesn't belong in this group, being the only one to not wear a serious expression in the crowd. Lastly, my eyes fall on Jordyn. I know that look he wears all too well. The king of wisdom is formulating an idea.

As if he heard my thoughts, Jordyn clears his throat. "I believe I have some insight on this topic." All eyes in the room turn to Jordyn. "When last we met King Mick proposed we begin a patrol to keep Fraun safe." Everyone nods their agreement with this statement, although no eyes move from Jordyn's face. He continues, "The disagreement came when we began to talk about what we would train this patrol for, and therefore where we would train them." Nods again.

"I believe I have an idea. By themselves, none of our traits may be suitable for a patrol. However, can you imagine how powerful a patrol would be that was strong, humble, quick, mirthful, and wise? Why they would be unstoppable." Jordyn's eyes travel the faces of his colleagues.

I take the opportunity to do the same. I see some smiles and nods, but Tin has turned his face to stone, revealing nothing. Jordyn and I lock eyes as he finishes his point. "Perhaps our solution is simple. Perhaps a troupe of the best Fraunians from all of our realms should train up together. The patrol group could spend a few suns in each realm, learning skills of that realm in turn. By the time they had visited all five realms, we would have a strong patrol who knew the Fraunian land better than any seated here. They would truly be the best protectors we could offer."

Here the young king stops talking and sits back, taking in the room again. There are many more nods this time. Larecio speaks first, "What a delightful idea, Jordyn. I could see my son enjoying his time training a guard."

"My son as well would enjoy his time with such a training," Mick states. "But what of Enchenda?" The older man turns to me. "Would you feel comfortable training a group of men in the ways of Enchenda and how to be humble?"

The question drips with something bitter I cannot name; he speaks as though trying to harm me with his words. "Why is it only Enchenda you worry about, Majesty?" I ask. I feel something grab my hand and give it a comforting squeeze. Without looking down, I squeeze back and hold on tight. At least someone supports me.

"You are the only one seated at this table with no male presence in your realm to train."

My defiance is obvious, I square my jaw and raise my chin. "You assume two incorrect things, King Mick." If it is confrontation the old man desires, I will gladly deliver it.

The man smirks at me. "Is that so? Well, straighten me out then, maiden, go ahead."

I make a calculated decision to let my voice ring out with all the authority I can muster. Still, my nerves set my body to tremble. I hold tight to the hand, the show of support helping me stay grounded. "One, you assume a lady like myself cannot possibly have anything to teach this patrol. In this, I assure you, you are sadly mistaken and outdated. I can bring a patrol up to speed on many things around and in Enchenda. Things I could teach that patrol you may even benefit from, good sir.

"Secondly, you assume there are no young men anywhere in my realm. Again, you are mistaken. Good King Jordyn did not suggest at all that the people training these patrols would need to be of royal blood. True, Enchenda has no young men with that in their veins running around. But I assure you, sir, we do have men in our realm."

Mick smiles. "I suppose I underestimated you, milady." He glances around the room. I take the opportunity to look down and see who the hand belongs to. It is that of King Tin. I smile at him shyly. He returns one of full force before taking his hand back. My next glance is toward Jordyn, as though my eyes were pulled there of their own accord. He is watching the exchange. My face reddens.

"It sounds as though our wise friend here has come up with a solution that we can all agree upon," Tin says. "What say the council?"

"I agree." Mick startles the room by agreeing with the king of strength. "Call the vote, Tin."

"All in favor of beginning a patrol that would spend time training in each of our five realms and serve all of Fraun say 'aye'."

"Aye." The room echoes with the word.

"The vote is unanimous," Tin notes. "Now the matter of details. How many men will each realm send and where should they report?"

I clear my throat. "As far as I am concerned there is no reason why the patrol should not begin training in the first realm and move onward from there." There are nods of assent around the room.

"As for the matter of numbers, I believe no more than two from every realm would be sufficient to begin," Mick adds.

"I can stand behind that number," says Larecio. "Call a vote, leader."

"All in favor of sending two men each to begin training for patrol in the first realm within five suns say 'aye'." A wide smile occupies Tin's face as he calls the vote.

"Aye."

"Again, the vote is unanimous. Send me your men," Tin glances at me, "or women within the next five suns. I will begin training them at that time. After a time, I will send them on to Enchenda for phase two of their training."

I cannot help but feel pleased with the way this meeting has transpired. In contrast to our last meeting, we have accomplished something today. Maybe I misjudged what it means to be a member of this council. Perhaps, although it has been a rocky lunar cycle, I am prepared to be the queen my kingdom needs. Perhaps—

"Questions of our policy regarding royal blood have been recently brought to my attention," Jordyn states.

My good feeling deflates instantly. We weren't supposed to bring this to them until I said I was ready. It was my choice to make. I cannot control the increased breathing, the redness that creeps into my face, or the glare I shoot across the table at the king.

Jordyn continues, "I think it befitting of the council to discuss the issue of unneeded relatives becoming common citizens."

"Where is this coming from?" Larecio questions, not unkindly.

"No specific place. As I mentioned, it has merely been brought to my attention. For example, I know it is not lost on this council that three of our members here have no offspring to assume the throne upon our deaths."

"Damn right you haven't. We need to speak of that," Mick says.

What are you doing, Jordyn? Why bring that up? Mick needed no inspiration to get fired up again.

"I thought we were discussing that. It has been brought to my attention that if the realms were to track their royal blood properly there may be other citizens fit to serve," Jordyn states.

"How would that be possible?" Larecio questions, propping his elbow on the table and leaning forward.

"I can give you an example," I blurt, eager to steer the conversation to safe grounds. "If my father had a younger brother, what would have become of him at birth?"

Mick plays along. "He would live among the common folk unless he is needed to serve the throne."

"Exactly." I offer him a smile for helping with the example before hurrying along. "Now let's say my Uncle continued to have children. I don't know about your realms, but Enchenda wouldn't know."

"Of course not, we don't track the legacy of every commoner in our realm," Tin agrees.

"Exactly," I continue. "Therefore, although I have birthed no children it is possible that upon the untimely death of my father and myself that my Uncle could have royal-blooded children ready and able to serve Enchenda."

The news silences the room. Likely the men are searching for flaws in my thinking, but they will find none.

"Fascinating," Mick breathes. "Jordyn, you among us are the smartest. Do you agree with this logic?"

"How could I not? There are no flaws there. Do you see why this issue was one I thought best to bring to the council?"

"I don't see what you want us to do about it," Tin says. Again the men around the room bob their heads up and down.

"I propose that our council select a representative of each realm to look into and update the lineage charts in our realms," Jordyn suggests.

"Jordyn, what a lovely idea!" I cannot help myself. Jordyn has discovered a safe way for me to have Charlotte added to the wall without having to tell her tale.

"It was a good idea, no need to get that excited," Mick chides. I offer him a shrug.

"All in favor of a representative from each realm updating the lineage charts say 'aye'," Tin bellows.

"Aye."

This time the vote is not unanimous. Tin continues, "All those opposed, say 'nay'."

"Nay." Mick glares around the table at those who did not vote with him.

"The motion carries four votes to one. Let it be known that Farcheda is not in favor of this new law, but will comply accordingly."

"So noted," Mick mumbles.

"Excellent." Tin smiles around the room. "Any further business?" He allows the silence to monopolize the room before he stands. "If there is nothing further, I call this meeting of the council of leaders adjourned for another lunar cycle."

Immediately the room begins to empty. Tin places a hand on my arm. "Can we talk?" he asks.

I notice Jordyn's steps falter as though waiting for my answer.

"Of course, Majesty," I answer. I think I notice a slight shaking of Jordyn's head, but then he is gone from the room.

Tin turns his chair in my direction. "How have you been?"

"Fine, thank you. How have you been?"

"Busy. I am sorry I haven't yet had the chance to speak with your father."

"Regarding what?" I ask. Immediately, I regret the question as the memory of Tin's promise at dinner comes back to me. "Oh, right. About … that. It's fine, really," I stammer.

Tin's face crumples. "You no longer wish to be courted?"

"No, it's not that. It's … well, this is hard. My father feels…" I stop, breathe, and start again. "My father and I feel that I should probably give Prince Carsen a chance. Kings of both realms have accepted this. We are actually meeting for dinner tonight. I'm sorry." The words rush out of my mouth quickly, before I can choose to stop myself.

Tin, for his part, looks devastated. His head and shoulders slump. "I understand. I should've acted with more urgency in the matter." He touches my hand. "Please let me know if anything changes."

"I certainly will. I'm sorry about this change of our plans, Tin."

"You owed me nothing, Princess. Think not on it."

It was easier to dismiss Tin's offer when I believed he was speaking in haste. I should explain to him that I had convinced myself his mind was changed on the matter. I never meant to hurt anyone. There must be a way to explain this. "Tin, let's be honest, we could never be." I shamelessly steal lines from Jordyn. "Sarcheda and Enchenda, they need us both to rule and be strong."

Tin gives me a puzzled expression. "What makes you think they would not have us both?"

I lay a hand on his shoulder, leaning toward his ear. "If we were to be together, our realms would lose one of us. A king and queen must rule together from their realm."

"Our realms could unite."

"Leaving four realms would be unwise." It is what I have heard but my confidence wavers under the king's austere expression. "Wouldn't it?" I question.

"I suppose so, but things could change." Tin grasps my hand. His hazel eyes flash greener today than I remember, hypnotizing me. "We would be the most influential Reign in years. I can't remember the last time a king and queen seated together both had royal blood. We could still both sit at the table for council meetings."

"We could?" Is that a rule? When was the last time that happened?

"Why not?" He leans toward me, our noses practically touching. Is that hope I see in his eyes?

"We could make the rules," he whispers.

"The council would vote for that?"

At this, the king bristles. He drops my hand and rises, the mood broken by his sudden anger. "The council is full of fools making decisions from their past." He grabs my hand again this time to pull me to my feet. "I want to make decisions for the future of Fraun."

"I do as well." Perhaps people misjudge Tin. Perhaps I did.

"Good." He moves closer until our noses are touching again. "You have this meeting with Carsen. You see which way he looks when speaking of Fraun. But if he is looking to the past as well, you remember that in Sarcheda there is one who does not."

I can find no words under the weight of this simple request. I nod.

Tin leaves the room and I am left with a puzzle of options spread before me. Jordyn, who says two seated royals cannot court. Tin, who argues that is an outdated rule that would not stop him. Carsen, the prince I have not met as an adult.

What is truly best for Fraun?

Chapter 33

Inside the carriage, I am wearing my finest clothes. My soft green gown, the color of Enchenda, reaches the floor. The long sleeves are tight to my skin but have caps on the shoulders. The bodice of the dress is black and tight, nicely showing off my curves. On my ankles, in my hair, and around my neck I wear matching silver chains. They are thick ropes, looped in a decorative way and catching the moonlight beautifully.

I have never been to Marchenda before. For this reason, when the roach-drawn carriage pulls into its borders, I am on full alert to take in new information. The homes are small, but well-lit from the inside. I can hear the sounds of laughter and smell food cooking. My stomach growls in response.

The front gardens of the homes are well-tended. In Enchenda one often sees small, low landscapes. In Sarcheda the homes were very dark and had much space between them. In Renchenda there were tall trees marring the vision from one house to the next. Marchenda appears to be the realm most closely resembling my own.

The carriage pulls to a stop in front of a small home puffing smoke into the air. The home is surrounded by a wooden fence and the front yard is immaculately maintained. This home looks like an inviting place. Like my own, this one is clearly repurposed from giant materials. I can see it in the unequal roof slats, the scratched doors, and the oddly sized lanterns. It doesn't detract from the home's charm in the least.

The front door opens and a man emerges. He looks to be about my height. He has brown hair and carries himself well. He is dressed in a pale yellow shirt and brown vest. He wears slacks of brown as well. By far the most handsome feature of the man, however, is his expression. He wears the most relaxed, comfortable smile that I have ever seen. It truly reaches all the way to his brown eyes.

The door of the carriage opens, and the man holds out his hand. "Princess Eselda, I assume," his voice is smooth like the Sarcheda chocolate.

"Prince Carsen?" I question, hopeful.

"That is what they call me. Please, call me Carsen." He reaches out his hand and I place mine delicately inside. I allow myself to be pulled from the carriage.

"You have a beautiful realm."

"Well, thank you. We are happy with it," he answers.

"You have reason to be."

"Are you hungry, Princess?"

"I am. But please, Carsen, call me Eselda."

"Alright, Eselda. Let us head into my home where we can eat." He turns and heads toward the home, leading me. The interior of the home also resembles my own, although there are more windows here. The hallway we travel is almost entirely covered in glass, a view that I would love to stop and take in were it not darkening outside. We do not stop at the dining room that we pass. Instead, Carsen leads us to the backyard where a table has been set for two people.

The backyard is unlike anything I have seen. Instead of grass or a garden, there is only a grey surface marred by symbols. "What is this ground?" I ask, stomping my feet on it. The surface has no pliability, holding fast under my heel. It is warm, hard, and echoes back the sound of my stomp.

"Isn't it remarkable? The scouts brought it back from an excursion.

The Giants used this material for everything. The scouts tell me there are spots beyond Fraun where this material is all you can see in every direction. Even the bravest scouts fear to cross it."

"What is it?"

"I know not its name. This chunk was found toppled and broken, they knew I would find it fascinating," says Carsen.

"What are the symbols?" I ask, gesturing to one colorful streak near the prince's feet.

"I am told they are old letters the giants used." Carsen points to the table, set flat on the surface. "Shall we sit here? I know there is a chill in the air tonight, but I find this to be my favorite spot."

Imagine being so large that this entire slab, which spans the prince's vast yard, would seem small to you. These large markings would be merely letters you used in communication. The rare glimpse into the world of the giants is alluring. "It is beautiful out here. Thank you for choosing this location."

The precise second my bottom touches the seat food is delivered to the table. The orchestrated delivery is flattering. Smells waft up from the bowl in front of me, garlic and onion filling my nostrils.

"I hope you like earthworm, Eselda. I am told this soup is delightful, the staff we have here are great chefs." Carsen's ever-present smile is infectious and I find myself turning on my own.

"Earthworm stew is something I'm very familiar with, it smells delightful." We each take up a spoon and begin eating. Soon, the silence grows uncomfortable. What should we discuss? How do I broach the subject of futures?

Timidly, I choose a conversational thread from my dinner with Tin. "Tell me what you do here in Marchenda for fun, Carsen."

Carsen puts his spoon down and gives his full attention to the conversation at hand. "Many things. We tell stories often, it's something we excel at. I enjoy going down to the school area and telling tales to our younger citizens. Each of us has a different style of story we like to tell. I personally am more partial to those with a good life lesson."

"I've never met someone who told made-up tales for the amusement of others. Would you tell me one?" Most of the tales used in the schools around Enchenda are those that really happened, like the story of the brothers. It is our practice to regal those old tales that have been shared time and time again. It is rare to find someone who makes them up, particularly with no notice or warning. I find the idea tantalizing. I lean on my elbows toward the prince.

"I suppose I could tell a short one. Let me think a minute."

I watch as Carsen stares up at the sky, eyebrows drawn together as he concentrates. His face is lean, his eyes are a startling dark brown, the color of the dirt in my garden. He has a strong jaw; he is certainly handsome in his own right.

"I have one," he states, returning his eyes to me. "Once upon a time there lived an old frog family."

"How many were in this family?"

Carsen laughs lightly, "Three children and two parents. But let me tell the story to the end before you ask more questions. The young boys grew up together, as close as brothers can be. The family often played in the pond outside their front door and their Mother doted on a beautiful lily that grew there. No one else could sit upon this lily pad, except for their Mother."

The prince's voice is soothing, a warm sense of calm washes over me as he talks. Although I have no brothers to speak of and no Mother at home to dote on anything, I find myself smiling at the idea. I lean closer still to the prince.

"As it came time for the boys to leave their parent's home and strike out on their own, their Mother was suddenly taken from them." The sentence is a brisk clip. I gasp at the abrupt sadness that pierces my heart.

"The boys were devastated," Carsen acknowledges. "In their grief, the oldest suggested they each take a part of the lily pad that their Mother had so loved to their new home. He reasoned that the memory would bring them joy whenever they saw it.

"Eager to preserve a part of her, the boys tore up the lily pad. Great care went into ensuring the pieces were of equal size. The boys each took their section of lily to their new home, around the further edges of the pond."

"That's rather sweet."

"It was, at first. The day came to pass that the lily, being a living plant, died."

"Oh no." I am surprised at how dejected I feel. I place my hand over my heart, I can feel it beating underneath the material. "The boys must have been so sad."

"They were unquestionably dismal. Here was the last piece of their mother, and each one thought that he had done something wrong to cause his part of the lily to die. No boy was willing to admit he had killed the plant. So each one continued to pretend that his part of the plant was alive and well, further upsetting the others who believed this strengthened their fault in killing it. The boys grew apart as a result. The father, when his death finally came, had none of his three boys by his side."

"How terrible." *Please make it at least to see me return home tonight, Father.*

"It was. From this sad tale, however, sparks a lesson we can all learn from. Sometimes our desire to share something beloved, no matter how equally we share it, can kill what we love and be our ruin."

The message hangs in the silence of the backyard for a moment. "Wow. You made that up?" I ask.

"I did. You couldn't tell?" Carsen chuckles. "I'm not even sure how a lily grows or if you could tear one up."

"It rang like a true tale." I flop back in my chair. "The Mother dying, it was so sad. Then the children lying to each other…" I trail off.

"Of course, I base it on things real people have done. That is the mark of a good tale. But the point, for me, is always the lesson." He smiles. "I fear the last of your stew has likely gone cold as you listened to the tale."

"You even added the part about the father dying alone. I only have a father. That thought pulled on my heart."

"You forget; I only have a father as well. That part was as personal to me as it was to you." The quiet quality of the prince's voice on this note snaps me back to reality. I take in Carsen's face again, there is a new dreamy quality to his eyes.

"Telling tales makes you happy."

"It does."

I reach out and take his hand, resting on the table. "Thank you for sharing it with me." I squeeze the hand.

Carsen squeezes back. "My pleasure."

"How old is your father, if you don't mind my asking."

"He just recently greyed. So he's barely forty annuals. Is it the same for King Gregario?"

"I suppose not." I shrug. "Honestly I do not even know my own age." The truth slips out in a whisper. "I know I have passed the fifteenth annual, but I cannot recall when that happened."

"I am nineteen," Carsen admits.

"You have one annual left." The statement trails up at the end, turning it into a sort of question.

"Less, actually." Fear looms behind Carsen's expression.

It is a fear I recognize. I wonder how long I have until I am waking up and facing the dark age head-on. "I fear the age markers." The honest statement slips out of me easily, offered to the prince like glass to be cared for.

His eyes meet mine and he nods. "As do I. My dreams carry such dark thoughts about what may be awaiting me." Carsen is speaking in a low voice. I am forced to lean closer to hear him. "At times I think it cannot possibly be as bad as I imagine. Other times, I fear I may be in for a nightmare."

"Have you known anyone who passes through this marker? Someone you can talk to?"

"Only King Jordyn."

The name, so often running through my mind, sounds strange from the mouth of the prince. "You know Jordyn?"

"He has had many a conversation with me about preparing to lead my realm."

"I suppose he has had the same with me," I offer.

"King Jordyn is a good man." Carsen smiles, squeezes my hand, and rises. "I am going to take our empty plates inside. Excuse me for a moment."

As Carsen traipses inside with an armload of dishes I stare at the giant's scrawl on the flooring. Imagine someone who was large enough that this writing came from a pen. The pen would have to be my size. I trace my toe along the writing nearest me. My foot could have made these marks.

"Fascinating isn't it?" I startle at the voice. When I turn to look at him, I see his cheery demeanor has returned. "I often wonder what the symbols were for," Carsen says. "Were they labeling something? Claiming ownership? Telling a tale?"

"I'm surprised and a little impressed with how long it has lasted. The Giants have been gone from this land for many generations and yet here it remains, preserved." I turn my chair to better face my companion who has moved his chair away from the table and slouched slightly. He is the picture of relaxation. "It makes you wonder," I muse, "what will remain of Fraun after we are long gone? What will whoever begins after us find of ours?" I return my gaze to the symbols in silence.

"Nothing."

I turn back to Carsen. He is still staring at the ground. Perhaps I imagined the single-word answer. "Excuse me?"

"Nothing will remain. A generation of people who live after us will find nothing of ours." He turns his eyes to me. "Isn't that our intention? We use only what we need and make nothing. Therefore, the next people to come will find exactly that."

"We have the Castle Fraun." I smile, trying to lighten what suddenly feels like a dark mood.

"That we do." He clears his throat and returns his voice to a lighter quality, the smile back on his face. "That will be our legacy then."

You are perplexing, Prince of Marchenda. You put on the mask of someone relaxed and happy, but there is much lying behind that facade. I would welcome the chance to see that hidden layer. Who is the man when he feels not the need to be mirthful for his realm?

"Carsen, I have had a lovely time. However, the night grows long. I hope you will call upon me again." Although it sounds like a formality, the sentiment is true.

The prince pulls me into a hug. "Count on it, Princess. It was refreshing to share my thoughts with someone so like myself. I will be calling on you soon."

I allow myself to be escorted out of the home and into the carriage. Once I am seated, Carsen places a warm kiss on my cheek. I smile at him before the door is closed and then I wave as the carriage pulls away.

Carsen is a good man but I must admit that kiss lacked the spark I felt in Renchenda.

Chapter 34

Having met with Carsen I feel I am no closer to knowing what needs to be done for Fraun. *What if I decided not to choose a husband? Could I lead my realm alone? Surely they will continue their friendships with me even then. I would not truly be alone, per se.* My thoughts are racing each other through my head as I pull open the door to Father's room. They are the very same thoughts that occupied the hours in which I should've been sleeping.

"I'm glad to see you well this morning, Father." I take a seat on the edge of the bed, patting him on the leg. In truth, he doesn't look well at all. Under his eyes there are dark circles, giving the impression his eyes are sinking into his skull. He is frail, blanched, and weak. I will my face to betray none of this.

"Tell me how went the council meeting and the dinner." His voice is a breathy whisper and is punctuated by a cough.

"The council voted to train up a patrol in all five realms, Jordyn's idea."

"Naturally." The king tries to chuckle, and another coughing fit ensues.

I wait him out, unsure how to help. "Yes. The vote was unanimous. I need to send two men to Sarcheda to begin training. I am going to head to the village today and find some willing volunteers."

"Check at the edge of town by the fields. There are many men there who are a young age, they often look for work."

"I will do just that, Father, thank you. The council also voted to update the lineage charts in all the realms," I say.

"For what purpose?"

"To help find all available citizens who may have royal blood within their veins. You know how concerned they are with the lack of heirs in some of our realms." I try to keep my voice worry-free. The last thing father needs right now is more to worry about.

"Did you tell them of Charlotte?" he attempts to prop himself up on one arm, but wavers dangerously and drops back to the pillow.

"Of course not, father." I pat his leg. "Fear not, that will be taken care of."

"What of the meeting with Carsen?" he asks, a glimmer of hope in his eye.

"It went well." A sparse blush begins on my cheeks. "Carsen is a good man."

"Is he courting you?"

The blush deepens. "I believe so. I asked him to call again."

"You make me a happy man, Daughter."

Am I an awful person for letting him root this small happiness in exaggeration?

"Father, I have business to attend to and you look like you could use some rest. I will visit again tonight." I kiss his cheek before leaving.

The trek to the village is uneventful this time around. The people of Enchenda seem to be holed up in their homes against the cooler air. I am wrapped in a warm cloak, my hands shoved deep into my pockets.

Not only do I need to find a few volunteers for the patrol, a task that may be harder than I anticipated because of the lack of people braving the cool air, but I need to find someone willing and able to update the lineage tree as well. How does one just stumble upon someone capable of good communication skills and an ability to write, a task not taught to all in school?

I reach the edge of the village square. Despite the cold, there are four young men, bundled up and fidgeting to stay warm. "Good morning, Princess," the tallest of the group greets. "Are you searching for something this morning? My friends and I can handle any household task and all we ask is for one warm meal each." Clearly the leader, he has stepped away from the huddle of the group.

My eyes search the faces of the men. The leader stands two clicks over my own head. His eyes are kind but his face is stoic. He looks to be older than me, but Father had mentioned the men here to be young and looking for work. Behind him, the other three men are shorter than I. To the far right, the last man has a sad expression, like a wilting flower. The middle man, the shortest of the bunch, wiggles continuously like a flag in the wind. The man to the left seems almost shy, turning his face away from me. I address their leader, "The task which I seek to fill today would require more work than a simple household chore. I need only the bravest souls; ones who are able and willing to travel all of Fraun. I search for someone who finds it in himself to be strong, humble, quick, happy, and wise."

"Something like that would require more compensation than a single warm meal," he answers.

"Three warm meals a day and a place to rest your head," I promise.

"You mention all five qualities of the realms, Princess. Would I be correct in assuming this job would require someone willing to work for other realms in our kingdom?"

"You would. Would such a man exist in this area of the realm? I am in need of two."

The man turns, facing those gathered behind him. "Kristopher, Michael you should head home." The man in the middle opens his mouth, taking a step forward. The leader speaks before he has a chance to object. "Michael you have family here. If the princess is asking for someone who can travel, that is not your lot. Who will care for your sister if you are gone?" The man, Michael, seems to agree. He hangs his head and leaves the clearing.

The man on the left, the one who had been looking downward instead of at me, speaks. "Thank you, Lance. I … uh … I am not ready for that."

“Kristopher you will be, someday.” The leader, Lance, uses an amiable tone.

I can hear emotion for the men he leads in his voice. Yet, when he turns to face me there is no trace of that emotion in his expression. “Tell us more about this job.”

I look to the man remaining, he continues to look dejected. “What is your name, sir?”

His cold eyes light upon my face, briefly, before returning to the ground. He does not smile. “Danyel.”

“Danyel does this seem like a task you would be willing to hear about?”

“There is nothing left for me here in Enchenda, Majesty.”

“Enough about him. I can handle him. He will not go if he is not willing, trust in that,” Lance interjects, stepping between Danyel and me. “Now tell us more about this position.”

I watch his expression as I explain. “Fraun is beginning a patrol. The men and women who make up this patrol will be from all five realms. They will travel throughout Fraun training with the various leaders, learning the skills and characteristics all realms have to offer. Once their demanding training is finished they will then be a patrol for the safety of all Fraun.”

Lance’s eyes betray nothing. “These men, this patrol you speak of, they will be expected to travel forever. Once they are a patrol they will be all over Fraun. Trained in all realms, living in all realms, these men would have no realm to call home.”

“That is true. They would be citizens of Fraun itself.”

“More prepared than any other, that is for certain.”

“Lance, who cares where we call home? Enchenda offers nothing for us.” Danyel steps forward. “I’m in.” He offers me his hand.

I hesitate. Should I accept a man who clearly takes this task to alleviate some personal sadness? Do I have a choice? I shoot out my dainty fingers and wrap them around his offered hand. “Excellent, Danyel. They will be lucky to have you. Do you have transportation that can take you to Sarcheda?”

“I’m sure I can procure some.”

“Good. King Tin will expect you by tomorrow. Please make

arrangements to be there on time." My smile is not returned to me.

"Will do, Majesty." The boy bows low before leaving the small clearing. I return my focus to Lance. "What are your thoughts on our patrol, Lance?"

"What is the council afraid of?" he challenges.

"What makes you think we are afraid of anything?" The personal pronoun was a nice touch. Perhaps I consider myself a member of the council after all.

Lance chuckles, the sound is hollow, dying at our feet instead of echoing around us. "You begin a patrol and train them more than any other in Fraun. You share them equally among all the realms. This speaks of a culture preparing for war."

I shiver at the word. "You have the wrong impression, sir. The council merely wishes to prepare for anything that may happen. There is nothing pending on our horizon, I assure you."

"Regardless of your reasons, I think it's about time Fraun organize something. I'm in." He offers his hand and I shake it. "I have transportation. I'll be at Sarcheda before sunset today," Lance says.

Look at me. I completed my first assigned task from the council in less than two suns time. As I turn to head home, I notice Sawchett drawing water from the town supply. "Good morning, child," I call.

"Hi, Princess."

"Can I carry that for you?" I offer my arm for the bucket, noticing how heavy it looks with water reaching its rim.

"Thank you." Sawchett transfers the bucket to me carefully, spilling only a few drops of the water. "We live right there." She points to Charlotte's house.

"I remember."

"You can leave it out here if you want. My aunt will bring it in."

"Actually I'd like to come in if it's alright. I really should say hello to Charlotte." I wait for the small child to step out of the way and nod before I enter the home. Inside a fire is warming everything, bringing a bright light to the crevices of the house. Is that dust covering the table? I run my finger along the surface. The motion leaves a line in the grey layer and my finger covered. That is concerning. "Is your Mother ill?" I inquire.

"She'll be alright, won't she?" Sawchett asks, her lower lip beginning to quiver.

I bend down until my eyes are even with that of the smaller maiden. "Where is she?" Sawchett merely points toward the closed curtain. "I'm going to go see her. Sawchett, whatever happens, you must trust that you will be cared for."

I leave the girl in the little kitchen and push the curtain aside. "Charlotte?" Beyond the curtain, the scene is much like that at my own home. The woman is up to her chin in blankets and looking worse for the wear; grey hair, sunken eyes, and sagging skin. "Milady, how are you feeling? Is there anything I can get you?"

"Princess, is that you?" Charlotte croaks out.

"Is it, Aunt. What can I get you?" I ask. Charlotte tries to sit up. Instead, I sit on the edge of the bed. "No, don't get up for me. I'll come to you. Tell me, how are you feeling?"

"Old," Charlotte chuckles.

She is the second person to make that joke today. I fail to see the humor. Can one truly feel old? "Can I get you anything?" I repeat.

The old woman shakes her head, no. "I'm all right child. What are you doing here? I fear I can't handle more questions about my past right now."

"I'm here for you and the girl. She was fetching water in the square. She seemed to need help. Once I got here it was clear we share concerns about your health."

"I am afraid of dying and leaving her to bear witness to that," Charlotte says.

"What can I do?"

"Take her with you."

There are so many reasons to deny that request: the king will not allow it, I am not ready to raise a child, and no one at home has prepared for it. The ferocity of Charlotte's gaze burns at me. I cannot turn the woman down. "I will."

Charlotte's eyes close. "Good. Tell Tutor that I have taken care of it."

"Tutor?" Curiosity piqued, I tap the woman to wake her. "Do you speak of Tutor the man or the profession?" When the answer is not immediate, I shake her slightly. "Answer me, woman."

Charlotte's eyes flutter open. "The man, silly girl."

"How it is you know Tutor?"

Charlotte's face registers shock for a moment. "Did I say that? What did I say?" Confusion flits across her tired face.

"You said you know Tutor. How is that?"

"He came here. When Sawchett was born he came to tutor her. Your father arranged it." The answer is clipped.

Is Charlotte lying? Why would someone lie about that? "You say Sawchett has some training from him then? She was not a child of the school?"

"No, no. She went to school as well. He only came sometimes. He helped both of us. I think your father did it from guilt."

"I will ask him of this," I promise.

"Your father or Tutor?"

"Whichever I find first. Know you where I can find Tutor?" I push to my feet.

"I do not."

"Is that honest?" I ask.

Charlotte's eyes lock on my face again. "It is the most honest I can be."

"Fair enough. I will send in the girl. You will take your time saying your farewells."

Back in the main room of the house, I lay a hand on Sawchett's little shoulder. "Your mother would like a word with you." When she departs, I find an empty wooden crate and begin tossing in articles of clothing that look like they must belong to the young one. The mention of Tutor's name has my mind working like a water wheel, constant and spinning. Why would he be worried about the girl? What does he have to do with Charlotte and Sawchett? I know the only person who can answer this to my satisfaction is the man himself. But where do I find him?

"Princess," the small voice breaks into my trance. I turn to find Sawchett standing in the room, her eyes filled with water. "I am ready now," Sawchett whimpers.

The small frame is shaking slightly, but Sawchett's shoulders are pulled back tightly. Her chin is raised. Taken as a whole her body language communicates a girl much older than her years and ready to face the world.

What impressive strength; where did she find that?

Without giving myself a chance to overthink it, I drop to my knees and open my arms to the girl. Sawchett runs to me, gladly accepting the hug. "It's going to be alright, little one," I coo, brushing the blond locks with my fingers. I feel the girl's trembling crescendo under my encircled arms. "It's alright to cry." The girl gives in to the urge and covers my shoulder with tears.

There is something about having to stand strong for another that makes you feel substantial. The sudden surge of power makes me feel more like royalty than I ever have.

Chapter 35

The door to my house flings back on its repurposed hinges faster than I meant for it to, slamming against the wall. My eyes take a moment to adjust to the darker front room. When they do, I see the small form of a servant bowing at me from the corner of the room. I recognize the woman I dined with and rush to her side. "Linchanta …" her eyes register shock at the use of her familiar name, "… this is Sawchett." I step aside to reveal the young child.

"Who is she, milady?" the servant asks.

"She is a friend of mine and she is to be treated as you would treat me. She will have a room of her own, we will need someone to fetch her more clothing, and I will see to her having a personal tutor." My heart flutters with doubt. How will I answer the questions that will likely follow these pronouncements?

But there are no questions. Linchanta merely nods, although her eyes do not leave the small one. "One more thing," I add, "my father need not be troubled with the news of another mouth to feed."

This pulls her eyes from the face of the child. They snap to mine. There is a question forming there, I can see it. Whatever it is, she swallows it down. "Of course, Majesty."

The new formal title slips into my ears easily and coaxes a small smile. I hide it by leaning down to the girl. "Sawchett, I have other business to attend to, but Linchanta will take good care of you. If you need anything, please ask. This is your home and you should be comfortable here."

"Can I play outside?" The girl's voice is weak and trembles slightly.

"Of course." I ruffle the hair of the little blonde. "Linchanta will take you out to my favorite garden once she has shown you the room you'll rest in. Sound good?"

"Thanks, Princess."

"Honey, call me Eselda."

"Thanks, Eselda."

"You're very welcome, Sawchett."

Linchanta offers her hand to the little one. "Sawchett, would you like to follow me to your room?" Sawchett places her little hand, and by extension her trust, in the offered palm. Together they leave, heading for the little room beyond the dining room.

Another order of business was taken care of.

As I turn towards my father's bedroom, I see Eee scurrying across the floor. "Eee," I call out, halting the roach in her steps. "Do you know the man who used to tutor me in my youth?"

"Yes."

"I need to speak with him. It's urgent."

"I could have him tracked down." Eee begins to move again, in the same direction she was previously headed.

"Eee," I again pause the roach merely with this word, "don't take 'no' for his answer."

"Yes, milady."

Chapter 36

"How is he feeling this afternoon?" I ask.

"About the same, Majesty. I am not sure how much longer he can hang on," the caregiver answers.

I bustle in like a hurricane wind, practically knocking the door off its second-hand hinges. "Father …" my voice trails off as I take in the sight of him sitting upright. "You look surprisingly well." I bend to kiss his forehead.

"You were expecting me to be gone from this world?" he asks lightly.

"I didn't truly know what to expect," I answer, sitting in the chair beside the bed.

"Tell me how your expedition went." He breaks into a fit of coughing that he cannot control. I hold tight to my stony expression, not wishing to show the fear he puts in me with this illness. I command myself to stay strong for my king.

When his coughing has subsided I continue as though

uninterrupted. "It went well. I found the two men who will represent Enchenda in the patrol. Both promised to be in Sarcheda by tomorrow nightfall at the latest. I have yet to find a scribe, but an idea has come to mind."

"What, pray tell, was that idea?"

"I am thinking it may be wise to request that Tutor fill the position." The idea had fleetingly crossed my mind, this much is true. But until I spoke the words aloud I had not decided what to do with the thought. Tutor is well-versed in both reading and writing. In addition, having lived among the common folk but worked among the royals he would be a wise choice for the conversations that must be had with Fraunians for this job. In truth, having now heard the thought aloud, I quite like it.

"That is one idea. Is he no longer providing tutoring services?"

"He is not. I felt as though he was no longer needed. He agreed with my assessment of the situation." I feel the pull and tug of my younger self wanting to ask if Father agrees with this decision as well. I bite back the bitter urge to ask him.

"It sounds like you have things handled."

"Thank you, Majesty." My eyes water at the unexpected praise. I blink too quickly, a fruitless effort to control the tides. "I'll let you sleep." I rush out of the room before he can respond.

Back in my chambers, I lean on the closed door and sigh. How regal is it to melt at every praise offered? I must learn to fortify myself against such praise if I am to be taken seriously as a queen.

I saunter to the window and place my palms flat on either side of the opening. In this manner, I am peering out over the walkway to town when I hear a loud crashing noise from the side of the house. Turning my head to the left, I see the head of a large creature come into my view.

A gasp escapes my lips and my hand sails to my mouth. The creature is brown, large, and leads with long hooked grippers. There are multiple legs, I count three on each side as the creature barrels toward town. I am numb with panic. Something in my mind screeches at me to move, get help, or aide in some way but my feet remain firmly planted on the flooring. I watch in horror as the creature approaches a group of boys kicking an acorn around in the street. From my room, I shriek, "Get out of the way." The voice is lost in the thin air.

I am left to watch in revulsion as the creature rapidly closes the gap between itself and the children.

Chapter 37

The town is busy. The king can tell children are playing nearby. He continues to see one or the other of the boys step into his line of sight from around a corner and then disappear again in a flurry of action and noise. According to the directions he received when he arrived in town, that is the direction to the princess' home as well.

Tin takes the corner at a reasonable clip. His eyes waste no time locking onto the ant progressing down the walkway. He takes in the whole of the creature, noticing its length is more impressive than its stature.

Instinctively, Tin steps into the path of the ant.

In his haste, he knocks one of the small boys back away from the road. When the ant collides with his body, Tin has already squared his feet to accept the weight. In this way when he stands under the creature he can lift the body and send the ant sprawling to its backside.

It takes effort for the being to right itself. In this time the king of strength never removes his eyes from the offending beast. He knows from his practice in the ring with different creatures that he must remain dominant to keep the pest moving. He holds his arms out at sharp angles in a show of size. He breathes heavily, being sure to make it sound like a war cry.

The showing is effective. The ant, once righted, scrambles away into the brush behind the houses. Thanks to his knowledge of the Fraun map, Tin knows it is heading for territory beyond their limits.

I regain my ability to move at the sight. I dash for the door and out of the house, all the while shrieking the name of the king of Sarcheda. From the end of the walkway on my front lawn, I see the king reach for the small boy. His eyes scan the child, looking for injuries. Finally, the boy rises. I arrive on the scene just in time to hear the boy thank the king, "Mister that thing would've killed me. Thank you."

Tin notices my arrival, his shoulders tighten and he stands a little taller. "If you were a bit stronger you wouldn't have needed me." His voice, hard and edgy, does not match the scene I just watched unfold.

Curious.

"Tin," I start. The king turns his head to fully look at me. "That was …" my mouth is unable to form adequate words. "It was … impressive." I settle for the first word I pull from the jumble in my brain. Once the word leaves my mouth I am disappointed in the choice. That wasn't the word for what I saw. Heroic would be better.

Tin waves off my compliment. "Ants are something we see our share of on the outskirts of Sarcheda," he says. "They can be dangerous when they are lost from their group, I think it's panic at being alone. Most of the time they mindlessly follow one another."

"I have never even seen such a creature. It could've hurt those boys if you hadn't been here."

"That's why we teach them strength in my realm. Boys that age could have handled such a creature in Sarcheda."

I think I just got a rare glimpse of what true character brews under the surface of this man, yet he tries to hide it from me now. Curious. "What are you doing in Enchenda anyway, King Tin?" I ask.

Tin visibly changes. His eyes and shoulders soften. He smiles at me and allows his eyes to trail my figure. "Actually, I came to see you."

I blush under the survey of the handsome king. "Oh? What can I help you with?"

"I know you had your meeting with the prince yesterday. I wanted to be sure you knew I was serious when I said I had the desire to court you. Clearly, I should've made it my priority in the beginning," Tin says. "What says the good prince? Does he look to the future of Fraun?" Tin asks.

I think of the giant remnants making up the back garden. Past. I think of the impressive story, not one based in past but one made up on the spot. One with even a lesson someone could learn from in the future. "I think he does," I answer. "But he hasn't yet forgotten the past. He seems to understand how to learn from it."

"What can we learn from a past full of old men who believed in outdated ideals?" Tin challenges.

"What ideals do you speak of?" I soften my tone in response to the sharp one taken by the king. I take a small step back. It would do me well to remember he is of a malicious age.

"This marriage fiasco. Do you know how many times I've been questioned by our council of leaders about my personal life and relationships?"

I shake my head. Although I'm sure I could guess.

"Who says a man is only really a man when he has a wife and children? Am I not fit to lead the council table because I do not possess those things? They talk of renumbering to remove me of my right, I know they do. What crime have I committed?" Tin asks.

That is exactly what I've been saying. I take a step toward the king and reach for his arm. "You are right. There is no crime in being alone. Certainly, if there is you are not the only one committing such a crime."

"They hold these archaic beliefs about meeting outside their council room, they undermine me when I speak out of turn, and if you need help with an issue in your realm they are not available." Tin shakes off my arm and turns away from me. "There was no one to guide me when I reached twenty annuals. No King, although they are all my elders, was willing to help me with that. I had to learn this on my own."

That's odd. Jordyn has initiated conversations with me on the same topic. Even Carsen mentioned meeting with Jordyn. "Not even Jordyn was able to offer guidance?" I quietly ask.

Tin wheels around to face me again. His eyes are troubled by anger. When he speaks his voice is low like thunder before a storm. It is a warning. "He is not the man you think he is."

I take a step back, feeling my heartbeat quicken. "You do not get along with King Jordyn?"

"We are different people both battling the same monster." The king shakes his head, rolls his neck, and looks back at me again. He takes a deep breath. "I am sorry. The state of the council gets me irate. Sometimes I wonder how we'll ever set Fraun right again."

"Do you truly feel there are that many problems here?"

Tin steps closer and takes my hand in his. He leans close until his breath falls upon my lips when he answers. "You've been there at the council table. Don't you see it?" I feel his need to have someone on his side pulsing through his body.

It must be so hard to sit there in charge of that group and remain strong. I squeeze his hand. "I think I see some of it."

At the show of reinforcement, the king leans in further until our lips touch. The sudden display of affection shocks me and the kiss is broken before I have a chance to recover. Tin straightens but does not step away. "I'm sorry, was that inappropriate?" He asks. Something in his tone of voice tells me he doesn't care in the least whether it was appropriate or not.

"Perhaps a little."

The king smiles and takes a step back. "Well, dear Eselda, I should probably head back. I have a patrol reporting to me soon. I merely needed to see you for myself to see where your prince's loyalties lie."

His loyalties?

Tin reaches for my hand, kissing the back of it lightly. "Until we meet again."

As quickly as he came, the king is around the corner and out of sight. I stand firm on the spot after he leaves. My head is fluttering with betrothal, kisses, councils, and rules.

Is it time for some of the rules to be reviewed?

Chapter 38

Our morning has been typically quiet. The clanging of the utensils on the plates and the snapping of the logs as they burn down in the fireplace are filling the awkward silences. Sawchett keeps yawning, likely because I continue to insist she rise at a decent hour of the morning even though I have not yet found her a tutor. I am interviewing another today, but if I don't stop comparing these men to the tutor I grew up with I will never find one.

"Your Majesty," a voice blusters into the room from the hallway. Two men enter. One is standing and dragging the other. The one in charge at the moment is clearly struggling, being the smaller of the two. He is pulling the writhing body of the other.

The body of the struggling man flips just right and his face comes into focus. "Tutor?"

"Tutor!" Sawchett exclaims, excitement lighting her little face.

Tutor must recognize the little voice. The fight drains out of him and he stops pulling against the stubborn foot soldier who insisted he come to see the royal family at the request of the princess. Not ready for the sudden stop to his protesting, the smaller man drops Tutor's weight to the ground. Tutor takes his time rising, never taking his eyes from Sawchett.

"Should I remain close lest he run again, Majesty?" the footman asks.

"No, you may go." I eye Tutor warily. This is the most unkempt I have ever seen the man. He is wearing grey pants that appear to be dirty, he is barefoot, and his brown shirt hangs loosely on him. I can see a small bruise on his left arm, half hidden by the shirt sleeve.

"Sawchett, what are you doing here?" Tutor asks, approaching the young girl.

"Missus Princess Eselda says I can stay here," Sawchett answers.

"I welcome the company," I explain. "Sawchett, why don't you go see to the garden and let me talk with Tutor." Sawchett rises, hugs Tutor briefly, and dashes out toward the garden.

In the girl's absence, Tutor braces for a fight. He does not turn around, so I have front-row seats to watch as the muscles in his back clinch. A bitter chuckle escapes. "Well isn't this a familiar scene?" He drops into the chair nearest him.

"How so?" I ask, coming back around in front of him and reclaiming my own seat.

"Many a time I entered this room to find two people dining. One who was tired and unprepared for the day," he gestures in the direction of the chair Sawchett has just vacated, "and one seated regally ready to lead this realm to great things." He sweeps his hand across the table, pointing to me. He allows his eyes to flit to the empty chair at the head of the table. "Why don't you occupy his chair?"

What is wrong with his attitude today? "My father lives, Tutor."

"I'm glad to hear it." He reaches for a strawberry, plucking it from my plate.

It is openly rude; he is asking me to get angry. I force myself to stay calm. I will not play your little game. Today we play with my rules. "Tutor, I have questions for you."

"I figured that out when I was summoned. Well, summon is not the right word. I figured that out when I was dragged out of bed in the middle of the night and forcibly brought here before you. What are you waiting for?

Ask your questions."

There is so much anger in him. I try to match his hard tone. "This time will be different. This time you will answer."

"Fine."

"How do you know Sawchett?" I begin with what I perceive as a safe question. Clearly, he was pleased to see the child, perhaps this is a good foot on which to begin.

"I've tutored her for the last three annuals since she could speak."

"How did you come to be employed in this manner?"

"Her mother asked me to do it." At this comment, his eyes flash dangerously.

I know how this will make him feel, but the time for treading carefully has passed. "Charlotte?"

"That's the one," he answers.

This attitude is so unlike what I recall of Tutor. He is slumped back in the chair and leaning on the arm of the furniture. He is sporting disheveled hair and wild eyes. It could be that the struggle with the man who fetched him for this meeting roughed him up a little. Or it could be something or someone else has changed the man I remember into this creature before me. "How do you know Charlotte?"

"She lives in the village. You've been there, it's hard to miss her house. She's right on the edge of the town square." He indicates the direction with one hand, but his tone of voice tells me he's being sarcastic.

"Tutor you are disrespecting a member of the royal family of Enchenda," I say without raising my voice in the least. "What relationship have you with Charlotte?"

For a beat, I am not sure he will answer. I watch the storm play out in his eyes. His jaw continues to work like he is chewing on a piece of tough meat and his right leg bounces like there is a spring below it.

Finally, he sighs. "Did you know I wasn't raised here?" The question is delivered in a whisper.

The familiar voice is back. I let out a breath I didn't realize I was holding and lean toward him. I'm thankful he is his old self, even for just a second. I'm afraid more movement, like a hug, would break the spell.

"My earliest memories are of Farcheda. I was in Farcheda until I was full height," Tutor says.

Ten annuals, I note.

"I lived with a nice couple, both old. As I understood it, my parents had died and I was being raised by the family that had lived alongside them." Tutor sits a little straighter in his chair, leaning his weight now on the right leg. In response, the bouncing is immediately resumed by his left. "When I had just reached full height, we were forced to flee Farcheda in the middle of the night. The old man had stolen something from a neighbor. We feared being caught so we fled. We ended up in Renchenda.

"I was given to another family, a younger one, to be raised. Honestly, I think the old couple was afraid they would grey and die in my presence and leave me with nothing. I attended school in Renchenda. I have to tell you, Eselda, their schooling is amazing. The things they have those children doing is …" he pauses while he thinks of a word, "… inconceivable for someone from another realm.

"During that time, I made friends with many a man who went on to become a Scout. At fifteen annuals I decided it was time for me to take my leave. I wanted to see Fraun. I wanted to travel. I wanted to join the Scouts."

The scouts are a daring and dangerous group. Their task of exploring what lies beyond Fraun and bringing back items that can be reused has always brought me equal parts fascination and fear. I pull my legs up on the chair in a childish show of my engagement in his story, settling in for the tale as I probably did many times growing up.

"The scouts wouldn't have me. They told me I first had to find a place to call home, then I could walk away if I liked. They reasoned that I was walking away from nothing in hopes of finding a home among wanderers. It was an argument with many flaws, but my youthful energy did not translate well to arguing my case. They took me on a tour of Fraun. We visited the realms in descending order, but I never made it out of Enchenda.

"When I arrived here, I fell in love with the realm. The houses are quaint, the people are so nice, and I really felt at home here. I stayed for a while in the group housing off the town square near the strawberry patch. I was staying there when I met Charlotte. She made a habit, apparently, of visiting there. She explained once that a child she had lost would've been the age of the boys in this group home and she liked to give back by visiting. She took me for new clothes, new shoes, and food. She came back to visit me four or five times. She was impressed with how smart I was, likely due to my time in Renchenda. When I had been here for an annual and was tiring of day labor, she told me of an opening at the royal house. Her husband, a wonderful man named Den, knew of an opening for a tutor here."

During his tale to this point, Tutor's eyes had flit between the fire roaring in the fireplace and the table in front of him. He nervously tells his tale, but he tells it as one would tell an empty room. At this time, he turns his gaze fully on me as though remembering I am here. "I doubt you remember, you weren't much older than Sawchett, but I was given the job when I was about sixteen annuals and I've been your personal tutor ever since."

"I don't remember having anyone other than you tutor me."

"You would've had someone else for a few years when you first learned to speak."

"Did Charlotte continue to help you?"

"She allowed me to move into her home after her husband died. I helped care for Sawchett and tutored her once she began speaking."

"You never knew Charlotte was royal blood?"

His knee speeds up in its jostling and his expression hardens again. "Not until you told me." He adopts his angry tone as easily as one would put on a shoe.

"Do you have any opinions on that subject?"

"I do not." His gaze is piercing. It is his turn to ask the questions that need to be asked. "Is it why you have brought the girl here?" He grinds his teeth as he awaits the answer. "Is she to be some kind of pawn for whatever you are planning?"

"I brought the girl here so she wouldn't need to see what is becoming of Charlotte," I snap.

"Are you grooming her as a princess?"

"It was not my intention, no."

"Then why summon me? Surely it was to tutor the young princess, prepare her to inherit the realm." His voice is thick with contempt.

Never in my life have I been spoken to with such hatred. "Tutor, I do not want you to be responsible for the education of the girl any longer. I had questions for you, that much is true. I had also hoped you had it in you to undertake another job, but now I fear it is too difficult a task for one so emotionally against royalty."

"I have spent much of my life serving your family. What makes you say I am against royalty?"

"I never had that thought before. But I realize you think less of Charlotte now that you know. This woman cared for you when no one else knew you. It sounds like you owe a lot to this stranger in your tale, and yet you seem enraged now that you know her truth."

"She lied." The words are spat from his mouth like seeds.

"She did. At the request of her king, for the betterment of her people, she lied." I look deep at Tutor, willing the man I know to be inside somewhere beneath the anger. "Can you honestly say you wouldn't do the same if I asked it of you?"

I find the scariest moment to be the one following this sentence. Can I, the future queen, ask things of my people? Will they follow me as they follow my father? Tutor rises and walks to the lineage chart painted on the wall. He stands ramrod straight, hands buried deep in the pockets of his grey slacks. I allow the silence to wrap itself around the room, a dark blanket on our scene. The silence stretches, folding over on itself until it has cocooned us both.

Deliberately, Tutor reaches his fingers out and caresses the black oval covering Charlotte's name. "She should be here," he whispers.

I want to jump for joy at the return of his familiar tone.

I walk across the room to stand behind my oldest friend. "How many others are missing, Tutor?" I ask. "How many, like Sawchett, never graced this wall?" I reach out my hand and lay it on his shoulder. "The council believes it would be wise to find out the answer to these questions. They have asked me to find someone capable of updating the lineage chart for Enchenda." I don't ask if he will undertake the job, I let the idea grow roots.

"She will likely die never knowing her name was once here," he whispers. "That is wrong. She should know."

"You're right, she should."

Tutor turns without warning, shocking me. My arm falls back to my side. Tutor is close enough that his foot lies between mine. "I would like to be in charge of updating this lineage tree, but I have one condition."

"I'll hear your condition."

"All names I find get recorded. No one can choose to leave one off the wall for any reason. I don't care if they were shunned, embarrassing, or dishonest. If I unearth proof of their royal blood, they get their names on that wall in gold ink." He gestures to the wall. "No exceptions."

I hold my serious expression for a beat as I pretend to consider his offer. Finally, a smile breaks out across my face. "I knew you were the right man for the job."

Chapter 39

Seven days and seven nights pass. I notice Sawchett is already blossoming under the attention of the newly promoted lady-in-waiting, Linchanta. I watch the pair pull weeds from the garden, the sun bouncing off their blonde heads bent low. Sawchett sits cross-legged on the ground, holding a stubborn green plant by the base and pulling with all her strength. The servant smiles at her, making light of the lack of upper body strength, before helping her to yank the offender from the ground.

I sip my lemon water and return my gaze to the papers in my lap. Although the people of my realm are not noted on the wall in my home, or in any place where the council will recognize them, they do feel honor in their lineage. It is tracked by the medicine men in the village. I requested copies of any death notices or birth notices that come their way. This sheet, prepared and sent to me this morning, includes the fourteen deaths of recent days and the twenty-three births. This is good information for a princess, such as me, to have as I plan for the future. This means there are nine more bodies to clothe, nine more mouths to feed, nine future students to train, nine more people to protect.

How many more people can the small realm house before it can do no more? Will we run out of food or shelter first? I shake my head. Certainly, the council will see fit to allow us to assemble more homes before people are without living quarters. I will see to it.

Sawchett's youthful giggle pulls my attention back to the garden where the two young ladies have managed to free the weed. Sawchett proudly holds it over her head, a sign of the struggle overcome. "Well done." I clap for the show.

"Would you like to help, Eselda?" Sawchett asks.

"Actually …" the voice floats from the far reaches of the yard like seeds on the wind. Gentle, calm, and beautiful. I turn toward it in time to hear the end of the sentence. "… I'd like to steal her away if it's not too much trouble."

My eyes light upon the brown hair glowing in the sun and I smile. "Prince Carsen, to what do I owe this pleasure?" I rise and stretch out my palm, which he wraps warmly in his own.

"I was hoping to speak with you a moment."

I notice the uptick in pitch at the end. Not an order, but a question. I nod once. "Let's speak over there." I point in the direction of the sideyard, away from the prying ears of the girls.

We walk in silence. Once we are around the corner of the house, Carsen sits down on the ground. He gestures to the space beside him and I sit as well. "How are you feeling today, Eselda?" he asks.

"I am well, thank you." What is he doing here?

"I have a proposition for you," Carsen blurts, reaching for my hand.

"I'm listening."

"I was speaking with King Jordyn."

My Jordyn? I mean my friend, Jordyn? I cover any emotions with a smile.

"He has offered his blessing and his castle should you choose to accept."

"Accept what?" I squint my eyes, trying to decipher the puzzle Carsen has begun laying out.

"I have been privy to the fact that your time to rule fast approaches and that the council is concerned. Were it not for this fact," he blushes, "I would never rush this."

"Carsen …" I spin my hand so it is now holding his as well as being held by him. I squeeze once. "… stop being apologetic. Let's have the thought on the table and we shall work around it."

Carsen leans in close. He veritably whispers, "Princess Eselda, will you be my wife?"

I wait to feel emotion. Warmth and love at the question, anger and frustration at the askant, anything. Instead, I feel nothing. It is the shock of this lethargy that holds my voice in its prison. My eyes drop to a spot on the ground and I freeze.

Carsen begins to panic, he presses forward. "I don't mean to be presumptuous. Like I tried to explain, I would never have rushed this were it not for the politics. But Eselda, I really do have feelings for you. Our date showed me what an amazing woman you are."

He squeezes my hand briefly, but I cannot react. His pulse quickens and his breathing picks up. "I played the scenario out in my head, you know, like a good story. I imagined taking you out on many occasions. We would grow to fall desperately in love and then we would wed. But when I talked with Jordyn," At this name my cheek twitches slightly, "he pointed out that this plan could take more than an annual. What if then we were unable to have children right away or that took annuals atop that? This is a long time to wait, he reasoned, if I already know how I feel."

Finally, I feel able to move. I turn my eyes to his face.

"You are beautiful," he blurts. "Your hair has this lovely red tint and your eyes are the color of a shamrock."

I shake off the flattering comment. "After one dinner, you already feel as though you could spend your entire life with me?"

"I do. You are an amazing person whom I am just barely getting to know."

I can appreciate that. But what of the future of Fraun? There is more to this than two people, one of whom may be falling in love. "Was this a business proposition or a proposition of the heart, Prince?"

"A little of both, I'm afraid."

"Then we better talk details of our business." I slide into the body language I have learned from Tutor; back straight, shoulders hunched slightly forward. Carsen will feel as though I am closing in. I will get honest answers. "Which of us is to rule Enchenda?"

"You."

"What is to become of you?"

"I will be your king, but this is your realm."

"What becomes of Marchenda?"

"They will need a ruler, but my father is not dying yet," Carsen answers.

As opposed to my father, he means to say. "He will soon. What then?"

"We will just need to have children."

Oh. Despite my desire to keep the pressure on him that one makes me sit back. I let my shoulders slump. "I am starting to think no one will be happy until I do just that."

Perhaps this is the only way to end this incessant focus on my love life. Perhaps this will allow me to actually run my realm without pressure. Jordyn … wait, that reminds me.

"What did any of this," I ask, "have to do with the king of wisdom?"

"What is he if not a good sounding board for all things logical and wise? Who better to help with a decision that needs to be analyzed?"

I can't argue with that.

"I knew how I was feeling, but when he explained the situation as the council sees it I knew it was unwise to wait. Both of our realms need more rulers quickly. I'm only trying to speed up what I know would've happened eventually, Princess," says Carsen.

It is this comment, delivered with such confidence, that finally brings the warmth. It begins in my stomach and slowly spreads. "We would've married eventually?" This time the question is playful.

"That's how the story goes." He sounds relieved. He reaches for me, placing one hand on either hip and scooting closer until there is no gap between us. There he freezes. I wait him out for as long as I can stand it before I close the gap and plant a kiss on the lips of the prince.

Carsen rests his forehead on mine. "I can love you, Eselda. If you will let me."

I think about my life as of late. A queen must make decisions for her realm. There must be a child, a child within wedlock, and it must come from someone who can serve Enchenda with me and not be tied to his own realm. It cannot be a king whose loyalties lie elsewhere in the Fraun. I begin to nod my head. "I will marry you, Prince Carsen."

A smile of pure happiness fills his face as he pulls our foreheads apart. This time, it is Carsen who kisses me and the kiss is deep. I cannot help but feel small tendrils of smoky sadness wind their way through the warmth of the moment.

When the kiss breaks, Carsen's smile is somehow wider. "Jordyn has offered us the castle Fraun for the announcement party."

"Announcement party?" What else did these two plan without me? Was there no doubt that I would say yes?

"Yes. It is customary to announce the engagement of any member of a ruling family. In this case, a special case, all of Fraun will delight in the news. What better reason for a party?" Carsen says.

"What else, pray tell, did you boys plan?"

"Nothing else, Eselda. Only that there is to be a party, and you are to be the star."

I smile a little as old dreams of dancing all night in the moonlight fill my head. "We are to be the stars, you mean."

"How could I hope to compete with you?" he teases. "Would you like me to work out the details of the announcement party with Jordyn?"

I shake my head. "No, I will handle that. You speak with your father. I will be in touch." I rise from the ground, and Carsen scrambles to get up in my wake. "I shall write to our friend now and begin planning."

"When will I see you again?" Carsen asks.

"Soon." I plant a small kiss on the cheek of my promised and head quickly to the house.

There is much to do.

Chapter 40

King Gregario of Enchenda
and
King Larecio of Marchenda
are pleased to announce the betrothal of their only children
Princess Eselda
and
Prince Carsen.

A Ball is to be held announcing this to all of Fraun on the next full moon in the Castle Fraun. We hope you and guests of your realm will join us for the celebration.

He crumbles the parchment in his fist and lobs it into the roaring fire.

Second place.

He doesn't even try to fight the dark malevolence as it takes hold, instead he lets it engulf him. As he rises from his chair, he swipes at it and sends the heavy wood smashing into the far wall. He stands, breathing deeply, and letting the anger grow roots.

This will not do.

I knew this was possible, but I thought I had more time.

No, this will not do at all.

I will fix this.

Chapter 41

Our house is bustling with activity. On the lawn, shivering from the cold, nine bakers sit with samples of their treats. In the front room of the home, thankful to be out of the elements, six musicians await their audience. They bear instruments and play soft notes to prepare. In the dining room, in front of a warm fire, seven dressmakers display their craft to an overwhelmed version of me.

I have already made decisions about the material to cover the tables, what time of day to hold this ball, and what beverages to serve. I am now trying to decide which dress would be just right. This decision, which would've been my favorite task as a younger girl, is getting lost among all the things to be done.

I finger the soft fabric of the simple pink gown again, smiling as it slips through my fingers. Pink is the color of a girl, immature and unprepared. I can no longer be that girl. I am announcing my engagement to a prince.

I look at the deep purple gown again, heavy and adorned with small white pearls. The sleeves are full length and would extend past my wrists to cover the backs of my hands with the small triangles of fabric. The skirt is shaped to flow out around me, brushing the floor and giving me the appearance of a large purple bell from the waist down. The top is cut very high, almost to my neck. I frown, I could never wear something that hot and restricting.

Next along the line is the blue gown. This one comes lower, dangerously so. What a fiasco I would be if too much skin were showing in front of the council and important members of Fraun. I sweep my eyes onward.

This next dress is yellow and has no straps or sleeves. The bodice is tight and wrapped with jewels. The skirt layers have been cinched to give the appearance of many layers although it may be only one. I reach out a finger and brush the fabric. It is cold but soft. "I would like to try on this one." I hear the other six dressmakers sigh as one.

The dressmaker, behind closed doors, helps me into the small gown. It is zipped up my backside as I face the reflecting wall. The bodice hugs my frame, giving focus to the curves I am learning to embrace. I run my fingers over the billowing skirt, smiling. The color plays well with my dark curls, cascading over the bodice. "Do I look like a princess?" I whisper to the mirror.

"No, Majesty, you look like a queen." The woman smiles and bows.

"I'll take it." I nod. "Now help me out of it and I will show you the girl you are to dress as well." As we begin working on zippers, I continue issuing directions. "She is to be in the same color, but something more simple. I want her to match my house, but she is to look like a girl. Light fabric, plain, soft. Then you will go to Renchenda and prepare my fiancé's suit as well. Use touches of this yellow among the black."

At this, the woman's hands freeze. "Renchenda, Majesty?"

My eyes widen. "Did I say Renchenda?" At her nod, I rush to rationalize the error, "My mistake, the party is in Renchenda. My betrothed is in Marchenda."

The woman widens her eyes, just once, and bends to gather the dress. I quickly slip back into my house dress, a more understated black garb. "Thank you, madam." I quickly leave the room, glad to escape the embarrassing error. In the hallway, I wave to Linchanta to bring Sawchett in for her fitting.

I dismiss the other dressmakers with my fondest apologies, then signal for the next group to be brought in. I close my eyes and run my hands across my face, trying to wipe away the exhaustion. When my hands come away it is a local medicine man standing before me. "May I help you, good sir?"

"I have news for you, your Majesty."

"On with it then, it's a busy day here."

"You may want to sit, Majesty."

"I am fine where I stand, thank you. What news do you bring?"

"The woman you asked about last time we spoke, Charlotte?"

I nod. I fear I already know why he is here.

"She has passed, Majesty."

Tears spring to my eyes. With much effort, I hold them in. It is silent in the room as I wrestle with my composure. My mind springs to the story Carsen weaved about the frog father. "Was she alone?" I ask, my voice shaking.

"A man named Tutor was at her side," he answers.

Well that, at least, is a comfort. "Thank you for the news."The man receives the hint, bowing gracefully from the room. I make a triangle out of my fingers and blow into it as I fight with my emotions.

I wish there had been more time to get to know Charlotte. After all, she is my Aunt. My blood relative. But I cannot allow myself to be selfish. There is someone else here who will feel this loss. Perhaps even more than I have felt it.

I trace my steps back to the dressing room, pausing outside the door to take a stabilizing breath. I can do this.

When the door opens I take in the sight of Sawchett as she is now. In front of the reflecting wall, a dressmaker beside her with a string wrapping around the girl's arm. Her excitement is palpable. It's a terrible feeling, knowing I'm about to ruin that.

"I need a moment with the girl." Without question, the dressmaker scurries from the room. I gesture to a bench along the back wall. "Let's sit."

The girl doesn't even question me. She drops to the bench. I sit beside her and take a deep breath. "I have some news for you, and it's not going to be pleasant."

Sawchett's smile falls. "Do I have to leave?"

I reach for her, slipping an arm around her shoulders and pulling her close into a sideways hug. "Never, my dear. I love having you here. No, the news comes from the village." I pull away enough to allow myself to look the girl in the eye. "Remember we talked about how sick your mother was?"

Sawchett nods slowly. She sits straighter and tears fill her eyes. She already knows the truth, but I must put it in words. There is no easy way to do this. "She has passed, Sawchett."

The tears are immediate. Sawchett flops down, burying her head in the folds of my black dress. Her sobs tremble her small frame and fill the little room. I stroke the soft sun-kissed hair and let her cry.

It is a struggle to contain my own emotions, but this is Sawchett's loss. I cannot lessen this pain by feeling some of it for her, although I wish I could. So instead, I maintain my calm while Sawchett falls apart.

Chapter 42

In the room that is becoming his prison, Gregario taps his finger impatiently on the bed sheet. "Try and stay calm, Majesty," the medicine woman coos.

"Where is she? Isn't this when she comes to see me?"

Growing old, he has come to realize, actually means shrinking. He no longer has the strength to rise from this bed. *For all intents and purposes, I am gone already. Is it too much to ask for an exit from this life worthy of the king I tried to be? Something honorable and graceful? Dignified even?*

A small knock on the door precedes the entrance of his daughter, bringing with her the smell of cinnamon. Eselda looks weary and tired. He recognizes the mask of strength she hides it behind, it is one he often wore himself.

"Good evening, father." She bends, kisses his forehead, and takes her chair beside the bed.

"How goes our party planning?" he asks.

"It went well; many decisions were made. I have other news to bring you tonight, father. News that will not be so pleasant." She winces at the thought of repeating the news but leans close to her father's ear so as not to be heard by the resident caregiver. "Charlotte has passed from this life," she whispers.

Internally the old man struggles to process the onslaught of memories rising within. *In recent years Charlotte and I had little to no contact. This is not what I want to remember.* He is smacked by the sudden memory of Charlotte, young and waif-like with hair like wheat, dancing in her flowing skirts in the field beyond the strawberries. She danced as though nothing in the world could break her happiness. *She was the most beautiful woman I had ever laid eyes upon.*

The memory changes, he recalls lying in a field alongside Charlotte. The tinkling of her laugh reverberates through his ears as though it is happening now.

Even after I learned who she was, I have always loved this woman. The one who never truly existed. The mere memory of the girl who was perfect for me. The one I never felt related to. The one I had no connections of blood to, but just wanted to be with. She will forever remain frozen at this age, in this way in my mind. Separate from the child of my father's dark secret.

Eselda can see Gregario is processing information, so she slips quietly from the room. The years rush at him faster now as he allows himself to remember things long buried.

My father's face the day he ran into us in the village is equally as clear as the memories of my young Charlotte. But that memory has sharp teeth which bite at my happy thoughts.

His face showed eagerness and excitement to meet the girl his son had spent so much time with. But that mask had cracked and hardened instantly when she came into view. Even the memory feels confusing as the true moment did back then.

Then came the unveiling. Charlotte was revealed to be the daughter of Stefan himself. The king had taken over the planning of the rest of the situation, including Charlotte's future. *Numbed by the turn of events and my father's bitter secret, I blindly followed his plan.*

In the wake of those events, Gregario had never spoken of them to a soul. The ache for the girl that no longer existed to him and never would again exist in the same way left him a changed man. He later married out of necessity and convenience for his realm. He forced himself to face forward and march onward.

Until today.

Today the old king finally glances backward and lets the sadness consume him.

Chapter 43

Candles burn and cast shadows upon my face in front of the largest reflecting wall I've ever seen. I am deep within the walls of Castle Fraun, wearing my yellow gown and readying myself for the evening.

I recall Carsen's promise … *there is to be a party, and you are to be the star.*

The gown picks up the light from the candles and reflects it, shimmering with its own beauty. My hair, wrapped around the diadem worn only when I am attending formal events, is flowing and light. I am the picture of royal beauty until the lights fall upon my face.

Don't get me wrong, I see the beauty there. My delicate features have been scrubbed until they are rosy. But the eyes … the eyes give away my true heart.

Tonight I announce a marriage of business, a marriage of convenience. The girl who once dreamed of a love story to end all love stories has accepted a fate absent of that. It is a fate I can resign myself to, but you cannot hide sadness like that from your eyes.

Enough. This is best for Enchenda and Fraun. Carsen is a good man. He is a good match. He will care for me, love me, and make me happy. "You will feel happy about this announcement," I command my reflection.

Behind me, the door opens. In the reflection, I see Sawchett enter. "Eselda, can you help me with my hair?" Sawchett asks, holding up a clip.

The dress for the girl was made in white with the yellow I chose as an accent color. The dress has long sleeves and a high neck, it complements the girls' blonde locks well. She wears it like a little princess. I beckon to the girl, holding my hand out. Sawchett passes me the small jeweled clip and watches in the mirror as I expertly flip the hair up into a twist that leaves only small ringlets framing the delicate face.

"You look beautiful, Sawchett." In the mirror, I watch her eyes sparkle like diamonds, an expression only a little girl playing dress-up can muster. I remember the days when ball gowns and dances held as much joy for me as Sawchett displays tonight. This is growing up. Not an end to my childhood but watching it through the eyes of another.

Sawchett twirls in a circle, her dress flowing out around her. "I'm going to go dance," she proclaims. I cannot even hope to answer before she runs from the room to do exactly that.

I turn back to my reflection. I take a deep breath and throw my shoulders back. I will go out and face the people. There will be many people here tonight. Each king was invited, and each will likely bring members of their realm with them. Those of Renchenda, who don't have to travel far, will likely be greatest in number. But even my own realm, farthest away, sent rows of people traveling on roaches to Castle Fraun this morning. My stomach flutters at the thought.

Again the door opens. This time in the reflection I see the king of strength himself. I talk to the reflection. "King Tin, can I help you find something?"

The king pushes the door closed quietly and closes the gap between us with remarkable agility. He stops just short of my body, his heat searing my back and shoulders. In the reflection I watch as he leans down toward me, closing his eyes and breathing in my scent. I close my own eyes as he whispers in my ear, his breath lightly brushing my skin and making the hair on my neck stand at attention. "I found what I was seeking."

My breathing quickens, my palms sweat, and my stomach flutters.

"Why did you search for me, Tin?"

"I had to see you one more time before the announcement is made and I can no longer stand this close."

I feel the heat of his hand on my hip, his palm lying flat where the skirt begins. "I had to touch you before you belong to another and I no longer can," he practically purrs.

I keep my eyes shut tight and swallow the rush of emotion at the flattery. "King Tin this is hardly appropriate." I try to sound confident. My voice quavers slightly. I hope he doesn't notice. "I am announcing my betrothal to another tonight."

The pressure on my hip increases and I feel his free hand light upon my other hip. I open my eyes and catch his in the reflection for just a heartbeat before he spins my body around. The motion is quick, almost painful, a shocking reminder of his strength.

"Do you choose him freely?" he asks. His voice is suddenly harsh and demanding.

Fear begins to creep up my spine. "I … I do. Carsen is a good man."

Something flashes in Tin's eyes but he drops his hands and steps back. It is a small step, but the space it leaves between us is enough to allow me to breathe again. "Then best wishes to you both." He traces his eyes down the length of my body, almost sadly. Then he turns to leave.

He is halfway to the door before he turns back. "Eselda, the rules could be changed." His voice is pleading. "It doesn't have to be this way. Just say the word and we can escape all of this."

My breaths are shallow as the comment echoes in the stone room. Reflexively I take a step toward Tin and the offered promise. Can the rules be changed? Is it this simple?

I stop myself. Think of what is best for Fraun. "Thank you for the offer, King Tin. I'm sorry. I'm betrothed to another," I answer.

Tin hangs his head, defeated. "So be it." His voice is quiet but somehow strong. He turns and leaves the room and all the air escapes me.

This is going to be a long night.

Chapter 44

He stands in the shadows at the back of the ballroom. People from all over Fraun fill the room, dressed in their best clothes. Four men with various instruments play music together along the side. Some of the younger Fraunians dance gaily in the center. At the front of the room, two of the five heavy thrones are filled as Mick and Larecio sit, smiling and whispering amongst themselves. Everything about this scene conveys happiness.

The king of wisdom quietly takes it all in.

This is logical, this match. They are the appropriate age for each other. They are of similar backgrounds. They need each other to bring a future to their realms. The match allows for five realms to continue to have representation. It makes sense.

When I listened to Carsen talk about Eselda I knew, deep down, I could not take this from him. There is no reason why I should object to this betrothal, and yet I feel the anger raging within.

For the first time in his life, Jordyn is at war with himself about a logical decision. This puts him in a foul mood. He remains hidden in the shadows, hoping with everything he has that this does not turn out badly.

The music changes to clipped noises used to get the attention of the crowd. A young man stands tall at the back of the room and speaks loudly into it. "Presenting, from Enchenda, Princess Eselda."

The doors to the ballroom open and Eselda glides into the room. At first, Jordyn can't look. He breathes deeply and keeps his eyes focused on the ground. A young Fraunian bumps into him and his eyes land on her in the shuffle. *That yellow dress … the woman wearing it … they both glow.*

Just that quickly, the monster is caged.

Chapter 45

I tremble with an old fear. The fear of making a mistake or of making a fool of myself in front of everyone. Walk slowly. Don't trip. I make my way to the front of the room where I shake hands with King Larecio and King Mick before standing beside the chair reserved for my father. The eyes in the crowd, which have followed me to this point, now turn back toward the door in anticipation of the prince.

The same man who announced me clears his throat and loudly speaks again. "Presenting, from Marchenda, Prince Carsen."

The doors open again. This time there is no one in the doorway. A gasp escapes the crowd. A few stray men run toward the door, looking left and right before shrugging.

Chaos ensues.

"What is going on?" I watch, confused, as people spread out to search the castle grounds for the prince. It seems like a lot of panic for one man who likely just changed his mind. I flop onto the floor near the thrones. As evidence of their focus on the prince, no one notices the decidedly unroyal act.

I turn my head as a pair of shoes stops beside me. "What is going on?" I ask again.

"People are worried. A prince is missing."

My spine stiffens at his voice. I turn my eyes up to the man I have been avoiding since the proposal. Questions I will not ask him fill my mind. Why? Can't we …? Will there ever …?

To add frustration to my sadness tears begin building behind my eyes. I feel them burning back there. I want to tell him about Charlotte's death. I want to tell him I doubt this marriage. I want to tell him that Tin seems to think the rules can be changed. If they can be changed for that king, maybe …

The desire to share this burden is so great, I have to physically restrain myself. I wrap my arms tightly around my drawn-up knees.

"Do you know where Carsen might be?" Jordyn asks.

I shake my head and feel my curls bob and dance. "I'm sure he's here somewhere." I shrug. "Perhaps he's changed his mind."

"He did not do that."

"How can you be so sure?" I don't add that I would have changed mine if another option had presented itself.

"The man I spoke to was clearly in love, just the way you described it to me once upon a time," Jordyn answers.

I blush at his words and cast my eyes to the ground. The guilt is overwhelming. Carsen really felt that?

"You don't run from that," Jordyn adds.

I whip my head back around to the king. "You don't?" Anger raises my voice. "That's funny, I thought someone wise once told me you must do what is right for Fraun and allow the system to work despite your personal feelings."

Jordyn does not shy from my gaze but meets it. He doesn't even blink. "In that particular case, the feelings did not befit Fraun. In this case, they do. The situation is not the same."

I rise. From here I'm close enough to touch Jordyn but I won't let myself give in to that desire. "I remember what you said and I haven't forgotten what I must do for my people." I can feel the tension crackling between us like lightning.

Without warning, there is a scream and a commotion at the entrance to the hall. Jordyn pushes me behind his tall frame and faces the doors. I peer around the king, annoyed at him for treating me like a child. A man has run into the front of the hall, terror writ plainly on his face.

"The prince is dead," the man bellows.

Chapter 46

Ever the responsible one in a crowd, the king of wisdom has managed to get all of the party guests into the ballroom to keep them occupied and in one place while we collect details. Now, in the center of a smaller room located just off the ballroom, he stands surrounded by the kings of Fraun and the man who discovered the body. I remain with this group as a representative of the House of Enchenda.

"Tell us what you discovered," Jordyn commands the man.

The man's eyes dance nervously around the outside of the room, taking in the varying faces that look on. King Larecio is sitting on the floor, wallowing in a misery none have ever seen him in. Jordyn, Tin, and I are in a small line directly in front of the man. King Mick stands beside Larecio, but his eyes are fixed on our conversation. The man swallows. "We were searching for the prince all over the castle grounds —"

"Who is we?" Jordyn asks.

"Everyone on your staff, Majesty," he answers. "I opened the door to the small room on the first level, where the prince had been getting himself ready for the announcement. I found him lying dead on the floor."

Jordyn jabs a finger at the servant. "Be more specific. What did you do? How did you know he was dead?" Jordyn's gaze is boring into the man, who shakes underneath it.

"I entered from the only entrance, and immediately saw him. He was laying on the floor and blood had pooled around him. I could tell it was coming from a long wound on his neck, which was sliced open."

At this, King Larecio lets out a long wail of pain. Jordyn remains focused on the man, but the attention of the other royals turns to the older king.

"We will look at this wound later, but what is your opinion? Could it have been something he did himself?" Jordyn quizzes.

Behind him, Larecio wails again.

"Jordyn…" I reach out and touch the arm of the king. He jumps as if slapped and looks down at my hand. "… take this conversation to the side of the room out of the earshot of the man's father," I request.

Confusion crosses his face.

"Please."

Jordyn and the man who made the discovery head for the side of the room. I follow and use my body to shield King Larecio from the view of this discussion.

"It was not one he could inflict himself, in my opinion. There was no weapon around. If he had cut it himself, what became of the weapon?" the man says.

"Was anything out of place in the room? Did you move anything?" Jordyn asks, his voice a little quieter now.

"No, Majesty. Nothing was moved and I moved nothing. I came straight to the ballroom to tell you and the others of the discovery."

"Did you shut the door behind you? Could anyone else have been down there since then?"

"No Majesty. I put a roach on guard at the door after I shut it with instructions to let no one pass without your permission."

Jordyn pats the man heavily on the shoulder. "Good man. Take us to the room."

I stand frozen just outside the open door. Jordyn and the servant have stepped into the room. I heard the king take a sharp and jagged breath when he entered. Fear for what must cause this noise from such a man has me grounded in my position. From this point, I can hear their conversation as it continues.

"I agree with your earlier assessment, good sir." The voice of Jordyn, shaky but ever professional, floats to my ears. "There is no way prince Carsen inflicted this injury upon himself."

"The wound is deeper than I remembered it being, Majesty."

"It is deep, someone used a sharp weapon to cause this. I cannot even look down at the body for clues. That deep gash and the awkward angle with which his body lies turns my stomach."

"I feel the same, Majesty."

"How long was Carsen absent before you discovered this?" Jordyn asks.

"Not long, Majesty. Perhaps three songs from the band. I had only enough time to search two other rooms before arriving here."

"Interesting." Jordyn's voice ticks up at the end and the word trails on. He is thinking.

"You are thinking that timeline will help us determine who may have killed the prince, Majesty?"

"I am thinking just that."

"So whoever did this must have been away from the crowd during that time," the man offers.

"That seems to be the case, yes."

"Who would do such a thing?"

I lean closer to the door, for this is the question I have as well.

"If I were to venture a guess, it is someone who has a reason to want the prince to not marry our fair princess there," Jordyn says.

My eyes slam shut. This is my fault.

"Who would not want them to wed?" the servant asks.

"I would hazard we are looking for a male, young, someone who perhaps thought they were a candidate for the princess if Carsen here were not in the picture."

A whimper escapes my lips. That cannot be, can it? What a terrible thing. My mind spawns a suggested culprit, but I will not acknowledge it.

"Do you know of such a man?" the servant asks.

"I can think of one or two such men," Jordyn admits. "More importantly, can you think of any?"

"Majesty, in the interest of being thorough, I must ask you something," the servant says. "Where were you when the prince here was killed?"

I cannot abide this. I burst through the doorway. "That is highly inappropriate, sir. The king was with me while you were searching the castle for the prince." The man steps back from me, fear written on his face. "How dare you accuse him of such an act?" I yell. "This man is a king, your king. Do you know what you are suggesting?"

Jordyn catches my raised hand, calming me.

"I only wanted to be thorough, ma'am," he answers, his voice quaking.

"He is not wrong to ask, Eselda."

"But you were with me. Perhaps it is good he is thorough, but tell him you couldn't have done this." I continue to trap the servant with my angry expression.

"I cannot do that," Jordyn says.

What? I turn my gaze to the king but not before I note the servant's mouth falling open in shock. Jordyn's blue eyes meet mine with pain.

No. No, stop talking before you say something that will forever change my opinion of you, Jordyn. Please.

"Carsen may likely have been killed before we knew he was missing. Until we know when he was last seen, I have no alibi. It could've well been me," Jordyn admits.

"Surely you would know if it was you, Jordyn." My voice is soft, a prayer spoken only to him. I close the small gap between us and rest my palm over his heart.

"I wish I could tell you I didn't do this. But things often happen in my dark states that I remember not." He reaches out a hand and caresses my cheek. "I was so angry with Carsen this morning when I saw him, the monster inside was hard to tame. I don't know what I may have done in a disassociated state if such a state were to have occurred. I'd like nothing more than to claim this wasn't me. I fear I just don't know that for sure."

"What do we do?" I ask as the first tear for this event finally falls.

"We let my man here investigate. He is wise, he will find the answer. Even if the answer is not the one we want him to find."

"Jordyn—"

"Eselda, it is what Carsen deserves," says the king. Jordyn turns his attention to the young servant. When he speaks again the earlier sadness is absent and he is all business, "Are you up for this task?"

"I have spent my life idolizing you, sir. I am seeing you in a new light today. If you had asked me yesterday if I thought you were capable of love, a feeling devoid of logic, I would have told you no. Today, after what I have witnessed here, I know that may not be the truth anymore."

I blush. Apparently, I did not imagine our spark.

"If you want objectivity, I can give that to you now. I fear I no longer know what you are capable of. Could it be murder? I am not sure. I consider it an honor that you trust me, Majesty. I will undertake this. I have a few questions for you though. Perhaps ones I should ask without the princess present."

"Ask me whatever you'd like. But I will make one suggestion. Do not let King Tin leave this castle without asking him questions as well."

Chapter 47

The king watches the sunrise through the window. He, as well as most of those in attendance at the party, has not been to sleep yet. Based on the questioning of the small servant man who has been put in charge of the investigation, he is a person of interest in this murder. As well it should be. *After all, I am the person who used the kitchen knife to slice through the throat of the prince.* He has to stop himself from smiling at the thought.

The lie I told earlier slipped so easily off my tongue, more so than I thought it would. I had dreaded having to lie about my involvement. I knew the questions they would fire: When was the last time I saw Carsen? Did I have any reason to want the prince dead? I wondered what I would say to such questions.

As it turned out, it was easier than I thought. Mostly truth with some small adjustments. I even had the foresight to talk about the darkness that is my age marker, just in case.

Ironically, were someone to outright ask me if I had murdered the prince I would probably take credit. However, no one has done that yet. For now, my lies seem to be holding water.

He glances around the room, eyes lighting upon the princess. This isn't over yet; it's only just getting started.

Chapter 48

Outside the large house, snow is softly falling. The rising sun tinges the sky a soft pink. People are inside their own homes, plumes of white smoke reaching for the stars. Sawchett knows the people are hiding from the cold as much as they are observing the day of grievance ordered by the council.

She overheard the conversation last night, this is "highly unprecedented" according to one lady. A day of grievance is often observed following the death of a royal. It is a day when Fraunians will not work. For one full sun cycle, they will not attend school or shop. They will remain in their homes and think about the life they have lost.

Today, however, differs from the previous days of grievance. At the Castle Fraun yesterday, as the sun was rising, the council made an announcement to the room. Sawchett had been seated on the floor, nearest the window, her eyes drifting closed on their own accord from the long night. The prince had been dead for the entire night and the sun was finally making an appearance. King Mick had loudly declared that all of Fraun would be observing the day of grievance by order of the council of kings.

The council would allow you to travel back to your homes and the day would be observed the next day, today.

Sawchett cannot help but be awed by such an act of power. King Mick's voice had boomed through the room and not a soul had questioned him. *Had Prince Carsen possessed such a power? If so, what could bring down such a man?* She finds she cannot come to an answer to this question. Instead, she fiddles with the hem of her dress and thinks of other things.

The girl, having nothing else to do today, is seated on the ground in the hallway outside the princess' closed door. Already this morning she has knocked and tried to coax the princess from the chamber to no avail. Her mind replays the comfort offered by Eselda just a short time ago when Mother passed. That thought leaves her grounded in this hallway. *The princess will emerge eventually and I will be on hand to comfort her when she does.*

Chapter 49

On the other side of the repurposed wooden door, I sit facing out my only window. I am watching the white dusting collect and slowly bury the front lawn. I sigh and a white circle from my hot breath mars the glass. Tomorrow morning, I must sit around the council table at the emergency meeting, as is tradition following a day of grievance.

Nothing like this has ever been experienced before, at least not since Oberian II. Never have all five realms observed a day of grievance together. In this case, it was needed. All realms were in attendance on this occasion, all realms will feel the shock and fear. The council will need to discuss this and proceed with caution from this point. Accidents can be explained; they are not something to fear. But outright violence …

I sigh again. This line of thinking is not productive. The council meeting has my stress level rising like the snow. What will they expect of me? Will they expect to see me fall apart as Sawchett did upon hearing of Charlotte or like Larecio when the facts of Carsen's demise were revealed? I am not sure I have that level of sadness in me, although I feel pain at the loss of my friend.

My thoughts turn to King Jordyn, almost of their own accord. What of this problem? I chew on my fingernail, taking out the tension on the inanimate and unfeeling object. Two seated kings are the main suspects in a murder investigation. Surely they will both be cleared, I cannot possibly believe either man is capable of such an act. But my assurance of their innocence may not be enough for the council. It may not be enough for King Larecio, who could demand justice.

A soft knock forces me back to reality.

"Eselda, there's a lady here who says your father asks for you," Sawchett calls.

I cross the floor in a few steps and yank the door open. The child topples inward. She must have been leaning on the door. Even as I right her my eyes fall on the medicine woman. "What is it? Is he …" my voice trips over my fears.

"He is alive, Majesty. He simply demanded I bring you to him, I couldn't delay him. I fear it is good for neither of you, but he insisted."

After a quick scan of Sawchett for possible injuries from her fall I follow the medicine woman to Father's chambers. At the present moment, the bed looks as though it is swallowing him. In fact, for the first time in my adult life, there is room enough on the surface for me to sit comfortably beside him. I do just that, sitting beside his legs and directing my head toward him.

"Daughter, I heard of Carsen's death." Father's voice is so low it is mostly air. I have to angle myself over his body to hear properly. I prop my arm up on the far side of his chest, so I can comfortably lean and appear to have an air of relaxation I do not feel. "When is the council meeting?" the king asks.

"Tomorrow morning."

"What happened to him?"

"He was killed." I hear the slight quake in my voice and cover it with a little cough.

"This is certain?"

I am afraid of the words not being adequate for the grave situation. Of the words bringing tears. Making it real. I merely nod.

"The council knows this?" he asks.

Again, a nod.

"Listen to me, Daughter. Mick will not stand for this. I know not the details of this death but I do know Mick. He will use this to scare you."

What does Mick know of my fears? "Scare me?"

"Yes. Find a friendly face to focus on and stay calm," he orders. It sounds strange, an order from the feathery voice. It is hard to believe I was ever scared of this man.

"Father, why would he try to scare me?"

"Because, daughter, the time approaches when the king of speed will call to renumber. This is something he needs support for. He will scare you and then offer you safety. In this way, he could earn your support." The longer speech leaves Father gasping for air.

I allow him a moment to regain his breath. "There's more you should know, but I fear it's not good for your health to inquire further," I say. Father cannot find the strength to form words but he can muster the energy to trap me with a gaze that means business. Despite his frail form, I squirm under such a gaze. "A small bit more, and only because I hope you can offer advice," I say. "There is an investigation that has been launched into who may have killed the prince."

"Good." There is no force behind the word, I barely hear it.

"They even have a few likely suspects, or so I hear." This time I see the mouth move but hear nothing. "I'm concerned about how this will play out Father because they suspect a seated king." No need to tell him they suspect two of them. The advice will be the same either way.

Shock marks the face of the old man. He shakes his head in disbelief, opens his mouth, and tries to speak. Words will not form. Instead, he holds up his hand and shakes it to draw my attention. I turn my eyes to the fingers. The first finger is stretched up tall, standing above the rest. He is asking me if the investigation focuses on the first realm. He is asking if King Tin is a suspect.

"How did you know?" I ask.

He merely shrugs.

"Yes, father. They suspect Tin. Will this cause more problems?"

A nod.

"They will call for the vote tomorrow, won't they?" I ask the question as quickly as it occurs to me that I already know the answer. This may be the proof Mick has been waiting on.

Another nod shows me my father agrees.

“Which way do I vote, Father?”

He shrugs. Then he reaches out with his hand and taps me on the forehead. It’s as if he is telling me to use my brain. "What if that is not enough?” I whisper.

Tears begin to fall, striking the blanket covering my father. “I’m scared,” I speak quietly, so quietly he probably doesn’t hear. Then I feel his arms, frail and thin, wrapping around my shoulders. He has pulled himself up into a sitting position, despite how much of his energy that must have taken. He is giving me the support I need.

I allow myself to fall apart, for maybe the last time. Tomorrow, I have to lead.

Chapter 50

The council is gathered, all except Tin. Larecio is barely holding it together. He is flopped over on the table, head on his arms, sobbing. His pain is filling the room, affecting everyone gathered. Jordyn is pulled back from the table, his jaw steeled shut. He will not meet my gaze. Beside me, Mick is annoyed. His jaw works dangerously as though he is chewing something or perhaps grinding his teeth. He is the only one present who doesn't appear changed by the recent death.

The door slams open and Tin saunters into the room as though nothing bothers him. He heads directly for his seat at the table and casually drops into it. He takes my hand, squeezing it. "None of us can take the pain away, Princess, but do let us know if you need anything," he offers. Then he drops my hand and turns his attention to the table.

"I call this emergency council meeting to order. Have we an update on the investigation?" Tin turns to Jordyn, but the answer comes from Mick.

"I asked the investigator to report to me," Mick announces.

Tin's head, along with all the others in the room, turns to Mick.

"Why? Did you find the king of wisdom incapable?" Tin challenges.

"The investigator explained to me that he had reason to believe that Jordyn may have been involved somehow."

The statement does exactly what Mick intended it to do, incites a reaction from all present. Jordyn's eyes close as though he is experiencing great pain. I slam my hand down on the table. Tin's eyes widen in shock. Larecio rises from his chair and squares his body at Jordyn. "You killed my son?" he bellows, his face reddening.

Mick rises from his chair, holding his own hands near Larecio in case restraining him becomes necessary.

"Jordyn, speak up. Defend yourself," I plead with the king from my seat. I can feel my body trembling. Jordyn remains frozen, his eyes shut and his fists clenched.

"Alright, enough," Tin barks. "I'm not one to stop a show of strength, but we need to hear the facts and draw our conclusions first."

King Mick sits, practically pulling Larecio down with him. Larecio keeps his eyes locked on Jordyn. "What says the investigator, Mick?" Tin asks.

"Well, he says the culprit is likely a male who would have reason to want Eselda and Carsen unmarried," Mick answers.

"I feel as though that is an unconfirmed suspicion," I argue.

"True, Princess," Mick concedes with a dismissive wave of his hand. "However we all know that the malicious age could cause one to do things they wouldn't otherwise do. Add to that the question of who had access to Carsen. How many of the people in attendance know the rooms of that castle well enough to get in and out unseen?"

"Actually that depends on just how long they had to do that," Tin interjects.

"Well, my investigator tells me that Carsen was last seen when his father checked on him whilst he was getting dressed. That would be a significant amount of time before Carsen went missing. The first guests were just arriving then," Mick says.

"It will be hard to find alibis for anyone for that entire period of time," Tin states.

"It isn't that hard for me or Larecio. I met him outside the same room, we walked to the ballroom together, and we were there until the announcement was made. We are each other's alibis," King Mick proudly explains.

"Did you see Carsen when you met up with Larecio?" Although he has not moved, the voice comes from Jordyn. All eyes in the room turn to take in the sight of him. As if he senses us watching his hands move up to hide his face.

"I did not. The door was closed," Mick answers.

"Are you implying I killed my son?" Larecio asks, his voice taking on an edge at odds with his title as King of Mirth.

Jordyn sighs, moves his hands, and opens his eyes, meeting the challenge. "No. I'm merely pointing out that your alibi isn't as solid as Mick would like people to believe. If Carsen was dead when you left that room it doesn't matter where you spent the next stretch of your time."

"Now see here, I stand to gain nothing from this death except for chaos and anger."

"I fear I stand to gain the same, good sir. Yet I seem to be enduring your wrath and doubt," Jordyn says.

Tin interrupts, "Alright gentlemen, settle down. What of the rest in attendance, did they not have alibis?"

"With a timeline as large as you're talking, King Tin, I fear no one will have a solid one," I say. "Are there facts beyond this? Is there anything about the crime itself that will lead us to an answer?"

"As I said, the investigator tells me it is likely motivated by jealousy from someone who wanted to be in the place of the prince that night." Mick's eyes fall back to Jordyn.

"Well, that's hardly reliable, especially considering it was the king you stare down who put that very thought in the man's head," I yell. "There are likely many who could come up with other reasons, but speculation does not indicate guilt."

"Who would want my son dead?" Larecio challenges, finally tearing his gaze from Jordyn long enough to turn it on me. "This is your fault, you know. Had you not agreed to marry him this never would've happened." He rises from his chair and points his finger menacingly across the table. "Someone killed my son to assume your throne."

Before anyone can get a word in or reason with the man he storms from the room. Mick, shrugging in apology, follows.

I drop my elbows to the table and cradle my head in my palms. "He's right. This is all my fault." I hope someone will correct me or point out a flaw in the argument.

I pick my head up enough to look at the two remaining kings. Neither has moved. No one will correct me, I'm not wrong.

This is my fault.

Chapter 51

When they are alone, Jordyn turns his gaze on Tin. The anger he is feeling becomes dangerously obvious, zapping back and forth between them. Tin matches the stern line of the mouth and the harsh body language.

"I cannot prove anything with certainty, Tin, but I fear as though one of the people in this room is responsible for the murder of the prince," Jordyn says.

"Is that so, Jordyn? Do you think I don't know what affects you today? Do you think I can't read the signs of the age marker all over your posture? You lose the battle against your demon today, friend. Perhaps this is not the first time you have lost control. Is there something you'd like to confess?"

"I have a moment I cannot seem to remember before Eselda's entrance into the hall. It is this missing moment, and this moment alone, that leaves me in doubt. Can you say the same?"

"I cannot. I know my whereabouts for the entire evening. Do you challenge me?" Something in Tin's eyes almost looks as though they'd welcome that challenge.

"I will solve this puzzle, Tin, and I will bring the killer to justice."

"Even if it turns out to be you?" Tin asks.

"Even then."

"So be it." Tin rises, shakes his head at the other man, and leaves the room.

Chapter 52

Outside the building, I flop down on a dry patch of ground underneath a large tree. I wrap my arms tightly around my knees and drop my chin on them. I am thankful the council did not have the presence of mind to call a vote on renumbering. I haven't decided how I will vote on such an issue. I try to take a deep breath and think logically, as Jordyn would. What is the purpose of having a first realm? Why does it matter what number your realm is or who is in charge of the council?

I think back through my old lessons with Tutor, reaching through the expanse of knowledge I've cataloged over the years. The king of the first realm leads all council meetings, maintaining calm and assuring all rules are followed. In the event of a tie, the first realm king can table his or her own vote in order to call for more discussion on the topic.

It's more than that, I am sure. There has to be a reason why the first realm is such a coveted position. I have a few more days to figure it out, the next council meeting is not planned for another half of the lunar calendar, about a fortnight.

"Eselda ..."

The voice belongs to King Jordyn. I turn to find him walking toward me, a cautious smile on his face. He looks shaken up and frustrated, an expression that is foreign on his face. "How are you holding up with all this?" he asks, drawing up to stand beside me.

"I'm doing alright, thank you."

"Can I sit?" he asks, gesturing to the ground beneath his feet.

I nod and scoot my bottom sideways to allow for space between us. "What do you think of this investigation so far? What do you think happened?" he asks.

Strange choice of topic, considering his obvious discomfort when it was brought up at the meeting. "I do not pretend to know the answer to that. I know you couldn't have done this, it is not in your character," I answer. I watch his face. Something is different in him. He seems somehow more like himself than he was during the council meeting. I turn my body more in his direction and lay my legs down between us. "What do you think happened?" I ask.

"Well, obviously I believe the idea that this could be someone after the throne of Enchenda is sound. It was my idea, after all."

"Are you completely opposed to any other ideas?"

"Such as?"

"I'm not sure. Thinking up ideas is something you are more suited to than I, Jordyn."

He adopts the expression he often has when he is deep in thought, unfocused but concentrating. "What if someone has a plan to remove a realm from Fraun all together?"

"What do you mean?" I ask.

"Think about it. If your Father dies and there is no heir, we would have to absorb Enchenda into the other realms. Perhaps redraw the lines of our boundaries. This would leave us with four realms, changing things for our council."

"Why would my Father dying cause this to happen? With or without Carsen I will be there to take on the throne."

"Unless the plan was to take you out as well," he says.

"You think someone may be after me?" My voice betrays the fear I'm feeling.

"In fact, now that I'm thinking this through if Larecio dies soon Marchenda would then be absorbed as well. This would leave our council with only three realms."

"But Jordyn, you forget, our council is in the process of updating lineage charts as we speak. I have already hired someone to work on Enchenda's." I rush to get the words out, eager to fall into a safety zone where I no longer feel like my life is threatened.

"Mine is in the process as well. I know this, you know this, and the council knows this. For that reason, we may be looking for someone who is not of royal blood. Someone who doesn't know the council is actively searching for members in the realms who have the blood in their veins who could rule in the event of the death of an entire line."

"That is a scary thought indeed. Do we have any way of knowing which commoners were in attendance at the event?" I know the answer even as I ask the question. I cannot even tell you who from Enchenda was in attendance. This would be an impossible list to compile.

"I wouldn't even begin to know who attended." Jordyn echoes the very thoughts from my head. "Besides, think on what we discussed in council, we are likely looking for someone who has knowledge of the Castle Fraun," he adds

"But as King Tin pointed out this isn't so much of an issue if the person had adequate time to make their escape."

"No. That logic doesn't track. If the person were new to the castle and having to fumble their way about for directions someone would have been likely to see them. I had my entire staff on the premises that evening." He pauses, again thinking. "What if the offender is someone I employ?"

I am grateful for his brain coming up with a possibility that doesn't include a seated king. "Could you supply a list of your employees?"

"Do you know the names of all who work in your home?" he asks, not unkindly.

"I know most, but admittedly not all."

"I do not know all either." He is quiet for a moment before yawning and stretching his long legs out in front of him. Suddenly he appears relaxed. "You have given me some new ideas to ponder, Eselda. I feel better just having something to occupy my brain."

"I'm glad I could help." My voice gives away a sadness under the surface.

"Tell me what bothers you then," he prompts.

I think about arguing. I think about denying my sadness. In the end, staring into the deep blue of his eyes, I am grateful for the friend. "Things feel so much harder than even I thought they would be. It's all wrong, Jordyn."

"You mean with Carsen?"

"Yes, among other things." Now that I have begun sharing I can almost feel him taking up some of the weight I have been carrying. The words tumble out. "I agreed to marry Carsen only for convenience. But he was truly a good person and I am sad for the loss of his life. I wish there was something I could do to comfort his father and his realm and I'm absolutely terrified that everyone will think, as Larecio does, that it's my fault he is dead."

"You cannot let that bother you." Jordyn reaches out and pats me lightly on the arm. "Larecio spoke out of pain and anger. He will come around to see the truth soon enough, he is a good and fair man."

"The most infuriating part of this whole thing is that it's all about royal blood. I am getting so tired of hearing how precious that is. Carsen had it and look where it ended him. It's like Fraunians are completely obsessed with those of us who have it. Yet I fear there are many out there who have it and know not. I just can't wrap my head around what it is that makes this such a precious commodity worth killing another person over."

"It's not."

"Clearly it is to someone, Jordyn. Doesn't that thought scare you?"

"It does. I have as much of it as you do. What if this makes us vulnerable? Is that what you're thinking?" he asks.

"Yes. If someone gets it in their head to wipe out all with royal blood in Fraun, haven't we made their job easier by documenting it on our walls?"

"I suppose so, but they are in our homes. It's not as though everyone has seen them."

"It can't be that hard to see them. I have seen two."

"I've seen four." Jordyn drops this fact lightly, but it is not received that way.

My jaw drops. "You've seen that many?"

"Yes, at one time or another." Seeing my expression, he laughs. The sound is so light and airy compared with the darkness of our lives lately that it offers refreshment which I gladly take in with a smile. "It's not as big of a deal as all that, you'd have to take very good notes to remember them all. Seeing them once is not enough," Jordyn explains.

"I suppose. I guess I'm being irrational. There are so many secrets coming out lately and I'm scared of what will be left of my life when they are all in the open. It's starting to seem as though nothing is what I thought."

"Like?"

The prompt is permission. Jordyn is giving me permission to share my secrets with a seated king without the presence of the others from the council. "My tutor, who has always been someone I consider a friend, is hiding something. He walks with a limp, he won't answer questions, he doesn't want to speak with me, and he has new bruises when I see him."

"This worries you?"

"Yes. It's more what we were discussing the first time he refused to answer questions that have me worried. Remember the royal blood I told you about, the one that wasn't charted?" I watch for signs that he will stop me here. The first time I tried to bring this up, he made his feelings very clear.

"I remember." He smiles.

"I mentioned her to my tutor, asked him about her. He got very angry and stormed out of my home. He hasn't been the same since."

"That is curious."

"He admitted he knew her, she took him in when he was first in Enchenda."

"He's not from Enchenda?" Jordyn asks, his curiosity piqued.

"Apparently he was raised in Farcheda and even spent some time in your realm before coming to Enchenda."

Jordyn stops me, reaching out a hand and laying it on my leg. "What is his name? How old is he?"

"He would be a few annuals older than I, his name is Tutor."

"I will look into his background a little, see if there are secrets buried there. Would you like that?" Jordyn asks.

"I would. Thank you."

"How fares your father?" Jordyn asks with his typical abrupt jump in topic.

"Not well at all, actually. Our last conversation, yesterday, was too much for him and his voice left him. I am worried about him, Jordyn." Unexpectedly, I feel ambushed by my feelings. The tears rush from my eyes unchecked. I wipe them, but it only makes them fall harder.

Jordyn recovers quickly from his shock and acts on instinct, pulling me into a hug and rubbing a small circle on my back.

I take comfort in the arms of my friend, my stomach fluttering at his touch. Over his shoulder, I watch as King Tin leaves the council building. I see him glance in our direction but I do not have the desire to move away. Not even when he pauses in his walk to look a second time. Not even when it looks, from here, like he is suddenly angry.

Chapter 53

The old study room is dark, lit only by the single candle I have brought into the room with me. I have spread out old parchment rolls on the floor around me. I carefully unroll one, trace my finger down the writing as I scan for important details, roll it back up and toss it into a new pile.

I have been sitting here on the floor long enough for my legs to cramp up three times. Each of those times I have taken a short break while the blood rushes back to them, causing me pain I don't think I will recover from. Each of those times the pain finally subsides and I resume the search.

The pile of already searched documents that do not talk about why it would be important to be the first realm is growing rapidly. The pile of documents left to search, in contrast, is dwindling. With each new parchment roll, I become more frustrated. My hair is collected in a messy knot atop my head and sweat mixes with grime on my body. I am aware what a mess I am becoming, but I care not. This information somehow feels like it will help me make my decision in a fourth of a lunar cycle and yet it continues to elude me.

Frustrated, I throw the scroll, another that told me nothing new, across the room. Glancing down at my pile I see there are only ten left. I sigh and reach for another.

Nothing.

Another.

Nothing.

"This is hopeless," I yell into the empty room as I lob the newest useless scroll into the black. I flop back to rest on my hands, staring up at the ceiling. The information must be locked in this brain of mine somewhere. It has something to do with war, that much I remember. Something about the king of the first realm's role during the war. Something that makes him different, somehow, from the other seated kings.

My shoulders begin to ache painfully from the stress. I reach up and rub one. Perhaps I could write to Jordyn, he would know. I stand up, intending to head to my room to grab some parchment with which to write him. Just outside the room I nearly crash into the medicine woman. The woman's frantic expression requires no more information. I turn on my heel and run directly to my father.

When the door opens I fear I am too late. My father, pale and small, lies buried in the pillows of the large bed as still as death. "Father …" I sob, suddenly finding I have no more words for the grief sitting on my chest. I rush to his bedside, taking his hand in my own and kissing him on the forehead.

As my lips brush his skin I feel it, the faintest of pulses in his wrist. "Father?"

I hold his hand as life leaves him. I sit close enough to hear the ragged last breath pass his lips. When it does, the sobs leave me and I cry long into the night, holding the hand of the man who was once my king.

Chapter 54

Enchenda is sad to announce the death of their king, Gregario. However, in his stead, we welcome Queen Eselda. Eselda, the only daughter of Gregario and Rubina, rest her soul, is a staple in our community. She is humble and will lead Enchenda to greatness, without a doubt.

The announcement arrived this morning by messenger. The king steeples his fingers over the paper, smiling to himself. *The queen will have people in an uproar. She is now one small accident away from wiping all royal blood from Enchenda. Yes, the business of finding the queen a suitable king will be in high demand now, that is certain.*

She must be in a tizzy. Surely she has noticed death seems to be tracking her everywhere she goes.

It's almost as if it stalks her.

Long live the queen, if she can.

Chapter 55

"A second emergency council meeting in one lunar cycle? This is getting ridiculous." King Mick's voice booms throughout the council chambers.

The day after the death of my father has passed. Yesterday, his day of grieving was observed only in Enchenda and Renchenda. If I were feeling normal I would probably appreciate the show of support from Jordyn. Instead, I barely acknowledged it. Now we sit around the table once again for the emergency meeting required after a day of grievance. This time, it is I who am barely present. I am focused on the table in front of me and have yet to respond to anything said.

"You know as well as the rest of us do that this meeting is required, Mick," Tin states. "Eselda is now Queen and will be welcomed by this council."

"True. Can we discuss other business during this meeting once that's settled?"

"What did you have in mind, old man?" Tin goads.

"What is going on with the patrol I have sent you? I want to know if they are being trained and what they are training on."

"The training progresses swiftly. They are quite a strong bunch. My boys have trained them in combat and on the various animals we encounter. They should be ready to progress to Enchenda for phase two of their training any day now. I fear this is not a good time for Eselda to be taking them on, however. Should we wait a few more days?"

"The hell we will," Mick bellows, rising from his chair. "I'm not giving you any longer than you should have with them. They are not to be your personal army." Mick turns his attention to Larecio. "Didn't I warn you he'd try and pull something like this?" His eyes are back to Tin before the king of the fourth realm can even nod. "I'll take my turn with them, we'll bring her back in later after they've been to all realms."

"She can handle it," Jordyn interrupts. "In fact, I'm sure it will give her something to focus on. It could be good for her."

"Kindly stop talking about me as though I'm not in the room," I say, quietly but forcefully.

"What say you, Majesty?" Tin prompts, his voice softer and kinder.

"Send them my way in two suns," I order.

Mick sits heavily in his chair, defeated.

"Then it's decided, we proceed as planned. What else have we to discuss?" Tin asks.

"I have another topic," Mick states. "What says the council to a renumbering?"

This time it is Tin who vacates his chair. "What reason have you to take this position from me?" His voice drips with hatred.

Suddenly I cannot stand another meeting like this. Another time when the people who are supposed to be leading Fraun sit around a table and fight. I push myself up, slowly, so all eyes have time to find me. "You boys accomplish little beyond arguing. Send word to me when you are ready to think about Fraun instead of yourselves." I turn and walk out of the chamber.

In the antechamber, my steps falter. What came over me just now? They are infuriating with their ceaseless arguing, but surely I can stomach it for Fraun. My father sat in that very chair and did his best each lunar cycle. Was the council different then? Was there ever a time when they could agree? It certainly is nothing like I once pictured it would be, sitting in that room with them.

"Eselda …"

I suppose I should be grateful that Jordyn has followed me out of the room.

"Are you alright?" he asks.

"Shouldn't you be in there arguing?"

I hear his steps cross the antechamber, I feel his hand lightly on my arm. Despite my anger and frustration, I feel the heat work its way through my body at his touch. "I'm sorry for your loss, Eselda. What can I do?"

"It's not just the loss of my father. It's the loss of the ideals I thought this council stood for. Do they ever do anything other than argue?"

"It's been tough lately, that is true. They mean well."

"Do they? I'm not sure anymore. Just once, I want someone to be honest with their intentions. Not hide behind stories or one-sided arguments," I say.

"Honest?" He steps closer, closing the gap between us and placing his hands on my hips. "Here's honest."

He is whispering, the secret offered to me alone. I am suspended on a cliff, hanging onto his words for safety, holding my breath.

"I never meant this to happen, but I have fallen for you despite my better judgment on the subject. It is not best for Fraun, it is not best for you, but I cannot help myself. It is not even logical, but I cannot turn it off."

The kiss warms me to my core. I feel it attacking the sadness that has filled my soul. I wrap my arms around his neck to keep him there. In recent lunar cycles, I have had my fair share of kisses, but none compare to this. Jordyn's honest revelation, the knowledge that my feelings are reciprocated, the permission and danger to share this intimate moment with the council just beyond a door, all add to the heat of the moment.

When the kiss breaks I immediately long for it again. "Court me," I whisper.

"Eselda …"

I open my eyes when I feel Jordyn pulling back.

"… I cannot do that," he finishes.

A sudden cold fills my lungs. "What?"

"I just told you, it is not best for Fraun or you." His voice wears the thick unspoken apology.

The anger rushes me without warning, hot and intense. “Then why did you tell me this?” I lay my hand on his chest and push him away, harder than I mean to. He stumbles a little.

“You asked for honest,” he answers.

“You are worse than the rest,” I scold. “You’re so …” I grapple to find the word, “… old fashioned." On my way out into the cold, I let out a wild scream.

The scream is a living embodiment of my anger. Anger at a system I no longer understand. This is it, the end of the fairy tale I thought my life would be. There will be no shining love of my life sweeping in to rescue me from responsibility and pain. There will be no following my king.

It is me. Alone.

Chapter 56

I know a servant is hiding in the shadows thrown by the lanterns in the dining room. I cannot even blame him. I know what I have been like lately, I've been impossible. I'm the dangerous ant charging full speed ahead at the children who are just trying to play. I see the problem, but I cannot find the strength to remedy it. This is what I have become. Deal with it.

The man rushes forward and drops into a low bow. "Your Majesty, your messengers have arrived with the daily updates," he says, handing me a stack of parchment.

"Thank you." I take the top parchment and begin to read as the man scurries out of sight again.

Death totals since my last update-seven (this number includes the two you are aware of)
Birth totals since my last count-twelve

Five more bodies to clothe, mouths to feed, people to train. My brain calculates this automatically. I flip to the next parchment.

Eselda,
I have given the royal painter a list of a few names I've found already. He will be coming by in the next few suns to paint them on the wall. Thank you for tasking me with this, it is good for me. I hope you are well.
Tutor

I glance at the lineage chart behind me and cannot find a change. The painter has not been here yet. I glance back to the parchment. Tutor doesn't mention my father at all. Perhaps he is unaware. I flip the parchment over, grab my quill, and jot a quick response.

Tutor,
I'm glad you find the job to your liking. I need to speak with you about changes in Enchenda as soon as possible, please. My father is no longer with us.
Eselda

Quick and simple. Perhaps he will not argue with that. I place the scroll in a new pile, to be sent out, and focus my eyes on the next parchment.

Dearest Eselda,
I remember what it was like when I was first ruling my realm, so many things to do and not always a clear idea of how to do them. I wish, at the time, someone had reached out and offered me help. Come to Sarcheda. You can ask me anything you'd like. I will help you with your new job. I'm also a great listener, we can talk about whatever you'd like.
Faithfully and Forever Yours,
Tin

I recall that during his visit to Enchenda he mentioned the same thing. A smile that has been all too rare lately graces my face. Fraunians misjudge Tin. I let Fraunians cloud my judgment of Tin. I flip the parchment over.

Tin,
I will come to Sarcheda, thank you for the invitation. In fact, I think I shall come tomorrow. I could use the company of a friendly face.
Eselda

I drop this with the other parchment in the pile to be sent cut and look to the next and last parchment.

Eselda,
We should talk, don't shut me out.
Jordyn

"You said plenty," I roar. I throw the parchment to the flames and watch as they consume the material completely. "There's nothing else to say."

Chapter 57

"Welcome back, your Majesty," King Tin calls as I disembark from the roach I have ridden. I offer him my hand to shake. Instead of merely shaking it, Tin uses it to pull me closer and wrap me in a hug. "How are you doing?" he asks into my ear.

"I am well, thank you." My stomach flutters again and I feel a blush begin on my cheeks. What is it about this man that always makes me feel like a girl again?

"You look beautiful." He smiles. "Now let's get you out of the cold before you freeze."

Tin, dressed in black and red as he usually is, looks incredibly handsome. I cannot stop my eyes from wandering to his backside, which is snug in the pants. I look away as he holds the door to his home open for me. I tremble with nerves when he lays his hand on my lower back to guide me through the frame.

"Let's head to my dining room, it's quiet and we can relax awhile. We have some time to chat before dinner will be served."

"That sounds lovely."

In the dining room, we take two chairs by the fire, away from the table. We are angled so that our knees are pointed toward each other. I sit up straight, trying to hold my body to the royal custom. Tin, however, slouches down comfortably in the chair and stretches his legs out in front of him. He crosses them at his ankles, throws his arms behind his head, and smiles at me. "How is being queen treating you?"

"It's fine, thank you."

Tin shakes his head and chuckles. "Why are you being so formal? There's no one around but me." His hands spread out beside his ears before reverting back to hold up his head. "You can be honest here, no one will judge."

I take in the king's relaxed posture and laugh a little, letting my shoulders slump. "Oh thank goodness," I sigh.

This earns a hearty laugh from Tin.

"I didn't know if you expected me to carry myself like a … like a …"

"Like a queen?" he offers.

"Well, yes." I laugh.

"Here's something I've learned, Eselda. You are Queen now. That means you can stop trying so hard. However you carry yourself is exactly how a queen would carry herself. You can do no wrong now because who could point out that you were mistaken?"

"I guess I never really thought of it that way before," I admit.

"Well then, you're welcome. I'm glad I could help." He winks at me and I feel myself blush again. To cover it, I glance down at my feet. If this is about comfort, I will get comfortable. I pull my feet up into the chair. "Now see, isn't that more comfortable?" Tin asks.

"It is."

"So, what can I help you with tonight? What issues have come up in Enchenda?"

"Well nothing really, I've not even been Queen for a fortnight." I chuckle. Now that I'm here and relaxing, it's hard to remember what had me so stressed. "Oh, one question I did have. Who handles your school visit here?"

"I do. Why do you ask?"

"The school teacher sent me a letter inquiring about who would handle that now that my father has passed."

"Yes, I suppose she did. They plan ahead at the school here as well." Tin smiles. "Don't let it bother you. Jordyn and I both handle our own visits. I personally enjoy it very much as ours often includes a feat of strength display." He flexes his bicep muscle and winks at me again.

I try to smile, but the mention of the king of wisdom's name makes it suddenly hard to focus. It's like black water is leaking into my eyes, clouding my vision. My head hurts again and a sharp pain throbs at the back of my skull.

"Are you that worried about the visit?" Tin asks. He is squinting at me as though trying to figure me out.

"What? No, I've handled it for many annuals, I'm sure I can take more." I fear I don't truly understand the root of his question.

"You looked suddenly distracted or upset. I had thought it was the school visit. Is something else wrong?" He sits up a little straighter in his chair, giving the impression I have his full attention.

"No. Nothing I can't handle."

"Eselda, please. Let's be honest with each other," he implores.

This time I feel the anger bubble up inside me. It's like water that has been set on a low heat has finally spawned bubbles. I open my mouth and release the pressure. "Honesty can be overrated."

Beside me, Tin looks shocked. "Now where in Fraun did that come from?" he asks in a light tone.

I fix him with a confused look. "Where did what come from?" I snap. Is he making fun of me?

This time, the smile fades completely from Tin's face. Suddenly serious, he leans in closer to me, pulling his chair with him. "How old are you?"

The question catches me off guard. "Over fifteen annuals, why?"

"How long until you are twenty?" he asks.

Something about his voice is all wrong, worried, or … oh no. The realization of where he is headed with this line of questioning starts to trickle in. "Oh, my … I don't know. I hadn't been counting. Do you think I'm there?" My breath is coming faster now.

Tin continues to stare at my face, cataloging my features. "Your eyes are lightening up again, back to their normal green. You are not there yet, but you approach it." He sits back in his chair again, offering me a small smile.

"What? How do you know?" I lean forward in my chair, toward the answers.

"Before my twentieth annual I had small bouts of anger often. I had trouble controlling them or even realizing what they were."

"But they weren't the real age marker?"

"No. I may have thought they were then, I don't recall. But nothing compares to how it feels when you lose yourself to the malicious age." He fixes me with a hard expression. "Nothing."

Jordyn said something similar, I remember. The thought does nothing to calm the panic threatening to drown me. "If this isn't the age marker, then can I learn to control it?" Give me answers.

"I'm not sure. Do you want to talk about what triggered it just now?" he offers.

"Jordyn." The name slips easily from my lips but I cannot look at Tin when I speak it. Instead, my eyes track to the flames dancing in the fireplace. I wish I could feed my troubles to those flames and watch them burn.

"Should we talk about it?" he asks, a sad edge to his voice.

"I'm not sure I want to."

"I'm not sure I want to hear it. But perhaps it would do you good to share some of the burdens with a friend."

The sadness in his voice draws my eyes back to him. He is staring at me, the firelight catching in his hair and making him incredibly handsome. But his face holds so much melancholy, it shocks me. "What brings you such great sadness, Tin?" I ask, always eager to put the focus on someone else.

"I saw you with Jordyn the other day, after the council," he admits. "I understand so many things now. How long have you two been secretly courting?" His eyes darken dangerously and I notice a twitch in his jaw. Signs of his age marker, perhaps?

Despite my best attempt, I cannot stop the laugh from escaping. Tin looks shocked, as though slapped by the laughter. "I'm sorry …" I say between chuckles. "I don't mean to laugh at you." I regain my composure with deep breaths. "I'm sorry. I laugh because that's what you thought this was." It comes out as a question. I rush on. "You thought I traveled here in anger to tell you that I am hiding a secret courting with the king of Renchenda?"

"Well," he thinks about it, "yes. I thought perhaps you were angry that you had to hide it from the council who surely wouldn't understand. I was afraid, perhaps, that you thought you had to hide it from me as well." He sits forward again, now using only the edge of his chair. "Is that not accurate?" he asks. Something that looks like hope lights across his chiseled features.

"Not at all. I will not pretend I don't have feelings for Jordyn. But clearly, it is unreturned. He continues to tell me that he cannot court me or be with me because of the rules."

"That's not surprising at all. Jordyn has always been a stickler for the rules," Tin explains. A small version of his smile tugs at the corners of his mouth.

"Yes, well … I suppose I had always imagined someone would fall in love with me and nothing would be able to keep us apart."

"So your anger is because you wish you could be with King Jordyn?" Tin summarizes.

"No, my anger is because I'm not good enough for King Jordyn to fight for." Perhaps because I am on guard for it now, I feel the bubble of anger within. My vision begins to darken at the edges.

"Now that is something I understand. I can see it angers you to think of it. Perhaps we should talk of something else, take your mind off of it."

"Fine by me."

"So, if I understand you correctly, no one is courting you at this time." His eyes flash in amusement as his smile deepens.

Not this again. I don't think I can handle another person telling me that they have the best of intentions, and are falling for me, but can do nothing about it. "No," I answer.

"I no longer need to ask permission from your king, as you are the highest voice in Enchenda. I know you feel as though rules, although they have their place, should not be used to stomp out emotions. So …" he leans forward and grasps my hand in his own, "… can I have your permission to court the beautiful Queen Eselda?To invite her often to dinner, to spend time with her, and to learn all the intricacies of her soul?"

I feel myself calming down as I stare into his eyes. He is pleading with me to answer him. His happiness feels contagious. "I see no problem with that." I swallow hard. "Are you sure it is okay with the council you run?"

Tin leans even further off his chair, so he is standing just over me. "I dare them to try and stop me," he answers, winking.

I feel instantly calm.

That is the exact right answer.

Chapter 58

Again, there is good food and entirely too much of it. A young servant girl enters now, carrying a tray of something small and dipped in what looks like chocolate. "What is this, Tin?" I ask. "I hope you don't think I could possibly have room in my stomach for another course."

"Now my dear, are you truly going to try and convince me that you cannot make room in there for some chocolate? After how you felt about it the last time?" Tin asks.

The servant drops the plate and I take a sniff, the sweet smell of chocolate wafting into my nose. "Oh, it smells divine. What is it?" I look to the servant, but it is King Tin who answers.

"Sliced bananas covered in chocolate that has been melted."

"You can melt it?" I ask as the servant leaves the room.

Tin laughs. "Quite easily, or so I'm told."

I lift a slice of banana in my hands and take a small nibble. A soft moan escapes my lips. "This is remarkable. I think I like it even better than the cookie from last time."

Tin chuckles. "I'll take your word for it, I don't enjoy chocolate nearly as much as you do." He gestures to his plate and I notice for the first time that his banana slices are not covered in the melted goo.

"You don't eat it?"

"I've tried it, but I prefer the taste of my fruit plain."

"Well, I can get plain fruit anywhere." I take another large bite of my snack. "I plan to fully enjoy chocolate whenever it's offered."

Tin laughs. "I fear the way to your heart may be paved with the sweet treat."

I take another bite and shrug. "Probably." This time I join him in his laughter.

When we have both finished dessert, Tin rises and offers his hand to me. "Now, what shall we do for the remainder of our evening? Is there anything you would like to discuss?"

I allow myself to be pulled to my feet and wrap my hand delicately around Tin's elbow. "Actually, there is something I'm curious about. I have developed quite a healthy appreciation for lineage lately. Could I possibly see your family tree?"

"Sure thing. Right this way." Tin leads me down a dark and long hallway, the occasional torch lighting our path. The hall is wide enough to allow me to remain beside him. My boots click loudly on the stone floor, echoing our every step back to me.

At the end of the long hallway, Tin turns to the right, and we enter a bedroom. Immediately in front of us, there is a large bed made up with a dark red blanket. The bed is easily the largest I have ever seen in my life. Likely four people could fit comfortably on it. In addition to the blanket, which looks thick and warm, there is quite an impressive mound of pillows at the top of the surface. Beside the bed on either side is a wooden table, each holding a candle. For some reason, both candles are lit although the room was empty when we entered.

"Is this your room?" I ask. I hear the admiration I feel for his lavish settings in my tone of voice.

"It is. The lineage chart is painted on this wall here." He gestures to the wall the door is on. The gold script matches that which I have seen in Renchenda and my realm. I drop the arm of the king and stand to look up at the wall, my eyes shining with excitement.

I begin at the top, where I note Renchenda is written as well. That matches with what I learned earlier, the ancient kings were brothers born of the same parents. My eyes trail down the tree. The names are circled and starred where necessary. This tree is considerably less complicated than mine. "Not many people in your lineage have multiple children."

"True. Is that not also true in Enchenda?"

"I suppose there are a few families that have only one, but you often see multiple children. Your line is different, I see no lines with more than one child." I trace my eyes back up the line again, having reached Tin's name, and find the observation holds up. Not one mother birthed more than one child.

My eyes stop at another spot. "What is this?" I ask, pointing to a place where three names appear in a straight line. Twane-Tron-Sharpei. Tron's name is circled and starred.

"Tron was the only son of Sarcheda and Alenda," Tin explains, pointing to the line showing this. "He took two wives."

I turn my head away from the wall and trap Tin with a quizzical expression. "What? I thought that ended with Second."

Tin shrugs. "My ancestors occasionally continued the practice." He gestures to another spot, further down the line, where it happened again. "They believed multiple wives helped to ensure them a male descendant to take the throne," he explains.

"Why male?"

Tin sighs. "Remember I'm explaining something other people in my lineage have believed, it doesn't mean I believe it."

I nod that I agree.

"Men are traditionally stronger than women. In a society that values strength, it's easy to see why some would want only male rulers." He shrugs. "What can I tell you? My ancestors were fools."

I turn back to the wall and feel Tin step closer to me. My eyes continue searching until I find two black circles on the far right of the wall. Here we go. "What is this covering?"

"A child born out of wedlock. The father is unknown but that covers the mother and child."

I turn to him. "So you could have royal blood outside of those marked on this wall as well?"

"It's possible, I suppose. As promised I have hired someone to look into that. But it won't be from that source. Both mother and child died during childbirth."

"Then why go through the trouble of blacking out their names?"

"They would've been shunned upon learning she was with child before they passed."

"So if you had royal blood not tracked here, where would it come from?" I ask, steering the conversation away from the topic of death.

Tin reaches over my shoulder, touching a spot with his left hand. I turn my body to face the wall again. His finger points to the left of the wall, to a circled name. "Roberta," I read.

"This line continued to birth females. They were not needed to rule." He points to the right side of the wall, nearest his own name. "My direct lineage continued to have male blood and people to rule. After a few generations, no one bothered to check in with them anymore. I'm out of touch with this line, I'm not sure if there are more children here or not. It is where the updater I now employ was to begin his search."

"How long ago did they stop checking on that line?"

"Roberta and my father, Todd, were about the same age. That's all I know."

I turn again. As he talked Tin has stepped closer so that when I turn we are nearly face to face. "What happened to your parents?" I ask, quietly.

A dark cloud settles over the king's expression. His brown eyes literally get a shade darker. I wince. "I'm sorry, I shouldn't have asked."

"No, it's alright. It's just hard to speak of." Tin places his hands on my hips. "My parents fell into the ravine along the edge of Fraun."

"Was it hard to lose them both?" I ask. I notice my voice quavers in response to how close he stands and the hands on my hips.

"Incredibly." He leans in close to me and whispers. "Do you know what else is difficult?"

"What's that?"

"Trying to focus on a conversation with you standing this close to me in my bedroom." He kisses me almost before the sentence is finished. The kiss is hungry, deep, and full of longing. I melt like chocolate under his fingers. He greedily runs his fingers up and down my back as we kiss, keeping me pulled in close. I wrap my arms around his neck in response. I feel myself giving in to the sensations, letting go of all my stress and pain.

Tin pulls away from me, physically pushing me back. "You should go."

"What? Why? Did I do something wrong?" I search Tin's eyes for answers.

His eyes are a little darker than normal, but he looks otherwise exactly the same. Perhaps a little flush from the heat of the moment.

"You did nothing wrong." He reaches out and caresses my face. "If you stay I fear we may do something we'll regret. Go home and get some sleep. I will come to Enchenda in a few days time and we will have dinner together. I promise." The king keeps his eyes locked on my face, but steps back to put more distance between us.

Seeing no other options, I leave the room and the house.

What just happened?

Chapter 59

The path to the unused building is long. I gladly walk it, enjoying the break from my routine. The air on this mid-morning is crisp but much warmer than days past. I welcome the freshness into my lungs and allow it to clear my head as I walk. Two sunrises have passed since my dinner and, by extension, my courtship with Tin. The thought brings a warm smile to my face and the memories of our passionate kiss bring a blush to my cheeks.

This morning I travel to visit with the patrol, who arrived in Enchenda yesterday. When they first returned I was showing a new servant around my home and I didn't have much time to spend with them. Instead, I directed them to the building here, which will serve as their accommodations, with instructions to settle in.

Ten men serve on the patrol and Enchenda has no place fit to house all of them together, including my own home. Instead, I was forced to offer them an old barn. I ordered some materials which could be used to fashion beds but even those were not the best quality. There is no kitchen in the building either. How do I expect them to enjoy warm meals? I will have to offer full access to my garden today. It is the best I can do.

As I approach I observe a young man tending to a fire in front of the building, smoke rising to the heavens. They've dug a fire pit, how creative. The man stands and waves. As I draw closer I notice the man is Danyel, the patrolman representing Enchenda.

He has changed in the lunar cycles since I last saw him. Already his shirt strains from the new muscles coming in underneath it. Tin has done well with these men. "Good morning, Danyel," I greet.

"Majesty, good morning."

"How did you fare last night? Were you terribly cold?"

"Not at all, we built a fire right in the middle of the room. It kept us warm all night. It was wise of you to offer us such meager accommodations, the boys are quickly learning humility already," Danyel says.

This boy has such strong faith in me. "It was my hope that we could provide you with something better, but you are a large group."

He laughs. "That we are. This is good, Majesty. It is a reminder to us all that the job we have undertaken is for others, not for ourselves."

"I'm proud of your humble nature, Danyel. You do Enchenda proud."

The man beams under the praise. "Thank you, Majesty. What plans have you for us today?" he asks.

"First, I believe it would be wise if you would show the patrol around Enchenda's boundaries. They need to know where Fraun ends. Would you feel comfortable undertaking this?"

"Absolutely, Majesty."

"Good. While you are here, it goes without saying that you may come to me with anything. You have full access to my garden, which is behind my home. Oh, and you'll want to pay careful attention to this area here," I gesture to the area behind their lodging, near the edge of Fraun, "because we had a stray ant near this area not long ago."

"We will keep that in mind, Majesty. Thank you."

"I will see you all tomorrow morning, sunrise. I'd like you to meet in front of my home for training."

"We will all be there. I'm sure they look forward to meeting you." Danyel bows low again. "Have a nice day, Majesty."

"I will, thank you. Goodbye, Danyel." I turn and head back toward my own home, a smile on my face. That went well.

I turn the corner to my garden and find Sawchett sprawled out on her stomach, a parchment in front of her eyes. Her bare feet are bent up behind her, swinging as though they hear music guiding them. "Good morning, child. What are you reading?"

"My tutor wanted me to read about age markers a little."

I freeze. "Age markers?" I try to keep my voice even. Does the girl realize her bloodline? "Which ones do you speak of?"

"My next one coming up, the tenth."

I let out a breath. "Yes, you will be full height in a few annuals. I've noticed in just the short time since you've lived here you have grown taller. I suppose your body is readying you."

"You only think that because you've stopped growing." Sawchett smiles.

"This is true."

"This says I will also have all my …" the girl consults the parchment "… reproductive parts." She turns her head and looks up at me. "What does that mean?"

I sit on the ground beside the girl and slip off my own shoes, wiggling my bare feet in the dirt. "It means, if you met someone and fell in love, you'd have all the parts needed to bring a baby into this world."

Sawchett gasps. "But I'll still be so young."

"Just because your body will be equipped for it does not mean you will have to rush to do it. Look at me, I'm past ten annuals and I have no children."

"That's true." Sawchett resumes reading her parchment. I recline back to rest, my palms flat on the ground behind me supporting my weight. "After that, I'll get nice full shiny hair, like yours."

"Well, no doubt yours will continue to be the yellow it is now, not brown like my own."

"I wish mine were red," Sawchett said wistfully.

"With luck, you will grow to love yours for the beauty it offers." I reach out and brush Sawchett's long hair with my fingers. "I wonder if your hair will cease to grow but remain straight like it is."

"I hope it doesn't. I hope I get curls like yours," Sawchett states simply, with a little pout.

"I covet your straight locks, actually. If I could find a way to keep mine equally as straight I'm sure I would do it."

"Are there other age markers, Eselda?" Sawchett asks, having reached the end of her parchment roll.

"Only for those of royal blood," I answer. Am I ready for this conversation?

"What are they?"

"Sawchett, let's go inside. I'd like to show you something." It's not right to keep a secret from the girl. I cannot allow Sawchett to be a stranger to the age markers when they arrive. I will not allow her to be blindsided by them like I was. I lead the smaller child into the dining room.

Instead of finding it empty, as planned, we find a small man standing on a ladder at the lineage chart. He is writing on the wall with a thin brush. His ladder, I note, brings him near the name of my grandfather. No time to waste. "Here child, sit," I direct the girl to the chairs nearest the fire.

"This wall here shows the history of my family. It shows where we come from and who came before us." Sawchett turns her head to look at the wall I gesture to. I continue, "This man here is responsible for tracking my family lineage, and our royal blood. Everyone on that wall experiences age markers beyond their fifteenth annual."

"What are they?" Sawchett asks, returning her eyes to my face.

"Your tutor can fill you in on that, I have something more important to share with you. What do you know of your mother's heritage?"

Sawchett wrinkles her nose as she thinks. "Nothing."

"Your mother's father, your grandfather, was once King."

"My mother was a princess like you used to be?" Sawchett asks, her eyes lighting up with the secret.

"In blood alone. Charlotte was never allowed to be called Princess or to live in this house."

"Wow." The word comes out with adoration. "Wait, what does that make me?"

"That means that you also have royal blood flowing in your veins, yes."

"I'm a princess?" The sentence is whispered, almost as if giving it volume would make it suddenly untrue.

"I suppose you are. Would you like to be a princess?" I ask. Why can't I rule that to be so? I see no reason to deny this further.

Sawchett's eyes grow wide. "I want to be a princess more than anything."

"Then that is what you shall be. I will inform your tutor myself so your training can be adjusted accordingly. Go and fetch him for me."

Sawchett pops out of her chair. "I will. Thank you, Eselda." She runs from the room.

I allow myself a moment to wallow in the girl's joy before turning my attention to the man at the wall. "How many names do you add today, good sir?"

Never once turning from the wall or breaking in his painting the man answers. "I unearth one and add one."

"Unearth?"

"Yes, I remove the black paint from this name covered here." He taps the wall with the end of his brush.

Fascinated, I cross the room to stand by his side. Charlotte. "You can do that? It doesn't remove the gold paint?"

"I can do it."

I watch him work for a moment. "I'm quite fascinated by lineage."

This earns me a look from the man. His hand freezes as he glances at me as if noticing who I am for the first time. He smiles before turning back to his work. "I am as well," he adds once he is back to his task.

"Can you unearth those two names up there for me as well?" I point to the two toward the top of the wall.

His eyes barely grace them before he nods. "I can and I will."

"Thank you." I turn to go.

"Majesty?" he calls.

"Yes?"

"Is that girl, by any chance, Sawchett?"

I smile, I suspected he was listening to our conversation. "She is. Do you add her name today?"

"I do."

"Well, I would kindly ask you to keep that which you learned here today between us until I have the chance to spread it throughout the kingdom myself."

"I wouldn't dream of usurping that power, Majesty."

"Excellent. Thank you." I turn toward the door in time to hear the running feet pad down the hallway. The noise, followed by a slower set of steps, brings a smile to my face. It seems Sawchett has found her tutor and dragged him to meet with me. It's good the child is so eager.

Sure enough, the tall man enters, practically shoved through the doorframe by Sawchett's small hands. "Good day, Majesty. You wished to speak with me?"

"I did, please have a seat." I gesture to the chairs by the fire. Once he is seated I waste no time getting right to business. "I feel I mislead you when we last spoke and I'd like to correct that error of mine."

"Very well, Majesty. What seems to be the problem?"

"It's no problem with you, rest assured." I pat the man reassuringly on the arm. "It is simply that I didn't make clear the nature of the child's education."

"The nature of it, Majesty?"

I take a deep breath, hold my chin high, and muster all the no-nonsense attitude I can. "Sawchett is a princess in the house of Enchenda. She has royal blood in her veins and wishes to be groomed to one day, upon my death, accept the throne. Her education should reflect this." I worry, for a beat, that the man will argue or demand answers.

He does not. "As you wish, Majesty."

"Thank you, sir."

"My pleasure. Am I excused to continue our lesson? We have other age markers with which we must discuss in light of this new information."

"You are, thank you again." The man departs and I relax a little in the chair. A small laugh floats to my ears and I turn to look questioningly at the man painting the wall, the only other presence in the room. "Did you just laugh at me?" I ask.

"My apologies, ma'am. Did you think he would argue with you?" He laughs again. "You are the queen, after all."

"I am, that is true." Perhaps I am still underestimating the power of my title.

The man steps off his ladder and wipes his hands on his pants. "I am finished here. Would you like to look it over?"

I practically leap from my chair and walk to the board. My eyes light first upon the reflection of Charlotte's name. I allow a small payment of emotion for the girl who is recognized at last.

Then my eyes move on. Underneath Charlotte and connected by a golden thread, I see Sawchett's name. Imagine the joy the girl will feel when she sees this.

Lastly, my eyes track to the two other names that have been uncovered. I speak their names aloud to the room, "Suzette and Margarite."

"Nice names," the man says.

"They are nice names. I am glad you uncovered them for me."

"I hope I get to uncover all those that we've had to cover over the years."

At this, I turn to face him. "Do you hold the job of painting for all realms?"

"I do."

"You may be busy lately. The council has ruled all realms must update their trees."

"Yes, I had heard that as well. I suppose I owe you thanks for that?"

"You are happy about it?" I ask.

"I am, as all who appreciate lineage should be."

"Actually the idea belongs to the king of Rencheda."

"I should've guessed. He's an expert at presenting good ideas, after all. I will be sure to thank him when I am there, I have an appointment to add two names to his wall as well."

"Well good luck with that sir. Thank you for your service to Fraun."

I turn my eyes back to the lineage wall and allow happiness to fill me. "They are all recognized at last."

Chapter 60

How did I never realize how busy my father must have been? The sun is just beginning its trek down the sky. I am enjoying a rare moment to myself, hiding out in my room and dressing for dinner. I hear the sound of a bold knock shatter the quiet of the house. Likely that'll be some other news that needs my immediate attention.

I finish tying the simple white belt around the waist of my red dress. I allow myself the luxury of an extra glance at the reflection wall. This dress, which bells out a bit more than my usual style, is not one of my favorites but it is a nice dress. The deep red accents the little tones of red in my hair.

I pull open the bedroom door and nearly trip over Eee, who is standing in the hallway. "Your Majesty, you have a guest."

"Thank you, Eee." The roach is gone before I can even put my bare feet in the hallway. Clearly, she has more important things to do than answering the door and fetching me. With everyone else treating me differently it's nice to know roaches never change. I nearly laugh at the attitude. As I draw closer to the entryway, I allow my annoyance at the intrusive visitor to creep into my features.

"You look beautiful in my colors, milady."

Tin's voice catches me off guard and melts my frown away. "I wasn't expecting you."

"You weren't? I promised to join you for dinner tonight." He crosses the space between us and kisses me firmly. "I hope it isn't too much trouble for your staff that I am here."

"I'm sure it's fine. I'm glad you're here."

"Good."

I lead Tin through the doorway into the dining room. Sawchett is already seated at the long table, in her customary chair by the fire. I smile at the girl even as anxiety begins to settle in my heart. How will I explain her? "Sawchett, this is King Tin of Sarcheda." I glance back at Tin. "This is Sawchett." How much more information should I give him?

"I'm a princess," Sawchett calls out.

Well, that answers that.

"Is that so?" Tin asks, masking a different question with his tone.

"Yes. They painted my name there and everything." Sawchett points her little finger at the lineage chart on the wall.

Tin's eyes follow the path of the girl's gesture. His jaw twitches. "Well, congratulations."

"We've been hard at work updating our lineage chart," I say with a smile. I lean in closer to Tin. "Her parents are no longer with us and the girl has no one else," I pass the secret quietly, meant for him alone.

"Shall we eat?" I ask, gesturing to the table and a chair Tin should take. I open the side door which connects to the kitchen. "Excuse me."

A young woman appears. "Your Majesty?" The voice reveals confusion. "Can I help you with something?"

"I'm sorry to trouble you but we've had an extra guest to dinner. Could I please get a serving for King Tin?"

"From Sarcheda?" the girl asks, her face lighting up.

I choke back my laughter at the cheery response. "Yes."

"Absolutely, Majesty. Right away."

I return to the dining room and take my seat at the head of the table. In this manner the lineage chart lies behind me, the fireplace and

Sawchett to my right, and Tin to my left. I smile at them both before focusing my attention on King Tin. "Our dinners are usually very laid back so we aren't typically served. I have someone bringing another bowl, please take this one," I gesture to the bowl before me.

Tin shakes his head. "I wouldn't hear of it, I can wait."

"Do I need to wait too?" Sawchett asks. "I'm starving."

"Sawchett, don't be rude," I say.

At the same moment, Tin offers an entirely different answer, "Don't wait on my account."

I laugh. "You heard the guest, go ahead and eat."

Sawchett keeps her eyes focused on me as she grabs her spoon and takes a slurp of the soup. When she is not chastised for eating, she drops her eyes and eats more quickly.

The lady from the kitchen arrives bearing a bowl of soup and a platter of rolls. "I found some rolls in the kitchen, Majesty, that should accompany the earthworm stew nicely. I hope that is to your liking," she says, dropping the bowl of soup in front of Tin and bowing low.

I open my mouth to answer before noticing it is Tin the woman addresses. This time I have to clear my throat to stop the laughter.

Tin, however, smiles under the careful gaze of the woman. "Thank you, milady. It smells wonderful." His voice is low and somehow seductive. The woman giggles and retreats back to the kitchen.

"I think my kitchen staff fancies you, Tin," I note, chuckling a little.

"I think you're right." He gestures to his meal. "I seem to have received a larger portion than you as well."

Sure enough, the bowl in front of the king is easily twice the size of my bowl. This time we both share a hearty laugh. As our laughter dies, Tin takes a spoonful of the earthworm stew. "This is good," he says, delving in for another bite.

Sawchett grabs a roll from the tray, practically standing on her chair to be able to reach across the table. "What is this?" she asks, holding it up to her nose.

"A roll, it's bread," I answer. "Sometimes other realms send us deliveries of it as a treat."

Sawchett breaks it open, smells it, rips off a chunk, and tosses it in her mouth. "It's plain," she critiques, wrinkling her nose.

"Try using it to sop up the stew remnants in your bowl," Tin suggests.

We watch as Sawchett does just that. "Delicious." She smiles. "What a grand idea." The girl resumes eating with renewed gusto.

"Did our patrol arrive safely?" Tin questions as he also returns to eating.

"They did. I've set them up in an empty building and they have toured Enchenda's boundaries. Tomorrow they are set to meet me at sunrise to begin their formal training."

"Sounds like you have it all handled."

I inflate under his praise. This is so much easier than deciding everything alone and wondering in silence if I've done right by Fraun.

"What does training in humility entail, exactly?" Tin asks.

"I wish I knew. I've been struggling with how to bring these lessons to them. I know what I want to show them but I've never been a natural leader." I sigh. "How do I impart the wisdom of putting others before yourself? Of thinking of the greater good above thine own? Of serving others, not for compensation but because it is needed?"

"Would you like help?" Tin offers.

My face breaks out into a wide smile. "You'd be willing?"

"I'm not afraid to lead," he answers. "Besides those sound like lessons I could benefit from learning myself. I could help at least until you are comfortable."

What a wonderful gesture. Too bad I can't take him up on the offer. "I appreciate the offer, Tin. Perhaps on a day when I haven't asked the patrol to meet me at sunrise. Do you realize what time you'd have to leave Sarcheda to do that?"

Tin locks eyes with me. His hazel eyes fascinate me. The light green at the edges is consumed in the center by a brown that spreads out like flames. He raises his eyebrows in question. "I could make it in time if I do not leave Enchenda tonight."

I swallow hard, suddenly feeling very flushed. "Ok," I manage to choke out.

"I'm done. May I be excused?" Sawchett calls out, already rising from her chair.

Glad for the interruption, I smile at the girl. "Yes, of course. See you in the morning." When the girl leaves the room, I sit back. My brain is desperately trying to think of another topic. I keep defaulting back to remembering the heat in my body when we kissed. I feel my face getting hotter.

Tin continues to watch me. "Did I make you uncomfortable?"

"A little," I answer sheepishly. Will the truth change his opinion of me? "I've never had a man sleep in my bed." My skin flushes under the admission and my stomach leaps.

Tin reaches for my hand. "I can sleep somewhere else if you'd like. I'm not trying to rush you. I just want to be here to help tomorrow and this seems to be the easiest solution."

Oh, thank Fraun. "You're right, thank you."

Tin drops my hand and resumes eating. I follow his lead. A comfortable silence wraps around the room as we finish our meal.

Finally, Tin pushes his chair back from the table and adopts a more relaxed posture. "Are we going to talk about the little princess?" he asks. His voice takes on a small breath of indignation.

I'm caught off-guard by the onset of the attitude. "Sawchett?"

"Is there another?"

"No, no. Of course not." I push back my chair from the table as well. "My grandfather had a second child in secret with a woman who was not my grandmother," I explain.

"And you judged my family for taking multiple wives?" His eyes darken slightly with the challenge.

I open my mouth to respond, then close it again when I can think of no argument. "You make a good point," I concede. "I hadn't thought of it that way."

"At least my relatives had the decency to marry both women," Tin points out.

"I'd hardly call that decent." Tin opens his mouth to push the point, so I rush to continue. "But I agree that it wasn't decent the way my grandfather handled it either." Tin closes his mouth. "Anyway, one woman married my grandfather and gave birth to my father. The other woman married a common man from the village and birthed Charlotte, who was raised as though she belonged to the man."

"No one knew of her?" the king asks.

"Not so far as I can tell. Charlotte and her husband later had Sawchett. When Charlotte died I took the girl in."

"What is your plan for the child?" he asks, resting his chin in his palm.

I expected him to be angry. I have misjudged him again. His interest is better than I hoped. "It is as much her right to rule someday as it was mine," I answer. "She should learn what options she has, learn the age markers that are our curse to bear, and decide for herself." Is he, perchance, questioning my decision? I bristle, ready to defend my choice.

"I agree," Tin says.

The uniformity squashes my anger. "Thank you."

"Do you intend to let her rule?" Tin asks.

"Perhaps, if she is needed and desires such a future."

"Were you given such an option?"

"No." I think about my fear of ruling and how quickly I would've given that up when my father first fell ill if I had been given the chance. Didn't I try to get out of it? I tried to convince myself letting Jordyn absorb Enchenda was best. I think how much work it is to be a good ruler now. Maybe I'm not cut out for all the pressure. "Perhaps the option would've been nice."

"I would've accepted the job even if the option to back down had been given," Tin states matter-of-factly. "It's the ultimate show of strength." He shrugs. "Do the people of Enchenda know about the princess?"

"Not yet. How should I tell them?"

"I'd just gather them all up and announce it. You keep forgetting that you are their queen, no one will argue with you." He offers me a smile. "It's nice, sitting here talking simply about life together. Somehow it makes us a real couple." He winks at me.

"It is nice." But he helps me more than I help him. "Is there anything going on in Sarcheda that I can offer my help with?"

"Can we take a walk? I think I'd like to see something out of doors in Enchenda." Tin expertly avoids my offer.

Though I notice the obvious derailment, I smile and push through on his chosen subject. He'll open up when he is ready. "We can. Let's go see my garden, it's my favorite place. You'll want a jacket. Did you bring one?"

"I did."

We don our jackets and traipse to the garden. The garden is a picture of beauty tonight. The ground sparkles with dew and plants are standing tall despite the cooler weather. The frost was minimal this season, Fraun snapped back to warmth quicker than in previous annuals. The change in the cycle is exciting, but that may yet mean a very warm contrasting season.

"Tell me why this is your favorite place." Tin's voice takes on an alluring edge.

"It's beautiful." I offer the simple answer first before delving into the more complex one. "Life happens right here below your feet annual after annual." I reach out and caress the leafy greens of a kale plant, which often survives winters here. "Something so perfect, something essential to life, grows from a mound of dirt and some rainwater. It's fascinating."

"You really enjoy this process."

I smile at his ability to make any conversation sound so personal. "I do love it."

"It is charming how you wear your happiness on your face."

"I do?"

"You have a face incapable of lying. It reveals your every thought and truth, even without your permission."

Something about this admission intrigues me. Rarely in life do you find an opportunity to see yourself as others see you. Somehow it seems truer than the reflection I see every day. I lean into him.

"Your green eyes and your smile tell a true story at all times." He reaches out and catches me under the chin, holding it between his thumb and forefinger. "I can read doubt, love, or truth here." He lifts my chin upward a little and my heartbeat quickens in response. He softens his tone again so that a fly would have to land on his very shoulder to hear his voice. "I can even tell your true feelings by the blush that oft takes up its roots in your cheeks. It reveals your discomfort with the thoughts in your mind."

As if responding to his very words the coloring tiptoes up my cheekbones and settles. "There, see. Now I wonder what it is that traverses that brain and causes you to redden." He bends to brush his lips lightly on the darkening circle of heat.

My defenses lower and a soft purring sound escapes my lips like a sigh. Tin's eyes flash at the sound, a carnal response in him set off by my pleasure. "You have such an effect on me," he growls, closing his eyes.

I feel a kind of power begin in my gut. A power that can only come from igniting passion in another being. I let the power flow down my limbs, relishing it. When it reaches my fingers, I don't hesitate to trace them along the muscles under his shirt, an act I would've previously restrained. When the king's eyes fly open, I recognize deep longing in them. It acts as a stimulant. I will do anything to see that longing again. Hungrily, I kiss him, pressing my body against him and feeling the muscles in his back ripple beneath my fingers.

Electricity crackles between us, warming the air. We paw at each other, hands roaming over clothing and grabbing for some piece of the other to hold onto.

Again, as it was in his home, Tin pulls away from me. I reach for him, confused, and try to pull him back to me. I feel the cold air rush into the void he has left. "Stop," he barks. The command, altogether angry and harsh, halts all my movements.

He softens his tone, but the hard edge remains. "Please, you are going to make me go somewhere you don't want me to go." He looks me in the eye. Finding something that frustrates him, he throws his hands up. "Sometimes your innocence is so taxing." He sighs. "Eselda, we are not wed. There are things that people do when they are wed that you would stop me from doing tonight. If we don't stop now, you will have no power to stop me later."

The truth of the statement carries much weight, having just felt his muscles underneath his clothing. The king of strength would be able to get so much from me if he desired it. Do I want that? My blush deepens. "You want that?" The thought races from my lips. As quickly as it escapes, I wish I could breathe it back in. I didn't mean to speak it aloud.

"I want you. In any form which I can have you." Tin steps closer to me, but not as close as he was before. "I want all of you," he breathes.

The admission leaves us both speechless.

It is I who recovers first, "I do not want to be apart from you. Will you still sleep in Enchenda tonight?" I ask. I do not add that my heart may not survive if he leaves.

"If you find me another bed, I will. Anything else would be too tempting, I fear." He bends, kissing me again. The kiss is softer but still filled with raw emotion.

After showing him an empty room, I lie on my bed unable to sleep. What would the council do if they knew of our courtship? Do I want to give into my base needs as Tin wants to? I warm at the thought of Tin's hands roaming my body, finding places no one else has seen or touched. Tin is right about the needs inside us. If we continue in this way, I will not be able to stop myself from giving in to my desires.

Chapter 61

He paces the room, anger raging inside his ribcage, beating on the bars to be free. His feet punish the floor with every step. *It was never supposed to be like this. The plan was simple, all I had to do was follow the plan.*

One ruler, like Oberian. One ruler to lead them without discord. One ruler to make all the decisions without all the incessant arguing. One ruler with royal blood in his veins.

He breathes deeply. When that doesn't calm him he crashes his fist into the thick wall. The pain has the opposite of the desired effect, it enrages the beast more.

Damn the woman for not following the plan.

His thoughts effortlessly flow to her death. Days ago he was so sure he would carry out that death. He is still sure he could do it. *But what if there is another way?* What if two strong rulers of royal blood could rule together on the throne if that throne was over one United Fraun?

Could the woman be swayed?

He drops onto the bed behind him, falling to its frame without a second thought. The mantra begins to pulse through his brain.

One Fraun. One Fraun. One Fraun.

He allows the thought to permeate the cloud of anger, sending its droplets back to whence they came.

One Fraun. One Fraun. One Fraun.

Soon, sleep visits, and in his dreams, he holds her in a way he has been denied in life.

Chapter 62

I grab a cup of tea in each fist and drag my tired body out of the front door. The sun should be rising soon and training will begin. As I cross the dark yard, enjoying the sight of the lights trapped in the dark expanse of sky, I sip on the tea in my right hand. For the first time in a long time, I wear pants today in preparation for a day of activity. I am hoping it will show the patrol I mean business.

I lower my eyes and take in the sight of King Tin seated on the wall that marks the boundary of my family land. My heart flutters at the sight. "Good morning," I call.

Tin turns in my direction. I can feel his eyes searing my skin. "You look ready to train," he says.

"As do you." I track my eyes down his chiseled and exposed chest. I have never before seen him without a shirt. I have never seen muscles like that on anyone. I find it hard to focus. It is better than I imagined.

"How did you sleep?" Tin asks as I perch beside him on the wall.

"Well. You?" I take a long sip of my tea and hold the other cup out to the king, which he gladly takes.

"I was a bit distracted by the thoughts of this woman I find myself falling for," he drops the comment lightly then takes a long sip of the tea.

I blush deeper and change topics. We must remain professional in the presence of the patrol, due to arrive any minute. "Can I ask you something?"

He picks up on the business tone and copies it smoothly, "Anything."

"What benefits befall the king of the first realm during a time of war? I cannot recall the lesson and it's been occupying too much of my time lately."

I cannot see his eyes in the dark, but his lip curls up in a snarl. "I can make decisions for the safety of Fraun without consulting the council."

His age marker scares me even more now that I have experienced my own small preview. I lean back on my arms, putting distance between us. I carefully select my next words. "I only wondered what power you hold that King Mick may be coveting."

"Do you side with him?" His fists clench between us.

"No," I answer. Suddenly all doubt is gone. I am sure this is the truth. "I do not support a renumbering at this time."

Tin breathes deeply once, twice, three times before his shoulders relax and he has some visible control. My support calmed him. This earns him a kiss on the cheek and a smile just as the patrol rounds the corner of the property.

I stand for the patrol and they form an arc facing us. If any of them are shocked to see the king of strength, they do not show it. Tin keeps his seat on the wall, but he flexes all the muscles in his upper body in an impressive display worthy of his title. The sun is just peeking over the horizon; the men are timely. "Please introduce yourselves, tell which realm you hail from, and explain how you came to be on the patrol," I order.

The first man, short and stocky but with muscles bulging under his thin black shirt, speaks. "I am Daijan from Sarcheda. I earned my place here by holding ten blocks high over my head with no sign of strain." He flexes an impressive bicep at me.

"I am Lance," the next man interrupts this show. "I was selected from Enchenda by my humble queen for being willing to serve all of Fraun above myself." I nod in recognition.

"I am Trep," the next man speaks, "also of Sarcheda. I held ten blocks over my head as well and outlasted all others, save for my counterpart here." The younger man looks to Tin as he speaks, but the king does not show any sign he is listening.

My eyes track to the next in line. "Morales here from Marchenda. Selected by Carsen. Who knows why for sure." The voice drips with disdain, which I was not expecting.

Next to him, a smaller man speaks up. "We can't exactly ask him, is what my friend here means. We can only speculate as to why we were chosen."

"And you are?" I question, turning to the new speaker.

"Vincente, Majesty. I am also from Marchenda." He bows just a little, as if afraid he might offend someone if he were to be caught bowing.

"Danyel, chosen from Enchenda. I am here to bring pride to our lovely host," Danyel speaks up from next in line, pulling my attention along the row.

"Charlez here, from Farcheda. I came in second place in our footrace to see who should represent our realm on this patrol. Glad to meet you, Majesty." Another man bows to me.

"I came in first, that's why I'm here. Breth is the name." The voice comes from the far end of the line, skipping a few in between. I nod once at him before returning my eyes to where we left off in line.

The next is significantly smaller than the others, he smiles at me with youthful exuberance. "Carthen, Majesty. It's a pleasure to meet your acquaintance."

"Yours as well, Carthen. I assume you hail from Renchenda?" I ask.

"I do. We won a logic competition, my strength being the category of geography. It's my passion," Carthen says.

"My strength is mathematics, lady," the last man states, smiling. This one is light-haired and handsome. "The name's Garven, also Renchenda."

"Well, it's a pleasure to meet you all. I am Eselda," I hesitate before offering my title, little use of it making the word rusty on my tongue, "Queen of Enchenda. It is my job to bring you lessons on being humble."

All eyes track me as I pace in front of the group, including those of King Tin who has yet to remove his eyes from my figure.

"Humility is not easy for one to learn. It literally requires you to put all others before yourself, to fight your instincts to be proud or arrogant. We expect this patrol to be respectful of all in Fraun, to not abuse the power given to you by this position, and to understand that you work for all citizens of Fraun at all times. None of you are better than anyone whom you serve." I eye the first man, Daijan, who had flexed his muscles at me. "Even though many of you won a competition to be here."

Daijan scoffs, making a noise that resembles a snort. Before I can react, Tin is up off the wall and in the face of the man. "You will respect the queen, or you will deal with me. Are we clear?" Tin asks.

I have never heard Tin's voice take on this edge. It is different than when he speaks from the depths of anger. He is fully in control of this situation, commanding respect with his voice. Despite being flustered that he interrupted, I am flattered that he felt the need to protect me.

The act leaves no lingering doubts with the patrol as to why the king of strength is here. Daijan deflates under the presence of his king and bows low. "Yes, Majesty."

Tin eyes the rest of the men as he returns to his place on the wall, offering me a smile once he is seated.

"Well," I stumble, "does anyone have any questions?" Possibly because of the impressive display of anger from my partner, no one speaks. I smile at them. "Alright, then we'll proceed. The plan for today is simple. We are going to travel around Enchenda as a group. Our goal is to complete no less than ten tasks for people in the realm without being asked or forced. If you come upon someone struggling with something, you are to offer to take it or help in some way. This is not about you. Should you expect praise or ask for repayment of any kind, you will not be able to count this act. When, as a team, we have completed ten tasks we can return home for the day." I search the faces. "Are we clear on this?"

"I have one suggestion, Majesty, if I may," Danyel speaks up. I acknowledge him with a wave of my hand. Danyel continues, "I would like to propose that you not count actions you undertake as part of our total." He steps forward, turning to look at the assembled men. "I have watched this woman move about this town, she cannot help herself from stopping to help others. It is her we learn from, so I want you to observe how easily she falls into what she is asking us to do." He turns to face me again. "But I do not believe we should earn our ten acts from things we watch you complete."

"Good point." This time the voice is from the king of strength, who jumps off the wall in one motion. "But you can count anything I do. This is a skill I would like to learn as well."

"Who am I to argue with that idea? Let us away, shall we?" I say.

When we begin walking, Tin and I lead the group. The king of strength pulls a shirt from behind his back and puts it over his head as we walk. I glance over my shoulder, seeing the men all grouped together whispering. "What do you think they discuss?"

Tin turns to take in the sight as well. "I've taught them to discuss strategy in any situation. To analyze the facts they've been given and create an action plan. I'd like to hope that's what they do."

"I notice you decided to put a shirt on."

"I worried you were too distracted," he teases. I laugh. "What is the plan?" he asks, curious. "How can you be sure they will encounter ten people who require help?"

"That's not the task at all, Tin. The task is to help ten people in the midst of completing a chore who could use the help. It would be cheating to wait for someone to ask for your help. All around you on a daily basis, there are people who are completing things that you are cut out to help share the burden of. We hesitate to help them because they are complete strangers or because it is not our struggle and we have our own. A truly humble person would never pass another person who they could help." As I explain, my eyes track to the surrounding village in search of such a person.

Tin stares at me. "You truly are a remarkable person," he says, honesty flooding his every word.

"Thank you," I state. I wish there were a way to adequately express my gratitude.

Our group walks in silence for a little while longer, as the sun continues to climb the sky. I spot a small child struggling to carry a large load of what appears to be potatoes toward a house. Here is a nice easy task for the group to begin with.

We gain ground on the boy quickly, and yet no one makes contact with him. I pause in the road. As I watch, the patrol walks right by me. I clear my throat loudly, earning the head-turning of the two men from Renchenda who had been at the back. The surprise moves through the group, each man stopping in his tracks as the message is received. I shake my head, point at the boy, and mouth "watch".

"Good morning, young sir. Could I help you carry those?"

"I'm not going far, Majesty. I'll be alright."

"Nonsense, I'd be honored to help you carry them and to say hello to your mother." I hold my hands out for the potatoes and the boy deposits half his load. I shoot a look of impatience at the patrol.

The look has the effect of sending Danyel and Lance to my side. "Here, Majesty, let me take some of the load," Lance offers. Danyel, for his part, merely puts out his hands and takes a few from the boy. Together the four of us traverse the road in silence carrying the root vegetable.

The patrol, unsure of what they should do and trailing the king of strength behind them, follow. When we reach a house, the little boy drops his load and runs in. "Mother, come see who is here," he says the second he is in the front door.

He returns a few seconds later followed by an older woman who smiles lazily at me before bowing low. "Your Majesty, how can we help you today?"

"We are not here for anything, milady. We simply came to help your son with his load."

"Won't you come in for a drink of water?" the woman offers with a smile.

"Thank you, milady, but we carry water with us." I gesture to the water container I carry, made of leather and strapped to my waist.

"Excuse me, milady," Tin calls, stepping from behind the group. Recognition dawns on the face of the older woman and she blushes deeply as she bows. "I notice you have a shingle there on your roof that has come loose. Might we be of some service with that?"

The woman's eyes follow the king's gesture up to the roof. "My, I hadn't even noticed. I don't want to trouble all of you."

Tin turns on all his charm, smiling at the woman. "It's no trouble at all. Keeps these lads busy."

"Well, in that case, be my guest." The woman steps fully outside and sits on the ground, evidently intending to watch the patrol fix her roof. Tin snaps his fingers and the men jump into action. I stand beside the woman and watch them, a smile forming on my face.

"What are all these young men doing in Enchenda anyway?" the woman quizzes.

"They are the new patrol for Fraun, two of them represent Enchenda actually."

"Yes, I recognize young Danyel." At his name, the boy turns and waves a little. "What is this patrol for, exactly? Surely they are for a more important purpose than fixing the roof of an old widow."

I sit down beside the woman. "This is their purpose. All over Fraun, there are people in need. I am teaching this group to be humble enough to serve Fraun, and those people, above all else."

"Your parents would be proud of your humility, Majesty," the woman says.

"Thank you." We watch in silence as the sun continues to rise a little and the men fix the shingle.

Finally, job done, Daijan approaches. "You are all set, madam." He smiles. "Have a nice day."

Back in the street the men immediately turn to me, "Do we get credit for that one?"

I laugh. "I'll give you credit for the roof since King Tin came up with that on his own. You do not get credit for the potatoes since that one came from me."

"I told you it came naturally to her to find people in need," Danyel tells the group. "We need to be looking for anyone at all completing a task that is too large for them."

"Do not forget what King Tin just taught you as well," I add. "Sometimes it is as simple as finding a small job they haven't yet noticed and offering to fix it first."

"Either way, one down and nine to go," Lance notes. The group heads off toward the town square, this time Tin and I hold up the rear of the group.

"Well done, your Majesty." I smile at my handsome companion. "I am proud of the selfless act you just demonstrated."

"I learned it from you." Tin winks at me and my stomach tumbles in excitement.

By midday, the group has completed six tasks and I am growing ever confident in the patrol. They are demonstrating not only ease with finding the tasks but also genuine excitement the likes of which can only come from putting people before themselves. There was a small incident when Breth, from Farcheda, asked for a slice of pie cooling nearby in exchange for helping. I let the boys finish the task and enjoy their pie without bursting the bubble. Once they were in the street and calling out, "three done, seven to go" I had set them straight.

"Actually," I had called from the back of the group, "you requested compensation in some form, that one does not count."

The boys had stopped dead in the middle of the road and turned on me. "Why didn't you say something then?" Breth challenged.

"What would have been the point? The gentleman you were helping didn't need to feel as though it was his mistake. I figured I would tell you as soon as I got the opportunity, which I just did."

The boys were not happy about it, but they must have learned the lesson. Now they are back in good spirits, having just helped a few boys retrieve an apple that had rolled under a fence they couldn't climb and earning their sixth task.

I take the opportunity to pull Tin aside. "Do you think you could supervise the last four tasks, Tin?" I ask. "I hardly slept last night and the fatigue catches up with me."

He smiles at me. "It would be my pleasure." He bends in and kisses me on the forehead, not wishing to be caught by the patrol in a more intimate gesture than that. "Sleep well."

In this way it came to pass that I arrive back at the house in Enchenda alone, yawning. "Your Majesty, your mail arrived," a young servant calls. I roll my eyes in frustration and hold out my hands for the parchments. The servant transfers two rolls to me. I take them to my room. Flopping on my bed I stretch the first roll out before me.

Eselda,

I looked into the man you asked me about. Tutor did live here for a while a few annuals back, although I cannot find many who remember him. I can tell you he was one of the top students at our school here. He would be about five annuals older than you, by my calculations. Kind of young to be your tutor, but not unheard of.
I will keep digging.
I hope this letter finds you well.
I miss you.
Jordyn

The last sentence stings my eyes briefly. It was his choice to miss me. He had the opportunity to be with me and he has made his choice. The news about Tutor is no news at all. This was an excuse to write to me in hopes of a response. I ball the paper up and throw it across my room. I will do no such thing.

I turn my attention to the next parchment.

E,
Thank you for the update. I am terribly sorry to hear about your father. I hope you are well. You know I believe you are ready to be Queen. Likely you are doing a remarkable job; I would expect no less.
I will visit soon. I have not forgotten your expectation that I answer a few questions for you.
Respectfully,
Tutor

I drop the parchment to the floor and lay my head on the pillow. With thoughts of a visit from my friend to bring me answers, I sleep.

Chapter 63

Time passes quickly and before I fully grasp how much time has passed it is the night before the next scheduled council meeting. I am in Sarcheda, we have just finished another filling meal together and are seated in a room I didn't know about until a few suns ago. The room is large and wide open like a dance hall. There are paintings of the former kings of Sarcheda hanging on the walls. The first time I saw the room I asked what purpose the paintings serve. "To remind us of where we come from," Tin told me.

Now we sit on the floor with a plate of fruit between us for dessert enjoying a comfortable silence. "Do you think they'll do it tomorrow?" Tin asks.

The question catches me off guard, I had been daydreaming about the sight of Tin shirtless as he had been days ago in Enchenda. "What?"

"Call for the renumbering. Do you think they'll do it tomorrow?" Tin repeats.

"I'm not sure. I don't think I can yell at them for fighting and distract them again." I try for a lighthearted tone, but the look on Tin's face tells me it wasn't received as such.

"I just don't know what to do about this," he admits. "I hate that they think I can't handle being the king of the first realm just because of my age. What have I done?"

He has a point. The last fortnight or so has taught me a lot about the king of strength. His anger, when it is real, is scary and dark. But it can be helped. Even if it still scares me to try. I reach for his arm now, calmly rubbing it to let him know I am there. "You're a good king. They have no reason not to trust you. They base their accusations on fear and speculation. Do you know which way the other kings will vote?"

He groans. "Larecio votes with Mick. You vote with me. Our wildcard is your man, Jordyn." The angry eyes turn on me, sparking dangerously.

This is when he is the hardest to tame; when the anger is directed at me. I swallow the ball of fear. "My man? Nothing about him is mine," I state forcefully. I swallow again and adopt a smoother tone. "I know not which way he will vote either."

"You act as though you have no contact with him."

"I don't. I haven't spoken to him since the last council meeting. There's nothing to say." My voice, and my anger, rise to my defense.

"You don't write?"

The accusation is lobbed like a bomb, ready to throw me off my game. I see it coming for what it is and pull my hand away from the king. "He writes to me. I have not responded."

Tin stands and leans over me. "Are you lying to me?"

The anger in his eyes is at a new level, one that has me completely unhinged. "No, Tin. I am not lying." Perhaps the honesty will help to defuse him.

Seeing that attempt fail, I rise in a show of strength he will appreciate and close the remaining gap between us in two small steps. I reach for him, wrapping my hand around his neck and pulling him down toward me. He could stop me if he wanted. I would be powerless against his strength. Tin allows himself to be pulled into the kiss.

Tin wraps his arms around my waist and gives into a short kiss. When we pull apart I see the anger dying down in his expression. "I love you," he whispers, hoarsely.

I recover quickly from my shock. "I love you, too."

This time, when the kiss heats up quickly neither of us pulls away.

"Eselda …" he whispers my name against my lips even as his hands continue to roam over my back. "… come to my room."

My eyes widen with shock at the comment. He is asking, not telling. I tell myself to think it through, but my body has already decided. I nod and allow myself to be led to his room.

Once the door is closed we fall to the bed. I feel the weight of his strength as he balances just above me. We resume kissing with fervor. I run my fingers over the muscles that have occupied my fantasies for a fortnight. Tin slips his shirt over his head, breaking the kiss only long enough to do it.

I feel his hands reaching for the hem of my skirt. It is this act that brings me to my senses. I try to sit up. "Tin, wait." I can see the struggle on his face as he pulls himself away from me, laying on the bed beside me. "I don't know if we should …" I trail off, the point pretty clear.

Tin nods. When he says nothing else, I swing my legs toward the side of the bed. I should go.

I feel his hand wrap around my wrist, squeezing. "Stay," he commands.

"But, we shouldn't —"

"Then we won't." He meets my eyes. "Just stay."

In his eyes, I see his struggle. He has it under control. I lay beside him, my head resting on his shoulder. He wraps his arm around me and pulls me close, turning to rest his chin in my hair. I close my eyes and let myself relax. It's not long before sleep overtakes us both.

Chapter 64

Back in Enchenda, the small princess sits on her large bed alone late at night. She hasn't been sleeping well lately. Likely this is due to the large stretches of time she has been spending alone. Eselda is often gone in Sarcheda. When she is here, he is here too.

I wish I could explain what it is about King Tin that I don't like, Sawchett thinks. *It's nothing concrete, nothing he's done or said. It's just a feeling I get around him. He makes me uncomfortable even when he is going out of his way to be nice. I can't exactly tell Eselda how I feel. She would never understand. He seems to make her so happy.*

But the queen is awfully angry when he's not around. I *caught her losing her temper with the servants. Then there was the time I left the door open and she screamed at me. Of course, she did apologize later. It's just not quite the same as I thought it would be. Perhaps it's my fault. Who wouldn't feel the stress of another mouth to feed and another body to clothe? Eselda has always been allowed to live a careless lifestyle and worry only about herself. Maybe her anger is with me, but she is afraid to admit that.*

The other thing that keeps the young girl awake tonight is the council. They meet tomorrow and Eselda intends to tell them of Sawchett.

Eselda intends to inform them that she will announce me to the realm soon. Tin says they will not argue with Eselda but I doubt that. Who would not argue the presence of a child that appears out of nowhere already eight annuals old? It's just strange.

Sawchett sighs and flops her blonde head around on her pillow in search of a more comfortable position.

Perhaps life would've been simpler if I'd never known I was royal blood.

Chapter 65

The journey to the council meeting is quite a different affair today. Normally, I travel alone on the back of a roach to the center of the Fraun where the council building rests. But King Tin's home in Sarcheda is closer to the building than my own home, so we walk.

It's probably unwise to hold hands with Tin as we walk through town. Fraunians in Sarcheda could see us. But no one is outside. So we hold hands, making me hyper-aware of each finger threaded through Tin's. I haven't seen a flash of anger out of him all morning. I know he dreads the coming meeting and must be harboring some anger. Why does he shield me from it? Perhaps the more important question is how does he contain it?

He holds my hand until the building is in sight. Then, he offers it a squeeze before dropping it. "Unless you want the council to see us as a courting couple?" he asks.

Is he leaving the decision to me? I think it through. Mick will be angry. This makes me want to grab the hand again. Jordyn will be angry. This makes me want to kiss Tin right in the middle of the meeting. Larecio will be hurt. It is this thought that makes me shake my head, no. "Not today, my love. That is business for another day. Today is about you leading your council as best you can."

"Today is also about Sawchett," he says.

"True. Today Enchenda gets an heir to the throne."

Chapter 66

The plan is simple. Eselda will tell the council about the girl first, to soften up the old kings. They will be pleased that there is a future for Enchenda. Then Tin fully expects the question of renumbering to be mentioned. He has already taken the liberty to contact Mick and tell him what will happen if he brings that up, but you can never be sure if the old man received the message. Besides, Larecio may yet call for it as well. That remains to be seen. Either way, there are things to discuss. It would certainly work in favor of Tin's plan if the council was feeling the stress and fear of something pending. So he has an issue he wants to bring forth as well.

He looks to Eselda, she wears the customary green expected of her for the meeting and he dons threads of red. But they have conceded to wear the colors of each other's realms in a silent show of support. Eselda wears a red ribbon holding her hair back. He wears a pin of green on his lapel. Likely no one will notice, but it keeps the woman happy.

Tin has to admit she is beautiful. He has not lied about being in love with her, that feeling came out of nowhere and surprised even him. He has been spending every day with her, but she doesn't know everything about him. *Would she be able to love me if she knew everything?* Despite his desire to not care what she thinks, the thought bothers him. He shakes it off.

As they approach the building, Tin notices Jordyn approaching from the right. He rides a bug of some sort and moves quickly. Tin feels Eselda change. Lately, that has been happening a lot. The queen is approaching twenty annuals. Her shoulders tighten, her jaw locks, and her eyes grow dark like a field of grass suddenly cast into shadow. He reaches out and brushes the back of her hand, but earns no response.

Tin shakes his head. *I knew this was a possibility. You'd have to be an idiot not to notice Jordyn is one of her triggers. There is something there. You can try to hide it from me, Eselda, but you are a terrible liar. Stew in your anger, perhaps it will turn out good for our cause.*

Jordyn stands on the steps, apparently waiting for them as they approach. "Did you come together?" he asks. His eyes are locked on Eselda.

Eselda meets the gaze of the king of wisdom, holds them for a second, and then enters the room without a word. Tin takes in her show of strength feeling pride and the exuberance that can only come from being the one chosen. Jordyn looks to Tin, expecting an answer from him instead.

"I couldn't let the lady walk the path alone," Tin answers, stepping through the door.

Jordyn follows them into the building and takes his seat. A glance around the room tells him he was the last to arrive.

Tin bangs a gavel on the table. "I call this meeting of the council of kings and queens to order. Does anyone have new business to discuss?" he calls out, his voice booming with authority.

"I do," Eselda says, following the plan.

Tin watches her. The anger continues to radiate off her in dangerous waves. For this reason, no one will challenge her in this business today.

"The council should be aware that an underage girl has been found to have royal blood in her veins. Her parents have passed and I have decided to raise her in my home and groom her to be a princess." She looks at Mick. "I'm sure that calms your fear about the future of Enchenda?" Eselda asks.

Jordyn is the first to recover from the surprise. "You are letting her live in your home?"

The look Eselda gives to Jordyn, Tin notes, *can only be described as one of contempt.* He rubs her knee, attempting to calm the obvious anger. *Should a renumbering be called today we need Jordyn on our side.*

"Yes, do you challenge that?" Eselda asks.

Chapter 67

Jordyn recoils from the words and the hatred that spews from Eselda. He has only the strength to shake his head, no. The meeting continues around him but Jordyn cannot focus on it. Fear clenches his throat, constricting his breathing. *Tin and Eselda arrived together, which cannot be good news. Is it a coincidence that Tin wears a green lapel pin?*

Eselda turns to look at Tin, offering him a smile for something he has said. Jordyn notes a red ribbon affixed at the base of her braid. *Not a good omen.* Jordyn's anger bubbles. *So it wasn't a coincidence then that the words Eselda offered me just now echoed the words of Tin after the last council meeting.*

The monster rages and Jordyn allows it to consume him.

Chapter 68

On either side of him, the anger pours out. For a heartbeat, although he would not admit it to anyone, Tin is scared. He looks from one to the other, in awe of the communication passing between the two of them although they are not speaking. He decides to take this opportunity to broach a new topic, perhaps his young companions will calm themselves before any renumbering is brought up.

"I would like to propose a capacity law to the council," Tin says.

"For what purpose?" Larecio questions. The man is unrecognizable from his former self. His hair has turned a deeper shade of grey since their last meeting, he is gaunt, and his face clearly shows that he is out of care for these decisions.

Why does he even bother to interject into this conversation? "There are more births than deaths every time I am updated. I grow nervous for the time when our food runs out," Tin says.

"Are you running low on food in Sarcheda?" challenges Mick. "We have the same problem with births to deaths but our food remains intact."

Tin looks beside him to the one person who could answer this question as well as he could. She continues to fume in her anger. He turns his attention back to Mick "I do have a shortage. We are having trouble feeding everyone." The lie slips into the room undetected.

Fear crosses the old man's face. "Truly?"

"Did you doubt this would happen? We feed ten more Fraunians every time I turn around. The numbers grow in leaps and bounds," Tin says.

"What would this capacity law entail, exactly?" Mick asks, entertaining the thought.

"One child per family."

"What of the families, like my own, who already have more than one?" Mick challenges.

"This will be a new law. I'm not a monster, Mick. Anyone already with a child can proceed to have their infant. This will affect only those who are not yet bringing infants into this world."

"See here, it's not the business of this council to tell people how many babies they should have," Larecio booms. "Jordyn, surely you see this for the foolishness it is."

Tin looks to his right noticing the king of wisdom is deep in the throes of agony now. His hands grip the table as though it is parchment he can tear in half. His dark eyes continue to stare down Eselda. *Jordyn cannot answer you right now, I'm afraid.*

"It's not illogical, Larecio." Tin keeps his voice even and calm. "I'm merely afraid that without such a law we will likely run out of food soon. Imagine if this isn't followed, where would that put us in ten annuals of growth as we've seen? Do you have the food for that many? Do you have the housing for that many?" Tin sees the fear register on Mick's face and has to bite his cheek to keep the smile from showing.

"Maybe it's not such a bad idea, Larecio," Mick says in a lower voice, head turned toward the old man. "Perhaps it's an issue we can side with the young king on."

"Fine. Call the vote, Tin," Larecio yells, shaking his head.

Tin pinches the leg of both royals on either side of him as he calls out. "Those in favor of the capacity law, limiting all to one child per household except in cases where more than one already exists, say aye."

Chapter 69

I come to attention at the pinch and give Tin a strange look. What is going on? I listen as Tin calls for a vote. Oh no, what are we voting on? I notice the almost imperceptible nod of his head. He is helping me. My heart soars with gratitude. "Aye," I call, fishing under the table for his hand and squeezing it.

Chapter 70

Jordyn wants to smack that smug smile off Tin's face. He hears the law called out for a vote, he hears all four of the other royals vote in favor. *I refuse to vote.*

"Let it be known that Renchenda doesn't vote in favor but will still adhere to the law," Tin says.

Jordyn grinds his teeth. "So be it," he mumbles.

Chapter 71

"Any other new business to discuss?" Tin asks. When no one says anything, Tin offers a small smile to Eselda. *They heeded my warnings,* Tin thinks. "Then I call this meeting adjourned. See you all in another lunar cycle."

Eselda immediately leaves her seat and jogs out of the building. Larecio is not far behind her. Mick takes his time gathering his things and heading to the antechamber. Before following, Tin steals a glance to be sure Jordyn is still locked in anger.

Chapter 72

Many minutes pass in the silent room. Jordyn fears he will not get the beast under control again, ever. He tries to think of Eselda, which has always calmed him before, but he can only call up images of her with Tin. He shakes his head.

No, no. I will not lose control.

He slams his hands down on the table, the anger burning his lungs.

Control. Control.

A capacity law? What is his game? Intending to catch the king and ask him, Jordyn finally rises from the chair and heads to the antechamber. He is almost at the door when he hears voices. He slows to decipher who they belong to.

"I didn't call it, calm yourself."

That voice is Mick. Jordyn leans closer to the doorframe.

"I just wanted to be sure that you knew I was serious about what I wrote in that letter," says Tin.

The anger flares again. Jordyn has to stop himself from bursting through the door and starting a fight he surely couldn't win.

"I got the message," Mick says.

"Good. You just be sure you don't forget. If you should change your mind and decide to threaten my seat with a renumbering, I'll just use the army you've provided me with and call for war."

"I didn't give you that army, I gave Fraun a patrol." Mick tries to sound confident. It falls flat.

"Yet I'm the only one who has trained them, aren't I?" Tin laughs and the sound sends chills up Jordyn's spine.

"Hasn't Eselda had her time with them?" Mick asks.

Tin laughs harder. "I've offered to help her train them. The army is loyal to me and me alone."

Jordyn hears footsteps moving away from the doorway. He risks a glance and sees Tin heading for the door. When Tin suddenly turns on his heel Jordyn barely has time to pull his head back in the door.

"Oh, and Mick…" Tin calls out, obviously not noticing Jordyn, "…If you get it in your head to tell the council about this meeting I'll kill you just like I killed that damn prince." The laughter follows Tin outside and leaves Jordyn frozen in place.

The anger fades completely until Jordyn is consumed by his fear. He drops to the floor and puts his head on his knees. His hands shake and his mind rolls.

Tin controls the council, Tin controls the patrol.

Does Tin control Eselda?

Redeeming Jordyn

Redeeming Jordyn was first published in the summer of 2019. It was Jordyn's story. Readers loved him in *Breaking Eselda* and we desperately needed a hero so he took over the telling of the story. Our big driving question in this one was: Would Jordyn be the king who would save Fraun?

Redeeming Jordyn saw our big, bad villain get worse. It also saw him have an epic showdown with our good guys. This showdown was one of the first things I planned when I came up with the series. I knew this would happen and I knew how it would end. It was just a matter of writing the series to get us to that point.

Originally this story was also in third person omniscient, like the original draft for what became *Breaking Eselda.* At that time I had planned to call this one Age of Maliciousness, a nod to the age marker plaguing many of our royal cast. In those drafts, the first book took us all the way up to Eselda's birthday and left the second book opening on her actual birthday.

However, once the point of view shift happened and I really took a look at what was going on, this needed to change. *Breaking Eselda* was really a dark book at its core. We're faced with the reality that our main character cannot save Fraun. She's simply not the person to do it. I made the choice to end that book the moment we learn that information.

That allowed me to make the sequel about redemption and strength. After that realization, the title was obvious.

Fun Facts about *Redeeming Jordyn*:

1. The scouts we meet in this one were inspired by one of my absolute favorite movies. If you have to live in the woods with friends it may as well be like merry men banding together in a 1991 remake of a classic tale.
2. My favorite character from *Redeeming Jordyn* is actually Tutor. His whole personality just comes alive when he meets people who accept him for who he is and I loved writing it.
3. My favorite scene from this one is the very first battle. It clearly showed what we were facing and how serious this would get. Everything got real in that scene.

That's your background information on *Redeeming Jordyn*. Look, I made it through the whole introduction before mentioning this is my sister's favorite book ever!

Prologue

"I know what hate feels like, it is the age marker I fight against each day. Hate boils in your heart, quickens your breathing, and drives your adrenaline to spike. Hate fuels your body to act on every indiscretion, to think about every mistake. You feel hate in varying degrees for different people, but one thing is constant. Hate dominates your mind if you let it. Hate I understand, but of its counter, I know not."

"Perhaps love is as strong as its antagonist. Love then could warm your heart. Love could quicken your breathing and spike your adrenaline as well. Where hate may feel harsh when this happens, perhaps love will feel soft and free. Love will fill our hearts to act on every impulse to be with the one we love, perhaps to ignore their every mistake and flaw. Perhaps, like its reverse, love is also felt to varying degrees."

"The power of hate scares me, Eselda. What if love has the same power?"

"I am sure it does. But how can I fear something with such promise?"

Chapter 1

Tin controls the council.

I just heard it with my own ears. He admitted he sent a letter to a seated king of another realm and threatened him. He controlled Mick easily, something I wouldn't have thought possible.

Tin controls the patrol.

He called them an army. It was my idea to train the patrol that would serve all of Fraun. I didn't expect him to turn them into an army.

I cannot be logical when I am afraid and logical is how I handle things. I allow myself to stay huddled on the cold stone floor of the empty council chamber, breathing deeply, until I can feel the fear draining from my body. I must come up with a plan.

What has happened to Fraun?

First, there was the issue that Eselda brought to me, royal blood being uncharted all over the realms. Then, a seated prince was murdered. Now, I find out that the prince was murdered by a seated king. A king who somehow earned himself an army. An army that I practically gave to him.

This is my fault.

I tip my head back, feeling the angry monster within me build up. I clench my fists. I put faith in Tin. I stood up for him. When other kings were trying to take his seat from him, I said they needed strong reasons. I let him keep that first seat.

This is my fault.

Then there's the problem of Eselda being wrapped up in this. How many times did Eselda ask me to court her? Two? Three? I forced her hand. I practically wrapped her up and delivered her to that monster. She has to know. She has to know what he has done, what he is planning, and what he is capable of.

Does Tin control Eselda?

It is that thought that propels me to stand my full three clicks. I will tell her what he has admitted to. She is not safe. She needs to see reason.

I cannot let something happen to Eselda.

Chapter 2

"Eselda, wait." Her shoes are punching the pathway with every fast step, her long hair trailing behind her. Even with his voice calling out, she does not slow.

"Please, wait," Tin pleads.

He picks up speed and the queen slows a little. This allows him to reach her. He grabs her right wrist, fully fixing the mask he must wear to his face before spinning her around. "Talk to me," he commands. "Are you okay?"

The pair of rulers are leaving the council meeting. Eselda is nearing the malicious age when she will be consumed by a hunger for power. "I'm okay now." She adopts a brave smile. "Tell me what happened in there."

"You had an episode. Should we talk about that?"

During the council meeting, Eselda had completely lost herself. Something or someone had triggered the young queen, making her angry enough to see black. "No, I don't want to talk about that." She turns and resumes walking toward Enchenda.

Tin follows, their hands still clasped between them. "There was no argument over Sawchett so we could discuss her pending announcement."

That's right. Sawchett, the little princess, who has been taken into the house of Enchenda. The council was told about her. She can be announced to all of Enchenda, giving her realm an heir to the throne. "Do you think we can announce her tomorrow?" Eselda asks.

"I don't see why not."

Eselda allows herself to be lost in the details for a moment, a safe place to be lost. *Sawchett can wear her dark green gown, she will be so cute. We can braid her blonde hair down the side of her head. We can stand by the strawberry patch in town, which will make a good backdrop.*

"Why did you say 'we'?" Tin breaks the cloud of dreams.

Eselda whacks him playfully on the arm with her free hand. "We are a 'we'. Aren't we?"

"Of course. But Enchenda does not see us that way."

"I'd forgotten." Her shoulders droop with a sudden sadness.

"We can change that if you'd like."

Tin is serious about this. It warms Eselda's heart to know he would not hesitate to tell Fraun they are courting if she would let him. It is such a change from Jordyn telling her it's impossible to love her. She sighs heavily. "No, that would become a big issue to shadow Sawchett's welcome. I want this to be about her." *Besides,* Eselda thinks, *consider what happened to the last man I announced a relationship with.*

"Alright, then we wait."

Is that sadness in his eyes? "Tin, I will tell people," Eselda says.

"I know."

It is silent for a beat as Eselda wishes she could give Tin what he wants. "Tell me what else the council discussed. I didn't know that you could black out in anger. It scared me. I heard nothing you talked of." Her voice is a whisper as she changes the subject.

"No one called for a renumbering." Tin sits in the first seat, a coveted spot for the kingdom of Fraun. There are rumors that Mick, King of Farcheda, wants to take this seat from him. The last time he called for a renumbering Eselda had just lost her father. She dashed from the room, refusing to participate in the vote.

"Really? Tin that's great news." Eselda looks confused at the sadness still lingering on Tin's face. "Isn't it?"

"I suppose so. I guess I wish they would just get it over with if they're going to do it. All this waiting makes me crazy." He shrugs. "But I'm glad they didn't, no one was in the mood to vote with me."

The stinging remark hits home, making Eselda wince. "I know, I'm so sorry. I don't know what came over me."

Tin stops. Still holding his hand, Eselda has no choice but to stop as well. Her shoulder aches from the quick tug. He is staring at her, the brown flames at the center of his hazel eyes flashing dangerously. His anger crackles between them. This is not the full anger of the age marker, which Eselda knows is burning under his skin. She has seen its effects. This is a short burst, like lightning. "That's not true," Tin challenges.

"What's not true?" she asks, rubbing her shoulder.

"You know what came over you. I guess I just need to know how deep this thing runs."

Her eyes squint as though he is speaking some language she cannot understand. "What thing?"

"Eselda every time we talk of him, your eyes cloud in anger. Now you see him and you fall so deep that you forget to listen for something as important to Fraun as renumbering." He steps closer to her, touching her cheek with the back of his free hand. "I know you love me, I feel it. But am I competing with Jordyn?"

Her eyes close and she leans into Tin's fingers. *I do not want to be torn between two men. I do not want to be so angry with Jordyn. I want to be happy.* She sighs and opens her eyes. "It bothers me that he did not want me, that I was not worth fighting for."

"You're worth it to me."

"I know." That's what bothers her most. If Jordyn was as willing to fight as Tin, they wouldn't be standing here. But it's not fair to say those things to Tin. Jordyn has made his stand clear. "I love you. Only you." She seals the promise with a kiss.

Tin resumes walking with renewed confidence, smiling as though this important conversation was merely a short interruption. "We also discussed the issue you heard the vote for. There is a new law in Fraun. Each couple can only birth one child."

"I did hear part of that." In truth, Tin had saved her from embarrassment at that moment. He had brought her around with a sharp pinch on the leg, nodding at her to show which way he was leaning. "Thank you, by the way, for helping me to know which way I should vote," the queen says. "Who proposed that law?"

"Larecio. Apparently, the new amount of births in relation to deaths has him nervous that food will not hold out. It is a good point." The lie slips right through Tin's lips, undetected by Eselda. In truth, the unnecessary law was brought to a vote by the king of strength himself.

"I suppose I have had the same fears. I hope people will not be outraged at the law."

"That depends on how you present it." He flashes her a full smile. "I'm sure you will present it well."

"Should I use the opportunity of Sawchett's announcement to mention it or would that bring the focus off of the girl?"

"I admit it would not be the most opportune time, but you don't want to wait too long. Perhaps just get it all done at once. In fact, I should journey home to Sarcheda tonight and bring the announcement to my people as well."

"Do you have to?" she asks, pouting.

"I do. But I will miss you greatly. If I am to head home, I really should go the other way. It's already quite far we have walked down the wrong path. You probably should find transportation home, this is a long walk for you. Head in the direction of River Fraun, but keep your eyes open for a ride. I will call on you in a few suns." He bends, kissing her lightly. "Be well."

"You too." Eselda watches his retreating form for a little while until she is sure he will not turn around. Then she continues in the direction of Enchenda. There is much to do.

Chapter 3

Sawchett's stomach is in tangles. She is jittery and nervous like a leaf in the wind, standing behind the strawberry patch and waiting for the time of the announcement to draw near. Her blond hair is loose and flowing around her in the slight breeze. Her dress, one of emerald green, has a rather large hoop at the bottom and continues to sway while she bounces nervously. Eselda told her she had to wear shoes, so she wears plain black leather ones. Her favorite part is the diadem atop her head that Eselda let her wear. It is silver and contains lovely green jewels all around it. It is small compared to the one perched on the queen's head, but it is lovely.

Sawchett peeks around the strawberries and spots the size of the gathering crowd. This does nothing for her nerves. She begins bouncing again, staring up into the sky to keep her eyes off the crowd.

"Are you ready?" Eselda asks, approaching from around the corner.

Sawchett looks in her direction. "I don't know. I'm scared."

"It'll be alright. Let me do all the talking. Wait until I've announced you to come out, okay?"

Sawchett only nods. She fears that if she opens her mouth to respond she will vomit.

Eselda steps out from around the bushes and clears her throat. Quiet trickles through the crowd as they turn to face her. All in attendance bow low. "Good morning, Enchenda," Eselda calls. Her voice echoes off the buildings.

"Good morning, Majesty," the town calls back.

"I've brought you here today for a few short but important, announcements. I will then allow a brief question period.

"First, and most important, is the matter of an heir to my throne. As you know, I have no children. However, it has come to my attention that my grandfather had another child we knew not of. That child also bore offspring. Her child, by her request, will be raised in my home and groomed as an heir.

"Please give your best welcome to Enchenda's new princess, Sawchett."

The little princess' shaky legs barely carry her to stand beside the queen, who she has to lean on for support. She closes her eyes, expecting the doubt and the boos to fill her ears. Instead, she hears a clapping sound. Opening her eyes she finds the crowd cheering and clapping, waving at her. She calmly waves back. *Suddenly I'm glad Eselda talked me into this.*

Beside the girl, Eselda continues. "Next, a piece of news from the council." Her comment silences the gathered crowd. "The council is concerned about how we grow in size. We have seen fit to instate a capacity law until we can ensure that there will not be a shortage of food. The law applies to all in Fraun, not only Enchenda. To be in accordance with the law, each family shall be allowed to only have one child."

Murmurs move through the crowd.

"I will now take questions." Immediately a hand raises. The queen points at the small woman in the second row, indicating she should speak.

"I have two children. What becomes of my youngest?"

"What an excellent question, I'm sorry that wasn't clear. This law applies from this date forward. Nothing becomes of your children, madam, but please do not have more until the council deems it otherwise."

Another hand flies up. "But I'm with child now, Majesty, and it is to be my third." The woman rubs a hand along her swollen belly as she speaks.

"Please complete your pregnancy and congratulations. But do not have more children until the council deems it otherwise."

"So our limit is really one more than we have now?" a man shouts from the back.

"No, no. The limit is one child. In the event that you already have one child or more than one child, you are allowed no more," Eselda answers.

Sawchett notices beads of sweat forming on the queen's hairline. Eselda reaches to brush it, making it look as though she is fixing a stray hair. *What is this capacity law? Do we support this?* Sawchett thinks.

"Do we have a food shortage? Should people be worried?" a woman calls out.

"I believe this is a precautionary measure at this time," Eselda answers.

"Will they be considering changing this back at any time?"

"I don't know the answer to that, but I will certainly ask them to consider that. Yes."

Sawchett's jaw drops. *The queen will ask 'them' to consider this. Isn't she one of 'them'?* The murmuring increases. This is not going as planned.

"The princess and I really must be off, there is business to attend to. Please, excuse us. Have a nice day." Eselda grabs Sawchett's hand and retreats in the direction of the house.

A single old man is heard over the din of the crowd, "That is sure not the way King Gregario handled things." Eselda doesn't acknowledge the comment, but Sawchett sees her wince as though she were slapped.

Once they have cleared the town square and are passing the rows of homes on the straight path to the royal house, Sawchett dares to speak. "Eselda, it seemed like you didn't really support that law. Is that one you voted against but had to uphold? My tutor tells me that is council policy if you are in the minority of a vote."

"No. No, I voted in favor."

"But we have enough food. I don't understand," Sawchett pushes.

"Every time I receive notice there are more mouths to feed, child. Fraun grows too fast. This is better." The tone of voice makes it clear this is not up for discussion. Sawchett allows herself to be silenced. But in her head, she is readying her arguments. *This is not right for Fraun. As a princess, shouldn't she fight against that which is not right?*

Chapter 4

Citizens with royal blood in their veins are cursed with age markers we must bear. The marker I am within now, the twentieth, affects us for five annuals. It is the curse of a hunger for power in the darkest depths of our souls. When the age marker is fed by anger or hatred it grows. It forces your very soul to become darker, angrier, and heavier.

Seeing Eselda and Tin arrive together for the council meeting in the colors of each other's realms awoke my beast. But nothing in the world has ever made my blood blacken like hearing his words from her mouth. "Do you challenge me?" I repeat the words to the empty throne room.

She really said that to me. It is the same thing Tin said to me when I first spoke to him of Carsen's death. I worried, in my darker states, that I may have harmed the prince. My malicious age has a tendency to consume me. Occasionally it causes me to have dissociative states where I cannot remember what transpired. Who knows what happens when anger takes hold during these times?

But no, it was Tin. Tin the whole time.

The throne room is the one room of Castle Fraun that no one enters but me. My servants know that I bring myself here when I need to be alone. Perhaps they think I work on Renchenda policy, but instead, I let my guard down here and try to get the beast under control.

I close my eyes and call up the memory from a happier time in Enchenda. Sitting on a bench under the warm sun with Eselda beside me I had described the age marker to her. I was trying to prepare her for what will come her way. I admitted I knew nothing of love, only of hate.

Eselda, the remarkable woman, had deftly defined love for me. *"Love will fill our hearts to act on every impulse to be with the one we love, perhaps to ignore their every mistake and flaw."* I can feel the warmth spread throughout my chest as though Eselda's palm were flattened there again, pushing back the monster within. I feel the warmth radiate across my body.

Love, it turns out, is the only counter to the malicious age. I probably should've known, considering it is the age marker that follows it. I have found the love that tames my dark side. I have seen the brightest parts of my soul, they are rooted in Eselda. It took me too long to see that and now the memories are all I have.

Chapter 5

"Sawchett, you need to focus. A princess needs to be able to answer these questions with ease." The tutor, a man named Marshawn, is growing increasingly frustrated with the girl's lack of focus this morning. She lays on her back, enjoying the uncharacteristically warm weather in the garden, and barely answering his questions. "Let's try again, please. What are the names of the current seated kings of Fraun?"

"Shouldn't you say Royalty, not Kings? Eselda isn't a king."

"Fine. Name the current seated royals of Fraun."

"King Tin, Queen Eselda …" Sawchett trails off. *I always forget the name of the third guy. I'd skip over him, but I know Marshawn will want them in order. It wouldn't do any good anyway. I can't remember the name of the fourth guy either.*

"King Mick, King Larecio, King Jordyn," the voice rings from the side of the garden.

"Tutor!" Sawchett calls as she jumps up from the ground and dashes across the yard, throwing her arms around the neck of her old friend.

Tutor lifts her into a spin with ease. "Good morning, child. How goes the lessons?" he teases.

"I cannot remember anything, I'm hopeless."

"Well, lessons are important. They are often easier when you focus instead of daydream." He turns his attention to the tutor. "May I borrow her for a moment? We are old friends."

"Be my guest, perhaps she'll focus better after a break." The man heads for the house, shaking his head.

"Let me look at you, little one." Tutor kneels to be closer to the level of the girl. She spins to allow him to see how much she has changed. "You're taller, stronger, and healthier I think," he remarks with pride.

"I am taller. Am I more regal?" Sawchett asks, wiggling her eyebrows.

"Regal? Why would you be regal?"

She cocks her head to the side. "I'm a princess, didn't you hear?"

Tutor's grin falls. "What?"

"Are you mad? Don't be mad."

"I'm not mad, sweetheart." *At you, anyway.* "What do you mean you're a princess?" Tutor pulls Sawchett down to the ground to sit beside him and gives her his full attention.

"Eselda says my Mom had royal blood but never had the title. Did you know Charlotte was a royal?"

"I heard that rumor as well, yes."

"Well then the painter guy he came and put my name on the wall."

"I knew he was doing that, I asked him to do it myself." Tutor begins to grasp where the conversation is going. He holds out his hand to the girl in a calming gesture and adopts a tone often used with Eselda when he conducted her lessons in the annuals before she became Enchenda's queen. "Sweetie, I think you misunderstood. You have royal blood, that is true. But to be a princess you would need to have a parent who is ruling the realm. Charlotte is not doing that, neither is your father. So you are not a princess," Tutor explains.

"No, Eselda says I can be a princess if she decrees it. She announced it seven suns ago. I'm a princess." Sawchett crosses her arms over her chest in a childish show of frustration.

"Is Eselda here, maybe I can clear a few things up with her?"

"You're mad, aren't you? You said you weren't mad. You can't be mad if you said you weren't."

"I'm not mad." Tutor softens his tone. "I'm excited for you if this is what you want. Being a princess is hard work, but I can think of no one better suited for it." He gives a small shake of his head as he recognizes the platitudes he often used to soften the last princess of Enchenda come spilling so easily out of his lips.

As it was with the girl before her, Sawchett beams under the praise.

"Now I need to speak with the queen, she has requested my presence. Also, your training needs to be handled like a princess. Find your tutor and focus that brain." He taps her on the skull as he orders this.

"Eselda's not here." Sawchett remains seated, shrugging.

"Where is she? When is she expected back?"

"Sarcheda, probably. I don't know when she'll be back."

"How long has she been gone?"

"This time? Since yesterday morning." Sawchett looks bored with the conversation, she has begun twirling her blonde hair around her finger.

"What do you mean, 'this time'? Does she travel to Sarcheda often?"

Sawchett traps Tutor with a look of disgust. "Yeah, all the time."

"Sawchett I haven't been around, what do you mean 'all the time'?"

The girl sighs dramatically and flips her hair back over her shoulder. "Probably every other day Eselda is gone. She sleeps in Sarcheda with King Tin. When she's not there, he's usually here. It's been that way for a while." Sawchett can see the question form. Before Tutor can even ask it, Sawchett waves her hand in frustration and answers the unspoken question. "It's been lunar cycles, practically since I came here."

"Are they courting?" Tutor asks.

She shrugs. "I guess so. I don't know."

"Wow." Tutor can think of nothing else to say. *This is not what I expected to learn upon arriving in Enchenda.* "What else is different around here?" he asks.

"Not much." She twists her mouth around and averts her eyes. "She gets angry sometimes."

The age marker. He tries to recall how old Eselda was when he began his post. Some quick math estimating the difference in their ages then and progressing her forward puts her age around nineteen annuals since he is approaching twenty-five. *Too soon, but it's close.* "Yeah? How angry?"

"She yells at people sometimes. It's no big deal," Sawchett says.

"Does she yell at you?" A protectiveness flares within him, one born from years of sharing a home with the girl and her mother.

"Sometimes. She always apologizes. It's not a big deal, Tutor."

"What does she look like when she gets angry?" he asks.

This earns Sawchett's attention. She looks at him like she wants to read his thoughts. "She looks the same, I guess. Sometimes her face gets flushed or her eyes get a little darker. Is she twenty annuals, Tutor?"

He smiles a little at the tutor who must have taken over for him. He has wasted no time in getting to all the age markers with the girl. "I don't think so, no. It's probably no concern."

"It worries me sometimes, how angry she gets," Sawchett confesses. "If that's not because she's twenty, then could it get worse when she is at the malicious age?"

"I'm not really sure," he answers, frowning at the girl. "How concerned are you? Should I take you out of here?"

The girl looks flabbergasted. "Where would I go?"

"We could find a place to take you, the kingdom is large. If you tell me that you need to leave I will assure you safe passage anywhere. I've made friends with the scouts in my travels over the annuals."

Sawchett thinks. "No, I like it here. Eselda means well. I like her."

"If you change your mind, many of the servants here know how to reach me. Or you could get on a roach and tell it to take you to the nearest group of scouts. They would all know how to find me."

"Okay," she draws out the word in annoyance and rolls her eyes.

Tutor stands. "I have to go. I'll stay in town for the night, if Eselda should happen to come back tell her to find me at Charlotte's old home." The girl nods her head, sending her blonde locks bouncing. "Oh, and Sawchett please remember to focus on your tutor's lessons."

"Yeah, yeah," Sawchett calls. Released from the conversation she is already on her feet and bounding into the house.

Chapter 6

In Sarcheda, Eselda sits on the front wall watching as Tin participates in a show of strength. Some of the young boys from the school have been brought here today to watch their king. The boys are seated in a group on the ground around him. You can tell by the way they watch his every move that they love him.

In the center of the circle, Tin is raising large wooden blocks over his head and throwing them. Each block sails over the heads of the boys, causing them to turn and see how far away the blocks have landed. After each toss, there is wide-eyed excitement. The boys clap as the last block is thrown. Eselda watches as the shirtless king crosses through the circle. The boys all quickly reposition to allow him to pass. Tin stacks all of the discarded blocks, twelve in all.

A patrolman from Sarcheda once told Eselda ten blocks was the number he won his competition with. She raises her eyebrows in a small show of doubt. *Those two men won a competition by hoisting ten and my lover here intends to lift twelve?* A murmur spreads through the small gathered crowd as they too count the blocks. Apparently, this is quite the feat, even by their standards.

Tin flexes his muscles in preparation for the task, closes his eyes, and takes a deep centering breath. Everyone watches, rapt, as he puts his arms around the bottom box. The silence in the clearing is complete. It's as though Sarcheda itself holds its breath.

Tin's legs tense and he rises with the boxes. There's a moment where time stops as all watch him with fear and awe. *Will he fall?*

Tin balances the weight. His legs straighten. He pushes his arms high, so they are extended fully. The boxes now stand high above his head. In this position, he freezes.

Eselda begins to clap and the gathered children follow suit. She cannot help but be highly impressed. Clearly, the king of strength is showing 'no sign of strain' as the patrolmen once claimed as well.

The blocks clamor to the ground. Their weight causes the ground to shake and the noise echoes off the house behind the queen. "Now you may have your time to try," Tin says. "But be careful, these are no toys you touch."

The boys dash forward and Tin retreats to the back to stand beside Eselda. His upper body is covered with a sheen of sweat. "Impressive," Eselda whispers.

"Well thank you. I had this amazing woman present today whom I needed to impress. I pushed myself to an extra block for that reason alone." He winks at her as he reaches for his water. He takes a sip and then pours much of it over his head, allowing the water to trail down his chest.

Eselda cannot help but find the entire display a little enticing. She clears her throat in an effort to hide the emotion before speaking. "You don't normally lift twelve?"

"No one normally lifts twelve." He chuckles. "Our previous record was eleven."

"Now I am even more impressed. Who held that record?"

"My father, although I tied it last annual."

The royals watch for a moment as the group of boys split up around the twelve blocks and try to lift them. Eselda becomes even more impressed as she watches them struggle to lift even one heavy block. One boy, slightly larger in height than the others, lifts one block effortlessly. The gathered boys work together to stack two. The tall boy proceeds to lift those as well, although Eselda can see his legs shake from the effort.

"Excuse me for a moment. I must get that boy's name."

Tin pulls the boy from the group and bends down to his height. The two have a whispered conversation. Tin cuffs the boy on the shoulder and rises. The boy returns to the group and is immediately surrounded by the other boys as Tin returns to Eselda's side. "I think you just made that boy a celebrity among his peers," she says.

"He is the strongest in the group, he should be their celebrity."

"Well, as much as I hate to leave this gathering, I should be home tonight to check on Sawchett."

"I will come by tomorrow and work more with the patrol if you'd like," Tin offers.

"Perfect. I'd kiss you but the boys are present."

"You owe me one." Tin winks.

"That is a debt I will gladly pay."

Tin watches Eselda's retreating form and lets the mask he wears for her fall away. He thinks through the plan again. *The time approaches when I will need to take the next step. Eselda must either become my bride to stand beside me as one or …*

He allows the thought to trail off. Suddenly he is sure. "She will choose that option," he says aloud.

Chapter 7

"King Jordyn, you called for me."

I look up from the parchment before me. My lineage updater has sent me a new name he will order added to the wall. It is nice to see him finding relatives alive and well. Any happiness I felt when this parchment arrived leaves my body with a sigh as my eyes land on the man bowing before me in the doorway to the study room on the first floor. "Yes, I did. Have a seat, please." I gesture to the empty chair beside me. I roll up the parchment and place it below my chair as the man sits. He will have my complete focus. "I asked you to come because I have more information for you about the murder you investigate for Fraun," I begin.

"More than you gave me when I conducted your interview, sir?"

I can see the doubt on his face. Believe me, I wish I never had to see that expression on citizens of my realm. It is proof that I am not the king they deserve. It would be easier to take if the man simply slapped me. "I do. First I'd like to explain the reason I could not simply declare my innocence."

"That's not necessary, Majesty. Really."

That answer tells me that part of him thinks I did it. I shake my head. "Citizens of Fraun who have royal blood in their veins suffer from an age marker the rest of our citizens do not. At twenty annuals we are met with something known as the malicious age. It makes us answer to a darker side of ourselves more than we should. It causes us to act on our anger. I was angry with Carsen, although I understand it is not logical to harbor such feelings."

"You are in love with the queen, Majesty?" he asks.

"The fact that you finally asked that question makes me know I employ the right man for this job. You are not afraid of the uncomfortable questions." He smiles under my praise. "I am in love with Eselda, but it is a love that cannot be. Nevertheless, during the evening in question, I became angry and blacked out. It is not something that happens often, but when it does it scares me to be around other people. When my anger faded I was in the dance hall. I have no reason to believe I encountered Prince Carsen during the time I cannot account for, or that I would've harmed him if I did. But I cannot be sure. Someone from Renchenda must be sure. It is our way."

"So you wished me to come here today to explain that you are innocent or that you do not know if you are innocent? I fear I am confused, Majesty."

"I wished you to come here because I now know I am innocent. I heard the confession of the murderer myself. Prince Carsen was killed by King Tin of Sarcheda."

The man closes his eyes and shakes his head sadly. "He was my prime suspect."

There is no triumph in the knowledge, for either of us. There is too much at stake here, for Fraun, to be satisfied in being correct. "You will report this to the council. They should be aware," I command.

"With all due respect, Majesty, it is not my finding to report. I did not hear the confession."

"You wish me to tell them?" I ask.

"I think it wise." The investigator stands from his chair. "I will consider the case closed." He bows low and turns to leave the room.

"Wait," I call. "What do you plan to do about this?"

He turns back to me and sadness is written all over his face. "For the first time in my life, I feel like there is nothing at all that can be done. More so even than when your mother …" he breaks off, shaking his head. "Fraun is not the place I thought it was. I am disillusioned."

I want to correct him, as a good king would. I want to alleviate his fears and promise him protection. But I cannot find the words. He has spoken my fears aloud to me. He has given them an audience in this room.

Fraun is falling.

Chapter 8

"Good Morning, Sawchett," Eselda calls. The queen has been sitting at the breakfast table for quite some time waiting for the girl to awaken. She has just come strolling into the room, rubbing her eyes and yawning.

Sawchett jumps in surprise. "Eselda, you're back. How was Sarcheda?"

"Good, thank you. I witnessed a feat of strength, which is something of a tradition there." Eselda begins eating the food before her as Sawchett picks up her spoon. "How fared your lessons in my absence?"

"Okay, I guess. I'm having trouble focusing, according to my tutor."

"Is that so? Have you tried a different location? My tutor used to suggest I study in the garden to improve my focus."

"Speaking of your tutor," Sawchett jumps in, "he was here yesterday. He said he would be at Charlotte's. He may still be there if you hurry."

Eselda's spoon clatters to the tabletop. "Don't think me rude. I will go see if he is there. We will catch up later." She doesn't wait for a response.

At the door to Charlotte's home, the queen's hope drains. There is no answer to her knocks. "Tutor, are you here?" she calls out, memories of the angry disposition she last saw on his face clouding her brain. She lays her head on the wood, disappointed.

"Can we talk?"

She whips around at the sudden voice, frantically hoping her ears deceive her. *Perhaps the voice belongs to someone else. Perhaps Tutor will be standing there.* She tilts her head up, past the carefully tailored clothing of a royal, past the thin chain that disappears under the neckline of the orange shirt. She takes in the shock of blonde hair perpetually falling into the ocean of blue in his eyes. Standing with his hands shoved deep in his pockets and looking more nervous than a prince on his first school visit, is not her former tutor but the king of wisdom himself.

Chapter 9

"I have nothing to say to you." She throws her chin up defiantly. She is angry. I can almost see her entire body hum with the feeling. It is not full-on anger, she is not at the malicious age. This is the anger of a woman scorned. It may be scarier than the beast.

"Please, Eselda. It's about Tin." I hate seeing how the name alone relaxes her shoulders a little. I hate myself for not being that comfort to her. She steps closer to me as if she senses I will speak ill of him and she can encourage me to keep my voice low. "We should have this conversation somewhere more private," I add.

I watch her clench her fists. "If memory serves there is an old bench over that direction." She indicates the strawberry fields with a tilt of her chin.

I turn and head toward the bench. She is punishing me, choosing this spot. This is where it happened. The conversation about love, the kiss. I wonder if she remembers the moment. Is she trying not to think about it? I never once allow myself to turn and check if she follows me. I can't turn around now. This is already hard enough. Maybe she will turn and run, I can still say I tried. Isn't that enough?

She sits on the farthest edge of the bench, her knees turned away from me. I breathe deeply and exhale, drawing strength from the sweet smell of the strawberries. Then I dive in. "I overheard something after the last council meeting. Tin and Mick were speaking in the antechamber."

She won't look at me. Her eyes are fixed on the ground. It's probably easier this way. "Tin threatened Mick. He claimed the patrol answers only to him. He called them an army. He said he would declare war if Mick called for a renumbering."

I wait for her to say something, anything. Instead, she leans back on a plant, tightening her delicate little arms under her perfect breasts. She turns her green eyes to my face and blinks at me.

"Have you heard a word I've spoken?" I ask, exasperated.

"Oh, I heard your tale. This is below you, Jordyn."

"What are you talking about?"

"I assume you've concocted this tale because it cannot possibly be true. The patrol reports to me right now. I provide their training each day."

I throw my arms up in frustration. She is not even acting like herself. "Where is this patrol today? Right now?"

"They are in training." Her voice trips on the half-truth.

"With?" I push.

She sighs in defeat. "Yes, they are with Tin. But it is not what you think. I have seen him with them; he trains them in my lessons in my way. They are not an army and Tin has never referred to them as such."

"Eselda, you have to believe me. I have no reason to lie. Tin is planning something, why else would he threaten war?"

She reaches up her fingers, brushing her auburn hair out of the way so she can rub her temples. "Look, Jordyn, I don't want to fight with you. Trust me when I say Tin desires not to war. He would've told me." She stands up, stomping her feet and sending a little cloud of dust around the hem of her dress. "You were right about you and me, okay? We were never worth fighting for. I'm not angry anymore, but this story you've told doesn't change anything."

"It's not a story." My voice hits a new high volume and rings in the clearing for a beat. I take a breath and consciously lower my voice. "He killed Carsen." The fact drops quietly, like a drop of water hitting a full bucket.

Her anger picks up. It is palpable in the little clearing. "That's out of line, Jordyn. You've gone too far."

"I heard him admit it. It fits, Eselda. You know it does. You were worried it was me—"

"You worried it was you," she corrects.

"For all the same reasons you doubted me it could be Tin."

Now it is her turn to yell, "You have no proof."

"I heard him say it. Ask him yourself." Suddenly I don't want to do this anymore. I have done my part. I told her. What she does with that is on her.

"You speak from jealousy."

I recoil from the word. "Jealousy? No, Eselda, I speak from fact."

"You just can't stand to see me happy. You know Tin and I are willing to fight to be together. You know we are in love and you just can't stand that." With each statement, she takes a small step toward me so that by the last word she can poke me in the chest.

I deflate as though she has burst my soul. My voice is barely a whisper. "You are in love?"

"Yes. Nothing you can say will change that." She turns and stomps from the clearing.

Eselda's footsteps can still be heard stomping away when I drop my head into my hands. "Tin controls the council, the patrol, and clearly he controls Eselda."

Chapter 10

On the other side of the plants the little eavesdropper whimpers in fear. What she just overheard has her so worried her sides hurt. *A seated king murdered a prince?* She quakes with the new knowledge. *What will happen next?*

Out of fear and confusion, the feet begin running. They do not stop until the edge of Enchenda when they nearly collide with a common roach. "I need to find a scout, it's an emergency. Can you take me to one?"

Sawchett climbs aboard the back of the roach and flees from Fraun.

Chapter 11

As the sun rises on Enchenda, people are already awake. There are some in the realm who head to the town square to shop or trade as though nothing is wrong in the kingdom. Others remain in their homes, readying their chores for the day. Still, some will leave the realm today to continue the search for the little princess.

In Eselda's home, anger is brewing. Sawchett has been missing for two full lunar cycles. They have searched high and low. They find no trace of the body, but yet no trace of the girl either. Tutor has yet to contact the queen. Her many letters alerting him to the missing child have been ignored.

What kind of safety is Fraun offering? Carsen was murdered at a council event. Sawchett has been kidnapped from her realm. People should expect more from their council.

Eselda releases the anger she has pent up inside herself in a roar that fills the small room. She grabs the nearest item, the bracket for a candle, and hurls it across the room. In the silence, she turns the anger inward. *I should demand more for my people.*

Chapter 12

"Good afternoon, King Jordyn. To what do we owe the pleasure?" The small servant woman who answers the door at Mick's family home in Farcheda is sweet-faced and young. She bows low to me.

"I'm here to meet with King Mick. I thought he was expecting me."

"He may be. I am specifically charged with her ladyship, I tend not to give much attention to his highness. I will bring you to his office. It is where he often holds these meetings." She steps out of the doorway to allow me entrance into the room.

The royal house here appears to be built for easy access to any room. We enter a long, narrow hallway that runs the expanse of the home. There are doorways off both sides. The servant girl immediately begins walking down the right side of the hallway. She travels up about three doorways and turns, knocking on the door.

"What is at the far end of this hallway, if you continue straight?" I ask.

She turns to look the way I point. "The back gardens."

"Who is it?" Mick bellows from within the room.

"Majesty, I bring King Jordyn for your meeting," the girl answers.

"Come in then."

Inside the little room, there is a single round table with four chairs. Mick is seated in one of the chairs, parchments being rolled back up with his hands. He deposits them at his feet even as he sweeps his free hand toward the empty chairs. "You may sit. What would you like to speak of today?"

"You waste no time getting to business," I note aloud as I sit. "We need to talk of war."

"You have shut me down every time I try and broach this topic. What has changed your mind?"

"I have reason to believe it may be worse than you even considered in your darkest musings, Mick."

"You do not believe, as I do, that Tin will declare war on Fraun?" Mick asks.

"The concern is not with just that anymore," I say. "I fear it goes deeper than even that. You worry that Tin will declare war on the rest of Fraun and I must admit I now agree with you there. My concern is that Tin will bring Eselda and the second realm to his side in this war."

"I do not understand why you think this. Explain it to me," Mick commands.

"I'll put it as simply as I can. I have reason to believe Tin and Eselda will wed soon," I answer. "I do not want to explain further. I do not want to answer questions about this at all. I'd rather not be having this conversation, truly. But someone must be aware."

Mick sits back in his chair and rubs his face with his hand. "With the little princess missing and no other heirs in either realm, this would unite Sarcheda and Enchenda."

"It would. You understand my fear."

"Then when he declares war …" Mick doesn't have the strength to finish the thought.

"It's the larger, new first and second realm combination against the remainder of Fraun," I finish.

Mick thinks out loud, "If he wins that war, he will control all of

Fraun. He is likely to win that war, I fear. He has an army and he is the king of a realm known for strength."

"Even if he loses, he could choose to never again be a part of Fraun. He could rule over his new kingdom and start again."

Mick bristles, "Surely Eselda wouldn't allow that, an entirely new kingdom."

"I don't know anymore. She's not the same person she was."

"What is our next move, Jordyn?" Mick leans forward again. "Tell me the smart thing to do and I will carry it out posthaste."

"I fear he will declare war on your realm personally. I wanted to meet with you today to tell you that Renchenda sides with you. I'm sure you will find the same in Marchenda. Your realm would not need to stand against Sarcheda alone. Fraun is behind you. We should begin training men as soon as possible for what may come."

"You think there is no avoiding this now, then? There is no plan for how to stop that which Tin has put in motion?" Mick shakes his head. "Never mind, don't answer. I can see in your face a misery that answers enough."

I rise from the chair. "If you want to be ready for this you need to stop pretending it won't happen and ready Farcheda for war."

Chapter 13

Everything has changed.

I sit at a table in my dining room inside Castle Fraun, awaiting a visit from someone I have never met. Someone who could further change everything. Lately, it seems as though the sky is darker, the clouds are heavier, and the entire world is mourning the loss of Fraun as I knew it. Dark days.

"Pardon me." A man enters the room, a tired expression on his face. The man is older than I, but not yet grey. He is wiry and tall; there is a remarkable physical resemblance to myself. I rise and offer my hand to the man, who gladly shakes it.

"Please, have a seat." I gesture to the empty chair. "I'll get right to business. I recently hired someone to update my lineage tree. In their investigation they came across you, alive and well. It is rumored you are my Uncle, Thometh. Is that accurate?"

"Your mother, Aine, was my older sister."

"You are not married, you have no children. Is this accurate?" I ask.

"It is."

"Can you tell me why you were not tracked on our family lineage tree?"

"My sister was already twelve annuals and well on her way to becoming the queen of Renchenda before I was even born. Our mother, Rose, passed in childbirth. My father with his royal blood continued to rule the realm, but he felt a great sadness at her passing. It is my understanding that anything dealing with me was painful. I'm sure it was an oversight, at first, to not have my name added." He raises one thin shoulder quickly like the events do not even warrant more than a half-shrug. "Once I was old enough I struck out on my own and I have made it a priority to never waste the time of those living within these walls since that day."

"I'll get right to the point then. I would like to formally accept you as a member of royal blood in good standing with Renchenda. The time may come when I am unable or unwilling to rule my realm. If this situation were to occur, the rule would fall to you. Are you up to such a task?"

"I'm older than you, Majesty. What makes you think I will outlive you?"

"The time may come when I am unable or unwilling, I did not say dead. Are you up to such a task? My research into your background tells me that you bring much to the table in the way of intelligence and level-headedness. Such a thing may prove to be an asset to Fraun in the near future."

"There's something you are not telling me." Thometh eyes me wearily.

"You're right, there is. If you accept the proposition, we will discuss the future of Fraun."

"I must accept before you will tell me?" The man's eyes come together in confusion.

"Sadly, yes." I rest my elbows on the table and lean forward on my forearms, intending to wait as he processes my offer. I don't have to wait long.

"You have ignited my curious nature. I'm in," Thometh says.

"Wonderful, then let's begin. What do you know of Sarcheda?"

Chapter 14

Eselda feels the rolling of the bed beside her alerting her that Tin is awake. She feels him rub her arm lightly. Her eyes open slowly like sleep is unwilling to let them part. "Good morning," she mumbles.

"I have something to ask you, are you awake enough for that?" he teases.

She sits up on her elbow and rubs her eyes. "I'm ready."

"I feel the council is no longer acting in the best interests of Fraun," he begins.

Her eyes open further and blink rapidly to fully wake her brain. "I've been thinking similarly. But what do we do about it?"

"I want to do something drastic." He takes her hands. "Hear me out before you think me crazy. I think they will not change their ways until they take us seriously. I think they need a clear message that what they do is wrong. We should start a realm where age does not matter. Where you are not pressured to have children. Where anyone of royal blood can rule. All the things that matter to you, my love."

"It sounds wonderful, Tin, but how do we do that?"

"Marry me."

"What?" Eselda pulls her hand free. "You have lost your mind."

"No, I'm thinking clearly for the first time. Marry me. Our realms would unite and we would be the strongest realm in the history of Fraun. We would have the power to change the rules. We could force them to vote for those changes."

"You want to marry me only for this purpose?" It is Carsen all over again. *Why* she wonders *does everyone who wants to marry her mean business and everyone else want to tell her why they cannot love her?*

"I want to marry you because I love you. I want to rule our realm with you for this purpose."

"We would rule side-by-side?"

"Absolutely."

"So this is a marriage of love, helped along by business?" she summarizes. It's already sounding better than her last marriage proposal.

"Yes. Eselda, will you marry me?" Tin's eyes sparkle in the dim light of the morning.

Joy wells up inside the queen and she finds she cannot answer. Instead, she pulls the king down on top of her and kisses him passionately.

Chapter 15

King Tin of Sarcheda
and
Queen Eselda of Enchenda
are proud to announce their engagement.

Please join them for a celebration on the night of the next full moon
in Sarcheda's town square.

I fold the parchment carefully, laying it back down on the desk. I take a deep breath and let it out. I rub my face. Then, with a grunt, I send my fist slamming down onto the folded parchment. The desk wobbles dangerously.

"Why can't you see that you are being used?" I yell to the empty room.

I reach for a blank parchment, scrawling quickly.

Uncle Thometh,

I must ask you to accept the plan we discussed. I am stepping down as King of Renchenda, effective immediately. I have no doubts that you will be able to lead the realm to great things during this dangerous time.

I will leave tomorrow at first light. My plan is to find out what is beyond Fraun and if we can count on any outside support during our time of trouble. Please stay in contact with me, as I will stay in contact with you, through the scouts.

You may move into the home as soon as you'd like. I'm sorry to leave this to you, but it must be this way. The next council meeting approaches, and you will need to notify them of the changes. They will not argue, there is too much else to argue about.

Jordyn

Chapter 16

Eselda's eyes fly open and search the room for what may have dragged her from sleep. Her eyes register colors all wrong, everything is darker than she remembers. *I am in Tin's bedroom, our bedroom, in Sarcheda,* she realizes.

A noise reaches her ears. Something loud, like banging. Acid slides up her throat and her vision darkens further. She launches herself out of the bed and to the doorway. In her hurry to wrench the bedroom door open the wood splinters. "What is that awful racket?" she screams at the top of her voice into the hallway.

Tin's head appears from around the corner. Eselda can see his mouth moving, but she cannot hear him. A buzzing noise has started in her skull, causing a headache that makes her squint. "What? Speak up, for Fraun's sake," she yells.

Tin is at her side in an instant. He slowly reaches for her, grabbing her face and staring into her eyes. Whatever he sees there causes him to frown slightly. When he speaks from this distance, she has no trouble hearing him. “Fascinating.”

“What is fascinating?” she snaps, clenching her fists.

“You are absolutely beautiful when you are angry. Your eyes are a remarkable shade of green, so dark it is almost black. Tell me, my dear, how do you feel about the council this morning?”

“Why do you ask me this? That council is garbage. They accomplish nothing.” Eselda raises her fist, intending to hit him in the shoulder.

Tin catches it in midair. A grin breaks out on his face. “What say you to war then, my dear? Shall we take our chances with it?”

“War?” For a second her anger falters, *war is bad.*

But murder is bad too and Carsen was murdered on that council’s watch.

Then Jordyn lied to me about that murder.

Jordyn sits on that council.

Her anger multiplies. She grinds her teeth. The headache deepens until the vision begins to tunnel inward. *That council wants me to have babies. Babies that will grow up with dreams of greatness only to sit at that table and learn what a mess we have made of Fraun. Babies the council will corrupt and exploit.*

The council only cares about royal blood.

Maybe they would understand if that blood were being spilled.

“War may be our best option,” Eselda answers.

Tin’s smile occupies all the real estate on his face. He wraps his arms tightly around her waist and pulls her to him. “Happy birthday, my love. Welcome to the malicious age.”

Chapter 17

The house in Sarcheda is always cold, despite the time of day or which lunar cycle it is. Each morning when Eselda drops her feet from the confines of the warm blankets onto the stone flooring, she feels the jolt of cold up her spine. She is tired of being cold.

Eselda has taken to wearing an overdress, shawl, or blanket every single day as she moves about the large home. In the lunar cycles since she has moved, she has never once been warm. Now, cold as ever and buried under a blanket, Eselda sits cross-legged on the frigid stone floor. Her back is to the fireplace and her fiancé sits in a position mirroring her own in front of her. Her long mahogany hair cascades down her back, curling softly at the ends.

"Eselda, come back to me," Tin calls, his voice soothing and careful. He can tell just by looking at her that she's lost herself in angry thoughts again. The king shakes his head and reaches out to touch her shoulder, trying to bring her attention back. She jumps under his touch but her eyes focus on him. "You have to stay focused, even when you are angry,"

Tin says.

"How am I supposed to do that?" Eselda snaps.

Tin takes a deep breath before answering. It goes against his nature not to snap back at the queen, but he manages to remain controlled. "Think of something pleasant. We cannot have you flying off the handle in front of the council. They already doubt your ability to control this age marker. You cannot be a slave to it."

"I'm no one's slave." He watches her green eyes darken until they are almost black. He has to take a deep breath and remind himself that it is her age marker that makes her talk to him this way. They have learned, in the fortnight since Eselda turned twenty and came of the malicious age, that she does not handle it well. Tin takes her hand in his. "Fight this, my dear. Breathe and control your age marker."

Eselda closes her eyes and tries to think of something pleasant. Tin's hand is warm in her own, she can feel his fingers trace over the smooth skin absently. *Love.* She smiles at the thought, the single word that springs to her mind. The buzzing in her head quiets, and the cold in her bones lessens. A sigh escapes her lips. When she opens her eyes, they are closer to their shamrock green. This is a sure sign that she has controlled her emotions, for now. "There you go," Tin praises. "Well done."

"Why does it affect me so? Do you have this much trouble controlling the anger?" Eselda asks. Even in her calmer state, her voice retains its new, hard edge.

"Everyone is different, as I understand. I had long fits that drove me to physical violence, perhaps because of my strength training. I've heard of some who experience blackout periods."

"Like I had at the council meeting before I was of the age?" Eselda asks. The memory is foggy. Eselda had small bouts with her age marker before she turned twenty. Tin explained it to her like a rehearsal. Her body had been practicing for the big show.

"Exactly like that. This may be harder for females. I don't know anyone we can ask." Tin shrugs an apology. Both royals have long ago lost their mothers and the branches of both family trees are sparse.

"What about you? Do you still feel it? How are you able to control it so well these days?" A thought occurs to her, one that sparks a seed of hope in her chest. "Does it get easier?"

Tin frowns, his dark hazel eyes squinting with the effort of recalling the past. "No, it was hard the entire time. I could not even hear over the buzzing in my ears sometimes. I think I had forgotten what color things really were because I spent so long seeing them through such a dark filter."

"You speak in the past tense," Eselda notes, cautiously.

"I am five annuals your senior, my love, I reached twenty-five already." The fact is delivered casually, but it weighs on Eselda's heart.

She thinks through the old memories, the age markers that are the curse of those with royal blood to bear. Twenty annuals, her age, the malicious age. An age where blood will boil and anger will be overwhelming. The age where a desire for power usurps all else.

Twenty-five annuals, the next marker. The age where a desire to procreate will replace the desire for power. An age where one can be consumed by a carnal act of love. "You have reached the age of the flesh?" she inquires, doubt wrapping around each word. Tin has postponed their wedding plans, for fear that she was unprepared for such an event in her malicious state. He has given her a bedroom of her own in his home to avoid any issues with sleeping arrangements. Surely this is not the act of a man who is within the throes of an age marker that would cause his blood to crave her body. This is more the act of a man who is repulsed by her age marker.

"I have reached that age," his answer is simple, his eyes daring her to challenge him.

Eselda watches carefully. There is no fire in his eyes. No angry flash, no burst of color to show her that he cannot handle himself. More truth lies in the eyes than in the statement.

"Why do you doubt that?" Tin asks, tilting his head to the side.

"It just feels like you are pushing me away lately, instead of pulling me close. Shouldn't you crave my love now?" *I crave yours to stop the beast that is my curse.*

Tin leans closer to Eselda, brushing his nose along her cheek as he breathes in the smell of her. He whispers his answer to her ear. "I crave you all the time. I don't know if it's my age marker, or how provocative your anger can be, but you consume my thoughts." *I simply cannot let you hold that much power over me.* Tin can admit this only to himself. Eselda is not privy to the darkness that lurks in the king's soul; the one that has not faded away with the end of his age cycle.

Eselda blushes under the compliment and shies away from his touch. "You restrain yourself so well." Tin sits back. When his eyes take in the sight of her they darken a little. *It's as if the familiar tell, signaling his anger brewing under the surface, now gives away something else that may be hiding there,* Eselda notes. *Does this show his lust?*

"Do you want me to stop restraining it?" Tin asks.

Eselda's heartbeat quickens under his steady gaze. "Why do you postpone our marriage?" she asks, timidly. *Why not wed someone you love and lust for so you can have all of her?* The buzzing in her skull resumes.

"Eselda we agreed it was smart to wait. What would happen if your anger flared in the middle of our ceremony and you blacked out?" *If you don't remember marrying me then everything is for naught.*

"I know, you're right." Eselda sighs. "Of course you are right. But how long must we wait?"

"It's why we sit here, day after day, trying to learn how to survive this age. You did well today." He reaches for her cheek, rubbing his fingers lovingly across its surface. Eselda leans into it, closing her eyes. She allows the calm to flow over her with the expression of his love. "Perhaps the time will come soon when you are ready for that kind of public ceremony," Tin says.

The small door to the room bursts open, banging loudly against the wall. The king spins to address it, dropping his hand from Eselda's cheek in the process. Tin stands, his arms clenched by his sides in a show of strength at the interruption. Height is important in their society. Tin stands at only two and a half marks, not remarkable. But he is the king of strength and his bulk is imposing. He often uses this to his advantage.

Eselda's vision darkens, her eyes narrow, and she feels the beast roar again. The buzzing, her constant companion now, begins to grow so loud she can no longer hear the voices, although the man's mouth is moving. It is like a chord on an instrument is being struck repeatedly in her head, but the instrument is out of tune and the sound only causes her a headache. *It's ridiculous, what brings on the anger,* she reflects. Despite her conversations about the marker, she hadn't truly understood until the morning she awoke in the state. It is not just normal things that set her off, it's everything. The way a leaf falls from a tree, the tone of someone's voice when they talk, the noise people make, the way people ignore her. *It's all such that I could explode.* "What is the cause for this interruption?" she veritably screams. Both men turn to look at her, her voice having been entirely too loud for such a small chamber.

"Your Majesty …" the man bows low to Eselda, his face reddening under his obvious embarrassment. "I didn't see you seated there. Forgive my intrusion, I only need to borrow King Tin for a moment."

Tin places his hand on the man's arm and practically drags him from the room. The man's feet struggle to gain purchase on the flooring. Once in the hallway, the king releases him. "What time does he plan to leave tomorrow for the meeting?" Tin asks.

The man he refers to, King Mick of Farcheda, is an important component of the council meeting and Tin's plan tomorrow. Tin, as is his custom, requires some information about arrival times to best upset the king of speed. Tin can either be the first to the meeting, upsetting Mick because he was not the fastest, or he can be late. Either act is sure to annoy the old king.

"The king plans to leave his home by sunrise."

"How good is this information?" Tin asks, eyeing the man warily. The man is of the house of Farcheda and has been a servant there for many annuals. He is also, as of late, Tin's spy. Spurred along by promises of pending changes under Tin's rule the man has changed his loyalties.

"It is flawless, Majesty. I want to earn my way into your graces."

"Good. As we discussed, once things begin you should come here immediately. Do not wait to find Mick. When you hear the word, you come to me," Tin commands.

"As you wish, Majesty." The man bows and backs quickly from the hall.

Tin watches him go, a smile stretching across his face. Although his malicious age marker has faded, he has not lost his touch. The blood that boils within him was never because of his age. Tin has long felt the pull of power. *Certainly, it was a little worse with age,* he reminisces. *It was harder to control how angry I got when I was young. But I have long wanted the same thing; one Fraun, united under my rule.*

Chapter 18

It is not yet sunrise in Fraun. The people are burrowed in their beds, dreaming of better days. Fraun lies in an area of land that is circular, divided into five realms not of equal size. Each realm is bordered by something different, separating them from the land beyond.

Sarcheda, first realm, is separated by a deep ravine that no being can see to the end of. During the time of the giants, it is believed that this ravine carried water from one area to another. No one knows if there is water at the base today, as no one dares to travel down it. It is this ravine to which the former king and queen of Sarcheda, Tin's parents, owe their death.

Enchenda, Eselda's humble realm, is bordered by a large forest of trees along the back. This area has been well traveled by the scouts, as it provides access to other areas that are not of Fraun. Far back in the woods the river known as River Fraun continues. No scout has followed it to its end, but they have walked some distance along its edge.

Farcheda, third realm, has a fence around its outside border. When he first became king, Mick ordered the scouts to build the contraption. They used old material known as chainlink to the giants and built a fence no Fraunian can climb despite many attempts. The fence extends a little way into Enchenda's land, just as the forest continues a little way into Farcheda.

Marchenda, fourth realm and home of King Larecio, is bordered by unexplored expanses of grassland. Oftentimes bird's nests are found a little too close to Fraun and have to be removed by scouts who are daring and brave enough to attempt such a task. Fraunians can likely venture out into the tall grass if they so desire, but few do.

Lastly, Renchenda is bordered along its edge by more trees. These are larger in height and in diameter than those found bordering Enchenda. These trees the citizens of Fraun cannot see to the top of; they stretch seemingly to the heavens. These trees provide a source of worry for Fraunians. You cannot trust what you cannot see.

This morning all is quiet. A group of scouts, having just delivered a package to a doorstep in Farcheda, slip quietly back around the fence and disappear into the woods surrounding Enchenda. No one is disturbed and no one is aware they were ever there. It is as they like it.

The only other souls in Fraun who are awake at this hour, before the sun, are on the other side of the kingdom in Sarcheda. Tin has just risen, dressed, and is slamming back a cup of tea in a remarkable hurry. His fiancé, having been dragged from her bed by him, is in a foul mood. "This is ridiculous. Why do we head to council so early? It is a short walk and the meeting does not begin for a while yet," she rants, her face going red with effort.

"Eselda, I am going early. If you would rather go back to sleep, be my guest." Tin's voice is short and clipped indicating this is not the first time this morning she has questioned his decision.

"No, I'll go with you. I want to arrive together," Eselda says. Tin nods and takes a strawberry off the counter. "Why can't we just go together at a decent time?" she whines. "The buzzing in my ears is already giving me a headache. The darkness of my vision is making my eyes unable to focus, so instead they water. I am tired, cold, frustrated, and in pain. Can't you just give me a little longer to get it under control?"

"Let's go now, we can eat as we walk and it will be just the two of us." Understanding that he will not win this argument with anger, which

Eselda clearly has in spades, Tin instead closes the gap between them in one swift stride. He wraps his toned arms around her waist and pulls her close to him. With their noses practically touching, Tin turns up the charm. "No one will be along the path to disturb us, it'll be quiet and romantic." He winks.

Eselda smiles and visibly melts in his arms. Leaning in, she kisses him. When they pull apart, she is still smiling. "Okay, you win." Eselda grabs a strawberry and the pair depart.

As expected, they are the first to arrive at the council building. The building is located at the center of Fraun, technically on the edge of the Marchenda land. It is an old stone structure with two rooms and an uneven roof. One room, an antechamber, is primarily for standing around and waiting for meetings to begin. Occasionally in the history of the council, a guest not of royal blood has been allowed to wait here before an audience with the council. The second room houses a table depicting a map of Fraun and five chairs.

Tin drops into the chair at the head of the table, farthest from the door to the antechamber. He props his heels up on the wooden depiction of Sarcheda, hooks his fingers behind his head, and smiles at his beautiful companion. "You know, there's no one here now. We could make use of our time together. I've never kissed anyone at the council table." Tin winks, feeling pride as he watches the blush creep up her neck and cheeks.

Eselda sits beside him, in a chair behind the Enchenda space. *That will never do,* Tin thinks. He reaches out, grabs her chair by the leg, and pulls it closer. There is a loud scraping noise of wood on stone. The muscles in his arm ripple under the task but the chair provides no challenge.

When the legs of the chairs are practically touching he stops pulling and drapes his arm around her shoulders. "There, that's better." He leans in and kisses Eselda, passing the fire he feels for her with every passing moment directly through his lips. This is not an act, he truly feels things for Eselda that nothing can satisfy but moments like these. Before his twenty-fifth annual when they kissed he often felt like he was losing control of the situation. Now, the feeling is multiplied infinitely. He cannot kiss her for long, he cannot hold her for long, without feeling like control is draining from him.

Today is no different. After a few minutes of passion, Tin is forced to pull back from the queen. His eyes are dark, his face flush, and his breathing quick. Eselda notes the changes in him. "Are you alright?" She brushes her hand along his cheek and the king's eyes close.

Immediately they pop back open, and Tin pushes back from her, resting on the opposite arm of his chair. "I'm fine. Don't worry …" his voice trails off as a noise in the antechamber alerts them to the presence of another king.

King Mick practically flies through the door, stopping short when he sees the seated pair. Mick is wearing blue, the color of his realm. The last time Eselda saw him his hair was an interesting mix of black and grey. Today the entire head of hair is grey. The king has reached his fortieth annual and the age marker Fraunians refer to as the death spiral.

Mick's eyes track to the moved furniture. *Oh good, he noticed.* "Mick, glad you could join us." Tin's voice drips with vexing sarcasm.

Mick rises to the bait. "Now see here, you are arriving earlier and earlier every lunar cycle. That is no business of mine, but I will not rush to get here as you do. I will not stoop to that level."

"Yet you are here early. Just not early enough." Tin smiles and resumes his relaxed position with his hands behind his head. Mick takes his chair, in Farcheda territory, and sits up straight. He glares at Tin. Tin acts as though he doesn't notice and fixes his gaze on the ceiling.

Eselda, uncomfortable, stares at the table. With her chair now moved she is sitting right behind the river Fraun, on the border between Sarcheda and Enchenda. She is looking at the blue line marking the river. It looks deep as though carved into the wooden table, a silent reminder that nature is permanent. She reaches out her slender finger and traces it along the deep curvy rut. The river wraps around Enchenda, but her fingers cannot reach that far. She traces the line up as far as her arm can reach and back to the edge of the table.

The trio sits in this frozen tableau for a bit before Larecio passes through the doorway. Larecio's hair is completely white, his face tired and sunken. If one was unaware that Larecio is from the realm where mirth is valued, one would never guess it. Larecio has been torn apart by the murder of his son and the fact that they have been unable to name the killer. The man darkly wants justice and this causes him much internal grief. The internal struggle mars his external appearance and he does not wear it well.

Eselda's eyes flit from Larecio, where they had fallen when he entered the room, to the doorway. In anticipation of the last arrival, her mood darkens. *Jordyn.* The lion inside her begins to purr softly, ready to roar when necessary. She waits, staring, knowing that the king of wisdom has been a trigger for her anger recently. She tries to focus her mind, to be controlled for Tin's sake.

Sensing her discomfort, Tin reaches for her hand absentmindedly rubbing his thumb across the back of her palm. Besides keeping her focused, this will keep her chair next to him. Jordyn is sure to notice that the queen sits in Sarcheda territory today and this is symbolic of something Tin wants to project.

The group hears slow footsteps on the stone in the antechamber. Eselda keeps her eyes on the doorway. Tin pretends not to notice and continues to stare at the ceiling. Larecio probably doesn't notice, his eyes remain closed. Mick turns his head and plasters a smile on his face.

The man who enters is bulkier than the group is expecting, sporting a slight belly bulging under his orange shirt. His eyes are light green and his hair yellow. His face is plump and ruddy. He looks around the room, nodding his approval. "Nice place you have here."

Mick rises. "Can we help you, sir?"

"My name is Thometh." He offers his hand to Mick, who eyes it suspiciously. "I am the newly appointed King of Renchenda." Sensing that Mick doesn't intend to shake the offered hand, the man shrugs and returns it to his side.

Tin, leader of this assembled group of powerful rulers, cannot continue to act as though he is ignoring the situation. Deliberately slow, Tin drops his feet to the floor and rises. "What happened to Jordyn?" The name alone sends Eselda's anger up a notch, it is now simmering under the surface.

"Jordyn stepped down from his position voluntarily." The man, Thometh, moves with grace to the chair behind the area on the map that would represent Renchenda. Lowering himself into the chair, he meets Tin's gaze. "I believe you will find my blood suitable. The former Queen Aine was my older sister."

Mick takes his seat in a huff.

"What caused Jordyn to reach this decision?" Tin asks, still standing but using a calmer tone.

Thometh fixes his gaze on Eselda, noting where she sits at the table. "I'm not sure. You'd have to find him to ask him," he answers.

After an awkward silence, Tin sits and directs his attention toward the room at large, careful not to focus on any one face. "I call this meeting of the council of kings and queen of Fraun to order. First business, we have been asked to welcome the new king of Renchenda, Thometh. Are there any objections to this change in ruling line?" The room is silent. "Excellent. Let's begin. Is there any new business to bring before the council today?"

"I have a question for our new friend here," Mick calls out. He fixes the new king with a cold stare. "You likely noticed that two of us seated here today are already sporting grey hair."

"Actually, I believe mine is white," Larecio rumbles.

Mick continues despite the interruption. "We are suitably nervous for the lineage following our rule for this reason. My own personal realm is quite prepared, as I have children and grandchildren with royal blood of my own."

"For Fraun sake, Mick, we are all aware of your bloodline." Eselda stamps the table with her fist. The table holds firm, but Eselda can feel it quake.

"Clearly that proves my next point, a few of us ruling are also slaves to a different age marker," Mick smirks.

"Actually, only one of us is," Tin states, being sure to show his most charming smile. "I've reached twenty-five annuals."

Mick's smile falters. "Regardless, my point is more about the lack of heirs to your realms than your age," Mick continues, waving his hand toward Eselda and Tin as though they are flies approaching his plate of food. "My question for our new king here is whether he has children of his own at this time, someone to lead Renchenda in the event of his untimely death."

Beside him, Tin feels the muscles in his fiancé tense. He doesn't dare risk a glance to see how much her anger rises. Instead, he continues to run his thumb in lazy circles over her hand, squeezing it to let her know he is still there. It would help his plan along if the queen were whole for the meeting today.

Thometh smiles. "What a good and important question to ask of me, Mick. I am not wed, however I am thirty-two annuals. With any luck, I will find myself a suitable mate soon and bring lovely children into this world. There is a maiden I have eyes on already, truth be told. I am confident you will be happy with my lineage in due time." The answer is delivered professionally and calmly.

"Who is to lead your realm if something happens to you?" Mick pushes the topic, leaning across the table toward the man. "Would Jordyn be willing to return for that task?"

Eselda's temperature rises and her breathing speeds up. She can feel herself getting angry. *Why does Mick insist on acting as though he has the power in this room? Are we not equals here? Balanced?* She squeezes the hand Tin has offered her hard enough to cause him to look out of the corner of his eye in her direction.

"Again, sir, I must tell you that you would have to ask him that question. But you would need to find him first. He expressed to me that he was leaving Fraun," Thometh says.

At this, Eselda turns to look at the newest king. "He left?" *Where would he go? His precious throne could not handle the threat of my brewing feelings for him, yet he can run away from it? Didn't Jordyn once claim Fraun needed him? Where is he now? He accuses Tin of evil doings and then abandons Fraun before I can clear Tin's name.*

"He did." Thometh nods solemnly.

"Let's move on," Tin commands, his voice ringing through the room. He speaks a little too loudly in an effort to cover the strange emotion bubbling in his gut. *Why does she still care about Jordyn?* "Thometh will update us if anything on his lineage or heirs is to change. What other business have we to discuss?"

"Let's talk of our patrol, shall we?" Mick smiles at Eselda. "When should I expect my turn with them? I believe they are late." The patrol has already been parceled out for training to Sarcheda, Tin's realm, and now to Enchenda with Eselda. The idea originally proposed had been to train the patrol in all five realms, creating men who knew Fraun better than anyone else; true Fraunians.

Eselda has allowed Tin to take over the training completely at the appearance of her own malicious age. *They are still with us?* Eselda knows she cannot allow herself to see this as a bad thing. Mick will be looking for a chance to accuse Tin of raising an army, as Jordyn did. "Are you questioning me?" Eselda leans toward the old man, menacingly. "I would not question me, sir. I have the patrol right now, they travel with me. When my time with the men is up, they will be sent your way."

"By my calculations, that time should have expired. What reason do you have to keep them?" Mick asks. If he notices the darkening of Eselda's eyes, the firsts clenching at her sides, he chooses to ignore it.

"You will have them when it's time. Stop trying to control everything; there are five of us here to share power equally," Eselda says.

"Now actually, that brings me to a question," Thometh says. Eselda snaps her head in his direction, put off at the interruption. "Am I to understand that you two will be wed soon? Will your realms merge at the marriage?"

The buzzing becomes so loud that Eselda cannot hear Tin's response. *Why do they doubt me? Are they sitting here waiting for the day when Tin comes alone? I bet they've already called someone who can repaint their precious table. They're already plotting what they will do with their council of four.* Eselda watches Thometh bobbing his head as though he agrees with something. *I have never before wanted to smack someone for nodding their head, but I could now,* she thinks.

If she could hear Tin, she would hear a composed answer. "Eselda and I have decided we cannot ignore our love. Yes, although it would be something new and scary for Fraun, we would merge our realms."

"What would you call this new realm?" Thometh inquires.

"I see no reason to decide that now," Tin answers.

"It wasn't so long ago that she loved my son. Are we to believe that this is really love?" The voice, quiet and distant, comes from Larecio. The look he is giving Eselda can only be called hatred.

"With all due respect, Larecio, I believe the marriage to your son was only to be a formality. I can assure you that what we feel is very real." Tin takes a moment to glance lovingly at Eselda.

He would not want to rule for me, Eselda thinks. *Tin wishes to rule with me. Tin wishes to change the laws.* The thought calms her a little, enough that she can breathe and hear normally again.

Tin watches her eyes lighten a shade. "Trust me when I tell you that Eselda and I will handle the situation with care."

"If you have children, would you be open to the idea of splitting back into two realms with one of your children leading one?" Thometh asks.

"Kindly stop planning my life for me," Eselda says.

"Eselda your life should be second to Fraun," Mick points out. A fit of coughing wracks the old king's tall frame. The council waits him out.

"This could all be solved quite simply," Eselda says, her voice like a knife blade through the men. "Will the council consider a ruler who is not of royal blood?"

"No," Larecio calls.

"Absolutely unheard of," Mick booms.

"I don't see why we would need to, am I missing something?" Thometh asks.

"This is ridiculous." Eselda rises, throwing her hands in the air. Frustration and anger that have been building in the queen since before she took the throne culminate. "I don't know how to work with you people. You are so old-fashioned and out of touch with everything. What makes a ruler good at ruling has nothing at all to do with the blood flowing in their veins."

Eselda's voice is so loud that Larecio uses his hands to cover his ears. Mick literally cowers away from her in his chair. Yet Eselda continues to rant. "I have met some of the most decent people in my life in Enchenda. They care for each other, they watch out for each other. They are better people than this group, and yet they have no royal blood." Her face reddens as she yells. *There is no fixing this.* "I can't believe I ever thought this council could make decisions that were right for Fraun."

Tin rises, standing beside Eselda in a show of solidarity. He places a hand around her shoulders, calming her instantly. She leans her face into his shoulder, hiding from the council. Tin speaks loudly and clearly in the silent room. *Finally, the time has come.* He bites the inside of his cheek to keep the smile he feels from showing on his face. *This couldn't have gone better.* "We both believe in this issue, as you can tell. Would the council reconsider their position on someone leading a realm who is not of the brother's blood?"

All around the room it is silent. Tin waits it out until he is sure their silence means they cannot. "Then you have made our decision easy," Tin says.

Eselda picks her head up from his shoulder but stares at the floor.

Tin continues in the booming voice he uses to call a vote at this very table. It is the resounding voice that comes from a speech that has been rehearsed. "We believe the council no longer has the best interests of Fraun at heart. For this reason, we challenge the council for control. Consider this your warning. Armies will be raised. War is coming to Fraun. We will fight for the right to make decisions in the best interest of Fraun. We fight for control of this land." Tin takes Eselda's hand. They head for the doorway together, brushing the wall as they skirt the table.

"What if we don't fight you?" Thometh whispers as the pair reach the door.

Tin tosses the words over his shoulder mere steps from leaving the room. "In time of war, as king of the first realm, I can decide for you. You'll fight or you will die. Either way, you will lose Fraun," Tin answers.

Chapter 19

Beyond the outskirts of Enchenda, near the edge of the river known inside Fraun's boundaries as River Fraun, the trees grow thicker. There are infrequent spots where you could find a clearing, and the scouts know each one. Along their travels, they will use these locations to set up camp, buried from the eyes of anyone who may be looking for them. The scouts have long been a group who like to travel lightly and alone. They are strong but not because they associate with Sarcheda. In fact, this group of little men and women do not consider themselves Fraunians at all. Wanderers by nature, they are loyal to none.

This particular day, a band has lain down their heads and set up their temporary camp in a small clearing about a day's walk from Enchenda's borders. They are on a mission, requested by King Mick, to find anything that can be used as weaponry. This particular pack of scouts is now nine members strong. Franc and his wife, Carlina, are the two who began the group. They met up with Lili and her son, Sieven, just after the lad was born about seventeen annuals past. Evelyn and her husband, Kurt, joined when the group they traveled with became too large for their liking. Their daughter, Abney, has traveled with this troop for most of her eighteen annuals of existence. Then there's Toby, who joined the group eight annuals back when he defected from Fraun.

The most recent addition to their group, a tall man who would reach three marks on the wooden rulers Fraunians measure themselves by, sleeps fitfully under a warm blanket on the floor of the forest. The other eight people in the group have risen, started a small fire, and are heating water for tea. They sit around the fire in a ring, in varying stages of awake, watching the newest scout thrash on the ground.

"Should we wake him?" a small woman asks. Barely two marks tall, her height often makes her appear young although she approaches forty annuals. She has long dark hair, which she keeps braided at her back. Her eyes, which are a bright blue that almost seems unnatural, are focused wearily on the new man.

"Carlina, what are you afraid of? A little nightmare can't hurt him," the man beside her chastises. His voice is deep and strong. The man himself is a startling contrast to the little woman he speaks to. He is large, wide, and strong. Although he stands only half a mark over her head he seems to tower over her.

"Oh of course you don't care, you big oaf," she teases, playfully slapping him on the arm. "He's just a child. I say we wake him."

"Alright, wife. I suppose what you say goes." Franc rises and walks to the younger man, lightly tapping him on the side with his foot. "Aye, man. It's morning," he calls.

Chapter 20

I wake, jumping a little with surprise. Immediately I feel the beast roar within me at the rude awakening. I struggle to get myself under control and remember where I am. I sit up, rub my eyes, and look around. It all rushes back at me: the scouts, Fraun, Tin, Eselda. "How late is it?" My voice comes out shorter than I meant for it to. I take a deep breath to calm myself further.

The woman known as Carlina approaches, kneeling beside me. "It's barely sunup, but we were worried about you. Do your dreams bring troubles?" Carlina is a loving woman. Although she has been wed for many annuals she told me they have not been blessed with children. She has been attempting to mother me since my arrival, possibly because of my young age. Of course, not knowing I am a king helps that.

Wait, that's not right. I am not a king. I was a king.

"Nothing I cannot handle." I smile at Carlina's care, which reminds me of Eselda. The thought of Eselda, as it typically does for me, brings rest to the monster. I rise, stretching my extensive limbs toward the sky. There are popping noises from my back and neck. "I do not think I am used to sleeping on the ground yet. It brings me strange dreams."

"It'll do that, yeah. We should try and find you a mat you can sleep on when we are at the home of the giants today," Franc calls over his shoulder as he walks back to the fire area.

"Is that our destination?"

"It is. One lays about another sun's journey that direction." Franc indicates an area further west of Fraun. "We should reach it by nightfall if we leave soon."

"The home is empty?" I ask. I reach for the hot water to pour myself some tea.

The answer comes from Sieven. "It is somewhat empty. We often use it to gather materials. It's very large, too high to see the top of. We have to hike up to the upper floors, it may take a few suns before we reach a new room."

"I am excited to see such a place. I have never been this far outside of Fraun."

"I have never really been inside Fraun," Sieven says. "We shall have to trade stories."

I pat the boy on the shoulder. "That we shall." I take a moment to look around the group I have joined. Three suns ago I met up with this group as they were near Renchenda. I had been out exploring, intending to do so on my own. This group took me in without question and I owe them much. It is this group who has taught me what you can and cannot eat in the forest. This group shows me where to get water. This group seems to know where they are going. Out here I am not a king. Here I am one of many traveling together, like a pack or a family. They love each other. I am not expected to lead. I am welcome with open arms. It is a feeling that brings me happiness I never knew I was missing.

After everyone has eaten and camp has been packed, the scouts head out. Kurt and Evelyn lead the pack followed closely by Sieven and Abney. Carlina and Lili come next, whispering between them. I walk beside Franc.

"What is life like inside Fraun?" Franc asks.

I focus on my feet to avoid tripping. "Simple," I answer.

Franc laughs. "Simple is the one thing I know it is not. Simple is what we have here, my tall friend." He gestures to the forest around him. "Simple is the pack on my back, the shoes on my feet, the staff I carry to walk. Everything I own is here. What you have is not simple."

"I suppose that is true. I guess I meant orderly. We have homes, food, jobs, and expectations. We follow the rules." That's not as true as I once thought. Apparently, I alone followed the rules. Tin made his own agenda and rules. How do I explain that? That truth is what caused me to turn my back on Fraun. Fraun has become something I never wanted.

"Rules like what?" Franc pushes, either not sensing my discomfort or not caring.

"There is a king in each realm," I begin.

"I knew that. We work for them. Farcheda and Sarcheda mostly, the others don't call on us much."

That explains my previous anonymity. "Yes, well the kings help uphold any rules. Fraun citizens are only allowed to build if it is absolutely necessary and only from repurposed materials," I explain.

"That's always been our job, to bring you the materials."

"Exactly. You bring only what is needed when it is needed."

"Are you all living close together? I've not been too far inside Fraun to know. But it looks like there are a lot of people crammed into each home."

I lived in a huge castle alone. How did my people live? I once saw a small home that slept seven, surely that is a lot. "I suppose it is getting a bit cramped, but we grow in size when needed."

"Why don't you expand outside of your little circle?"

My feet stop and I stare at the older man. "What do you mean? Aren't we closed in on all sides?"

Franc laughs again, a deep resounding laugh that echoes off the trees around us. "Does it look like you're closed in? No. Oberian only made it seem that way to you. Nearest I can figure, it keeps you in line." He shakes his head and speeds up, leaving me behind to ponder this new information. Obviously it is true that Fraun is not as closed in as I believed, I am clearly outside those borders now. What are the implications of that? Is it true Fraun could simply expand? What keeps us from that?

"Don't I know you from somewhere?" Toby interrupts my thinking. "I've been meaning to ask you. You look familiar somehow."

I look down at him. The man is younger than me, but not by much. His hair is very dark and close to his head, his clothing is all black, and he carries weaponry. "Are you from Fraun?" I ask, noting the clothing looks more tailored than most in the group.

"Originally, yeah. Sarcheda. I left after Tin took the throne."

"Any particular reason?" Even with my long legs, I notice I have to walk quickly to keep up with the pace Toby is setting.

"Tin gives me a bad vibe." Toby shrugs. "I can't really explain it."

"I understand. He does the same for me." Of course, I know why. King Tin is a murderer. A murderer who controls the kingdom I once loved. I feel the beast begin stretching his limbs, awakening. I am glad no one here would likely know of the age markers to recognize the signs; I am sure my eyes are darkening now. Then again, even if they did they probably can't see my eyes from their heights. I tower over everyone here.

We reach a steep incline that requires silence and concentration to hike. I find I am glad for the interruption. The questions about Fraun somehow feel too personal. Soon the sun is directly overhead and Carlina is calling out, "Lunch break."

Everyone stops and drops their packs to the floor. I desperately want to sit. My legs are burning and my feet are incredibly uncomfortable. But, when the rest of the group remains standing, I do as well. All at once, everyone begins unpacking food items and getting to work.

Sieven and Abney grab bows and head off to hunt for meat. Lili, Carlina, and Evelyn each grab a pot and begin to hunt through the trees for edibles. Kurt and Franc pull out empty bottles and turn to me. "We are heading for the river to get water. Would you join us or help the lad?" Kurt calls.

I turn to look at Toby, who appears to be finding wood to prepare a fire. "I'll help here," I answer. When the men have left the little clearing, I begin to move the brush away from one spot to prepare for a fire. I use small pebbles nearby to ring out the pit, as I saw Toby do yesterday. By the time he returns with armfuls of wood, the pit is ready.

"Nicely done," Toby says, dropping the load. "That will certainly shave off some prep time." I watch with eyes that take in all detail as Toby strikes a piece of wood from his pack along a rock. Fire roars from the red head of the stick, Toby drops it into the pile and the wood ignites. Smoke reaches for the heavens as Toby bends to blow on the flame a little. He sits back in a more comfortable position once the flames are even. "There, a fire for lunch."

As if called by the fire, Sieven and Abney return. They are laughing lightly and Abney carries a dead ant. "Look what we found," Sieven calls.

"We? I don't remember your arrow striking the heart," Abney teases.

Sieven reddens. "She's a better shot than me." He shrugs.

"Did you hit anything this time?" Toby asks, getting into the rhythm of the ribbing.

"The tree just behind the ant. I was able to recover the arrow," he smiles, holding up the prize.

"Well that's an improvement, I'd say," Toby says.

The older men return to the clearing then, hoisting a container of water between them. They set it over the flames as though it belongs there and smile at the younger scouts. "Nice catch, Abney," Franc says, nodding in approval.

"How do you know it was her?" Sieven asks.

The group laughs. "You'd be doing a lot more crowing if it'd been you, boy." Franc pats him on the shoulder. "It'll be you soon enough, you keep up the practice."

From my seated position beside the fire, long legs curled beneath me, I smile. This casual banter is not something I am accustomed to. I am from a realm where wisdom is taught and honored. In Renchenda they do not believe in talking just to fill the silence. I am also from a family that took up an entire three-story castle for only three people. There was a lot of spreading out and not a lot of time spent together. This way of the scouts is an entirely new way of living for me. I find it to be one I could get used to.

Before long lunch is served and everyone is silently devouring the food. I eat the roasted ant and vegetables like a starving man, shoveling the food into my mouth with my bare hands. Traveling works up an appetite. It is quiet in the clearing while we eat. The only noises are the sounds of eating and the crackling of the wood as it burns and falls into the fire. When the bellies of the troop are full it is Franc who breaks the silence, "We should move on or we'll never reach our goal today."

His voice is a call to action and all follow. The first day I was with the group I struggled to get my feet under me at this command, such as it is. Today I am on my feet as quickly as everyone else, cleaning and packing. The food remnants, although there are not many, are scattered on the ground for animals to consume. Reusable pots are washed in the water that had been set to boiling. The fire is put out, dirt piled upon it to ensure it doesn't reignite. The ring of rocks are returned to their rightful homes. In this way when I turn my gaze back over my shoulder to the clearing it is as though we were never there.

Chapter 21

After many more steps, my feet are pulsing in pain. I would think my feet would grow accustomed to the journey; perhaps they will eventually, but they have yet to do so. Instead, with each pounding of my foot, anger slowly pours back in until I am inwardly cursing my nemesis, the king of strength. Tin has caused chaos in my life. I like things orderly and safe. It is Tin who killed Prince Carsen, although I cannot prove this fact to Eselda. Tin managed to win Eselda's heart. Tin causes the threat of war. Tin has taken control of the council of kings through threats and coercions.

"Are you alright?" I feel a small hand on my elbow.

I glance down and into a sea of green that brings me instant peace. "You have eyes like someone I once knew," I tell Lili. The woman is less than half my size, but age weary.

"Do I? Well isn't that interesting? My son inherited them as well. I hope it's someone you have good feelings for," Lili says.

"The best." The honest answer slips out, precluding the sigh.

"Well, then I'm glad I could bring you good thoughts." Lili keeps her hand on my arm, using me as a sort of crutch as we walk.

I notice my anger has faded completely with the good company. "I'm glad as well," I say.

The trees we travel through part and in front of us looms a

building unlike any I have ever seen. The reddish brick facade is wider and taller than any in Fraun. Taller even than I had imagined. I crane my neck to see the top. No matter how much I lean I still cannot see where the building meets the sky. "Is this a single home?" I ask, awe tinting my voice.

"It was something for multiple families," Lili answers. "There are many homes within, sharing a common hallway. We have not explored them all."

"Can we?"

"Well many have been emptied of all useful items by now. Some are occupied by roaches, so we stay out of them. Some units have a terrible odor coming from them, perhaps from rotting food. Still, there are others we can explore. You will see." She smiles at me.

"You've been in here before?"

"Many times," Lili answers.

The group approaches a doorway and a new thought occurs to me as I track my eyes up to the top of the door, a significant height above my head. "How do we get in?" I ask.

Franc points to the ground where Abney is now laying on her stomach. "We fit underneath." We watch as Abney sends her pack of gear and her bow under the door. Then, flattening herself completely, she slides under.

I eye the round belly of Franc doubtfully. "We will all fit?"

"She will open a vent, there." Franc points to a metal grate on the side of the building. The group begins heading toward it, walking among rocks. As I watch, Abney emerges. She is a little dirtier, but her smile is wide.

"Come on in," she calls. She holds the grate wide over her head, standing on her toes to allow access to all. Even with this height, I have to duck to avoid conking my head. Seeing that I was the last to enter, she drops the gate and follows me in.

"Where does this lead?" I ask the girl.

"Well most of the rooms on the first floor connect here, but we will need to climb up. We'll enter all the rooms through their ceilings."

"The ceilings?"

"Yes. We use ropes."

Sure enough, I can just make out the silhouette of broad-shouldered Kurt ahead of us pulling a rope from his pack. The group stops and watches as the rope is thrown up to a ledge. It takes two tries before the rope stays firm when tugged. Kurt wraps his right arm in the tangle of rope and pulls, hard. The rope holds steady. Kurt then plants his feet on the wall in front of him, sitting back until his legs are perpendicular. I watch in awe as the man uses his arms and planted feet to walk up the wall.

One by one the group repeats Kurt's actions. I take careful notes. Feet planted, sitting position, pull with the arms. Each member makes the task look easy, even with their large backpacks. But I have my doubts. Soon I am the only one at the base of the tall wall.

"You're up, Jordyn," Franc calls, his head appearing over the ledge. "Don't keep us waiting."

Hands trembling, I repeat the actions of the scouts. I am surprised when I place my foot on the smooth wall and there is no give. Footwear has its purpose after all. Almost to the top, I feel my foot slip, but my hands hold tight. When my foot finally steps onto the ledge, I realize I have been holding my breath. I eagerly pull in fresh air, allowing myself to be pulled away from the edge by Franc.

"Easier than it looks, ain't it?" Franc asks, slapping me genially on the back.

"Easier than I expected, maybe. But not as easy as you all made it seem."

Franc laughs. "We have practice, friend. You will learn." The group resumes walking, now using hand torches to light the path. The tunnel is narrow and silver, made of a metallic material I have never seen before. I run my hand along the wall, it feels cold to the touch.

Toby falls back until he is keeping pace beside me. "I remembered where I know you from," he whispers. "I delivered rice to the castle about an annual back." He hits me with a cold stare, daring me to challenge the memory. I remain silent and focused on the path we travel. The beast within me is awake but surprisingly calm. I wait to hear where this will go. "You are a king," Toby challenges.

"I was. I gave up my title."

"Gave it up or had it taken?"

I meet Toby's dark eyes and his steps falter. "Gave it up." When I speed up my steps, Toby matches my pace.

A tunnel opens up to the left and Sieven is standing by it, torch in hand. When we draw even with him he jogs to keep up. "I thought you'd want to know this hallway leads to the group of roaches who live here. If you need to make a quick delivery or something, come right back here."

"Thank you." I smile, touched by the boy's gesture to make me feel comfortable.

We walk a few more steps in silence. Sieven clears his throat and picks up his pace, moving out of earshot. Toby continues the conversation as though never interrupted. "You gave up a royal title to be here with us?" His voice drips with skepticism.

"Things I know and love about Fraun have changed."

"Are you aiming to change them back or turn and run?" Toby asks.

I take a moment to think. My brain fills with the image of Eselda, her warm smile reaching her enchanting eyes. My heart aches at the thought of her still there in Fraun. Before I can even smile in memory my vision changes. Tin is by her side, his arm protectively around her waist, glaring. My anger flares. "I don't know yet," I answer.

Toby grimaces. "We've had many people flee to us from Fraun since I've been here. They come for all kinds of reasons, as I once did. I wonder if you're our first royal though. The group must know; we keep no secrets here." Toby looks pointedly at me and adopts a sterner tone. "You will tell them or I will."

"This is where we camp tonight, gang." Carlina calls in a singsong voice. We gather at an intersection of tunnels. Four directions are possible here, including the one we have just traveled. In the faint light from the torches, I can also tell there is another ledge above us, likely meaning more tunnels.

I turn to Toby as we close the gap on the others. Quickly, before we can be overheard, I answer. "I will tell them. Tonight."

Chapter 22

The sun is already set, the realm is quiet, and he is barely arriving home. On the empty streets, his weary feet stomp quietly. Dirt flies into the air with each step and coats his baggy pants. Tutor reaches the building he has rented, a small one on the edge of Farcheda. His steps slow instinctively. The stones in front of the door support a large brown package. Cautiously he approaches it. *What could this be?* His brown eyes spy a parchment tied to the top of the package. He frees the parchment.

Tutor,
I am safe. I reached a group of scouts who have supplies and food enough for another. I can wait for you here. How are things in Fraun? I really need to tell you what I overheard, but I shouldn't write it out in case this is intercepted. Here is a little clue instead.
Sawchett

Tutor flips the parchment over but finds nothing else written. He tears open the box. Inside the box, there are two items. The first is an ordinary can like the ones used by the giants, only smaller. It appears to be empty. Tutor reaches in, freeing the can from the box. It reaches about to his waist and is too large for him to hold. He places it on the ground. He walks around it but can see nothing unusual about its appearance.

He turns his attention back to the other item in the box. Holding it up he can tell that it is an arrow. He has seen many of these in his time; it is small and manufactured by the scouts. Arrows from the giants would be too large, likely taller than Tutor himself. The scouts fashion these to use for hunting. He has seen it in practice. But it eludes him what kind of clue it may be.

Turning his eyes back to the can he notices a parchment lying at the base. Tutor puts his hands along the edge and propels himself over the lip and into the can. The scrap of parchment has been torn from a roll. It is small and contains only three words.

Patrol
Council
Eselda

Is this a clue? Tutor's frustration builds. *The last time I saw the girl she was living life as a princess in Enchenda. I told her to seek scouts only if she was in danger. What danger lies in these clues?* Tutor grabs a quill and a spare bit of parchment from his travel pouch and scribbles a note to the girl.

Sawchett,
Your clues are strangely cryptic and help me not. I will find you soon and we can talk. Stay safe.
Tutor

He leaves the empty box outside the home but carries the can and arrow inside with him. Grabbing a grape and a cup of tea left on the table this morning, he settles into a hard chair and lights a candle. From his travel bag, he pulls a small leather notebook, a quill, and a large parchment.

In his job to update the lineage tree for Enchenda, he has been traveling and speaking to a lot of people. He rereads his own tidy scrawl, the fruit of many lunar cycles worth of interviews and notes. Tutor unrolls the long parchment on which he has copied the entire family tree from the wall in his former realm's home. He finds the branch on the far right. Queen Laurina's nephew, Tometh, ends that branch presently.

Tutor's quill writes quickly. Tometh married Lyn. He adds her name and connects it. Their four children are also mapped out in his careful handwriting. The eldest child's husband and her child are also recorded. Tutor smiles at the drying ink. The painter will add these to the wall. *Seven total names.* This thought pauses Tutor's hand.

There should be another. But that name Tutor cannot bring himself to write. He should write it. He once swore that all secrets he discovered would be unveiled. But this secret …

I meant to stop the hiding. I meant to find their lies.

A knock at the door saves Tutor from his internal struggle. Grateful for the interruption he yanks it open to find the friendly face of a Farcheda grocer. The chubby man is bearing a basket of fruit. "For me?" Tutor inquires, stepping out of the way to allow entrance.

"You don't eat enough," the man answers. The fruit is dropped on the table and the grocer's eyes turn to the can. "What is this here for?" He runs his finger along the dull edge.

"A friend sent it to me," Tutor says. He heads to the kitchen to brew hot water and offer his guest some tea that is not lukewarm from a day on the table. "Do you know its purpose? I fear they were being coy."

"I know the giant's used such things for storing food. The tin keeps it fresh."

A clatter sounds from the kitchen. "What did you call the material?" Tutor is frozen over the dropped lid of the teapot.

"Tin. It's a metal. The giants used it a lot. I've heard the scouts often cut these babies up and make things from them." The grocer flops into a nearby chair at the table, oblivious to Tutor's discomfort.

"What kinds of things did they make with it?" Tutor asks. He makes a conscious effort to keep moving, adding leaves to the water.

"Weapons mostly: swords, arrowheads, knives, things for hunting. Although I suppose they wouldn't be sharp enough to pierce the hide of some things. They'd be good for plants or softer flesh."

"Like Fraunians," Tutor mumbles. The clue is starting to make more sense and churn his stomach contents. Tutor finishes making the tea and sits across the table from his informative companion. "Do you think this arrow was made of the tin?" he asks, brandishing Sawchett's other clue.

The grocer takes it and turns it over in his hands. The flame from the torch catches the blade and sends rays reflected across Tutor's glasses. "It sure looks that way to me," the grocer says. He places it back on the table and sips his tea. "Enough about old materials. Have you heard the news?"

"What news?"

"Sarcheda declared war on Fraun."

The sentence falls on Tutor's ears like a bomb, shattering his hopes for the future and igniting his eyes. "What?" It is the only word his lips can form in the shock.

"Yeah, at council I suppose. Prince Hector was in my shop today rounding up men for an army." The older man fixes Tutor with a fatherly look. "Will you fight for Fraun?" his voice rings with concern.

Tutor is touched by the gesture but the question vexes him. *Will I fight?* He believes the ideals of Fraun are worth fighting for. He would not argue that Tin is a man to fight against. *But what issues do they battle over?* "Sarcheda alone against all of Fraun? For what purpose?"

"Well I don't rightly know but it sounded as if Enchenda may have sided against us."

Tutor's face falls. Sawchett is a princess in Enchenda. Enchenda … "I cannot fight against Enchenda."

"You will side with them?" the grocer challenges.

"I will not choose sides."

Silence envelopes the room. The grocer finishes his tea as Tutor's brain works to process the news. *A can of tin holding patrol, council, and Eselda. A weapon forged of tin. A war where Sarcheda and Enchenda unite against Fraun.* Tutor's exhaustion and his fear war within him and yet his exhaustion causes his eyelids to droop.

"Well, I don't want to overstay my welcome." The plumper man rises and heads for the door. "Good night, friend, and good luck." He allows the door to click softly behind him as Tutor's head falls to the table. "We will all need it."

Chapter 23

From her seat on the dirt lawn, she can clearly see him. The scene is Sarcheda, the lawn belongs to the royal home. Eselda wears a dress of green, but with a red sash. Her legs are splayed out before her, her arms stiff behind her supporting her weight. She watches Tin standing on the rock wall surrounding his home and facing away from her. She can see the sun catching the sheen of sweat along his bare back. He has been working with the men he has assembled for the coming battles all day. The setting sun now marks the end of their training time for more than just today.

Tomorrow the men will leave for the first fight of the war, and their nerves make them restless. Eselda cannot see the men who her fiancé will address from this vantage point. But she knows they are there, ready to heed his call to arms. She lets his words wash over her, as they empower the men.

"My men we have shown ourselves to be ready. To be worthy of the battle to reclaim our land." The power of the king's words strokes Eselda's inner beast. She closes her eyes, enjoying the sensation. "At our current size, with your strength and training, those old men stand no chance." A roar goes up from the other side of the wall. Eselda can picture Tin's bare chest rippling. She can see an image in her mind of him raising his arms to quiet them. Sure enough, their noise stops.

"They will fall. With them will fall all the useless laws. They will no longer tell you what you can build, where you can live, or how many children you can have." Another roar goes up. Again, it is silenced quickly. "They will hold no power over you any longer. When I am King of Fraun you, my loyal and faithful army, will be rewarded with land and stature."

Eselda's eyes pop open as the roar grows deafening. She watches Tin hop from the wall, a fluid and carefree leap. She stands to watch him, eager to see all of the power he is displaying. Tin throws his arm high in a fist. "Tomorrow, you battle for Fraun," he bellows. The noise grows even louder as the men begin to celebrate.

Eselda can see them all now. The sea of black and red clothing stretches beyond the little clearing, crowding nearby homes. The men are dressed in thick armor and carrying weapons. They throw their arms about, yelling and shouting. Eselda feels overwhelmed just by their presence.

Tin waves her over. She rushes to his side and he drapes an arm around her waist. He leans into her ear to ensure she hears him over the noise. "My queen, what did you think of the rally speech?"

"There are so many men here," Eselda says in lieu of an answer.

"They are here to support your ideals, to fight for what you believe." Tin kisses her cheek.

She recognizes a few faces at the front of the crowd. "The patrol is here as well?"

"Of course. They helped me to train this group. I would never have been able to prepare this many men in time."

A rational thought tries to edge its way through the buzzing and the cloud that have become Eselda's brain. She blinks rapidly, trying to place it. "The patrol was trained for this?" she asks, her eyes squinting.

"I trained them for strength. It didn't take much to train them for battle beyond that." Tin notices the line of questioning. "Do you have a problem with that? I personally saw it as lucky that we had people to help me. You want to win this war, do you not?"

Eselda pushes the thought aside, smiling at Tin's handsome face. "Of course. I want to change Fraun for the better."

"This is how we do that. This army is for us, for our future."

"Army?" she asks. The word triggers fluttering in her gut.

"Yes. Would you have me call them something else?"

"No. It's just …" she trails off, unable to call the memory back. "How long have you called them that?"

"I have no idea. Why do you ask?"

"I just …" Eselda tries to smile at him but the gesture looks forced and fake. "I can't remember."

"It's the age marker, love. It caused me to forget little things as well. It's temporary. It will come back to you." Tin kisses her on the forehead. "I must be off, there are some last-minute things to discuss. Will you be alright here?" Eselda nods and watches him pass through the sea of people effortlessly. Many pat him on the back or shoulders as he passes. She smiles, her thoughts now only on Tin.

The queen's eyes miss the sight of the slightly shorter man just on the other side of the wall. The man who has watched the king and queen a lot lately. The man is not at all happy with what he sees.

Danyel shakes his head. "I cannot be a part of this any longer," he says, although no one is listening to him. He grabs his weapon, a sword sharpened himself a lunar cycle ago when he was given a promotion to Sergeant of this army, and quietly slips out of Sarcheda.

No one sees him leave, no one questions him.

Danyel heads aimlessly toward Renchenda. In his mind, he cannot decide which course of action to take. Should he fight for Fraun? A battle like that, with him an obvious traitor, would surely equal death. Should he flee and head out of Fraun? He turns around, watching the people he has just left. Could he leave them?

The plan comes to life in his mind, and he latches onto it. He will escape Fraun through the woods around Renchenda. Perhaps he will find people, scouts or something, to help the real Fraunians support their battle. He will wait it out.

Surely Tin cannot be successful in this war. Surely Fraun will not fall.

Fear grips Danyel. Then the man who refuses to admit he is being cowardly begins running.

Chapter 24

Late that night in the comfort of an extravagant bed in Sarcheda, Eselda dreams of an open clearing surrounded by trees. At first, when the dream begins the queen is confused. She attempts to get her bearings by looking around. The cold wind whips at her hair. She shivers. She starts to cross the clearing just as a man charges in.

It is Tin. Dressed in battle armor, weapon drawn, he is running. He crosses the clearing and bends down, searching the trees he emerged from for something. *Is he being followed?* She sees panic written on his red face, his breathing is heavy. Eselda's fear kicks up. *What could cause a reaction like this from such a strong man?*

Eselda tries to approach Tin, but a sound from behind her stops her short. Tin has heard it as well. He turns his gaze in the direction of the sound. Another man charges into the clearing, but in the haze of the dream Eselda, cannot make out his face. The man draws his blade as he runs. When he meets with Tin the blades crash and spark. Tin holds his arm straight, his eyes locked on the other man's blank face with hatred.

Eselda shivers. Panic has a hold on her, keeping her feet where they stand. She watches in agony as the men fight around the clearing.

Tin stumbles.

The faceless man raises his sword high overhead and begins to plunge it toward the king of strength. Eselda shrieks and covers her head with her palms.

Suddenly she is awake, hands over her face in her bed. Eselda looks around the dark room, listening for sounds or movements. Her breathing is quick. She tries to calm herself. "It was only a dream." She sends the words into the darkness. Her pulse continues to race, beating against her chest. *I need to be sure he is alright.* She swings her legs free of the covers and goes to Tin's bedroom, down the hall.

The room's darkness makes it difficult to see him. Eselda squints as she wanders into the room. When her shin collides with the bed she softly calls his name, "Tin." It comes out as a question. She hears the rustling of sheets.

"Eselda? What are you doing in here?" His voice is a low growl.

"I …" she trails off. She cannot explain the bad dream for fear of sounding like a child. "I wanted to see you."

"It's the middle of the night," Tin says.

His voice sounds close but her eyes will not register in the dark. *Where is he?* It does nothing to calm her racing pulse. Eselda feels his hand on her arm and jumps a little at the surprise.

"But since you're here …" Tin pulls her down to the bed.

Eselda allows him to trail kisses down her neck and onto her shoulder, feeling the warmth rush over her. She loses her fear to his touch, melting under the attention. Tin's hands race over her body, leaving heat in their wake.

For Tin it is hard to separate the dream he was just having from reality. They are too similar. For this reason, he allows the age marker to take him too far. When the passion ignites he cannot be close enough to her body. Tin kisses her deeply, and feels her tremble in his arms. He reaches for the hem of her nightgown, intending to free her from it.

"Tin, no."

Her voice cuts through his reverie. *Not a dream, then.* He pulls back from the queen. "You came here to me, Eselda," he growls. *No one ever turns me down.*

"Let's get married. Then we can be truly together," Eselda offers.

In that moment, Tin finds it very difficult to recall why he doesn't want that ending. He closes his eyes and breathes once, twice. Sane thoughts enter his brain. If they wed, Eselda controls half of his kingdom. Of course, without her he doesn't have Enchenda. *There was a time when I thought we could rule together. In my present state, I have realized I follow her too blindly when in the throes of passion. It is as I feared. A man in love can be led astray by the woman he follows.*

No. The wedding must be delayed. I will find another way to keep the queen happy. One Fraun. "We will wed soon, my love." *One Fraun. One Fraun.* It is the only thing that gives him the power to resist her and maintain control. *One Fraun.*

Chapter 25

If you were a citizen of Fraun on this dreary morning, you'd be unable to sleep. Nerves would be bundled in your gut like a quarry of rocks, heavy and oppressive. Young men you've known your entire life would be bundling up into makeshift armor, quaking at the very thought of what they undertake today. You would watch them, some not even old enough for their hair to have ceased growing, and you would lie to them.

You would tell them they will be safe. You would tell them they can win this fight. You would tell them it is a noble cause they battle for. You would tell them they will come home to you. You would kiss or hug them and then lie to their faces. Because the truth is no one knows what will happen in this war; but we cannot afford a soldier to think that way.

A two-day journey outside of Fraun in an abandoned giant's home on the third huge floor of an old brick building the men and women of the scout pack have no idea what is transpiring. We are separated from the tension growing as each soldier mounts a roach. We are cut off from the pain of Fraun.

Toby and I have been lowered into an apartment and set loose to find 'anything useful' to bring back. The sheer size of the room is impressive. I stand in the center, turning in circles and attempting to get a clear path mapped out. "It feels like most of Fraun could fit inside this room," I note. From somewhere deeper in the house, Toby laughs.

"Where do I even start to look, Toby? There is so much here." Things are scattered along the floor and piled along the walls. I even see what appears to be large cabinets in the distance. Truly this home is massive.

"Just pick a spot and get started. Don't start where I am standing," Toby says.

I walk to the table closest to me, climb up the legs, and begin sorting through the items on the table. The work is exhausting. Turning over items, looking between things. As the day progresses we sort through drawers and piles. We climb on items too large to move and search around them.

As the sunlight starts to shift marking the end of the day, we convene at a basket that has been lowered to the center of the room. We have been piling the collection next to it and now we begin loading the basket. Franc, in the vent above, will pull the haul up when we are ready. Rice, beans, fabrics, and some medical wrap are loaded until the basket is full. Toby tugs on the rope and we watch from below as the basket slowly rises. "Good stuff there," I say, pointing up at the retreating basket.

"I found some weapons to send up as well." Toby holds up some pointed metal objects. "They have two bent ends each but I think we can straighten one." He tries, straining against the material. The metal concedes and straightens. Toby grasps the end that remains bent, almost as though it were a makeshift handle. He lunges holding the straight end out toward an imaginary enemy.

"That's creative. I think it will work," I say.

"There are many of them. I took a whole load." The shorter man holds up a row of metal. I eye it curiously. It is hard to believe this row, which is nearly as tall as Toby himself, is the same item. "You break them apart." Toby demonstrates, freeing one from the bunch.

"Fascinating construction." I would like to explore that idea further, but I am cut short by the basket again arriving at our feet. We load the weapons, some more fabric, and a small sword. Lastly, I hand Toby two small pots to put in.

"Where did these come from?" Toby inquires, tugging on the rope to have the basket raised.

"There's a house through there." I gesture to an adjoining room. "It's filled with items that are our size."

"You think giants may have kept some of us as pets?" Toby asks.

"The thought had crossed my mind, yes," I answer. "I cannot imagine what life would've been like then. I assume you'd be fed and clothed, but what kind of life is that? You are contained to the house they own and nothing more."

"I don't know. It sounds a lot like Fraun to me," Toby shrugs. "Is there anything else in that little house we should take?"

"Nothing that would be small enough for our return journey."

"One more?" Franc calls down, his voice booming off the walls.

Toby cups his hands over his mouth, "Aye."

"There's nothing left down here. Why send it again?"

Toby laughs. "For us."

The sensation is odd and I do not like it at all. I am seated on the floor of the basket and basically flying through the air. All of my trust is currently in the hopefully capable hands of Franc, a man I have not even known for a fortnight. I keep my eyes firmly closed and refuse to move my body at all.

"It's easier the more you do it," Toby offers. His tone is lined with unshed laughter at my expense.

"I'm finding you scouts say that about everything."

"True." The laughter escapes. When the basket bumps flat against the vent floor Toby taps my shoulder to get my attention. "Safe to open your eyes now."

"For a king, you sure are afraid of much, my friend," Franc teases.

I am not offended. I have learned that good-natured ribbing is a way these scouts show someone belongs. Instead, I smile. They have accepted me and, by extension, my past. "Former king," I correct.

"Aye, free to be poor and dirty like the rest of us." Franc offers his hand and pulls me from the basket.

"Oy there. Is that Franc I hear?" An unknown voice reverberates through the metal hallway. I turn in its direction to find three strange scouts approaching. In the lead is a man similar in size and age to Franc himself.

"Kristof, my old friend. How are you?" Franc pulls the man into a hug. Both men slap each other heartily on the back. Everyone else in the opening looks as uncomfortable as I feel. I offer an awkward smile to the woman and smaller girl who have come along with Kristof. The woman doesn't notice and the girl merely turns her eyes down to the floor.

"I am well, Franc. We grow in numbers lately and we search for more clothing and bedding today."

"We grow as well, actually." Franc gestures to me. "This is Jordyn, a defect of Renchenda." As I shake hands with the man I am silently glad Franc had the presence of mind to keep my former title to himself.

"This is Sawchett, a defect of Enchenda." The man, Kristof, gestures to the girl.

My eyes lock onto her little round face. "Sawchett? I know that name." Eselda told the council she was training up a new royal-blooded girl to take the throne. I have never met the girl, but the name is the same. The girl shies away from my gaze. I step to the right in an effort to see her better. Her blonde hair falls almost to her waist. I see enough of her face to know she is young. I step to the right again, the child mirrors my move to further hide behind the woman. "Stop moving, child. Are you the little princess?" I ask.

The question causes quite a stir. The two traveling with the girl spin and close her in, backing her against the wall. "Are you a spy?" the woman demands menacingly.

"No. I am not a princess." Sawchett's voice is muffled around unshed tears. "He is a king," she accuses, pointing her finger at me.

The two turn again, this time directing their angry glares at me. "What is the meaning of this, Franc?" the man demands.

Franc steps forward. "Now don't make a big deal here, old friend. Jordyn was once a king but he stepped down of his own accord. He's chosen to defect from Fraun, same as you and I. That's his choice."

"Can I talk to the girl?" I ask, ignoring the anger and tension surrounding me.

"I'll do better than that." The man seizes Sawchett above her elbow and shoves her toward Franc. "You can have the girl. Franc seems to want royals defecting to him. You're his problem now."

Franc catches the stumbling child, steadies her, and waits for the pair to storm off. He even raises his hand to silence Toby when the young man opens his mouth. The quiet rings in our ears and the tunnel. Finally, Franc speaks. "We gladly take on new scouts, especially young ones. My old companion there has long run a troop that detests Fraun. It's why we left and started our own group." He addresses Sawchett, "If you are to join us, you will need to clear the air with Jordyn here. I'll leave you two to talk and we'll introduce you around to everyone if you are staying." The girl nods.

I take a seat on the ground, facing Sawchett. The girl is nervous. She is twisting her hands around and around each other. She tips her head toward the ground in the start of a bow. "Don't do that. I'm not a royal any longer," I chastise.

"I guess I'm not either." Sawchett flops down beside me. The floor vibrates a little underneath us. "What is this place?" she asks.

"An abandoned giant home. They keep calling this place a vent."

"It echoes."

"That it does." I look directly at her. "Are you going to tell me what you are doing here? You are the little princess Eselda spoke of, aren't you?"

"Why are you here?" she asks.

"Out of fear for the future of the society I love, I left Fraun. I hoped that I would find some help to bring back. Someone to support Fraun if a war were declared." The honest answer softens the girl. I can see it in the way her hard shoulders relax a little.

"I heard you talking to Eselda in the strawberry field and I got nervous. It scared me to hear you say she was controlled by him. I don't like Tin. I don't want Eselda to be in his control. I was afraid of what would happen to me if I stayed." Her voice is quiet, but it carries in the metal tube.

Memories of the confrontation with the queen of humility flood me. The despair I felt when I learned how deeply she followed Tin flow back into my heart. It was a mistake to push Eselda away. That mistake has already cost us both so much. I hang my head; the weight of one more person suffering from my bad decision pushing it down. "It is my fault you are here, then."

"It's alright. I suppose it's better than being in Fraun when a war breaks out. That would be scary," Sawchett says. A small shake passes through her body.

I smile at the girl's positivity. It reminds me of Eselda. Eselda would never stand by and watch another in pain. I have been on the receiving end of her assistance once or twice. I take a page from her book. "I will watch over you," I tell Sawchett. "I will make sure nothing happens to you. I feel as though it is my duty since I drove you here."

"Thank you."

"Do you have any family at all?" I remember, as soon as I ask, that her parents passed. It is why Eselda brought her into the house of Enchenda.

"No, just a friend who looks out for me." She smiles. "I guess two of them, now. If I can count you as a friend."

"I'd like that. Now let's go meet everyone else." I rise and begin to head back toward where we left Carlina and Lili this morning.

"Jordyn?" Her questioning voice turns me back to her, she is seated right where I left her. "Do you really think they will war?" she asks.

I believe in the quest for knowledge. I believe all questions deserve a straight answer. "Yes."

"Who will win?"

"I do not know that."

"Will Fraunians die?"

I sigh and return to sit beside her. "Yes. Both sides will likely have losses."

"I like that you tell the truth. Some people lie to me because I'm barely full height." Sawchett offers me a sad smile. "But I needed to hear the truth." She turns her attention to her feet; cleaning dirt from the shoes she wears. "Do you think Eselda will die?"

"Sawchett I want to be able to tell you she will be safe more than I want anything else, but I do not know the answer to that."

"I hope she will be safe. I liked her before Tin."

"Was she different after Tin?" I ask. Of course, I have my opinion, but I restrain it.

"She's a different person whenever he's around. It's like you said, he controls her. It's really scary."

I feel the beast, who has been calmer recently in my time with the scouts, rear up inside. Eselda cannot be allowed to become a bad person for this man. "Perhaps I can talk to her, make her see reason."

"Didn't you already try that?" Sawchett asks.

Yes. The painful conversation in the strawberry field. I told Eselda what Tin really was. I tried to warn her. She cannot be warned. She chose this. "I suppose I did. I refuse to believe someone like Eselda can turn into a bad person overnight."

"Did he kill the prince?"

"Yes." I harbor no lingering doubts about my nemesis' guilt. Have I left Eselda in a dangerous situation? Should I have tried harder to get her out of the arms of a killer? Guilt begins to rise inside me like the acid that rolls up after you eat bad meat.

"Don't give up on her, Jordyn." The quiet plea breaks through my musings.

I smile at the girl. Her face is dirty and her yellow hair is matted. She is wearing clothes that do not fit her and she looks exhausted. Her ability to care for someone else even in this state surprises me. Then again this is a power Eselda has as well. This girl will be my calming reminder of Eselda at her best. Of love. "Never," I promise.

Sawchett rises, brushing off a layer of loose dirt from her pants. "Let's go meet my next family." She plasters on a brave smile. "I'm starving."

The group of scouts welcome Sawchett easily, as I knew they would. Carlina is instantly drawn to the small girl like I am drawn to Eselda; as though they are the perfect completion of each other. The girl in need of someone to care for her and the woman who wants only to care for others. As the meal is wrapping up, Carlina pulls Sawchett down to the ground in front of her and begins brushing her hair with a course brush. "Tell us your tale, child. Where are you from?" Carlina prompts.

"Enchenda."

"How is it you came to be with us?"

"My father passed before I could talk. My mother passed just recently." Sawchett shrugs. "I have no one else."

"My husband tells me you know Jordyn here. What is that connection?"

"We have a mutual friend," I answer. "The queen of Enchenda took in Sawchett after the girl's mother passed."

“Is that typical behavior for royals now?” Lili asks, skeptical.

“No. Queen Eselda believes in doing what is right, despite what rules get in her way.”

“I think I would like this Eselda,” Carlina says.

“We all do.” Sawchett smiles.

“Well I, for one, am glad you left Fraun. It’ll be nice having you around. You have spunk, kid,” Toby pipes up. “How old are you anyway?”

“I’ve just turned ten. How old are you?”

“Nineteen. A few lunar cycles shy of twenty if my Math is correct.” Toby’s chest puffs out with pride.

Franc laughs. “Well, another spunky mouth to feed is fine by me.”

“Speaking of Fraun, how much do we have to deliver this time around?” Kurt asks. Kurt is often the voice of reason in this group.

“A lot,” Toby says.

“Shall we travel downstairs and find a roach or two for the journey then?” Kurt asks.

I’m curious what has been happening in Fraun in my absence. I stand. “I’ll be happy to go with you. I would like to see if a roach is available to take a message to someone for me anyway.” Kurt nods and we silently trek down to the roach’s corridor. Outside the room, I sit to pen a note while my companion discusses arrangements with a few of the many-legged friends.

Uncle Thometh,
I am curious about the state of affairs there. Nerves flit through my brain; since I haven’t heard from you I always fear the worst. I have found a troop to travel with and am safe. Send word of what supplies you require, I will do my best.
Jordyn

“Jordyn …” I look up to find Kurt smiling down at me. “They have three roaches who will take loads for us and another who will take your note. The supplies should be in Farcheda before nightfall tomorrow. Let us hope that is timely enough for King Mick.”

Chapter 26

Without question, her favorite time of day is that fraction of an instant when she first opens her eyes and everything seems beautifully possible. That one minuscule moment before the dirt of reality starts trickling in to bury her. *Father is dead. Charlotte is dead. Charlotte was alone, except for the boy she befriended in her sadness and loss. Carsen, the prince of Marchenda, was murdered.* Eselda's eyes begin to water. That, however, is only the beginning.

Memories of Jordyn come next. *"We are both smart. You are humble." Jordyn let me fall for him. He kissed me with such passion. But he dismissed me.* Anger builds, replacing her sadness slowly. That moment in the antechamber of the council building still stings like a slap to the cheek even after all this time. *"I cannot do that … it is not best for Fraun or you."*

Her thoughts flit to the most depressing of topics. The queen's tears flood her eyes as she thinks of her little cousin, Sawchett. The little princess went missing from Fraun more than five lunar cycles ago. Half an annual later Eselda still feels consumed by her guilt and pain. She knows people have stopped the search. The council Eselda used to be a part of asked the roaches, scavengers by nature, to keep feelers out for bodies. *They think she is dead.* Eselda's shoulders slump forward and her eyes cloud.

Now that she is fully buried alive by her reality; the anger uses her dismay to gain footing. The buzzing in her head picks up, vibrating her spine and making her head ache. *The council assumes Sawchett to be dead but they do not care. Their precious royal blood has everyone close to me dying and yet still they tout the worth of the plasma. It's a disgrace.*

Tin understands. Tin is the only person who stands beside me and fights. Tin stood up to the council for me. When I could no longer stand to be in Enchenda without the memories of Sawchett turning me into a useless mushy mess of tears it was Tin who took me in without hesitation.

Eselda propels herself from the bed, throwing the sadness off as best she can. Dressing for the day and putting her long locks back in a ribbon she attempts to don a brave mask. *I will bear this pain again. I will shoulder it all and carry myself through it. I will force myself to be strong for the people.*

A gasp escapes Eselda's throat and her brave mask crumbles.

They war today.

More people will die today. Tears begin to build in her eyes again. *Who am I to ask people to die for my cause?* Her hand flies to her mouth. "I am as bad as them," she whispers to her reflection.

"Tin," she bellows his name as she flees from the image of herself. "Tin." Her voice, shrill and panicked, draws him to her.

He emerges from his study and slips beside her. Instantly he begins searching her face and cataloging the emotions he sees. "What is it?"

"We are making a huge mistake." Eselda trembles under his strong grip on her arm.

"What?" He finds her eyes to be their normal, emerald green. She is not speaking from anger. Tin squints in confusion. "What are you talking about? What mistake? What happened?"

"The war, Tin. It's a mistake. Please, you have to stop it." Tears slip down her cheeks and her voice quakes.

"Eselda, where is this coming from?" Tin asks. Anger enters his voice.

Eselda jumps in shock. *He has not spoken like that to me for quite some time.* She swallows hard against that ball of fear that takes its home in her throat at his tone. *I must remember his strength and step lightly.* "I have seen enough people die, Tin." Her voice is barely a breeze. "Innocent Fraunians cannot die for me, too."

Tin clenches his jaw and tightens his grip on her arms. His eyes, however, stay light. The anger is the same despite the faded marker. Her fear builds and a whimper slips past her lips. "This is not about you," Tin growls. "This is about what is best for Fraun."

"But death is not best. It cannot be."

"If people have to die before the council is ready to realize their errors, then so be it."

Eselda's tears pick up their speed. "Tin can't we find another way?"

"They will never see reason, you know that." He softens his tone, but his grip remains firm. "Trust me when I say this is the only way to get what we want."

"I'm so scared, Tin. What will be left of our kingdom when this is done?"

Tin tugs her arms, pulling her close effortlessly. There is now only a thin gap of air between them. He slips his hands from her arms to her waist. The fit is familiar. His heartbeat quickens until he can feel the flutter in his neck. *Damn my age marker.* "Whatever is left of it we will rule fairly. The leaders could actually listen to the people, Eselda. The people could be given what they want." He kisses her forehead, suddenly eager to feel her skin. Inside he leaps at the contact. "Decisions could be made instead of arguing to no avail in council. Think about it. Close your eyes," he orders. The queen complies. "What do you see for Fraun?"

Eselda speaks without hesitation, allowing her instincts to guide the answer. It brings a smile to her face to imagine their world this way. "Leaders who are good people, leaders who care. Fraunians that are happy. Laws that make sense. No more battles over royal blood. No more deaths that spill the blood." Her eyes pop open. "I see peace."

"I want to give you that, my love." Tin kisses her warmly. "Do you want that so much that you would fight those who keep you from it?"

Tin has taught her this lesson. Some things are simply worth fighting for. *Clearly, Jordyn does not believe this.* Almost instinctively Eselda tips her head up as though craning to see Jordyn towering over her. Her eyes slip closed as she recalls that kiss, the deepest and most passionate she has ever felt. It floods her brain full force. The memory is so strong she can almost feel the pressure of his lips on hers. The adoration that passed through their bodies was so palpable she finds she can still feel it warming her. For a second all the humming in her brain subsides. She is painless, in a real and calming way. She draws a deep breath.

But he would not fight for that.

Just as real, Eselda can recall the moment Jordyn pulled away. Her eyes had fluttered open to see his handsome face. *I asked the king of wisdom to court me. I asked him to throw aside his belief on this one issue for me. To put faith in what we felt and what we could have.*

The anger rushes back in full force and the humming resumes. When Eselda's eyes open now, they are black. Tin smiles. Whatever Eselda has been thinking about, she is back. *The age marker makes her radiant and so willing to see my point of view.* "Love is worth fighting for," she states forcefully. "I love Fraun."

"Good. Then let me handle this. I will show you what the future can be." He finds he cannot help himself and kisses her again. His hands spread out on her waist, greedy to touch more of her.

Eselda pulls back. "Can I ask you something?"

Still feeling the pull of her, his breathing quick, he answers with a sigh. "Anything."

Eselda feels the lion in her chest roaring in anger. She has never willingly allowed the beast full reign and yet she often feels like it is beyond her capacity to control it. She glares at Tin. "Do not lie to me," she warns. "Do you believe this war is the only way to the peace I speak of?"

Tin grimaces, looking forlorn. "I do."

"Will you be fair like I envision our leaders being if we win?"

At this, Tin smiles. "When we win," he corrects. Eselda kisses him, happy to hear him promise her the world she wants. Tin, on the other hand, is merely glad the queen doesn't notice he didn't answer the question. "Eselda, I have to go. The army rides today and I need to be there when they depart." He kisses her again, but quickly. "Will you be alright?"

At her nod he turns to leave. Halfway to the door an idea forms. *What if it is as simple as asking for that which I want?* "Eselda, one more thing. I hate to even bring it up, but the army needs it official. Could I have control of Enchenda lands by virtue of my royal bloodline?"

"You mean, I give up Enchenda?" Eselda asks. The roaring is loud in her ears. *Perhaps I misheard him.*

"No. Merging our lands. We would do it anyway when we wed. I don't think it's a big issue but it's a formality. The sergeants tell me I need to have that power to command things for both our realms. Otherwise, you'd need to speak with them as well and I know how that vexes you." Tin has the forethought to look sheepish.

"I guess that would be alright." *Whatever stops this discussion. My head aches.*

"So you give me control of Enchenda? I can make decisions for that realm?" Tin is careful to mask his excitement.

"Sure." Eselda fails to grasp the importance of this simple act, the weight of her one word.

"Wonderful." Tin slips from the room. He searches the hallway for a servant. Finding one hiding in the shadows he calls the man over. "Find me an artist and a map of Fraun posthaste."

"I am somewhat of an artist, Majesty. I can draw. There is a map on the wall in your office. Would these suffice?"

"Follow me." Tin leads the man into the aforementioned office and stands before the wall map of Fraun. "I will need a rendering of this map with a very important change." He slowly circles the lands of Sarcheda and Enchenda with his fingertip. "You will redraw this as all one territory." He faces the man, his happiness showing on his face. No longer wearing the careful mask of the attentive lover the king is almost unrecognizable.

"Enchenda has fallen willingly. Sarcheda lands now include everything inside River Fraun. You will draw this new map for me. Tint all of Sarcheda lands in the red color chosen by our brother. Deliver this parchment directly to the council chambers. Leave it on the table for all to see. Do this today and you will be compensated handsomely."

"As you wish, Majesty." The man bows.

Tin rubs his hands together, smiling as he turns back to the map. "It begins."

Chapter 27

"Tell me about this other friend of yours," I prompt. Sawchett and I remained behind when the group split into two yesterday. Toby, Kurt, and Sieven rode roaches loaded up with materials to Fraun. The rest of the crew stayed behind. Tonight we are perched on large rocks surrounding a clearing watching the setting sun paint the sky a variety of beautiful colors.

"Tutor? He is a great man," Sawchett answers. Her blonde hair is braided around her head in a wreath. It is a sign of the maternal relationship that has continued to blossom with Carlina.

"Again with the names I recognize. He is a friend of Eselda's as well, is he not?"

"He was her tutor when she was young."

"Is that the capacity you know him in as well?"

"Sort of." Sawchett wrinkles her nose as she thinks. "I remember him always being around. My earliest memories match up with him already living in our home." She shrugs. "I'm not sure how he came to be living there."

"That is strange. He is not a relation?" I ask.

"Not that I know of. Charlotte always took care of him and he lived with us but they referred to him as my tutor." Sawchett shrugs again.

"People in Enchenda seem to take stray people into their families a lot," I note.

"I suppose it's the humble thing to do."

"That's a valid point. You are a smart little one. Did I hear you tell Toby you were full height?"

"I am." The smile Sawchett offers squints her eyes with its size. "I reached ten annuals shortly after I left Fraun. I noticed the day, but I had no one to celebrate it with."

"You are a good size." Truthfully the girl is now probably a mark or two taller than Eselda. She has the appearance of one stretched to excess, as many in our society often do once they reach ten annuals. She will likely fill out a lot in the next five or six annuals.

"Thank you." The girl blushes under the praise. "Jordyn, do you think the scouts we travel with have always been scouts?"

I look around at the others. They are in various stages of relaxation. Evelyn and Abney sit with their heads together looking over a parchment. Lili and Carlina seem to be braiding some vegetation. Franc leans against a tree with his eyes closed. "I get the impression that the older scouts all left Fraun of their own accord."

"But Sieven and Abney?" Sawchett pushes.

"I believe they were likely born as scouts. Sieven hinted to me that he knows nothing else."

"What do we call them? They are not Fraunians, are they?"

"No, they have no Fraun loyalties. I suppose we call them simply 'scouts'."

"Did our people not have a name before Oberian united us?"

"None that I am aware of. There was no society to name, everything was a bit …" I tilt my head up to the darkening sky as I try to think of the appropriate word. "… individualized."

"I think I would like to ask. Do you think anyone would be offended?" Sawchett begins biting her thumbnail in anticipation.

"Let's ask together." I rise and approach Evelyn and Abney, closest to us. "We have an odd question for you," I prompt. I turn my head to look at Sawchett, hopefully demonstrating I want the question to come from her.

"I don't mean to be rude," the girl begins, shuffling her feet nervously. "I was just wondering what an appropriate name would be for you since we cannot call you Fraunians."

"We cannot call you that anymore, either," Abney points out. Her voice comes across as cold, but she smiles.

"What my daughter means," Evelyn begins, shooting an admonishing look at Abney, "is that you are no longer of that society either." To Sawchett she smiles. "We simply call ourselves scouts, dear."

"That is what Jordyn said." Sawchett offers me a grin as a reward for solving the puzzle. "Did our people have any other names before Fraun was created?" Sawchett asks.

"Well, I am not that old, child." Evelyn laughs. "But I suppose they didn't. At that time our people lived in the houses of the giants. The only other little people you ever saw were people who lived in that same house. Unless, of course, you were a scout or a wild."

"A wild?" I interject.

"Yes. Scouts had no permanent home, much like now. They traveled among the house dwellers trading supplies. The wilds, on the other hand, stayed away from all giant civilizations."

"Do wilds still exist? Why have we never heard of them? How many are there? How do they survive alone?"

Evelyn scoffs at me. "How can anyone hope to answer you if you don't pause to breathe, Jordyn?"

"I'm sorry. My curiosity often runs away with my mouth."

"Wilds do exist to this day. They travel in small packs, similar to how we travel. I'm sure Fraunians haven't heard of them because they want nothing to do with the organization and rules of Fraun. I am not sure how many there are now." Evelyn smiles and takes a dramatic breath. "Did I answer all of the questions?"

"How can they possibly survive on their own?"

"They are no different than we are, Jordyn. Do you think this troop would have any trouble surviving alone?"

I have seen no evidence that this troop requires anyone for anything, except travel. Then again the only reason they need to travel quickly today is for the timeline put on them by Fraun. "I suppose not," I answer. “Wait, Franc said something about the other man we met having a group that wants nothing to do with Fraun. Are they wilds?”

“They are. They do not deliver to Fraun or associate with Fraun.”

“So in an emergency, they could not be counted on to provide assistance?” I ask.

“No, I don’t suppose they could.”

I frown. “Could the scouts?”

“Perhaps. What kind of emergency do we speak of?”

“War.” The answer jumps from Sawchett’s lips before I can answer.

Evelyn’s eyes fly to the girl’s face, scrutinizing. “That word should not be thrown around, young one. It has many implications you cannot fully grasp.”

“I’m not throwing it around,” Sawchett whines. “It is what they talk of.”

“She is not wrong,” I say. “The council is at odds with each other. It is why I had to step down. I fear it is inevitable.”

“No one benefits from a war,” Evelyn declares, shaking her head.

“I know. I fear it cannot be stopped.” The comment rings in the clearing as though strong enough to provoke an echo.

Evelyn shakes her head again. “I don’t want to talk of this anymore. Perhaps you should talk to Toby when he returns.”

“Forgive me for pushing, but why Toby?” I ask.

“He predicted a war when he defected eight annuals back. It is why he left as well.”

Without warning the ground beneath us begins to tremble and shake. I hold my arms out to steady myself. I look nervously at Sawchett. “What was th—” my voice is swallowed up by another rumble. This one lasts much longer. The trees shake and sway with the oscillating. I have to reach my arms out and catch Sawchett, who topples.

When it finally stops, I look at Franc. The man’s eyes popped open in the confusion. There is fear on his face. “What was that?” I ask.

“I have no idea,” Franc says, his voice a menagerie of panic.

“It has never happened before?”

“Never.”

“Could it be coming from Fraun?” Evelyn asks, glancing sideways at the former king. “He mentioned they are at each other.”

"We are too far," Franc answers.

It is true. We have traveled out of the home of the giants and made camp in the woods but we are still at least two suns of travel outside of Fraun. "Could a tree have fallen?" I ask, my brain working out possible scenarios.

"Perhaps." Franc thinks, his face scrunching under the effort. "That is the most likely explanation." He nods. "I'm sure that is what it was."

Evelyn, Sawchett, and Abney visibly relax. I feel no such relaxation from that answer, but I do not push it. The logic doesn't line up. If a tree fell, what was the second rumble?

Chapter 28

Despite the warm air blowing throughout the lands, Lance shivers. Standing in the tent that has been erected for him and the other newly appointed sergeants of the king's army, he has to close his eyes and remind himself why they do this today. Fraun is threatened. It is no longer a safe place to raise a family. Lance's own wife and son cannot hope to be safe within the boundaries of Fraun any longer without peace. King Tin and Queen Eselda seem to recognize that this war will bring peace. *They want the same thing I want.*

Lance is the last one remaining in the tent today. The rest of the leaders of the army, formerly known as the patrol, have gone outside to hear from their king before they ride into battle against Farcheda. Lance hears Tin's voice boom out over the open field and rushes to leave the tent.

"My men, we undertake a dangerous and important battle today. Before you leave I want to bring you one piece of good news to take with you." The power of the voice, resonating throughout the field, awes the men into silence. The smattering of chatter that occupied the morning dies down and all eyes turn to Tin who is perched on some throwing blocks, shirtless and flexing muscles to illustrate his strength.

"I know how you feel about this war," he bellows. "Fraunians will be pitted against Fraunians and it is dangerous. But I must remind you that it is this battle that will finally bring us peace. I can prove this. Enchenda has fallen willingly and without a fight. We are one step closer to a united Fraun."

A cheer goes up from the crowd of assembled men. Lance feels a strange quiver in his stomach as though he has swallowed an angry fish. *Enchenda has fallen? Weren't the two realms uniting? Doesn't Eselda speak for Enchenda?*

"To win this war with little death and little fighting, we must win King Mick." Tin's voice takes on a solemn tone and a responding hush settles over the army. "King Mick stands between you and freedom, between you and rights, between you and your land. King Mick will not concede. I know you desire to see as few deaths as possible, so this is our way. We attack Farcheda today." Nods of assent greet Tin's comments.

"If we want the other realms to fold willingly and without a fight, we must have Mick unhinged. If you want Mick unhinged you must make him feel we are serious. When you see someone in royal armor today, you take them out." He allows the comment to resonate with the men. "Long live Fraun."

"Long live Fraun." The call is echoed back to him.

"Long live the king." A voice from the front calls.

"Long live the king." The voices of the army meet together in a crescendo, repeating the phrase. Tin closes his eyes and raises his arms to the voices as they continue the chant.

Lance thinks about his past, about the pain, death, and confusion that has led him to follow this man today. He believes the council is out of touch with the citizens of Fraun. Citizens are leaving Fraun for a chance to live without the council's rules. If this can be done as Tin promises, maybe all of those people don't have to leave. Lance allows his head to nod to the beat of the army's chant until he is swept up in the promises. "Long live the king," Lance chants, shaking his fist. "Long live the king."

The ride into Farcheda is long, but the army maintains its fire. The energy practically hums from each soldier as they march or ride across

Fraunian lands. Few among them have been given helmets, but all have weapons. Lance carries a sword. He was responsible for the training of each swordsman. He glances around him, seeing the faces of the men he had a hand in training, and his chest swells. *We have a solid chance of winning this today. If we scare enough people today in Farcheda, perhaps they will carry that fear to their precious council. This could be over tomorrow as soon as the word spreads.* Lance smiles at the thought. *A united Fraun as early as tomorrow. A safe Fraun for my wife. No more of my sons will die.*

The army approaches the border between Sarcheda and Farcheda. The fog that has plagued their morning sends tendrils floating upward with each stomp. As they come to where they know the border to be, they see a line of soldiers awaiting them. Lance pulls his sword from its sheath. He hears the unmistakable sound of others around him doing the same. Arrows are notched and bow staffs are held high. Lance waits for the cue from the generals, Daijan and Trep. The Farcheda army comes into focus more clearly as they draw closer. There are men as far as the eye can see, but their armor is of lesser quality. The weapons the Sarcheda army faces are makeshift and repurposed. Lance holds tight to the hilt of his sword. Finally, the call comes: "Charge!"

Lance enters a trance-like state. He is conscious enough to hit those around him only to wound, not kill. Shoulders, upper arms, legs. He is careful to avoid hitting heads or major arteries. He will send them running home to tell of the fierce Sarcheda army. He keeps his eyes carefully on the sea of men surrounding him. It seems as though they are not lessening. Everywhere Lance turns a hastily thrown-together garment of protection catches his eye.

He wounds a man in the shoulder and watches him retreat toward the houses. Another man takes his place, and Lance sends the blade slicing through his upper arm. Turning, he sees a man clad in Farcheda armor notching an arrow. He follows the man's line of sight to find a Sarcheda boy in the line of fire. The boy is young, too young. *Why is one so young fighting for our army?*

Lance feels immediately pulled to help him. With renewed vigor, Lance charges through the crowd between them. He lashes out with his sword, slicing the arm of the Farcheda archer clean through. The bow clatters to the ground and the two stand face to face. "Run home," Lance orders, his voice hoarse.

"Never." The man lunges at Lance, an arrow held firmly in his hand. Lance, seeing no other option, buries his blade into the man's chest. He falls to the ground, blood spurting from the wound.

Lance turns to check on the younger soldier. "Are you alright?" he asks. The boy merely nods before returning to his battles. *The men in Farcheda are child killers.* With hatred anew for these men, Lance resumes the fight. No longer content to merely injure, the sergeant leaves bodies in his wake.

The Farcheda army begins to dwindle. Some lay dead on the ground, serving as tripping hazards to those who remain to fight. Others retreat to their homes, locking their doors and praying they were not followed.

As the field begins to clear, Lance takes the opportunity to look up, taking stock of the progress as he has been taught. A man in a helmet depicting the lightning bolt that serves as a seal of Farcheda is on his knees before Daijan. The men in the Sarcheda army watch with a mix of fascination and awe as Daijan raises his battle axe. The words of their king ring in their heads. "When you see someone in royal armor today, you take them out." The command was simple. Knowing what will happen, Lance watches. He is amazed that he feels nothing. *King Tin has commanded this, the act which has the power to end the war as quickly as it begins.*

Just before the axe falls, the Farcheda royal slips the helmet from his head. Perhaps the act is to accept death. Perhaps the act is to show the assembled crowd what is transpiring. Either way, it sends shockwaves up the spine of Lance. Underneath the royal helmet is not the face of the devil himself, it is not the face of hatred.

It is the face of a child; innocent and young.

"No." The word escapes Lance as a scream. It is wrong. No cause can be worth the death of a child who has not earned the right to a full life. He plummets toward the pair, dropping his sword as he runs. His throat burns.

"No." The word turns to an agonizing garble as the axe slices easily through the neck of the child. Lance lands beside the body as it drops to the floor. Around him, the Sarcheda army celebrates their victory as the last of the Farcheda army makes a hasty retreat.

Lance gathers up and holds the body of the boy in his arms,

rocking. Although he knows it is not so, his body reacts to the weight as if it is his child. His grief doubles and tears fall from his eyes. He weeps for the child, for the family, for any children who have been lost to this war or any other. The pain he feels is more real and deeper than the moment requires. He does not know how much time passes with him being the sole mourner of the lost youth.

"What is this here?" The voice is soft but draws Lance's attention. A common roach has entered the field. Lance looks around. The field is empty save for him and the boy. His own body is covered with the blood of the child and of the lives he has taken today.

"A Sarcheda soldier crying over the body of a Farcheda prince?" the roach says. "That is highly unlikely." Lance has no strength to explain his anguish over this stranger. He hangs his head. "Do you know this boy?" the roach inquires.

"No." Lance's voice is merely a cough.

"Why do you weep for him?"

At this, Lance fixes the roach with a glare. His eyes are red and the blood and dirt on his face are streaked from tears. "Someone should," he answers.

The roach draws closer. "You will come with me. Leave the boy. His family will take care of him. You must not be here when the people of Farcheda arrive. You are Sarcheda army, they will kill you on sight."

"Where would you have me go?" Lance asks, the reality of his situation setting in. He will not be welcomed back by his army. The word of his deception is sure to have spread.

"I have a place. You will be safe. You will tell your story and you will hear more. Come, we must go now."

Unsure of where else he will find such an offer and exhausted from the emotions that have attacked him today, Lance climbs aboard the back of the roach. "Thank you," he mumbles. As the forest chugs past his vision, Lance allows himself to drift off to sleep.

Chapter 29

The trees provide Sawchett with solace from the droplets of rain that fall heavy on the branches. She keeps her back flattened against the sturdy trunk, her knees drawn up against her chest. It is late at night and to her knowledge, the former princess is the only one awake. This leaves her with some much-needed alone time to get her thoughts organized.

What do I believe? Jordyn believes Eselda is a good person. Tutor believes in loyalty. Carlina believes in choice. Franc believes in hard work and independence. Eselda believed in serving others in Fraun.

What do I believe?

Do my beliefs match those of the scouts, free to roam about in the dangerous world unhindered by rules? Or do my beliefs match the safety of Fraun where all choices seem clear? Sawchett feels a shiver climb up her spine. *Will Fraun survive long enough for me to choose?*

The crunch of feet on stones causes Sawchett to draw and hold a breath. *Who is out there?* In the darkness, the girl can make out no shapes. Time ticks by in absolute silence. Sawchett lets out a breath, relaxing her shoulders. *I imagined it.*

A giggle floats on the wind next and Sawchett again straightens her spine. "Sieven we'll be caught if you are too loud," Abney's voice dances through the night.

"Me? I didn't laugh," Sieven answers.

"No, but you force my hand. You cannot tickle someone and expect no reaction," Abney counters. Her voice is light, teasing. "If my father wakens it'll be you who has explaining to do."

Sawchett maneuvers her body to allow herself to push off the ground and stand.

"Don't worry my dear, no one knows we are awake. You needn't fear it," Sieven says. His voice drops until it is low and somehow sexy.

Sawchett freezes. *Oh no, have I tiptoed into some intimate moment? Is this a secret? Why do I have such a knack for being in the wrong place during secret time? I will have to wait them out. I can't exactly be caught spying on them now. How would that look?*

"Sieven what do we hide for? Are you not proud to be seen with me?" Abney asks. "Surely everyone would understand."

"They forget we are grown, Abney. You and I are children to them. They would see our love as naive, a phase. I don't want to endure that."

Sawchett's eyes widen. *Love? I did not see that coming.* She suppresses a giggle at the thought. *I should get out of here. Where are they now?* She listens for seconds, but the pair have fallen silent. *They're probably kissing.* The thought brings the giggles back. Sawchett's hand slips to her mouth to hold them back.

"Did you hear something?" Abney asks.

There is the unmistakable sound of a blade being unsheathed. Sawchett sighs. *I'd rather be caught than stabbed.* She rises. "It's me, Sawchett. I couldn't sleep. I wasn't eavesdropping. Not on purpose anyway."

A flame sparks. It touches a torch and lights the trio with an orange glow. Sieven and Abney are both soaked from the falling rain. Their eyes are wild and their hair is plastered to their heads. Between them, their hands are clasped without care. Sieven lowers the sword in his free hand to his side.

"What did you hear?" Abney asks.

"Not much." Sawchett shuffles nervously from foot to foot. "Nothing that I will repeat. I promise." She tries to smile at the lovers, but it falls flat. "I think I'll just head back to camp."

Everyone finds love, I suppose, she thinks. That is the same here and in Fraun.

Chapter 30

Larecio hangs his head in the meeting room, frustrated and angry. *My son is dead.* It's unusual how much his future and his livelihood focused on his child. It's as though a limb is now missing; one he finds he cannot live without. Each morning he finds he no longer cares about anything without the boy there. *How can I sit at this table, a representative of the realm renowned for Mirth, when I cannot even find the strength to smile? I am nothing but an old hypocrite.*

The door to the room opens, allowing entrance to Thometh. The younger man pauses in the doorframe. He grimaces at Larecio. "How are you holding up?" he asks, by way of greeting. Larecio merely nods, never taking his eyes off the table. Taking the hint, Thometh sits in his customary chair silently. He busies himself looking around the room. Spying a sheet of paper in the area known as Sarcheda, he points. "Is that yours?"

Larecio follows the outstretched finger. He shakes his head. No, it does not belong to him. Thometh rises, walks around the table, and surveys the parchment. "Larecio, look at this," he orders. He hands the crudely drawn map to the other king.

Larecio takes in the site of the shaded red area. It encompasses all that the men in the room know as Sarcheda and that of the lands formerly known as Enchenda. Larecio would not have thought it possible for his sadness to deepen. He would've been wrong. The parchment flutters back to the wooden surface. "At least we have one answer we sought," Larecio asserts. "They will call themselves Sarcheda."

The door to the council chamber bangs against the stone wall, startling both kings. Looking up, Thometh sees a younger version of Mick. He stands at almost three marks tall. The clothes of royalty, a head of black hair, and fierce brown eyes greet the kings. "Are you the prince of Farcheda?" Thometh asks.

"Not anymore. My name is Hector. I am King of Farcheda."

"He is Mick's eldest child and only son," Larecio clarifies.

"Has your father passed? I wasn't aware that he was—"

"I have overthrown him," Hector says. "I came here today in his stead to find what this council intends to do about this war. Will you cave and side with the evil King Tin? Do you believe the garbage my equally evil father has been feeding you? Or do you have a third option that we could entertain?" His eyes radiate dangerously, a challenge to the council. Hector is past his thirtieth annual and therefore not captive to the age markers. This anger comes from years of battling with his father's temper and dangerous ways.

"What causes you to accuse your father of being evil?" Thometh asks. He makes his way back to the chair in Renchenda territory, sits, and rests his chin on his fist. He fixes the newcomer with a curious gaze as though ready for a story.

"Let me answer you this way." Hector remains standing but leans on the table. "Why did my father claim Tin was evil?"

Larecio answers, "Tin breaks council laws."

"My father broke council laws. Be more specific, which laws?" Hector asks.

"Their men take multiple wives to ensure male rulers."

"Is that all? Surely there are larger problems. If not, this will be an easy contest to win. My father is more corrupt than that."

Thometh peeks at Larecio before revealing one dark truth. There is no way to know how this comment will be received by the old king. "It is probable that Tin murdered the prince of Marchenda," Thometh says. Larecio's head hangs lower as though a block has been placed on his neck. The old man's eyes close.

"This makes him a bad man who is unfit to rule, in your opinion?" Hector challenges.

"Murder? Yes, I believe it does. Do you not agree?" Thometh says.

"I absolutely agree. It is why I am here today." Hector sits, leaning forward on his elbows. "My father had a twin brother, are you aware of this?" Thometh shakes his head, no. "Well, he did. Antony was a little older and therefore was given the throne which my father coveted."

"He served for exactly a fortnight, I recall," Larecio's voice is hollow as though he is barely interested in the conversation.

"He did. Do you know why he stopped serving?"

"You said he 'had' a twin. I assume he died," says Thometh.

"He did." Hector fixes the king of Wisdom with a cold stare. "My father killed him. For the love of the throne, for the love of power alone, my father killed his own twin. Is this a man you see fit to rule?"

"Are you sure of this?" Thometh asks.

"He admitted it to me himself. He does not hold secrets from us. When I realized what this council is doing, I knew he was behind it. This council has allowed two men who want power and recognition to lead us to war. I overthrew my father and I am here now to find out if you are willing to see reason. If not, I will be forced to leave Fraun as well and begin a new kingdom of our own. One where our people can be kept safe." Hector stares down the other kings.

"What was the catalyst for this change?" Thometh pushes.

"We were attacked at our borders three suns ago."

"We heard, yes. I am sorry for the loss of Farcheda men."

"Although I mourn the loss of our men, it is not what finally drove me to usurp my father's corrupt power." The new king of speed turns his eyes to Larecio. "My son, Patt, wore my helmet and rode into battle. When the army of Sarcheda saw him in royal armor, they beheaded him. My son was not even fifteen annuals."

Larecio's attention is captured by the shared loss. He turns his eyes to Hector. "This did not sadden you?" he questions, thinking of his depression.

"It saddens me to the deepest depths of my soul." Hector's voice breaks as though sobbing, but no tears fall. "Our people deserve better than kings who want power so badly they will kill innocent children for it. Our people deserve kings who will have the courage to put aside their egos. My father was not that king. Tin is not that king. Because of people like them ruling this kingdom, my son is dead. Will you help me change that?"

Larecio, in the first act of compassion and courage since that dark day at Castle Fraun, rises from his chair. "I will help you. What do we do?"

Hector turns to Thometh. "We hold our ground and we fight back. We will not attack them, but we will defend our land. Do you agree, King of Renchenda?"

Thometh smiles at the pair. "I do agree. For the first time since I became King, I am proud of what I see before me. We will be stronger than ever when this is said and done. We will not give in. Has Farcheda enough men to raise the army to the borders again?"

"We do. More weapons arrived from a group of scouts. I will send some your way if you require them."

"We set our troops up along the borders of Fraun." Thometh gestures to the line he speaks of on the parchment that was left on the table. "We hold our boundaries tight day and night. We will be ready for all attacks."

"We hold our ground." Larecio nods. "We cannot let him win."

Hector turns his head to read the map. "Where did that parchment come from?" he asks.

"It was on the table when we arrived," Larecio answers.

"Who knew you were meeting? Who would have access to the table?" Worry stains the face of Hector.

"The door to the antechamber is always open. I assume Tin himself either placed it here or had it placed here," Thometh reasons.

"Then we will place some men here as well. If he comes back, we will be ready. This is not going to be over until Tin and Eselda have fallen." Hector punctuates his statement by slamming his fist down on the parchment. "We didn't ask for this war, but we accept it as an opportunity to better Fraun."

"Cheers to that, friend." Thometh bumps the fist of the other king. Silence follows the gesture. The kings keep their eyes fixed on the parchment and the challenge it represents. Each man is wondering if they truly have what it takes to keep Tin's influence from spreading.

"Do we need a First Realm to call an adjournment to this meeting?" Larecio asks, uncomfortable with the sudden silence.

"No more outdated ideals. Have we discussed all we have to discuss?" Hector asks. The men around the room nod. "Excellent. Send word if you need me." As quickly as he came, the man is gone. The door slams shut as he departs.

"What do you think of this, Larecio? You are the oldest king present and you have seen the most change," Thometh says.

"I suspected Mick of the death of Antony, I recall that. If it is true that this council held two kings both who had murdered royals, one on each side of the war, we were doomed. Perhaps this new lineage is the only way out of that," Larecio answers.

"But we cannot avoid more deaths. Tin will attack again."

"That he will. Somehow I feel as though I will be more prepared for that now. We face this together, for the first time."

"Excellent. Please alert me if you need anything, friend."

"I will. It has been a long time since the men in this room bonded together like this." Something resembling a smile settles on Larecio's face. It seems out of place to Thometh, who has only known the other man to wallow in enveloping sadness.

"It is good for Fraun."

"It is good for me." Larecio nods. "I will see you soon." The old man leaves the room.

Thometh glances around at the empty chamber. He flips the strange parchment over and writes on the back.

Jordyn,
This was left at the council chambers. I thought you'd want to see it. The council has undergone many changes, but I feel they are for the best. Fraun is set to be better than ever should we come out of this on top. We could use the support of armor, weapons, and men. If you find any of those things please send them my way.
Uncle Thometh

Chapter 31

Eselda,

I take a dangerous chance writing this. I hope you understand that. If your husband were to get his hands on it … let's just say I'm not sure how he would react. For starters, I suppose I owe you congratulations on the wedding. I hope it was everything you hoped it would be. I received word that Enchenda and Sarcheda have combined and taken the Sarcheda name. I don't want to pry into business I am not fit to pry into any longer, but for what it's worth I think that is a mistake. I sincerely hope you are not turning your back on the good people of Enchenda. They need you, Eselda.

I meant what I said. I always mean what I say to you; I've never lied. I certainly hope your husband can say the same. Have you thought to ask him about Carsen yet? Sorry to bring it up again. The future of the kingdom we love hinges on you understanding the truth in that scenario. Please ask him, if you haven't already.

I miss you.

Jordyn

Eselda feels a tightness grow in her chest as she allows her eyes to trace back up over the letter. *Jordyn assumes the wedding went off as planned. What reasons would he have to doubt that? But where is he? Why has he not contacted me before this? How does he know I gave Tin control of Enchenda? She turns to the roach who has brought the letter.* "The man who gave you this, where was he?"

"I cannot tell you that," the roach answers.

"I am a queen in Fraun. You will answer my question," Eselda demands.

"I am not a citizen of Fraun. Even if I were, you are not a queen."

Eselda bristles. "What do you mean I'm not Queen? Of course I am. I am royal blood of Enchenda."

A sound that can only be described as a laugh escapes the shorter creature. "Enchenda has fallen. That blood would mean nothing."

"What?" Eselda's brain begins to ache as the humming deepens. Her anger turns her face a dangerous shade of red.

"The king known as Tin assumed control of Enchenda. At least that is what he told his people. I have this from someone who was once a sergeant in his very own army."

"But I only gave him the right to make decisions for me," Eselda whines.

"I don't assume to know how the politics of your kingdom work. All I know is what I was told." The roach turns to leave. "I've delivered the letter. Do you intend to write back? I could wait."

"Where will you be returning it to?"

"Quite a distance. That is all I care to tell you."

"I will not write back at this time. Thank you." Eselda is left alone to ponder this new information. Her anger radiates from her and her hands shake from the building emotion. "Tin," she bellows.

The door opens to allow the king entrance. "I'm growing tired of being summoned by you with a yell." He fixes her with a stoic expression, jaw hardened.

"What is this I hear of our lands combining?" Her anger pours out of every word.

Tin rolls his eyes. "This is not news. You gave me control of Enchenda."

"We control it together."

"No. We are not wed. You gave me control."

"I did no such thing. You asked to make decisions for my realm. I gave you that right. I did not give up Enchenda."

Tin smiles, turning up his charm. He closes in on her, dropping his voice. "You should really study policy more. During a time of war, you gave control of your realm willingly to a king who was raising an army. You have avoided a battle, that much is true. But I control all of the land now known as Sarcheda."

Eselda's stomach plummets to the floor. "You have no intention of making me your queen?" she asks.

"I would gladly make you Queen once this is all finished."

"What is your end goal?"

His smile turns up. "One united Fraun."

Eselda pulls back as though burned. "You will do away with the five realms?"

He splays his fingers alongside his head in frustration. "Why do we need them, Eselda? One kingdom will work for us as it did for Oberian." Tin steps closer to her, holding his arms out. "We can do this together. One Fraun under our rule."

"Together?"

"If that is still what you want. I love you, Eselda." Tin's eyes darken as his smile reaches them. *Make your choice,* he thinks. *Choose me and we can be together.*

"I love you as well." A small smile dances on her lips. Just as quickly, it falls. She squints her eyes. "Why did you keep this from me? I feel betrayed. You took my lands."

Tin bristles under her doubt. He balls his hands and bangs them down at his sides. "I told you what I was doing. It's not my fault you didn't understand."

Eselda rubs her forehead. "You still seem so angry. Why is that? If you are no longer limited by your age marker, shouldn't your anger have faded?"

Tin scoffs. "I can still feel anger. I have always been someone who wears his emotions. It is not my fault you anger me sometimes. I do my best to control it." He closes the remaining space between them and brings his hands to rest on her waist. The physical contact darkens his eyes further, weakening him. "I try not to inflame your age marker by instigating. We would be a volatile pair in matching anger."

"It doesn't always work. You make me angry as well," Eselda says. A note of teasing enters her voice.

"I know and I'm sorry. Nothing has changed. I will still seek your input." He kisses her lightly. "I will still come when you call for me but you could try not to always yell for me like you are being murdered."

"What does this mean for Enchenda?" Eselda asks. Her brain struggles to process around the distractions being thrown up by the age marker and the closeness of Tin.

"Nothing. The people will not feel a difference. You trust me, don't you?"

Eselda looks deep into his eyes. She feels a little seed of doubt has been planted in her gut, but it is not yet growing roots. *Disappointed as I may be in his decisions lately, he is still the same man who offered me so many things when I needed them.* "I do trust you. But I want to be a queen, for Enchenda."

"You will be. You once told me that you weren't sure you would have chosen this path if an alternate had been offered to you. Do you remember that conversation?"

"I don't know." She closes her eyes to think back to those lunar cycles after her father got sick but before he passed. *I had been learning so much so quickly. I was petrified of my future.* The buzzing increases and her head throbs. *If someone had offered me an out then, a chance to step down, I would've taken it.* A rational part of her brain breaks through the fog. *Am I letting Tin think for me because I am scared?* She shakes her head and as quickly as it came the thought is gone. "I think I remember," she says.

"Then this is your chance to find out what you want. Right now you get to focus on other things, like planning a wedding." Tin smiles at her. "When the war is over and we are triumphant, you can again be Queen. This time one who is Queen of a peaceful kingdom united under a pair of strong rulers."

When their lips connect, they linger for a while. Tin feels the warmth she brings to him ignite. He pulls her even closer. Eselda's head tips back allowing Tin to deepen the kiss. He runs his fingers along her back and tingles race each other up her spine. "We will be the best rulers Fraun has ever seen," Tin purrs, his forehead resting against Eselda's.

"Aren't you worried about the balance?" Eselda asks. The topic change breaks the mood entirely. Tin's eyes return to their normal hazel and he stands up straight again.

"Eselda, I'll make this simple for you." His voice has dropped an octave, it has a dangerous edge to it. Eselda shivers. "You are either with me or you are against me."

Eselda gulps and swallows. "I …" she fades away, unsure of what to say.

"I would do anything to rule Fraun, Eselda."

"Anything?" her voice squeaks on the question.

"Anything." He allows the answer to resonate. "Nothing will stand in my way." He turns to leave the room again. At the door, he hesitates. "Choose sides, quickly."

Alone the confusion takes hold. *Why must I choose?* Sudden tears stop Eselda's throat and she doesn't try to hold them back. She drops to the cold floor and cries until her eyes are swollen. She wipes her hand along her face. "Why can't I remember everything?" she moans. *It would be so much easier if I could just remember everything. This blasted age marker causes me to have such a headache that even forming coherent thoughts is impossible. Remembering things makes my head throb.*

Eselda reaches for a nearby piece of wood whose purpose she doesn't know. She turns it in her hands, trying to figure out what it is used for. The buzzing increases. Eselda has to close her eyes to process, the light in the room suddenly seems too bright. Frustrated, she throws the wood as hard as she can across the room. It lands with a resounding thud against the far wall. She drops her head into her hands. *I am hopeless in this state.*

The parchment from Jordyn, which Eselda hid upside down on the table when she bellowed for Tin, catches her eye. She pulls it toward her and rereads it. "*Have you thought to ask him about Carsen yet?*" Her mind whirrs; she grips it in her hands, squeezing it tight. *What am I supposed to ask him about Carsen?*

Like a switch being flipped, the buzzing stops. Eselda's eyes pop open and she freezes, afraid that any movement may cause the memories to turn off. "Jordyn thinks Tin killed Carsen." The words echo off the walls of the empty room which suddenly feels smaller.

Eselda rises. "I have to ask him." The buzzing returns, bringing anger and darkness with it. Eselda allows it to overtake her, feeling its power. She will find the king of strength and demand answers from him. The simplicity of it baffles her. *Surely it will not be this easy, or I would've done it sooner. My fiancé is the strongest man in Fraun. His anger is that of legend. I have seen these things myself. This will not be an easy confrontation.* She steels her chin and takes a deep breath. "I will fear him not. I will find the answers."

The silent room does not answer, but Eselda can feel the strength oozing from the building and into her. Her back straightens. "I have challenged him before, surely I can do it again." Her fists clench.

What will I do with the knowledge? If Tin is innocent, and that means that Jordyn is incorrect, how do I proceed? She shrugs. That is Jordyn's problem to bear.

But what if Tin is guilty? The seed of doubt suddenly grows roots, reaching rapidly for her toes. "What if he's guilty?" she asks the room. "What if I'm living in the home of a murderer?" The fear weakens her knees and she falls back to the floor. "What am I going to do?"

Chapter 32

The clearing looks oddly familiar, but Eselda cannot seem to remember why. She shivers from the cold. The gown she went to sleep in, frail and wispy, is the only thing between her and the blowing wind. The edge of the circle she stands in is rimmed with trees, thick and green. The ground is wild grass, but it is not too tall for Eselda to stand in. She has the distinct feeling she is waiting for something, but she cannot recall what.

A man dressed in battle armor crashes through the trees, running with his weapon drawn. Eselda's breath catches as she registers the face of Tin. Fear grips her as he runs in her direction, weapon raised. Eselda cowers back from him, wincing. It takes her a second to notice he cannot see her. That second is enough for her to realize how deep her fear of him runs.

His face looks different. She is standing in front of him when he stops running and turns to look over his shoulder. His face shows something she doesn't regularly see on it; fear. She moves her head around, trying to get a better angle. "What is it you fear? How it is I know so little about you after all this time that even I do not know what would give you this look?"

She lets any further questions die on the air when it becomes clear that Tin cannot hear her any more than he can see her.

Another man charges into the clearing and just that quickly Tin's fear is gone. Replacing it is the hard shell of determination, Tin's look of power. Eselda shivers again and steps out of the way. It occurs to her why this is familiar. *This is a dream. Tin and the man will fight and the man kills Tin.*

Eselda tries to pinch her cheeks to wake herself. "I don't want to see this again," she says aloud, hoping the sound will wake her. Nothing works.

Powerless to stop it but unable to look away, Eselda watches the blades clash and the men strain. Again the other man has no face. Where the face should be, Eselda sees merely a blur of peach. *It's as though something in my subconscious blocks this image.*

As she watches, the swords meet above Tin's head. He holds his arms straight, locking with the other man's blade. Tin stumbles. Eselda wants to close her eyes and keep herself from seeing it, but she cannot. Fear has her frozen in place. The man raises his sword high overhead and plunges it toward Tin.

At the last second, Tin reaches his sword and brings it up to parlay the move. Eselda gasps. *Tin wasn't killed?* He rises and the men continue fighting, Tin with a renewed hatred. He is charging at the man, continuing to back him up toward the edge of the clearing. The man takes another step back and hits a tree. He is now stuck between the tree and Tin. Eselda puts her hands up to her lips, scared of what will happen.

Tin's face breaks out in a smile. Eselda hears his voice fill the clearing. "Well isn't this interesting? I seem to have you backed against a wall here, old friend." Eselda has only a moment to wonder why he sounds pleased before Tin lets out a roar and plunges the sword forward.

When she wakes this time, she is covered in sweat and tangled in blankets. She breathes deeply, trying to calm her racing heart. Her breathing grows jagged as she fights back the tears. Eselda rubs her eyes. This time, unlike the last time she had this dream, she has no desire to run to Tin. Instead, she lies back on her pillow and tries to take relaxing breaths. The thought of running to a man who even in her dreams triumphantly kills another scares her. *Who takes such pleasure from death?*

Eselda's feet hit the cold floor almost of their own accord. Before the buzzing in her head can fully begin, before the reality of her situation can bury her again, her feet head toward the door. Her hand hits the doorknob. The metal will not turn.

Frantic, she tries again. The door is locked tight. Eselda drops to the floor, sitting with her back to the doorknob. It is this challenge of being locked in a room that fully makes her realize her predicament.

Stripped of her title, lost in a new realm, part of the pair who brought war to Fraun; Eselda is buried by the reality she has created.

Chapter 33

Outside the door, the king sits with his back against the wood. He struggles to get the feelings surging through him under control. *It was wise to order her room be locked.* He cannot recall which staff member he ordered to do it, which means he cannot get the key even if he wants to. Tin refuses to allow himself to be a slave to Eselda. He can feel his body craving to hold her as if his skin knows how close she sits. He trembles as he tries to get it under control. This age marker, more than the last one, is torture for Tin. It is a source of powerlessness he hates feeling. He rises, determined to head back to his room and get some sleep. Through the door, he hears her sharp intake of breath. The sound drives him right back down to the ground. He presses his ear against the door, tortured by the knowledge that her voice was so close. Try as he might, he hears nothing more.

He presses his back against the door again, realizing that she must be doing the same. He feels some comfort in knowing that they are that close. It is this comfort that allows him to drift off to sleep at last.

Chapter 34

Outside the entrance to the house of the giant, I pace. I have no eyes for the beautiful day today; the sun shining and birds somewhere chirping. The full scout troop is back together and most of the members are scattered around the grassy area in various stages of relaxation. Toby is inside the giant's building, tending to our newest guest. I have not been allowed an audience with the man for two suns, since his arrival.

When the roach brought the man to the troop he was bathed in blood. The man was wearing black and red, the colors of Sarcheda. He was in armor. He was tired, beaten down, and emotionally drained. The roach brought us snippets of conversations she had with the man along the journey, but not enough to satisfy my intense craving for answers. Toby took the man into the giant's home. After a short conversation, Toby emerged and declared that the man was unfit for any interrogation. The group ordered me to stand down.

Today, as he did yesterday, Toby has risen first to check on the man. I also continue my behavior from yesterday, pacing outside the door that houses the stranger. I need answers. Why the colors of Sarcheda? Why the armor? What is happening in my absence?

The door opens and Toby emerges, arms held high like a surrender. "He is still very weak. I'm not sure he will tell you everything you want to know, but I've determined that he is not a threat to you. He has nothing in there he can use as a weapon."

"So I can enter?"

"If you must." Toby steps aside.

I hurry into the room before Toby can change his mind. The man is lying prostrate on the floor, his head propped up on a pillow. He manages a weak smile. I notice the clothing was removed and the blood cleaned off. The man is now wearing simple clothes in varying shades of brown. I drop into a comfortable position beside the man, on the floor. "My name is Jordyn. I am from Renchenda. I have many questions for you regarding the state you were in when you arrived and what little information I was able to glean from the roach who brought you did nothing to satiate the curiosity that is my nature. I hope you are up for talking," I say.

"I will do my best, Majesty." The voice is weak.

As proof I am becoming comfortable in my new role, the title shocks me. "I am not a king," I answer automatically. "Do I know you?"

"No, sir. I once worked for the patrol of Fraun. I know you only by name."

"And yet you know not that I have stepped down? What kind of training are they offering that patrol?"

"We are more of an army now than a patrol, I fear." The man hangs his head as though ashamed of this change.

"That explains the armor you were wearing when you arrived. What is your name?"

"Lance. I am originally from Enchenda."

"The roach explained to me that Enchenda and Sarcheda have combined. Is this accurate?" I feel my anger spark at the thought, I fight to control it.

"Yes, sir."

"Tell me more of this army. What is your purpose? What do you do?"

"Since war was declared—"

"It was officially declared then?" I cut through Lance's sentence, manners be damned.

"I'm afraid so."

"By King Tin?" I physically swallow to control my anger, imagining the foul beast that is my age marker slipping down my throat. Too late I realize that act would bring it closer to my heart. How much longer can I hold it in without it exploding?

"Yes, sir." Lance waits to see if another question will be fired. When it is not, he continues with his earlier answer. "Since war was declared we have been working to build our troops. The members of the patrol were given titles befitting their position in the army. I was called Sergeant. We were asked to train the new members in fighting techniques. Each of us was assigned a specialty, mine is sword fighting."

"So it is all in practice. No one has been harmed?"

Lance hangs his head even further, so his chin is practically touching his chest. "No, sir. I'm afraid the first battle happened just before the roach found me. We were told to attack Farcheda. Many Fraunians were killed."

"From both sides?"

"As near as I could tell, yes."

"That explains the blood that was covering you," I state. Lance merely nods. "What happened with Farcheda? Did Tin seize control there?"

"I'm not sure about the outcome. The roach pulled me out of the battlefield before I could be found and killed."

"Found where? Why would you be killed?"

"A boy was killed during the battle. He was young. Too young to have been fighting. He wore a royal helmet. The Sarcheda men acted on their orders to kill any royals they found. The child was beheaded. I have lost two children of my own, I could not bear the death of another child." He pulls his head up and meets my eyes. "I fear I lost control and wept for the boy. The roach pointed out that if I, in Sarcheda clothing, were found weeping over the body of a Farcheda child I would be killed."

"Your sons were killed in battle as well?"

"No. My sons have been gone for annuals. It is unrelated to the war. But seeing another young boy taken out violently brought them to mind."

"I'm sorry for the loss you suffered." I allow a moment of silence to permeate the room. "Do you know anything about Tin's goals concerning this war?"

"All I know is what he shared with his army. He wants a united Fraun. He promises positions of power for those who stay loyal to him. He promises to give his supporters large sums of land, to ensure safety and justice for all those under his rule."

"One Fraun under him and Queen Eselda?" Saying her name physically hurts. I have to close my eyes to get control. The pain is like an animal inside, pushing to get out. Eselda has made her choice, she is not the same person who I first met.

"She is not Queen." The answer is whispered, quiet.

My eyes fly open. "Why not?"

"Enchenda fell without a fight. Her lands were turned over to King Tin."

"Her husband?"

Lance visibly pulls back from the angry tone. "No. They are not wed."

My mind begins whirring away, working hard. If Eselda forfeit her rights to land by giving them to Tin then there are only four realms in Fraun. Tin controls the largest section of these realms, which matches the map Thometh sent me. From the sounds of that letter the remaining three realms intend to fight Tin for control. What will become of Eselda if Tin wins? If Tin loses? "Are they to be wed?" I ask.

"That depends on who you ask."

"I'm asking you." I fix the sergeant with a stare that makes him squirm and drop his gaze.

"No, they will not wed. Tin does not need her any longer, he already has her land."

"That is what I feared you would answer." I take a deep breath and ask, perhaps, the most important question of the day. "Is she in danger?"

Lance meets my piercing stare directly. "Tin's quick temper has never appeared to be aimed at Eselda, but Eselda has never challenged him either. Were she to stand up to him …" He gulps and nods his head slowly, like the act alone is condemning her. "I believe she could be in danger, yes."

The thought of Tin hurting Eselda is too much for me to bear. I must act. “Then you will teach me to fight.”

“What? Why? I wasn’t planning on staying with the scouts.” He shakes his head. “I wanted to be alone once I was back on my feet.”

“Eselda is in danger. We have no choice but to learn to battle and join up with the true Fraun. Tin must be stopped at all costs, I see that now,” I say.

“Why do you believe that one side or the other is right? When I was listening to King Tin everything he promised seemed to make sense. All his points about the safety of citizens make sense,” Lance argues.

“Of course, they would make sense. Tin is stealing ideas from other people. Those were Eselda’s words or the council’s words being thrown back at you. I’m sure of it. Tell me one thing that he promised you.”

Lance thinks. “There was a law passed about how many children one family could have. A lot of the guys were worked up about it. He promised to repeal it.”

I scoff. “Did he tell you that he was the one who suggested that law?”

“No, he must have left that part out. There was more though. He talked about useless deaths. Carsen, for example, or the little princess from Enchenda. He said that with a strong army and a strong leader, those could be stopped.”

“Interesting.” I sit back, leaning my weight on my palms. “I don’t want to pretend that every citizen of Fraun is completely safe at all times. That would be insensitive of me, considering you lost two children. What I do know is that Tin’s specific examples are worthless. Tin himself killed Carsen, I have this from Tin’s mouth. As for Sawchett, your little princess, she is alive and well.” I point to the window nearby. “She’s sitting on the lawn right now inventing ridiculous stories about creatures that fly and can carry her away.”

“She is?” Lance’s shock is apparent in his eyes. “Eselda would be happy to hear that. She searched high and low for that little girl. She hasn’t been the same since the princess went missing.”

“We don’t refer to her as a princess any longer,” I say.

“Good to know.”

“Perhaps I will suggest she write to Eselda.” I smile at the other man. “All these things you tell me convince me I was right about Tin. He is not a good man. He knows how to put on the face a good man would wear, but he is dangerous. We have no choice but to fight back against him and what he stands for. One man craving all that power is dangerous. Lance, will you do me the honor of teaching me to fight? Will you train me to stand for Fraun?"

Lance's eyes take in the full expanse of my appearance. "You are easily the tallest man I have ever met, but there is almost no fat on your body. Then again, the boys who joined with Sarcheda in the last round were younger, scrawnier, and weaker than even you. If those boys can be taught to brandish a deadly weapon for a kingdom they do not truly understand, surely I can teach you to wield one for the kingdom you love. I will do that, sir. It will be an honor to stand beside you and protect Fraun you value."

I am humbled by the honest assessment. "I believe I have something to discuss with our little scout troop. You rest up and let me know when you are ready to begin my training." I open the door and find Toby perched nearby on a small tree. He was ready to rush the room should our conversation go awry. It is a touching show of his loyalty and support. "Toby, a word?"

"What's up, Jordyn?" Toby comes to my side immediately, searching my face for signs of the news I may have gleaned from my time with the new guy.

"You were right about the war," I begin.

Suns past I followed Evelyn's advice and sat Toby down to talk with him about a pending war in Fraun. Toby had explained that, in his opinion, it was likely to have already started. A man like Tin, Toby reasoned, doesn't wait longer than he must. He would strike the second he thought Fraun was weak. Eselda's father dying and me leaving would both be signs that Fraun was ready for the taking. "I knew it." Toby's voice conveys the fact that he takes very little pride in being right. "Lance was dressed as if in an army."

"He was a sergeant for Sarcheda."

"What's the plan, then?" Toby asks, crossing his arms across his chest.

"I will fight for Fraun. Lance is going to teach me to battle and I will return to Fraun to join the fight. It was wrong of me to abandon them. I believe in Fraun too much to leave them to be butchered by Tin."

Toby doesn't even hesitate. "Excellent. When do we start training?"

Despite my hope for support I am surprised at the show of solidarity. "We?"

"Absolutely. Those people in Sarcheda are a dangerous bunch. They put too much emphasis on strength alone. Those who are weak are often left to die or mysteriously disappear. I could never abide by someone like that ruling all of Fraun. I will stand beside you and help you fight for what is right."

"Do you think I can expect support from the other scouts?"

"We will never know until we ask," says Toby.

I wear a solemn expression as we close in on the peaceful clearing. Although I have accepted my new role, I have trepidation about going forward. Are we too late to help the battle? Toby follows me, providing the image of a united front. Once we are before the other scouts, I clear my throat and everyone looks up. "I have something to tell all of you. I have decided to join in the fight for Fraun. Someone I care for very much is in grave danger, it has become personal for her and therefore for me. Lance, the man who was brought here, was a sergeant with army training. He will teach me to battle. Toby has offered his services as well," I explain. Toby nods his head in a gesture almost like a small bow. "We will leave you if you want no part of this, but we would also accept your help if it is offered."

"I'm not sure what kind of help an old codger like me can offer, but I am willing to find out," Franc calls out. I smile at him.

"I would venture that you can count on us all, Jordyn. We have grown rather fond of you and we never let a friend down," Lili says, without rising from her seated position under a tree. Nods of assent follow her words.

"Thank you all. It means a great deal to me that you are willing to support me in this."

"Can we all get training?" Sieven asks his face lighting up with excitement. A splattering of laughter fills the clearing.

"Yes, if you are to help we will provide training to you all," Toby answers. He reaches over and grasps me heartily on the shoulder. "I believe," he states quietly, "you officially have yourself an army."

The words, delivered to help boost my confidence, leave me instead feeling cold. Am I just as bad as Tin? The worry slips down to my stomach, hardening into a tight ball. What have I gotten myself into? "Excuse me for a moment." I slip quietly from the group, wrapping around the side of the building. I drop to the floor and hold my head in my hands. "Eselda." Her name falls from my lips and deepens my worry. In all the ways I imagined this playing out, I never would've thought of this. I am going to join in the fight for Fraun. Is this a mistake?

It can't be a mistake. For once in my life, I am standing up to fight for something that I love. That feels right. But, what then, is this worry in my gut?

It's the scouts. Do these people follow me to their deaths? I rise and return to the clearing. Everyone has resumed their previous activities. It is too much to bear, watching them lead normal and relaxed lives. I cannot bring this fight to them. I cannot destroy their sense of peace. "I cannot ask you to join this war." The words burst forth, emotion propelling them past my lips.

Everyone looks at me. "What?" Franc is the first to recover from his shock.

"This war. This is a war for Fraun. I cannot ask you to join us. You owe Fraun nothing."

"We don't fight for Fraun, mate. We will join this fight for you," Franc explains as if that answer is perfectly logical.

"That's the problem. Don't you see? I cannot ask you to risk your life for me and my causes." My frustration grows deeper. "Thank you for the offer of support, but I must do this alone. I believe in what Fraun can be but I cannot ask you to do the same."

Toby rises. "Jordyn I am from Fraun. This battle is as much mine as it is yours. I have dreams of what Fraun could be as much as you do. With all due respect, my friend, you cannot keep me from it."

"Same with me." This voice is from Kurt. "My wife and I left Fraun because we never felt it was safe. Our rulers never looked out for us. The kingdom you speak of, the one you envision, it's what we always wanted. I will stand beside you to help create that Fraun. You cannot stop me."

Evelyn nods her agreement with her husband's statement all the while smiling as though it is poetry. "Your Fraun is our dream, Jordyn."

"Mate, we don't fight this war for you," Franc explains. "We fight it with you. The cause is noble and your way is just. We believe in you and agree with you. We fight because it is right."

Emotion rushes at me, choking me up. "I don't know what to say."

"Say 'thank you' and go get some rest. We will start training you tomorrow and you will want to be well-rested," Toby calls out.

I nod, my emotions blocking anything further. "That I can do. Thank you."

Chapter 35

Instead of a once bustling city full of merchants and children, there are empty streets and disturbing quiet on Tutor's walk home. Residents of Farcheda are hidden in their homes, behind doors that contain newly installed locking mechanisms to keep the Sarcheda army, rumored to enter homes uninvited and cause havoc, at bay.

It's more than the strangely quiet streets, though, that bother Tutor. Along his route he sees men of the Farcheda army standing guard against the new border. The men are young. It breaks Tutor's heart to see them lined up like that.

He turns a corner and spies a home that has recently burned. This too is becoming a sickeningly familiar sight. The Sarcheda army is not above burning lands to the ground. Tutor finds the practice to be barbaric and unnecessarily cruel. If he had any doubt about which side his loyalty fell before, it faded once the fighting began. Although it puts him at odds with his old friend, he cannot stand with an army that behaves like Sarcheda's.

Tutor rounds the final corner and fixes his brown eyes on the stoop of the home he is renting. Another sigh escapes him. An older gentleman sits on his stoop and Tutor does not recognize the man. "I don't want whatever you are selling today, sir," he calls out, drawing close to the home.

The man rises. "Oh, I'm not selling anything. If you have a minute, I need to speak with you about your lineage."

This sentence captures Tutor's attention more than a stranger at his home ever could. He stops walking and takes in the full appearance. Like himself, this man is carrying a bag bulging with parchments. The man has a writing tool tucked behind his left ear. He looks as though he may be as tired as Tutor feels. "What about my lineage?"

"I update a tree and I need to speak with you about your parents. Could we step inside your home?"

Tutor thinks about what he knows of his birth family. He shakes his head. "There's nothing you could tell me I have not already learned myself. I update the tree for Enchenda."

"Enchenda?" The man's blue eyes blaze with curiosity. "Enchenda has fallen, sir. Surely you mean that you update for Sarcheda."

Tutor rolls his eyes and opens the door to the home. "My business is none of your concern." He moves to shut the door. "If you'll excuse me I have work to do."

The stubborn man sticks his foot in the door, preventing it from closing. "Was your father the man known as Den?"

Tutor pulls the door open again, his face registering his surprise. "Who do you work for?"

"Was that your father's name?"

Tutor steps to the side. "Perhaps you better come in after all." The man enters the home and glances around. The surroundings are meager since Tutor does not spend much time there. There are parchments depicting lineage charts scattered on the table. Tutor hastily puts them in a pile. "We can sit here." He gestures to a chair, which the man drops into.

A sheaf of parchment is pulled from the bag around the man's shoulders and the quill is freed from the tangle of his curly hair.

Tutor eyes him warily. "Who do you work for?" he repeats.

"Marchenda," the man answers.

Tutor's shock is absolute. "Why is a lineage updater from Marchenda interested in who my father is?" he queries. Tutor has, of course, looked into his heritage in his travels. Ever since Eselda let that name, Charlotte, drop from her tongue during a visit to her home he has not been able to get the truth of his lineage out of his head. But a man from Marchenda should know nothing about Charlotte.

"What do you know about your father, sir?"

"Call me Tutor. I don't know much about him at all, in truth. I was raised by other people. Why don't you tell me what you know about him? I'm sure you are more informed than I am." Tutor sits back, a vain attempt to give off the air of one disinterested. In truth, his heart pounds.

"Marchenda had two sons," the man begins. *We are going way back,* Tutor thinks. He chooses to keep this thought to himself and not interrupt. The visitor continues, "The youngest child, Larent, married and had two sons of his own. His eldest had a single daughter, Spanz." The man produces a parchment showing this much of the lineage tree.

Tutor leans forward and finds the line the man speaks of, in the middle of the parchment. It appears to end with Spanz. "Is this the tree you work from?" Tutor asks.

"This is a replica of what is on the wall in Marchenda, yes. I have found it continues from here."

"Go on then." Again Tutor sits back in his chair and this time he crosses his arms over his chest.

"Spanz became pregnant out of wedlock. As is our custom, the royal family asked her to live among the commoners and shunned her. The child, I have come to learn, was named Sean."

"I fail to see what this has to do with me." Tutor clouds his voice with impatience.

"I am getting there in due time." The man clears his throat. "Sean was raised as a common citizen of Marchenda. He never knew the truth of his birth. In due time he moved to Enchenda for work." A bead of sweat forms on Tutor's brow. The mere mention of that realm clues him into what may be coming.

"Sean prospered in Enchenda. He found a good job, he married a beautiful woman, and they had a son," the updater explains. Tutor's breathing quickens. "They named their boy Den. Den grew up never knowing his father had royal blood in his veins. He took a job working as a tutor in the house of Enchenda. He married a woman named …" Here the man pauses his tale to consult a parchment. "… Charlotte."

Tutor's eyes close and breath escapes through his nose. *No, this isn't possible. A mistake has been made.*

If the man notices Tutor's discomfort, he does not acknowledge it. Instead, he rushes on with his tale. "Now, this is where I have had trouble finding the full story, as both Den and Charlotte have passed on. I hear from varying people that they may have had a son, but for some reason, they did not raise the son themselves. It has been brought to my attention that you may be that son. Could you shed some light on that for me?"

Tutor pushes his palms into his eyes and groans. *This is exactly what I have been trying to avoid by refusing to put my name on Enchenda's wall. The implications and responsibility of having royal blood in your veins … it's too much.* He looks at the man sternly. "Who else have you talked to about this?"

The man is put off by the question. "I have only talked to people who may be able to tell me more. Why do you ask?"

"Do not write my name there, please. I know how important this is but I'm begging you, do not write my name there."

"Are you the son?"

Tutor sighs the weight of his past fully upon his chest. "I am."

"Sir, I must insist I be allowed to write your name. You have royal blood in your veins. In a time of need, Marchenda could call upon you to lead."

Tutor groans again and opens his eyes to the lineage chart that still lies in front of him. He draws his eyes along the left-hand side, tracing along the line that will eventually end in Larecio and his deceased son. Alongside them, there appears to be a healthy line of similar age. "What of this line? Are Alerta or Stef still with us?"

"Well, yes. They are both alive and well. I fail to see what that has to do with your lineage."

Tutor eyes the man carefully. *He looks like a smart man. Clearly, he has been entrusted with the secrets of Marchenda. Perhaps he can handle more secrets.* Tutor reaches for the parchments he had hastily stacked upon their entrance to the room. He finds the one he looks for, the Enchenda tree, and unrolls it before the man. He speaks as he works. "There is more to this than you understand, good sir." He drops his finger on the spot without even having to search. He closes his eyes as the man reads, unable to watch as the excitement reaches the eyes of the stranger.

"What does this …" the man trails off, his surprise temporarily stealing his voice. "You are of Enchenda blood as well?"

Tutor speaks through clenched teeth without opening his eyes. "My mother had royal blood of Enchenda, yes."

"And your father was of Marchenda?" The man's glee is evident. "This is magnificent. The blood of two brothers is rare indeed. You could assume the throne of either realm. You would have the right to—"

"I know my rights." Tutor's voice, dangerously loud, silences the poor man. Tutor forces himself to draw a calming breath and open his eyes. "I'm sure you can agree that in these uncertain times this information, in the wrong hands, would be dangerous." As he says the word 'dangerous' a realization dawns on him. He vacates his chair. "I have to go. Keep this information to yourself for now." The words fall like a threat, heavy and deadly.

"But sir …"

The words reach deaf ears for Tutor has already fled the house carrying nothing but himself. Tutor runs straight into town, searching for any animal that can support his weight. The first he finds is a roach. "Excuse me, sir. I am looking for a girl known as Sawchett. She travels with the scouts off the western border. I must find her. It is a matter of life or death."

"I know the troop. Climb aboard," the roach clicks.

As Tutor rides, his leg jostles from nerves. *If Tin were to find out what Sawchett and I hold within our blood, he would come for us. The girl is not safe. The blood of two brothers flows in her veins and mine.*

This is, without a doubt, the most insane thing Tutor has ever learned. He feels as though his brain could explode from the implications. He has one thought and one thought alone running on repeat in his head.

I must find Sawchett before Tin finds learns our truth.

Chapter 36

King Tin walks the campsite for the Sarcheda army in the early morning glow. Half the men are just rising, stoking fires, and preparing food to carry them through the day. The other half has been on guard all night and is due back at any minute. Although he believes in the battles and wants the war to go his way, Tin has yet to fight. He is careful to arrive in time for the changing of the shifts each sun and has armor that fits him, but he dons it not. Instead, no matter the weather, Tin arrives in the same outfit. Pants the color of burnt wood and no shirt. There is no doubt among the men that he possesses the necessary strength to take on any opponent. He uses this argument to justify saving his fight for the moment in which it is most needed. After all, if he were to die the cause would die with him and that helps no one.

This morning as he moves lithely through the camp his dark hair glistens and his muscles ripple. He is proud of these men. They have taken their roles as higher citizens of Fraun seriously. They pillage homes, they take what they need, and they do not take no for an answer. Tin supports this behavior. The soldiers believe they are better than Fraun, above Fraun. This distinction allows them to do what needs to be done.

Tin stops beside the tent he has erected for his leaders, those men formerly known as the patrol. He smiles slyly. Most of these men are not from Sarcheda originally, and yet they follow him to battle and lead his army. It is a symbol of the control he has over them. The control he believes he will one day have over his entire kingdom. "Good morning Garven," he greets the young lieutenant who emerges from the tent.

"Oh, good morning your Majesty. What brings you by this morning?"

"I am merely checking on the troops. How went the guard yesterday? I don't think I saw you upon your return to the camp."

"It went well, sir. We are short a few men now, so it is becoming difficult to rally the troops effectively. Would it be possible for us to promote another soldier to sergeant?"

"Did we lose a sergeant? That title was given to the men from Enchenda, I believe."

"We did and it was Majesty. Actually, we lost them both."

"Both?"

"Danyel disappeared mysteriously a while back before the fighting even began. We thought he would return, but he has yet to do that." Garven shifts from foot to foot. "Lance was seen reacting strangely during the battle of Farcheda but hasn't been seen since."

"Strangely? Strangely how?"

"Someone thought they saw him coddling the body of the dead prince, Highness."

"That is strange indeed. I will look into this." A man defecting from his army, if that is what these men did, cannot be excused. "Garven I permit you to promote two soldiers. I also need you to find someone you can spare to strike out and look for these men. I want them brought before me. I have questions I'd like to ask them about their loyalties."

"I understand, Majesty. I will get right on that." Garven bows to his king before scurrying off toward camp.

Tin seats himself on a log to await the return of the overnight guard. He takes the opportunity to review his plan. The army managed to get King Mick to step down, his spies tell him that Farcheda is now under the rule of King Hector. Letters to Hector to discuss possible routes for peace have gone unanswered. They will attack Farcheda again, eventually. In the interim, they look to Marchenda. Larecio is old and has no immediate heirs. Tin knows the army will have little trouble taking out this old king. Then the new blood in charge of Marchenda, assuming they have some, will be scared enough to turn over their lands to him without further incident.

Once he controls Marchenda he will be able to use the council building to hold his meetings. The generals can meet to discuss battle strategies and the entire war becomes more efficient and professional. *Farcheda will fall after Marchenda. If I cannot convince Hector, then I will have to take Hector out. The remaining two children in that line are women, they can be won over like my own little woman was.* Tin's hollow chuckle rings off the trees.

That will only leave the lands of Renchenda to fall. Renchenda is important. *Castle Fraun will be mine, but Thometh is a wild card.* Tin has spent his time analyzing the movements and the ambitions of the other royals, but Thometh seems to have appeared on the throne out of nowhere. It is unnerving. *I don't know if the man can be bought. I don't know the man's fears or concerns. I don't know what I can use to win him. How can you talk someone into being on your side if you don't know what they want to hear?* Yes, Renchenda will require more time.

Tin rises when he hears the boots of the army approaching. He solutes his generals, the men who represented Sarcheda in the patrol, as they crest the hill. "Daijan, Trep," he calls, "good morning. How was the evening watch?" The men are leading the troops back from the Renchenda border where they have been holding their ground against the opposing army.

"It was boring." Trep laughs. "They didn't do a thing all night."

"I don't know why you won't let us attack, Majesty," Daijan complains.

Tin likes Daijan, he gives the man a lot of leeway. At this comment, the king leans into the man. "That sounded a lot like someone questioning my commands, General," he whispers.

"Not at all, Majesty. I am sorry it sounded that way." Daijan's face reddens and he makes a show of stretching his shoulders and yawning. "It must be that I am tired, Highness. I know not what I'm saying."

"I'm sure that was it." Tin backs up from the man and offers a smile for the benefit of the troops. "Well done, men. You have earned your breakfast and rest. You'll need your strength for tomorrow." At this clear dismissal, the troops behind the generals disperse.

"Majesty, what will they need their strength for?" Trep asks once the army is far enough away to not overhear.

"We attack Marchenda soon. I want them at their best for that fight."

A glimmer of excitement reaches Daijan's eyes. "Excellent choice, Majesty. Are we to attack the home of the king?"

"You are." Seeing the worry on Trep's face, Tin addresses him next. "Is there a problem with that, General?"

"No, Majesty. I have small concerns but no problems."

"Tell me the concerns, then."

"I recall on the map you drew up that the home of Larecio lies to the back edge of Marchenda. We will have to break through their front line and travel quite a distance to make it to the home." Out of fear for the verbal challenge he is issuing, Trep's voice is low.

"Not if you attack from behind." Tin's smile is crooked and the brown center of his eyes flashes wickedly. "You leave tomorrow for Enchenda. There you will enter the forest and track around the ravine skirting our lands. You will then trek up through the forests surrounding Renchenda. Once your men make it through that forest you will reach the grasslands that mark the edge of Marchenda. The grasslands will be no trouble for your men at all." Smiles stretch out over the faces of the two generals as they begin to grasp the plan. "From that side, I'm sure you will find Marchenda unguarded. The home of Larecio will be close by and the battle simple. Even if the old king is guarded in his home, your men should have no problem."

"Brilliant, Majesty." Daijan smiles. "Absolutely brilliant."

"Thank you." Tin tips his head to the men. "I have my moments." He smiles at them. "Long live Fraun."

"Long live Fraun," the generals repeat, bowing low to Tin. "Long live the king."

Chapter 37

Out of habit, what remains of the council of kings will still meet in the council building today. Despite the Marchenda citizens in haphazard armor lined up along the nearby border, despite the smoke rising to the sky from homes burning in Farcheda, despite their sour attitudes, the kings will arrive.

The men enter at approximately the same time, dragging their feet and skittering their eyes to the borders like prey moving too close to enemy territory. "What has transpired since our last meeting?" Thometh asks once they all sit. Larecio sports large circles under his eyes and his skin yellow. Hector's face has aged in the lunar cycle since he took the throne of Farcheda. His face holds new wrinkles and his eyes a level of sadness that takes Thometh's breath away.

"The Sarcheda army crosses River Fraun and enters our lands from Enchenda," Hector answers, his voice gruff. "We cannot hold the entire border, it is too large."

"What do they do when they cross?" Thometh inquires.

Hector sighs. "Burn our homes. Kill our citizens." He shakes his head. "It's terrible."

"Can no one stop them?" Thometh asks. He notes the question could be taken as condescending. Clearing his throat, he tries again. "How can we help?"

"My men send the soldiers scurrying home or kill them. But finding them is proving difficult. Perhaps men to help hold that border would help." Hector gestures toward the blue line showing his newest enemy front.

"I can spare men. The army has stayed out of Renchenda so far," Thometh states. "Does anyone know why that is?"

"The castle," Larecio answers. "They fear it. No doubt it will be the last thing that Tin takes control of."

"You speak as though you think he will win this war, old friend," Hector challenges.

"None of us have fallen yet, that gives me hope." Larecio sighs. "Do you think Tin loses hope?"

"No. According to my sources, Tin has yet to battle. If he were losing hope he would be out there himself trying his best to keep control. He doesn't think this is over yet," Hector answers, solemnly.

"Have they attacked Marchenda?" Thometh inquires, eyeing the oldest king.

"Only here at the border." Larecio gestures in the general direction in which he speaks. "They have yet to breach our realm."

"Well, that's good." Thometh attempts a smile.

"Yes, but how long can we continue to hold them? Our troops grow thin and weak. I fear Sarcheda will break through soon. Have you two considered what a challenge it will pose for you if Marchenda falls?" He catches the eye of each king in turn before continuing. "You already have trouble holding your large borders. Imagine if Tin controlled my lands. Your borders would become impossible to hold."

Fear crosses all three faces. "We have to try," Thometh states.

"You cannot give up hope, Larecio," Hector chides.

"I am not giving up hope. I just want you to be aware. He has always been a smart strategist. Tin will recognize the power it would give him to control Marchenda."

Hector slams his hand down on the table, shaking it dangerously. "Then we cannot give it to him."

"Are your citizens being taxed by this fight as mine are?" Larecio challenges. "Are they tired, dying, and scared? Why are we doing this to them? Someone tell me why it would be dangerous for us to give Tin what he wants. What happens if we all sign a treaty with him together? He only asked for citizens not of royal blood to be allowed to rule. Is what we are doing worth that argument?" Larecio's voice echoes through the room. A cough punctuates it.

Thometh waits out the cough before answering. "He would not stop at that, friend. You know that as well as I. Tin wants control of Fraun for selfish reasons, he doesn't plan to make us privy to those reasons. We cannot allow him to gain the power which he seeks."

Thometh rises, the passion commanding his legs. "King Tin would be a dictator who uses the people of Fraun for his whims. He would do worse than our last dictator, I can promise you that. Tin has a way with Fraunian, they listen to him. Look at the army the boy was able to amass. Can you imagine if this power extended to all of Fraun? People would be enslaved by the thousands."

Thometh begins to move about the room as he continues, gesturing to the table as the words pour from him. "Imagine if we gave it up, gave Tin the control he wants. He would erect statues and buildings in his honor all over Fraun. He would pass laws that benefit only him.

"He wouldn't listen to the people, he wouldn't care about the people. He would do what he has already begun to do. He would boss them around and manipulate them." He stops walking and shakes his head. "No. This cycle has gone on for too long. We end this, we fight him, we better Fraun." He slaps the table. "We better all of Fraun."

"You intend to get Sarcheda and Enchenda back from him?" Hector asks.

"Don't you?" Thometh challenges. After a beat to think about this question, Hector nods. "Those people inside his borders are as much Fraunians as the people around this table. They deserve better than what Tin is giving them. We will stand up to him and take those lands back."

"You talk a good game, Thometh," Larecio interjects. "But you admit that he has yet to attack your lands. What will you be saying when it is Renchenda blood being spilled? My son is dead." Larecio points to Hector. "His son is dead. We have given everything to fight this man. What will you be saying when you have given it all as well?"

Thometh nods. "That is true, you have given much. But I am

willing to give it all. I am willing to join my men and fight Tin if that is what it takes. He cannot say the same. He is not battling side-by-side with his soldiers. I believe in Fraun enough to die for it, and that makes me dangerous to Tin." Thometh's voice resonates in the room.

"I have not yet given everything either, Larecio. My son was taken, true, but I will not rest until I have paid Tin back for that. Tin will have to kill me to stop me from fighting. We will fight until one of us is dead." Hector slams his hand on the table again to prove his point.

Larecio holds up his hands. "Alright, alright. I'm not against you, boys. I merely wanted to point out that there is a reason why I feel more dejected than you. I will continue to amass troops and we will fight."

"Thank you, Larecio." Thometh nods. "We appreciate you holding in there. Should we send you troops to help?"

"I can always take more men."

"I have written the scouts to request more. Perhaps they will come through soon. Perhaps they can offer more than weaponry."

"I must get back." Hector rises. "My wife is alone at our house and I need to send her guard away soon. Larecio, please write and request anything you need." He rests a hand on the old man's shoulder. "Do not give up hope, I feel we can still win this." He offers a weak smile before leaving the room.

"As long as you two feel it is not hopeless, I am with you." Larecio sighs. "Forgive an old man his sadness."

"You have the right to be sad, good sir. Tin took your son." Thometh heads for the door, pausing when he reaches it. "But Larecio, don't let him take your optimism, for then you've truly given him everything."

Alone in the room, Larecio's head falls on the table and he coughs again. "Sometimes I wish you were still here." As the days progress, the pain of his loss does not fade. "You would know what to do, you would know who to speak to. You were always a better man than me. I wish it had been me who died that day, Carsen." Larecio stands and casts his eyes on the ceiling of the old room.

"It should've been me."

Chapter 38

"Do you think they maintain their hope?" Sawchett asks. She is seated across the blossoming yellow and orange breath of the fire from me. There is a cool breeze blowing, sending her blonde locks back off her sweaty neck and providing much-needed tranquility.

"The council?" I ask. At her nod, my eyes track up with thought. "They have to keep that hope or they will fail."

"What happens if we lose?"

I keep my eyes toward the sky watching the grey clouds promising rain move slowly and faraway birds race them. "He will not stop until he controls it all or until someone stops him."

"What does Tin want with all that power?" Sawchett asks. "It seems like so much work to rule it all. It would be terrible to have all that responsibility."

"Tin doesn't think about that. Tin thinks about being the ultimate ruler. The infamous name that goes down in history. The one name that all Fraunians know. He fails to think rationally. For them to speak his name with reverence there must be Fraunians who survive. Those survivors must prosper and grow under his rule. The people will want a voice. We don't remember rulers fondly because of their strength alone. We don't need a ruler to build more. We don't need snap decisions or empty promises," I say.

"What do we need?" Sawchett asks.

This answer requires no further thought. It has occupied much of my time lately to find that exact answer. I have already learned so much, yet this answer has been right before me for so long. I bring my eyes down to her face. "We need balance," I tell her.

"But that's so simple," she answers, wrinkling her little nose.

"Simple to say, hard to obtain. The brothers had the right idea, one kingdom, one goal. I am starting to doubt the twists it has taken over the generations."

"You would change council rules?" Sawchett asks. "Isn't that blasphemy?" She chokes on the hard word with a little cough.

"I am not proposing throwing them all out. I merely think it may be time for the council to reevaluate what it truly means to be a member of Fraun. We need to make it worth belonging to again."

"Even for Tin, when this is all over?" Sawchett asks.

The question shows the girl's naiveté. Tin and Fraun cannot exist together, not the way I envision it. One of the two must fall. I know that, but the girl cannot handle that. Not yet. Death is too new a concept for her. Instead, I nod slowly. "Yes, even for him."

I wonder if she can tell I have just lied to her.

Chapter 39

Her footsteps resonate through the empty kitchen as she paces, angrily stomping her feet. Eselda has commandeered the large room in the Sarcheda home. She knows, no matter how hard he tries to avoid her, he cannot avoid the kitchen if he wants to eat.

The door opens and a servant enters bearing an empty tray. The woman is not familiar. She has not filled her tray in this kitchen this morning. "Where does that tray come from?" Eselda demands.

"From the troops." The woman's voice trembles in fear.

"Was the king among them? Did he accept this food?" She rounds on the woman, her eyes sparking dangerously.

"No, Milady."

"Good. Drop the tray and leave me. I am waiting for the king."

"As you wish." The woman drops the tray and turns to go. "If I see him would you like me to send him this way?" she timidly asks from the door.

"Yes." Eselda resumes her pacing, her footsteps somehow even louder. She has been trying to find time to meet with Tin. She wishes to speak with him about things: Carsen, the war, things Eselda is starting to remember. He locks her in her room at night and avoids her during the day. As much as she wants to trust the man she's fallen in love with, she finds it increasingly hard to do that. He is behaving like someone with a secret held to his bosom. Today, Eselda allows her anger to smolder and get the better of her.

The woman who was once queen catches her reflection in a metal pot hanging upside down on a rack near her head. Her dark curls are a tangled mess around her shoulders, her eyes are wide and frantic. She leans closer to the reflection. *My eyes are so dark.* Once green and sparkling, they are closer to black now. She knows Tin's eyes used to cloud when he was in the throes of his age marker. Perhaps her anger controls her now?

Eselda closes her eyes and takes a deep breath. She wills herself to be logical and sane. When she opens her eyes again, they are a little lighter. She smiles at the change. *I'm not completely hopeless, I can control this thing.*

"Eselda, you were looking for me?"

Eselda turns on her heel to find Tin standing in the doorway. For a moment she forgets her anger at the sight of his bare chest shining with sweat. Those amazing eyes are alight with passion. "I have been searching for days. Where have you been?" the question comes out breathy.

"Running an army." Tin practically rolls his eyes. "What did you need?"

"I just want to talk with you. Can we please sit?" Eselda can see from the expression on his face that Tin has no desire to sit here and have a conversation with her. *What happened to us?* "Please, Tin. I will make us some tea."

She turns to make the tea and hears the scraping of a chair on the floor. When she spins again he is seated but he has plastered a condescending look on his face. Clearly having a conversation with her is not a priority. "Thank you for sitting. I needed to ask you about a few things that have been slowly coming back to me." Eselda quickly rushes on before Tin can interject and make her start to forget things again. "First the lands. Will you consider giving control of Enchenda back to me?"

"No," Tin barks.

Eselda is shocked at the immediate refusal. She expected him to ask why, she expected discussion. "Not at all? Tin, they are my lands by birthright. I know you were worried about my age marker but I've learned self-control." She is thinking, of course, of the way she controlled it just before his entrance.

"I have as much royal blood as you. They were given to me legally and I will keep them. I'm trying to grow my lands here, Eselda, not give them away."

"That is cruel. You are being cruel." Eselda works as much insult into the sentence as she can. Her anger begins to sneak back in.

Tin sees the black swirls start to swim around her eyes like smoke. He laughs. The sound sends shivers down Eselda's spine. "I've been called worse," he says.

"Why are you being so heartless?" Tears work their way up Eselda's throat and threaten to fall from her eyes. She is aware that she sounds whiny and young, but it is the sound of heartbreak. *Who is he? Which is the true Tin: the one I love or this cruel version?*

"We are in the middle of a war. If I allow myself to be full of heart then it will break it that we are killing innocent Fraunians. Heartless is the only way I can survive right now." The answer has an air of honesty that makes Eselda's heart ache for the man she thought he was.

"I will not take much of your time, then. I have only one other question."

"Is it important for the decision of your loyalty?" The ultimatum he gave her the last time they spoke is clear although he does not repeat it; choose sides, quickly.

"Yes. Do you know what happened to the prince?" Eselda asks meekly.

"Yes."

Eselda waits for him to elaborate. He does not. Instead, he puts his hands on the table as if to push himself up.

"Did you kill him?" The question leaves her before she can stop it, in a rush.

He freezes, his palms still flat on the table. He leans toward her, staring at her as though trying to categorize her age marker's characteristics. A smile breaks out on his face. Something in his expression snaps with that smile and his mask falls away. "I was beginning to think you were never going to ask me that." Even his voice is different. No longer does Tin purr at Eselda with control. This is the Tin of her nightmares.

"You're pleased I asked?" she asks. Her voice quakes on the question. For the first time, Eselda is aware she choose a room full of knives for this confrontation. Her adrenaline spikes. She can feel her heart in her wrist beating below the surface like thunder.

"Yes. I hate lying. I killed him," Tin answers. Eselda feels the room start to spin. "I slit his throat with a kitchen knife and watched him bleed all over the floor." Tin sounds proud of the act. Eselda's hand flies to her mouth in an attempt to contain the vomit that threatens to come out.

"You know something else, my love?" Tin asks. Somehow he makes the last two words of the question ring with contempt. He leans closer still until he is practically whispering into her ear. "I would do it again."

Eselda whimpers. "Why?" It is the only word her mouth will form.

"I needed you. I could not let him have you."

The comment holds no romance, it confuses Eselda. "You did this for love?" The idea that such a disgraceful act could be done in the name of love has her stomach turning. She wants to close her eyes, to disappear from this. Instead, she allows her anger to flood in so she has the strength to stare straight at him.

"I didn't do it for love." Tin rises. "I did it for land. I needed Enchenda and I got it. So I guess I should say thank you."

The dam holding her beast back shatters. Tin watches as Eselda's eyes turn dark and her jaw clenches. Although her head is buzzing, she finds she can ignore it if she tries. She takes a step toward him and her hand brushes the handle of a knife nearby on the counter. Without thinking, acting only on instinct, she wraps her fingers tightly around the shaft of the weapon. She brings her hand up beside her.

Tin grabs her wrist. "You judge me?" he asks quietly, fixing her with a deadly stare. "You think me a bad person for what I did to Carsen when I was of a malicious age, but here you are intending to do the exact same to me." He uses his strong grip to bring her knife-wielding hand up between their eyes as if to show her what she had been trying to do.

Her eyes register the light bouncing off the blade. *Is this what revenge feels like?* "I wasn't …" Eselda stutters. "I didn't want to … I don't …" In truth, she can't imagine ever actually killing anyone. *It would make me a terrible person.* She opens her hand and the knife clatters loudly to the floor between them. *What does that make Tin?*

"You don't have the strength." He drops her wrist and turns to go. At the door, he knocks twice. "I'm glad we've had this conversation, Eselda." He smiles as the door opens and a soldier steps into the kitchen. "Everything between us is out in the open now and you have chosen sides. Of course, you chose wrong. But that is the beauty of choice, I suppose." He turns to the soldier. "Take her to her room and lock her in there. No one is to let her out without word from me."

"What do you intend to do with me?" Eselda asks, raising her chin in challenge. The soldier snags her arms and pulls them behind her back. Afraid of her violent anger, Eselda lets the soldier restrain her.

Tin steps forward until their noses are practically touching. He feels the age marker flare up at her proximity, but he combats it. Eselda notices the change in his eyes, which darken as they used to in anger. "I don't know yet, but I need you out of my way."

"Will you kill me?" she asks.

"Perhaps."

Eselda leans a little closer to Tin, showing him she is not afraid. "You don't have it in you to kill me yourself, that's what this is." She knows the challenge will anger him. She watches his eyes carefully, they do not darken further. They actually lighten. Knowledge files itself in her brain. The eyes show the age marker. He wanted to touch her then but now it has passed. She swallows in a gulp. This anger before her now is all Tin.

"You're a fool. I will kill you myself when I no longer need you." He pushes her back and steps toward the door. His heart pounds. That small touch as he shoved her was not enough. He has been starving himself from physical contact and now his body demands release. He balls his fists, focusing on the pain of digging his nails into the fleshy palms.

"Do you even fight with your army or are you too much of a coward for that too?" Eselda yells. It feels good to channel her anger at something, even if that something could easily overpower or kill her.

"Why do you care?" He reaches for the door to put space between them.

"I've had a dream about you fighting, you know. I see you for what you really are in the dream." This stops him halfway to the door with his hand out for the knob. "I see fear all over your face, you are running from an attacker," Eselda says. "You put on a strong face, King of Sarcheda, but inside you are just weak. I see that now."

The words slice Tin worse than the knife would have. He turns to glare at Eselda. "Your dreams mean nothing." He spits. "Take her to the room and lock the door."

Outside the kitchen, Tin takes deep breaths. He knows he should've killed her right then and there. He was terrified that his body wouldn't let him complete the act. The age marker forces him to feel such power from her touch that he fears he could not overcome that. *What would that have looked like to the soldier watching?* The soldier brings up a new problem. Tin flags down another soldier passing the hallway. "You there. Eselda from Enchenda is being locked in her room. See to it that it gets done right. Then kill the soldier with her."

"Majesty?" The word is a question, a chance to back out.

"You heard me. The man questioned my authority. You will kill him, make an example of him. Are we clear?"

"Yes, Majesty." The soldier bows low.

"Thank you. When it is done you personally will take the post outside her bedroom door. She is to be fed twice a day. Do not talk to her, do not feel sorry for her. If anything out of the ordinary happens, you have my permission to kill her. Are we clear?"

"Yes sir." The soldier bows again.

"Good. What are you waiting for?" Tin bellows. Tin closes his eyes, breathing in the one idea that can calm him.

One Fraun. One Fraun. One Fraun.

Chapter 40

"No no no no no." Toby steps in between us, stopping the practice blade with his left hand. "Jordyn when you step toward the other fighter you put your feet close together. This puts you off balance." Toby twists his arm and pulls the sword out of my grasp. Flipping it he demonstrates; mirroring the move but keeping his feet shoulder-width apart. "Now when Lance comes back with his move I'll be ready to parry."

"Got it." I take the blade back, sigh, and prepare myself again. "I'm ready." I plant my feet like I watched Toby do, matching his arm motions as well. Toby claps me on the shoulder, smiling.

"There, see. You're a fast learner. We've earned a break," Lance says. The three of us move to the side of the clearing and take a seat. I take a pull from a cold water container and pass it around.

The sun is directly overhead and we are sweating through our shirts. We have been at the practice since we woke today, just as we were yesterday and the day before. My arms hurt in places I didn't know I had muscles. The sword is not heavy, but the amount of time you spend holding it upright is exhausting. I have picked up the basics quickly, although not as quickly as Toby.

"I thought you said I wouldn't really be combating for long during a sword fight anyway." I address Lance. "You said most sword fights are over with a single blow."

"True. Against inexperienced fighters, you will be able to injure or kill on the first attack," Lance answers.

"So why do we worry about me being able to fend off the next blow? Shouldn't our focus be on learning where I want my first strike to land?"

"Yes," Toby says. I turn my head to face Toby. "But if you fail to land your first strike you have to be ready to fend off the next attack. Otherwise, they will end it with their first strike." Toby gulps the water. "And trust me when I tell you Sarcheda will not be trained to injure rather than kill."

"Besides …" Lance cuts in, "… Tin is anything but an inexperienced fighter. He trained me."

"You two aren't exactly making me feel confident," I say.

Toby shrugs.

The sound of footsteps crashing through underbrush saves the men from having to boost my confidence. All three of us rise, Lance grabbing a sharpened blade from the ground beside him and holding it by his side. His muscles tense, ready to raise the blade at the first hint of trouble.

A roach enters the clearing bearing a small man with light brown hair, some kind of twisted metal on his face, and a frantically worried expression. "I'm looking for Sawchett," the man calls, leaping from the back of the roach.

Toby steps between the man and Lance's expertly wielded weapon. "Tutor? You need to calm down, friend. What's going on?"

"Sawchett, I need to find her. I know she's here, Toby. Where is she?"

"She's fine, calm down." Toby reaches for Tutor to restrain him. Tutor ducks under the arm.

Lance, glad to have Toby clear of harm's way, holds the blade out toward Tutor. "Hey now, my friend asked you what you're doing here. Care to answer that question?" Lance holds Tutor's gaze and the blade steady.

Tutor puts his arms up. "Not exactly the welcome I was expecting."

"Yeah, well, there's a war going on out there. Tell us why you're looking for the girl," Lance demands.

"She's in danger," Tutor answers, his eyes flashing.

"From who?" Toby asks.

Tutor turns his head slightly to the right to answer without impaling himself on the blade. "King Tin of Sarcheda."

"Do you work for him?" Lance asks, the blade twitching slightly.

"No." The men stand as still as an engraving; Tutor with his arms up and breathing heavily, Toby behind Tutor with his arm still reaching toward the man, and Lance with the blade pointed at Tutor's chest. I take a step forward into Tutor's line of vision.

"The girl is fine, I assure you." I can feel control of the stalemate pass to me. Lance lowers the blade but makes no move to put it away.

Recognition dawns on Tutor's face as he looks me up and down. He tips his head in a low bow, almost from habit. "How can I be sure you don't lie for him?" he asks.

"For Tin?" I laugh out loud. "I would rather die than lie for that man." I grab the water bottle. "Now why don't you sit down here and tell us what's going on." I take a long sip of the cold liquid.

"I need to see Sawchett," Tutor repeats.

"Perhaps you will, once we hear your story." My voice leaves no room for doubt. Shrugging, Tutor sits on the ground facing me. The other men remain standing, all eyes on Tutor.

"My name is Tutor. I am from …" Tutor hesitates, "… Fraun," he finishes, lamely.

"You know Eselda." What probably should have been a question leaves me as a statement. Tutor merely nods.

"He's spent some time here with us as well," Toby offers.

"Is that so?" I ask. "When was this?"

"I was in the service of Enchenda, tutoring Eselda, for many annuals. That service had gaps toward the end. I spent some of that time among the scouts." Tutor tries for a weak smile. His nerves about his new situation get in the way and the expression comes off more like a scowl.

"Tell me what you're doing here," I demand.

"I have learned something about the girl's heritage that cannot be ignored. It makes her vulnerable to Tin." Tutor's voice quavers.

I exchange a glance with Toby and then Lance. The man is hiding something he will not reveal with all of us present. "Jordyn, I'm going to go check on the girl. I'll inform Franc of our friend here. If you need anything, just yell." Toby leaves the clearing, clearly understanding my nonverbal message.

"Do you need me?" Lance inquires.

"You're welcome to stay if you'd like. I have no secrets," I answer.

"We know that, Jordyn. But I think this man would feel better telling whatever it is he's hiding to a smaller audience." Lance pats me on the back on his way out of the clearing.

"Alright, you heard them. What's going on?" I prompt when we are alone.

Tutor shrugs. "I suppose I can't outrun this forever."

"Outrun what?"

"My past." He wipes his face with his hand. "Do you know who I am? I mean, do you know anything about me at all? You know that I knew Eselda, that tells me that you have heard of me. I only wonder what you already know so I don't have to repeat things and waste time."

I smile at Tutor. If we are to have an honest conversation, we will need a catalyst. Clearly, it will have to be me. "I know you were raised by a family that is not your own. I know you were brought to Renchenda when you were around ten and given to another family because of something your first adoptive family learned about your past. I know you excelled at our schools. I know you wanted to join the scouts and the scouts took you on a tour of the realms. I know you've never been to Sarcheda. I know you took a job as a tutor in Enchenda. I learned all this from my research of you, which I conducted for Eselda," I say.

Tutor is impressed. "All that is accurate, but for our purposes, we will need to discuss my birth family."

"Fair enough."

"My mother fell in love with the prince of Enchenda when she was a girl." Tutor settles himself in to give voice to the hidden story. "She knew he was the prince, of course, but she never knew her secret. For lunar cycles they traipsed around the town, completely infatuated with each other. Prince Gregario became so sure he loved my mother that he decided to introduce her to the king." Something like a chuckle bubbles out of Tutor's mouth.

"The king took one look at her and lost his cool. Can you imagine how shocked you would be if the secret you buried came home with your son? You see, annuals past the king had impregnated two women. My grandmother and Gregario's mother. He had kept the child a secret. Yet here was his son bringing home the one woman in town that he simply could not have. The king was beside himself with rage.

"The king sat Prince Gregario down and told him the truth. I won't pretend to know how that story went. What I do know is that my mother was introduced to a man working in the royal home. His name was Den. They fell in love, got married, and promised never to have children because of her bloodline." At this, Tutor looks up and meets my eyes for the first time. "I am proof that they lied about that." He drops his eyes back to the dirt.

"You are their son?"

Tutor nods. "I never knew. My father was fired a few annuals before I took the job in Enchenda. By the time I arrived there, they were just a nice family who offered to help me out. I took the job working with Eselda. After Den died Charlotte eventually admitted she was my mother but I kept that pretty quiet. I still never knew about her blood."

"How did you find out about that?" I ask, unable to contain my legendary curiosity.

"Eselda."

My smile is genuine this time. "Her curiosity pales only when compared with mine."

This earns a chuckle from Tutor. "Eselda met my mother. She heard the whole tale and then asked me for my opinion." Tutor's eyes trace up to the sky as he leans back on his palms. "I still remember how shocked I was when she told me the name that was missing from the wall was Charlotte. I felt like a bomb had exploded right there in the royal dining room." He looks at me. "It was the second most shocking thing that has ever happened to me."

"The second?"

"Believe it or not, the first came just a few days ago." He sighs. "A man came to see me. He was tasked with updating lineage charts."

"I can't imagine that would still be necessary, Enchenda has fallen," I state, adding up the facts and concluding that Tutor must have been visited by someone from that realm.

"Actually, I was hired to update for Enchenda. This man was from Marchenda." He chuckles. "That shock you are showing on your face is exactly what I felt myself. As it turns out, my father's grandmother was shunned in Marchenda. She had royal blood in her veins that she never told her son about. Her son, not knowing he wasn't common, moved to Enchenda. He got married and had my father."

I lean on my elbow and rub my face. "You have two bloodlines in you."

"Marchenda and Enchenda."

"You are aware of what this means?" I ask.

"I think so. I have within me the rights to overthrow any seated king from either realm by virtue of my majority blood. Is that right?"

"Yes." I nod solemnly. I easily read the expression on the face of the shorter man. "Am I correct in assuming this is something you don't want?"

His sigh is deeper than River Fraun. He puts his fingers on his forehead, pushing as though relieving pressure. "My grandfather threw my mother out like common trash. My mother gave me away to a strange family to hide me. My adoptive family passed me off to another when I became a burden to them. Enchenda may be family, but that word means nothing to me. I owe Fraun nothing." Tutor's jaw is squared, he is daring me to argue with him.

"You won't find disagreement from me."

"Thank you." When Tutor slips into silence, I match it. The silence wraps around the clearing. Around us, the sounds of leaves waving in the light breeze pick up. "How rare is this?" he quietly asks.

"Rare, but not unheard of." I clear my throat. "I have the blood of Renchenda and Farcheda in my veins." Tutor's eyebrows raise in shock. "It is generations removed, unlike yours."

"That explains the charm." Tutor indicates the small silver coin at my throat. The symbol of a lightning bolt is scratched into the round surface.

I glance down at the object. "The symbol of Farcheda on one

side." I flip the coin to reveal a crude tree hastily etched. "Renchenda on the other." Out of habit, I slip the charm below my shirt collar so only a thin chain is visible.

"Do you think me a coward for wanting to hide this from Fraun?" Tutor questions.

"How could I? Look around you, Tutor. I have as much royal blood as you and yet here I sit. I ran from my title as well. You will find no judgment here."

"Do you know what I hate the most?" Tutor asks. I shake my head. "They were so quick to throw me away, to hide me. But when my sister was born they kept her." He shakes his head. "My sister was raised by our parents. When my mother became too ill to care for her, my sister was brought into the royal home and raised as a princess."

Sister? I begin adding the clues but do not interrupt the emotional tale to ask for confirmation.

"No one ever told me about the age markers. No one ever told me that what I was feeling was because of them. I battled my dark age in secret, exactly like my family condemned me to battle it."

"You have every reason to be upset by that." I know that my own tale would help Tutor feel close to me, but it is not the time to share it.

"I almost fell into the same trap my poor mother fell into." He chuckles again, an empty sound. "I never admitted that to anyone before."

"What trap is that?"

His eyes land on my face. I can clearly read his anger and sadness etched in all his features. "I started to have feelings for her. No one told me she was my cousin. No one told me it wasn't acceptable. I mean, I knew I was her tutor, but I didn't know …" he lets his voice evaporate.

"Eselda?" It comes out as a question, but I already know the answer. There is no one else in our kingdom who would fit this bill.

"Yeah." The word is a sigh, sad and deep. He returns his gaze to the woods.

"I'm sorry. How old are you now?" I have seen no sign of darkening in the brown eyes behind the glass even as Tutor's anger has built. He should be out of the malicious marker.

"Twenty-six."

"Do you feel the pull of the next age marker?" I ask from my desire for answers as much as from my desire to help.

"Not as much as the last. I felt constant desires to fight or punch something, although I didn't know what it was. This one is more mild, controlled."

"That's good to know. I have time left in this one, I fear."

"You handle it well, from what I can tell," Tutor says.

"Thank you. That means a lot. It is a lot of work some days." I offer a weak smile. "Tutor, my friend, you have unloaded a lot today. Tell me, what would you like me to do with this information? Do I bury what I know of your blood?"

"Marchenda has other heirs, a cousin of the king and her daughter. Enchenda has fallen—"

"Enchenda has been absorbed," I say.

Tutor meets my gaze. He must read my excitement, but not understand it. He squints in confusion. "Does that distinction matter?"

"It absolutely does. A ruler from Enchenda with a blood majority over the present ruler of that land could still stake claim to that throne."

A flash of lightning bursts through the darkness of Tutor's past and illuminates everything. I see the moment he grasps the knowledge. "I can overthrow Tin?" It is a question as much as a comment, and for the first time since sitting down to speak with me, excitement trickles into his tone.

"You could and, if I'm correct in my assumptions, Sawchett could as well."

"We could fix this?" Tutor asks, leaning forward.

"We could." I smile at the use of the shared pronoun.

"I would be a terrible king," Tutor starts, shaking his head. "But I would be better than him."

"I think I agree with you on that last point."

"What do we do?" Tutor asks, suddenly on board with the plan. "What happens next?"

"We meet the scouts. We get their opinion. This is not a one-person operation, Tutor." I clap the older man on the shoulder as we both rise. "That's what makes us better than him."

Chapter 41

Eselda's eyes flutter open to reveal the clearing that is becoming familiar. She looks down to find she is wearing the simple black dress she fell asleep in, her bare feet touching the cold grass. "The dream," she mutters. This dream keeps coming back to her as though it is trying to unlock something in her brain. A determination grips her. *I will learn something new this time.* She closes her eyes, breathing in the clues in the air.

The wind has that familiar burning in her nostrils signaling cold weather. She can smell the vegetation but it smells different than the woods around Enchenda. Her eyes open again. *Perhaps this is not the same woods?* She ignores Tin as he crashes into the clearing. *He is a part of the dream I have paid attention to before.*

Eselda crosses the clearing, focusing her eyes on the spot where the other man will emerge. This time around she fully intends to learn something from the other fighter. She waits in silence, listening for the sound of crashing footsteps. She does not have to wait long.

As before the fighter is faceless, but there are other things to notice about him. Eselda takes in all she can as the fight commences. He is not wearing the colors of Sarcheda. He wears armor that is somehow more shoddy than Tin's. She can see the brown clothing underneath, it appears to be thin and patchy.

The fight approaches the point where Eselda remembers it ending, with Tin backing up the other fighter to the tree. Eselda almost wishes she could control the dream and move the tree. The man's back hits up against it directly next to where Eselda is standing. Tin delivers his line, "Well isn't this interesting? I seem to have you backed against a wall here, old friend." He plunges the sword into his opponent.

This time when Eselda wakes, it is a bit calmer. She takes one deep gasping breath and then her eyes adjust to her surroundings. She is on the floor near the door of her bedroom in Sarcheda, where she has been locked for some time. She cannot tell the time in here, as there is no window.

She has tried everything. Banging on the door, screaming for help, begging the man who brings her food. Once, in desperation, she even tried seducing the man who brings her food. It didn't work and he hasn't been back. Which means she is now hungry and locked up.

Eselda glances down at her bloody hands. Her knuckles split open some time ago whilst she was banging on the hard wooden door. There is nothing in here with which she can clean it off, so they continue to bleed and dry up. Eselda tries to spit on the back of her hand and wipe off the newest layer of blood, but she is too dehydrated and no water falls from between her lips.

She sighs and drops her hands to her sides again. The dream will give her something else to focus on besides self-pity. She thinks it through. *Somehow the forest was different than what I grew up with. Where else in Fraun is there a forest? Renchenda has one. Perhaps this dream is happening outside of Renchenda.*

The armor of the other man tells her he is a representative of Fraun, not of Tin's army. This gives her hope for a second until she realizes that twice in this dream she has seen Tin kill the man. *This cannot be good. Tin does not enter into fights, he allows his army to do that. If Tin were in a fight, surely this would mean that the other man was important.*

I continue to dream about an important man being killed for Fraun in Renchenda. How depressing.

Perhaps I know the man. Could I warn him? Would he need to be warned?

Eselda shakes her head against the buzzing that is beginning. She is finding it possible to overcome the distracter that is her age marker when she has a clear task and she approaches it logically. *Focus, Eselda. Something must have given you a clue about who this man could be.*

She can recall the exact moment in the dream when the sword plunges into the stranger. Tin, leaning back on his right leg, had used all his impressive strength to push the sword upward into the man's chest. She shudders at the memory. The look of determination on Tin's face from the angle she saw it this time was nothing short of abhorrent.

Tin stabbed upward. She closes her eyes and brings the images back. She had been standing beside the man, taking in his appearance. *Yes, he was taller than me. Much taller. I came up to only his shoulder, perhaps.* Tin as well, when he approached, was a full head shorter than this mystery man.

I search for someone tall and important in Renchenda.

Eselda's mind drifts, obviously, to Jordyn. She shakes her head at the empty room. "No, Jordyn doesn't fight for anything," she reminds herself, feeling the frustration grow. *Thometh is tall,* she recalls. *Not as tall as Jordyn but tall enough to be the man in the dream. Perhaps it is Thometh. Thometh will challenge Tin to a duel.*

Could Tin be that afraid of Thometh? Eselda has a hunch that he could be. The man resides in the castle and could well control the council fighting against Tin. She wants to be excited about this turn of events, but how can her excitement hold up when the dream continues to end with Thometh's death?

"There has to be a way out of this," she whines. Eselda has spent her time coming to terms with her involvement in this war She has learned that she cannot forgive herself for what she has done. At this point, it would be in the best interest of Fraun if Eselda and Tin were both taken out of their future. She has already decided that if she can find a way out of this room she will end it for Tin, even if it means she takes herself out with him.

The dream tells her what she already knows. Thometh and his council, the true Fraun, fight against Tin at all costs. They will battle with their lives. Without Eselda figuring a way out of this room and intervening, they will not survive. Her dream tells her that her subconscious believes Tin will be triumphant. Eselda silently vows to do whatever she can to change that. *But what can I do?*

Her brain, usually adept at feeding her ideas and thoughts, goes silent in response to the question. *What can I do?* There are literally no ideas.

But Tin is afraid.

That is something else her subconscious is trying to tell me and it could be important. Tin is afraid of the real Fraun. He may put up a good front, but deep down he is terrified of what they will do to him if they win. If she can only find a way to get him face-to-face with her, she could use this fear. Isn't that what she has learned from Tin; how to play up someone's fear to your advantage? She merely has to get to him.

But that is a problem. Tin hasn't been to see her since the kitchen. *When I wrapped my hand around the warm handle of a knife and thought it could be the end of my problems. When my subconscious tried to tell me that Tin is better off dead than at the helm of the army he controls.* "I should've listened to my body then." She allows herself the fantasy of imagining how different things would be right now if she had just followed through. The soldier could've been bent to listen to reason upon the death of his king. She would've controlled the army and could have made them fall back.

Of course, that would also mean I would be a murderer. The weight of that is crushing. It's not the act of actually killing Tin, which she has learned she is perfectly capable of if it serves Fraun, it is the guilt afterward. *Could I continue to wake up every morning remembering the face of Tin as I killed him? The face of him from my dream striking his sword into someone else is bad enough. Can I really stoop to his level?*

That is why she hopes someone takes her life after she takes Tin's.

Chapter 42

The silence of the night slips into the circle of scouts following Jordyn's recounting of the tale. Tutor found that he couldn't bear to share the story of his lineage again, and Jordyn offered to take that part of the explanation. Now Tutor can feel the judgment from the others falling on his chest. He swallows and forces himself to look around the circle.

To his immediate left sits Toby, whom Tutor knows from previous excursions. Toby is a good man. He has a quick temper when something doesn't fit his sense of loyalty, but he is hard to shake once he trusts you. Toby and Tutor have had their skirmishes in the past, but he knows he will find support from this man today.

He turns his head to his right, where Jordyn sits. Jordyn is the epitome of confidence, sitting up straight and smiling toward the flames of the fire warming the cool night air. To Jordyn's right in the circle, Abney restrings a bow. The blonde ringlets that frame the delicate face are in contrast to the speed with which she expertly strings the bow. She proves that it is dangerous and deadly to judge by appearance. Tutor cannot tell her reaction to his news, but she looks deep in thought.

To her right sits Sieven. His tan face looks eager and he offers Tutor a smile when their eyes meet. To his right, Lili sits absentmindedly braiding something. Tutor is not sure the woman has even been listening to the tale. He can hear someone lightly humming and highly suspects it is her.

Lance reclines next to Lili, leaning back on his hands. His eyes are turned up to the night sky and his feet are stretched out before him toward the fire. Lance will support him as well, Jordyn has assured him. Lance was a former member of the Sarcheda army who has recently defected to be with the scouts.

Next his eyes take in Evelyn and Kurt, sitting side by side and holding hands. Tutor smiles at the couple. *To know love like that* … he muses. Shaking his head to relieve it of such thoughts he looks to the next pair, Carlina and Franc. She is resting her head on his shoulder. Her thick braid is pulled to the front and she uses it like a pillow. She chews her fingernail in thought.

Lastly, his eyes fall on Sawchett. The girl sits with her skinny knees drawn up and her head resting on them. She looks as though the news shocks her. Tutor is seized by a desire to wrap her in a comforting squeeze. He puts his hands on the ground beside him, intending to push himself to his feet. "Well, I say welcome to the group, boy." Franc's booming voice startles Tutor, causing him to jump.

He decides to remain seated. "Thank you," he stammers.

"What's the plan?" Lili quietly asks, her eyes never leaving the braiding.

"The first thing we should do is talk to the council." Jordyn's voice echoes with authority.

No one argues his point. "They need to be aware that we support them. The only way to do this is to discuss our plan, in its entirety, with them. I do not want to rebuild Fraun on secrets."

"I agree," Toby speaks up. "King Mick is pigheaded. We need him to see that we don't work against him."

"Oh." Tutor is the only one to catch the mistake. "Mick is no longer King of Farcheda."

"What?" Jordyn looks aghast.

"His oldest son Hector assumed the throne after the death of his son," Tutor explains.

"How exactly does one assume the throne of a king?" The question comes from Evelyn. "I feel, in light of your lineage story, this is something we all need to learn."

Tutor decides to take the answer here to show the troop that he plans to be as much a part of this as Jordyn. "Normally anyone of royal blood in a realm can challenge a current seated king for his throne. The king is under no obligation, however, to give it up. He can do one of two things. He can willingly give the throne to the challenger—"

"Why would he do that?" Toby asks.

"Either because it's best for Fraun, as I did," Jordyn answers, "Or because they were coerced into doing so by the challenger."

Tutor continues, "For whatever reason, the king could give it willingly, or it goes before council. If it goes before council then the two present their case and the council votes on it. A majority vote takes the throne."

"But in your case, we wouldn't need to do that?" Evelyn prompts.

"No. If a challenger has what we call majority blood, more bloodlines than the current seated king, the king has no choice but to abdicate his throne," Jordyn answers.

"We are sure, then, that Tin has only one line?" Kurt asks.

"Positive. No one from Sarcheda would taint their blood by mixing it with another bloodline," Toby answers.

"How did this Hector character assume the throne then?" Franc asks.

"In Farcheda we heard he challenged his father and the old man backed down," Tutor answers.

"That seems out of character for Mick," Jordyn states.

"I thought so too. Perhaps there is more to that tale," Tutor answers quietly. "Either way, you'll be seeing Hector at council when you go there."

"We will go together. I believe it would be best to send at least two of us," Jordyn announces.

"Tutor and Jordyn will go," Franc says. "If there are no objections." After a beat, it becomes clear there are none. Tutor feels a swell of pride at the show of support and faith in him.

"Well, then the next thing I think we should do, once we've gone to council, is rescue Eselda from the home in Sarcheda." Jordyn's intensity sucks the air from the group. Everyone turns to him.

"Our biggest concern is the girl?" Abney asks.

"As far as I'm concerned, yes. If we do not get her out, Tin will kill her." Jordyn tries to conceal the emotions building, but the anger shows in his eyes which darken. Even in the firelight, Tutor can see the change.

Lance sighs and turns his chin downward, away from the sky, so he is facing the assemblage. "I fear that may not be possible. Eselda seemed to be in favor of this war. She seemed less like a slave to Tin's whim and more like a willing party. Have you considered that she may not want to be rescued?"

"I had heard, as well, that she sides with Sarcheda." Tutor's voice cracks, although whether with emotion or lack of use, he's not sure.

"We rescue her," Jordyn barks the command and his eyes flash again. The comment echoes through the small clearing, bouncing off trees.

"Does your age marker—" Tutor is intent upon questioning this turn of emotion.

Jordyn waves him off dismissively. "We owe her the chance to get out," he says, his voice somehow softer and more controlled.

"Alright, assuming she can be pulled away, what comes next once we have her?" Carlina asks.

This time it is Tutor who answers. "Tin must be challenged, publicly."

"How will you accomplish that?" Toby asks.

"It will need to be in front of his army. We should challenge him to a duel or something, get him in front of all his men, and then challenge his throne. Maybe we'll be able to win a few over to our side. The rest we fight. Tin has to be taken out," Tutor explains.

"That'll be harder than you think. Tin doesn't fight," Lance reveals.

"Bloody coward." Franc looks appalled.

"He can't even fight his own war?" Kurt's disgust fills his every word as though the actions of Tin are poison in his mouth.

"How are we to draw him out then?" Sieven asks his first interjection into the conversation. Tutor notes the boy's voice rings with confidence.

"He won't back down from me," Jordyn's voice is quiet, yet undaunted.

"So, Jordyn will challenge Tin to a duel and Tutor can talk to the army. The rest of us should be ready to fight those that remain," Kurt summarizes.

"I will fight," Sieven announces.

This, finally, draws Lili's eyes from the braid. She sensibly looks her son up and down. "Do you fight for the honor of Fraun?" she inquires.

"Yes, mother."

"So be it." Her eyes track back down as her fingers resume their weaving.

"You can't be serious," Abney says, her eyes rolling. "You're terrible with a bow, what good will you be? You'll only get yourself killed, Sieven." A trace of fear creeps into her voice.

"I'm good with a sword, ask Lance," the boy grumbles.

"He's not wrong," Lance says.

"What happens if you die?" Abney pushes.

"What happens if anyone of us dies?" Sieven counters. "The rest of us will just have to pick up and move on."

"But that's not the plan, Sieven." Abney's voice grows uncharacteristically shrill.

"What plan, dear?" Evelyn asks, leaning toward her daughter.

"The plan was for all of us to take up arms for Fraun. Sieven seems to be following that," Kurt adds.

"No, Sieven was supposed to stay safe. He has to survive," Abney yells, her eyes beginning to fill with tears.

"Abney, I'll be fine." Sieven reaches a calm hand out in Abney's direction. "It'll be even better because I will be there to make sure you survive. Nothing has changed." Tutor can tell there is something more passing between the pair than their words imply but their parents seem baffled.

"Sieven I cannot live in Fraun alone after the war. I'm scared," Abney says.

"Who said anything about living in Fraun?" Evelyn asks. "You can live wherever you'd like."

"Abney and I have decided we want to live in Fraun after this is over." Sieven reaches out and grabs the girl's hand, squeezing tight. "Together."

It takes a second for the news to be processed. When it finally is, Tutor sees excitement light up the eyes of all in the group. As if they share one brain everyone rises and wraps the two little lovebirds in a bone-crushing group hug. Tutor awkwardly stands on the outside, rubbing his arms. He notices Lance, similarly standing on the other side of the circle.

"I guess this is why we are fighting." Lance smiles, once the hug has dissipated. Abney and Sieven, a little redder than before, still have their arms wrapped around each other. Lance raises a bottle of water. "To the future of love and Fraun," he calls.

It is a good reminder for Tutor that this is not about him or his family issues. This is about the future. As the celebration builds Tutor looks to Sawchett. Although he was told the truth, the girl knew him only as a tutor, never as a brother. Her shock must be deep. He pulls her aside. "What are you thinking, Sawchett? This was big news for you today." Tutor offers her a smile.

The girl raises tired eyes to her brother. "I'm okay." She smiles. "I guess I don't feel like much has changed for me. Except that I have a brother."

"Do you think of me that way?" He thinks of all the years he had grown up without anyone. It is hard to accept that Sawchett is a part of him when it took so long for her to come into his life.

"I've always thought of you like that. Now I just have a reason," she answers.

"That's nice to hear. I guess I have always felt like it was my duty to protect and care for you."

"Now you have a reason as well." She shrugs. "Although I can take care of myself."

Tutor laughs, glad for the release. "I have no doubt that you can." He bends, kissing the hair at the top of her head. "Good night little sister."

Chapter 43

"Good morning, Tutor." I am unsurprised to see my tortured new friend has arisen before me. We are scheduled to head to the council meeting today, which I know will begin at high sun. This morning the sun has not yet risen in the sky, and the fire Tutor is building will be our only source of light or warmth as we get ready for the journey.

"Morning, Jordyn." Tutor looks up from the budding flames only long enough to smile quickly.

"Are you feeling alright about our journey today? Are you nervous at all about speaking to the council?" I ask, taking a seat by the flames and starting to pull some grapes off a nearby bunch.

"I'm not nervous. It's a good plan we came up with, I'm sure the council will be glad for the support."

"Is Hector a good man? I don't recall much about him."

"I don't know much about him either. He was often seen about the realm, which means he's likely a very hands-on ruler. The death of his son may have changed him though."

"It's why Lance left, you know," I drop the statement casually.

"What?" Confusion fills Tutor's face.

"He watched the Sarcheda army kill the young boy and felt immense grief over the death. It is wrong to kill such a young child. Lance could not be a party to that," I explain.

"That is an interesting fact."

Sawchett enters the clearing from the direction of her tent. She is yawning and rubbing her eyes. "Good morning boys." The words are pushed out of her mouth on the exhale of her large yawn.

"What are you doing up so early?" I ask, turning around to see who approaches.

Sawchett flops down onto the ground beside me and yawns again. "I'm going with you two."

"No, you certainly are not." Tutor rolls his eyes. "You will be safe right here in the forest."

"Look, Tutor, I appreciate your concern but I need to go with you. The fact is I have as much royal blood in my veins as either of you has. If something should happen to you two they will need me to challenge Tin for his throne. I want to find someplace safe to stay in Fraun while I await my part in all of this." Sawchett's words are devoid of her usual whine.

Tutor opens his mouth to argue with her.

"I know a safe place you can stay," I state, deterring any squabble Tutor had been preparing.

"She isn't going." Tutor's attempt to remain the deciding factor in this waivers under my calculated gaze. "It's not safe."

"Castle Fraun is perfectly safe. The walls are among the thickest in Fraun and my Uncle will watch over her. I trust him with my life." I communicate my understanding in my crooked smile. "I know you worry, but you would worry even if she were here."

"Besides," Sawchett pushes, "your choice is either to let me go along and stay at the castle or make me stay here. If I stay here I'll force Lance and Toby to train me and I'll join the fight. This is my war too, Tutor."

"You can't argue with that ultimatum." Despite Tutor's obvious discomfort, I have to appreciate the girl's moxie. "She speaks like someone who will be a good queen. Actually, I quite like the idea of starting you in training. Perhaps you can travel under the cover of night."

Tutor sighs heavily, sensing that he cannot win this argument. "Fine. Get yourself ready to go."

Sawchett smiles. "Well chosen, brother." She pauses at the edge of the clearing, just outside the light cast by the fire's glow. "Can I ask you two something?" We both nod and she rushes the words. "I hate that I don't understand all this yet. But, here goes. If all it will take is for someone to challenge Tin's throne, why are we gearing for a fight?"

I roll my neck around like my shoulders are causing pain. "That is a good question. We challenge him for his throne for the council and the citizens of Fraun. I know Tin will not accept that. Tin will fight us to keep it. He long ago gave up on Fraun's rules."

"Are you willing to fight him?" she asks, her voice a whisper.

"I'm willing to do what must be done."

Sawchett accepts this answer. She retreats toward her tent. When we are alone again, Tutor sits back from the flames. The fire has taken on its own life and is giving off plenty of heat. "Are you worried about challenging Tin to a duel?" Tutor picks up Sawchett's line of thinking.

"It would be stupid not to be afraid of him. He's the king of strength. By default, this makes him the strongest man in the realm." I meet Tutor's gaze. I find no judgment in my admission of weakness. "I'm terrified," I admit.

"He's not only strong, he's also unpredictable. That is a dangerous coupling." Tutor winces.

"You refer to his anger? Some of that may have been due to his age marker. Unless my calculations are wrong …"

"Not likely," Tutor mumbles.

"… then he's already moved on to the next marker."

"What if his age had nothing to do with his temper?" Tutor asks.

"What reason would you have to suspect this?"

"They're not my reasons, just something I overheard once. I arrived in Enchenda for my training with Eselda and headed to meet up with her in the dining room, as usual. Instead of finding her, I came upon a door slightly ajar and the voice of Gregario broadcasting into the hallway. From that hiding spot, I overheard Kings Gregario and Mick having a conversation I will never forget. Mick believes that Tin is responsible for the death of his parents," Tutor reveals.

I recall when Tin's parents died, although I was young myself. By now, that was eight annuals ago, when I was fourteen. One night, Tin had been a prince, content to learn the ways of Fraun from a tutor like the rest of us. The next night, he'd been attending council meetings with my mother; a king in a prince's body. At the time it was all incredibly sad. Could a boy really have caused those deaths? "Did Mick have reasons for that accusation?"

"A young boy in the house of Sarcheda was traveling with the royal family one day."

"A servant?" I ask.

"Yes. The boy claims to have seen the events unfold. According to him, Tin ordered the ride be halted near the ravine that circumvents the realm. The boy watched in horror as Tin confronted his parents in anger. His father said something and gestured to the mother. The boy had no memory of what the father said." Tutor swallows hard around the pending truth, the next part of the story is difficult even to retell. "For whatever reason, the boy claims to have watched as Tin put his hands on his mother's shoulders and shoved her to her death."

"What of his father?" I ask, unable to think of anything else to say.

"Evidently, there were more words exchanged before the father fell similarly."

"By his son's hand?"

Tutor nods. "Do you think there is truth to that, Jordyn? You know Tin better than I."

"If this tale is true then I know him not. Killing a man whom you believe to be your competition but have no love for is one thing, monstrous though it is. That act pales in comparison to taking the lives of your own parents, people who raised you and brought you up." I sigh. "Either way, we had better prepare ourselves to visit the council. This rumor only serves to remind me how important it is to take Fraun away from such a man."

"I agree completely, friend." I feel the cold morning air close around my body as I step away from the flames. "It is a relief to share that burden with someone." I hear Tutor say behind me. I smile. Lies are exhausting. I understand that.

Chapter 44

If Thometh, Hector, and Larecio are surprised to see the three scouts enter the stone council building they hide it well. All three faces turn to the newcomers and smiles break out. "Nephew, you've come to join the fray?" Thometh greets me, pumping my hand and smacking me on the shoulder.

"We have come to discuss the plan for the future of Fraun," Tutor answers.

I take in the room, noting that not much has changed. I am glad to see the council has decided to keep the tabletop as it always was. The curved markings surrounding Enchenda still shine a blue that evokes thoughts of River Fraun.

I gesture to the empty chairs which rest against the far wall. Turning my head to address my cohorts, I offer the chairs with a simple nod of my head in the appropriate direction. "Sawchett and Tutor sit, please." I turn back to the kings. "Today I bring with me two members of the scout troop I have been traveling with. These two have learned something interesting about themselves and they'd like to share it with you. Following that, I'd like to share my plan for the future of Fraun. I am pleased to introduce Tutor and his sister, Sawchett." As I walk to take the final empty chair, I gesture to the pair who have seated themselves in Enchenda territory.

Around the table, handshakes are exchanged and I fall into the chair beside my Uncle. This, appropriately, leaves six people crammed around the table and Sarcheda symbolically empty. "Scouts, this is my Uncle, King Thometh of Renchenda." I indicate the tall, weathered man beside me. Uncle Thometh wears royalty well. His blonde hair is a shade darker than my own. This makes it go much nicer with the orange of his realm.

I gesture next to the old man at the table. "This is King Larecio of Marchenda." The cheekbones now stand out from the man's face and his skin has taken on a grey hue. It pains me to see the once great leader as this new shadow.

"I assume, by process of elimination, that you then must be King Hector of Farcheda." I smile at the man. Tall, with dark hair, and brown eyes that tell of his clarity. I like him instantly.

"I assume you are Jordyn, former King of Renchenda." Hector delivers the statement in a careful tone and waits for my nod before continuing. "Pleasure to meet you. What can we help you with today?"

"Actually," Tutor answers, drawing all eyes in the room to him, "we are here to offer our help to you. It has come to our attention that my sister and I are of an unusual bloodline."

"Unusual how?" Hector asks, leaning his cheek on his hand as he puts his elbow down on the table.

"Our mother was royal blood of Enchenda." Tutor holds the gaze of the king, daring him to question.

"How does that help us?" Thometh asks.

"Our father was royal blood of Marchenda," Sawchett speaks up in a clear voice, offering a childish smile to Thometh.

"Who is your father?" questions Larecio.

"Den, grandson of a shunned woman named Spanz," Tutor answers, holding his chin up and facing the old man. Larecio merely nods.

"You have majority blood then." It is a statement, not a question, from Hector.

"We have come to understand it is this majority blood that gives us the right to challenge Tin's throne." Tutor's comment and the substance it carries resonate with all in the room.

"Your blood contains the lines of Enchenda and Marchenda. Tin is ruling in Sarcheda. I fail to see how this helps us." Thometh's voice is not at all rude. He speaks around his broad smile. Excitement tints his tone, he speaks as one would speak about a promised gift but one they are afraid will be stolen soon after opening.

"I have it from sources close to Tin himself that Enchenda was given to Tin to control. This is a different thing entirely than falling under his control. He absorbed Enchenda," I explain. I smile at the kings, an invitation for them to enjoy this gift I have brought. Recognition lands lightly on their faces like butterfly wings and their smiles turn up a notch. "Tin keeps Enchenda whole; he is King of both lands."

Sawchett sits forward and speaks loudly. "This gives us the right to challenge him to control and by virtue of our majority blood, he has no choice but to back off."

"This is a promising turn of events indeed." Larecio smiles warmly at Tutor and Sawchett. "I think I'm happy you joined us today."

Ever practical, Hector's smile is more subdued. "What is the plan then, Jordyn? Surely you do not expect Tin to adhere to that rule and step down from this war immediately."

"Not at all. In fact, I plan to challenge him to a duel myself. If need be I will battle with Tin while Tutor and the scouts do their best to handle what remains faithful from Sarcheda's army."

"When is all this planned to take place?" Hector asks.

"Before we can challenge him our priority is to get Eselda out of Tin's deadly grip," I answer.

Inwardly, Tutor sighs. I hear it only a fraction of a beat before the council bristles. "Why would she be a priority?" Hector asks, sudden anger seeping into his words.

"Jordyn," Thometh lays a calming hand on my arm, "she stood beside him as he declared war on this council. She made no move to stop him. What reason would you have to rescue her?"

Chapter 45

Tutor notices the change. Jordyn's eyes darken as though twilight has descended upon their depths. His fists clench where they sit on the table. Quickly, Tutor dives into the conversation. "Jordyn and I both know Eselda well. We have trouble believing she is behind this war."

"She's different when Tin's around," Sawchett offers. "Perhaps if they can get her alone she would see reason."

"We have to try," pleads Tutor. Seeing Jordyn's anger has made him question something important. *There is a chance that Jordyn will not fight in this war without Eselda on our side, safe.* "It's a condition of the scouts helping," Tutor tacks on the claim.

"I will agree we can try and reach her," Thometh concedes. "But you must agree not to sacrifice any of you if you are wrong about her."

Hector nods his agreement. "I can stand behind that plan."

"Don't you need to vote or something?" Tutor asks. He is aware of the customs of the council which would require an official call to vote and a majority ruling.

"We are being more informal lately." Thometh grins. "I'm sure you can understand."

Tutor risks another glance at Jordyn. The anger has not ebbed. Thometh follows Tutor's gaze and taps his nephew lightly on the arm to get his attention. "They've agreed, Jordyn."

Jordyn shakes his head. He squints as if the voice is reaching him through a fog. "What?"

"There's no need to worry, the council has agreed to let you try and get Eselda out," says Thometh.

Some of the anger leaves. "Good." Jordyn attempts a smile. "It is important to me."

"What other plans do you have?" Hector asks.

Chapter 46

Tutor explains the plan we laid out with the scouts without interruption from the council. I use the time to get a grip on my anger. I have done so well with that lately, since being in the forest. Perhaps the mention of Eselda was a trigger. Perhaps being back in this chamber holding decisions for the future of Fraunians in my hands is the trigger. I shake my head. No matter the reason, I hate that they witnessed my struggle today. I will have to try harder in the future. I take a deep breath and force myself to sit upright at the table.

Sawchett leans forward. "Tin will not come out to a public place to have witnesses to his throne being impugned unless it's for a substantial reason. It seems as though the personal vendetta he has amassed with Jordyn will serve as this. Then there's the matter of the challenge. The council will know that the challenge alone makes Tutor the rightful heir, but some Fraunians will need more. Tin will need more." She blinks at the men in the room who seem shocked by the big plan coming from the smallest in attendance.

"You think that is the best course of action? How old are you, girl?" Hector fires the question at Sawchett.

"Over ten annuals. Why, exactly?"

"You'll certainly be among the youngest ruler we've had," Larecio notes.

"Ruler?" Sawchett asks.

"Remember, gentlemen, this is only a failsafe if Eselda is not well enough to have Enchenda returned to her reign," I cut in.

"Oh, you're giving Enchenda to me?" Sawchett turns her attention to Tutor who blushes under her shocked expression.

"We can talk about that later, Sawchett," he mumbles.

"Let's assume this all goes as you have laid out," Hector speaks loudly to ensure he will not be interrupted. All eyes in the room turn to him. "Eselda is rescued from Tin's home and is found to be of sound mind to rule a realm. Tutor here challenges Tin for the throne and Tin backs down or is convinced to do such by some epic battle Jordyn miraculously wins. Control of Enchenda falls back to either Eselda, Tutor, or Sawchett. What becomes of Sarcheda? What becomes of the council we are all a part of at this new time? How do we clean this up with the Fraunians?" Hector does not sound upset. On the contrary, he sounds as though the very idea of planning all this has zapped the energy from his core.

"Someone will take Sarcheda until we can determine if the tree there can be updated," Tutor offers.

"Farcheda can be first realm in your new council," I offer.

"That is gracious of you, Jordyn. I feel as though numbering is not going to be nearly as important after this is over. Perhaps we have put too much emphasis on it up until now." Hector's honesty is refreshing.

"I am relieved to hear you say that, Hector." Tutor smiles. "I believe the same. I think the new kingdom can and should include many changes, but I feel they are best made together. Now is not the time for making all those decisions."

"Wisely spoken, Tutor." Hector acknowledges the man with a nod. The reverence these men use to speak to each other gives me great hope for the future of Fraun.

"Well then, we have no choice but to carry out the plan as my nephew and his scouts have laid it out," Thometh says, standing. "I will take the girl with me today. I will give her a safe place to rest her head. I do believe Jordyn is correct in her need to train. We will be sure to send her with a guard at night occasionally to train with your men in the forest."

"Excellent, thank you. Tutor and I will return to the scouts and prepare for our coming part in this." I rise to stand beside my Uncle. He seems so tall from a seated position, but I have at least a mark on the older man.

"Perhaps it would be wise for Tutor to stay in the castle as well until such a time as he is needed," Larecio interjects. "He is our last hope of taking Tin's rule away from him."

I watch Tutor's face as he swallows his anger and fear in one large gulp. He raises his chin, rises, and speaks clearly for the assembled men. He points one finger at Sawchett. "She is your last hope. I am just a baby someone once abandoned who happens to have more royal blood than most of you. Don't hang your faith in me alone for I am not worthy of such confidence. I only seek to play my part in our plan." Before anyone can question him, Tutor leaves the room, looking much more regal and ready than anyone in attendance can recall seeing in one person before.

Chapter 47

Two suns following the council meeting the plan is already set in motion, a runaway boulder speeding down a mountain that no one is capable of stopping. Toby has contacted someone to relay the message that Jordyn wishes to duel to Tin. The scouts travel closer to Fraun in order to get some clues regarding the whereabouts of Eselda and await a response from Tin.

Today the scout troop, no longer sleeping without a guard to watch the camp, lies along the far side of the ravine that encloses Sarcheda. From this location, they can see if someone approaches on either side and remain separate enough from the army for their safety.

Lance is awake and watching the sun rise along the horizon from beside the fire. He sharpens his sword, the long scratching sounds reverberating through the silent forest. He uses a rock this morning, although he carries a strap that can be used as well. For battle, it is necessary for a very sharp blade, and therefore a rock is his choice. Lance is facing off in the direction of Renchenda, toward the larger trees.

Today they are between the two forests in a more open setting and Lance's nerves are strung tighter than Abney's bow. He had requested they travel to the trees before setting up camp, but the women were too tired to travel more and Jordyn wanted to be nearer to Sarcheda. Secretly, Lance is afraid that Jordyn believes if they travel too far they will forget about Eselda's rescue. Actually, that is probably the case. The scout troop seems to be on Lance's side in this; Eselda was a part of the pair that declared war. Lance is not sure she can be rehabilitated in the way Jordyn seems to hope.

Lance rises and squints into the tree line. He thought he saw a person peeking out from behind a tree. He watches, silence filling the void left when the sound of sharpening stopped. Again he spots it, a face peering out from a nearby tree. It is gone before he can fully process it, but the shoulder was certainly clad in black. Lance cautiously heads toward the area, stopping only long enough to kick the tent which houses Franc and Carolina. "Someone is in the trees," he says, an answer to the mumble issued by Franc at the rude awakening.

"Show yourself," Lance calls to the trees as he approaches. "Surely you know the sound of sharpening a blade. You would be foolish to hide from me now." His voice portrays a bravery perhaps greater than he feels. If this is the Sarcheda army, they could already be surrounded. His heartbeat takes off like a race roach at the starting line.

"Don't do anything stupid. I'm alone. I'll come out now."

The voice sounds oddly familiar, Lance thinks. A set of empty hands sticks out from behind the huge tree. Lance raises his sword, ready for an attack that may never come. The arms and then the body emerge. Lance lowers the sword immediately.

"Lance?" the voice questions.

Franc rushes from the tent carrying the closest weapon, a dull blade used for practice. He arrives on the scene just in time to see Lance drop his blade and pull the stranger into an awkward embrace. The round man shakes his head. "I suppose the danger has passed?"

Lance turns. "Sorry, Franc. False alarm. Go back to bed."

"Who is this man?" Franc asks, slowly approaching the pair.

"I am Danyel, of Enchenda." Danyel offers his hand to Franc, who shakes it.

"Well good morning, Danyel. I am going back to bed if you have no objections."

Danyel waits for Franc to move back toward the tent. He looks Lance over carefully, searching for an injury that would explain his presence here. His old friend is wearing brown, having disposed of the army uniform. There are no obvious signs of trauma but the once calculating gaze has gone softer, sadder somehow. "Who was that?" Danyel asks, pointing to the tent where Franc has retreated.

"Franc. He's a leader of sorts for the scouts who have taken me in." Lance turns and heads back toward the center of camp, signaling that Danyel should follow with a flick of his hand.

"So you're a scout now?" Danyel's voice is cautious. "What happened to the army?"

Lance takes his time adjusting himself comfortably in a seated position before answering. "I left."

The simple answer does not satisfy Danyel. "Why?"

"I could no longer support what they were doing."

"Did something happen? Is the war still going on?"

Lance nails Danyel with an accusatory glance, easily slipping into the role of prosecutor. "Where have you been all this time?"

"I couldn't watch him control all those people any longer. He was turning so many into something they're not, me included," Danyel is whispering. His chin shamefully drops to his chest. "I've just been camping out in the woods here hoping to find someone ..." his voice trails off as he thinks about the long days of hunger and hope.

Lance allows the silence to settle around them. He goes back to sharpening his sword. For a while, the only sound is the shink of the rock over the blade. "The war you asked about still goes on."

"Is that why you sharpen your blade?"

"It is."

"But you fight not for Sarcheda?" Danyel's puzzlement clouds his voice.

"No." Lance meets the eyes of the younger man who once followed him around Enchenda in simpler times. The man he took into his gang of hapless workers; able of body but broken of heart. "I have realized Tin has an agenda only for himself. I will not help with that agenda. I fight against it," Lance explains.

A smile that contrasts the darkness of the current time alights on Danyel's face. "Took you long enough." He laughs. The sound breaks apart something in Lance's chest. Despite himself, he chuckles as well.

Chapter 48

The tent flap signals my arrival into the clearing. I see the face of the new man fall, his laughter fading into the cold morning. "Good morning, Lance," I greet. "Who is this?"

"Danyel, formerly of Enchenda patrol and Sarcheda army, meet Jordyn, formerly king of Renchenda." Lance gestures between the two of us.

"Things must be really be falling apart if a king defects to the scouts," Danyel mumbles.

I am sure he intends to goad me, perhaps start a fight. He looks dejected and pained, a look I can certainly relate to. Instead of offering him the reaction he is expecting, I grin. "We intend to fix that. Can we count on your support as well, friend of Lance?"

Danyel's eyes look me up and down. Likely, he notices I no longer wear the colors of Fraun, having traded them in for the brown worn by most scouts. My muscles have been developing during my days in training, but I do not rival the enemy we fight in that category. Danyel nods at me. "I certainly don't support your competition, sir."

"Please, call me Jordyn." I take a seat and roll my neck around to stretch.

"You'll like him, Jordyn. He will support you in your blind ambition to rescue Eselda," Lance reveals.

Danyel and I turn to look at each other, assessing each other anew. "Is this true?" I ask.

"I support the idea that she must be rescued from Tin, yes."

"I do as well. You believe she is being kept against her will?"

Danyel's eyes pinch closed as he thinks. "Eselda was never a prisoner in Sarcheda."

There goes one theory.

"But there was something unusual about the way they communicated."

"Explain," I command.

"I hadn't known her long before she met Tin, but something is wrong with the way they interact."

"Her age marker would've occurred right around that same time, Danyel." Lance's irritation is evident in his tone. "I know you both want to blame Tin for all this but it could easily have been Eselda's malicious age."

"You know of the age markers?" My head whips around to face Lance.

"Yes." Lance does not elaborate.

"She's the best woman we've ever met," Danyel simply states.

"Perhaps she was once, but she sides with him," Lance says.

"So did you, once," Danyel says.

There is too much truth to Danyel's statement for Lance to argue. Instead, he shrugs. "I already said I would support her rescue, and I will. I just wanted Jordyn to be aware that you believe as he does. It seems as though not many around here do."

"More people for us to prove wrong when we find her," I say. "Speaking of which, do you know where we can find her?"

"Last I saw, she was staying in the royal house in Sarcheda. I have seen nothing that would indicate that has changed," Danyel answers. "It may be safe for us to try now, I saw the army leave a few suns ago in that direction …" he points toward the Renchenda forest "… and they have not returned."

Why would the army risk that terrain? I hide the worry from my face quickly. "We shall have to try today, then."

Lance merely shakes his head. "I will rouse Tutor and we will head toward the royal house to scope out the territory." We watch him stomp off in the direction of the tents.

"He doesn't argue with you, even though you are no longer a king. How does that work out?" Danyel asks once we are alone.

"We make decisions together here, this troop. Trust me, he argues with me plenty. I think this is simply a case where the arguing has already been done." I laugh lightly. "Lance isn't one to repeat a losing argument."

"That is true."

"What is your relationship with Lance? How do you know him?" I ask.

"We were friends in Enchenda before we joined the patrol. He was someone I looked up to. I lost everything I thought mattered to me and Lance helped me get on my feet. He helps a lot of citizens in Enchenda, people who are consumed by loss."

I find this interesting, I lean toward the younger man. "What led to your sadness, if you don't mind my asking."

"A woman I loved chose another man."

He whispers the truth but he may as well have yelled it for the power it brings. I have to take a deep breath and sit back. "Oh." I cannot bring myself to tell him of our shared pain. It brings me closer to Danyel, this stranger from Enchenda. If nothing else, the sadness on his face now makes sense. This man understands, possibly better than most.

"Lance lost two children. It kept him going to work with the men from Enchenda who had also lost something. He made us confront our sadness and find jobs to keep ourselves moving. He would not let us wallow in self-pity," Danyel says. "He is a good man."

"I do agree with that assessment. I believe I am going to enjoy having you around, Danyel." I stand and stretch my limbs to the sky. "Let us prepare ourselves to free Eselda."

Chapter 49

At the edge of Sarcheda near two homes that are currently empty, there is a patch of wild grass. It is tall enough that I can easily lay flat on my belly and be completely hidden from view. From this vantage point on my belly, I can see the home of the royal family. Granted, I have to look beyond their rock wall, but I can see the home nonetheless. Here we are concealed from the army. It is far enough away from where the forces have erected their tents, yet it is within your sightline to watch them come and go.

"Jordyn, we've been staking out the house all day. We have watched Tin come and go. We have seen servants and soldiers trek in and out. It pains me to say so, but she's not here." Tutor sighs. "I'm all for finding Eselda but the sun is warming the back of my neck so much I feel the skin sizzling."

I hold back from pointing out that it's making him grumpy. I know Eselda is in there as sure as I know Tutor is beside me. I cannot see either of them, but I can feel their presence. I stare at the empty front yard until my eyes begin to water, begging me to blink.

Beside me, also pressed flat on the ground, Tutor and Lance exchange whispers. I ignore them. I no longer care what they think. With Eselda this close I cannot process much else. It is taking all of my energy to keep myself here on the ground instead of racing forward to inspect the house. The only reason I stay here is that I forgot my sword and would therefore be unprepared for a battle.

"Majesty!" The man dashing from the front door we have been watching is shrieking for Tin. "Majesty, come quick!" He runs toward the army camp. Before he can enter the camp, Tin saunters into his path.

My reaction is animal; a snarl escapes me and I try to push myself up off the ground. Tutor's arm hits my calves hard, holding me to the ground.

"Wait," Tutor orders.

Lance, for fear of being caught and swiftly murdered, attempts to flatten himself lower to the ground.

I begin sucking air at a faster rate. "The house is unguarded," I mumble. I try again to rise, placing my palms flat on either side of me.

Tutor shoves me, hard. "Stay here," he commands. "All in Sarcheda know your face. I will go." Tutor jumps to his feet and sprints for the fence before I can argue.

Time passes impossibly slow. Tin and the soldier continue to talk in voices that cannot be overheard. Occasionally, one of them will gesture toward the home. Tutor carelessly leaped over the fence and boldly walked right into the home. I have talked myself out of following Tutor twice already. I prepare myself for a third round of the mental battle, placing my palms flat on the ground again.

"No, stay here," Lance commands. His tone leaves no room for argument. I let myself be convinced.

Tin wraps up the conversation with a loud directive. "Deal with it!" The soldier turns and walks toward the home. I watch him close the gap and mentally calculate the short period Tutor has to get himself out.

"C'mon Tutor," Lance mumbles. The gap grows smaller. Smaller.

The soldier's boot hits the lawn inside the fence and the front door flies open, banging against the brick house. Tutor appears in the opening, the huge smile on his face making him appear foolish. "Who are you?" the soldier barks.

"I was interviewing for the new kitchen position." The lie rolls off Tutor's tongue as if it has been rehearsed. He offers a smile to the soldier as though his heart isn't pounding with fear.

"Alright then." The soldier begins walking and Tutor breathes out a dramatic sigh of relief. He locks eyes with me and begins to scuttle in our direction.

The soldier turns around. "Did you get the job?" he asks, just before the darkness of the house swallows him.

Tutor is momentarily confused, as one often is when lying. "I'm not sure yet." He stumbles over the answer. "Put in a good word for me?"

The answer must satisfy the soldier. He nods and disappears into the home. I can see the tension leave Tutor at the man's disappearance. His shoulders slump and he turns, smiling again. He runs to us. "She was here. No one has seen her in almost a fortnight. The staff thinks she went back to Enchenda." I sit up in the grass. "She's safe," Tutor adds.

The relief is instant. The weight on my chest dissipates, I take a deep breath and rise. "Then why are we still here? Lance you will send Danyel to the house in Enchenda to retrieve her. Tell her the scouts can offer her safety during this dangerous time. He may tell her I am with the scouts, and Sawchett also, she'll likely be glad to hear that."

I may be with Eselda soon. I can tell her I made a mistake. I can beg for her forgiveness, for a second chance.

"Now, let's get back to camp, we have some training to finish."

Chapter 50

He stands outside the heavy door panting and trying desperately to win the internal argument. Of course, he's not sure which way would indicate winning, and therein lies the problem. Does he enter or does he leave?

In his right hand balances a tray burdened with fruits and vegetables from the kitchen. A pitcher full to the brim with cold water is set carefully at the center of the tray. In his left hand, he holds the key that will open the door and grant him access to his desire. Should he give in to the marker that plagues him?

Tin has avoided Eselda for almost a lunar cycle. His servants tell him that it has been some time since she was visited with food and water. She has been surviving on whatever is in the room. Therefore, she is as desperate for the food he carries as he is for her touch. He has not been himself since she has been locked in that room. He should hate her. He wants to hate her. Yet, he cannot ignore her.

His body, a servant to his age marker, craves her touch. He can feel the lack of that connection as a cold void all over his skin. He has tried to be with other women, visitors to the army. But they do not fill the void and they leave him with a pang of bitter guilt. *No one else's touch is enough.*

That answers it. Tin slides the key into the door and turns it. The click frees the wood and the door swings open. He moves quickly before he can talk himself out of this, approaching Eselda with intense longing.

She is crouched on the ground beside the bed like an animal. Snarling, she leaps from the ground toward the open door the second she hears the key. The face of the intruder causes her to falter, but only for a beat. Anger greater than anything she has ever felt washes over her. She charges full speed at Tin. Her hair is wild and matted. Her hands are covered in blood. Her eyes are dark and full of hatred.

Tin holds the plate of food up. "Stop," he commands.

The sight of the tempting meal forces Eselda to draw a shaky breath. The smells fill her nostrils and the ceaseless rattling in her stomach becomes unbearable. She clamps her hands around her middle and groans. "Eat first, you can attack me after you have had a meal. With how withered you are it wouldn't be a challenge for me to win the fight." Tin keeps his voice controlled and calm.

The hunger in Eselda's gut wins. She eagerly grabs the tray and drops to her knees. She digs into the food with her hands, shoveling it into her mouth in large globs. All the while her eyes remain vigilantly fixed on Tin; her guard is up. She does not trust him. She drinks half the jug of water in one gulp and uses the rest of it to clean her hands and face. Only once everything is consumed does she allow herself to fall back into a seated position and think clearly.

This is my chance, she realizes. *Tin is here. Now is the time to keep my wits and take control of this situation any way I can.* "Why are you here?" she asks. Her voice is like fallen leaves, drying out until they crack under any pressure.

"I missed you," Tin says.

He almost sounds sincere, Eselda notes.

"Don't you still love me, somewhere deep in there?" he asks. Eselda cannot, will not, answer. "What happened to us?" Tin clouds his voice with the thick weakness that he knows Eselda adores. He inches closer to her, reaching for her, and donning the mask again.

Eselda knows now what she should've known all along. Tin is weak, internally. His age marker seeks satisfaction. She pulls back to keep him from touching her. If he cannot satiate that hunger then she controls him. She slips into the role of hurt lover, wearing an exaggerated pout. "You lied." The anger singes her facade.

Tin realizes this was a foolish idea. He turns and begins to head back for the door. Eselda knows if she lets him leave the room she has wasted her one chance to fight for Fraun. Her fight is here, now, in this room with Tin. For Fraun, Eselda drops deeper into the role of her old self. She is ashamed of how dirty this skin feels. "Wait, I'm sorry. It's my age marker. It makes me say things I don't mean. Please don't leave me alone in here again." She swallows, a scowl lighting on her lips to give her the strength for the next lie. "I need you."

Tin turns to gauge her sincerity. She is back on her knees, groveling at his feet. The sight is tantalizing. Eselda notices the darker color the of eyes. *It is working.* "Tell me of our war," she practically gags at the pronoun. "How does it progress?"

"It's going well." Tin's voice is a low purr. "Our men should've circled Renchenda by now. Any day I expect to get word of Larecio's downfall."

Larecio, Eselda notes, is not the right build to be the man in the dream. "You don't fight alongside your men?" she asks.

"They need me not. I hold things down here." Tin steps closer to her. His body has taken up an odd humming, starving for a touch of her skin. He feels it like a million tiny feet, stomping every inch of his body. *Enough small talk, stop this feeling. Quench my body's thirst with your skin.*

"What are you afraid of?" Eselda knows fear is a trigger for him and yet she pushes the sore spot anyway.

"Nothing." But his face shows a flash of anger, a crack in the mask he wears.

"Surely you don't think they can win in a battle against you." She flutters her eyelashes to keep up the innocent routine, hating herself.

"You know I am the strongest in Fraun." He throws his bare shoulders back.

Is that fear I hear? Eselda savors the taste of the small victory. She rises in one quick motion, shocking Tin into taking a step back. "Is strength enough?" she needles him. "Is it enough against the wisdom of Renchenda?

They will have strategy on their side. You will never surprise them." The daggers of her words contrast with the seductive curves of her body. She further confuses him by stepping closer, swinging her hips. They are now only a few marks apart. Tin's eyes darken to black. Eselda pauses for a fraction of a second before she remembers the darkening will indicate lust now, not anger.

Tin swallows against the desire choking him. "We do alright in strategy, my love," his voice cracks. He reaches for her and Eselda bats his hand down with a playful slap. Tin can feel his skin scalding where she hit. "What will it take to get you in my arms?" Tin growls.

Eselda licks her lips. "Tell me your age marker controlled you. Tell me it forced your hand when you killed Carsen. Tell me you can be the man I once thought you were."

Tin moans. "I can give you power, I can give you Fraun. I cannot give you those lies."

She tries one last time. "Then tell me you'll give up this war before anyone else dies. Give it all up right now. Then you can have all of me." Eselda allows the words to sink in as she traces her hips with her hands.

Tin wants to give in. He wants to satisfy this pain. But at what cost? To give up now would give her the power. Eselda cannot have the power. He shakes his head. "This was a mistake. I should go." He bends to retrieve the tray.

"Back down now," Eselda pleads. "Beg forgiveness of the council. Blame your age marker. They'll believe you. Then you and I can be together and all this goes away." The thought of being with him makes her skin feel as though slimy fish are living under it, but it would be a small price to pay for the end of the war.

"One Fraun, Eselda." Tin stands, now holding the heavy tray and pitcher. "Like Oberian had. It's what I want more than anything."

"Are you willing to die for it?" She tries to push the button again, playing on the fear she saw on his face when she mentioned Renchenda. "Are you willing to die by the hand of Thometh, fighting for the power you crave? I have seen a vision of this." She wavers a little under the weight of the lie. "You can end it before it gets to that point. They already hate people of this age, they will believe you."

Tin freezes her next words with a dangerous stare. Eselda gulps air as she notices his eyes have somehow lightened up, as though her presence no longer draws his age marker out.

"I won't have to die for it." Tin steps close to her again. This time it is her fear and not his lust filling the gap between them. "What you forget, my dear, is that only royal blood will feel that pull to power. No one else wants power as badly as I do. No one else would take another life for that power."

"Others with the blood exist," Eselda stammers.

Tin's hand moves fast. Eselda flinches and closes her eyes, ready for the slap. Instead, Tin caresses her cheek. He feels the connection spark and send warmth traveling up his arm. "I have always felt the pull of power, Eselda. I felt it at twenty. I feel it now, at twenty-five when it should've faded. I felt it at seventeen when I killed my parents so I could be King." The statement and the revolting touch cause the bottom to drop from the room. Eselda clenches her teeth to keep from vomiting. "I will be in control of my kingdom because I want it more than anyone else in Fraun." Satisfied that the burn of her touch has finally reached his heart, Tin severs contact and turns to go.

Eselda throws herself at the door, wailing in misery. As the door clicks and the lock tumbles into place, she screams. *No one will come for me again. I just missed my chance to make a difference for Fraun.*

Tin has won.

Chapter 51

I chug from the jug of cold water. When the jug is lowered I take equally greedy gulps of air. I use my forearm to wipe droplets of the liquid from my chin. Then I lean back on my arms to relax, sigh deeply, and watch the training sessions.

To my left, Abney stands straight and tall between Sawchett and Evelyn. Her blonde ringlets catch the sun as she nods her head in approval. Sawchett's equally yellow hair has almost reached her waist now. Today it is tied back to keep it from tangling in the bow she is using. I watch as she empties her quiver expertly into the target. Her shooting is straight, and her hands steady. On the other side of Abney, Evelyn wears her signature brown ponytail. Her shots also hit the target. Her form is different from that of the younger girl, somehow Sawchett gives off more confidence when she shoots. I watch Abney stand behind Evelyn, wrapping her arms around the older woman and modeling something. When she backs away, Evelyn's arrow is loosed to hit the bull's eye square on. Abney offers her a smile and another nod that sends the blonde hair bouncing. It is remarkable how their skills progress.

My focus turns to the men directly in front of me. They have cleared the dirt to make a small ring. Inside the ring, they have graduated to practicing sword fighting one on one. The pair practicing now, Sieven and Lance, no longer have to hold back when they spar. I watch Sieven attack, forcing Lance to stop the thrust he didn't see coming. Lance immediately goes on the offensive, striking thrusts that back Sieven up toward the edge of the circle. The boy has progressed far in a short time, proving himself to be a better sword fighter than even I had hoped to be. Sieven is a good match for Lance in the ring.

Across the ring, Toby sits gulping water and relaxing, a mirror image of myself. We have just finished sparring. It ended with Toby stopping his sword just above my heart, holding his arm steady to keep from hurting me. I had no parry for the attack. Had it been a real sword fight I would be dead. The thought brings me a mix of fear and excitement. It is a good thing Toby is on our side.

Directly behind the ring, Lili and Carlina are seated on the ground with a pile of material in front of them. The women have shown themselves to be adept at making arrows. Lili even knew of a plant that was poisonous and grows in the wilderness. They make some arrows that are dipped in the poison harvested from the plant. These, they explain, are to be used sparingly and only in desperate situations. The poison arrows have wingtips that are red, instead of the traditional black. I watch Carlina carefully cut apart some kind of metallic container to make an arrowhead. Her thick braids fall in her face and she bends closer to the material to watch the lines. The shape be correct if we are to use the arrow as a weapon in the coming war. The arrows are the same ones that are being used by the girls in target practice. Abney has explained that many more will be required for the war, as it is not practical to assume you will be able to retrieve them all for reuse. That is just one thing that makes what we are doing here so real. The weight of the deaths that will surely come with our battles is constantly on my conscience. I can feel myself bending under the pressure.

To my right, the two eldest scouts practice battling with long sticks. The sticks have been honed to perfect cylinders. Kurt and Franc each grip one in the middle and use them to battle. They have proven themselves to be skilled at handling the weapons in many contexts. Yesterday, Kurt demonstrated his ability to deflect Abney's arrows with the weapon. Franc has battled against Lance's sword. Now, they turn the sticks against each other, the sound reverberating through the entire woodland area each time they strike. Franc has worked up quite a sweat, and I can tell that Kurt is taking it easy on our jovial friend. Tutor is on the ground beside the pair, sitting alongside his stick. He has been picking up this ancient battle technique in the suns since he has been a part of the troop.

A grunt from the center ring brings my eyes back to the sword fight. Sieven has managed to knock Lance to the ground and is holding the point of his sword directly over the fallen man's chest. "You bested me, young man," Lance calls out. The words are an interesting mix of resentment and pride. Sieven moves his sword to his side and offers Lance a hand in rising, which the older man takes.

Toby rises and cracks his neck. "I suppose we are up again," he says.

In answer to the call, I stand and stretch. My muscles are much more developed than they were lunar cycles ago when I fled Fraun. I recently had to borrow some shirts from Kurt, finding that my former tailored clothes were too tight fitting on my biceps. I now wear the loose-fitting brown clothing of a scout at all times. I shake my hair out of my eyes where it has fallen since it stopped growing at fifteen annuals. Although my sword fighting grows better with each passing day, I dread entering the ring again. I am tired and worn out. I know better than to mention this. Lance would have nothing nice to say. I can hear it already, Tin is not likely to allow me the opportunity to rest up before attacking.

Taking up my sword, I enter the ring and assume the stance. "Jordyn." Lili's always calm voice draws my attention. "A roach approaches." This statement has the effect of halting all training. Twelve pairs of eyes track in the direction of the sound of movement through the forest. I can hear the strings of three bows being drawn back as the girls ready the weapons. Out of the corner of my eye, I see Kurt adopt a fighting stance. In front of me, Lili wraps her hand around the shaft of an arrow with red wings. We stand, silent and ready for whatever approaches.

"It is Danyel, returning from a scout mission, I mean no harm," the voice calls out. Everyone visibly relaxes.

"Are you alone?" I prompt.

"I am." The roach enters the clearing, bearing Danyel on his back. Danyel's face is dirty, his clothes are tattered, and he looks distressed. "I need a word with you, Jordyn," he calls out. Immediately the rest of the scouts return to their training. Tutor jumps up to take my place in the ring. I follow Danyel to a quiet section of rocks often used for conversation. We both take a seat.

"I have news from Fraun," Danyel speaks quietly and stares at the ground. "I visited Enchenda first. The house of the royal family looks abandoned. It is quiet there, no one is around, and layers of dust cake everything." He swallows back emotion and continues. "Enchenda is not the same as I remember. People are in their homes all the time, shutters are drawn. There are Sarcheda men in the streets, I had to hide from them as I traveled." Danyel's eyes track up to my face. I am sure he sees a sadness on my face that matches the one he is showing to me. "Dark days rule Fraun now, I fear," he adds.

"Eselda?" I choke out the name, all I can manage of the important question burning in my soul.

"No sign of her, I'm afraid. I took it upon myself to travel to Sarcheda again. I asked around with a few of the servants who I once knew. They say they have not seen her, but there was a fight between Tin and Eselda. I don't know the details."

"What of my messenger who was sent to call out Tin? Did you hear anything of him?"

"The servants say a man brought a message to the head of the Sarcheda army. Rumor has it the captain killed this man on orders from his king."

I shake my head. Nothing goes as planned. "So Tin will not meet with me?"

"I'm not sure if that was your messenger or not, no one seems to know what message he brought. Perhaps this was a messenger from some other realm."

"This is bad news you bring me." I sigh. It is dangerous to try, but I must find a way to get Tin to meet my challenge. The last messenger was told to use my name, but perhaps he didn't have the chance. It sounds as though the messenger never had an audience with Tin. "We must get the message to Tin directly. He will not back down from a public challenge. We will send another scout with a personal challenge and orders to deliver it to Tin in front of his army."

"There is other news, sir." Danyel's sadness has not ebbed.

I assumed the sadness was for the loss of the messenger, or the lack of progress on finding Eselda. Clearly, this news that Danyel has yet to deliver is worse. I brace myself.

"Sarcheda army took Marchenda," says Danyel.

Cold fingers squeeze my spine. If this news is accurate, Tin controls more than half of Fraun. We have lost too much time already. "How?" I ask.

"They entered from the side of the plains. They attacked the royal home at dark." Danyel's eyes water. "They killed King Larecio."

"There is still more royal blood in Marchenda, is there not?" I ask, my mind working hard to process details.

"There is. Alerta, Larecio's cousin, has fled to Castle Fraun. She will be safe there until such a time as she can assume the throne."

"So the people of Marchenda are under the Sarcheda army's control?"

"I suppose so. I would imagine the scene there to be much the same as what I saw in Enchenda."

Fear grips me. "He will attack the castle soon." There is no more denying it. This war has gone on long enough. I rise. "We will tell the scouts and take a vote, but I propose we close the remaining distance to the castle tonight."

Chapter 52

Seated in a circle on the ground that has been cleared for sword training, the scouts are silent as I summarize the new information. The news is not as shocking to them as it was to me. Fraun is under attack, they knew this. The scouts have no loyalty to Fraun and no kinship with Larecio. They feel pressure with Tin gaining a stronger foothold, but they do not mourn the king or the falling kingdom as I do.

"I am in favor of mounting up and heading to defend Castle Fraun," Sieven announces. "We are ready."

"We should take a vote," I say.

"All in favor?" Sieven calls out. All around the circle hands reach for the air. There is a silence, deep and clear which speaks louder than any response I could give. Thirteen hands are reaching for the sky. Thirteen people are ready to stand up to Tin.

One by one the hands drop. "Mount up, scouts. We leave as soon as dusk falls." It is Tutor who makes the call. No one argues.

Slowly the clearing empties until only Tutor and I remain. "Is this a fool's errand, Jordyn? Do we lead these good people to their deaths?" Tutor's voice is barely above a whisper.

"I know no other way to take back Fraun and save Eselda," I answer.

"What if he kills her before we can get to her?"

"I will not lie to you, that is my greatest fear. But we fight for Fraun, not for Eselda."

"What if we can only save one?" Tutor asks.

"Then we save Fraun. Even if the decision kills me," I answer, quietly.

As if the answer itself is a call to action, Tutor rises and leaves the clearing. I sit alone for a beat, feeling sadness to my core. Tutor has hit upon the darkest part of my soul where my doubts live. There is no question that Fraun as a whole is worth more than one person's life. But that one person means more to me than my own life.

I can only hope that I never have to make such a choice.

Chapter 53

This time when the dream comes Eselda is expecting it. Her eyes open and she is standing in the familiar clearing, smelling the trees and feeling the cold wind thrashing her body. The first emotion to find her is relief. In the dream, Eselda feels no hunger, no agony. She closes her eyes and breathes deeply, enjoying the sensation of being whole again.

Her eyes snap open. *Why does my mind keep bringing me this dream? What more can I learn from it?* She bends down and runs her fingers along the soil. It is cold to the touch, but loosely packed. This means nothing to her. She rises again as Tin barrels into the clearing.

Losing her mind with agony at what he has done to her, Eselda runs to him. "You are a monster!" she bellows. She tries to hit him with her fists, but cannot connect. Her hands pass right through him. The momentum almost carries her to the ground. "I can't even kill you in dreams," she howls.

Eselda watches Tin as his face adopts the panicked look. The sight offers her little comfort this time around. *What is it that I need to see this for?*

She sits on the ground, hard. "Forget it, I'm not watching this again. I will just sit here and enjoy feeling normal for a change."

She hears the other person, Thometh, crash into the area. She knows that behind her stubbornly turned back they are fighting. She keeps her chin raised in defiance, refusing to watch this again.

"Well, isn't this interesting? I seem to have you backed against a wall here, old friend." Tin's voice rings through the clearing. Eselda counts to five in her head, hoping that is long enough for Tin to finish murdering the man. She does not wish to watch the triumph on his face as he kills an innocent. *I already know he's a monster, I don't need more proof.*

When she finally turns, the air is squeezed from her lungs. Tears spring to her eyes and cascade down her face. The agonizing scream starts in the dream, but when it ends she is awake. The image cannot be erased from her brain. It is seared into her darkest memories.

Tin, triumphantly standing over the bloody chest of the fallen soldier for Fraun. The crumpled body at the foot of the tree Tin had backed him toward. His eyes closed, the blonde hair falling into his handsome face. Eselda has seen the death of Jordyn in her dreams. Trembling, she has only enough energy to scream out his name as she slips to the floor.

Chapter 54

Tin hears Eselda scream out Jordyn's name from his office. He can feel the tug of his traitorous heart at the sound of her voice. *Why does she scream for Jordyn?* An emotion Tin is not used to feeling flares within his chest. *Jealousy? Is that what this is?* His fists ball up into deadly weapons. *I will kill him.*

Tin propels himself to the door intending to head for the army and the weapon stock they secure. Turning the corner quickly, he literally crashes into a young soldier. "Majesty, I was searching for you." The soldier bows low. "I bring you a message."

"From where?" Tin barks.

"Danyel approached me along the border." The soldier gestures toward the river as he rises from his bow.

"Danyel? Everyone was under orders to bring him to me if he showed his face here again. The man has defected from our army." All of Tin's jealous rage is now being tunneled into this confrontation.

"He was armed and he surprised me, Majesty. I'm only grateful he didn't kill me." The voice of the young soldier quakes with fear.

"What message did he bring?"

"He bade me tell you that Jordyn, formerly King of Renchenda, calls you out for a duel."

"A duel?" Tin asks. He has already heard this message once. Someone showed up and brought the same message almost a fortnight ago. Daijan relayed the message personally. Tin ordered Daijan to have the matter taken care of. The messenger was killed, as was Daijan shortly thereafter.

"Yes, Majesty. Apparently, Jordyn intends to meet you at Castle Fraun tomorrow, where you will duel until one of you is dead."

"Who else knows of this challenge?"

"The entire army heard him, Majesty. He made sure of it. Your soldiers were giving chase as I ran here to tell you the message."

The entire army knows I have been called out by a former king? I will kill him. "I will mount up and head to meet the challenge." Tin offers a small smile. "Let us hope they killed the traitorous Danyel." The boy continues to stand before his king. Frustrated, Tin waves him off. "Be off with you, I have a duel to prepare for."

Tin turns and stares at the door holding his former fiancé. There is silence on the other side. He reaches into his pocket for the long key that holds her freedom. The key represents a small path to the man she always hoped he would be. His foolish heart, trapped by the age marker that ties him to Eselda, wants him to follow the path. The leader within him that yearns for power fights for the right to remain strong. If he does nothing, she will die behind that door.

For once in his life, the weaker side wins. Tin bends down and positions the key on the floor. Standing again, he pushes it with the toe of his boot until it is concealed by the door itself. Either the key is now sticking out toward Eselda's side, or it is hidden below the door. Tin groans under the weight of the decision. *That is the closest I can get to being the man you thought I was, Eselda.*

He stands guard before the door for a full thirty count. There is no noise or movement. "We could've been a good team." The words are a sigh on the wind, lost in the hallway. She will never know they were spoken and perhaps it is better that way.

Chapter 55

In the army camp that night, Tin finds everyone has returned from battle. He stands before his men, atop a wall that surrounds their camp, in the fading light of the sun. He is dressed in full armor and the rock drawn upon the helmet nestled under his right arm indicates he is a royal from Sarcheda. The troops fall silent as they take in the sight of their leader in his gear. "My men, a challenge has been issued." Nods meet his opening statement.

"A former king, one of the men who sat beside me on the council and voted to take your rights away, has publicly challenged me to a duel. I have led you to victory over Enchenda. I strategized with the generals in a move that earned us control over Marchenda." A chorus of cheers rises from the crowd. Tin uses his hands to calm the tide.

"Until now I have remained behind the scenes, directing your every move but trusting you to carry them out. With this challenge, I must saddle up and join you in battle. I urge you to remember where your loyalties lie as we travel to Renchenda tonight. We must stick together. We must look toward the future. Remember what we stand to gain by triumphing over the former kings. I can tell you that this duel means they are desperate, we have them scared. Join me on our ride tonight, men. Tonight, we take back my castle!"

Cheers erupt from the army as they wave their weapons and close in around their king. Tin jumps from the wall, landing expertly on the back of a roach who has agreed to carry him into battle. High over his head the broad sword he has chosen catches the last of the fading sunlight and glints dangerously.

I'm coming for you, Jordyn. One Fraun will be mine.

Chapter 56

The sun slips below my line of sight. I watch as it drops like a duck looking for a meal below water, quietly disappearing from view. My eyes adjust quickly to the lack of light. Before the darkness engulfs the top floor of Castle Fraun I have already accustomed myself to seeing into the depths of the forest.

The scout troop is divided tonight. Each member has taken a post skirting the edge of the property line and peering into the darkness so as not to be surprised. We sit. We wait.

Inside the castle, the assembled men and women who will stand beside us in the name of Fraun await their chance to prove their loyalty. They have come in surprising numbers, fleeing from what has become of Enchenda and Marchenda. They have come from Farcheda where the boundaries have been abandoned in favor of this fight.

Young, old, strong, determined. We wait.

Sawchett has proven handy. She has learned to speak with a small species of bird that roost in the trees surrounding Renchenda. Is it a skill she has been successful teaching to a few others. This makes the group able to send short messages or warnings to each other quickly. We will send the location where Tin appears from when the coward appears.

Tutor rounds the corner of Castle Fraun and nods in acknowledgment as he approaches. "No sign of him yet?" Tutor asks.

"None."

"It is the same at all posts. A roach arrived near the front door not long ago. Word has it that Tin leads an army in this direction."

"We thought as much."

"It's good to know you predicted his actions well." I continue to watch the woods. It brings me no pleasure to acknowledge that any part of me understands Tin.

"What about Eselda?" Tutor asks. His voice carries the hesitation that comes with knowing you are broaching a sore subject.

"Maybe he'll bring her," I say.

"Do you believe that?"

"I hope it."

I can feel Tutor's eyes on me in the silence that follows my statement. He is cataloging my tight shoulders and my squinted eyes. It won't take him long to assess the problem. "Is your age marker worse when you are inside Fraun?" he asks.

I close my eyes and drop my chin to my chest. I allow myself two deep breaths. The beast has done well these past lunar cycles. I have easily fought it off the few times it has raised its head. I knew my friend would have no trouble sensing the truth, tonight I battle and lose. "It seems to be harder here, yes."

"Why do you suppose that is?"

"Here in Fraun, they expect me to lead. The pressure of being in charge of so many other lives takes its toll. Today, seeing all of those Fraunians … they could die, Tutor."

"Is there anything I can do to help? We need you at your best. What aids you when you are battling the marker?"

I could lock myself in a room of the castle and allow one outburst of anger. I could break something, yell, or throw things. But those things only held the anger at bay temporarily. There was only one thing that ever truly worked. "Love," I practically whisper the word.

The memories are instant. Sitting on a log in a field of strawberries with Eselda beside me. Her long hair tickling my arm. The feel of her small hand flat against my chest, warm through the shirt. The pressure of her lips upon mine.

The love flares in my chest and beats the monster back. When I open my eyes they are clear, blue, and focused again. "Love does it every time."

"You were thinking of her?" Tutor asks. "Does she know how you feel?"

"I once told her, but I fear I handled it poorly." My tone makes it clear that this conversation will go no further.

"Did I ever tell you about the time I got in a fight with Toby?" Tutor expertly changes subjects.

Glad for the shift, I chuckle. "No, you did not. Do tell."

"Annuals back, I decided to take a visit out to see the world. I traveled to meet up with a scout troop I had once known. Toby was among them." Tutor eases into his story. "I had been with them a few nights and we were all camped out around a fire just enjoying life. The men were all chattering away about this and that. I happened to be sitting by Toby. Well, Toby was carrying on about Fraun and how much he hated the royals there."

"Was this before you knew of your blood?"

"Just before, actually. I didn't take it too personally. But I had been tutoring Eselda and nursing a sad version of a crush. I knew it was wrong and she was, after all, a bit younger than me."

"And out of your league, of course." I good-naturedly rib the older man, mostly to show I am okay with talking about her.

"Of course." Tutor laughs. "So, when Toby attacks the royals, I take offense to it. I stand up, in the middle of this group of large men, and declare that he doesn't know what he is talking about," Tutor says. I laugh and Tutor continues the tale with vigor, egged on by the show of support. "I tell him that some of the royals are better people than anyone in this group of deserters. Of course, Toby won't stand for that. He gets right in my face." Tutor holds his hand about one mark from his nose. "He tells me that if I want to argue with him, I'll have to back it up with my fists."

I laugh, imagining the scene. "What did you do? Tell me you ran away as you should have. Tell me you backed down."

"No, sir. Think about this, I was fully in my malicious age at the time."

"Oh that's right, but you didn't know that."

"I didn't, but it sure makes sense now." Tutor laughs. "In my state, I was sure I could take on anyone and I was not about to be wrong. So, I picked up my hand …" as he talks he demonstrates the action "… and I slapped him in the face."

My laugh is long and deep. "What did he do then?"

"What do you think he did?" Tutor joins the laughter. "He hit me so hard I landed on the other side of the clearing on my rear end."

"Did you learn your lesson?" I ask through laughter.

"Yes. I learned never to stand up to Toby." Both of us laugh heartily.

I wipe stray tears from the corners of my eyes where laughter has squeezed them out. Then I take a deep breath. "Was it strange, going through the age marker without knowing what it was?" I ask.

"You know what I think? I think the age markers are kind of an excuse. I think once you know what they are, it's worse. They can be controlled. I controlled them and I watched you control them well tonight. I think it's like the pain I had in my leg after that fight with Toby; it's there and you know it, but it doesn't keep you from walking."

"Wise words, friend. Are you sure you aren't from Renchenda?"

Tutor fixes me with a serious expression. "I am Fraunian. When this war is over, that is what we will all be."

"I like that idea. We can all be strong and humble."

"We can all be fast, mirthful, and wise as well. Imagine how powerful we will be then." Tutor smiles into the darkness.

My mind recalls similar words being spoken about the patrol. "Tutor, you need to speak about that with the army when it comes time."

"You think?"

"That will be the idea they can stand behind. That will be the thing they are looking for. It will be the promise you can make that Tin could never offer them. Well-rounded lives in all skills." Suddenly, I am sure that is the answer. "We will all be Fraunians."

"Fraunians, it is." The words ring through the night, a simple solution to a messy problem.

Chapter 57

Across Fraun, unbeknownst to the two men discussing what it would mean to be Fraunian, Tin leads an army with a different purpose in their direction. Atop a roach, the king of strength rides proudly. Perhaps none in the army see a difference in their king, but fear is slowly easing its way into him. Fear makes him vulnerable. Being vulnerable makes him angry. Anger makes him dangerous.

Behind him sprawls the army of Sarcheda. They are vast now, owing to the promises Tin has been making. When your choices are to join the army or die of hunger, many join the army. They ask very few questions about what their mission entails because to question the king is to be an enemy of the king. There is no doubt about what this king does to his enemies.

Directly behind Tin rides his only living general, Trep. Trep eyes his king warily. It has been a while since the men have seen Tin outside of the Sarcheda home. His coloring has changed. Perhaps the fight with Eselda was a bigger issue than they thought. Trep shakes his head sadly. Tin could've been a great leader. Immediately Trep chastises himself for thinking in the past tense. That is no way to enter into a fight. Surely the great king is in there somewhere. The man whom Trep followed into battle. The man whom Trep would die to protect. The man who promises riches and fame for all his followers. Riches and fame to be surpassed only by those of the king himself.

Trep has been inside the resplendent home, he has seen what money can buy. Never again, after this war, will the general's own family have to live in squalor. He will not have to share a room with three children, sleep on the floor, and eat rotting food just to survive. The king will give fame to the army. Since all of Sarcheda has someone enrolled in the mass of fighters behind him, the king will have no choice but to give honor to all of Sarcheda.

The roach Tin rides on pulls to a stop in front of a home with three women standing outside, hanging wet clothes on a line. "Good evening, ladies," Tin says. He turns on the charm instantly and without thought, melting into his old ways. The youngest girl giggles and turns her eyes down, hiding behind her hair.

"We are traveling to Renchenda," Tin explains. "Are we headed along the right path?"

"You are not welcome here." The oldest woman stands her ground before him. She uses her arm to push the giggling girl behind her and stares him down. "We want no part of this riff you have created in Fraun. You will not get directions from us."

Behind Tin, Trep's eyes widen. This woman has guts, even if she is a fool.

"Madam, perhaps you are unaware of who you are speaking to. I understand that men in army uniforms may seem like easy targets for your anger. I am no ordinary army man." Tin drops his voice to a dangerous growl. "I am King."

"I know precisely who you are."

Tin feels the shock of the information. For a heartbeat, he thinks about riding away and forgetting this conversation ever happened, returning to his war without worrying about the few people who do not support him. Instead, he turns his head and takes in the sight of the countless men behind him whose support he does have. These men cannot be allowed to see him ignoring problems like this. Not supporting the true king of Fraun must not be an option.

He steps off the roach and moves until he is at arm's length from the woman. She does not move except to flick her hand toward the door. The woman left to the side takes it as her signal to pull the giggling girl by the arm into the house. The click of the lock echoes through the front yard.

"If you know who I am then you know, precisely, what you have invoked with this show of disrespect," Tin says.

The woman nods. "I do." She looks him up and down. When her eyes reach his face they stop and a smile spreads across her lips. "I have invoked your fear."

The reaction is pure instinct. Tin backhands the woman across her cheek. She sprawls to the ground. He stays frozen like that, his arm in the air, as he watches her. She props herself on her elbows and gingerly touches her cheek where the blow fell. Still on the ground, she turns her face up to Tin.

She laughs. The sound, hollow and out of place with the times, echoes through the army. "I cannot be so easily beaten down as your queen. You will have to try harder with me."

The laughter is what sets him off. Tin pulls the sword from his side and holds it to her throat. Immediately, the woman freezes. "You are out of line, woman."

"I walk the line you have created." She makes no move to shy away from Tin's blade.

He doesn't wait for her to say anymore. He pulls his arm back and stares into her eyes as he slices cleanly through her neck.

As he watches the woman bleed out a few thoughts run through his mind; he hopes this shows his army he still has power, he hopes killing Jordyn will be as easy as this, and he hopes this was the last of the openly defiant citizens. One thing is certain, the woman who literally raised her chin in the face of death and kept her eyes open wide to greet it will not soon be forgotten by the king of strength.

Chapter 58

One Fraun. One Fraun. One Fraun.

It is all I have ever wanted. How can they not see that this is the answer? One Fraun united under a single king that will lead them to greatness. No more fighting about decisions. No more proving your point to four other kings. No more majority rulings.

One king. One Fraun.

As they draw closer to the castle, a tall shape comes into view. Tin's anger deepens. *Jordyn. Of course it's Jordyn. How fitting. The person who stands between me and one united Fraun stands alone to stop me from taking it.*

Jordyn is not trained to fight someone like me. I will take him down and then there will be no one to stand in my way. Tin glances at the soldiers behind him. *First, the woman who dared to question me fell and now the king who stands for old Fraun will fall. No one will ever question my authority again.*

Chapter 59

The army does not draw weapons. They approach and fill the lawn of the castle. The scouts and I take position on the stairs facing them. Tutor, leaning on his long stick, stands beside me. He looks equal parts deadly and yet calm with his stance. It's a mix that I worry I am not projecting, as my insides are quaking for the coming battle. Do I have what is needed for this within me?

Tin rides up through the center of his army, most of whom walk. Another man rides directly beside him. They draw up close to the steps and stop.

Anger, which has nothing to do with my age marker, ignites. I reach for the hilt of the sword at my side and wrap my hand around it. I make a conscious decision to let the anger wash over me. The rush of power is a drug. It floods my system and changes everything. My eyes and vision darken. My limbs feel longer. I stand to my full, impressive, height. "Step down from that roach," I command. My voice booms through the assembled army.

Tin dismounts and wraps his hand around the hilt of his sword. He smirks. "What is your plan here, Jordyn? My army is vast." He gestures to the assemblage with his free hand. "Surely you don't intend a dozen men to hold off the army of Sarcheda."

I step forward to the edge of the stone steps and gesture back toward Tutor. "This man lays stake to Sarcheda by virtue of two bloodlines in his veins. He is a rightful descendant of Enchenda and Marchenda. By absorbing Enchenda into the ranks of Sarcheda, you have given him the freedom to take your title." My eyes burn into Tin's face. I don't care about any other bodies in the clearing tonight. This is personal. "You are no longer the king of Sarcheda, Tin. Stand down."

"If you want my title, you will have to take it by force."

A dangerous smile takes over my face. "I thought you'd never ask."

Chapter 60

Tutor watches the exchange between the two former kings. He lets them have this moment, knowing it is as personal and raw as they need. When the talking is over, Jordyn is the first to attack. Tutor watches nervously as they clash blades a few times. Suddenly, Tin turns and dashes from the clearing toward the woods on the left. *Why would he flee?* Tutor turns to look at the scouts and finds Sawchett has notched an arrow. *He ran to keep it between the two of them. A fair duel.*

Tutor fights his instinct to follow Jordyn and help, knowing his fight is here.

"Fraunians," he shouts to the army. "What Jordyn spoke was true. I am the bloodline of two great kings. You have been led astray by your leader. He spoke lies to you and made promises he never meant to keep. Think about it. Have you been given the food and accommodations you were promised? My friend and former patrolman, Lance, tells me that you have been sleeping in tents and eating slop.

"Tin has no intention of treating you differently once you are united. Fighting and war are his only truth. What has he done to convince you that this will stop when he is the one king of Fraun?" He pauses here, but no one answers. Tutor considers it positive that they are listening quietly instead of drawing weapons.

"I cannot promise you riches. I cannot promise you fame. I can promise you a king that will listen. I can promise you representation at the council table. I can promise you that the Fraunians who lead the five realms of Fraun will work together to make the right decisions. I can promise you that we will listen to you regarding what is wrong.

"I can also promise you a Fraun that is balanced in a way Fraun has never been. Imagine a Fraun where you can be strong, humble, fast, mirthful, and wise. We plan to educate all Fraunians in every trait. We plan to represent and display them all.

"I have made my choice, as have the people standing here with me. We want a balanced Fraun and we will fight anyone who wants otherwise."

Behind Tutor, the assembled scouts and Fraunians draw their weapons. Abney, Sawchett, and Evelyn are on bows. Sieven, Lance, Toby, and Thometh with swords. Lili and Carlina holding daggers. Kurt, Franc, and Hector sporting long sticks. They are a small group, but their determination shows. King Hector flings open the doors to the castle, revealing more Fraunians with weapons ready to step up.

"Today is your chance to choose," Tutor says. "Do you follow the empty promises of Tin and risk dying for his cause? Or do you accept me as a rightful king of Fraun and join us today for balance?"

Chapter 61

Tin runs through the trees at full speed. Branches sting his face and arms as they leave their marks. *That girl, the little blonde one, was readying to shoot me with an arrow. That is hardly fair play.* Instead, he dashed off into the woods. At first, he fully intended to stop and fight, but the trees do not allow for such.

The trees give way to an open, grassy area. Tin slows his running to a jog as he crosses it. He stops at the far side and bends down to catch his breath and listen for Jordyn. *How can I no longer be King? Who cares what the council says? Once I win this battle, it will all be over. My men will dispense of that traitor and I will be King.* He rises as he hears Jordyn's footsteps crashing through the trees, renewed anger showing on his face.

Chapter 62

I have let the blade fall to my side as I run. Now, entering the clearing, I draw back to a fighting stance. I see anger on Tin's face as he rushes toward me. I use everything I have learned from Lance as we battle. But the pain in my arms, a result of the strength of my opponent, is like nothing I have experienced. Tin is strong, there is no question about that.

I strike out high, forcing Tin to put the blade over his head. The motion puts Tin off balance, he stumbles and falls to the ground. I plunge at Tin, but the blade is pushed aside. He jumps to his feet. Something in his eyes changes, a flash of something. With his next attack, he comes harder at me. He steps forward with each thrust, pushing me backward. I meet his attack, content to let him tire himself out.

Until I feel my back hit a tree. Then, panic wells up inside me. This is how it all ends.

"Well, isn't this interesting? I seem to have you backed against a wall here, old friend." Tin roars and pushes the sword forward.

The pain is instant. It rushes from my body with a groan. I drop to the foot of the tree, squeezing my eyes shut as my hand clamps down on the wound. I watch Tin raise his arms in triumph.

This is how it all ends.

Chapter 63

Not everyone steps up to join Tutor and the scouts after the rally speech. The front line of the army charges them without further hesitation. They are met with the weapons of the team, and most lay in a heap at the foot of the stairs within minutes. Sawchett earns herself a sword across the cheek when she misses with her arrow, but Sieven kills the offender shortly after.

This quick dispense of the first round leads many of the soldiers to step forward, turn, and face the Sarcheda army. Tutor acknowledges the shift in their allegiance with a quick nod.

The rest of the former army of Sarcheda seems to divide before their eyes. The fighting is instant among them. Shouts of "traitor" and "coward" ring through the clearing. Tutor shrugs at his friends and charges into the fray.

Chapter 64

I open my eyes to see Tin standing over me, arms raised in celebration. I glance down at the bloody spot on my armor. The sword tip has pierced right through, but the wound is above my heart. I am alive.

Tin notices my eyes open. He adjusts his stance, ready to continue the fight. "You are wounded, but not out yet?"

"You'll have to kill me to stop me," I say.

"That was the plan, old friend."

Our blades clash again and the fighting continues. The wound, thankfully, is on my left and I am right-handed. Still, every thrust forces a grunt or groan. I am beginning to lose hope that I will ever win this battle. I can only hope that enough true Fraunians remain to dispense of Tin when he returns to the battle there.

I take a step and my ankle twists painfully. Unable to stop myself, I fall to the ground. Tin stands over me, triumphant. A smile stretches over Tin's face as he raises his arms high overhead. I notice the weakness he has exposed. I use my long arms to lean forward and put the tip of my blade at

Tin's exposed throat. "Drop the sword," I command.

There is a pause before the sound of the blade crashing to the ground echoes off the trees. Holding my sword steady, I slowly rise to my feet.

Tin puts his arms up in surrender. He breathes deeply and keeps his eyes glued to mine. "Tell me you can be redeemed," I command. "Tell me that there's hope for you."

Tin smiles. "You're a coward, Jordyn." He leans closer to me, pushing his skin against the blade enough to send a trickle of bright red blood down his neck. "You don't have the guts to finish this."

"You taunt the man who holds your life in his hands?"

"I will tell you the same thing my father once told me," Tin says. "Prove you want it badly enough to kill for it and I will only feel pride. I wanted that dream enough to push my parents, who I loved, to their death. You only have to kill your competition to end it." He takes another step forward, grunting as the tip disappears into his neck. "I'm making it easy for you."

"There is no redemption in you?" I'm angry to hear how my voice quakes. Taking this man's life will stay with me forever. Despite everything I have practiced, despite everything I have seen, that is something I cannot bring myself to do. My grip slackens on the sword.

"None. Jordyn, if you show me mercy I will kill you," Tin states. He smiles. "Either way, this is almost over."

I back the sword up until I can again see the tip of it, gleaming red in the fading sunlight. I cannot do it. Tin smiles. "Well, at least in death you may finally have the heart of the woman you could never have in life." He takes a step back from me, toward the fallen sword. "Say hello to Eselda for me in the afterlife."

My eyes darken until they are blacker than the sky in the dead of night, I can tell in the way the clearing is plunged into total darkness. "You killed her?" All rational thought leaves my brain. Before Tin can make another move, I charge at him. I scream as I plunge the sword into the chest plate.

I am smart enough to know exactly where the heart is.

Chapter 65

"Jordyn." The name reverberates off the trees. It is dangerous to be out this way calling his name, not knowing which of them still stands from the battle. Toby shakes his head and calls again. "Jordyn." They've been gone too long. "Jordyn."

Toby cautiously approaches a clearing in the trees. There are no sounds and two bodies on the ground. *Two bodies is not a good sign.* He speeds up, rushing into the clearing. Tin lays in the dirt, legs crumpled as though he fell. A sword sticks straight up from his chest. He is not moving.

A short distance away Jordyn lies on his side. He is bleeding from somewhere on the left side of his chest and there is a lot of blood running down the breastplate and pooling under him. He is staring at Tin. Toby hears ragged breaths as he draws closer. *Thank Fraun, he breathes.*

"Jordyn?" Toby takes a step closer to his friend, kneeling to tap him lightly on the shoulder. Jordyn does not move. "Jordyn, you need medical attention for that wound. You'll have to come with me," Toby prods.

Jordyn nods his head once, without removing his eyes from the fallen enemy. Toby waits as Jordyn gets his feet beneath him. When he turns his face to Toby, the breath leaves the younger man's lungs. There is no trace of the faint blue in Jordyn's eyes, they are completely black. "Are you okay?" Toby asks.

"No." Jordyn begins to walk slowly in the direction of Castle Fraun. Toby has no choice but to follow.

Chapter 66

Medicine men and nurses travel through the fallen Fraunians for both sides looking for any who can be treated. Tutor sits on the steps, nursing a sore arm and watching, hopeful. During the battle, his shoulder had been popped out of place. Although it is back in place now, the pain remains.

He glances down at a gash on his right side, courtesy of a sword from the remaining general to Tin's army. "Hold still," the medicine woman hisses. She is stitching quickly, trying to close the wound.

"I'm trying," Tutor speaks through clenched teeth. "It feels like you're sewing it with hot coals."

She meets his eye. "Stop watching. Think about something else." She looks back down at the work. Strands of her long brown hair are blowing on a light breeze and getting in her way. "Of, for Fraun sake. Chop this braid off," she commands. She turns her head slightly to allow him access.

"What?" Tutor asks. "You're past ten annuals. If I cut it off, it's not growing back."

She grunts, rolls her eyes, and closes her hand on the hilt of his sword. "It's not clean to have my hair coming out of this braid and into your blood." With one hack along the thick braid, she shows Tutor one more sacrifice he never thought he'd see.

He turns his eyes away from her and out toward the people of Fraun. Really, he is surprised that so many men and women joined the scouts in battle. He was fearful all along, although he wouldn't have admitted it. Fearful that they would all be killed by the mass numbers they faced. Something he said or did must have been important enough to sway them. Now, they sit or stand on the lawn of the castle nursing wounds they sustained while fighting for his cause. He makes a silent vow to himself to make sure their sacrifices are all worthwhile.

"I'm done here," the medicine woman says. "Keep it clean and bandaged until it's fully healed. You'll have a scar." She turns to walk away and Tutor turns his attention to the rest of chis crew. His eyes fall on the crumbled body of Lance. The medicine woman who sewed his gash closed in within shouting distance. "Hey," Tutor yells. "Help me." He runs to Lance's body, falling beside him. He hears the medicine woman join him at his side.

Part of him already knows. Still, he has to ask. "Help him, please." He leans back out of her way.

She leans her head on Lance's chest now, closing her eyes to listen. Tutor looks at the blood pooling underneath the great soldier. The medicine woman's head rises, she catches Tutor's eyes and subtly shakes her head. Tutor watches her reach up and close Lance's eyelids through watery tears. She whispers "be at peace" before she pushes herself off the ground to deal with the rest of the injured.

Tutor lays a hand on the shoulder of the man who taught him how to wield the sword that saved his own life today. "I'm sorry," he whispers.

"Mom? Mom?"

The voice belongs to Sieven. Tutor is sure of it. He pushes up from the ground, leaving Lance's body where it fell, and hurries off toward the sound of the voice. Sieven is on his knees, bending over the fallen body. Cold fear wraps around Tutor's heart. *Not another one.*

"Is she—" Tutor starts.

"She's breathing. I need help here," Sieven yells.

A young man is beside them in an instant. Tutor steps away to allow him space and turns his eyes to the woods where Jordyn and Tin disappeared. *Who else will fall today?*

Chapter 67

The darkness in my vision is so complete that it is like navigating the woods in the pitch black of night. I can barely see through the obscure filter before me. I have stumbled a few times. Unfortunately, I have not fallen and cracked my unworthy head open on something. I keep walking. My throat burns from unshed tears that just won't fall. I'm too much of a monster to cry now. I am a murderer. I'm no better than Tin. Compared to the guilt weighing on my soul and my broken heart, the pain inflicted by Tin's blade is nothing.

Chapter 68

"Tutor, they're back!" Sieven, closest to the woods, calls out.

Tutor turns his head, interrupting his conversation with King Hector, to see. Sure enough, Jordyn has emerged from the woods with Toby in tow. There's a second of happiness at seeing his friend triumphant. It does not last. Something is wrong. Tutor jogs to meet them. He stops at Jordyn and takes stock of what he sees. His eyes are darker than Tutor would've thought possible. There is a wound somewhere on his chest. "Jordyn, it's Tutor. How bad is it?" he asks.

Jordyn tries to focus on Tutor's face, but through the filters it is difficult. He wants to form words, he wants to tell Tutor of the battle.

The wise former king whom Tutor has grown to admire crumbles in front of him. It catches Tutor off guard and he only has enough time to keep Jordyn's head from striking the ground. "Get me a medicine man, now," Tutor yells at Toby.

Tutor drops to the ground beside Jordyn. "It's going to be alright. We will fix it," he promises. He only hopes he's not lying.

Chapter 69

"What is our next course of action?"

"We need to get you settled in Sarcheda."

"I'm more concerned about keeping our promises."

"So, what do you suggest?"

"We need to immediately have a council meeting. Can you step outside and find everyone?"

"Right now?"

"What would we wait for?"

I lay on the cot and listen to the exchange. I recognize the voices of Tutor and Hector. I keep my eyes squeezed shut. The pain in my body is down to a twinge. Likely, this is owing to some kind of herb for pain management. My thoughts turn to Eselda and I draw a shaky breath. Dead? I had hoped, more than anything, that the resolution of that story would be different. What is left for me in Fraun now?

Hearing footsteps leave the room, I sit up. I find Tutor standing alone. The newest king rushes to my side. "How are you feeling? They have stitched the wound closed. You were triumphant in your battle. Toby tells me Tin is dead, no pulse."

"She's dead, Tutor," I answer. I feel my eyes fill with tears.

"What? Who?"

"Eselda."

The air leaves Tutor in a rush. He sits on the edge of the cot and his shoulders slump. "I think I thought we would be successful with her rescue."

"As did I."

"We were successful on all other ventures, Jordyn. Surely you can see it is wise to focus on that." Tutor offers a crooked smile.

I can only nod. It may be wise, but I cannot.

"We are meeting with the council in a few moments. I have sent for them all. You will join us, yes?" Tutor asks.

There is much to be done for the future of Fraun. Many changes are coming. I cannot be another corrupt king of Fraun, murdering for my cause and then sitting at the table like I know best. If I had the gumption to choose Eselda, would any of this have happened? If our realms had united, would it have been enough to keep Tin from this war? "I will not do that, Tutor."

"You are not resuming your throne in Renchenda?"

"Thometh is a good king. He fits with the council you are creating. He will lead Renchenda to great things."

"You would as well, surely you are aware of this."

"I am aware of my strengths. I am also aware of my shortcomings. I will not be King again."

"So be it. Where can we find you, should we need you?" Tutor asks.

"I will travel with the scouts who have accepted me fully as I am. I regret that I may not always be easy to find, but that is my desire."

"I would argue with you, but you have changed. Your eyes have gone black and your posture slumps. Either the loss of Eselda or whatever decision you were forced to make in that wood has changed you." He leaves his agreement on my inability to lead Renchenda unspoken. "Jordyn, I wish you the best on your travels. Stay safe and check in with us." Tutor claps me on the shoulder as he walks out the open doorway to find Hector.

"Give her a proper burial."

Tutor is already in the hallway and has surely shifted his focus to the pending meeting. My voice is quiet. He could ignore the request. Yet Tutor once loved Eselda like a brother loves a sister. He even admitted he once felt something more serious for her. This is how I know he will do it.

Chapter 70

The meeting is not at all what the previous council would condone. The leaders of Fraun are convening in the hallway of the castle. Tutor and Hector stand leaning against the wall, but the rest of the royals have seated themselves comfortably on the floor. Sawchett herself is propped up against her older brother's legs. They all wear weary expressions after the recent battle, but no one is arguing the importance of this meeting.

"We need to dispense with the formal appointments of leaders for all realms. I suggest a roll call of sorts," Tutor begins.

"I will lead Farcheda," Hector says.

"Under King Hector's rule, I propose Farcheda be named as first realm," Tutor says. "Assuming there are no objections." The Fraunians filling the hallway silently nod their accordance.

"I will lead Marchenda, I assume that's why I'm here." Alerta is a beautiful woman with tantalizing dark skin. Tutor smiles at her almost without meaning to. She is likely around his age, a fact he does not miss.

"Am I to remain in my position?" Thometh asks. He is looking to

Tutor, who merely nods. "Then I accept that fate. I will lead Renchenda."

"I will lead Sarcheda until someone with that blood can be located," Tutor says.

The hallway falls silent. Tutor shifts his leg to alert his sister to her cue. He glances down to ensure she is awake. When she still doesn't respond, he bends low. "That would be you next, Sawchett," he says, annoyed.

"Things need to change around here before I agree to this," Sawchett says, her voice loud enough for all.

She rises. Perhaps it's her bold statement or the way she suddenly carries herself with a dignified posture. Perhaps it's the blood on the hem of her shirt that came from battling for Fraun. Perhaps it's her age, which even Tutor has lost track of in the confusion. Whatever the reason, she suddenly appears more like a queen than anyone was expecting from a child of her age.

"I am not agreeing to be a part of a council that continues in the way it has been. We need representation from all realms. A representation that is not royal blood." The statement rings in the hallway, bouncing off the stone. "I propose we hold something of an election for a representative to attend council meetings with royalty. What says the council?" she asks.

"I find I like that idea. Would you continue to bring ideas like that to the table, Sawchett?" Thometh asks.

"I am full of ideas like that."

"Then I propose we accept her proposal to keep her on board with us. We could use her ideas. Who among us should call for a vote?" Thometh says.

"All in favor?" Sawchett's voice rings clear in the chamber. All the hands in the room rise, Tutor offering her a crooked smile and a little chuckle with his vote.

"Then I will gladly lead Enchenda."

Although the meeting doesn't look like the meeting the old council would've approved of, there is a council that would have been proud of what they are seeing. It's not Mick's council, Gregario's council, or even Larecio's.

Once upon a time, at the beginning of Fraun, five brothers sat on the steps of this very castle and created the realms. They spoke like brothers, they were informal, and yet they created everything our heroes have known and fought for.

If they could see it, those brothers would be proud of this group. They would know that, under this crew, everything is going to be alright.

Epilogue

As the days pass, it gets easier. Easier to forgive myself, easier to stop imagining what her life would've been like, and easier to move on from Fraun.

The sun is rising over the hillside, painting the sky with its vivid blend of purples and pinks. I am the only one of the scout troop awake. I take a bite of the strawberry I have picked and take stock of what remains of my crew.

Franc and Carlina sleep in a tent nearby. Franc has grayed and seems to be sick, but he is still alive for now. It is hard to imagine what Carlina will be like once Franc is gone. I have been planting the idea in her mind that it may be wise to move her to Fraun.

Sieven and Abney have married and moved to a home in Farcheda. Sieven was recently elected to be Ambassador to the council. They seem to be doing well. Sieven misses his mother, who died on the battlefield. We miss her around camp as well. It is something we discuss often in our letters, which Sieven and I exchange regularly.

After Lance's death, I learned that he had a wife and young son living in Enchenda. I often send care packages to them directly. I feel the weight of his death of my shoulders often. Lance was a good man and his family needs someone to help care for them. I hate that I have cost them that.

Danyel has taken up residence in Sarcheda. I have made a few deliveries there. The young man seems to be flourishing under the new balanced teaching. He seems happier than he did before the war.

Sawchett and Tutor, of course, have moved on to represent royal blood in Fraun. I am careful to avoid personal deliveries to their residences or read letters from them. Although they are two of the few I consider to be friends it is hard to face them. I am no longer a part of Fraun, and it hurts too much to be around people who remind me of her. The queen and king who reside in the homes she once lived in, who knew her when she was young … surely that would be too difficult.

Toby has returned to Fraun for treatment of an infection he sustained during the fighting. He hopes to return to our camp after he is healed. The medicine man who treats him tells me that the wound is serious. He is not sure if Toby will survive, let alone be allowed to return to the life of a Scout.

Evelyn and Kurt round out the remaining crew. In truth, it will likely be only this couple and me wandering the outskirts of Fraun together, exploring the world left by the giants, once Franc passes. It doesn't matter. I would wander it alone if they all moved back. I am not fit to be in Fraun any longer.

Out here my age marker has less control over me. When it does gain a footing, I can fight it off easily. No one out here should be threatened by my ability to lose control. Carlina has taken it upon herself to check in with me each morning and let me know what happens with my eye color. In the time since the war, I have decided to ensure the crew all know what royals battle. Eye color has been a significant indicator of the markers. Once I allowed the beast to win and took the life of another, my eyes became black. Slowly, in the annual since, my eyes have lightened a little each day. They are still not back to their clear blue.

I wonder what her eyes looked like darkened in her age marker. I drop my head into my hands. Why can I not even allow myself to think her name? It's as if I have allowed her memory to grow even stronger in her absence. Perhaps I'm giving it too much power.

I raise my head to the sky. "Eselda." I allow her name to echo off the trees around me. The wind whispers back to me, bringing the memories with it. Her small hand on my chest, teaching me about love.

Love.

I have never loved another, Eselda, and I never will. I travel with women who are married and my seniors as I approach the age of the flesh. I made a mistake, I pushed you away. It is my deepest regret.

That memory rushes to me as well. I had lost all control and confessed my feelings to her outside the council room. We shared a kiss that I will remember forever. That is the day I broke her heart and forever became a monster.

My eyes track to the edge of the forest. The memories pop like a bubble as my attention is fully on the shifting shape between the trees. We are no longer weary of war and under constant attack, but wild animals travel out here. I reach for my sword with small movements, never moving my eyes from the shadows. A figure stumbles from between the trees, clutching something in its right hand. My breath catches in my throat before I faint away, falling to the ground beside the log I had been sitting on.

When my eyes flutter open I have to squint at whoever is above me. The sunlight is shining around behind them, blinding me. Features start to come into focus; long hair slowly falling out of a side braid, round pale face, large green eyes. It's impossible. "You're alive?"

"As are you, evidently," Eselda answers. She grabs my hand and pulls me up to a seated position on the ground, sitting down across from me. "I have been tracking you for lunar cycles, Jordyn."

"I thought you were dead. He said you were dead." My brain cannot process what I am seeing. My heart hammers away in my chest. Unable to help myself, I reach out to touch her arm. She is really here, this isn't a hallucination.

"Should I tell you what did happen to me?" she asks. I merely nod. "He had me locked in a room of his home. Then one day the key was just there, on the floor, waiting for me. I opened the door and ran. No one stopped me. But I was exhausted and underfed. I didn't get very far before I collapsed. A nice lady brought me into her home and fed me. I kept ranting to her about the dream I'd been having and how the man I love needed to be rescued."

I cannot correct her right now. This is not the time to explain to her that Tin was a monster. This is certainly not the time to tell her I killed him myself. What will she think of me?

"The woman and I went outside her home when we heard the sounds of roaches returning toward the Sarcheda home. Imagine our surprise when it was Tutor leading the pack. My former tutor, a royal. I spent a few nights discussing things with him. I've been officially pardoned for my part in the war, although I have been banished." She shrugs her thin shoulders as though this is nothing to worry about. "Tutor was writing to you for me. He told me he was explaining my story, explaining how I was searching for you. He was to let me know when he found your exact location. When I was banished I headed for the last place you were seen. I've been nearby here for over a lunar cycle, hoping you and your scouts would return."

"Why … why me?" I croak.

Eselda reaches for my hand. She rubs her thumb across the back of my palm. "I need your forgiveness, Jordyn."

That is backward. "Why?"

"I have been punished or forgiven by everyone in Fraun that I wronged. I have come to terms with what happened and my part in all of it. But you are the one person left who I wronged. The one person remaining who knew me better than I knew myself. I owe you an apology for turning my back on you. You tried to tell me what I was facing. I realize now, Jordyn, that I always loved you. I wanted to come and tell you that, in person. It was never Tin, not in the same way. I see that now. I'm sorry I didn't see it then."

My heart soars. Love. Love fixes everything. "Eselda, that is the most amazing thing I have ever heard."

Eselda's entire face lights up with her smile. "Truly?"

"Truly. But I'm afraid I can only forgive you on one condition." Here goes nothing. "You have to forgive me as well." Seeing the confusion flit across her beautiful face, I rush the explanation. "I never should have refused to be with you once I realized the depth of my feelings. But it's more than that.

"Eselda, I killed Tin. I gave into the age marker so completely that it turned my eyes black, but I was conscious of the act. I chose to kill another Fraunian. I'm not sure if that is as easily forgiven as what you ask me to forgive you for."

Eselda squeezes my hand. "I had noticed your eyes are darker, actually. Jordyn, I already knew about Tin. Tutor told me." Her voice is quiet. "This bothers you, doesn't it?"

"I'm as bad as he is, Eselda. I took a life."

"You listen to me, Jordyn. You will never be even half as bad as that man. He locked me in a room to die, he killed his parents, he murdered a prince, and he cared for no one but himself. He needed to be stopped. Frankly, you are my hero for bringing an end to the misery he brought to Fraun. You do not need my forgiveness." She reaches out her free hand and lays it on my chest, running her thumb along the new muscles underneath the thin shirt. "You need love to help you learn to forgive yourself."

The warmth radiates from where her palm lies out toward the rest of my body. I reach for her shoulders and pull her forward. My breathing quickens at the thought of being able to touch her again.

The kiss I had been remembering before she returned, the kiss that went down as the best kiss either of us had ever had? This one was better.

This one was the beginning of our forever.

Training Tutor

Training Tutor was first published in the summer of 2020. It was Tutor's story. Readers had been on quite a journey to this point and Tutor had been faithfully there since the very first scene of the very first book. It made sense to give him a chance to tell his story, especially considering what we'd learned about him in book 2.

For this book, things were changing. I had made the decision to take this series beyond where a fantasy series normally goes. We were going past the war, past the happily-ever-after. The driving question now became can Fraun rebuild and accept the new lineage?

This one, unlike the previous two, never had another title. It was never in third person, it was never longer or shorter than it is now. The basics of this one were decided early on and I was able to keep it.

In *Training Tutor* we see the addition of a new bad guy. When I was drafting the early stories, I already knew this guy existed. He's in my early notes, actually, but he never made it to the page until book 3. I'm not sure that he's worse than Tin, per se, but I know he's the reason Tin is the way he is. That's all I'm saying about that.

Fun Facts about *Training Tutor:*

1. The very first scene I ever wrote for this one was actually the sunburn scene with Tutor and Alerta. I almost never write things out of order but this one just came to me and I had to write it down. It's also how I decided early on that Tutor and Alerta were going to have a very different relationship than Jordyn and Eselda ever did.
2. My favorite character from this one is Danyel. When we first meet Danyel in *Breaking Eselda* he's this shell of who he could be. Writing his growth as he comes back to life and finds a purpose has been amazing.
3. My favorite scene in this one is probably that first chapter back with the Scouts. Something about the way you just drop out of the stress of living in Fraun and back into the slow moving camp of the Scouts is so refreshing.

That's your background on *Training Tutor.* Enjoy this one. It's the one you don't get in most fantasy stories, the one that probably wouldn't have happened if I followed the "rules". It's what happens next.

Prologue

"Fraunians, what Jordyn spoke was true. I am the bloodline of two great kings. You have been led astray by your leader. He spoke lies to you, made promises he never meant to keep. Think on it. Have you been given the food and accommodations you were promised? My friend and former patrolman, Lance, tells me that you have been sleeping in tents and eating slop.

"Tin has no intention of treating you differently once you are united. Fighting and war are his only truth. What has he done to convince you that this will stop when he is the one king of Fraun?

"I cannot promise you riches. I cannot promise you fame. I can promise you a king that will listen. I can promise you representation at the council table. I can promise you that the men and women who lead the five realms of Fraun will work together to make the decisions that are right. I can promise you that we will listen to you in regards to what is wrong.

"I can also promise you a Fraun that is balanced in a way Fraun has never been. Imagine a Fraun where you can be strong, humble, fast, mirthful, and wise. We plan to educate all Fraunians in every trait. We plan to represent and display them all.

"I have made my choice, as have the people standing here with me. We want a balanced Fraun and we will fight anyone who wants otherwise.

"Today is your chance to choose. Do you follow the empty promises of Tin and risk dying for his cause? Or do you accept me as a rightful king of Fraun and join us today for balance?"

Chapter 1

I am King of a realm I have no right to represent. This thought runs through my head as the man before me kneels to be recognized. He has lived in Sarcheda his entire life. He has served Kings of Sarcheda before me. Yet he bows to me. Before he is fully erect again the thought has been chased from my mind and all traces of it expertly wiped from my expression. I have earned this seat. Not just through bloodlines, of which I have a majority, but through battle.

"King Tutor," he begins, "I am here before you today to offer my services to your throne." He is not a tall man, although neither am I. I land a few clicks below the mark that is two inches on the ruler in the medicine tents. This man would likely fall at exactly two inches. We value stature around most of Fraun. But I have learned it is the muscles that matter in Sarcheda. Despite his age, obvious in the white hair that rests in tight curls along his head, he would probably best me in that category as well.

"What services could you provide me, Marcus?" I can see the shock in his face at my using his name. He must think little of me. Of course I have used my resources to learn all about him in preparation for the meeting, only a fool would come unprepared.

"I am a tutor, Majesty. I tutored the great King Tin, among others, in the ways of Fraun. Surely I can be of assistance."

I hide my shock at the reverence in which the former king's name is delivered. A man who declared war on Fraun just two short annuals ago should not be spoken of in such a manner. "I was a tutor myself before the war. If I recall, those of royal blood are given tutors only until they rule. Why, good sir, would a seated King require a tutor?" I ask.

Marcus tilts his head to look up and down my form. When his eyes land again on my face I cannot help but notice they appear to find me lacking. Sarcheda citizens are used to dark skin, strong bodies, and muscles. My underdeveloped set of biceps, pale skin, dirty blonde hair, brown eyes, and glasses are not likely to be what he is looking for in a king of strength. "I only assumed, since you have no blood of Sarcheda within your veins and were never seen around our realm before the war, that you would need to know more about daily life for our fine citizens." He clears his throat. "I had heard," he adds, "you had trouble acclimating."

I cross my arms over my chest. "Be careful what you imply here, Marcus. I am your King. Do you have a challenge you'd like to issue?"

Marcus lowers his chin, a sad excuse for a full bow before a king. "I have no royal blood in my veins, Majesty. Certainly not enough to claim majority over someone with the blood of Enchenda and Marchenda in their veins." Somehow the names of the realms that hold my ancestry sound like vile words from his mouth.

"Then you have no rights with which to challenge my throne."

"I do not."

"Then there is only one thing left to say to you." I take calculated steps across the stone floor until I am within striking distance of the man. I lean toward him. I am not a fool. This man is threatening me. If I have learned anything from my time training with the scouts and living in Sarcheda since the war, it's how to use my body to intimidate. I puff out my chest and raise my arms slightly, so they hover away from my body giving the impression I may hit him at any time.

"If you have a problem with my bloodline, you are welcome to find a living heir of Sarcheda himself and bring them before me to challenge my throne. Until then, I will not be needing your services or your suggestions."

He drops his chin again. I turn to walk back to the front of the meeting room. From behind me, I hear his voice. "I apologize if I have offended you. I did not mean it to sound like an insult."

I do not turn around. "Yes, you did. However, I accept your apology."

"I would be honored if your Majesty would consider me for a seat on the council of representatives, to show there are no hard feelings."

I freeze where I am, halfway to the exit and my escape from the meeting in the royal home where I listen to the grievances of my realm. I answer him without turning. "Sarcheda's Ambassador has never given me any reason to doubt him. He has served us well for two annuals. Why would I replace him?"

"I have heard that Roland plans to step down."

Now I turn. "Excuse me?"

"The rumor is that he wishes more time with his family. In his place, I would be a good candidate for Ambassador to the council representing Sarcheda. I am sure you can see that I have deep roots in Sarcheda. I would like you to put my name in the election."

"I will consider it," I say. My voice pushes through clenched teeth.

"Why do I get the impression that is a no?"

I smile at him, thinking he is a smart man to have garnered that impression. "I have no idea, sir. You are dismissed."

Chapter 2

I am the last to arrive at Castle Fraun. As I approach the home of Thometh, King of Renchenda, I take a moment to enjoy the building that holds so much history for Fraun. Not only is it the largest building in Fraun, rising three stories high, it is also one of the only buildings that our ancestors took the time to create for beauty as well as function. Most places around Fraun follow the rules set forth by our first leader, build only what you need and waste nothing. This building, this tower, was commissioned under the hand of a ruler who believed in power. You can see it in every facet of the building. The door even has elaborate carvings in the wood, something that would have wasted precious time from the builders. Time our council policies tell us would have been better spent on other projects.

But the tower also holds a fascination for me that goes beyond its beauty. We defended this building with our blood and our lives during the War for Fraun. These steps symbolize everything we wanted to accomplish, everything Fraun could be. We took our stand here. As I pull open the wooden door, letting myself into the castle, that is the memory that replays in my mind. Because of this, when I enter the full room for the council meeting, I am in the right mindset to start the meeting. I am ready to forget the frustrating meeting with Marcus yesterday that has occupied my thinking all morning.

I am greeted by the warmth of a fire and the sound of laughter on the warm air. "Good morning, friends. What joke did I miss?" I ask, shaking a dusting of snow from my coat as I hang it on a peg by the door.

Thometh, holding hands with his beautiful new wife, Lucinda, smiles up at me from his seat near the fire. "It was a joke that loses something in the retelling, I fear. Welcome, Tutor. We have saved you a seat near me." He gestures to an empty chair beside him.

The full council is present today. Thometh and Lucinda, King and Queen of Renchenda, are joined by their ambassador, Garven, who once served the patrol which became an army for Tin. Garven considers this position his personal repayment of the debt he owes Fraun. Beside the empty chair left for me sits my ambassador for Sarcheda, Roland. I nod at him in greeting as I take my seat. Queen Sawchett of Enchenda and her ambassador, Annabeth, are seated on the other side of the room.

During the war for Fraun, Annabeth was a healer who tended to wounded fighters. While she was stitching an injury of mine, she cut her hair very close to her head. Since our hair doesn't grow past our fifteenth annual, her hair has stayed at that length, barely kissing her chin, even as it turned gray.

From Farcheda King Hector and Queen Saren are joined by Ambassador Sieven. I offer a smile to Sieven. He has grown so much in the annuals since the war I almost wouldn't recognize the former Scout and friend who fought beside me in the War for Fraun if I didn't see him at every council meeting.

Finally, Queen Alerta of Marchenda is joined by Ambassador Olivia. Olivia may be our most intriguing story since she is only ten annuals. Her striking red hair makes her hard to miss in any crowd, despite her small size. Little Olivia's name was put down on the ballot for Ambassador against an old farmer who had lived in Marchenda all his life. We were a little shocked she won. Secretly, I was also pleased. Olivia is energetic and fresh, two things we need more of during the council meetings.

Thometh clears his throat. "Ambassadors and Council Members, I call this meeting of the Council of Kings and Queens to order. What business have we to discuss today?"

Around the room, the conversation draws to a close and everyone sits up more in their chairs. We are not around a table here, we are seated in wooden chairs spread in a sort of circle across a room in Castle Fraun. Before the war, Queens like Saren and Lucinda who have no royal blood and are married to Kings that do, would not have been allowed at these meetings. This, along with the ambassadors who sit in our circle and the servants from Renchenda who remain in the room for the open-to-the-public meeting, helps me remember how far we have come. We are truly living in a better Fraun. Our hard work was not in vain.

Saren leans back in her chair, placing her hands on the swollen belly of the newest heir to the Farcheda throne. Her straight black hair swishes over her shoulder in the act. "I checked yesterday and it appears our new council building is almost complete. We should be meeting in it within two lunar cycles, I'm told." In the annuals since the war, we have outgrown the old council building with all whom we invite, but we are working on a solution to that problem.

"What features will the new room hold?" a young servant asks from her spot on the wall behind Thometh.

Saren smiles. "There is a new table, the old one was simply too small. It is larger to accommodate more visitors who may wish to sit. The map of Fraun will still be painted there, but it will be smaller and not run the length of the table. As we discussed, the map will be colored and labeled with names of realms and not numbers."

Beside her King Hector shifts in his chair, leaning forward to rest his forearms on his knees. He then takes up her description. "The room itself is larger. More chairs will be present. Today, for example, we have twelve members of the council present and five visitors. In the past, we had only room for about seven bodies."

"So there is room enough for citizens to view the proceedings?" Sieven asks.

"Absolutely. We are also including a viewing area. It is sort of a second room that connects to the main room by cuts in the wall. Citizens may be more comfortable being separated from the proceedings and that is an option as well. It serves as a sort of antechamber," Saren answers.

"Wonderful, thank you for that update," Thometh says. "Next, I'd like an update on the education of our younger Fraunians. Queen Sawchett, I believe you've been handling that?"

My younger sister, silent until now, speaks up from her spot on the opposite side of the circle from me. "All across Fraun the new curriculum is going well. Our teachers tell me the balanced instruction in speed, mirth, wisdom, strength, and humility is going exactly as planned. The children are enjoying their visits from leaders in each realm. We are working on a sort of travel plan that would allow a group of students from each school to visit the ruling family home in each realm like we did last annual. Are we still in favor of that?"

There are nods and calls of ascension all around the room.

"Excellent, I will proceed with that schedule." She sits back in her chair. Almost as soon as she hits the back, she springs forward again. Her blonde hair, starting to curl slightly at the end, swishes across her chest. "Oh, I almost forgot." Eyes in the room are drawn back to her youthful face. "The symbol of the new schools that I brought to you last time has been finished." She fishes a sheet of parchment out of her pocket and holds it up for the room to see.

The parchment shows a blending of the five symbols that represent the realms of Fraun contained within a black circle. A full tree whose branches reach out and tickle the circle represents Renchenda. Each branch stands for knowledge gained, connected at the roots and yet possessing its own strength. The bright sun can be seen peeking through branches and representing Marchenda. I imagine citizens of the realm of mirth are taught of the happiness and warmth symbolized here. A small streak of lightning can be seen in the top left of the circle. This symbol of speed will represent Farcheda. Along the lower arc of the circle water flows, representing the humble substance that gives life and, like Enchenda, asks for nothing in return. Lastly, my eyes fall to the rock sitting at the base of the tree. Sturdy and whole, the rock should represent Sarcheda.

Perhaps because of my lack of Sarcheda blood, I feel no connection there as I stare at the parchment. I don't feel stable. I don't feel an inanimate rock, for Fraun sake, is even a good symbol for a realm at all. Who decided that? But what would I suggest in its place? What can be found in nature to be strong at all costs if not a rock? Beyond that, who would I even admit my feelings to? Likely students in Sarcheda are taught the symbolism of this rock as soon as they're old enough to have speech. I know students in Renchenda learn of the tree and Enchenda students learn of the water. It would not be fitting of the king to admit he isn't aware of the importance of this symbol. At a loss for what else to say, I try for polite. "It looks great, Sawchett."

She smiles. "I cannot take credit. The designer did a remarkable job. With the council's permission, he will create a wooden sign for each schoolhouse depicting this image. Are there any opposed?" No one is opposed. Sawchett folds the parchment and slips it back into the pocket of her green dress.

"Would it be possible, do you think, to order an extra sign for the council building?" Lucinda inquires.

"I will ask him," Sawchett answers. "I rather like that idea."

Thometh speaks up again. "Thank you, Sawchett. I appreciate that update. The symbol of Fraun was a long time coming and I appreciate you handling that."

A silence wraps the room. We are meeting more frequently now, two or three times in a lunar cycle, in an effort to keep all Fraunians on the same page. This means our meetings are often shorter. In addition, the meetings are no longer led by a single king. Instead, we shift the norms from one to another almost seamlessly to ensure the balance is obvious. Today Thometh has stepped up, although Hector is technically King of the first realm. Next will be my turn.

Our council meetings today are also more relaxed than the ones I studied before I knew of my bloodline. If you have an issue, you present it. Speaking of that, I lean forward. "Are there issues any present would like to bring before the council?"

Roland, the representative from my own realm, stands. "There is an issue from Sarcheda, Majesties. I have done my best to quiet the voices over the last two annuals. But there remains a concern that the food shortage, which was brought before the council by our former king, may he rest in peace, may have been real. It is one of the issues that continue to come up. We understand the information that was brought before us in the past when we mentioned this. We know King Thometh believes the food shortage was a tool Tin used to gain power and footing with the council.

Despite my attempts to dissuade our citizens, the fear remains. I am wondering, Majesties, if there is another way for me to convince citizens there is nothing to fear once and for all."

Embarrassment burns my cheeks. Why is it always my realm? "Are Fraunians in Sarcheda going hungry, Roland?" I ask.

"No, sir. As I say, it is just a fear. I believe they are afraid there are, perhaps, other realms where there are hungry citizens or hungry children."

"I have a suggestion." The voice comes from the shadows to my right, just beyond the light of the fire. It takes a second for my eyes to register Alerta, Queen of Marchenda. "I would love to host a tour of the Fraun gardens, many of which lie within Marchenda. Anyone who wants to attend would be welcome. Surely the amount of food available to feed citizens would help to dissuade the fears. Would that be something that you would be interested in attending?"

Roland pauses for a beat, his brow furrowed in concentration. "I think it would, Majesty. I would love to attend something like that. Thank you." Issue settled, he returns to his seat.

"I would attend a tour as well," I say. I don't have to force a smile. Something about the simple solution makes my cheeks twitch with the gesture on their own accord.

"Wonderful. Anyone else who would like to attend, simply let me know before we leave today. I will be sure to contact you all when a date and time have been set with the gardeners."

After a peaceful round of silence, Hector rises. "Alright, productive meeting my friends. I will see you all in a fortnight or so. Meeting adjourned." He offers his hand to Saren and helps her stand. King Hector raises the index finger of his free hand. Everyone in the room matches the gesture. "One kingdom," he calls.

"One goal," we echo. Meeting adjourned.

Chapter 3

In another part of Fraun entirely another man also sits around a table with a fire burning in a fireplace. Smells from the public kitchen he lives behind waft into his home bringing with it a memory. The memory is so clear. A young king standing in the hallway outside his kitchen in the royal home of Sarcheda. He was dressed in black pants fitting of battle, arms crossed over his bare chest. Pants fitting for battle on a king who hasn't seen a fight? Annoyance at the king had been tamped down with a scowl as the man approached him. "King Tin, a word?" he'd led with.

"We're in a war. I don't have time for your nonsense. Make it quick," Tin answered. His voice had been hard and angry. Either the war was taking a toll on him, he was playing a character, or he'd been growing annoyed with his old friend.

The man played his part well. He pretended to cower before the mere boy with the position of power. "I merely had an idea that I wanted to share with you." He dared to cast his eyes up to the king's face then had to mask a smile when it appeared as though the king was, in fact, listening. "I was thinking that the old king of Marchenda would be a good target for you. I'm sure you had already thought of that." In a stroke of genius, he had then turned his face to the king as though in awe of the radiance he saw before him. "You're such a wonderful leader for our army, after all."

Even now the man chuckles at the memory. He was really layering on the lies there. Because, in truth, Tin had been a terrible leader. He guided others into war without being willing to fight. But the older man had never told the king that. He had always played along as if he agreed with every decision Tin made.

This particular memory was no different. In the shadows of the hallway, away from the eyes of the army, he had fed King Tin information. He had pulled the strings on his personal, royal, puppet. "King Larecio would be unguarded in his own home."

"Of course he would be," Tin snapped. "His home is safely tucked away along the back edge of Marchenda. He's untouchable and he knows it." Tin's impatience had seeped into his words. Then he'd turned his back on the man, ready to end the conversation. The disrespect had stung, made the older man want to lash out.

Instead, eyes squinted in the effort to control his anger, he'd spoken softly. "Of course, I'm sure you're correct. Perhaps I am mistaken, I've never been there myself. I just thought the grasslands could be crossed. I'm sorry to have wasted your time." He had turned on his heel and strode from the hallway, unwilling to let the young king walk out on him.

Less than a fortnight later, King Tin had directed his soldiers to carry out the plan he claimed was his own. Perhaps, by that time, he even believed it was. The mind is a tricky thing. The soldiers of Sarcheda had crossed the grasslands, just as the man had suggested. They'd killed King Larecio in his own home, leaving Marchenda without a leader for a few suns. It was just one more example of how the older man had triumphed in this war, leading his puppet king.

They'd been so close.

Sarcheda should rule the kingdom. Sarcheda should be synonymous with Fraun. They should hold the power, wield the fist of justice, make the decisions. The rest of these traits, what do they have when pitted against strength? Nothing.

This time, he will remain strong. His mistake was always trusting the boy-king to do this on his own. The boy was too easily swayed, too weak.

It won't happen again.

Chapter 4

"Tutor, can I speak with you a moment?" I am just outside the castle, heading for the roach who brought me here today. I left him warming himself by the fire to wait until the council meeting was over so he could bring me back to Sarcheda. I turn toward the voice, finding Alerta running at me. "I'm sorry to keep you, I know it's cold. I just wanted to ask whether you thought the garden visit would bring the peace-of-mind your ambassador seems to be searching for."

"I can certainly hope it will," I answer.

"Wonderful." When this woman smiles, my heart feels like it is going to pound right out of my chest. She has the most enchanting eyes I have ever seen, they're speckled with a color like rays of sunlight. I can't help but smile back at her.

"I haven't taken a tour of the gardens since the war. I know they've grown, but I'm curious to see them myself," I say.

"They really are magnificent. The fields are so much larger than they once were now that we are using the grasslands that border Fraun. We employ many Fraunians. Even with the snow staying later this annual than it usually does the fields are likely to be full whenever we decide to host the tour." She shivers as if simply mentioning the cold weather has brought her temperature down. I watch as she tightens the coat, fastening it around her neck.

"We should get home before the snow resumes," I say. The ground is covered with a light dusting right now, but the pink-tinged clouds promise more to come.

"Probably," she agrees. I notice she makes no move toward the fire and the waiting roaches. Somehow that observation warms me.

"Did you have something else to discuss?" I ask. I don't know what I'm hoping for in her answer. I hope I don't offend her by asking. I certainly don't want her to run off. "Not that I'm eager to be rid of you," I add.

She laughs lightly, reaching out and touching my arm in a friendly gesture. Despite the warm jacket I wear, I feel her touch. I look down at her hand, surprised by the flames it causes. When I look back to her face, I see the same shock mirrored there. "Are you ..." I trail off, unsure how to ask her age without sounding rude.

She pulls her hand back. "I should probably get home." Her eyes look different now, frightened.

"Is everything all right?"

"Of course." She straightens her collar, pulling it a little tighter, and shivers again. I can't help but notice this time the gesture seems forced. "I look forward to your visit to Marchenda and our plentiful gardens. Good day, King Tutor."

I reach down and take her fingers almost without thinking. I feel the flames again and they're just as shocking, even though I'm expecting it. Is this the age marker? I am twenty-seven annuals and in the age marker known as the age of the flesh. I know only what I have been taught, which is that it will bring a desire for love in all forms and affects only those born of royal blood. I have been in this marker for two annuals and I have never felt this before. Interested, I bring Alerta's long fingers to my lips, kissing them lightly. Even after I sever the contact I feel the fire on my lips like a sunburn. "Until we meet again, Majesty," I say, hoping to pass the kiss off as a goodbye gesture instead of an experiment of sorts.

She lowers her head, a gesture that makes me think I may have embarrassed her. Then she hustles off toward the waiting roaches. Although I have to go in the same direction, I stand there watching her retreat. I'm full of questions about the age markers and wishing, not for the first time, that I had someone I could ask.

Chapter 5

King Tutor,
I am writing to request a meeting regarding a new building in Sarcheda. I would like to come before you in a fortnight to present my case. Please respond.
Angel

The door to the sitting room is open, a fire crackling behind me as I open all the parchments that have arrived today. Many of them will be citizens asking for time before me, as this one has. Many of them will be citizens providing me with information they think I need. I always knew the number of requests a king gets in a day were plentiful, that is one of the many reasons why I originally relished my ability to tutor the royals without dealing with their burdens. Of course, that has all changed for me now. It's my responsibility.

A man enters and clears his throat. "Pardon me, King Tutor, I hope I'm not interrupting. The door was ajar."

I drop the parchment onto the table and rise in one motion. Roland, the representative for Sarcheda, is standing before me in the customary red and black of our realm. I walk around the table and hold out my hand. "Good morning. Come in and have a seat."

After the handshake, Roland drops into a chair on the far side of the table. I pull out one beside him and sit, turning my body toward him. "What can I do for you this morning, Ambassador?" I ask. Over the annuals, I have learned that Fraunians will respond well to a king who gives them their full attention. I do not want to give him the impression that anything else is more important to me than the citizens of Sarcheda.

"Majesty, I have come to a decision. I feel as though I am no longer the best choice to serve as Ambassador to the council. I am stepping down."

I'm not sure if the sudden frustration that hits me like a fist to the gut is because Marcus was right or simply because the fear of this moment had already taken root deep down. I take a deep breath and shake my head. "I had heard this rumor, Roland. I must admit that I hoped it was just that, a rumor. Our citizens like you, they feel comfortable bringing issues to you, you have a good head on your shoulders, and you speak with a classic intelligence that suits our realm well in the company of Kings. I hope everything is well at home and that there are no emergencies that led you to this decision. Is there anything you need from me?"

Roland shakes his head. "It is nothing like that, sir. I have a comfortable situation at home now that my children have grown. You may have noticed that I grayed since the war. I wish to enjoy my annuals remaining quietly with my wife. I will still be active in the realm, but this allows me to control my time. I'm not sure that I'm explaining this well."

"You absolutely are." I reach out and lay my hand on his shoulder. "You will be missed but I wish you well."

"Thank you, Majesty." He rises from his chair and begins to head for the door. "Actually, if I'm stepping down from my post I realize that means I will not be seeing you as often in this sort of meeting. It may be a good chance for me to ask questions I've had floating around in my head. Would you mind?"

This man has done a lot for Sarcheda and meets with many Fraunians to hear their complaints before they feel the need to come before me. He has saved me time and kept everyone happy. I owe him much.

When I first accepted the throne of Sarcheda, Roland was one of the first to greet me and sit down to listen to me. He has been at every meeting of the citizens. "Ask me anything," I say. "I'll answer anything I can for you."

"It's about Tin, Majesty."

My smile falls. "Not my favorite topic."

"I understand." Roland takes a step back toward the chairs. "It's just that our former King, when he proclaimed war on Fraun, did not speak for all of Sarcheda. You must understand that."

I nod. "I do understand that. I have never held what he did against this realm."

"But at the same time, you must understand that we did not see him as an evil man."

"He was an evil man, Roland." I punctuate the statement by slicing my hand through the air between us as though I can cut that thought right out of his head. "Tin should not be someone who is revered by Sarcheda, even in memory. This is obviously something you agree with. I noticed you referred to him by his given name and not his title when you suggested we speak about him."

"I do agree, Majesty. But I, and many of the citizens of Fraun, merely saw Tin as a leader that won strength competitions, was kind to our children, handled school visits with grace, and provided all that we needed. It is hard, even now, to merge that truth we understood before with the things we are learning he did."

I try not to cringe. This is not a message I want to be hearing. Fraunians should not be speaking of Tin with kindness and yet I can't be heard speaking out against him if this is the man they remember. My stomach churns as I think about it. Part of me wants to ask what it would take to convince them he was a monster through-and-through. Part of me suddenly, irrationally, wants this conversation to be over. "I thought you said you had questions, Ambassador."

"I did. I do. My question is this: was there truth to anything Tin was telling us before the war?" He sits on the edge of the chair. I sigh and roll my neck, tilting my eyes first toward the ceiling and then down to my chest. He rushes to explain in response to my obvious frustration. "It would be easier to give doubters little truths they can remember than to try and claim everything they'd ever believed was a lie. I'm finding push-back because I have nothing to offer them."

I decide not to pretend I don't know what Tin was telling them. Over the annuals since the war, I've learned this information. Tin told them the system was broken. He told them the only way to fix the system was to follow a single ruler, conveniently him. He told them he would listen to their demands, he would be the voice of Sarcheda. I turn my eyes back to his face. "Roland, I'm going to be real with you." He nods. "Tin was out for one person, Tin. He told you exactly what you needed to hear to convince you to follow him blindly. He did the same with Eselda. He did the same with anyone who was listening. When he was done with them, like with his sergeants, Lance and Danyel, he dumped them. Make no mistake, if Tin fed you any truths, it was by accident. He would've made up anything to get citizens on his side."

He nods. "However, I will say that Tin wasn't wrong about Fraun being broken." I clench my fists in front of me and move them down like I'm banging a gavel. "You can tell them that he was right about that. The council needed to reevaluate the ideals we followed and how we upheld them. Letting Ambassadors be in those meetings is just an example of how we have done that. If it helps to hear me say that he was right about some things, say that with my blessing," I offer.

"I trust you, Majesty. You have been a good king here and have done good things for our realm. I feel as though you lead us with honesty," he says. "I hope you don't feel as though I am stepping down because I cannot trust you. I just want to leave this role better than I found it I want to continue to spread the word about the council. I want to be able to answer these questions, when I am asked them, in the same way that you would."

"Thank you." Despite the uncomfortable questions, which I am tired of facing, I appreciate Roland's support. I lay my hand on his shoulder. "Truly, thank you. For all you have done for Sarcheda and will continue to do when your role as Ambassador comes to an end."

Roland's eyes drop to the ground and his cheeks redden. "Did you kill King Tin, Majesty?" he asks.

The question catches me off guard. I pull my hand back as though flames have suddenly shot from his shoulder. "No, I did not." I do not offer the name of the man who brought an end to the former king. I do not offer the story. It is not my story to tell and it never will be. "Is there anything else, Roland?"

This time his eyes slip closed as though the next thought will bring him physical pain. "Just one more thing, Majesty. I think Marcus should be accepted as the next representative."

If he were looking at me, he'd see shock written all over my face. I lean back from him and cross my arms over my chest. "Why?"

He leans forward, pleading his case. "He attends every meeting I hold, he is deeply rooted in this community. I know he doesn't always support your ideas, but you don't need someone who always supports you. You need someone who is Sarcheda through-and-through. With all due respect to your title and position, Majesty, I feel as though nominating Marcus for Ambassador sends the right message to the realm."

"This is not your decision." My frustration right now is with Marcus, not Roland. I force myself to take a calming breath and speak in a gentler tone. "But I have faith in you and I will consider this. Thank you for your opinion." I turn back to the table, reaching across to grab the parchments I had been reading. "If there's nothing else, I'm going to get back to answering the citizens."

"I'm sorry to have taken so much time." I hear him stand up but I do not hear footsteps to indicate he is walking away. I turn to find Roland still standing beside me. When he sees that he has my attention again, he speaks in a tentative voice. "Is it true that you have no blood of Sarcheda? If you did, it would make the explanation —"

"It's true," I interrupt. "As far as our lineage expert can find, Sarcheda's bloodline has ended."

"That is unfortunate."

"It is. Sarcheda was a good man. Strength of body and mind should never be underestimated. I am doing all I can to learn these ideals and keep our realm alive." I rise so I am face-to-face with the former ambassador, someone who I know will bring this information to the citizens. "I know we rely on the birth line of Sarcheda and his brothers. But I have blood of Oberian in my veins. In the absence of Sarcheda lineage, the other rulers and I may be the closest you will find."

Roland nods. "That is true." His eyes light up as if he is remembering something. "It is that blood which you have a majority of, as well."

Majority blood. The reason I was allowed to overthrow Tin in the eyes of the council. Both of my parents had blood of Kings in their veins, from two different realms. It is the best and worst secret of my life. The smile I attempt probably comes off as more of a grimace. This is a past I am still not fully comfortable with, despite annuals of trying to be. "I have the blood of Marchenda and Enchenda within me, yes." Although the story has probably been widely told, especially after I announced it during the final battle of the great war, I'm familiar with the look that passes over Roland's face. It is the look of reverence associated with this truth.

"Roland, you should know that majority blood is not as special as you were once led to believe. Four out of five of our sitting rulers have the blood of two brothers in their veins. The original brothers were all descendants of Second. The bloodlines are not as separate as we once thought." I lay my hand on his shoulder and hold his gaze. "One Kingdom, remember?"

"All that is true, Majesty." He offers me a smile. I remove my hand and straighten, drawing a deep breath. "It will be my last act as Ambassador, at our meeting tonight, to remind Sarcheda as you have reminded me today. I appreciate you taking the time, again, to discuss these issues with me. I know it must often feel as though Sarcheda is questioning you. That is not the case, Majesty. It simply bothers us to think our realm is not well represented."

"As it should. It bothers me that they worry," I say.

This time it is Roland who reaches out and lays a hand on my shoulder. The gesture feels intended to comfort. I try to accept it like that, although I don't feel comforted. "You are a good King. Thank you for all you have done for Sarcheda, in the war and since. It was an honor to serve with you," Roland says.

"You as well."

I watch him until he is out the door. Then I drop my head into the palm of my hand. Will I ever get to stop answering for my bloodline?

Chapter 6

The house in Enchenda reserved for the royal family has been Sawchett's favorite building for as long as she has had memories. She and her mother lived nearby, in a small house in the center of the realm, for many annuals. Sawchett can still clearly remember the day Eselda, a princess at the time, took her into the house. She never even hesitated to follow Eselda. *Because she was my princess?* Sure. *But I think it was also because, if I followed her, I would be able to see the inside of that house.*

Speed forward to today, when Sawchett is living in this large place basically on her own. It is sadder, somehow, than she ever imagined it would be. She keeps the place filled with workers but somehow there always seems to be enough emptiness to permit stress and over-thinking to enter.

Sawchett reaches the dining room, where she's meeting today with the man who paints the family trees on the walls in Fraun, Erick. After the war, he was commissioned to paint over all the depictions tracing the royal blood through the annuals in the royal homes, something he was not happy about. Then he was asked to paint a large one showing all the families, but the location was to be determined. Today, Sawchett gets to be the bearer of good news, the location is ready.

"Good morning, sir," she greets.

He rises from his seat before the empty wall that once housed the family tree in Enchenda. "Good morning, Majesty. I was just admiring all the work I did here once. I can still see it in my mind." The sadness behind his words stains the air in the room.

"I'm sorry that is the way it had to be. You understand our reasoning?"

"I understand that you want history covered. Until the time when you allow me to repaint it, that is all I see."

"Well, fear not. That day has arrived. Have you brought the parchment I asked to see?" She wraps her hand around the back of a wooden chair and begins to drag it over toward him.

"Stay there," he rises and drags his chair to the wooden table. "This document won't fit in our laps. I'm still not entirely sure why you wanted to see this." He drops a parchment roll that is almost as large as he is onto the table and begins to unroll it. As he approaches the middle point of the table Sawchett takes over holding the beginning, which is starting to return to its original rolled state.

Her eyes drop down to the document he has presented, which swallows the entire surface of the large table. Tiny names scrawled in that gorgeous handwriting that once decorated the wall in this very room take her breath away. "Wow," the word leaves her mouth on the last exhale of breath in her body. She leans closer to the parchment.

"It's all here. From Oberian," she tilts her chin upward to the top of the parchment, "to the last of the descendants." She lets her chin drop toward the bottom of the parchment. "It's amazing to see all five brothers charted on one document. It is larger than I thought it would be." She turns her attention to the small man across the table from her, responsible for creating this lineage tree between them. He is smiling at the parchment not unlike how someone would smile at their own children. "How many names are here?" she asks.

"Well, now, that is an interesting question you ask. Remember some of these names appear in more than one spot. Like this one," he points just to the right of the middle, to Sawchett's own name. The queen's name is circled in gold as it will be on the wall. This indicates that her blood is those of the royal ancestors. She runs her finger over it, happy to see it beside its brother Tutor's name for the first time in history. A smile plays along the corners of her mouth. "You'll find that same name here." He points just left of center to the same pairing of names.

Sawchett's eyes follow both spots up to see that these are, as she would guess, the branches for Enchenda and Marchenda. Her name is identical in both locations, except for the small star near her circle in Enchenda, signaling that she served as Queen in this realm. "I understand. How many unique names are here then? How many are represented?" As she asks her eyes grow large. She realizes this document is huge, there is no way someone could have all that counted. "On second thought, that's probably not something —"

"One hundred seventy-four," he answers.

"Wow," she breaths.

"Sawchett, why did I bring this before you today?" he asks.

She pulls her hands back off the table and the parchment rolls itself back up, protecting its secrets again. "The time has finally come when all this information is ready to be put up in a space where every Fraunian can see it," she answers.

The man's face changes. His jaw goes slack and his head tilts to the right. He recovers from the shock quickly, blinking fast and shaking his head. "I never thought I'd see the day."

"The new council building is almost ready. They tell me there is a wall large enough to house this entire tree. The plan is to allow the tree to grow out to all sides, you can have use of all four walls if necessary, but all branches must connect. We want it like this, with all the realms being represented. We will use the same rules King Tutor once applied when he updated for us; if someone is found to have royal blood their name is added."

Erick rubs his hands together. "This is putting some faith back in these old bones. Perhaps Fraun needs another chance."

"Another chance?" Sawchett squints in confusion. His age is obvious since he has white hair atop his head. But why choose that particular phrasing?

"I was once Fraunian, Majesty, but it has been many annuals," he answers, picking his scroll up off the table.

"So, you are a scout?" Sawchett is familiar with this notion, of course. She and her brother spent time with a group of scouts before the war. They were a group who didn't live in Fraun and didn't claim Fraun as their home, only venturing inside the territory to deliver goods. Yet, when it came time to take back Fraun from the grip of Tin, those same scouts fought side-by-side with the royal defects. The scouts made it possible for her to return to Fraun and make it what it is today. Two of Sawchett's greatest friends and mentors are even now leading a scout troop beyond the southern end of Fraun's borders.

"No, I wouldn't say that." He clears his throat. "My dealing with Fraun begins and ends with this document here. I have no loyalties for them at all. I am interested only in lineage, no matter whose lineage it is. Fraun of old exploited that interest and compensated me enough that I could do my work despite my personal feelings on your kingdom." He turns his cold eyes to her. "I have no love for this kingdom."

The memories of another hard man who spoke like this flood Sawchett with fear. "You are a wild?" It comes out as a question but she already knows the answer. The group of travelers who avoid Fraun, who openly despise Fraun. There have long been rumors about their existence, but few have met them. Sawchett traveled with one small troop for a while before finding Jordyn and his scouts. They were nice right up until they learned where she was from. As Erick describes, these wilds have no love for Fraun.

"That is closer to true, I'm afraid. There is no title for my kind of existence but Fraunians need to label me and that is what you call me." He clears his throat. "Although I must say that what I have heard you discussing in the last two annuals has given me hope. Perhaps this is no longer the kingdom I defected from. Perhaps you are moving in the right direction."

In the time that Sawchett has known him, Erick's hair has gone gray. She wonders how many of his annuals have been dedicated to the tracking of her kingdom's ancestry. She suspects this is, for him, a true labor of love. "So you will paint our tree? The new building is being erected right in the heart of Fraun. They know to expect you there and to give you time and space needed. We want you to give this living history a voice." She lovingly strokes the parchment as she speaks, imagining this as it will look when finished.

"I will paint it. I will give those one hundred seventy-four individuals the recognition they deserve. Then you will sit under it to meet and remember the thousands who aren't being put up there. The ones being tracked only in the medicine tents." He picks up a bag he had dropped to the ground by the old wall, slings it over his shoulder and hoists the rolled parchment up over the same shoulder. "You will remember that those citizens are as important to what you do day in and day out as the names I will paint. You remember that and maybe Fraun has a chance."

He leaves out the back door, the one to the garden. The young queen of humility sighs at the now empty room. "Actually, those citizens are more important," she whispers.

Chapter 7

The sun has barely risen in the sky and I have easily ten things I need to do today. That list includes uncomfortable tasks like deciding if I will recommend Marcus as the new Ambassador for Sarcheda. Yet instead of working, I'm standing underneath the largest tree outside the house in Sarcheda, looking up into the branches. Danyel has gone so far up the tree that I can barely see him. "Do you see anything?" I call up to him. Early this morning a young citizen claimed to have seen a nest in this tree here. Nests mean birds and birds can mean danger to Fraunians, due to our small size. I tried climbing the tree myself, but I didn't get very far. For that reason, it is a good thing my friend Danyel tends to come by for breakfast some days.

"I see it. I'm almost there," his voice floats down to me on a breeze.

I pull my jacket a little closer around my body. "I really hope there are no eggs in there," I mumble. That seems like a level of complication I'm not willing to deal with.

"There's definitely a nest," Danyel calls.

"Can you reach it?" I ask, feeling useless down here. Maybe I should get water or something, for when he comes down. Part of me feels like I should be here in case he falls. Although that's ridiculous. What would I do about it? It's not like I'd be able to catch the body of a grown man who is the exact height as me as he fell from the top of a tall tree.

"It appears to be empty."

"Thank Fraun," I answer. "Should we remove it?"

"Way ahead of you."

An untidy bundle of twigs and things falls from the tree. Although it catches me off guard, I flinch for it like I'm going to catch it. Of course, I miss. This proves my theory that I would never have been able to catch a full-grown man. "Be careful coming down," I say as a warning.

Danyel descends the tree as easily as he ascended, with grace and quickness that surprises me. Before I can even worry about his safety or think about offering unnecessary advice he's dropping in front of me and brushing his hands together. "Well done," I say. Then I turn my attention to the bundle. "It feels wrong, somehow, to remove the home of whatever creature used this. Doesn't it?" I ask, never taking my eyes from the nest.

"If it makes you feel better, I don't think it was being used. The nests we see along the banks of the river are much more complex than this." He kicks the bundle with his toe and it begins to fall apart. "Probably a small bird started it and was startled away by the presence of all of the fraunians coming and going."

I clap Danyel on the back. "Well, it will give the kids who found it peace of mind that you removed it. Thank you. Let's get some breakfast."

Although we are technically at my house, Danyel leads the way into the kitchen. As soon as he crosses the doorway, his body language changes. He freezes. "Where did that come from?"

"What? You're blocking the doorway, I can't see anything." I push on his upper arm and he steps into the room and to the side. There's a loaf of freshly baked bread, already sliced, sitting on the counter. I take a big sniff and close my eyes with pleasure. "Excellent. Bread would be much better than fruit." Danyel and I didn't grow up in Sarcheda. The making of bread is common here where citizens often have the strength to form the loaves, but not in other realms. For this reason, it is my favorite gift to receive.

I grab two cups and fill them with water from the bucket Danyel brought me from the river. He grabs two slices of the bread. "Hey Tutor," he says. "There's a parchment under this loaf."

"Bring it to me," I say. I settle myself in a chair by the wall and put the water down. Danyel crosses the room, takes the chair opposite me, and hands me the parchment.

Dear Council of Rulers,
As the newly appointed Overseer of Education, I have a few questions that will help as the teachers work out the kinks in the balanced curriculum we are bringing to the students of Fraun. We recently met to discuss the upcoming lessons and have found there are two topics with which we are not all on the same page. Please add your notes or assistance on the following lessons and pass this parchment along to the other members of the council.
Much thanks,
Marthisa

"It's from the head of the teaching council," I tell Danyel. "It appears she's requesting feedback." I glance ahead and notice several different handwritings. "It looks like I'm not the first member of the council to receive it."

"It looks long," Danyel comments between bites.

"It may take me a bit," I agree. "I had better get started."

History of First Realms:
Enchenda was first realm in the beginning of Fraun.

This note matches the handwriting at the top of the parchment. I squint my eyes to read what has been squeezed into the margin beside that.

This is not accurate, I believe Renchenda was first. -King Hector

In entirely different handwriting, on the opposite margin, another note.

Renchenda was only first realm for about two suns before

Enchenda was named first. This was largely because of the castle and was not appointed. Here in Renchenda, we consider Enchenda, the eldest brother, to have held the title first. -King Thometh

This is something I am aware of since I attended school in more than one realm. Renchenda does not teach that this period of time, two suns, even had a first realm. The way they tell it, the brothers decided on five realms and then eventually had a meeting and elected a first realm, Enchenda. Everywhere else, it is taught that Renchenda was first realm until the election. I cross the room and grab a stick from the fire pit to scribble my own opinion with the ash.

In the desire to teach one curriculum, we need to settle this. Let us say that Renchenda held the responsibility and the castle until the election. -King Tutor

I put the stick back down on the table and continue reading.

Enchenda held the position of first realm for two generations. Queen Selena (Enchenda) had an older sister who was shunned, disgracing her reign. For this reason, King Marcher of Marchenda became King of the first realm.

Marchenda held the position of first realm for two generations. King Shen (Marchenda) grayed with no heirs and it was voted, unanimously, to pass the title of first realm to King Freth of Renchenda.

Renchenda held the position of first realm for three additional generations. Queen Alep (Renchenda) had some shame brought to her house and the title of first realm passed to King Stan of Sarcheda.

Here, I notice another note carefully scribbled into the margin.

In the issue of being thorough and honest, that shame was that my father, the seated king, was suspected of murder. Nothing I can confirm, however. -King Thometh

Another murder in our history? I'm sure there's a story there. I wonder if there is anyone alive who could tell it. I keep reading.

After the death of King Tin and the War for Fraun, Farcheda is given the title of first realm under the direction of King Hector.

New handwriting, this one lighter as though someone used a device low on color.

This makes him seem rather blameless. Perhaps it should say, "After declaring war on Fraun, King Tin (Sarcheda) was stripped of his title and the council elected to give the honors of first realm to King Hector of Farcheda." Just a suggestion. -Queen Alerta

Good suggestion. -King Thometh

I pick up my stick again, adding my vote into the mix.

I am in favor of Queen Alerta's method of delivery. -King Tutor

Here, I notice we are jumping to the second topic mentioned in the preamble. According to the careful heading, we are now talking about "Building Process".

Please help me understand the process of requesting to build new. We seem to have some who disagree. I will not write anything here but await your input. Thank you! -Marthisa

The handwriting changes.

1. Schedule a meeting with a representative of royal blood in your realm

or the realm in which you hope to expand.

2. Bring to the meeting answers to the following questions: why would you build, is there space available, how much space are you asking for, where will you get the materials.

3. The ruler in that realm will take the issue under advisement. If they believe the issue warrants granting, they will bring it before the council for a vote where majority rules.

-King Hector

I am suddenly glad King Hector received this parchment first. It leaves little else for us to add. I do notice that there are small notations on the right-hand margin near the bottom.

The project should not be started until the council has ruled. -Queen Alerta

An emergency session can be called to vote quickly in the event of a project that affects safety or security in a realm. -King Thometh

I start to roll the parchment up and my eyes catch some handwriting on the back. I flip the entire roll and find a little bit of what I now recognize as Thometh's handwriting.

Perhaps King Tutor can weigh in on the building that was happening in Sarcheda before the war, I'm sure that is the reason we are confused about the process. -King Thometh

I sigh. I was so close to being able to roll this up and call it done. I reach again for my stick.

The building in Sarcheda appears to have been conducted without adherence to these rules. Rest assured, Sarcheda follows these rules, as written, now. I expect that the rules are taught following the letter of the policy in Sarcheda schools, as they should be taught in all other schools in Fraun. -King Tutor

I check both sides of the parchment again to ensure I have missed no other notes. Finding none, I roll it back up. "I'm done with this," I say, noticing Danyel is done with his breakfast. "Are you going anywhere near Sawchett's home today? It appears this parchment may have been traveling through the realms in order beginning with Farcheda and ending with Enchenda. She will need to give her input as well."

"I can. I'm working on the river today. It's not too far out of my way to pop into her house." He takes the parchment from me. "Thanks for the bread."

"You're welcome. Take the rest of it with you." I wave my hand toward the counter. "Give it to your friends on the river crew. I'm sure they'll appreciate it as well."

Without hesitation, Danyel grabs the loaf. "See you later," he says.

I wave and take a bite of the breakfast I've left abandoned while I worked. My brain wanders back to the parchment. I'm glad we're trying to get all of this cleared up. I'm glad we're finally answering the questions about ruling lines that every Fraunian really should've already known. But I can't keep myself from being irritated that they had to call out Sarcheda again. I have been ruling this realm for two annuals. Yet at every single turn, I'm answering for the monsters that ruled before me.

Will this ever end?

Chapter 8

Roland and I have piled into a carriage manufactured in Sarcheda and hooked onto the back of a roach. These carriages are specially made using repurposed wood and wheels. This particular one has enough room for two of us and has no roof, meaning we're open to the elements and the air as we ride across Fraun. The air blowing across the top of the wood makes me shiver. I pull my warm jacket closer.

"Have you ever been to Marchenda?" Roland asks.

"I've been through a few times," I answer. It's strange that I don't feel more connected to Marchenda than I do. I have never lived there, although the blood of the ancestor who shared his name with this realm runs through my veins. "Have you?" I ask.

"Never. I hear it is beautiful."

"We will certainly find out," I say.

As the sun reaches its highest point in the sky, we pull up to a single-story house. This particular house is very similar to the ones all around it. It seems low to the ground but long, like the houses in Enchenda.

There is one large tree on the immaculate front lawn. There are also about twenty citizens spread out in various forms of relaxation, apparently waiting on our arrival.

Alerta meets us just as the roach comes to a stop. "King Tutor and Ambassador Roland, welcome to Marchenda," she greets. She is covered in a yellow cloak, fitting of Marchenda royalty, and is wearing an impressive smile. Her hair is pulled back in a way that makes it straight on her head, but curly at her neck. She is radiant.

I accept her offered hand as I step out of the carriage I have been riding in. "Thank you. This is a beautiful section of Fraun," I say, shaking her hand. Truly, it is. Perhaps because of its similarity to Enchenda, this realm feels comforting.

"We have good quality soil here, it allows us to grow many things." She sweeps her arms out to gesture to the area around her home. There are houses, neatly tended gardens, and flowers lining the dirt streets. "As you can tell, we are presently inside the section of Marchenda where our citizens live. But we will be touring the fields where we grow food for Fraun. I'm waiting on a few more members of the tour group to join us and we will begin."

Roland, having walked around the back of the carriage, joins us. He bends at the waist to greet the queen. "Majesty, thank you for hosting us." Around us the other carriages from Sarcheda begin arriving, bringing concerned citizens who wish to see the gardens.

"My pleasure. Come this way, I'll introduce you." Alerta turns and heads toward the house beside her royal home. This house is smaller than my own, but not by much. I recognize Queen Saren from Farcheda among the crowd seated on the lawn and acknowledge her with a nod. She smiles in return.

"Ladies and gentlemen," Alerta calls. Heads turn in her direction. Talking stops. "It is my pleasure to welcome King Tutor and Ambassador Roland from Sarcheda."

I try not to grimace. I hate being in the spotlight. I would've been perfectly fine had she not introduced me. I raise my hand kind of awkwardly and drop it again to my side. I quickly cross the lawn and fall to the ground under a large tree beside Queen Saren. I'm grateful when the talking around us resumes. "Good afternoon," I greet. "Was I the last to arrive?"

Queen Saren squints and looks around the lawn, searching for someone. "I don't see Ambassador Sieven and his wife, Abney," she answers.

"Wonderful." My love for Sieven runs deep. Before the war, Sieven was traveling with a troop of scouts outside Fraun. I'm sure his life was peaceful. When things began to heat up here in Fraun and Tin declared war, I left in search of Sawchett. I found her among Sieven's family who welcomed us and our strange cause with open arms. There was no hesitation from the young man to join our fight. It didn't surprise me when he came to live in Fraun after the war. It was in his heart, I could tell.

I don't have to wait long before the pair I was waiting for turn a corner into our line of sight. I rise to greet them. "Abney, you look radiant," I greet, kissing the back of her hand after shaking it. "Farcheda agrees with you."

"It certainly does, Tutor. I am volunteering with the school a few times a lunar cycle. I thoroughly enjoy it."

Alerta joins us. "Wonderful, I'm so glad you made it." She speaks in a louder voice for everyone assembled, "Let us begin the tour." She starts down a neatly trimmed path, leading us away from the houses. She moves at a quick pace, but I notice none of the group struggle to keep up with her.

We crest a small hill as a group. When I reach the top I see the land before us open up into rows of green peeking up from among the deep brown soil. The air hangs with the smell of fresh vegetables, clean and slightly sweet. There are Fraunians among the rows, walking or crouching low attending to plants.

"You'll notice," Alerta says "the citizens of Marchenda take great pride and care in handling our crops." She resumes her walking at a slower pace down toward the rows. I follow, as does the group. Unlike them, my eyes remain on the beautiful queen.

"There are some here watering crops, planting seeds, cultivating vegetables at their prime, and moving insects that threaten the food source," she explains.

"The fields keep many employed," Roland notes, his eyes taking in the numerous bodies moving about the crops.

"Is it Marchenda's primary source of employment?" Abney asks.

"At this time, yes. However, it is not only Marchenda citizens who work in the fields. Occasionally we get scouts helping, they are paid in food for their time. A few Farcheda citizens travel here daily to work as well." Alerta turns her head to offer a warm smile for Saren, Queen of Farcheda.

"This is substantially more food than we grow in Farcheda," Saren responds.

"Sarcheda cannot produce this much either," I say, "and before this, I thought our production levels were impressive."

"We didn't make this much before the war," Alerta says. She reaches the edge of the dirt marking the start to the gardens and stops walking. When she turns to face us she creates an impressive picture. Beautiful queen, arms out, garden and sunlight providing a backdrop. I am drawn to her skin, shiny like autumn leaves having turned before winter. Her eyes shine with passion.

I know, once upon a time, this land was wide open. Tin, in his effort to take Fraun, sent soldiers out along the outer edge of our Kingdom. They approached over this land until they reached the royal house. Tin was able to have King Larecio murdered because this field was open. It can't be a pleasant memory for Alerta to spend time thinking about. Although it is how she took the throne, no one wants to lose a cousin that way.

"How long could this garden provide Fraun with food?" Sieven asks, a note of admiration clear in his voice.

"My estimate is two lunar cycles," Alerta answers.

Sieven peels his eyes away from the crops. "Every single citizen could eat for that long? That is impressive indeed."

"That number changes all the time as we are always cultivating and planting," Alerta says.

"How does the food get to the other realms?" a short man asks. I don't recognize him but I note that he stands beside Ambassador Garven from Renchenda and conclude that he must have also traveled from our realm hailed for their wisdom.

"There are carts just there," Alerta points to the left of the fields where wooden carts are lined up beside the garden. "We fill them and roaches help us transport. They take some vegetables of their choice as simple payment."

The group spreads out, down aisles of acorn squash and carrots. I watch them finger the tops of the plants and talk with workers. I walk myself to stand beside Alerta at the top of the rows. She smiles at me. "It's nice that Fraunians can create so much food here," I offer.

"Food is the one thing we are allowed to create. It's a necessity."

"Necessary things can still be impressive," I say. My answer must please her because her smile pulls her cheeks up, making her eyes wrinkle slightly at the edges. A small dimple appears in her right cheek. Her eyes sparkle. I feel my age marker like a flame in my gut. I have to look away. This is not the time to get wrapped up in fantasies.

Without warning, I feel her hand burning through my long sleeve shirt. I keep my eyes on the crops mostly because I'm afraid if I move she may take her hand away. The fire burns right up my arm, I can feel it move through my body. The pull of this age marker is unbelievable. I feel her hand lightly start moving up and down my arm and the embers smolder everywhere her skin hits.

When I can't resist anymore, I look at her. Alerta is almost the same height as me, maybe a few clicks smaller. This means when I turn my head, I'm looking almost directly into her dark eyes. Something about them is different today, they're swirling with black like smoke. "Alerta, are you twenty-five annuals?" I ask, knowing the eyes are the window to the age markers we are slaves to.

"Twenty-six," she answers. Her voice is husky, low.

I feel a tug at my center, like a string being pulled inward. The heat follows the string, setting me aflame. I turn my body and lay my hand on her shoulder. I reach up and brush her hair with my other hand, tugging a loose strand back behind her ear. Just as I'm feeling like I'm going to explode, Alerta's eyes slip closed and she lets out a soft moan. My heartbeat quickens. "This age marker is powerful," I say.

"It appears so." Her eyes pop open again, now a full shade darker than they were. I recognize the darker hue to everything around me, meaning my own eyes have likely darkened as well. It's as if the sun has disappeared behind a cloud, although that is not the case. "I have never felt this before. It feels like …" she trails off, thinking of a word.

I step closer to her. Our bodies are almost touching. I can feel the flames jumping between us. "Fire," I offer.

"Yes. Exactly. Fire." She leans toward me and tilts her head upward. Her lips are marks from mine. So close and yet ...

She closes the gap, pushing our lips together. Everything melts away: the gardens, the noise, the sunlight, everything. It is just the two of us and this fire that we have started. I am aware of her arms wrapping around my back, her nails scraping along my spine. I'm aware of her lips, softly parting.

She pulls back, separating our skin but not stopping that wild zapping of energy. Her eyes are black. "I'm suddenly aware of the fact that we are not alone out here," she says. She tips her chin, slightly, toward the fields.

I take a step back, trying to honor her implied wishes. I take a deep breath. We can't be doing this kind of thing, not here. Alerta has a daughter. We are royals of different realms. We both have the blood of Marchenda. That thought causes me to cringe and a little of the fire goes out. I take another step back, angle my body toward the gardens again. I should probably look into that lineage. "Sorry about that. I think my age marker got away from me."

"As did mine. Are you in the same marker?" she asks.

"Age of the flesh, yes. I'm two annuals into it." I swallow, feeling more of the fire extinguish. "I've never felt anything like that before." I shrug. "Strange feeling." I turn and look at the queen again, noting that her eyes are lightening back up to show the rays of sunlight among the brown. "It almost felt like I was being consumed by you. I was hyper-aware of your body and mine. I'm surprised you remembered others were around, I couldn't focus on anything else."

"I heard a noise, it brought my attention back." She touches my arm again, lightly. "It doesn't take much to feel it. My fingers are barely on your arm now, but …"

"It's like someone put out a fire, let it drop to barely warm, then took a stick from the ashes and uses it now to get my attention."

"Yes, exactly." She pulls her hand away. I feel the absence of the heat and hear her palm slap down by her side. Then she takes a dramatic breath and blows it out. "Well, I have to admit that kiss was electrifying. The age marker certainly intensifies the pleasure of a good kiss. If it's not a problem for you, King Tutor, I would like to propose we try something like that again. Perhaps in a more private setting."

I know I should disagree, I can think of a lot of reasons why that is not a good idea. I risk a glance at her, she offers me a smile and I'm struck again by how beautiful this woman is. I nod, once. "I have no problems with that," I say.

Chapter 9

King Tutor,
In the last lunar cycle, we have buried seven Sarcheda citizens and delivered four babies. In addition, we have treated a serious injury from a bird which may result in death shortly. A group of scouts also made a trip to be treated in our medicine tent. There were six of them. One scout woman birthed two babies while under our care. Those numbers were not included in the four Sarcheda births I spoke of.
Until the next lunar cycle, be well.
Jeanette, healer

The report has low numbers this lunar cycle, I note. In the annual following the war, we saw extraordinary numbers of deaths, births, and treated scouts. So much so that Jeanette, our healer, was before me requesting we expand and bring in another healer. I hope that she isn't seeing that request as an error now that our numbers are dwindling.

"Majesty," a voice interrupts my musings.

I turn my head to the doorway even as my hands busy themselves rolling the parchment back up and dropping it to the floor below my chair.

"Marcus," I resist the urge to groan. "You are early."

"I apologize. Should I wait in the hallway?" Marcus asks. He is, again, wearing the colors of Sarcheda. Does this man own anything that's not black and red?

I summoned Marcus this morning, but he is early. I'd like nothing more than to make him sit in the hallway as punishment for not following the time I set forth. But that is immature. Besides, I have no comment on the numbers from the medicine tent to write up on the parchments. I have no other meetings scheduled today that could delay this one. I raise my shoulders. "No, come in. Please, have a seat." I gesture to the chair opposite mine. The two identical wooden chairs are angled before the fire, forming the three endpoints of a triangle. I do not rise from my chair as Marcus sits.

"I regret I was shocked to be summoned before you today," Marcus begins.

I wave my hand, stopping what I am sure was a perfectly practiced speech. "I asked you here to discuss the Sarcheda Ambassador position — "

"So you've decided to consider my offer?"

I widen my eyes, showing my shock. "Do not interrupt your King, Marcus," I warn. He lowers his head once, quickly. Somehow I doubt the show of embarrassment is sincere. I wait until the silence is uncomfortable before continuing. "Roland has decided to step down as representative. It is a decision I am sad about but can support." I lean forward in my chair, resting my arms on my knees. "I should be clear," I whisper the words as though they are something I shouldn't admit. "Roland, who I admire and respect, recommended you for this position. Had he not done so, you would not be here."

I return my posture and volume to their previous positions. "Am I correct in assuming you will take the position?"

Marcus' eyes narrow and he begins to move his jaws as though he may be grinding his teeth. "I will." His voice is too light, too cheery for the facial expression. "I am honored you would even consider me, Majesty. I plan to serve Sarcheda with strength of character for as long as you will allow me."

"Excellent." I rise from my chair and offer him my hand. "I will bring your name for a vote. I believe no others have stepped forward to throw their names on the ballot. So, congratulations."

There is actually a brief hesitation before he rises and accepts my handshake. As he leaves the room I can only hope I have not just made an irreparable mistake.

Chapter 10

One second Eselda is asleep on the blankets that make her bed and the next she's standing in the center of her troop's campground at dusk. She blinks, feeling the lashes flutter against her cheek, and turns slowly to take in all the details. The clearing is familiar. Although her scout troop often travels, this is the same clearing they are sleeping in now. There is one obvious difference, an extra tent is set up. Eselda takes cautious steps toward the extra tent. A breeze blows through the camp, sending the leaves of the nearby trees spinning. Her hair doesn't move.

This is a dream, just like the last time. She's suddenly sure of it. Her heartbeat speeds up in response to the realization. The last time she dreamed about a moment like this someone died. That last dream represented a moment that Jordyn calls the worst moment of his life.

Jordyn.

The need to find Jordyn, wherever he is in this dream, surges through her veins.

As if called by her thoughts, Jordyn's tall frame emerges from the tent before her. She feels a quick calm rush her body like warm tea on a cold night. He is safe. Dreaming of death is never comfortable. Dreaming of death when it is someone you love is impossible.

"It's time," Jordyn calls. His voice booms through the clearing. He sounds sad. His eyes are pulled down at their corners, she notes. He is positively melancholy. That observation solidifies her fears. This is a dream about a death.

"Who are you talking to?" Eselda asks out loud. Of course, she's not really in the same moment in time as Jordyn, so he doesn't respond. She turns and spies two forms seated by the fire. Their knees are turned in toward each other as if they are deep in conversation. Neither of them moves or acknowledges Jordyn.

Eselda turns just in time to see Jordyn duck back into the tent. Sure that the answer to this mystery must lie within that fabric, she follows him. All the while her brain is screaming one question: who dies in this dream?

There are blankets spread out across the floor and a pail of water sits beside them. A woman wearing clothes befitting a scout lies atop the blankets. The woman's face is blurry in Eselda's vision, just like it was the last time she dreamed of death. Eselda takes in the woman's soft curves, looking for a clue to who she may be. As she watches, the woman shutters with a painfully broken breath. There are no medicine men in the tent. There are no other scouts in the tent. The body is not one that Eselda recognizes. *Who is this woman?*

With a final release, the woman's chest falls silent.

Tears spring to Eselda's eyes automatically, despite not knowing who this woman is. She looks to Jordyn. His outward appearance remains stoic, arms crossed and face impassive. But his eyes, those blue orbs she knows so well, reveal his sadness at this loss.

Whoever this woman is, no one is here to hold her hand. No one seems to care that she is gone. Jordyn is here, but he feels as though he needs to hide his true feelings. That feels wrong, somehow. Shouldn't everyone have someone who will mourn them when they die?

Eselda kneels beside the bed, putting her lips where the ear should be on the face she can't see of the woman she doesn't know. She knows the woman can't hear her now because she's not here, this hasn't happened yet, and her soul would have left her body if it was happening. Eselda knows that what she is about to do isn't really for this woman. Yet something in her soul compels her to do it.

"Goodbye," she whispers.

Eselda's eyes open as the echo of the word fades in the darkness of her own tent, back in her reality. There are tears on her cheeks as if they followed her from the dream.

Chapter 11

"Ladies and gentlemen, welcome to the annual strength competition." The voice bellows over the clearing, easily reaching my ears. The crowd lets out a roar. "Please put your hands together for our reigning champion, standing at one mark and eight clicks, with a respectable age of seventeen annuals, Kristoff." This time the answering roar is louder, thundering up to the clouds.

I pace behind the tree, waiting for something that may clue me into what's happening. While I wait, I shake out my arms. I need them to stay loose. There has only been one other competition like this during my reign as King. I was there. I know how they go. Competitors will step into the clearing and lift stacked stones straight above their heads. They will hold them steady. A competitor must show no sign of strain. Each contestant gets two tries to lift their personal best. The person who holds the most blocks is crowned champion. In the event of a tie, competitors will return to the clearing to lift against one another and the duration of the hold will determine the winner.

The crowd groans with defeat. Kristoff must have tried his first lift and failed. That gives me hope. Maybe he'll try a smaller lift for his second attempt and give me a chance at this. I pace for a bit longer and then I hear the crowd explode with applause. I hang my head. If the roar of the crowd is any indication, he must have put up impressive numbers.

"Now welcome, for his first-ever strength competition, standing at one mark and ten clicks, twenty-seven annuals in age, our ruler, King Tutor!"

I jog out from behind the tree. I try to look confident and comfortable. My solid exterior, which doesn't look much different than the rest of the citizens' thanks to two annuals of daily training, hides an interior that is positively quaking. Even the act of being out here with my bare chest on display is fraying my nerves.

I center myself behind a stack of stones. This stack holds eight bricks, my personal best record in training. I close my eyes and take a calming breath as the crowd quiets. I try to push all thoughts out of my head. I draw a deep breath in, bend at the knees, and wrap my arms around the bottom block. Then, on an exhale, I use my legs to push upward. The crowd cheers as I extend my arms over my head.

I hold long enough for the judge to check for signs of strain, counting to five in my head before dropping the stack. I look to my trainer, along the right of the crowd. He offers me a thumbs up but he doesn't smile. This is our signal. It was a good lift but it won't win.

I wave my hand at the pile as I take a step back.

The crowd cheers louder at the signal. I'm calling for another block.

The trainer pauses with the block over the pile, his doubt obvious in his posture. I have never successfully lifted nine blocks. My appearance in this competition is important today. If my ambassador is to be believed, citizens are doubting my ability to run this realm. I have to show that I can compete here. I have to try nine. I shake out my arms and roll my shoulders back. Last annual Kristoff won with nine. Nine is more than most in the realm can lift.

When I step up to the blocks again a sudden silence surrounds me. I imagine the whole of Sarcheda holds its breath with me.

This time when I straighten the added weight causes an instant pain in my left knee. I fight it, willing my leg not to wobble. I pray I don't drop anything. The five-count seems to stretch into infinity, but finally, it comes. I can't help but feel pride at the enormous cheer that rises from the crowd. I look around, taking it all in, chest out.

My eyes lock onto a face I wasn't expecting to see and my smile grows. She is clapping and returning my smile. It's almost enough to make me miss the signal; thumbs up, no smile. But even Queen Alerta's smile can't distract from the comment murmured behind me. "King Tin could lift twelve."

I force myself to keep the smile affixed and wave at the crowd as I leave the clearing. I just beat my own personal best in front of the whole realm. Why isn't that enough?

Kristoff is already standing in the trees to the side of the arena when I approach. He gives me a nod of acknowledgment before turning his back on me and crossing his arms. It is forbidden for competitors to have conversations in this waiting area. We stand together in silence while three other competitors from around the realm compete, each one joining us when their lifts are at an end.

Finally, the announcer speaks again. "Ladies and gentlefraun, let's bring our top two competitors out to the arena," he bellows. "Kristoff and King Tutor, please join me on stage."

I almost cannot believe it. I already know, based on the signal from my trainer, that I didn't win the competition. But this means I have made second place, respectable for my first competition. I shake hands with each of the other three competitors in turn before jogging out to the arena. One young man, who looks like he may barely be full height, whispers "good job" as I shake his hand. So, when I'm standing beside Kristoff, the reigning champ, with the announcer between us I am smiling.

"Ladies and gentlefraun, with nine blocks lifted, your runner up, King Tutor of Sarcheda." He holds my hand up and a cheer fills the arena.

Then he drops my hand and silence falls over the assembled crowd. He lets it reign for a heartbeat.

"And your champion this annual with eleven lifted blocks, Kristoff of Sarcheda." I can't help but notice the resulting cheer is louder and longer. I join in, politely clapping.

When the noise fades, I take a step toward him with my hand

outstretched. "Well done," I offer. "Two extra blocks is something I cannot imagine. A wonderful display of strength."

He shakes my hand. "It's not a record," he says as if that is all that matters.

"It's only one away from the record," I offer. In the annuals since the war, I've been fed this information. The current record of twelve blocks was set by King Tin before the war. Before that, the record was eleven and that record was held by King Todd, Tin's father. In fact, as far back as lifting challenges go, the ruling family of Sarcheda has always held the title. That is, until last annual when I didn't even compete.

"Someday I will set a new record," he says. Before I can respond, he's walking away from me to greet the crowd.

I'm left watching him walk away and wondering if I'll ever be able to give Sarcheda the champion they want.

Chapter 12

The strength competition today took everything I had. I can see it in the muscles that tremble and spasm at my shoulders. My red shoulders. In my life before the war, I wouldn't have walked around in the oppressive sunlight without a shirt. As King of Sarcheda, it's expected. It was worth it with my realm, I could see it on their faces, but it cost me.

A scout friend of mine, Evelyn, sent me a tub of oil from a plant that grows in the wild which is supposed to soothe burns. It's somewhere in this room. I hear the door open as I'm rummaging in the cabinet. I don't even bother to turn around and look. As a citizen of Sarcheda, Danyel was probably in the crowd to witness the strength competition. He's probably worried about how I'm taking the loss.

I find the oil hiding toward the bottom of a cabinet. "Aha!" I'm already standing and turning, holding up the prize. "Will you be so kind as to help me apply this to my shoulders and b—"

Alerta. I wasn't expecting Alerta. I was expecting Danyel and instead, I see the queen of Marchenda's perfect skin and smile. Her eyebrows are raised in question. My skin tingles and I feel my hands start to tremble. "I'm sorry," I stammer, "I thought you were someone else."

But she's reaching for the jar, wrapping her delicate fingers around it. "What are friends for?" she asks.

I watch her scoop a gob in her fingers, drop the container, and rub her hands together. Then her hands are lightly pressing on my shoulders. I can't look at her anymore, so I turn my eyes to the ceiling. Everywhere her fingers touch is burning, and not like they were burning from the sun. It's a burning that lights up my entire body. My face flushes with embarrassment. I know we've talked about the age marker and our reaction to each other, but she cannot possibly know what thoughts are running through my head. I feel her hands run down to my chest and risk a glance at her.

Her eyes are locked onto my skin, her hands gliding along the pectoral muscles. I can tell her hands are running dry, and her touch is lightening like she has noticed the same, but still, she runs them along my body. I swallow the lump that is forming in my throat.

Her hands move back up to my shoulders and start their way down my arms, which are at my sides. To reach my wrists, she takes a step closer to me. Her eyes turn toward my face, so I put mine back on the ceiling and take a deep breath. Our agreement extends to our age markers, physical contact. We never discussed the feelings I feel fluttering in my heart. I swallow again and resist the urge to close my eyes, which would only heighten the feeling of her skin on mine.

Her hands run back up my arms, to my shoulders. She takes another step closer. Her breath is falling on my neck as her hands wrap around to my back and lightly rub. I could offer to turn around, I should offer to turn around. It would provide her better access. I should give her the oil and insist she reapply it to her dry hands. But I don't want this to end. Her breath falling lightly on my neck, her hands gently brushing my skin. It's magic.

"How is that?" Her voice is low, sensual. I take a step back.

"Good." I take another step back, letting her hands fall to her sides. I let my eyes fall to hers. She smiles.

She reaches her hand up to her own shoulder, pulling back the fabric near her neck. "Do you think I need some?" she asks.

No. Her shoulders are absolutely perfect, the color of the chocolate stored in the kitchen downstairs. I want to kiss them. I would be a fool not to take the offer to touch them. I have no words for this. I don't want to tell her she needs the gel, as she doesn't. But I also cannot tell her what I'm doing. Instead, I reach for the oil and scoop some out. I throw the canister and step close to her again, rubbing my palms together.

When I touch her skin, I watch her face. Her eyes instantly slip closed. I wonder if the electricity I feel is mirrored on her own skin. It is almost instinctual, the way my lips find hers. She throws her arms up around my neck and returns the kiss. I feel the flames ignite again, burning away at my doubts.

Chapter 13

There is one small tavern in the center of Sarcheda. The night after the strength competition, there are only four patrons huddled in the bar. Three of them are barely able to hold their heads up after consuming large amounts of the fermented grapes served here. The fourth man sits in dark shadows at the far corner of the tavern with a glass full to the brim with the deep red liquid at the center of his table. Besides the employee wiping down bottles and counters, this stranger appears to be the only sober one on the premises.

The door to the tavern opens, allowing a cold blast of air and a tall man to enter. The employee cleaning the counters nods in his direction. "Wine?" he offers. The tall man waves his hand in front of him like he's signaling to throw away a bad hand of cards.

The stranger in the shadows watches the tall man look around the room. His eyes dart right past his target the first time. But, eventually, the eyes track back to the little man in the shadows. This time he is spotted. The tall man crosses the room in three strides and drops into the empty chair.

"Make it quick," he orders as if he were the person in charge of this clandestine meeting.

"The king who sits on the throne of Sarcheda is a disgrace. He has no Sarcheda blood. We need to find a way to replace him, immediately." The stranger in the shadows speaks with a low voice, harsh and raspy. He makes sure to keep his head back out of the lights of the candles burning in sconces on the walls.

"The way I hear it told there's no one left with Sarcheda blood," the taller man says.

The stranger feels a scratching in his throat but doesn't clear it. He allows it to disguise his voice even further. "Then we replace him with someone who has been trained in the ways of Sarcheda. Someone who won't lose a strength competition at the hands of a teenager. Someone strong. Someone we could be proud to have representing us at the table of that outdated council. Someone who will fight for us."

The tall man chuckles, drawing the gaze of the employee. "I suppose you're suggesting you are such a man?"

"Not at all. I'm putting you in charge of finding such a man."

"Me?" The tall man recoils from the surprise, tipping the chair back onto two wooden legs. "What if King Tutor can be trained—"

The stranger slaps his hand on the table, interrupting the question. "Do not call him that," he commands. "He is an imposter sitting in the seat of a Sarcheda king. He used a sword to take the life of the last true king of Sarcheda. You will not use that title in conjunction with that name in my presence. Do you understand?" Venom drips from the words and hangs in the air.

The tall man's hands go up palms toward the stranger, creating a wall to split them and show he means no harm. "Have it your way. I was merely about to ask if you think Tutor can be trained in our ways. He's been working with our trainers. If you have no one else to suggest we put on the throne, why can't it be him?" He swallows and lowers his hands. Then he pushes his chair back down onto four legs. "But I understand how you feel. Did he really kill King Tin?"

"Of course he did. He'll deny it, I'm sure," the stranger answers. "But when it came time to take the life of the last of the great Sarcheda line, he didn't even hesitate." The stranger leans forward until his face falls into the light. "What kind of man hides in the shadows and doesn't take responsibility?" He lets the question linger for a beat. "Tutor is a coward who doesn't belong on our throne. Find me someone who does." Again, he sits back, plunging his face into darkness.

If the taller, younger man is surprised to see the identity of the mysterious stranger, he hides it well. He nods once. "I will do my best."

"Sarcheda will be strong again," the stranger vows.

The tall man recognizes that he has been dismissed. He nods to the employee as he leaves the tavern. Back at the table, the stranger is silent until the door closes. "Sarcheda will be stronger than it ever was," he whispers. Then he slams the full glass of wine before him in one swallow. "Sarcheda will be unstoppable."

Chapter 14

The nightmare shocks Sawchett awake with a sharp intake of breath. Her heart pounds in her chest as she looks around the room, convincing herself that nothing is out of place and she is safe in her bed in Enchenda. She sits up and forces herself to take three calming breaths. The nightmare was so realistic. She was standing on the steps of Castle Fraun, Tin bearing down on her with a sword drawn, rasping out the same phrase over and over again: "One Fraun." She has to remind herself that the threat of war died with Tin. They are safe now. They are making a better Fraun.

After the nightmare, she forces herself up out of bed early. She takes her time eating breakfast and dressing, yet still, Sawchett leaves her house earlier than she needs to. She's supposed to be meeting with Tutor at the new council building to see the lineage tree painted there for the first time. The letter from Erick arrived yesterday morning, telling her the tree was ready for her viewing pleasure. Tutor wanted to wait, she did not. She wanted to rush straight to the building and see it first thing. She resisted the urge. Now, she walks quickly along the path, eager to lay her eyes on the full lineage tree on the wall of the council building for the first time in Fraun history.

The kingdom of Fraun is basically a circle, as all the citizens know. The five realms are not equal size and the borders are not exactly straight. They are divided along natural boundaries, like the river which makes up the borders of Sawchett's own realm, Enchenda. The old council building was located just east of the center of the circle, technically in Marchenda territory. The new council building will be a little closer to the center of Fraun. This puts it more squarely in Sarcheda territory. Sawchett doesn't worry much about that, she trusts Tutor. But she can't help but notice if the building had been there before the war, it would've been Tin's building to use as he saw fit.

Of course, none of that matters now. They fought back against him, they won the war. Now they're rebuilding Fraun in the way it should've been done before. Allowing citizens to represent themselves at the meetings, documenting all royal blood on one tree, and living in harmony with each other. All of the realms are represented evenly. They're working together as one Fraun in a way that no one ever remembers seeing before. Sawchett is truly grateful to be a part of it.

Of course, out here alone, she can also admit that it all makes her a little uncomfortable. Two annuals ago when the war was over, she barely hesitated before taking her position as Queen of Enchenda. She was Queen at only ten annuals. Barely even old enough to have passed the age marker that is marked for Fraunians by reaching their full height. Even now, her hair is still growing. It won't stop until she reaches her fifteenth annual. For now, it's just a constant reminder that she isn't really an adult and yet she's ruling an entire realm.

What does someone like her know about real life? She shakes her head side to side twice, stopping the negative thoughts. She chose her side, she fought a war. That, more than her blood, makes her worthy of the title of Queen. Fraun needs rulers who want balance, rulers who know the safety of the citizens needs to be their top priority at all times.

She can be that ruler.

She will be that ruler.

She is that ruler.

Chapter 15

I arrive at the new council building intending to be early and, instead, discover my younger sister has beaten me to our meeting. She is intently looking at the newly painted wall. Her straight blonde hair skims the belt at her waist. It often seems longer every time I see her, as if reminding me how close she draws to the fifteenth annual. Today she wears the green of Enchenda and looks every bit of her title in the skirt of her Realm's colors flowing around her ankles.

It is still difficult for me to see her as a queen. Although she was not aware of our relationship until I was already an adult, Sawchett and I have always been close. Before we knew of our bloodlines, I was her tutor. I was hired by the woman who claimed my sister as her own. The very same woman, it turns out, who couldn't or wouldn't claim me as her own.

Sawchett turns and spies me watching her. "Tutor, you've arrived," she calls. She runs to me and I wrap her in a hug.

"What were you studying on the wall there?" I ask.

She releases me and looks back at the wall. "Lineage."

My eyes follow hers to take in the painted tree. Automatically my feet pull me closer to the painting. The tree begins at the top of the longest wall in the new building but it still needs to spread out to the walls on both sides. The tidy script list names I recognize among some I don't. The vast number of entries is staggering.

"Isn't it impressive?" Sawchett asks.

"I have never seen it all together before. What is this denoting?" I point to a name, Tawn, which has a faint box around it. Circles, which denote those with royal blood, I am used to. Boxes are new.

"These names are in two places on the wall," she answers. She searches near Renchenda, to my left, until she finds the same name. "Here it is."

Sure enough, Tawn appears there as well. I let my eyes track to my name and find the same indicator. "That's confusing," I chuckle. I point to my name, nestled beside Sawchett's, "Starred because we're ruling, circled because we're royal blood, and squared because we are on two trees."

"I think it's amazing." She smiles. "Look how many names are boxed." I do as she asks, taking in the full tree. I have to pace in front of it to do so. She's right. It makes me wonder how early my sister arrived today and stood here studying lineage.

"Is there anyone on this tree with three bloodlines?" I ask.

Sawchett scrunches her little nose. "Not directly, at least not that I've seen. But then Sarcheda and Renchenda were brothers with the same mothers. I guess that means Jordyn kind of does."

"That's a stretch."

"I know." Sawchett shrugs her shoulders. "It's just that both Sarcheda and Renchenda had the same parents. They were true brothers. If you go back that far, they would have been next in line to rule each other's realms," she explains.

"That's interesting logic." I pause to consider what she is presenting. "But I don't think it is true. The brothers considered each other unique. They broke their kingdom into five realms to honor each other individually. If something had happened to Sarcheda then, I think the brothers simply would have absorbed the land." I rest my hand on her shoulder. "Even with his logic, Jordyn himself would never claim to have Sarcheda blood."

"You're right," Sawchett agrees. "Then I don't think three bloodlines exists. Still, it is amazing how many had majority blood."

We stand in silence for a beat longer, both staring at one of the points where our names are written side by side. I can't see what's happening in her head but I know I'm thinking about the topic that means so much to Fraun. Majority blood, after all, is why I'm here. This secret of our births, buried for so long, gave me the right to overthrow Tin. Everyone was convinced it was so rare. It's a strange feeling, being confronted with proof of that lie.

"All of these names came from Oberian," Sawchett sighs.

I turn and look at her. The starry-eyed reverence makes me think of Eselda. Someone else I once discovered spending time studying the secrets locked in this lineage. "Sawchett, is something bothering you?" I ask. I remember the pain the former Queen of Enchenda was feeling when she took to studying the wall.

Sawchett turns a confused look on me. "No."

"Good." I purposely turn my back on the wall of my ancestors and put myself squarely in front of the young queen. "Lineage is fun, but we are much more than those who came before us. We make our own destiny."

Sawchett smiles. I cannot help but notice it falls flat at the edges. "What do you think of the progress of the building? That is what we actually came here to discuss." She opens her arms and spins in the empty room. "We should be ready to hold a council meeting here in a quarter of the lunar cycle."

The building is spectacular. The rocks have been hand-trimmed and filed so although they are repurposed they fit well and look nice. The room is just as it was described to the council, large enough for all of us. "I can't wait until our council is meeting here." I smile at her. "The builders have done a great job."

"They've brought life to the council's vision."

"It was really your vision," I point out. Sawchett shrugs. I almost laugh at how quickly she wipes away my praise. Humility is second nature to her now. Once upon a time, she would've lit up at that kind of comment.

"Hey Tutor, can I ask you something?" she asks. I nod in response. "The malicious age, what really happens when I reach it?"

"You have a while yet," I begin. She nods her agreement but I can see in the knotting of her hands at her waist that the question still holds. I remember how it felt to face that alone, not understanding what it was because no one had ever told me I was royal blood. I wouldn't wish that surprise on my sister. I wouldn't wish that on anyone. If I can help her understand what she is facing, I will do it. I step closer and speak softly. "You will feel angry with little or no provocation. You will be able to feel that anger boiling away inside you, waiting to strike. Your eyes will darken when the boil becomes too great," I explain.

"They will become black orbs if I give into the feeling completely," she adds. I know she's thinking of Jordyn and how dark his eyes became after the death of Tin.

"That is what I heard as well." I reach out and lay a hand on her arm. "But love conquers it, Sawchett. Thinking on a feeling of love, focusing on that, can calm the boil."

"That is good to know." She sighs and walks around me so she can face the lineage again. "All of them dealt with that."

I move to stand beside her. That is something I never really considered before. All of them must have gone through all of the age markers. "I would assume so," I tell her. To myself, I wonder why they never bothered to share their experiences. Did each person on this wall truly believe they were the only ones battling with the malicious age and the age of the flesh?

"Do you think they all knew love helped?" she asks.

The question catches me off guard. I have to pause for a breath cycle to give it some thought. "I don't know the answer to that," I finally tell her. "Jordyn is the one who told me and not until I was out of the age."

"I wonder about the ones who wouldn't have been allowed to love. Like the unwed mothers who have no father for their children listed on the wall."

I consider this and decide it can't be any worse than the ones who went through the age without even knowing they were royal blood. But I don't want Sawchett to feel sorry for me, so I keep that thought in my head. Instead, I choose a different way of rebutting her claim. "Just because they have no one listed doesn't mean they didn't love. You can love someone you are not married to." That makes me wonder if Alerta ever loved her daughter's father. Does she still? That is a story I'd be interested to hear.

"I just hope I find love before I'm buried by hate," Sawchett sighs. "So many secrets." She turns to me. "I'm glad someone figured out our truth. It could've been buried with Charlotte."

I have been waiting for an excuse to tell my sister a secret I'm harboring. If I was waiting for an invitation I just got as close as I'm going to get. "Sawchett, I need to tell you something." I swallow. This truth, this little secret, is something I have been hiding. I never liked secrets. Growing up they were something that made me irrationally angry. This is the last one I'm harboring. Ironically, it was also the first one anyone ever gave me to hold.

Sawchett scrunches her nose up like there's an unpleasant smell in the room. "That sounds serious. We better sit." She directs me toward a piece of wood that has been laid in a sort of bench on the side of the room. I clasp her hand and lead her there, hating that I have to tell her this truth. "Alright, get it out. What's the big secret?" she asks.

"When I came to Enchenda I had no family. I had been raised as an orphan for fifteen annuals. Charlotte found me, let me live in her home. You were a baby. From the first day I met you I knew that you were Charlotte and Den's baby. But it was a secret, no one was supposed to know."

"Because of my royal blood."

"That would be my guess, yes. Although I honestly never knew that. I never even suspected it." I take a deep breath, hoping for a little strength. She's not going to like this. "Charlotte told me she was my mother."

She yanks her hand away from me and her head snaps back as if I slapped her. I see her scrambling to rationalize this for me. She's trying to find a way to let me stay trustworthy. I love her for that. "Before she died?"

I close my eyes so I don't have to watch. "Before Den died." I can hear the exhale through her nose, like a grunt. I open my eyes. Her arms are crossed across her chest, sealing herself off from me. Her eyes are no longer looking at me, they are focused on the floor. I shake my head. "I'm sorry. I swear I didn't know about the blood." I reach out for her arm. She twists her torso away from me. It's the most childish thing I have seen her do in many annuals. I rub my hand along my forehead, trying to push out the tension that is suddenly there.

"You knew you were my brother for most of my life?" The words are violent, angry.

"I'm sorry." It's not enough but what else can I say?

She stands up from the wood and whips around to face me. She is standing perfectly straight, starring at some fixed point over my head. Her arms are still crossed but her face is expressionless. All traces of that childish reaction are gone. "What's done is done," she says. She spins on her heel and heads for the entrance to the building. It's the worst thing she can do. No reaction is a terrible reaction.

"Sawchett, don't leave it like this." I spring off the wood and run to her. "Let's talk this through. I should've told you. I'm sorry. What can I say?"

She tilts her head to the right and leans closer to me. "Would you have ever told me if it wasn't for the war?" Her words, meant to attack, cut deep.

"I probably … I meant … I'm sure I would've …"

She grunts and swipes her hand between us, ending my sad attempt at finding her an answer. "What's done is done," she repeats. She turns again and heads for the door.

This time I don't chase her because I don't have anything to say.

Chapter 16

The breeze blows lightly, bringing the smell of nature. This is a smell Jordyn never learned to enjoy in Fraun. The crisp smells of vegetables, the sharp smell of animals somewhere in the distance, and the slight tang of cold weather on the horizon. Jordyn and Eselda haven't set foot inside Fraun for two annuals. At first, it was strange. But now, watching the fire flicker as the campground sleeps, there are no pangs of longing or sadness from the once king. This is home.

The scout troop has changed over the annuals since the war. Eselda, of course, joined them when she was thrown out of Fraun for her part in the rebellion. She is sleeping in the first tent to his right. Franc, the lovable father figure who ran the group before Jordyn, took his wife, Carlina, and returned to Fraun. Franc has entered the age marker known as the death spiral, marked by his gray hair. He won't last much longer. They live in a cottage next door to Queen Sawchett of Enchenda who can help Carlina now and when Franc passes. Kurt and Evelyn, Abney's parents, are still around. In fact, they are sleeping soundly in the first tent to Jordyn's left.

Evelyn thought about moving back to Fraun to be with her daughter and Sieven but changed her mind after one night in the noise that is Farcheda.

Almost an annual ago, Kurt was delivering in Marchenda when he happened upon a young couple who was interested in seeing what scout life was all about. They came for a night and have never left. This is how the tent beside Kurt and his wife came to be filled by Mario and Nina.

The last tent, beside Jordyn and Eselda's own, belongs to Toby. Toby grew up in Sarcheda. At some point in his past, which he staunchly refuses to talk about, he defected from Fraun in favor of traveling with the scouts. Toby took up travels with the same group of Scouts who devoted loyal support and fierceness for Jordyn's dream of what Fraun could be. It was Toby who first agreed to fight alongside Jordyn. Toby who ventured out into the woods and found Jordyn after that terrible battle. Toby who helped bring him back to Castle Fraun for treatment.

But they almost lost Toby that day. Shortly after Jordyn left Fraun in favor of the woods, Toby spiked a fever. He was under the care of a medicine man for an infection that was ravaging his body for a fortnight. It is a miracle he survived at all. He still has a permanent limp in his step from the wound on his leg that became infected. Despite that limp, he is the same strong-willed, fierce Toby he always was.

Jordyn reaches out and stokes the fire, watching as the embers dance to the sky. He lays the water kettle in the flames to heat. Tea will be desired as the sun rises higher over the horizon. These quiet moments are the only time Jordyn allows himself thoughts of Fraun. He is careful not to tread onto their grounds, in solidarity with his future wife who cannot. He supports the changes to Fraun. He writes often to Tutor, Sawchett, and his Uncle Thometh. But that life is simply not his life anymore. Were the war to happen today Jordyn is not sure he would fight their battles. That fact alone tells him how much he has changed.

The flap to Kurt's tent opens and the man emerges, arching his back and craning his neck alternately left and right. Jordyn looks up from the flames and his hands freeze at the sight. Kurt yawns and rubs his eyes. When he lowers his hands and looks to Jordyn, confusion fills his face. He looks over his shoulders, first the right and then the left. "What? Why do you look as though you have seen a ghost?" he asks.

"Your hair," Jordyn answers, pointing.

Kurt's hands reach up to his own head, running his fingers through the soft locks. "What about it? It feels fine. I could probably use a wash."

"It's white. When you went to bed last night it was still yellow. Now it's white."

"Oh." Kurt drops his hands to his side, relieved. "That makes sense, yeah. I suppose it's the anniversary of my birth."

"You are forty annuals. Happy Birthday," Jordyn offers. He tries to focus on the fire but continues to steal glances at Kurt.

Kurt rolls his eyes. "Come on, Jordyn. You've surely seen someone go gray before. Your parents, perhaps."

"I suppose my father did. I just didn't remember it happened in one night all at once like that," he answers. He abandons the stick he was using to stir the fire and leans his elbows on his legs. "Does it always happen instantly like that?"

"I don't know. I suppose it has to do with the darkness of hair to begin with. I'd imagine my light yellow hair doesn't take as much to change. Your parents, did they have dark or light hair?"

Jordyn shifts around, clearly uncomfortable. "Dad's was lighter than the queens."

Kurt either doesn't notice or doesn't care about Jordyn's discomfort. He reaches for the abandoned fire stick. "There you have it. Did hers take longer to gray then?"

"I don't know. She didn't live long enough to gray," Jordyn answers. Kurt opens his mouth to comment and then shuts it again. He clears his throat.

Without warning, the ground beneath them trembles. Jordyn has to throw his arms down to the ground to brace his body and avoid falling from the log. The trembling lasts long enough to wake the rest of the troop. The blankets on all the tents pull back. Almost simultaneously Toby and Eselda are by the fire as the trembling stops. "What was that?" Eselda asks.

"A tree falling," Jordyn answers, but his words trip on the lie.

Evelyn emerges from her tent, shaking her head. "That explanation was not believable three annuals ago when I first heard it. It was less believable an annual ago when you tried again. Then, last lunar cycle, when you spoke it I knew it was a lie. Today I know even you don't believe it," she says.

Jordyn wants to argue, but he cannot. The tremors have happened as she says and he truly doesn't know what they are. "We need to investigate this," Kurt states. "Everyone who is coming should get dressed and wield weapons in case of danger." He turns and disappears into his tent. Silently the troop obeys until only Eselda remains, standing before Jordyn.

"You are worried," she says.

"I cannot explain the shakes."

Eselda laughs. "You hate things you cannot explain." She reaches out and lays her palm flat on his chest. She can feel the shirt underneath her fingers but it has been lunar cycles since the coin of his ancestors lay underneath that. "You will lead them to investigate. I will stay here and keep an eye on the camp. Be safe." She leans forward and kisses him before taking his abandoned seat by the fire.

He knows better than to argue. He takes his sword, well cared for and sharp, out of their tent. He straps it to his side, and memories of that terrible night return. At the height of the war, Jordyn had come sword-to-sword with King Tin. Tin, who was the cause of all the troubles. Tin, who had kidnapped Eselda. Tin told Jordyn he had taken Eselda's life. Jordyn, deep in the malicious age, had made a choice that changed him. He drove his sword through Tin's body, leaving him lifeless in the clearing. With the sword making him equipped for anything and the shameful memory burning his cheeks, he leaves the tent. "Eselda, how is it today?" Jordyn quietly asks.

She knows exactly what he means. She rises and crosses to him. In the light of the fire and the rising sun she searches his face. His eyes are the blue of the sky on a sunny day. But at the edges, like an eclipse in reverse, the ring of black is still there. "Better every day, my love." She leans in and kisses him again. This time the kiss is deep and long. Jordyn wraps his arm around her waist, holding her close.

When they hear someone clear their throat, the couple pulls away. Eselda blushes and drops her eyes. Jordyn feels the pull of his new age marker. This time, he knows his eyes will be clouded in a darkness that is nothing like the black ring at the outer edge. He knows the darkening of his eyes in the center is temporary, a result of his twenty-fifth annual. He cannot help but lust after Eselda. Jordyn has entered into what is commonly known as the age of the flesh, a time when someone of royal blood will be pulled to act on love in a physical way.

Despite this age marker, Jordyn has never felt even a hint of love for any other woman. The age marker seems to crave only Eselda, which is interesting, scientifically speaking. He often wonders if it is this way for everyone. Do they get only one love? If so, he must admit he is worried about what will happen in a few annuals when Eselda reaches the age of the flesh. She can reassure him that she never truly loved Tin and Jordyn knows she loves him now, but what will the eyes say?

Eselda drops back down to the log and strokes the fire. She can hear the water in the kettle boiling and uses a cloth to move it off direct heat. "Eselda, we will return shortly," Kurt says. He gives a little wave and the group, all but Eselda, travel away to the south. This direction, away from Fraun, is the most likely spot to hide secrets or dangers. The instant decisions made by her troop are Eselda's favorite part of being a scout. Everyone knew right away they would explore, no one questioned it. Just as no one questioned her decision to stay behind. She will cook breakfast when they are returning. This way she doesn't have to walk long distances and they don't have to wait for her. They can all get their curiosity or their need to be moving fed today. More importantly, she doesn't have to make decisions. It has been a long time since the war and yet Eselda's guilt remains. She simply doesn't trust her own decisions, not anymore. Maybe that will change when the malicious age ends.

The sun shifts in the sky, changing the shadows in the clearing. Eselda knows her family will be returning soon and they'll be eager to fill their bellies. She has the water for oats and tea reheating in the flames. Nearby she stands at a tree stump cutting strawberries to lay atop the oats. She hears the sound of someone returning and a smile plays at the corner of her lips.

Wait, something about the sound is not right. She lays down the small sword and turns toward the noise. It's coming too fast, crashing through the forest. She rises.

"Eselda," Jordyn's voice carries through the trees. He is panicking. She steps toward the sound of his voice, nerves sending her stomach plummeting to the ground. "We need a roach," he says as soon as he sees her.

"Wh—"

"Now, Eselda!" he interrupts. "The giants are back."

Chapter 17

Birds make Fraunians nervous. It's a natural reaction, considering most birds are large enough to pick them up and fly away with them. There are stories, myths told to keep children away from birds, about Fraunians being flown toward the sky and dropped from a great height. Sawchett has never believed such tales. In fact, during her time with the scouts, she learned that birds are not altogether interested in them at all. While she cannot directly speak to them, she finds ways to communicate.

She holds her hand up and out to the bird at the edge of Enchenda territory, near the woods. The bird hops forward, tipping his beak down to her hand. He quickly moves his head back again. Sawchett can still feel the weight of the little grains. "It's okay," she whispers. "You can have them. Go ahead. They're for you. I won't hurt you."

The bird tries again, moving his beak down quickly toward her hand. This time she feels the soft nip of the beak and the weight of the grains disappear. "There you go. You're such a pretty bird." She knows better than to try and touch the feathers. This bird may be the same one she met yesterday but he is skeptical of her. If she startles him, she will have reason to worry.

Sawchett whistles a note, changing pitch halfway through. The bird cocks his head to the side. The queen repeats the whistle. The bird tilts his head in the opposite direction. She repeats the whistle again. This time the bird takes up the call, mimicking her whistle. She laughs. "Well done." Her hand darts into her pocket and pulls out the last of the grains, which she holds out to the bird. This time, he doesn't hesitate to take them.

Sawchett rubs her empty palms together. "That's all I have today, my friend. Come back tomorrow, I'll bring more." She takes a step back and waves her hands. The bird takes to the air. Sawchett tilts her head up and repeats the whistle. From somewhere in the trees above she hears the call echoed back.

In the silence that follows she hears the sound of the water in River Fraun churning. She decides to head for a quick swim, the weather is just starting to warm up and the last of the snow has melted. The water will be cold, but it may not be too cold for a quick dip.

Her steps take her through the grass and away from the trees at the edge of Enchenda. She is headed south, toward Sarcheda. Toward Tutor. Sawchett sighs. How many more surprises and lies will she have to face in her lifetime? At only twelve annuals, she has already endured a lot more than her share. Her mother had the blood of a royal in her. Her grandfather was so quick to dismiss her family and yet he accepted his other child, raising that line to lead the realm. Her mother may have loved a man who was her half-brother, if the rumors there are true. Her father, who she doesn't even remember, had the blood of a royal he didn't even know about. Then, she learned that her tutor was really her brother. Now, the worst truth comes out, her brother knew about their relationship the entire time and never told her.

How old was she when Den died? Four or five annuals? She wasn't even speaking at the time. If what Tutor said was the truth, finally, then that means he has known they were siblings for that long. He can say whatever he wants but Sawchett knows if it hadn't been for the war he never would've told her. He would've been content to go on with his life as a lineage updater and let her live on as the princess of Enchenda, clueless and carefree.

She reaches the bed of the river and slips off her shoes. The water is meandering along here, no rocks or white caps in sight. She takes a nose full of the fresh, cool air tinged with the smell of water. Dropping her shoes on the shore, she wades out into the stream. The frigid water comes up to her ankles and takes her breath away. It is still too cold for swimming, she realizes. Her feet will be the only thing wet today.

She takes a few steps around, swirling her toes in the water and kicking up the dirt underneath. Sometimes, when it is quiet outside like this and she is free to enjoy nature, Sawchett misses being a scout. There was something so easy about that way of life. *It certainly felt like the life of a scout held fewer secrets.*

She sighs. Maybe, she thinks, there's a reason Tutor kept this to himself. *Maybe it's not so bad that he kept this secret.* Sure, it hurts to know that he was one more person in her life who felt like he couldn't let her in. One more person who hid the truth from her. But, if her situation was a mess, wasn't Tutor's worse? He doesn't talk about that time in his life, not really. But Sawchett knows it must have been awful to feel so detached from a family who claimed he was rightfully theirs. She wonders if she would have had the strength to support her mother or tutor another child after annuals on her own. *Could she have stepped into such a role after practically being abandoned?*

She turns her head in the direction of the royal home of Enchenda, her home. She cannot see it from this far out, but she knows it is there. She sighs again. Yes, the truth is, she would've been able to support Charlotte. She can understand that. It is the same reason why she is now the Queen of Enchenda. Sure, sometimes ruling a realm is a burden. But that burden is hers to bear for Enchenda. It is in her blood in the same way that it was in Tutor's to accept the role and do what he could for Sawchett.

She climbs out of the river and grabs her shoes, deciding to carry them for the walk home. She likes the feeling of the grass on her toes as she picks her way back through the realm. The sound of the river becomes softer and softer as she walks. When her house is in sight she tries the whistle again, wondering if her new feathered friend is still around. It takes a few beats and comes from a great distance, but the call is answered.

Chapter 18

The training area is crowded today. Besides my trainer and myself, Kristoff has come to practice his lifting. The presence of the king and the champion in one practice arena has drawn a sizable crowd. My trainer watches my form carefully as I raise and lower the weighted bar. “Good,” he says. “Ten more and you can stop.” I groan. “Twenty if you insist on complaining,” he chides.

I raise the bar again and again, silently counting. This bar isn't heavy, not really. Two blocks would be heavier. But when we raise and lower it we are expected to slow our form and repeat the action multiple times. By the second or third round of lifts, it starts to feel heavy. By this, my fifth round of lifts, it starts to hurt.

“Majesty,” his voice sounds different. It is coated in panic.

I open my eyes. “What is it?”

“A ladybug approaches.”

I drop the bar and look along the path of the trainer’s gaze. The flashing of the sun on the red coat tells me the bug approaches fast. There is a shadow atop his silhouette. He carries one rider. "Do you require security, Majesty?" I do not answer right away. Instead, I take a moment to examine the rider. Impatient for my answer, the trainer bounces on his toes beside me. Whoever the rider is, they are the size of one fully grown. As the ladybug draws closer, I can make out dark hair and the brown clothing of a scout. I can feel the tension radiating off the trainer beside me, nervous for who this intruder may be. But something tells me we are not in danger. Finally, the face of Toby, a scout I know, comes into view.

"No, he is a friend." The trainer's shoulders relax and his arms fall to his side. I pat him on the shoulder before walking away from the clearing. For reasons he has never shared with me, Toby is not comfortable inside Fraun. He has occasionally met with me but always outside Fraun or near the border where he can quickly leave again. I keep in touch with my connections from the old scout troop. From my location here, bordered by the ravine, we are not a direct path to the scouts' last known location. Toby has ridden through the forest surrounding Renchenda and around through Sarcheda town to get here. He will be anxious to deliver whatever vital message he is carrying and leave.

"Greetings," I call out when the rider is close enough to hear.

His feet hit the ground beside the ladybug before the creature has drawn to a complete stop. The bug scurries to the shade under a nearby tree, panting. "Greetings, Tutor." I do not insist he call me King. The scouts are not of Fraun. Instead, I offer my hand. Toby shakes it vigorously.

"I'll be quick here. I have been sent to relay a message. Jordyn has found a giant. It is alive. He told me to rush straight to you."

The shock leaves me breathless. For a beat, I consider sitting on the ground. I'm suddenly glad I left the clearing to meet Toby and didn't stay near all the citizens watching the training. I shake my head slowly. I realize I'm holding my breath and take a few ragged ones. Then I look Toby in the eyes. "A giant?" I ask, my voice sounding breathless. I cover my eyes with my palm like I can hide from this and push on my face, welcoming the pressure that reminds me this is real. This is not a nightmare, no matter how surreal it feels.

"Yes," Toby answers.

I drop my hand from my face and force myself to focus. "How far from Fraun?"

"I left the area nearly two suns ago on a roach. I have only paused long enough to change animals. The giant was spotted due South of here." He indicates the direction he speaks off, out beyond the ravine edging Fraun.

Two suns is a decent distance to travel, especially on the back of a fast moving creature. I use my hand to cover my mouth. I have no idea what this could mean but my stomach clenches. The uproar this could cause physically hurts. "How did you come to find it? Did the giant approach you?"

"We have felt tremors more than once. This time we investigated and saw the giant," Toby explains. "It did not appear to see us."

"There was only one?"

"That we saw, yes."

I want this to not be happening. Just last night I was worried about my ambassador, the citizens of my realm, Alerta, and my age marker. Now I want things back to that normal. But I also know I must face reality. I run my hand along my face, trying to wipe away the shock and stress. "I will tell the council," I decide out loud.

"What message should I return to Jordyn?"

I take two full breaths before answering. "Jordyn has my utmost respect but he is no longer a leader in Fraun. Thank him for the news and give Eselda my best."

Toby's features tighten. "That is the full message?"

"For now. We do not act alone in Fraun. We have felt no tremors here. I conclude we are not in immediate danger. We will await the decision of a full council." I speak with a calm that is at war with the lump in my gut.

"I knew this was a waste of time," Toby spits the words. "Fraun will do nothing in the face of a giant large enough to crush everything Fraunians have built?"

"The giant knows nothing of our existence. We are in no immediate danger. These are the facts you have given me," I say. Toby shakes his head in response. It is not disagreement with the facts, but open contempt at my actions. "What would you have me do?" I ask.

"Ready an army." His answer is quick, not requiring thought.

So is my laughter. "An army? What army could we raise large enough to take on what you have seen?" I ask when the laughter dies. "We cannot battle even one small giant."

He must agree with my logic because his face falls. "Surely you must support some action," he says.

"I do, but I don't have ideas that are better than yours. The council will hear the issue and propose ideas. Better ideas, with any luck. You are welcome to stay and attend." The mere act of offering this comfort reminds me that I do not govern alone. I may not have ideas but I can put faith in the council. A little feeling washes back into my extremities.

"I can't wait. I will report back on your lack of action to Jordyn now," Toby says.

I nod. "I understand. I will send a messenger to you once the council has made a decision."

"Fine." Toby turns and stomps off toward Renchenda.

I turn my attention to the exhausted ladybug he has left behind. "You require food and water which my home will provide. Should you so desire you will find shelter there as well."

"Thank you," the creature answers.

"Can I ask, have you seen the giants our man there speaks of?"

The ladybug turns his head in my direction and his antennae move rapidly. I wonder if he sniffs the air to sense danger. "I have only heard rumors," he answers.

"Are we in danger, in your opinion?"

Again, the antennae move. "Not today." He scurries off, ending the discussion.

Chapter 19

I am pacing the large formal dining room in Castle Fraun. Emergency meetings are not something I enjoy attending, let alone calling. A fire is blazing and chairs are set up in a circle beside the large table. This time, to be quick, there are only enough chairs for the royals. Ambassadors are not required to attend emergency meetings. Should they, or other Fraunians, choose to attend they will stand around the outer edge of the room. I don't want to think about what a panic I am about to cause for Fraun particularly if there are citizens in attendance. I need to just focus on getting through this meeting.

Hector blows into the room. "Tutor, an emergency meeting? Is everything alright?" He drops into a chair beside me, the one immediately before the fire. Saren enters and quietly takes the chair on his left.

"An urgent message from the scouts came through to me. I'd rather wait for the full council," I explain.

"Jordyn?" he asks. I merely nod. Hector sighs. "Well, I guess we should be grateful we had two annuals of quiet."

I have no response. It's the same thought I've been having. Part of me is happy the giants didn't make an appearance while we were busy fighting a war. But isn't this a little too much excitement for one lifetime? My thoughts are interrupted by the door opening and ushering in a breeze. Alerta, her dark hair in tight curls framing her delicate features, walks into the room. Her face brightens with her smile. "Hello, gentlemen." Her arm is twisted behind her. As her skirt shifts, I can see her hand is wound tightly around a small girl. The girl shares her mother's hairstyle but her skin is a full shade lighter. She has brown eyes that dart nervously around the room.

"You must be Stef," I greet. "I'm Tutor. It's a pleasure to meet you."

The girl shuffles her feet. "Mama, where do I sit?"

"Stef, say hello to the kings," Alerta says.

"Hello, Kings. Where do I sit?"

Alerta sighs. "There, on the floor will do." She gestures to the side of the room farthest from the fire.

I drop into the chair I am standing in front of. From my seat, I can clearly see the door to the room and the place where the child flops down onto the floor. She sighs and places her chin in her hands. "How old is she?" I ask.

Alerta sits in the chair on my right. Her face takes on a dreamy quality. "Six annuals. Before I know it her hair will be full length. Then it'll feel like I blink and she will be full grown."

"Have you warned her about the markers of royal blood?" Hector asks.

"It's such a delicate conversation to have. Her tutor has talked of them to her but she hasn't spoken to me about the details." Alerta doesn't ask us for our opinions or experiences, which is wise. Of course, I have no children to make those decisions for and Hector's only son died during the war for Fraun. It's only recently that Hector and Saren have proven themselves able to even consider another child. As if remembering the same thing, Saren's hands run along her pregnant middle.

The awkward silence is broken as the door opens to allow a group to enter. Thometh holds the door as Queen Lucinda, Queen Sawchett, and Ambassador Annabeth file into the room. "Sorry we are late," Thometh says in place of a greeting. "Lucinda and I were speaking with the new lady-in-waiting we had brought in when she moved into the castle." He indicates an empty chair with a sweeping gesture. "Lucinda, please take my seat." He walks around behind the chair, leaning down on the back of it. "I would prefer to stand."

His new wife, lovely in the orange of her realm, takes the seat. She flips her blond hair over her shoulder and sits up straight. "I feel so important, joining you all here in the center of the room."

"You are the Queen of Renchenda, Majesty," Hector offers.

"That title is still so new to me. Honestly, I remember a simpler time before everyone felt the need to bow before me."

"Don't we all," I say.

I try to catch Sawchett's eye, but she's not having it. She is seated directly across the circle from me, but her arms are crossed across her chest and she is pointedly avoiding putting her eyes on my face. The door opens again and Marcus enters. I suppress my urge to groan. "Alright, Tutor. Enough small talk. Tell us why we are here," Thometh says. That reminds me that we are here for bigger things than my new ambassador.

I harden my face into a serious mask and dive in. "I received a message from Jordyn. It's an alarming message, you may want to prepare yourself." I look toward Alerta's daughter, Stef. She is still leaning her head on her hands and looking bored. Her eyes have glossed over and she may be humming quietly. With any luck, she's not paying attention. I lower my voice, just in case. "The scouts have felt tremors in the ground. Recently they went to investigate the tremors and found a real giant."

Alerta gasps.

"Oh c'mon," Marcus calls from the shadow behind Alerta. "What proof do you have?"

"The scouts saw the giant with their own eyes. I spoke to a scout named Toby myself." I try to hold my anger in. I tell myself Marcus is shocked by the news and it only appears that he is angry with me.

"You're just trying to stir up trouble. After all, you earned that seat you sit in by stirring up trouble. Surely you figure you stand to gain something by bringing in more trouble now," Marcus continues.

I stand up. "I think you misspeak, sir. Tin caused trouble." At the mention of his name, Stef finally turns her attention in my direction. I'm not sure if fear of the former king's name or my tone of voice draws her attention. Either way, the idea of being overheard by the small child makes me lower my voice a little and proceed with caution. "I was part of the group that brought peace to Fraun. Many of the Fraunians seated here with me fought for that. Don't make this about trouble."

"I'm just going to bring us back to the topic," Hector says. "How large was this giant?" He leans forward to place his elbows on his knees.

I sit back down in my chair and address Hector with my answer. I can feel my heart racing. I force the action into my foot, tapping it erratically. "I didn't ask. But suffice it to say it was a giant." I notice the angry edge of my comment and intentionally soften my tone. "It would be large enough to cause damage. The good news is that it appears the giant is not aware of our existence. It didn't spot the scouts. Basically, we need to decide how best to proceed here."

"Wow," Hector breaths. "That is not at all what I expected you to say when this meeting was called."

"What are our options?" Sawchett asks.

"We could attack," Hector says.

"We wouldn't be able to fend off a real giant." I make the same point I had to make to Toby.

"We could run," Alerta says.

"What?" Hector sits up again. "The entire Kingdom of Fraun is supposed to run? How do we rebuild everything?"

Saren speaks up from beside him. "How do we replant all the food you showed us? Surely running is way down the list of options. I would hate to abandon lunar cycles worth of good food."

"As would I but it needs to be on the list," Sawchett points out. "So does wait it out and hope they never find us."

"So, do nothing?" I ask. Sawchett shrugs.

"We can approach them," Thometh offers.

"I feel as though a group of us approaching a giant is as dangerous as a group of us attempting to attack. We must remember the giants are not only significantly larger than us but also an angry group with a history of violence," Hector says.

"Now wait, what makes you say they have a history of violence? After all, the giants haven't been seen or heard from in many generations," Thometh says.

"They disappeared because they killed each other in a war," Hector says. You can see the moment he realizes what he has pointed out would also apply to us. His shoulders slump and he snorts out a breath. "I suppose I don't know for sure. But it's a risk we need to be aware of."

"So, the choices I'm hearing," I summarize, "are attack, do nothing, reach out to the giants, or run. Do we have any other suggestions?"

"Those are all terrible ideas," Alerta points out, her voice breaking.

The room falls silent. I let the silence reach to every corner of the room. I hope that in the silence a better idea will spark an explosion. I'm rewarded with an idea from my own sister, mumbled quietly from her chair. "I guess we can send a group to keep an eye on them."

"That's actually a good idea, Sawchett," Alerta says.

Marcus crosses his arms across his chest. "The group could obtain some proof to bring back to the council as well," he says.

"Proof—"

"Solid proof from real Fraunians," Marcus interrupts me to add.

"All in favor of sending a small group of Fraunians to observe the giant and report back, raise your hand." Thometh speaks in a loud, clear voice that cuts through the tension between my ambassador and I. I wait until the hands go up around the circle. When they are all up in the air, I send mine up, completing the vote. "So be it. Meeting adjourned."

Before anyone can leave, Hector leans forward and grabs my arm. "Do we need to vote about replacing a representative before we leave for the day?" His eyes move to the right, indicating he means Marcus.

Before I can answer Thometh steps up behind me. "No. As unpopular as his opinion may be in this room, it still appears in Fraun."

"You think there are citizens who believe that I do not deserve my throne?" I ask. Of course, I have the same doubts. But there is a big difference between believing you are not good enough and having someone you respect give voice to that same fear.

"No, that's not what I mean," Thometh says. "I mean there are citizens who question your motives. There are those who question my motives. They are as outnumbered in Fraun as they are in this council room, but they do exist. I think we keep him to solidify that in our minds."

"Plus," Hector adds, "if we can ever sway him we'll know we're doing a good job." He lays his big hand on my shoulder. "We remember how you earned this seat, Tutor. You're one of us, Sarcheda blood or no."

King Hector raises his arm, index finger toward the ceiling. "One Kingdom," he calls.

From our spots around the room, we match the gesture. "One goal," we answer.

Chapter 20

Everyone should have something in life that can instantly change their mood and put a smile on their face. As I walk out of the castle feeling undervalued and stressed my eyes land on one of those things. She is sitting on a log, talking to a dark-haired man who is a few clicks shorter than she is. Her dark legs are delicately crossed at the ankles. She looks up, spots me, and waves.

I cross over to them, feeling my mood lift. "You haven't headed home yet?" I ask. After my conversation with Hector and Thometh I stayed behind in the room thinking and watching. I expected I was the last to leave.

"Not yet," Alerta answers. "Stef had to run in and use the little Princess' room." She gives an uncomfortable giggle.

I turn my attention to the man. "You look familiar, have I met you somewhere?"

He offers his hand. "My name is Vicente. I was once in the patrol representing Marchenda."

I shake his hand but eye him warily. The patrol had shifted their allegiance to support Tin during the war for Fraun. I don't recall this man specifically, but I wonder where his loyalties fell at the battle right here on this very ground where Fraunian blood was spilled.

As if sensing my discomfort, Vicente grimaces. "I know what we became. I'm not sure I ever took the chance to apologize to you for my part in all that, sir. I am merely a roach trainer for Marchenda now."

"That's good to hear. What are you doing here today, in Renchenda?"

"Queen Alerta and Princess Stef rode in on a young roach today. I came along to ensure his training holds strong." He indicates a pair of roaches, one clearly younger than the other, under a tree behind the queen. "I'll just be checking in with them." He ducks off in that direction without another word.

Alerta smiles at me. "He is a fine roach hand. I have no reason to distrust him. His former patrol partner is a wild now, I hear." She shrugs. "I heard you talking to Thometh and Hector after our meeting. Does Marcus concern you?"

"I don't know. It's nothing against Marcus personally. He represents a pocket of Sarcheda citizens who disagree with my reign. I have no blood of Sarcheda." I shrug. "Of course, no one does."

"But how large is that pocket of dissent?" she asks.

"That's exactly what concerns me."

She purses her lips and draws her brows together, studying me. Then she relaxes the muscles in her face and nods once. "You've been a good ruler, Tutor. They'll come around. Besides," she brushes her fingers along my elbow. I feel sparks dance up my arm. "You don't rule in isolation."

"True." I run my hands through my hair. It's a sad substitute for running them through her hair or along her body, but it's more acceptable. I am not sure how she'd feel about physical contact with an employee in her home watching nearby. I clear my throat and try to keep our conversation going. "Have you ever felt rejected by Marchenda?"

"Absolutely." My surprise must show on my face because Alerta laughs, the sound bouncing off the trees surrounding us. "You thought they loved me?"

"I assumed." I swallow. "You're very lovable." I hope that didn't come off as creepy.

"Tutor, I had Stef out of wedlock. My realm shunned me and hid the truth of my blood. Raising Stef as I did was not typical. Becoming their Queen was —" she trails off.

"I hadn't thought of that." I realize how similar our stories are. Both of us rejected by a family we should've been loved by. I step closer to her and let myself reach out for her hand. She smiles and slips her fingers into mine. "There is so much of your story I'd like to hear," I tell her. "Will you share it with me one day?"

"Everyone has a story," she squeezes my hand with her fingers. "Someday I will be privileged to hear yours and share the burden of my past with you."

"Mom," Stef's little voice breaks through the fog of the moment. I drop Alerta's hand and take a step back. This time I run my hand through my hair to cover how awkward this feels. "Is it time to go?" Stef asks.

Alerta ruffles the girls' hair, sending a few wisps straight up from her head. "It is. Say goodbye to King Tutor." Alerta waves in Vicente's direction and he leads the two roaches toward us.

Stef barely glances my way. "Bye."

"Goodbye, Princess Stef." I make a show of bowing theatrically to the girl.

She giggles, hiding her face behind her little hand. "You're funny."

I act surprised, drawing a dramatic breath and splaying my hand on my chest. "Me? Funny? No." She giggles again.

Alerta's hand drops onto the girl's shoulder. Her laughter echoes Stef's. "C'mon, climb aboard the roach. It's time for us to head home."

Stef does as she is told, climbing in front of her mother onto the back of the waiting creature. As the roach begins to scurry off in the direction of Marchenda, Stef turns around to face me. It's the first time she's fully looked at me all day. The smile is firmly on her face. "Bye Tutor," she calls.

Just like that, I feel great.

Chapter 21

This time when Eselda opens her eyes the first thing she notices is that the clearing is warm. To her recollection, it was cold last time. Perhaps she was wrong about this dream being another vision of the future, another death. Perhaps it was just a coincidence. Just a regular dream. In her dream, or whatever this is, Eselda turns in a circle taking in the entire clearing. It's dusk, there's a fire burning in the camp circle. Again, two bodies are seated on logs, knees toward each other as though in conversation. This appears to be the same camp location the scout troop is in now, but with one extra tent.

Despite hoping the weather change means this isn't a vision, something in the back of her brain is buzzing with the knowledge that it is just that. Her brain is showing her this scene, just like before. Something important will occur. Something related to that death she witnessed the last time. She is meant to gather information.

The first time something like this happened she was shown the battle between Jordyn and Tin. That time the dream revealed little truths each time she had it. She's not sure why she's been chosen to see these things. She's not sure what she's supposed to do with the information. She only knows she should pay attention.

With that in mind, Eselda begins walking around the camp. She's looking for clues she may have missed or skipped the last time she had the dream. A cold breeze blows across her arms, just like last time. The tent flaps move slightly, revealing soft whispers from inside. There are lights glowing in each tent. This tells Eselda that every one of her scouts is accounted for. They seem to be enjoying their quiet time.

Jordyn steps out of the extra tent. "It's time," he says.

This time Eselda does not follow him. Instead, her feet guide her to the pair having a conversation by the fire. The pair Jordyn appeared to be speaking to. She pays attention to their body language as she draws closer. They are comfortable with each other, friendly. The clothing indicates a male and a female. She watches the male, who is facing her, reach out and touch the hand of the female, offering some kind of comfort.

Eselda walks faster, unsure of when the dream will break and send her back to the reality of her own tent. The man's face comes into focus and Eselda smiles automatically. Danyel of Sarcheda. *What is Danyel doing out here with the scouts?*

Perhaps he knows the woman in the tent. Perhaps he knows why this woman is important. Why, then, does he sit here instead of being by her side when she draws her last breath? Do they not realize how sick the visitor is?

Visitor. The word comes automatically to Eselda's brain, but she cannot disprove it. It cannot be one of her scouts. The body is the wrong size and the scouts seem to be accounted for. Where has this mysterious sick woman come from? Did Danyel bring her? When did he arrive? Surely whoever she is, Eselda and the scouts are caring for her.

So why do they let her die alone? Who would do such a thing?

Eselda is close enough now that she could reach out and touch the woman on the shoulder. She steps around her so she can see her face.

Her heart sinks.

Just like that, she is awake in her own tent feeling her disappointment like a weight on her chest. She has more questions after this dream than she did before it. The face of the woman talking to Danyel was her own.

Who is the visitor?
More importantly, why does Eselda let them die alone?

Chapter 22

It has always been customary in Fraun to have at least four days in a lunar cycle dedicated to an audience with the king or queen of the realm. In my time ruling Sarcheda I have them more like seven or eight times in a lunar cycle. Today happens to be one of those days. It was previously scheduled and I cannot justify canceling it. So, although my mind is on giants and danger, worrying about the group we have sent off into the woods to gather evidence of something that terrifies me to my very bones, I am here. I am sitting in a room of the Sarcheda home which I honestly don't know the purpose of. When I took possession of the home it appeared to be entirely composed of a few padded chairs, a small table, and a fireplace. We don't waste things in Fraun. We don't build new things; we repurpose. So the presence of a useless room loaded with things that appear to be carefully crafted shocks citizens who are used to things being done in the way of Fraun.

My first appointment of the day is a small man who owns a business in the center of Sarcheda. His store specializes in the manufacturing of outerwear, such as jackets and hats. Apparently, they recently began manufacturing gloves, which competitors often wear during strength competitions. This, according to the man, has caused a boom in business. When he enters the room, I notice right away that he isn't shocked by the opulence. He walks right past the ornate carvings in the door without pausing to run his hands along them. He drops into the plush chair without seeming to relish the comfort for an extra breath. This is a man who has done business with the previous rulers of Sarcheda. He has seen this room before.

"Good morning," I greet. "Let's get right down to business. Why don't you summarize for me why you are here before me?"

He nods at the request to get to business, seeming pleased. "Basically, Majesty, I'm going to need more space. We would like to request a second room be added to the back end of our building. We counted it out. My sons can all lie down in the empty space end-to-end with more than enough room before the neighboring business. This means we have at least twelve marks of space back there we can build on. I'd like permission to add a room that is the width of the existing building and only ten marks long."

The man's tactics are not unusual. In the time that I have been ruling, I have noticed Sarcheda citizens will bring requests to me in this same manner. First, convince me your business is deserving. Oftentimes citizens will take care of this step in a detailed written letter before they arrive at this meeting. Second, explain how you know the request is possible. Third, give me a number. Fourth, ask for something smaller than the number. I smile at the man. He won't hate me less for my answer just because I smiled, but it makes me feel better. "I will take your request to the council."

His face registers shock and maybe disgust. "You need to consult the council of Kings for a small building addition?" he asks.

"The council of Kings and Queens of Fraun," I emphasize the additional words, "is consulted in all matters of building or growth. This is our way." I sweep my hand side-to-side in front of me as if I could sweep away this very conversation. I don't know this man but I know that this conversation should be over with such a decree.

"I don't understand, Majesty. You are King." He leans closer to where I am seated in one of the overly padded chairs. He smiles. His voice drops as though we are sharing a secret. "This is your Sarcheda to rule. You don't need a council to tell you how to rule in Sarcheda. Just allow me to build the addition."

"No." The answer is curt, simple. I try for direct. I don't drop my eyes from his.

He shakes his head and lets out a breath through his nose with a groan. "I don't know how things are done where you are from, but in Sarcheda we are allowed certain liberties. You are King. Just rule on it."

That's enough of that. I rise from my chair. I am taller than this man. In Fraun, owing to the fact that we are all small, we take size seriously. Normally, I am among the smallest in any room. But my extra clicks on this man amount to much. He visible leans back. "I will consult the council because Fraun is about balance. This Kingdom is balanced in the palm of a hand of five." I hold out my hand at his eye level to emphasize, palm upward and fingers splayed. "We are not balanced on the tip of one finger." I drop my hand with a resounding slap on my leg that makes him flinch. "That is the end of this discussion. Should you wish to continue the discussion I will not take the matter to the council and your answer will be a simple no. You will not get the addition you want by pressing this issue."

"I didn't mean to offend, Majesty."

Yes, he did.

"I just know," he continues, "previous Kings would've just ruled on the issue without making a citizen of Sarcheda wait an unnecessary amount of time."

"Believe me, you will wait only the amount of time that is necessary. Now, I suggest you take yourself out of my house before I consider your lame attempt at an apology a way of pressing the issue."

The man opens his mouth as though he is going to continue to protest. I tilt my head to the side, waiting. He snaps his jaw closed, tips his head downward in a bow, and leaves.

I glance up at the ceiling and let out a breath. This should get easier, right? Instead, I'm being questioned at every decision and being told there are giants outside of Fraun. "What next?" I ask the empty room. What next indeed.

Chapter 23

The typical sounds of life fill the clearing. Somewhere in the distance birds are taking flight and the wind is whispering through the leaves on the trees. The scouts are not without noises of their own, which mix with those of nature. Jordyn listens to the sound of Toby chopping wood, the decisive and final blow preceding the sounds of the broken wood falling to the ground. This technique, chopping the pieces that have fallen into more manageable logs, is one of the things Toby has taught them.

Mario, Nina, Eselda, and Evelyn sit nearby chopping and separating vegetables for dinner. Jordyn can hear the sound of their small swords cutting through the various skins. Jordyn is cleaning the meat from a small fish Kurt brought back from a trip to the river. Kurt himself is off —

Jordyn's thoughts are broken by the sound of a hand-clapping three short bursts. That's the signal they worked out this morning. Someone in his group has reason to believe someone is approaching.

Jordyn rises from his place around the fire. He wraps his hand tighter around the handle of the knife. The group surrounding Eselda freezes in place, watching Jordyn for some kind of signal for how to proceed. "Toby," he calls.

"I heard it," Toby answers.

"Was it Kurt? Do we have eyes on the visitors?" Jordyn asks.

There is a shuffle following the question as Toby moves around, presumably to get a better angle. "I've got three bodies approaching." More shuffling following this comment as Toby scrambles up the branches of a nearby tree to get a better look. "It looks like they're on foot and carrying light loads. No weapons in sight. One in red, two in shades of green. Look to be male," Toby calls.

"Fraun?" Jordyn asks.

"Likely. Do you want me to head them off?"

Jordyn looks around the clearing. Everyone is alert and armed in some way. He knows his troop can defend themselves if it comes to that. "Let them come to us," he declares.

Toby forces the chopping tool into the log he uses as a base and comes to stand beside Jordyn. When the men enter the clearing they'll see a united front. Jordyn lets the blade hang by his side, hating that he can remember a time when he may have had to use it and how easily he slips back into that sense of dread and doubt.

They don't have to wait long before the men pass through the trees. The man in red, in the middle of the group, is none other than Danyel. A smile breaks across Jordyn's face. "Danyel of Sarcheda, you have returned to us." He steps forward and wraps the shorter man in an embrace. "Are you joining us permanently? Who are these friends you have brought us?"

Danyel shrugs. "Not staying, Jordyn." A sadness clouds his features. "The council sent us." Danyel's eyes track over Jordyn's shoulders toward the noise that tells Jordyn the rest of the scout troop is coming to stand behind him.

"I don't understand," Jordyn says. "Why would the council send you? Are you an ambassador now?"

"No, King Tutor told me the council needed a few volunteers. I joined up." Danyel indicates the men behind him with his chin. The two men in green are average height and build for Fraunians. They're both taller than Danyel and yet he could best them with the muscles he has developed. "This is Tom and Marco. They live in Enchenda near the border. We all work on the river."

"Danyel, hello!" Eselda runs to joins the assembled group, hugging her old friend. "Are you well?"

His sadness, almost always evident on his youthful face, cracks under the full smile. "Very," he answers. "And you?"

Eselda steps back, drawing even with Jordyn. "We are wonderful. How is everything in Fraun?"

"I hear we may be under threat by giants, but otherwise…" he trails off.

"I didn't know that was common knowledge," Jordyn says.

"It's not. At least not so far as I know. That's why the council sent us. We're to collect evidence and report back," Danyel explains.

Eselda's eyes wrinkle as she draws her brows together. "Evidence?"

From somewhere behind Jordyn, Mario laughs. The sound doesn't make the group feel pleasant and light, it is awkward and forced. "They don't believe what we have seen."

Danyel oscillates on his feet under the accusation. "I was only told they desire evidence."

"You've seen the giants with your own eyes?" The words burst from the Fraunian known as Tom as though he has been holding this question for a long time, waiting for the right moment to drop it in. He has lost his patience. Jordyn looks at the speaker as though noticing him for the first time. He is younger than Danyel but looks strong enough to handle his time in the woods.

"I have," Toby answers, stepping toward the trio. "What evidence would your precious council accept?"

"I don't really know," Danyel stammers.

"How are you to collect what you don't know they want?" Toby challenges, stepping toward them again.

"This is absurd," Eselda offers. Jordyn watches as she lays a hand lightly on Toby's arm. The younger man instantly calms at her touch, leaning back away from the strangers. The aggression, so plain on his face a beat ago, fades. "Why send three men? We can watch the giants ourselves and report back if that is what your council wants," Eselda asks.

"Our council?" The man called Marco speaks. "You are not of Fraun?"

Jordyn eyes this man skeptically. Has Fraun changed that much since they have been gone? Does this man not know his tale and Eselda's? "Not anymore," Jordyn answers. These two words address the question asked as well as the musings of his mind.

"The council wants Fraunian proof," Marco suggests. "Someone who is of Fraun seeing the giants with their own eyes."

Danyel speaks loud enough to cover the insult. "We don't want to impose. If you can spare men then come with us. We'd be grateful for the experience and your knowledge of the surroundings."

Jordyn eyes Marco even while responding to Danyel. "I will join you."

"Have you been watching the area since the sighting?" Tom asks. He is looking at Toby.

"We have," Toby answers. "If you are ready we can take you there now."

"I'll get my stuff," Mario says, ducking out of the group and toward the tent he shares with Nina.

"You will come too? Does no one need to stay to protect the ladies?" Marco asks. He tips his chin in the general direction of Eselda and Nina.

Nina scoffs. Eselda, practiced in self-preservation around men who assume her weak and out of patience with this conversation, has Jordyn's knife freed from his hand and buried in the tree beside the man before anyone can react.

"We'll be fine." She winks. "I can handle myself." She turns and walks back toward the vegetables, hips swaying with confidence.

"Ok. I suppose we are ready if you are," Tom says. He clears his throat and tries to hide his smile.

Jordyn lets a laugh through his nose at the expression on the face of the fraunians. "Let me grab a few things, then we'll head out." He turns and heads off to his tent.

Back at the vegetables, Eselda stops to think. She's entirely sure the person she's been dreaming about is a woman. The soft curves of the body do not match the men she's just met. But then, what to make of Danyel arriving? Surely that means the death she is dreaming of draws nearer and she is no closer to knowing who she dreams of.

Perhaps it's time she stop keeping this dream a secret.

Chapter 24

The royal house in Enchenda hasn't changed much, if at all. In fact, the whole realm is still very much the same as it was when I lived here. I walked by Charlotte's old home on the way in. It's still hard to think of Charlotte as my mother. Yes, she told me who she was. Yes, I've come to terms with it. But missing out on being raised by her makes me feel as if I somehow don't deserve to call her my mother. Or maybe it makes me question whether she deserves the title. Either way, I walked quickly by her house.

There are still children playing in the main streets between the town square and the royal home. There are still adults at work in the yards that line the main road. This realm is always alive with citizens. Ever since the first time I walked these streets I have loved Enchenda. It's a strange twist of fate that brought me to live in Sarcheda, but my heart is and always will be part of our most humble realm.

I raise my hand and knock on the wooden door to the home where I used to work. The home where I came to tutor the then princess, Eselda.

Before I knew who I was, before I knew the truth of my blood.

Sawchett flings open the door. "Tutor, thanks for coming!" Sawchett says. "I wanted to tell you there are no hard feelings about … you know." She steps aside to let me in. "I've forgiven you completely and I don't want to hear a word about it." She pulls her hair back and fixes it at the base of her neck with a length of ribbon. "Also, I need your help. I just can't possibly get these things all ready to send to Abney by myself. They're all jammed into a room and I want to get them all out of there." She starts to walk off in the direction of the bedrooms.

I hurry to follow her. "I appreciate that you are forgiving me. Are you sure you don't want to talk about it?"

"I'm sure," she calls over her shoulder. Her voice is cheery and light.

"Your letter said there were things you needed help moving. What kind of things are we talking about?"

"I found some furniture and things they'll want." Sawchett stops outside a room and turns to face me. "I'm so excited. Go on, take a guess about what I'm sending."

I squint at her. She does look excited, what would cause that? I haven't been in the room behind her before. It's not Sawchett's room, which has always been the room the ruling royal sleeps in. It's not the room that Eselda slept in when she was a princess. It's not the spare room off the dining room for those in need. We are near the study room but it's not that room either. "I have no idea. Something you are storing that you have no urgent need for."

"True." Her eyes sparkle with the secret.

"What am I missing here? Just open the door, let me see what we're doing."

Sawchett sighs. "You used to like games. Never mind, I can't wait." She flings the door open. There is a window along the back of the room. It is closed but still it allows the light to filter in. There is a lot of wooden furniture in this room. I look around, wondering if Sawchett expects me to help her move it all. Where does she even want it moved? There are piles of boxes, a small table, none of this seems important. Is that piece broken? "Why are we … " I trail off when my eyes land on something toward the back of the room. I take a step closer, look again. "Sawchett, is that — "

"Yes! That's the surprise. I have to get it out of here but all this other junk is in the way. Now do you get it?"

I laugh and turn to look at Sawchett still standing in the doorway. Her radiant smile makes sense. "Abney and Sieven are having a baby and you're sending them this crib you found?"

"Yes, isn't it wonderful?"

I laugh. "It is wonderful." I also strongly suspect it is the reason Sawchett decided to forgive me. "Now, let's get all this junk out of here."

We work side-by-side. It's nice to be absorbed in something simple, something that really can't be done wrong. We wipe down pieces of furniture that have become buried under dust. We move them out onto the front lawn where they can be taken by families that will put them to use. We wipe down the broken items and move them to the dining room. Someone from town will come pick them up specifically to repurpose them into something needed. Sawchett explains that she's been meaning to clean this room out since she found out about it. Really it's odd that the room even exists. Fraunians don't waste and Enchenda is supposed to be the home of our most humble Fraunians. Why is there a random room of unused furniture that could be out in other homes? I don't even have a guess.

Finally, after moving countless boxes and items, we can actually reach the crib. Sawchett and I begin wiping down the surface. Sawchett sighs. I notice she's moving more slowly. "What's on your mind?" I ask.

"What if the giants ruin everything we've created? If we have to abandon Fraun and start over, what happens to all the families?"

"Families like ours?" I ask, thinking how hard it would be to separate from Sawchett now that we finally have each other to rely on.

"Like ours. Like Abney's." She stops cleaning all together and sits back on her heels. "Did we fix this just to have the giants stomp all over our peace?"

I don't correct her. I don't point out that not everyone feels peaceful. I don't tell her that there are those in Sarcheda who preferred it the way it was before. "Everything will work out. It always does. You need to quit worrying. Find happiness."

"What makes you happy?" she asks.

I laugh uncomfortably. "Lots of things." But the one thing that pops into my head is a face, framed by tight curls. I drop the fabric I've been using and stand fully. "Ok, I think it's clean. Let's get this out of here." I move myself around to one end of the crib and grab hold. "You get the other end."

Carefully, we move the crib out of the room and down to the entryway. A young man, perhaps a servant, is walking toward the kitchen. "Hang on," Sawchett calls. He stops and turns. There's surprise on his face for a second, but that melts into something completely different as a smile breaks out on his face. "Can you take my spot? This is so heavy." Sawchett sets her end of the crib down.

"Of course, Milady." He immediately steps up and takes the end she has been holding. "Where are we taking this?"

Sawchett rubs her hands together, wincing as though it causes her pain. "Out to the cart. It needs to be delivered to Farcheda."

She follows us out to the cart and helps us to get the crib loaded. I shake hands with the man. "Thank you for your help."

"No problem." He is still looking at Sawchett. "Anything for my Queen."

I try not to laugh at the look he's throwing my little sister. I wait until he has taken a few steps away before turning to look at her myself. I suppose, in the annuals that have passed, she's grown into a woman right before my eyes. The fact that I'm inside of the age of the flesh means Sawchett has passed her tenth annual. "You know you're passed the age marker where Fraunians consider you an adult," I share. "You'll be in the fifteenth annual before you know it and many will expect you to start courting." I clear my throat. "Your station in our Kingdom doesn't mean you cannot choose any mate your heart desires." There's a note of teasing in my voice.

Sawchett turns to me. "I know." She looks utterly clueless.

"Good," I say. I turn away from her to hide the smile. She may be more mature and considered an adult by our customs, but there are some things my little sister is truly naive about.

"Why do you mention that?"

I look behind me, toward the house where the man was just a second ago. "No reason." I laugh. "No reason at all."

Chapter 25

"It's just me," Jordyn's voice bounces off the trees and echoes into the clearing.

Eselda and Nina let out the breaths they were holding and lower their weapons. "You scared us," Eselda says when he is in sight. She meets him halfway to the fire, wrapping her arms around his neck and kissing him. When she pulls back she can tell, even in the dim fire, that his eyes are clouding with his age marker. She smiles at him. "You missed me." It is not a question.

"Always," he answers.

"How's it looking out there? Did you find anything new?" Nina asks. She is still seated beside the fire, weaving something. Her black hair is pulled over her shoulder in a braid that reminds Jordyn of the one Evelyn used to wear back when Jordyn joined the troop.

Jordyn steps around Eselda and heads to the fire, holding his hands out to warm them. "We returned to the same place where we saw the giant before. There's nothing there right now. The group decided to set up camp in the nearby trees where they can keep an eye on the spot. At first light tomorrow they will head out to continue further south."

"You aren't going with them?" Nina asks.

Jordyn yawns. "Let's see how I feel tomorrow. Tonight I need some sleep." He gets up and heads toward his tent. "I'll see you all in the morning."

Jordyn is halfway to his tent when the sharp blast of two whistle trills shoots through him like an arrow. He freezes mid-step.

"Wait," Nina calls. "Did you hear that?"

It is quiet in the clearing as the three scouts practically hold their breaths while they listen. Faintly, Jordyn can make out the unmistakable sound of footsteps. He sighs. "Not again." He turns back toward the fire, brandishing his sword. He looks pointedly at Eselda. "We may need to move our camp." She nods and allows him to stand in front of her. "Who goes there, identify yourself."

"I mean no harm, I search for the former Queen, Eselda."

Jordyn glances over his shoulder. Eselda shrugs. Taking that as permission, Jordyn calls out to the voice. "Enter the clearing and drop your weapons on the ground." They wait, listening to the footsteps get closer.

A tall man, almost as tall as Jordyn's impressive three marks, enters the clearing. He is dressed in the brown clothing associated with a scout, carefully chosen to avoid any color loyalties to realms in Fraun. The stranger drops a sword on the ground and kicks it away from himself. "There are six more scouts with me a few steps back. They are unarmed and mean no harm. I search for the former Queen, Eselda."

Eselda steps out from behind Jordyn. Her eyebrows draw together. "I know you. How do I know you?"

"Marshawn." He points at himself. "I was once the young princess Sawchett's tutor."

Jordyn stands straighter, his sword comes up just a bit. "Excuse my protector if he scares you with his weapon. You have not been seen or heard from in many annuals and it is, after all, nightfall. This is an odd time for a reunion visit," Eselda explains.

"I haven't been seen in Fraun since the princess went missing, true. I'm sorry about the late hour." Marshawn casts his eyes down to the forest floor in shame. "I knew my arrival here would be rude." His glance dances over Jordyn's blade. "I knew it may even endanger me to come here." Now his eyes raise to the faces before him. "Yet still I felt it was better to not wait until morning."

"You have an important message?" Eselda asks.

"I have a delivery."

"From who?" Jordyn's voice is crisp, short.

Marshawn's eyes dart back to the ground. "It will become clear. I have been traveling with various groups around these parts since I left Enchenda. The group I have been with for more than an annual recently elected me to be their leader. In this position, I was treated to the truth of an old lady who travels with us." His eyes find Eselda. "Once I learned that truth, I had to come." Marshawn waves his arm and two more enter the clearing behind him.

A man, strong and sure, supports the arm of a frail woman with long white hair softly curling around her shoulders. Something in Jordyn's face changes. If he were still in the malicious age, Eselda has the impression his eyes would've just darkened. He wields the sword fully, taking large steps across the clearing until the sword is threateningly close to the man. "You?" Jordyn barks. "Explain yourself," he commands.

"Jordyn, who is that?" Eselda asks. Seeing he doesn't intend to answer, Eselda steps to the left so she can see around him and address the man. "Speak quickly, he is good with that sword when threatened. Who are you?"

"Carthen, defect of Renchenda, Majesty," he answers.

"Defect of Tin's army," Jordyn yells. His voice echoes off the trees. "I send you to him as part of the patrol and you never returned. The patrolmen from Enchenda returned. They stepped away from the fight and joined our cause. They fought for Fraun. Where were you in all that?"

Eselda walks forward slowly, her empty hands out. When she can reach him, she lays her hand on Jordyn's shoulder. "Let's not overreact. The man isn't armed." She gestures to Carthen's hips, which Jordyn notices are not bearing a weapon.

Jordyn's shoulders sag and he drops the sword to the dirt. "I'm sorry, I don't want to fight again." He takes a step back but keeps his eyes glued to Carthen as though he refuses to trust him.

"I'm not here for a reunion," Marshawn says. "I wasn't even aware he fought for Tin." He glances menacingly at Carthen. "We will discuss that later." His attention falls back on Eselda. "We bring the woman."

"I don't understand," Jordyn says. "What does she have to do with us?"

Marshawn turns to her. "Tell them," he commands.

"No," the woman delivers the word like venom.

Eselda takes a hesitant step closer, screwing up her eyes to see clearly. "Tell us what? What are you hiding?"

The woman's chin lifts, thrusting her face into a stream of moonlight. "Everything," she whispers.

Eselda draws ragged breaths and backs up, shaking her head. "No. Not possible." She turns to Jordyn, her eyes wide with panic. "No. This isn't happening. I can't face this, Jordyn. No."

"Eselda," he reaches for her. "What's going on? Who is this woman?"

Tears slip down her cheeks as she continues to shake her head. "No," she repeats. "It's not possible."

Jordyn grabs her shoulders. He bends at the waist so he can look her in the eye. "Talk to me, what's going on? Who is she?" he whispers.

Eselda shakes her head again and then looks directly into his blue eyes. "I think she is my mother."

Chapter 26

It's late when I arrive back at the royal home in Sarcheda. The sun has set, it's dark and quiet around the realm, and the breeze is the only thing making noise as it meanders through the trees. I want to climb into my bed and sleep until long after the sun rises. I want—

My thoughts are interrupted by the sight of a man-shaped shadow in front of my door. "Hello," I call out.

The shadow rises. "King Tutor, I need a word."

The voice sounds familiar. It brings an odd chill racing down to my toes. "At this hour of the night? Is there an emergency? Surely whatever it is can wait until sunrise."

"I'm afraid I am the only one treating this as an emergency, Majesty."

I draw close enough to see the face of the speaker even in the dark. Marcus. I have to fight my instincts not to roll my eyes and make a disgusted grunt at the sight. What is this about? "Marcus, I'm sure I have no idea what you are so concerned about but the concern of an ambassador warrants the concern of his king. Please, come inside." I open the door and step aside to allow him to enter the home. I step away to light a candle before closing the door, otherwise, darkness will consume us like a tomb.

Marcus waits in the entryway eyeing me as though he has all night and is in absolutely no rush. "Don't you have servants to handle that, Majesty?" he asks.

Holding the candle in my hand I push the door shut and head to the nearest place to sit, which happens to be the dining table. I refuse to light a fire in the fireplace. He can speak to me by candlelight at this ridiculous hour of the night. Then, when he leaves, it's easy to snuff the candle and go to bed. I drop myself into the closest chair and place the candle on the table. "It doesn't seem necessary to have servants keep up a home for just me," I say in response to his comment.

Marcus shrugs. "I'm not sure they'd mind. There were many citizens employed here when Tin was the only one living under this roof."

I refuse to continue talking about the way Tin did things in the past. I tap my fingers on the table before me in frustration. "I am sure you did not come here with concerns about my lack of staff. You had something to say? Let's hear it, Marcus."

"I'd like to speak of the emergency that you brought before the council. What is happening with the giants? Have we heard anything else corroborating your tale?"

I allow myself to yawn, tipping my head back and opening my jaw as wide as it will go. Perhaps this is less rude than openly showing my annoyance. "Why do you doubt the story so?"

"I don't doubt, Majesty. I am just curious."

"The men left a few suns ago to head to the scouts. From there they were instructed to find the giants and observe for a few suns. I do not expect to see them for a fortnight at least," I explain. I place my hands on the table as though I am going to push myself up. "Is that all I can help you with?"

"Honestly, it just seems convenient. Doesn't it?"

I relax back into my chair. Apparently, we are not done here. "Convenient?"

"I've spoken with all the other rulers of Fraun, Majesty. It appears you are the only source of this gossip."

"I don't even know where to begin with that, Marcus." He starts to open his mouth to answer. I raise my voice and my hand simultaneously. "No, listen. You are a representative of Sarcheda. That allows you an audience with your king, it allows you to attend council meetings, and it allows you to hold meetings to gain information from others in Sarcheda." I tick off the points on my fingers. I pause with them raised for a breath before dropping them to the table with a satisfying smack of my palm. "I do not believe it extends to meetings with the other rulers on your own. That is unnecessary and time-consuming. We will bring that before the council for clarification but if you need something you come to me. Are we clear?"

"Clear as glass," Marcus says.

"Good. Onto the next point. I am not a source of this information about the giants. I received notice from the source of the information. Likely, based on the area the scouts have set up camp, this is owing merely to the fact that I was the closest realm to their location. It could easily have been Thometh or Sawchett who were alerted had the scouts been located in a different area of the forest. I have no information beyond that which I shared at the council meeting. The council voted to send a group out to collect data and that group has not reported back. You are reaching when you assume I have anything more than I say I have. Do we have a problem here?"

"I'm not sure, Majesty." The final word drips with cynicism.

I show my exhaustion by running my hands down my face and sighing. Perhaps he will remember the late hour we are having this conversation. "Look," I say, "this is a discussion we should bring before the council at the next meeting. If you have doubts we can discuss them all together. If we wait for the next scheduled meeting the group we sent off may even be back. If you'd prefer, I can call an emergency session again and we can all talk through this. I don't understand why you say this is convenient, but—"

"You rose to power on a large issue that you needed to rescue Fraun from." The way he says those final words, with his lip curled and sarcasm dripping from his lips, it is clear he does not agree with the assessment.

The double insult of the doubt he just lobbed that sentence with and the interruption have my tired brain buzzing with anger. I stand up, intentionally slow. I place my palms on the table in front of Marcus and lean menacingly toward him. "I am warning you, Ambassador," I say. "We are done discussing this issue in private. You will wait until the next council meeting to call up any doubts or issues you have. You will not discuss any of this in any official capacity, with any ruler or citizen, before the council meeting. Do I make myself clear?"

Marcus nods once.

"Good. Now I've had a long day and I would like to get some sleep." I point to the door. "Get out of my house."

Chapter 27

Jordyn has managed to get everyone else out of the clearing and coax Eselda to sit. She is rocking back and forth a little, like a small branch swaying in the wind. Her arms are firmly crossed across her chest and her eyes have glazed over as she stares into the flames of the fire. But she is no longer crying or yelling and she's agreed to have a seat. He takes that as positive progress.

On the other side of the fire, the woman with the long gray hair sits equally silent. In fact, she hasn't spoken a single word since Eselda surprised them all with her assertion. Jordyn stands between them, eyes flitting from one to the other. In the light of the fire, he cannot see a strong resemblance between the women. He's not sure what gives Eselda the impression that this stranger is the former Queen Rubina. The old woman's eyes are darker than Eselda's and since she was not royal born it won't indicate any age markers. She is frail and small, even shorter than Eselda who only stands at two marks. She is thin and sickly, but Jordyn knows that could be because of her advanced age.

He sighs and runs his hands through his hair, tugging the long strands behind his ears. "Alright, ladies. We need to talk." There's no response from either woman. "I've got everyone else in bed and it is late. The only other issue that needs handling can be handled tomorrow morning with the rest of our men and those Fraun has sent."

He sees the flinch. When he said "Fraun" the old woman recoiled and her blink was long. *Interesting.* He shakes himself clear of the distraction and moves on. "We either have to agree to go to bed and deal with whatever this is later or talk right now."

"Bed," the old woman croaks.

Eselda's eyes snap to the woman's face. "You don't get to choose that." Her voice is edged with anger.

"Fine," she answers.

"Eselda, do you want to talk about this now?" Jordyn asks. He keeps his voice calm. Something like this is bound to have triggered Eselda's malicious age marker. He knows she can occasionally blackout during periods when the anger is at its worst. It has been a long time since that happened, but who knows what this shock has done to her system.

"Yes," she answers.

Jordyn finds a log nearby and drags it to a location where he can shoot up and reach either woman if that becomes necessary. Then he sits. "Let's talk." He turns his attention to the old woman. "Are you the former Queen of Enchenda, Rubina?"

Again she flinches. This time it was either at the title or the name of the realm, Jordyn isn't sure which. She lifts her head. The gesture, Jordyn notes, is almost regal. "Yes," she answers.

Jordyn readjusts himself to sit up straighter. "I must admit that is shocking. We presumed you dead. I thought I heard you had drowned in River Fraun. I'm sorry I don't remember the details, I was young."

"I was eight annuals," Eselda says. Her voice cracks a little on the sentence. It breaks Jordyn's heart. He wants to reach out and comfort her, but this is not the time. "I needed my mother."

"What can I say?" Rubina asks.

"Talk. I want to hear it all," Eselda answers.

"Yes, I do as well. Start at the beginning," Jordyn prompts. "I am not from Enchenda, your history is not familiar to me."

"I don't want to talk about this," Rubina crosses her arms.

Across the fire, Eselda stands in one quick motion. "I don't really care what you want, do I? I didn't want to lose my mother before I even stopped growing. I didn't want to find out the age markers from my tutor. We all have things we don't want. Now, talk."

Jordyn grabs Eselda's hand, trying to comfort but also preparing to restrain. She glances down in his direction and he notices her eyes are very dark. He wants to ask about her age marker, but fears doing so may make it worse. Instead, he squeezes her hand.

"Fine, I'll talk. Please, sit down," Rubina says. Her voice is soft, resigned. She runs her fingers down the length of her long hair like a nervous habit. Then, catching herself in the act, she throws it over her shoulder and drops her hands into her lap.

Eselda squeezes Jordyn's hand, drops it, and sits. She clasps her own hands and rests them in her lap. Her eyes turn to her mother.

"I'm going to start at the beginning because this man here doesn't know my history and I'm not sure how much you remember. I was ten annuals when I was hired to work in the royal gardens in Enchenda. My mother worked there, in the kitchen, and got me the job."

"Just to be clear, you do not have royal blood, correct?" Jordyn asks.

Her eyes close as if she is in pain. "I do not." She takes a slow breath in through her nose and then opens her eyes again. "While working in the gardens, I met Gregario. I was around eleven then, I imagine. King Stefan arranged for Gregario and me to wed. I was too young to care about such nonsense, I had no interest. Gregario was older than I was, he was closer to fifteen. It was an appropriate age for him to be married, but too young for me. I didn't even know what I wanted in life. How was I to be expected to become a princess?"

"I was a princess from birth," Eselda says. Her anger has not dissipated. "Enchenda has a phenomenal Queen now, one who is barely twelve annuals. Don't blame your age for anything."

Rubina leans forward. "Do you have a daughter? Who is this Queen?"

Eselda's laugh is dark, not at all like the laugh Jordyn has grown to love. "I am twenty-two annuals. I did not bring a daughter into this world at ten. She is not mine. She is Charlotte's daughter."

"I know that name," Rubina says.

"I'm sure you do. If you knew father at a young age then you knew Charlotte. Sawchett is the daughter of Charlotte and Den," Eselda explains.

"A girl? A Queen? That is unexpected." Rubina drops her chin and her eyes take on a dreamy quality. Jordyn clears his throat and her eyes snap back to his face. "Let me finish my story."

"You were expecting a boy of Charlotte and Den's?" Jordyn asks. "You are not surprised they had children, you were only surprised it was a girl." He turns to Eselda. "She knows of Tutor."

"Let me finish my story," Rubina repeats. "When I'm done you can ask questions." A cough racks the woman's body. When it finishes, she spits something from her mouth into the dirt beside her. "Excuse me, I am ill."

"You are not just ill," Jordyn says. "According to your math, you are four annuals younger than Gregario. The king died…" he trails off, looking to Eselda as if she will insert the time. When she does not offer it, he continues. "Over three annuals ago, possibly closer to four. You are in the death spiral."

Rubina clears her throat and starts again, ignoring his interruption. "I was promised to Gregario when I was eleven but we were not wed until I was fifteen. Even in Fraun," she scowls when she says the name of the kingdom, "girls are not wed until that age."

"Did you love him?" Eselda asks. "He always told the story as though it was true love."

"Maybe a part of me did." She shrugs. "Shortly after we got married Gregario changed. He was angry all the time. He was violent. He threw things and he yelled. Our servants cowered before him." She shakes her head, drops her voice. "I cowered before him."

"You said he was four years your senior," Jordyn notes. "If you were married at fifteen, he would've been nineteen. Only one year from the malicious age. That's a likely cause of the anger. It may not have been him, not really. That could've been the result of the age marker he, and any other born of royal blood, is cursed to bear. The very same ager marker that effects Eselda now."

"I have heard that, yes. But I didn't know anything about it at the time. I just knew I married a man who had become a monster."

Eselda, of course, can sympathize with finding yourself tied to a man who is a monster. After all, isn't that what happened with Tin? Her anger softens just a little. Jordyn can see the difference in the loosened grip of her fingers and the sympathetic tilt of her head. Rubina may well be winning her over.

"Anyway, I stayed with him. He became King, he outgrew the scary age marker, and entered another one." She smiles at her daughter. "You were born when I was twenty-two. The very age that you are now. I'm sure you can imagine how wonderful it would be to bring a daughter into your perfect little world."

Eselda shrugs. Truthfully, she can't. *Someone who cannot trust herself to make decisions shouldn't be raising a child.* "I'm in no rush."

"Sure, because you're obviously no longer a royal. There was nothing but rush and pressure for us."

"We understand," Jordyn says. "Continue the story."

"You mentioned Den. Do you know anything about him?" she asks. "Besides the fact that he is the current queen's father."

Jordyn shrugs. "He was the husband of Charlotte, that's all I know."

"He worked in our home," Eselda says.

"Yes, he was a foot soldier for Gregario at first. When you were five annuals and needed a tutor, he was promoted to handle that. He lived nearby in a little house on the corner of the square and he came every day. You were young so I often sat in on your lessons, sometimes I sewed while you learned. I thought it was peaceful and innocent. Gregario did not." She adjusts herself and clears her throat. "Shadows of the man he was in anger started to creep into our lives. He would accuse me of doing things with Den. He would accuse Den." Rubina begins working the thumb of one hand into the palm of the other hand as if working out the stress of the memory itself.

"You were scared of him?" Jordyn asks.

"Sometimes." She closes her eyes and draws a breath, gathering strength to continue her tale. Jordyn resists the urge to lean closer to what feels like an important moment. "When Eselda was eight she fell sick, nothing serious. Den showed up for the tutoring session and I told him she was going to sit this one out. We chatted for a little while. Gregario came into the room, thought that the two of us being alone was proof that we were having an affair on the side. He shoved Den. He wouldn't listen to my side of things. He fired Den and sent him out of the house."

"I heard something about that from Charlotte," Eselda says. "It was right before you di—" She shakes her head, "...before you disappeared."

"Yes. Gregario would not let it go. For days he shouted at me and accused me of indecent acts. We stopped speaking. It was uncomfortable. I started cowering from him again, fearing for his retaliation. One night, when he was particularly angry, I left."

"Left where?" Jordyn asks.

"I went to the river. At first, I was just going to put my feet in and enjoy some quiet. But then I got an idea. I could leave Fraun." She looks up from the ground and her eyes land on Jordyn. She latches onto the hope that he will be reasonable, logical. "You have to understand that I hated everything about that kingdom. I hid it well, but I hated it. I thought, for a while, that I could change it from the inside. I thought when I was Queen I could make a difference. I would make them see how they treat servants is wrong. I would make sure everyone knew about these age markers." She turns her eyes on Eselda. "You are in an age right now where you are dangerous to everyone around you. Fraunians need to be warned. They need to know that you cannot control this anger."

"If I couldn't control this anger you would have a bigger problem," Eselda says. Her voice is oddly calm.

Jordyn clears his throat. "I can't fault you for leaving." He gestures to the trees and campground around them. "Clearly, I did the same thing. But in my case, I had no family that would be negatively impacted and I left my realm in capable hands. I think you'll find she has a big reason to fault you." He points at Eselda. "I don't think this is a forgive-and-forget kind of situation."

"No, I imagine it is not," Rubina whispers, dropping her eyes back to the ground.

"You've just been out here all these years?" Eselda asks. She shakes her head. "He died, you know. I was there. He wasn't perfect but he was never violent towards me. He did a damn good job of raising me. It's not his fault I wasn't a good queen." She stands up. "I think I'm going to bed."

"Are you sure?" Jordyn asks. "You don't have any other questions?"

Eselda stands perfectly still as though considering his offer. Then she shakes her head. "I made it this far without her. I don't even know her. She made her choice. I'm going to bed."

Jordyn and Rubina wait in silence until the flap of the tent where Eselda sleeps stops moving. They listen to the sound of the fire crackling for a long time before Jordyn shrugs and speaks, his voice sounding loud in the echoing silence of the forest. "I guess you can sleep out here."

"Do you think she would've been a better person if I had brought her with me?" Rubina asks.

Jordyn stands up. His eyes track up to the night sky as he thinks. "I don't know." He looks back down at her. "But I do know that your choice defined her." He turns toward his tent. "Have a good night."

Alone in the clearing the once Queen sighs. "Night," she whispers. She certainly wouldn't call it good. She wouldn't call anything good. She hasn't used that word for many annuals.

Chapter 28

I'm early for the council meeting because my head isn't in the right place for this meeting, not by a long shot. I'm hoping to give myself a little time to get ready. I called the meeting. After some sleep and a day to think about it, I realized I had no choice. Marcus is claiming to represent everyone in Sarcheda when he accuses me of making up this stuff about the giants. If that even has a little bit of truth behind it, the council needs to know. So I called an emergency session of the council. Again.

The new building is basically done. The builders have allowed us to have the meeting there. As the roach I'm riding draws closer I can see that they're still working, taking a coat of paint to the sidewall. I also notice I am not the only one who arrived early for the meeting. Alerta is sitting on a rock across from the building watching the men paint. I disembark from the roach when I pull up beside her.

"Tutor, good morning," she greets.

"Good morning." I turn my attention to the creature. "Thank you, sir. I will require a ride home when the sun starts to drop from its highest point. Would you be so kind as to wait?" My annuals outside of Fraun have shown me what life is like for the roaches when they are not in service to us. We owe them for taking on this burden. There certainly is more for them outside our boundaries. The roach promises to return and scurries away. That leaves me to sit beside the beautiful Queen of Marchenda.

"You look distracted," she says. "Is something on your mind?"

"Nothing overly concerning. I grow tired of calling these meetings."

"I am sure you had your reasons. Would you care for a friendly ear to hear your troubles?"

I appreciate her offer, but suddenly I don't want to talk about all of this. "Not really, if you don't mind. I think I'd rather sit here on this rock with you." I relax my posture, resting my hands out behind me on the rock and watch the men paint.

They are using rolls of something like cloth. They run the roll through the paint color nearby in a bucket and then roll it along the wall of the building. Where before it was brown and traditional the paint gives it a fresh, lighter color. Still brown, but more like dry infertile dirt than tree bark. There are two of them, one standing on a ladder and one working on the ground. Soon they will need to be working in the same section, I wonder how that will work itself out.

"Have I ever told you the story of Stef?" Alerta asks.

I turn my head so I can see her. She certainly hasn't told me that tale. "I don't believe so," I say.

"Would you mind if I told you now?"

"I would be honored."

She shifts her legs toward me, scooting herself back a little on the rock. She pulls her right leg up between us, bending her knee and leaning on it. "I was about twenty annuals when I met Lucas," she begins. "He was charming and smart. He was everything I was supposed to be looking for in a mate, in a prince. He was from an important family in Marchenda. My mother was always looking for an excuse to get me married off, so when she heard I thought he was a nice guy she immediately set me up on a dinner date with him." She brushes her hand along her clothes, swatting at some imperfection only she can see. "We went out to dinner in town at a place that cooks for citizens. We had a quiet table but we were not the only ones there.

"Afterwards, Lucas invited me to someplace more private. We went to a barn near the fields. No one lived there so it was empty. He told me he knew the citizens who had lived there and that they allowed him to use the barn whenever he wanted. I never asked what he had used the barn for previously." She chuckles. "Isn't it funny that I only wonder that now after all these annuals?"

I don't see the humor. Her eyes have that far away look to them like she's losing herself in the story. I let my instinct guide me, placing my hand over hers. She smiles at me before continuing. "Anyway, one thing led to another and before I knew it we were… " she casts her eyes downward, nervously. Her toes start wiggling in her shoes.

"Kissing?" I offer.

She nods. "He was really charming." She shrugs, puts her smile back in place, and looks back at my face. "Anyway, whether it was my original idea or not I couldn't resist Lucas. I think I spent every waking minute with him for the next fortnight. Then one night we were alone in the barn again and we went too far." Her voice breaks a little. She clears her throat. "I'm not saying he forced anything, I agreed to it. But now, more focused and mature, I'm not sure I would've made that choice."

"Why not?" I ask.

"I didn't love Lucas. I loved the attention." Her amber eyes trap me. "Does that make me a monster?"

"No." The answer is fast but honest. "He is Stef's father though. Where is he now?"

"Gone."

"Dead?" I push.

"No. Just gone. When I found out about the baby, we were already done with each other. I knew that night was a mistake. I told him it was a mistake. I told my mother I didn't want anything to do with Lucas anymore. He seemed to agree, I didn't speak with him again. Then I found out about Stef. I went to his parent's house. I told him about the baby."

"What did he say?"

"Nothing. I wanted him to say something, you know? Anything." She slips her hand out from under mine and wipes her face although she's not crying. "Once I had done my part and told him, I left. I told him he knew where to find me when he found his voice. I went home. Three suns later his father showed up at my parents' house and told my parents everything. He had a letter Lucas had written telling them about the baby but Lucas was gone."

"Where did he go?"

"They're not sure. He left in the middle of the night. The next morning they found the note."

"That's crazy. Did anyone look for him? He's the father of a baby who will be Queen," I say.

"That's not how they saw it, Tutor." I remember the time period we're talking about would have been before the war. Before the update to the lineage chart. When shunning was still a practice of our council. The sadness on her face makes me want to wrap her up in a hug.

"My parents told me there was no option but to release me of my royal burden. That's how they put it. I could live in Marchenda but I could tell no one of my blood. I could have Stef, and live with her happily, but my part in their history was done. I never spoke to them again. My parents died not long after Stef was born, my older brother told me about it. He was the only one I spoke to right up until he died. When they came to update my tree and told me they were adding our names, I still didn't believe they'd need me. Larecio was my cousin and he was a good man, a good King. I let them add our names, but it didn't feel real."

I completely relate to that, of course. I reach out and touch her shoulder, hoping the contact will show her my support. She smiles. "When Larecio was killed and they called me, I was shocked. I wanted to help make Fraun better. For Stef, for my brother Sven, for all of us. I was there when you gave your speech, I was there when you fought for Fraun. But when you brought me into that room of the castle and asked me to lead Marchenda, that was the greatest moment of my life. There's nothing I can say to explain how good it felt to be acknowledged by the royals and invited to the table I thought I'd never be allowed to sit at. Fraun is so much better for what you … we … all did against Tin, Tutor."

Alerta stands up and wipes her hands down the front of her pants. "I hope you are not doubting that," she says.

"Not anymore," I answer. As I watch her walk away, toward the building, I realize that Fraun is full of these stories. It's what we fought for. I stand up knowing I will not let Marcus downplay what we did. A strong, balanced Fraun is what I have helped to create and it will persevere.

Chapter 29

Jordyn knows he needs to go check on the progress at the site where they spotted the giant. He needs to report to Kurt and the others about this new development. He needs to warn them there's another mouth to feed. There are more important things to worry about right now, and yet the sight of his beloved in pain steals his attention.

Eselda is sitting on the ground with her head in her hands. A cup of tea sits in front of her crossed legs, sending tendrils of steam up into the morning air. Jordyn walks quietly so as not to disturb her and rubs her back as he takes a seat beside her. "Good morning."

She turns her face to him, dropping her hands into her lap. Her eyes are mostly green with little wisps of black smoke swirled like a bucket of water after cleaning a campfire. She smiles but it doesn't reach her eyes. "Good morning."

"Do you want to talk about it?" he asks.

She catches her lower lip between her teeth and considers everything she learned yesterday. Finally, she shakes her head. "No, I truly don't. Let's talk about something else."

"Like what?" he asks. He slips his arm over her shoulders and she nestles into him, laying her head on his chest. From here she can feel his heartbeat. It's something she can count on. Something that will not change. Jordyn is her comfort and she lets that comfort wash over her.

"Nothing is what I thought it was. I don't know what we should talk of that will make that feel better," she admits.

"It was a shock, but you'll recover. This doesn't change anything. You are who you are already. What she did is in the past."

Eselda picks her head up. "That's easy for you to say. My past is full of confusing history that everyone keeps lying about. I hate to say it but you don't understand."

Jordyn sighs. "You're right. My past is not full of lies, but it is not pleasant. I wasn't raised by a perfect little family any more than you were."

"You had both parents."

"Until I was seventeen, yes." Eselda opens her mouth to make a likely valid point about the difference between being seventeen and being eight. Jordyn rushes on before she can. "I was very close to my father until he turned gray and died when I was seventeen. I won't pretend that was harder than what you went through. But my mother killed herself less than a lunar cycle after that." He reaches for her far shoulder with his free hand, caressing it. "Eselda, what you went through was terrible. But everyone has a past. It defines us but that is different than letting it control us."

"I keep forgetting how Queen Aine…" She pauses, sighs. "…how your mother died. I'm sorry."

Jordyn shrugs. "As I say, it was a long time ago and it doesn't control me."

She puts her head back on his chest and takes a deep inhale of his scent, clean and calming. "Tell me about King Thometh. How is he related to you again?"

"He is my uncle." Eselda feels the rumble of his voice on her cheek. "He is much younger than Aine. When I found him to be alive we sat down and had a conversation. His mother died during his birth. In his grief, my grandfather didn't add Thometh's name."

"How does one forget to add a baby to the family tree?"

"I don't know. Thometh seemed to think it was an oversight."

"But eventually he would've been added," Eselda pushes.

"That's what I would think, but I never saw his name there. Either way, once Aine became Queen she left him off intentionally. Thometh says they never had a good relationship. The day my mother became Queen Thometh left their family home. He didn't step foot there again until I summoned him."

"That's crazy."

"There seems to be no shortage of crazy stories flowing around Fraun," Jordyn agrees. He kisses her lightly on the top of her head.

Eselda pushes upright again so she can see his face. "Things are certainly simpler out here in the woods."

"I am not sure I can agree with that. After all, I'm about to head out to the site of a camp where I can monitor the appearance of a giant."

Eselda slaps a hand to her forehead. "In all the commotion I actually forgot." Her eyes meet his and he sees fear widening them. "This could get worse," she whispers.

He leans in, kissing her on the cheek. "Let's hope not."

"Should we take our troop and leave?" Eselda asks. "Somewhere further away from here, away from the giants?"

Jordyn looks up at the sky as he thinks. She gives him silence for a few breath cycles, loving the way he approaches every question with logic as if it were a puzzle with a correct answer. Finally, he looks back at her and she reads sadness in his eyes. "I do not think that is our best course of action. Something tells me we need to consider the citizens of—" He stops himself short of talking about the kingdom that has abandoned her. "We need to consider all the others," he amends.

On this matter, she decides, she will trust his judgment. After all, the last time lives were truly threatened Jordyn acted admirably while she only humiliated herself. "Do you still put the safety of Fraun above yourself?" she asks.

This time, the wait is barely two heartbeats. "I do," he answers. He pulls away from her, leaving a warmth that he can still feel burning along the length of his arm and torso, and stands. "Now, I really should go. I love you."

"I love you," she answers. Jordyn is four of his large steps away when she calls out to him again. "What if the safest course of action would be to move farther away? Could you bring yourself to do it? For me?" she asks.

She knows he hears her because he stops. His shoulders rise as if he's taking a deep breath. Then they fall again. His back still to her, he answers. "If it comes down to safety we will move." He turns his head so Eselda can see the profile of his handsome face against the forest beyond the clearing. "But we should take as many Fraunians with us as we can."

Chapter 30

He sits in the darkening room as the sun slips down the sky, feeling his anger deepen with each breath. *Giants. What are the odds that giants would appear again?* Out of all the carefully weighted outcomes he considered, giants never even crossed his mind.

He slams his fist into the table, feeling the uneven wood waver. He stands, pacing from one side of the small room to the other in the darkness. His footsteps echo loudly. *Giants. This is not acceptable.*

The giants will scare Fraunians. Tutor will offer them an ear to hear their fears. *That's all he's doing, listening. He cannot do anything about a giant. Nothing.*

But still, Fraunians will bend to his side because he's listening.

Listening!

A king of strength shouldn't listen. He should act.

So what should the action be?

He paces the length of the room, again and again, turning this question over in his mind. *What should the action be? What actions can be taken against a giant?*

It is imperative that he come up with something. *Something must tip the scales back in favor of a strong kingdom, one ruled by Sarcheda.*

Failure is not acceptable.

Chapter 31

Alerta and I sit in comfortable silence inside the new council building. I watch her observe the tree painted on the wall; her eyes tracking from the top, where the names patter through our past, to the bottom, where the names hold our future.

It's not long before the door opens to give entrance to King Thometh. He is alone today. He is wearing the orange that is expected of Renchenda royalty, but he looks weary. "What is the purpose of this emergency meeting, Tutor?" he asks.

"There have been questions raised about the validity of the claims I brought to your attention. I would like the assistance of the council in handling these concerns. Simply put, if it is my validity that is being questioned I feel it isn't in the best interest of Fraun for me to address those alone."

"Of course it's not," he says. "The council supports you."

I simply nod, unable to adequately find words that explain what that means. Support, such a simple concept really. But in Sarcheda that idea is easier spoken than given. Still, there is indeed no shortage of support from this group. "We cannot start the meeting until Ambassador Marcus is here," I say.

"We also need to wait for Sawchett and Hector," Alerta points out.

As if called by his name, the King of Farcheda sweeps into the door, half-heartedly waving before dropping into a chair. He looks distracted, disheveled. While those are two adjectives I am used to seeing when I glance in the mirror, it is not something one associates with King Hector.

I steal a glance at Alerta. She raises her eyebrows at me and tips her head toward Hector. My own unanswered questions are signaled in that expression. What is up with him?

Before either of us can get up the courage to ask, Sawchett enters. "I'm the last one here," she notes. "I guess we should begin." She perches herself of the arm of the wooden chair closest to her. She crosses her bare feet at the ankles.

"Actually, we need to wait for Ambassador M—"

"I have something we can begin with," Hector interrupts. "If you don't mind, King Tutor." I nod that he should continue. "If you hadn't called this meeting, tradition would've compelled me to." He takes a moment to look around the room. He looks as though something he is preparing to say is stuck in his throat. Finally, he clears his throat and speaks. "My father is no longer with us. He has died."

"Oh," Alerta lays her hand on his arm from the other side of his chair. "I am sorry for your loss."

Mick, former King of Farcheda, was gray the last time I saw him. In Fraun, that signals the last of the age markers. A citizen who has already grayed has less than five annuals of life left in them. For this reason, it is not entirely shocking that Mick has left us. Of course, that doesn't make the loss of a family member any easier to swallow, at least it didn't with Charlotte.

"In truth, we were not close," Hector reveals. "There was not much love between us. But he was my father and he was once King. It is important for the council to be aware that he has passed."

"Did Farcheda already observe a day of grievance?" Thometh asks.

"We will observe it tomorrow. He passed this morning." That is in accordance with Fraun policy. Citizens will be asked to cancel appointments and mourn the loss of the former king for one full sun following his death.

"Would you like the other realms to observe the loss with you?" Alerta asks. Such things have been done in the past, per the wishes of the council. There was even a time in recent memory, at the death of Prince Carsen, where all five realms observed the day concurrently.

Hector shakes his head, no. "My father was a murderer and a liar. If I didn't need to observe a day of mourning in his name I would not. There is no need for any other realms to give him that attention which he craved." His tone rings with finality.

At that moment the door opens, bringing Marcus and five other men all wearing the red associated with Sarcheda. "It appears you have begun without us," he calls.

I wince at the tone, somehow so selfish against the seriousness of the room. "Actually, we hadn't begun on Sarcheda's concerns. King Hector was bringing us news about the death of his father, the former King Mick."

"My condolences," Marcus says. He bows. I can't help but notice it is nothing like the shallow ones he passes off to me. "I was unaware Mick was ill."

"He was in his death spiral," Hector answers. "That is all I wish to say on the topic."

"Well, then allow me to change the subject." The men who arrived with Marcus spread out and take seats in various chairs around the circle we have naturally created. Marcus remains standing, throwing his arms outward and speaking as though the room is packed to the seams. "Ladies and gentlefraun, I wish to speak of the problem with the giants. It concerns me and the men I have brought before you today that this council sees fit to send innocent men out into the forest on only the word of a single king with no corroboration."

"I have two questions already," Thometh says. "Firstly, I was under the impression the men were sent to obtain corroboration, is that incorrect?"

"I suppose that may be the case, what says the council?" Marcus asks.

"The purpose of the group was to obtain proof of the existence of the giants. Their purpose was also to bring us more information with which to make further decisions," Sawchett answers. "They seek that which you seem to be looking for. Until they return, no one will be able to give you anything else."

"My second, and possibly more important question, is why do you doubt the word of *your* King?" Thometh emphasizes the adjective, narrowing his eyes and drawing out the word. He leans forward, resting his chin in the hand which is propped on his crossed knees.

"That is a very intelligent question, Majesty. We doubt the word of the king who has no blood of my realm. We doubt the word of a king who rose to power in questionable ways. I understand—"

"Enough." Thometh waves his hand like he is swatting a fly. He smiles at the room. "All who question the blood of King Tutor and, by extension, Queen Sawchett, please raise your hand." I watch as Marcus and four of his friends raise their hands. I cock my eyebrow in surprise at the man who keeps his hands clasped firmly in his lap and feel a smile tickle the corners of my mouth. The royals in the room keep their hands down as well. "There you have it, this is not a concern of the majority in this room at this present time."

"I understand that, sir. But, simply put, you cannot ignore the opinion of Fraunians simply because it is not the majority opinion," Marcus says. He drops his hand and the raised ones in the room fall in echo.

"True. However, I can assure you that the royals who run this council have accepted the bloodline of your king. That should please you. I am sure he grows weary of having his bloodline, which he was not even aware of five annuals ago, questioned at every turn. I grow tired of the conversation myself if I'm being honest." Thometh stands up at his chair and plants his fists at his waist. "Marcus here are the official answers from the council, who will amend or correct me if I am mistaken." He smiles. "The council believes in the message King Tutor received because the messenger is one who has earned our trust. The group of innocent citizens you mentioned is a group of volunteers who welcomed the opportunity to head to the forest and gain information for the council. We are concerned about the giants. We are doing the best we can by gathering more facts. Meetings such as this one stir up tension and serve no real purpose."

"Trust your king, that's my advice," Hector grumbles. "I understand how hard that must be for Sarcheda, after the path you were led down previously. But if Farcheda can trust me, Sarcheda can trust Tutor." I notice he seems to be speaking to the citizen closest to him, instead of to Marcus.

"If there is nothing else, I vote to adjourn this meeting," Thometh says.

When there are no objections, Sawchett raises her arm. "One Kingdom," she calls.

"One Fraun," we echo. I notice the guests join in the call. Marcus, looking like a child on the verge of a temper tantrum, does not.

"Marcus," Hector calls, "you will politely refrain from speaking ill of someone from this council. If you, as an ambassador, have concerns, you are welcome to bring them to your king or a regularly scheduled meeting. Consider this your formal notice that we do not tolerate Fraunians who cannot follow the rules. They exist for a reason."

Marcus pinches his lips together and narrows his eyes at the king of the first realm. But he doesn't argue. A beat passes, while I wonder what he will say. Finally, he nods once and turns on his heel to leave the room.

I let out an audible breath. "That was uncomfortable," I say.

Hector's answering smile is completely false. "He's no worse than the threat of giants, I suppose."

"No, I suppose he's not. It's still hard to believe they've found actual giants, isn't it? I never thought I'd see the day," I say.

"Do you suppose Marcus' shock is what is causing him to doubt you?" Thometh asks, still standing in front of his chair.

I don't even need to think about that one. "No," I answer. "Marcus has had a problem with me since before we knew of the giants."

"Do you suppose there are more giants out there, or is it just the one?" Alerta asks.

The question has the effect of silencing all noise in the room. "That's the fear, isn't it?" I ask. "If there's a community of them wasting resources and creating technologies we can't even dream of, what chance do we stand?"

The silence wraps around the room again as I watch the color drain from everyone's faces. "Let us hope it's just the one," Hector says quietly.

"If it's alright with you, I'm also going to hope that one is old and sickly," Alerta says. I think she's trying to make a joke. But no one laughs. No one even smiles. Because we're dangerously close to discussing what we're really afraid of. We're afraid that it's already too late for us.

Chapter 32

"This is not at all what I was expecting." Danyel's voice is a whisper. It barely carries across the small fire. They are all on edge. Every little noise jars them. Every light is questioned; can they do without it?

Jordyn nods agreement. "Nor I." Even the roaches they met along the way, the ones who took them out this far, are restless. Roaches are notoriously nosey creatures so it makes sense that they stayed. But they have as much to fear as the scouts if this situation goes badly.

So far, going badly does not describe the mission to view the giants. Jordyn thinks out loud. "We have been here for four suns." Which is true. Someone from the scout troop as well as all three of the men from Fraun have been right here at this campground for four sunsets. They have no tents, they have only blankets on the ground. They sleep in shifts and monitor the camp they have found.

The camp, as it turns out, is a circle of buildings off in the distance housing more giants than anyone expected when they asked roaches to bring them here. Secretly, they were all expecting a single giant or, at the very least, a single-family unit.

Jordyn ticks off the important points they've noticed so far on his fingers as he speaks. "The giants are farming the land. They are staying within their area and they haven't ventured outside of the circle they've created. They do not appear to be building to excess, making new technologies, or fighting with each other."

"It looks like Fraun, only bigger," Danyel summarizes.

That is exactly what it looks like. Nestled at the foot of the mountain the scouts have climbed, south of the ravine skirting Sarcheda, the giants have set up their own little community.

Toby approaches the group, having been recently relieved of duty at the ledge of the mountain overlooking the giant camp by the boys from the Fraun. "Afternoon," he says as he drops onto the ground.

"How did it go out there? Anything new?" Danyel asks.

Toby shakes his head. "Nothing. I count twenty-eight giants this time. Another smaller one emerged from a dwelling near the farm. I don't think we'd counted her before. Obviously a child, yellow hair, almost looks like Sawchett did when I first met her."

"Queen Sawchett," Danyel corrects.

"She's not my Queen," Toby mutters.

"I don't recall seeing one who matched that description," Jordyn says, speaking up before Danyel and Toby can launch into an argument about politics. "We can agree twenty-eight is the total right now then?"

"I think so," Toby says. "Every dwelling has at least one occupant. Of course, if more small ones are staying indoors we may never get an accurate count."

"What must be happening indoors to keep them there all day? Children in Fraun hate to be inside. I see them running around all the time, playing and such," Danyel says.

"If the stories and rumors are true, they'd be on some kind of technological device," Jordyn answers. "Spending hours plugged in to something glowing, ignoring everyone around them."

At his elbow, Toby chuckles and shakes his head. "Have you seen any such devices?"

Jordyn sighs and takes a sip of his water. "I can't say that I have."

"Neither have I. So that doesn't track."

"Maybe the kid stayed inside before this because it was sick?" Danyel offers.

Toby nods. "Could be. Or could be that the kid is planning some kind of war, isn't that what we'd heard they did in their spare time?" Toby's voice drips with cynicism. He is looking at the fire but Jordyn knows the words were meant for him.

"I'm the first to admit it, Toby."

Toby's eyes turn to the former king. "Actually, I haven't heard you admit anything out loud."

Danyel senses the change in energy. He raises his hands. "Look, guys, let's just—"

"What do you want me to say?" Jordyn asks.

"Admit that your precious council was wrong about the giants."

"We're back to this? For Fraun sake, Toby they're not my council." Jordyn's shout stops the conversation. Danyel catches it before Jordyn does, dropping his hands and shaking his head. Toby visibly pulls back. It takes a beat before Jordyn realizes what he's said. When he does, his chin drops. "Oh no," he breathes. It was the stress of the situation, it's a phrase they throw around in Fraun. He didn't mean it as it sounded. He doesn't believe in doing things for the sake of Fraun. He wasn't trying to push Toby to do something for the sake of Fraun. But none of that will matter immediately. None of that will smooth this over. That was the worst possible time to let that phrase slip out.

Jordyn returns his eyes to Toby. "I know it doesn't matter or excuse it, but I didn't mean that. You have to understand that I grew up saying and hearing that phrase." All trace of frustration or anger is gone from Jordyn's voice. He shakes his head. "The message was the same. They're not my council and haven't been for quite some time."

"I've been at a council meeting," Danyel offers. "They don't even talk about Jordyn or Eselda."

Toby rises. He throws his left arm out in the general direction of Fraun. "That council is wrong about those giants." He shakes his head and takes one step away from the fire.

"You're right." At the sound of Jordyn's voice, Toby freezes. He slowly turns back toward Jordyn, keeping his leg extended as if ready to run away if he doesn't say something Toby wants to hear. Jordyn clears his throat and speaks in a normal volume. "The official report to the council of Fraun will say that these are not the giants we've heard tales of."

Toby nods once and walks off toward his sleeping area. His voice carries over his shoulder as he saunters away. "If the council that created Fraun was wrong about the giants, what else were they wrong about, Jordyn? Ask yourself that."

Chapter 33

"Don't take this the wrong way, I love every single one of you as if you were birthed by my mother but isn't this our fourth meeting inside a lunar cycle?" Hector says, in lieu of a greeting. He is the last royal to arrive at the council building. He takes an empty seat between Alerta and Sawchett, to my left.

"I believe your count is accurate," Alerta answers.

"I know it's important," Hector says. "I hear the spies have returned their report."

This meeting was called by Danyel, who sent a roach ahead of his arrival. As if called by my thoughts, the door to the new council building opens to allow Danyel to enter. "Good morning, Majesties and Ambassadors," he calls.

"Good morning, Danyel. We are eager for your report. Please begin when you are ready," Thometh says.

"No protocol or call to action necessary today?" Danyel asks.

"This is an emergency meeting. All of that wastes time," Hector explains.

"Got it." Danyel wrings his hands in front of him as he speaks. I recognize the nervous tic and try to offer him a comforting smile. I am sure it comes across as a grimace. No one wants this report to go badly.

"We watched the giants' camp for a fortnight. We were accompanied by two men from the scout troop and three roaches. We spent nights atop a hill inside a copse of trees with a low flame to keep from being seen. At all times there was at least one of our group at the edge of the mountain watching the village below where the giants have made camp." Danyel's voice is clear, hard. He is delivering prepared facts and showing no emotion.

"How far outside the Fraun were you?" Hector asks.

"It took me three full suns riding on a roach to reach this council building." Hector nods once and Danyel continues. "The camp the giants have created is large. There are various tents set up, farmland, and many fire pits. The settlement appears to be permanent. They do not uproot the tents and move daily as scouts have been known to do. The fire pits haven't been cleaned and are rarely seen unlit."

"They're not moving and are therefore getting no closer than three suns worth of travel from Fraun at all times," Thometh summarizes.

"Exactly. We established the protocol of counting the giants twice a day at the beginning of each watch shift. Like us, the giants have obvious differences in their appearance. The tents serve as family bases. We were able to use these facts to help us gather an accurate count, we believe. At last count, we had twenty-eight giants in all."

There is an obvious reaction around the room, like a collective intake of air. Twenty-eight is a lot. If one giant alone could squash Fraun under his or her boot, what could more than twenty do? "That is a large number," I say.

"They are not all full-grown," Danyel says. "They appear to be in various stages of growing up."

"A community, not unlike Fraun," Alerta says.

Danyel beams at her. "Exactly what we thought. The similarities are remarkable. They don't appear to have a king, but we couldn't be sure. Jordyn is interested in whether one particular tent may be a council room of sorts. The men seem to gather there occasionally. We obviously can't see what happens when they are in there, but it is certainly interesting."

At the mention of Jordyn's name, Marcus scoffs. Danyel, obviously into this part of his telling, doesn't seem to notice. I shoot a warning glare at my Ambassador. He casts his eyes downward.

"What do they spend their days doing?" Sawchett inquires.

"Farming, talking to one another, or hunting. They seem to hunt in pairs off in the direction further from Fraun. Never once, in all the time we watched, did they venture anywhere near Fraun or the mountain we were watching from."

"You keep saying mountain," I say. "Mountain to us or mountain to them?" If the stories I grew up with are true, those two sizes would be vastly different.

Danyel clears his throat. "Well, um, let's see…" The stuttering is not good. I know Danyel well enough, after fighting side-by-side with him, to know that this is indicative of bad news. "Probably only to us. Um, they don't come near enough to it to be sure but it maybe would fall at…um… let's see…their waist, maybe." He holds his hand up near the top of his own pants to indicate where he means.

Again, the room collectively draws air. The size difference between us and them is just as we feared. "There's one more thing though," Danyel continues. "Something I've been asked to tell you. I have been asked to deliver this message word-for-word."

"From whom?" Hector asks.

"Jordyn."

The assembled royals nod. The respect for that name is great in this room, but perhaps not so outside of these walls. It is hard for Fraunians to forget that Jordyn abandoned Renchenda in their time of need. Granted, if it wasn't for his joining the scouts and bringing them to our side we would've lost the war for Fraun, but everyone is not always aware of that part of the story. To some, Jordyn is seen as a defect, someone to look down upon. This is evident in the mumble of Marcus. "I knew he was involved in all this."

I turn my head in his direction and pointedly whisper back. "Enough." To Danyel I use regular volume, "Let us hear the message."

"Majesties, these giants we have come upon are not the giants we have spent our lives hearing tales of. The giants we are witnessing are aware of their place in the world. They are tending gardens, they have no technologies. They are using flames to see. They are reusing materials and wear clothing similar to ours. These giants appear to have learned a lesson from their ancestors as we have." Danyel's voice rings out with confidence in the silence of the room. "These giants do not appear to be anything we have to fear." He nods once. "That is the message."

Alerta is the first to break the silence that follows the message. "I trust the judgment of the former king. I propose we allow the group, if they are interested, to continue to monitor the situation. A fortnight is not a long time, we would feel more confident with a lunar cycle or more of watching. It appears to me that no further action is necessary at this time."

"I second that notion," Thometh says. "All in favor?"

Aye's fill the room.

Marcus stands up, his chair scraping along the floor. "You will do nothing in the face of thirty giants? I demand action on behalf of Fraun," he shouts.

I throw my hands up in frustration. "What would you have us do?" I ask, without looking in his direction. Silence. I turn my head, finding his face. "What action do you propose?" Again, silence. Now I turn and address the council. "In the absence of any other ideas, with a carrying vote in favor of monitoring the situation, we will proceed in the council's proposed direction. Danyel, are you willing to return to the group and continue your part in the surveillance of the giants?"

"I am, Majesty."

"Excellent. Meeting adjourned, I believe."

"The citizens of Sarcheda will not be happy with a report that this council proposes to do nothing," Marcus says.

Again, I address the council without looking in his direction. "I will hold a meeting in two suns on my lawn in Sarcheda. All are invited. The topic will be this report, the council's decision, and a call for other ideas if any are present. Join me if you are able." This time I decide to end the meeting, raising my hand and pointing one finger. "One Kingdom," I call.

"One goal." The answering call is at least one voice short. I hear the grunt from Marcus followed by shuffling and a slamming door. Apparently, we are done discussing this.

Chapter 34

Eselda taps her fingers along her dress, nerves tightening knots in her stomach. She is waiting for Jordyn to return from bathing in the stream nearby. He returned from the giant camp a short while ago, long enough to get some food in his belly and get himself cleaned up. Now, she waits. Waits to hear the update on the giants and waits to bring him the news of her dream. Neither part of the pending conversation gives her hope for comfort.

By the time Jordyn steps through the fabric the sun has begun to track down the sky. Eselda pops up from the blankets to greet him with a kiss at the entrance. "I've waited as patiently as I can. Please give me the update," she says.

Jordyn drops onto the blankets, stretching out on his back and hooking his hands behind his head. "There are more giants than we thought," he says, getting right to the point. Eselda lets out a little gasp and drops onto the blankets beside him. "Toby counted twenty-eight."

"Oh my," Eselda whispers.

"But it's not what you would think." He turns his blue gaze to her face and she reads a calm there she can't quite understand. "They're nothing like the old stories, Eselda. They have permanent structures up and they're farming the land. They appear to only be building, planting, and killing what they need."

"They're doing nothing to excess?" she asks.

"No, nothing like that. It's like they've learned from their mistakes."

Eselda shakes her head on an inhale and then tips it back to the ceiling on her exhale. "That is not what we heard the giants were like." Something occurs to her then and she drops her eyes back to Jordyn. "Do you think these are different? Could this be something else? Were we wrong to assume the giants were back?"

Jordyn shakes his head. "No. I think this is them."

"Well, then what do you say to the differences?"

It's quiet for a few breaths while Jordyn thinks. Eselda considers asking the question again or maybe saying his name to get his attention. But she can tell by the way his eyes track to the ceiling and his breathing slows that he is thinking about it. She lets him think. "We're different too. Fraun was started on the lessons that we learned from the giants. Perhaps this little group, whatever they are calling themselves, has learned as well. Perhaps this little group of theirs is starting again."

"Should we fear them, Jordyn?"

He turns his eyes to the love of his life and sees her fear plainly written on her face. He pushes himself up and wraps his arms around her, reveling in the burning across his torso that comes from holding her close. "No. I am starting to think we don't need to," he answers.

When he pulls back from her to kiss her, the fear is still there. "Something else troubles you," he notes aloud. "Tell me what it is."

Eselda decides the time to pretend has passed. Jordyn already knows about her previous dreams, the ones before the war. They've talked about them in great length. She sighs. "I have been dreaming of another death. I've had it twice. At first, I didn't know who it was."

"The face blurs when you dream, yes?" Jordyn asks, scrunching his eyes to recall details she has told him in the past.

"Exactly. I didn't recognize the body of the person. But, with the recent changes here, I think I know." She swallows audibly. "It's her. I'm dreaming of the death of my mother."

The part of Jordyn that has learned to let himself feel emotions wants to reach out and hold her again. But the logical part, the part that wants to solve this puzzle, needs more answers. He settles for rubbing his hand in small circles along her back. "Tell me what you know so far," he prompts.

Eselda leans into him a little. "It's dusk when she dies, I know that. You are in the tent that has been put up behind ours. She's in there. You come out and tell me that it's time. I'm sitting at the campfire having a conversation about something with Danyel. We hear you, I'm not sure how we could miss it. You go back in the tent." The breath that she draws in rattles along her back, he can feel it under his palms. She is trying not to cry. "I don't go in with you. You stand in the tent and watch as my mother takes her final breaths. No one else is in there with her. No one holds her hand. No one comforts her." Her eyes turn to Jordyn and he sees the flash of black smoke swirling through the irises. "Not even you," she accuses.

Eselda's hand flies up to her lips. "That's not what I mean," she stammers. "I'm not mad at you." She drops her hand, letting it rest on Jordyn's thigh. "I'm upset I'm not in there. Especially now that I know who is it. If that woman in the tent truly is my mother, how can I possibly—"

"Maybe you don't hear my voice," Jordyn offers. "Maybe you don't understand how sick she is. Maybe you two are talking about something important and you think you have more time. What are you talking to Danyel about? How much time passes between me warning you and her last breath? How do I warn you?" His questions are rapid-fire, typical of Jordyn. It forces a small smile from Eselda, despite her sadness.

"I'm not sure what Danyel and I are talking about. I don't come into the dream near us. I have to kind of hurry to get there and by then you're already warning us so the conversation slows. I know we hear you. I also know we already know how sick she is. You don't have to tell us what it's time for, just that it's time." She shakes her head. "I appreciate the pass you are trying to give me here, but it's time to face what we already know." She rubs her eyes. "I'm a bad person."

"Stop," he kisses her on her forehead. "You are not."

She pushes on his chest, just enough to make him lean back a little. "Then what is it? Am I that angry with her?" she yells.

"I don't know. Are you?"

The tears are instant. Eselda has no answer to this question because she cannot admit to the best person she knows, someone who would never let this happen to his family, that she is. She's already decided, deep down, that she cannot be there for Rubina when she dies. She's already been through this grieving once. She's already lost her once, at least she thought she did. She cannot do it again.

Jordyn pulls Eselda's head to his shoulder and lets her cry. He rubs little circles on her back and makes soothing sounds. "If you can't be there when she dies, then I will be there for you. I will do whatever you need me to do," he whispers. "You don't have to be sorry. Just tell me what you need."

"I need to be weak right now," she whispers.

"Then I'll be strong," Jordyn answers and he squeezes his arms a little tighter around her body.

Chapter 35

"You can't let him bother you," Sawchett says. She is standing directly behind my left shoulder, whispering. But it irritates me that she thinks he bothers me. I tried to keep my face stoic during this meeting, I tried to shake it off.

"He doesn't." I watch the room continue to empty, Fraunians ambling out into the new antechamber. They're in various forms of conversation, no one paying any attention to the pair of siblings having a chat by the table.

"I'm only checking. Don't be annoyed."

I turn and give her my best annoyed face. "Don't be annoying."

She laughs. "He's one man, Tutor. Nothing is saying his opinion really belongs to others in Sarcheda or that he is spreading that opinion around. I certainly doubt he is having the effect he'd like to have outside of Sarcheda."

"If he isn't representing Sarcheda, then why are we allowing him to stand as Ambassador for Sarcheda?" I ask. My voice has a hard edge to it, betraying how annoyed I am. "It seems to go against everything we said we wanted at this council table. I've put up with it because everyone says this must be an opinion that exists in Fraun and we need to honor it."

"You're right. We will discuss it again at the regular meeting, not at a special session." She lays her hand on my arm. "Try to let it go, brother. He is not worth this kind of stress and tension."

I don't want to talk about this. I shake my head and smile at her. "You're right. How's life? Did Abney enjoy the crib?"

"She did. I received the nicest letter from her. They've already chosen a room for the little darling and have the crib all set up in there with blankets Evelyn has sent."

"How long until the baby joins the family?" I ask. I'm thinking I just saw Abney and didn't notice any sign of a baby growing in her.

"Oh they still have quite a few lunar cycles yet, but it's good to be prepared. Don't you think?"

"I suppose." In truth, I have no idea. "What's your thought on this news from Danyel?" I change the topic to something safer, something I have an opinion on.

"I trust Jordyn and Danyel. If they say we have no reason to fear, I believe them."

"Agreed. What do you make of this new phase of the giants? Do you think it's possible they learned from their past mistakes and have stopped wasting resources?"

Sawchett wrinkles her nose while she thinks. "It's possible." She shrugs. "I guess I just imagine them as really large versions of us." She starts to head toward the door. "We have proven we're capable of change, why would they be any different?"

I follow her as she heads out of the room. "That makes sense," I say. Sawchett pulls the door open and holds it for me so I can walk through before letting it close behind her.

The antechamber is not empty. A group of representatives is standing around, leaning in as though they are deep in conversation. Sawchett heads directly for the door, ignoring the group. I try to follow her lead but a piece of the conversation drifts up and out of the din. "… his lack of leadership is at an all-time…"

I snap my head around to the group. Sure enough, my eyes catch on Marcus in the center of the assembled men. My eyes travel the faces of the rest of the group, I see other Ambassadors and a few other Fraunians who were merely attending as citizens. One thing is abundantly clear, Marcus has found an audience outside of Sarcheda.

I take a step toward the group, letting my feet hit the floor loudly. The talking stops. "Is there some business being discussed here?" I ask. All around the group eyes fall to the floor and nervous shuffling starts. The citizens between Marcus and myself take a step back. Marcus, however, raises his eyes to my face. "Should we call back the full council?" I ask, my voice a controlled challenge.

Marcus' face breaks into a smile. "Of course not, Majesty." He bows deep. The gesture looks ridiculous. When he stands back up, his smile is gone. "We were merely discussing a common roach cart businessman from Sarcheda. He claims to be the head of a shop there, but the discourse he spreads is evident. You can't trust a man like that."

I know the story is a lie. I look to the faces of the others present. To challenge this right now, have it out with him, may do more damage to their impression of me. If I were still in the malicious age, it would be tempting to scream at him right here and now. But I'm older and possibly wiser. I know the council needs to handle Marcus and his insubordination within the proper channels. But I also feel my resolve slipping. If something is not done soon I know I won't be able to restrain myself from some kind of darker and more primal form of confrontation.

I push myself to take a step backward and take a deep breath, forcing a calm I do not feel. "Interesting story. Just remember, all of you who are Ambassadors to Council for your realms, it is still our policy to have discussions about Fraun at official meetings. Standing outside an official meeting holding a meeting in secret is not within policy." Before I say too much, I decide to leave. "Have a great day."

Outside the door, Sawchett shakes her head. "Maybe it is more of a problem than I thought," she says.

The breeze blows, kicking up the smell of flowers growing somewhere. I smile at her. "Thank you." It's not what I wanted to say, but somehow it feels more polite than "I told you so".

Chapter 36

I watch the group assemble on the lawn of the royal home in Sarcheda the day after the council meeting. Word has spread quickly. I recognize colors from every realm represented among the group. There are old and young, dark-skinned and light, tall and short all represented among the crowd. The only thing they have in common is the look on their faces when I share the news of the giants. Shock, fear, and stress show on every face. The expressions give me pause. I am bringing the citizens of Fraun all of these emotions. I have no idea how to battle back against these.

"Now it's important to note that the scouts along with the fraunians we have sent to observe report that there is nothing to fear from this group," I say. I'm hoping to ease some of the pain I am seeing.

Danyel, who stayed in Fraun particularly for this meeting, stands up from the wall beside me. "That's right. I have seen them myself. They do not see us, they don't seem to know we are there. I felt no threat even when watching the giants move about their society in the daytime." He sits back on the wall again, his feet just off the ground.

We are inside Sarcheda territory for the proposed meeting with short notice. The invitations were informally passed along by word of mouth and yet there are a lot of citizens here. Of course, Marcus is among them, as are Kings or royals from every realm.

"The point of us gathering today," I explain, "is to listen to any proposed ideas for the next steps. There were some concerns at the council meeting that our observe and wait approach was not something Fraunians would agree to. So we are bringing it to the citizens." I am careful not to look at Marcus. No point in calling him out right now.

"Do we have any weapons that would be effective against the giants if they were to come after us?" a man in the front of the crowd asks.

"I think I'm the right person to address that one." Danyel rises again. "I have seen the weapons Fraunians had at their disposal in the war for Fraun and I have seen the giants up closer than anyone else here." There are nods around the clearing from citizens who are accepting the conjecture that Danyel is as close to an expert on this topic as we will find. "In my opinion, no. Nothing Fraun has used or made would be effective against something the size we are dealing with." Instead of sitting back down, he leans on the wall this time, perhaps more ready to rise again should he need to.

"Worth mentioning, again, that no one sees a situation where this would be necessary at this time," I offer.

"But it could—"

"We should just run." The man is interrupted by a woman at his elbow. "They said there are no weapons. If you're afraid there's even a chance they'll attack then your answer is to run. That's all there is to it."

"What if we all wanted to run together?" another voice asks. This one is from the back of the crowd and I cannot see whom it belongs to.

"The council had discussed that as well," I offer. "I admit we have not looked into it further."

Sawchett, seated cross-legged on the ground in front of me, rises and turns to face the crowd. "There has been talk of finding a space large enough to relocate the entire kingdom," she says. "Is this something you believe we should pursue further?"

"I would be in favor of that," a man says. "Should we take a vote or something?"

"We can if you'd like," Sawchett says. "What would we be voting on? Would you like us to vote on relocating at this time?"

"No! I'm not leaving if there's nothing to be afraid of," a voice calls.

"What if we send another group to go explore in the other direction, away from the giants? See if there's even a space that can hold us all," someone suggests.

I take a step forward. "This could be arranged. All in favor of sending a group north of Fraun to look for a space large enough to accommodate the kingdom, raise your hands."

There's no need for me to count. Almost every hand goes up. Those that don't eventually join the raised hands, sometimes with a shrug. It's almost as if the entire assembled group decides it certainly can't hurt to explore our options. "Let it be done," I say.

"See me if you would volunteer for this mission," Sawchett says before dropping back to the ground.

"Are there any present who have further actions they'd like to see taken?" I ask. Silence is my answer. "Alright, then it sounds like we all have our missions. Please see Queen Sawchett if you are interested in being part of the group scouting for new land options. Otherwise, thank you for coming." I raise my hand, pointing at the sky. "One Kingdom…"

"One goal," they answer. Slowly, the crowd starts to disperse. I remain nearby, watching the group gather around my sister. She remains seated as though waiting for an appropriate time to rise. Among the group, I recognize only the man who painted names on the wall of the council building. For some reason, I am surprised to find him there.

Finally, Sawchett rises and addresses the group. "Thank you for your interest. We should discuss what you will be searching for and how we expect you to report back. Other than that, I see no reason why you all cannot undertake the journey should you so choose."

"We need to find a place with water and farming land," one man offers. "That much we know. What else would we require?"

"Building materials," a younger man answers. I nod at the suggestion.

"Lack of animal waste. We don't want to be barging into a more dangerous situation than the one we are leaving," someone points out.

Again, I merely nod.

"How large a space are we talking?" Danyel asks.

"Fraun is a circle," the painter of the wall answers. "We don't have any tools that would measure the distance now." He strokes his chin, looking as though he is trying to recall a fact. "You can cross the entire kingdom in about three suns on a fast roach," he says after a beat.

I am shocked by this information. Judging by the looks on the faces of the crowd, I am not the only one. I have never tried to cross the entire kingdom. Three suns is impressive. It is larger than I thought.

"Should we travel by roach then, do you think?" someone asks.

"That's the way I would do it if you can get some to help," Danyel answers. "As an added bonus, many of the roaches know what is beyond Fraun. You may find some who can help point you toward a place to begin your search."

"We do not know how long you will need to be gone from your families," Sawchett says. "We do not know what dangers will face you north of our borders. If you are still willing to undertake this journey, you will meet at the Farcheda border in two suns time with whatever you require for the journey. That will be all."

As the group starts to break up, I speak to my sister and Danyel. "I will draft a letter to the council with the time of the departure and the notes from this meeting."

"I will report to Jordyn and the Scouts," Danyel says.

"Sounds like you boys have it all under control," Sawchett smiles. She turns and starts to head in the direction of Enchenda.

"Sawchett," I call, "isn't this what you wanted us to do from the beginning?"

She turns and smiles. "Basically, yes."

I shrug at Danyel. "I guess she got her way."

"Those Enchenda women usually do." He laughs.

As Danyel walks away, I notice Sawchett has stopped to talk to the man who tracks the lineage and paints the wall. I approach them, waving so as not to appear like I am eavesdropping on their conversation.

"King Tutor, meet Erick. Erick, King Tutor." Sawchett sweeps her hand between us.

"I am familiar with the name, of course." Erick offers me his hand, which I shake.

"Are you of Fraun?" I ask.

"No. Erick is what you would call a wild," Sawchett says. There's a note of reverence I cannot help but pick up on. This man, already sporting gray hair on the top of his head, is much older than my sister. That leads me to believe her reverent tone has more to do with attraction for his lifestyle than an attraction for the man.

"If you don't mind my asking, what interest did you have in this meeting today?" I ask.

Erick narrows his eyes at me. "Giants threaten all little beings, surely you see that."

"I suppose I hadn't thought of it that way." I shrug. "I'm sure we appreciate your knowledge of the woods and your expertise."

He nods. "You certainly will."

I have no retort this for. I try for a smile and it comes across as awkward. "How long have you been a wild?" I ask, trying to steer the conversation back to something that doesn't feel uncomfortable.

"A very long time," he answers. He blinks a few times as though waiting for me to ask another question. When I don't, he shrugs. "I suppose that's the end of the interview, yes?" He smiles at Sawchett. "I will see you in two suns."

"It's good that something brought wilds and Fraunians together," I say to my sister.

Her eyes go wide. "Did you just try to claim finding giants still alive outside of Fraun is a good thing?" Before I can answer, she laughs a little and shakes her head. "I know what you meant, I'm only teasing." She sighs and the sound captures exactly how I'm feeling deep in my soul. The weight of the entire kingdom is in that sigh. "This isn't how we expected the future to go when we won the war, is it?" she asks, her voice softer.

I shake my head, wincing at the pain of the thoughts. "Not at all," I agree. "I never expected giants."

Chapter 37

When Danyel is in sight of the scout camp, he instantly feels a calm wash away fears he didn't know he was harboring. He can see everyone gathered together, heads focused downward as they eat. Laughter keeps floating out toward him, light enough to be carried on the breeze. This is what he couldn't find words to express to the citizens in Fraun. This normal life, laid-back and easy, is all the proof he needs that there is nothing at all to fear.

"Hello Danyel, welcome back. There's extra ant if you are hungry." Eselda gestures with her free hand at the pot over the open flames.

"Thank you." He stirs the food around taking mental stock of how much remains. "Can I share this with the roach who brought me?" he asks.

"Of course." Eselda turns to the creature. "Thank you for returning our friend safely. Are you hungry?"

"I could eat," the roach replies. That is answer enough for Danyel who loads up a nearby leaf with a full hand scoop of the meat and lays it before the bug. Only when the creature is eating does Danyel scoop himself a portion and sit among his friends. "Any changes?" Danyel asks between bites. His eyes flit around the outside of the circle, perhaps cataloging the camp and the faces of the scouts for changes.

"None," Jordyn answers.

Danyel allows his eyes to land on Eselda, taking stock of her slightly tortured expression, before falling back to Jordyn. "Rubina still lives?" he quietly asks. He was told about the former queen, of course, when Jordyn told all who watched the giants. He has yet to meet her.

"For now," Eselda answers. "You know how it is, I'd rather not talk about family."

"I have no family to talk about." Danyel shrugs. "I can respect that."

"Let's talk of something else, what news do you bring us from Fraun?" Eselda asks.

"Let the boy eat," Kurt says. "He can tell us when he is finished."

Danyel feels their expectant eyes on him. He gulps down one more bite to calm the roar in his stomach. "It's alright. The council meeting was first. They seemed calmed by your reassurance that we are safe, Jordyn. They decided to have my group rejoin you to keep an eye on the situation."

"That's all?" Eselda asks. Her right eyebrow cocks up toward her hair. "I find the council has changed a lot if the meeting was that simple."

"Well, there was one who didn't agree with the decision. An ambassador seemed to blame Tutor—"

"King Tutor," Eselda corrects. "You are not a defect, friend."

"Right." Danyel shuffles a little under the correction, clears his throat, and tries again. "King Tutor decided it was best to hold a meeting where citizens could provide alternatives."

"Citizens?" Jordyn asks. "Every time I start to forget how much it has changed there, something like this reminds me. Kings before the war never asked for citizens to come together. Kings never presumed the citizens had any ideas to bring to the table."

"You don't agree with them inviting citizens, my love?" Eselda asks.

"On the contrary, I do agree. It's a wise choice, indeed."

"I figured I should stay for that meeting as well," Danyel explains. "That's why I am back a little later than we discussed." He takes another large bite of ant and washes it down with the bottle of water he carries.

"Loads of Fraunians were at the meeting."

"Where was it held? What realms were present? Were the royals all there?" Jordyn fires the questions quickly.

Danyel, possibly because of their history, doesn't react to the rapid questioning except to answer. "Sarcheda, it seemed like all realms, and every royal blood was represented."

"Except Sarcheda himself," Jordyn mumbles.

"What?" Danyel asks. He thinks he heard the former king but since Danyel is not privy to the fact that the Sarcheda bloodline has ended, the comment means nothing to him.

"It is my understanding no one in Fraun has Sarcheda's blood. Isn't this the reason Tutor is allowed to lead that realm?"

"I guess I hadn't thought of that," Danyel answers.

Jordyn watches the consideration of this new fact play across Danyel's face as if it is being filed away for further questioning. Then he holds his hand out toward his friend. "Please, continue. What was discussed at this meeting you attended?"

"Right. They talked about fighting the giants."

Kurt's laughter explodes out of his mouth and echoes around the clearing. Before the echo can even die the entire group has joined in. Even Danyel laughs until tears are squeezed out of his eyes and drop down his face.

"Yes," Danyel says, wiping his tears on his sleeve. "They came to that same conclusion. There is no weapon Fraun can effectively wield against the giants."

"Even giants couldn't banish all giants," Kurt points out.

"That is true." Danyel finishes the last of his food. "Then they discussed leaving Fraun."

"Leaving all together?" Jordyn asks.

"Yes. Someone inquired about it. I believe they asked if the kingdom as a whole would run together," Danyel explains.

Eselda rearranges herself on the log, stretching out her legs in front of her. "They know this is not necessary, yes?"

"They do. But they're sending a group to the north to look for a decent plot of land that could support Fraun in the event that they ever do need it."

“So they make preparations,” Kurt says. “This is good.”

“Whose idea was this?” Jordyn asks.

Danyel thinks about the meeting. He can no longer picture the citizen who asked about running. No matter, thinking about the comment Tutor made as they were leaving gives him the answer Jordyn seeks. “It was Queen Sawchett’s idea.”

Chapter 38

This time, Eselda is expecting the dream. Danyel is now at the scout camp, intending to spend a few nights. Knowing that it's Danyel she's speaking to when her mother passes means the death is drawing closer.

The breeze begins and Eselda makes a decision. She will find out more about the conversation happening around the campfire. She runs to get closer to herself and Danyel. Their expressions are serious. Danyel, actually, looks almost sad.

"I don't know what to say," Danyel whispers. The pain in his tone makes Eselda sad. She's coming to him for advice, perhaps, and he wants to be helpful.

"It's time." As expected, Jordyn's voice echoes through the clearing.

The dream version of Eselda stands up and pours something out of a cup over the fire pit while the dreamer watches. "That's alright," she says, addressing Danyel and sounding fake, "neither do I." Her eyes flick to the tent Jordyn emerged from almost sadly.

"That's right," Eselda chastises the dream version of herself aloud.

"You feel guilty for letting your mother die alone." She steps closer to herself. That's how she notices the sadness that crosses her own eyes. It's like she can see the heavy weight sitting on her own shoulders. She watches herself shake off the pain and affix a smile to her face before turning back to Danyel.

"That's my cue," she says. Her voice doesn't give away any of that pain churning underneath.

When the dream ends and her eyes open she's completely conflicted. Obviously, it will be soon and obviously, it hurts her to be out of the room. *What prevents her from going to Rubina when Jordyn calls her?More importantly, can the dream be changed?*

Chapter 39

I can hear voices inside the dining room. Instantly my mind flashes back to the annuals spent in this house working for the royal family. Once I even stood outside this door and heard two seated Kings discussing the overthrow of Tin. Would anything have been prevented if they had? The thought makes me shudder. Today, it is not two Kings discussing policy that I hear. It is two queens and it sounds as though they're discussing dresses.

I push the door open and enter the dining room. "I wasn't aware you invited others to join us," I say to Sawchett as I swoop to where she is seated at the end of the table to plant a kiss on her forehead. At the other end of the table, Alerta sits in a relaxed position with her elbows resting on the table. Stef is seated in front of the fire, between the queens. There is one empty chair opposite the little princess. I drop into it and wink at the child. "Hello again, little Stef."

"Hello, Mr. Tutor."

"King Tutor," Alerta corrects.

I wrinkle my nose, making a funny face for the child. "Ew, don't call me that here. That title will be our little secret in this room."

Stef giggles. "Then you can't call me Princess in here."

"Deal." I reach across the table, offering my hand to Stef. Giggling louder, she reaches out and takes it. I pump our connected hands together once and then release them.

I look to Alerta just in time to see her exaggerated eye roll for the sake of the child. "Hello, Majesty."

"Oh sure, you two can shun your titles but I am still Majesty here?" she teases.

"You can be whatever you want, Mommy. Isn't that what you tell me?" Stef says.

"Yes, whatever you want," I echo. "We shall call you…" I try to think of something besides beautiful, which would surely not be fitting in this crowd.

"How about if we just call me Alerta," she says. There's a smile on her face that is bewitching. The fire, which has the slow burn of a fire that has been at its task for some time, is throwing off enough light to catch in her eyes.

I clear my throat and force myself to look back at the others in the room. "Now that we've all been properly introduced, I heard I was invited for a meal."

"You were," Sawchett says. "Let me just grab our plates." She disappears into a door behind her which I know houses the kitchen. She returns after a beat with a cart on wheels. The cart is loaded up with four plates of food. She stops the cart beside the table and hands plates around.

The dish she hands me is loaded up with a creamy stew of some kind, the smells are familiar and pleasant. I reach for my spoon. "It smells lovely Sawchett," I tell her. My sister recently began trying her hand at cooking in her own kitchen instead of having a chef on staff. She claims that it's calming to cook, and unnecessary to have someone else doing all the work when it is usually only her eating.

"What is it?" Stef asks.

"Vegetable stew. The vegetables are grown right here in the garden. I tried to learn how to grow them myself, but I'm terrible in the garden. I have a gardener now who handles that for me. They grow zucchini which gives the stew its heartiness," Sawchett says.

"You speak like a chef," Alerta says.

"I have been tinkering in the kitchen lately. It's fun."

"Don't let her fool you," I interject, "she's a wonderful cook."

Stef sloshes the stew around her bowl as she fills a spoon. She leans over the bowl to avoid dripping and slurps up the first bite. "This is really good," she reports.

A comfortable silence falls around the room as the four of us dig in. I almost didn't come to dinner today. I am used to being alone in my house. I eat when it's convenient. I do have a chef who prepares meals for me but he only comes four times a lunar cycle. He prepares things for me to eat and stocks them in the kitchen for me to heat on the days when he isn't coming by. It's been a long time since I sat at a table with what feels like an entire family and had a conversation and comfortable silence. I am struck by how much I could enjoy this feeling.

I hear the unmistakable sounds of spoons scraping along the bottom of bowls. We are coming to the end of this meal. "I'm finished," Stef announces. She pushes her chair back from the table. "Are we staying longer?" she asks.

"Stef—" Alerta chastises.

"You should stay long enough to see the garden I was telling you about and maybe even my kitchen. Would you like that?" Sawchett asks. I have to smile at this. We may not have grown up together, but even I can recall times when my sister was the child and not the adult in situations exactly like this.

"Momma, can I go with Sawchett?" Stef asks. I notice she is already standing, bouncing a little in her excitement.

"Of course you can." Stef drops her little hand into Sawchett's and the pair head for the kitchen, the shortest route to the garden. "Mind your manners," Alerta calls as an afterthought.

Suddenly, I'm very aware that we are alone in the room. I turn to her and smile, pushing my empty bowl away from me. "I am glad you two could join us tonight. It brought so much energy to dinner."

"I find you fascinating, Tutor. Sometimes when we speak I feel as though you have real feelings for me. Other times I feel as though I repulse you," she says. Her voice is quiet, softened under the weight of a truth she is afraid has consequences.

"Never the second one."

"What is it then? How do you feel?"

I push my chair back away from the table. I don't push it evenly so it ends up turning toward Alerta, which is a happy accident. I take a slow and shaky breath. "Honestly? I don't know what I feel. I do know we are both rulers of different realms. I know we both have the blood of Marchenda in us, however distantly. These are the things I have to remind myself when I think of how the kingdom would perceive us." These are the facts I can give her. The reasons why my brain has never let me admit how I truly feel about her. I smile. "You can tell I have put thought into this." I reach across the table, my palm up toward the ceiling. She glances down at my hand and brings her own to rest on top of it, palm down. She closes her fingers around my hand. I do the same, watching as my fingers curl up to the top of her wrist. "I have told myself all the reasons we shouldn't be together, all the reasons Fraunians will bring up. But still, I find myself thinking about how beautiful you are."

"The Marchenda family tree splits up near the top," Alerta says. I had expected our conversation to drift into something more personal and the sudden switch to lineage has me silent. "Marchenda himself had two sons. It is back that far, Tutor, where we have a connection. My side of the family sprouts from Annex and yours from Larent. For me, that was seven generations ago." She turns her head, just a little, and the fire ignites in her eyes. "For you, it was six, I think."

She has clearly thought about this too.

"What do you really fear?" she asks. "Lineage and ruling, that is something you were not raised to worry about. Those are the fears of previous rulers. There's another fear for you, you can be honest."

Something in her eyes is calling out to me, daring me to give her the honesty she is requesting. I feel my head slowly start to nod. "You loved someone before. Enough to bring Stef into the world. I watched a good friend be torn apart by the competition that can be born of unrequited love, even when it only feels unreciprocated. I don't want to go through that. I don't want to put you through that."

Alerta leans over the table, drawing her face closer to me and into the light of the dying fire. "Listen to me, Tutor. I did not love Lucas. I thought I did. That feeling, that was something else. Whatever that feeling was, lust maybe, it's dead. I promise you that. I don't know what I feel for you. I don't know if you want to take a chance of finding out or not, because I cannot promise we will not get hurt. But I can tell you that if we decided to give this a chance, you wouldn't have to fear competition."

I don't answer right away. I don't even answer when she pulls her hand away from mine and stands up. She has a child. An actual child. Sure, I think Stef is great, but doesn't that take the level of stress and responsibility up a big step? I don't think I am ready for whatever this is. My silence must tell her that.

"Thank you for being honest with me, Tutor. I am going to grab Stef so we can be back in Marchenda at a decent bedtime for her." She lays her hand on my shoulder as she walks by and I feel it warm to my core. Without turning I know she is headed for the hallway door. I have walked that distance many times. I know I have only a short time before what has become an awkward discussion is over.

I push my chair away from the table and turn around. She is only halfway to the door. "Alerta, wait." I close the gap between us. "You are the strongest woman I know. The way you stuck by Stef is nothing short of amazing to me. My past…"I trail off because I don't want to talk about that. I shake my head to clear that line of thinking away and try again. "It shouldn't matter to you what I think, but I'm proud of how you are raising her. The fact that you have Stef isn't a reason to not be with you. It's one of the many reasons why I know you are strong, amazing, and compassionate."

She takes one step in my direction. That's close enough. I reach out and lay my hand at her waist. She takes another step closer. I let my hand curl around to her lower back. "I am sorry I hesitated. You are the most beautiful—"

I cannot finish the thought because Alerta leans into me and pushes her lips into mine. I pull her closer as the kiss heats up. I run my fingers through her hair and feel the energy flow through my blood. When she pulls away I feel alive. "Alerta, may I court you?" I ask. It's a formality, but the royals in Fraun are nothing if not formal.

She smiles at me, it's playful and somehow sensual. "You better." She steps back until my hands have no choice but to drop off her waist. "I really do need to get my daughter home. I'll be in touch." She steps closer and plants a quick peck on my lips. It's a gesture that seems to indicate she needed a quick kiss for the road. It makes me smile.

Chapter 40

The sun has set, the fire is burning down, dinner is cleaned up. Now is the time when the scouts can relax. Some return to their tents. Toby and Kurt are out on giant duty. Danyel, Jordyn, and Eselda decide to stretch their legs out and relax near the fire. Danyel yawns and leans back to take in the sight of the stars, shining brighter out here than they do inside Fraun.

"What changes did you observe during your shift today?" Jordyn asks.

Danyel spent the day on watch at the edge of the mountain. Although he has been back from his shift for some time, Jordyn ate dinner with Rubina and they haven't had a chance to talk. "None. The count remains at twenty-eight. A group of five men went out on a hunt and came back with about ten of the things they call rabbits. I'm still not sure how far out they are going to get those." He turns his head back to look at Jordyn, instead of the stars. "They were gone from sunrise until just before I left at sunset."

"Their steps are larger than ours," Jordyn notes.

"True. Since we don't journey the same direction we don't know how it compares either."

"Are you worried about the rabbits?" Eselda asks.

Danyel smiles at her. "They're larger than us, so it makes sense to worry."

"Of the two things you're discussing I would think giants would rank higher on your worries," she notes.

Jordyn rubs his hand along her back. "You should come with me tomorrow and see for yourself. They are not the giants we heard of. Something about them feels..." he trails off, eyes up, thinking of a word, "normal," he finishes.

"No, thank you." Eselda leans forward and stirs the fire around with the sword beside her. Embers fly up and Danyel watches them until he cannot see them any longer. When he returns his gaze to the fire, she is still leaning forward. Her arms are resting on her knees. "I should be here in case she dies." She turns her head, resting her chin on her shoulder and looking at Jordyn. "In fact, you should probably get back in there and make sure she hasn't already left us."

"I can do that." Jordyn kisses her on the forehead before disappearing behind the blanket to where Rubina is resting.

"Why don't you visit her?" Danyel asks.

"It's complicated."

"Will you be in the tent with her when she dies?"

Eselda sighs. "How do I explain this?" she whispers. A small chuckle escapes her and she turns her eyes to Danyel. "I thought she died a long time ago. There's a part of me that wants to be with her in her final moments because everyone should have someone. But I have already come to terms with her death."

He frowns a little but nods. "This time you could say goodbye."

She shakes her head. The curls that are falling over her shoulders tremble with the gesture. "I said goodbye to my mother many annuals back." She reaches for the large cup of tea at her feet, wrapping her hands around it. She takes a long sip and then rests the cup on her knees.

Danyel rubs his hand along the back of his neck. It looks like an absent-minded gesture, one that comes more from a desire to move than because of an itch or a pain. His voice is quiet on the cold breeze that kicks up, bringing the scent of the trees with it. "My parents died a long time ago, too. There was a fire, I don't know if you remember. It was in the kitchen my parents ran. Our house went up in flames and my parents died. I was only spared because I was a grass cutter at the time so I was awake and at work early." He takes a deep breath. "It was the hardest time of my life."

"That must have been before I met you." Eselda offers him a small smile. She remembers when she first met Danyel. He was with a group of young Fraunians looking for work on the outskirts of Enchenda, by the strawberry patch. He was sad, dejected. He took a job on the patrol because it offered him a safe way to run away. Maybe this is what he was running away from. "I'm sorry for your loss."

"Thank you." He clears his throat. "It's so strange to be sitting here talking to you now. Back then, before that happened, you were just my princess." He chuckles. "I knew your face. I saw you all over town. You were like a dignitary to me."

Even in the firelight, he can see the blush that takes up residence on her cheeks. "That's awkward," she says. "I hated that part of the lifestyle. I'm not more important than you. My history and my life shouldn't be more important to Enchenda than yours." She sighs. "All of Enchenda knew my story." When his eyes land on hers he is shocked to see them filling with unshed tears. She reaches out and grabs his hand, squeezing his fingers. "Your princess should've known your story. I'm sorry I wasn't there for you when your parents died. I'm sorry that I didn't know."

He returns the squeeze, reveling in the feeling of warmth generated by the contact of skin on skin. "You would've been a good Queen, you know. We believed in you."

"That's sweet of you to say, but no." She drops his hand, wrapping hers right back around her teacup. "Everything in my body was telling me not to rule. Everything." She swallows with an audible gulp. "I couldn't catch my breath when I thought about being Queen. Just someone bringing up the topic made me want to cry. I would wipe away the tears or hold them in, but I hated how it was an automatic response to the topic. I could feel myself panicking. I was so against the idea of ruling Enchenda that I was looking for any excuse not to do it." She traps him with her eyes. "Any excuse at all."

"But why?" he asks. "You would've been a great ruler."

Her head shake is vehement, hard. "You can't say that. Great rulers don't run from ruling. Whatever I may have had inside me before all of this, it's been killed by what I did. I can never be a great ruler in Fraun because I was not willing to be one. I couldn't do it." She pulls her shoulders up near her ears. "The first chance I had to run from it, to hand it over to someone else, I took." She lowers her shoulders and shakes her head more slowly. "That's not something a great ruler does."

Danyel hates the tortured expression on her face. He hates how he can feel her pain in his gut. "You made a mistake. Don't let it bother you so much. It's eating you up inside, I can tell."

She sucks in air, holds it in her lungs for a beat, and lets it out loudly. "That's the worst part. It doesn't bother me as much as I know it should. I made a bad choice when I chose to give control of my realm to Tin." Danyel nods, that is not a statement he would even dare disagree with. It's the one action she took before the war that even a true supporter, like he was, questioned.

"I had suspicions about his true character even then. But I did it because I was looking for a way out." Eselda can see on his face the moment it happens. The old picture of the perfect princess shatters. He is no longer looking at her like she's fragile and someone to protect. She's just like everyone else now. She's normal, flawed.

"I don't know what to say," he whispers.

Her heart pounds. Those words. Those are the words. She stands up, looking around her for more signs. The tent flap opens and Jordyn emerges, exactly like she knew he would. Her breathing quickens. "It's time," Jordyn calls.

She pours the rest of her tea on the embers of the fire and decides not to fight the words that are already bubbling in her throat. The line from the dream. "That's alright, neither do I."

Eselda wonders how to admit to Danyel that she's supposed to stay here. That in the dream she sat right here and let Rubina die. She knows the arguments for it: she's angry, she's already been through this once. But on the heels of their discussion of her last big mistake, she realizes she doesn't have the heart to make another one. Instead, she points toward the tent. "That's my cue," she says softly.

Danyel nods and smiles at his former princess. He sees the struggle on her face but reads the decision he sees there as well. "Tell her goodbye for me. For Enchenda," he says.

"I can do that," she answers. She heads for the tent, knowing that she's about to change the dream once and for all.

Chapter 41

"Although we have met many times recently, this is our regularly scheduled meeting of the council of rulers in Fraun. Thank you all for your attendance today," Hector greets. His voice booms through the very crowded new council building. Perhaps because of the sighting of the giants, citizens from all realms are filling every space around the room and in the attached viewing space. I have my chair pulled up close to the table to allow for someone to be standing behind me. "Let's get started," Hector continues. "First up, let's have Queen Sawchett update us on the new patrol."

Sawchett rises as Hector takes his seat. "There was a meeting in Sarcheda to discuss ideas for further action on the issue with giants. It was proposed that we send a group out to the north, opposite of where the giants have been spotted. They are looking for an area large enough to hold the entire Kingdom of Fraun, one with access to food and water and displaying, at most, a little evidence of animals. They departed a few suns ago and I have no updates from the group at this time. By the time we are scheduled to meet again, they are scheduled to have sent me an update. They are traveling with three roaches who have experience outside of Fraun. They are headed toward a location they believe may have many of the things they are looking for."

"You expect everyone in Fraun to just run?" a woman asks. I notice the scarf around her neck is orange, the color of Renchenda.

"This is merely an expedition of learning. We are curious if there is even space that would allow this to be an option if we feel it is necessary later," Sawchett answers.

"That tells me you think we could be in danger," the man behind me speaks up. I can't see him now but when I saw him earlier the muscles in the exposed arms indicated Sarcheda.

"We don't know what will happen in the future," I say. "But the group we assembled seemed to think it was wise to keep our options open."

"Was this your idea?" a man asks. He is standing to my right, behind Thometh. I've never seen him before but he wears a green shirt, the color of Enchenda. He looks like an average Fraunian, nothing about him would stick in my memory later, except for the hatred in his expression right now as he glares in my direction. My heartbeat speeds up, suddenly I have a bad feeling building in my gut.

"No, I don't believe it was." I look to Sawchett for confirmation.

"This idea was proposed by a citizen, I don't remember which realm they were from." Sawchett looks around the room. "Many of you were present, perhaps someone else will remember that detail?"

There are slowly shaking heads all around the room. Either no one remembers or they don't want to admit it.

"Well, never mind. It should suffice to say a citizen of Fraun proposed the idea. I called for the vote myself. If there are no other questions I can answer…" Sawchett waits for a few breaths before smiling and sitting back in her chair again.

Thometh clears his throat. "Next order of business, a shop in Renchenda is experiencing a lot of new sales. They have asked for permission to expand their business. There is enough room behind them to allow for this growth. Does the council have a problem with me granting the request?"

"Should we be building more if we will have to abandon

everything and run north?" a voice asks. I cannot see the speaker.

"Well, I suppose I don't know that," Thometh says. "I heard Queen Sawchett say this was only a precaution. In my opinion, it seems as though we should go on with life as we know it until this becomes something more serious. But I am only one man. What says the council?"

"I agree," Hector says.

"I agree as well," I say. "Call for a vote on the expansion."

"Now wait just a second." It's the angry man and once again his eyes are on me. "We are a Kingdom made up of five realms. Only three have had their opinion heard. You will wait to call your vote until all realms have had their say. Isn't that the way of the council?"

I'm surprised to hear voices shout up in agreement. What is happening? It's probably in my mind, but this group seems openly hostile today. "The vote would be for that purpose," I explain. I hold my hands flat in front of me in what I hope is a placating gesture. "I'm sorry if I gave the wrong impression. I'm afraid I don't recognize you, sir. What realm do you hail from?"

"Enchenda. One of the realms you didn't let speak on the issue. What if we don't want you to allow life to continue as normal? What if we think it would be wise to wait for the patrol to report back? What if we don't want to just blindly follow Sarcheda?"

"We were discussing Renchenda," I say. I see my confusion mirrored on Thometh's face just before the older king turns around to face the man behind him.

"Do you have a problem with the king of Sarcheda, good sir?" he asks.

The man shakes his head and pulls back a little. He puts up his hands in front of him as if to indicate he is done. Beats pass with the room frozen, Thometh staring at the citizen who looks ashamed with his hands up. Thometh breaks the image, turning back to the table. "Would the other realms please weigh in on the issue?"

Alerta raises her hand. "I see no problem with continuing life as we know it."

"Sawchett?" Thometh prompts.

"Although some citizens of Enchenda have mixed feelings on the issue, I am seeing it this way." She is pointedly looking at the man who spoke out earlier although he is now staring down at the floor, his arms crossed in front of his chest. "If we change the way we have done things and then nothing comes of the problem with the giants, we will have changed for nothing. That will be frustrating to businesses who have not been allowed to prosper. It will be frustrating for citizens who have changed their way of life for nothing. It will make children nervous."

She now allows her gaze to travel around the room. "If, on the other hand, we continue life as normal and then find it is necessary to leave Fraun, our building or buying didn't make the loss greater. The loss will be great either way. For this reason, I am in favor of continuing life as we have done. All in favor of allowing the business in Renchenda to expand to the land present, say aye."

"Aye," all five rulers call. Five hands reach into the air. The room stays silent.

"There is a business in Sarcheda experiencing similar growth who has made a similar request," I say.

"What kind of business?" a woman about three back from the lady in the orange scarf asks.

"I don't see how that is relevant," I say. It's also not something they asked of the Renchenda business. I look around the room and find a lot of angry sets of eyes focused on me. As I think about it I realize the hostility today has only been directed at me and only after I speak. Interesting. My eyes continue to travel the room, searching for someone. Someone I expect is connected to that hostility. While I search, I answer. "However, if you care to know I see nothing wrong with telling you that it is a clothing business. Specifically, the man makes gloves that are used in strength competitions." My eyes land on the man. Marcus is standing behind Alerta, wearing all black. He is watching the conversation with an odd smile on his face. His arms are crossed. He turns his head and catches me looking at him. He winks.

"Does he have the space to expand?" Thometh asks.

"Yes," I answer.

"Has this been confirmed?" someone calls.

I don't even know how to answer that. Before I can process what I should say to this, Hector speaks up. "It has never been the practice of the council to seek out the requesting business and confirm this for ourselves.

First of all, that would be time-consuming. Secondly, it would mean that we were saying we cannot trust you to tell us the truth in matters such as this. Do you really want the council to confirm all such requests themselves?" Silence stretches. "That's what I thought," Hector says. "All in favor of allowing the business in Sarcheda to expand, say Aye."

"Aye." Again all five rulers speak the word in unison and five hands rise.

"Any other business for us to discuss today?" Alerta asks.

"You'll find nothing else on the agenda, but this is not the way we let meetings end," Hector says. He stands up. "Something is going on here today. We cannot bury this contempt and still keep a healthy Fraun. We fought too hard to get where we are today. We are not leaving this room until we talk about what is going on. What is causing this harsh feeling?" Little pockets of mumbling around the room start, but nothing concrete. Nothing I can hear. "Come on now, speak up if you have something to say. We are all on the same journey here," Hector encourages. Still, there are rumblings, but I can't seem to find the source of the talking when I search the faces. No one is speaking up.

I know the source of the discomfort is somehow rooted in me. I have a feeling Marcus is behind this, but he continues to stand there looking smug. I decide to speak up. Maybe I'll calm some of them. Maybe I'll incite the conversation. What can it hurt? "There cannot be dissension at this table. We are one Fraun. We are balance and strength and open meetings. We are stronger than our past."

A hear a snort and a chuckle from somewhere behind me. I turn toward the sound and find a small woman shaking her head. "He only mentions our strength, did anyone else notice that?" Her eyes lock onto mine. "What about our humility, speed, mirth, and wisdom? Why didn't you mention those?"

"Because he only thinks of himself," someone calls.

I push my chair back and stand up. "I am not more important than this vision, not one among us is. I would gladly step down from my post in favor of another ruler if it would bring you peace of mind."

A man I recognize as the ambassador from Renchenda places a hand on the table and leans toward me. "But no other rulers exist now. You've killed everyone with Sarcheda blood, haven't you?"

Suddenly my ears are filled with the sound of conversation all around us. I'm aware of Sawchett's and Hector's among them. But I lean into the man. "Is that how you truly feel?" The room falls silent at my voice. "You think this was a choice? Perhaps you need more time with your Fraun history, friend." I straighten my body and give one more glance around the room. I'm done. I can't keep having this conversation. I make my way to the door of the council room. It's easier than I thought it would be as Fraunians are parting to make way for me. At the door, I turn back to the room. "I'll let the rest of the council finish rehashing history with you but I do want to make one thing clear. I have never killed anyone with the royal blood of Sarcheda in their veins. Never."

I hear the voices rise again as soon as the door is closed. Then I hear Hector's voice boom out over the din. "Stop talking and listen up. I'm only going through this once."

I shake my head and walk faster so I don't have to hear it. I'm tired of trying to convince everyone I'm worthy of this title. I know the council thinks I am. I know they believe I deserve the post and they support my throne.

Maybe that's part of the problem.

Chapter 42

This time the tavern holds seven men from various parts of Fraun all dressed in the colors of their realms. The man who works the tavern, serving wine to the patrons, is near the gathered group with his arms crossed over his chest, staring at the stranger who controls the meeting.

The various men in attendance stand in a sort of circle with the stranger in the center. He is not the tallest man in the group. He's not the youngest. He's not even the strongest. But his voice is deep and strong. Everyone in the group is silent, listening to what he has to say.

"You heard how the meeting went, some of you were there." Sounds of agreement echo around the circle. "You saw that false king and heard the stance on the giants yourself. You saw, when the conversation got heated, a king step away from the table and abandon the discussion. Is that truly what we want in a leader of Sarcheda?"

Many heads are nodding now, like branches in a steady wind. But the man who tends to the bar squints a little in confusion. The barman clears his throat. "But you all heard King Hector speak up for King Tutor.

You all heard what he said at the end there, right?" the barman asks. He looks to the men standing around the circle. "He told us to make our own investigations if we must. He told us they have no secrets, that everything they've done is out there for any citizen to see."

"I've done the investigation, my friend," the stranger says, drawing the eyes of the surrounding men back to him. "I am telling you that the problems are not imagined. This man who sits on the Sarcheda throne has killed."

"So have a lot of us," the bartender pushes. "Anyone who wielded a sword for Fraun a few annuals back has blood on their hands. You cannot undo that which has been done." He shakes his head. "Honestly, I'm starting to wonder why you want to. You are aware of what Tin did, right?"

He entreats those gathered near him with his eyes, willing them to hear reason. "You all know he lied, right? There wasn't a bit of truth in what that man was saying."

"Be careful," the stranger's voice crackles with the warning. "Do not speak ill of our last great king."

This time the man who works in the tavern fully focuses on the faces in the crowd, ignoring the man trying to take charge. "Why does he even talk of Tin like that?" he asks them. "Someone tell me what was so great about him." He slowly and deliberately looks at each face before speaking again. "He lied to us, he brought us to war, he damaged the name of our Realm in the eyes of Fraun." He throws out his arms in exasperation. "I'd rather have King Tutor than Tin," he says.

The silence in the room expands. The men can practically hear the eyelids opening and closing as the stranger blinks at the bartender. "Well," the stranger finally says. "That is an interesting point." He also turns his attention to the other men who have assembled. "Let us remember his opinion when the time comes to again choose sides."

"Choose sides?" the bartender squeaks. "What are you talking about? I thought we came here to discuss a plan for the giants." He shakes his head, sadness taking over most of his expression. "You all want to follow him into making a mess of things, fine." He turns his back on the group and heads back toward his bar. He's thinking he really should've turned in these little meetings when they first started happening. He's thinking he certainly won't allow them to use his tavern for the next meeting. He's thinking he can't believe what he's hearing out of these citizens who call themselves Fraunian.

He's not thinking about the enemy he's just made or how dangerous such a man can be.

Chapter 43

Ruling was not supposed to be like this. The thought comes into my head suddenly, like lightning. But then it stays. I feel it growing, wrapping around my other thoughts. Getting stronger. The giants, the doubt from my realm, the doubt from myself, the bold hatred. It wasn't supposed to be this way.

A man enters the room and bows before me. I smile at him, but the thought is still nagging away. How can this meeting go wrong? I wonder. It's not a productive thought.

"King Tutor, my family home is run down. Our roof is caving in. We need permission to rebuild," the man explains.

"Citizens do not need permission to rebuild broken structures," I say.

"We do if we'd like to build from scratch. I don't want another thrown together roof that will collapse again on my family. I don't want it to be uneven. I want a roof that is made for my house."

"That is not the way of Fraun," I say.

"I want a roof like yours. Why is it allowed for you?" he challenges.

I'm seated in front of my dining table, the back of my chair is pushed flat against the wood. I am facing out, toward the man. I am tired. I have heard three requests already this morning. For that reason, I reach my hand up intending to rub it along my face. I freeze. The man flinched.

Fear. I never wanted to run a realm on fear. I put my hands back on my lap and speak in a calm voice. "I inherited this house, as I'm sure you are aware. I have problems with the way it was constructed and doubts that it followed policy. But that does not mean that we should abandon those policies."

"King Tutor, I'm sorry to interrupt," an employee of mine has been stationed outside to help keep our waiting citizens in some semblance of a line. It's intended to keep things moving. Now, he is standing in the doorway. "Queen Alerta of Marchenda is here, Majesty. Should I let her in?" He glances at the family man in the middle of the room as though trying to determine if we are close to being finished.

"She can come in. We are discussing policy," I answer. I turn my attention back to the man. "Sorry for that interruption. As I was saying—"

"You won't let me build. That's what you were saying."

I force myself to take a calming breath. "No, I will not let you build brand new. It is not our way. What I will let you do is take the materials that made up your roof before and repurpose them with more care. They can be cut, they can be resized, they can be refinished. They cannot be wasted." The door opens again and Alerta enters like a summer breeze. She is wearing a yellow shirt and black pants, her hair is held back by a yellow ribbon, and her smile is large. She waves delicately at me and skirts the room, heading in my direction. It takes me a second to remember what I was talking about. "So, in summary, I am denying your request to build a new roof but reminding you that there are options."

"I'm not a builder by trade. How do you expect me to know how to do these things you speak of?" he asks.

"Ask a builder. I don't know the name of one offhand, but I can ask around for you. I'm sure we can find someone. I know you'll require assistance with the task. For that, be thankful you live in Sarcheda. There is no better place to find strong hands to help than here."

"Is there anything I can say to get you to change your mind?" he asks. His voice is calmer.

"What you ask sounds like a simple question. But in reality, you are asking if there is anything you can say to get me to allow you to break Fraun policy and build something new." I shake my head. "I'm sorry, there's nothing that will get me to do that. Even for a good family man like yourself."

"Fine. Thank you for your time." He turns to leave.

"Sir, one more thing," I call. He stops and turns back to face me. Alerta has dropped into the chair at my side. "Let me know, by letter or in person, when you are scheduled to begin the build. I would be honored to help."

The ghost of a smile crosses his face before he bows. By the time he straightens, it is gone. I turn my attention to Alerta as the door closes again. "Good morning."

"Sorry to interrupt," she says. She reaches out, grabs my hand, and squeezes it. "I thought you'd be finished by now and I wanted to see you."

"There were a lot of requests today or I would be done. Never be sorry for visiting, you are fresh air on a hot day." I lean in and kiss her lightly. I right myself just as the door opens. Alerta lets go of my hand, returning hers to her lap.

I let out a long breath and clench my jaw when the man in the doorway is visible. The man from the council, the angry man from Enchenda, is standing in my dining room. Again he wears the green of Enchenda, this time in the form of a cap he is holding and twisting in his hands. He stops halfway between the door and my seat and turns his attention to me. "King Tutor, I hope it isn't an inconvenience that I am here today," he says.

I squint at the man, confused. That is a different tone of voice today. Gone is the angry man. "It is fine, what can I help you with?" I ask.

"I wanted to apologize for the way I acted at the council meeting. I was given some information that I believed without researching it myself. It made me angry and I acted on that."

"I appreciate the apology."

"I wanted you to know that I have done the research myself now. I have talked to citizens who fought in the war for Fraun. I have talked to Fraunians who knew you before the war and even some who know you now.

The information we have been fed about what kind of person you are..." He shuffles his feet and looks uncomfortable for a second. Then he meets my eyes. "They're all wrong, Majesty. The things that they're saying."

"Who is 'they'?" I ask.

"What kinds of things are they saying?" Alerta asks, her voice overlapping with mine.

"I don't feel right giving you names, but I can say that they are citizens who attend more council meetings and are closer to you than I am. For this reason, many Fraunians are believing the accounts they are hearing." He turns his head so that he is looking at Alerta. "As for what kinds of stories we are hearing, they are many but they all have the same idea. The stories paint King Tutor as a violent man who brings death to his enemies. There are stories of bloodshed during his time in Farcheda before the war broke out. There are stories that he killed scouts who didn't want to join the fight. Rumors that he came for Tin's head the second he learned of his majority blood and took Sarcheda's throne by delighting in killing the former king. There is even a story that he carried the sword with the blood of the former king through the streets of Sarcheda after the final battle." He drops his chin to his chest. "I'm ashamed to admit I believed these things because the source seemed credible."

I stand up and take a step toward the man. Perhaps a stronger proof that he believes the truth he has uncovered is here when he remains in the same position as I approach him. He does not flinch and he does not step back. "Let us hope that more Fraunians will do the work you have done and seek the truth," I say. I offer him my hand.

He picks his head up, smiles, and shakes my hand. "I am doing my best to be as vocal as I can about what I have learned."

"You need to be more vocal than the other side, good sir. We appreciate you on our side," Alerta says.

"After the real stories, Majesty, how could I not be?" He drops his voice to a whisper. "What Tin wanted to do to Fraun is terrible. We don't need a dictator and he would've won that war if you hadn't been waiting there on the steps of the castle. I know that now."

I'm overwhelmed by this change of heart. I step to the man and do something I know he isn't expecting. I pull him into a hug. "Support can mean everything to someone," I tell him. I pull out of the hug and shake his hand again. "Thank you."

"Thank you," he says. He turns his attention to Alerta, waving one hand. "Thank you as well, Majesty. I hope you both have a wonderful day."

When he is gone I turn to Alerta and widen my eyes. "Well, that was unexpected."

"Do you feel better?" she asks.

"I do." I take my seat again. "I needed that little bit of faith, that little support, I think."

"Do you think we should do something about the rumor spreader?"

"I think we have no proof that Marcus is behind this."

"But you believe it is him?" she asks.

I think for a minute. The man said it was someone close to me. "Yes."

"Are you going to try and find proof?"

"If I am right, the proof will have its day." I'm in no hurry right now. For the first time in a long time, I feel content.

Maybe everything will be alright.

Chapter 44

Sawchett walks out to her garden just as the sun is reaching its highest point in the sky. She expects to be alone, expects to take some time to sit and enjoy the sun. Maybe read over the letters that were sent with business to address, which she carries in her hand. But, more likely, to enjoy the sun and then regret that she never looked at those letters.

Instead, there are two young citizens the queen recognizes from town sitting in her backyard garden. Her time with the scouts in the past has made her wary. Her guard is instantly up, her nerves pulled tight like the strings on the bow she no longer carries. "Hello," she hesitantly greets. "Can I help you with something?"

The woman rises and bows. "Majesty, my name is Tanya and this is my brother Jeff. A servant in your home let us in. I hope that is alright."

If these people were here to harm her, it wouldn't be acceptable. But Sawchett isn't sure how to explain that without offending them if they have good intentions. "I'm sure he had his reasons for allowing you entrance. What can I do for you?"

"We live along the border of Enchenda, over by Farcheda," the man, Jeff, says. With his left hand, he gestures in the direction he speaks.

"Yes." Sawchett draws out the syllable, trying to make her confusion and mild annoyance clear.

"A roach arrived yesterday with a letter for you. He was sick, Majesty. We told him we would take the letter ourselves. The roach is resting up in our backyard, the medicine man doesn't really know much about how to treat them. The roach could die," Tanya says.

Sawchett's eyes widen. "A letter for me? From whom?"

"We aren't sure. We didn't open it. That wouldn't be proper." Jeff takes the rolled parchment from somewhere behind him, holding it out to the queen.

Sawchett glances down. She will have to step closer to him to reach the letter. She returns her gaze to his face and watches him carefully as she takes slow steps until she is close enough. Finally, she latches her hand onto the parchment. She tugs lightly and he lets go, offering a smile. Sawchett steps back again before allowing her eyes to look over the roll. One can never be too careful, even among Fraunians she recognizes. "Why isn't this sealed?" she asks. Her voice is sharp with the edges of the accusation.

"We don't know," Tanya says. "It arrived like that, honest. We have done nothing with it."

"It came from the woods," Jeff offers. "Perhaps whoever sent it didn't have access to a seal or wax."

"Perhaps," Sawchett says. She grasps the top of the letter and unrolls. The parchment isn't long, perhaps a click in length. She sees a name at the bottom that she recognizes, Erick. She slackens her grip, allowing it to roll back up as she smiles at the faces before her. "This letter is from a dear friend of mine who travels with a patrol north of Fraun. Thank you for bringing this to me."

Tanya bows again. "We will leave you, Majesty."

"Is there anything you can do for the roach?" Jeff asks. His voice is timid, suddenly.

The fear that they may be here to threaten or endanger her is gone now. In its absence, Sawchett takes a moment to study the pair. Tanya and Jeff, although Fraunians she recognized, are not citizens she has seen much of. They have never been before her to ask for anything, they are not business owners that she regularly deals with. The only reason she recognizes them is that they volunteer at the school like Sawchett does herself. She has seen them leaving a few times as she is arriving. Both appear to be barely older than Sawchett herself. The siblings have skin like cinnamon and arms strong from hard work. Their hair is dark. Tanya's flows down to just below her armpits but is as straight as a blade. Jeff's locks lay back in loose waves as though he constantly runs his fingers back through it. They are both, Sawchett decides, beautiful.

"I'm afraid I don't know anyone more adept at working on roaches than our medicine man. I have a stable here in Enchenda where a few of the employed roaches sleep and eat. There is a man who works back there." Sawchett points off in the direction of the stable. "You are welcome to ask him, but I'm not sure what he can do to help."

Tanya's dark eyes sparkle. "Wonderful, we will visit him. Thank you." She rushes toward Sawchett, offering her hand to shake the queens. When Sawchett is too slow to realize what is happening, Tanya reaches down and grabs the hand herself. She wraps both hers around it and shakes. "Honestly, thank you. We couldn't bear to watch him die without at least trying to help."

"I understand," Sawchett answers. "Good luck."

Jeff grabs his sister's arm and pulls her away from the queen. "Let's go find him now."

The siblings head off in the direction of the stables leaving their queen frozen in her garden, watching them walk away. She smiles to herself, thinking about what Tutor told her. Thinking that, perhaps, a mate for her will have to come from an ordinary citizen. Perhaps from a caring-for-all-creatures, cinnamon-skinned, citizen.

Her attention refocuses on the scroll in her hand once the pair is out of sight. Sighing, she unrolls it again and reads.

Sawchett,
The area the roach led us to is large enough to house the entirety of your Kingdom.
As you requested an update, we will send this letter. Honestly, this is all we know at this time. We have yet to determine if the rest of your conditions will be met inside this space.
Will report back soon.

Erick

She re-rolls the scroll and frowns. The truth is this was her idea. Sure, the citizens supported it and even suggested it, but this idea was cultivated from a version of her idea. She wholeheartedly supports this planning if things with the giants escalate. But having the idea come this small step closer to reality has her stomach dropping. Sawchett doesn't want to leave Fraun. She did that once. Then she realized how important it was to her, how great it could be. Now she's here, building that. For a heartbeat she thought abandoning all of it and starting over could help. They'd have no reminders of the agony and misdirection that came before them, no reminders of the pain they endured if they ran. But doesn't that thought make her as bad as *him*? She shudders at the thought even without allowing herself to think his name. Tin always frightened her.

She looks around the large garden, the seats that have been placed there, the house her family has lived in for generations. This kingdom has built so much. They have grown together. She doesn't want to start over. She doesn't want to leave.

With any luck, they won't have to.

Chapter 45

"Has Sawchett always been in your life?" Alerta asks. Her head is resting on my stomach. We are splayed out among the plants in Marchenda enjoying the smell of the garden and the feeling of being invisible amongst all the bustle of work. My eyes are closed to further enhance the heat radiating through my body from everywhere her skin touches mine. Her question is out of nowhere after beats of blissful silence. I scrunch my closed eyes in confusion. "What?"

"Sawchett is your sister, yes?" she asks.

Now my eyes open. I pick my head up off the ground to look at the beautiful Queen. Her head is still resting right where I left it, her hand still tracing lazy lines up and down my calf. "Yes, why do you ask?"

"You've just never talked about your childhood or your past."

Oh. "It's not something I like to talk about."

"That's fine." I cannot see her face but I get the distinct impression it's not at all fine. She sounds hurt.

"But you told me about Lucas and Stef. Would you like to hear about my past?" I offer. She pushes herself to a sitting position and turns to face me. Her dress is black and accented with yellow ribbons and stitching. It clings to her in a distractingly seductive way.

"I would love to hear about it," she says, all hints of sadness dissolving from her tone.

I force myself to focus, to not be distracted by the feelings I have for her. The feelings that get stronger with each passing sun. "I was born in Enchenda. My mother was the secret half-sister of the seated king at the time. King Gregario knew who she was, but no one else did. She was ordered not to have children so when I was born I was sent to live with a family in Farcheda." Alerta leans to the side, propping her arm on my legs. I take a deep breath and enjoy the burning for a beat before continuing.

"The family I lived with knew only that no one could ever know of my birth parents. One day the old man was in a shop and overheard someone whispering my mother's name. He focused in on the conversation and thought he also overheard some other words. The story I heard from the shopkeeper was that the old man got spooked and ran out of the shop without paying." I sigh. The digging I've done into my past over the annuals has been painful. Somehow sharing it with her is easier than I thought it would be.

"We moved to Renchenda. I finished school there and then I was expected to figure out what to do with my life." I reach out and run my fingers through Alerta's hair, no longer able to contain the urge. She closes her eyes and tips her head toward my hand. She is as much a slave to this age marker as I am, but we are learning how to control it together. "I thought I wanted to be a scout. I spent some time touring with them. Somehow, I ended up in Enchenda. Have you ever spent time in Enchenda?"

"No, I can't say that I've ever been there for a long period of time. I've passed through once or twice and, of course, I've had dinner with Sawchett," she answers.

"Well, it's beautiful there. I fell in love with the realm and the citizens who call it home. On the edge of the realm, there is a group home where Fraunians without family connections can live. It is free room and board but you have to be a productive member of the realm. I stayed there for a while, worked in a few local shops. The group home is where Charlotte found me."

"Charlotte is your mother?" she asks. This is something she knows. The question is a test. Can I admit that? Her eyes turn up to watch my face.

I smile. "Yes. She found me at the group home and took me under her wing. She got me a job tutoring the princess of Enchenda. Sawchett was already one annual by that time. She told me the truth about the girl, although she swore me to secrecy. So I was one of a few citizens who knew she was Charlotte's daughter. Eventually, Charlotte told me the truth about who I was. I guess I never spoke it out loud, but I knew that made Sawchett my sister."

"What did the citizens think? The neighbors and such. Did they know anything about you?"

"Not that I know of. We didn't tell anyone about our relationship. I knew and she knew." I shrug. "We never talked about it again after she told me."

Alerta sighs, the sound heavy. "I can't imagine how much guilt she must have felt. There you were, alive and well, but she had nothing to do with it. All that pain of hearing how you had to run to Renchenda…the fact that you wanted to join the scouts." She puts the hand not supporting her weight on her chest and shakes her head. "I cannot imagine how much it would pain me to see Stef living in a home for children with no families. That feeling that I failed her would bury me."

I'm too shocked to speak. I've never thought about that. Charlotte was a regular visitor to that group home, I know that. The boys all recognized her when she came in. Was she searching for me? Was she hoping I would come back? "Do you think she regretted sending me away?" I ask.

"How could she not?" Alerta sits up and scoots closer to me. "You were her child. Her first child. That is special, I promise you."

I have talked about this before. I explained parts of this story to Eselda. I explained parts of it to Jordyn. But today, for some reason, I feel the pain in new ways. My heart is breaking. "She threw me away," I whisper. "Why didn't she fight to raise me herself?"

Alerta touches my cheek. "She was scared. I bet she regretted it the second you left Enchenda. I bet she wished she could take it all back."

"I don't understand what I'm feeling right now," I admit. "There's always been this anger inside of me. I knew that the couple who raised me was not my family, they were good to me but they made that clear. When I learned who Charlotte really was, I was angry because it took her that long to claim me. Then, when I got to her house and saw that tiny baby lying in blankets in a basket, I was so angry I saw red."

"Because they kept her?" she asks.

"Yes." I nod. "What made her so special?" I shake my head. "No, that's not what I mean. Sawchett is special, even I know that. She is smart and creative. It's not about her, it's…" I trail off because I can't explain it.

Alerta kisses me on the cheek. I don't know when she got close enough to be able to reach me that way but I appreciate the shock of heat. "You wonder why you weren't enough?" she offers.

I have thought that before. I have said a version of that before. But to hear her whisper it hurts all over again. I close my eyes against the sudden stinging sensation. The feelings running through me are not ones that I relish confronting. The pain is still so fresh, even after all these annuals and everything we have been through.

"I never met Charlotte. I am only speculating here, but I imagine Sawchett got the life she did because of you," Alerta whispers. My eyes open and narrow. She has my attention even if I don't know where she's going with this. "Charlotte regretted how she behaved when you were born. She was in pain, Tutor. When Sawchett was born she couldn't allow herself to do that again. She couldn't let another baby have that life. Sawchett didn't get to spend her childhood with Charlotte because she was more special than you were. She got that childhood because she was just as special as you and Charlotte could not give her special child away again."

I don't have words to explain what is happening inside me at that moment. The anger dissolves and leaves me feeling lighter. I smile and it's a real smile. More real than most of the ones I have been giving lately. Maybe, just maybe, I can make peace with this past. I reach up and bury my hands in Alerta's hair, pulling her close. Then I lean in and kiss her. Without all the anger still pent up in my belly, the inferno we generate is even better.

Chapter 46

Tutor,

I received another update from the patrol. They can confirm there is a sustainable food source already growing wild, although they were unclear what it was. There appears to be good soil for farming as well. They are drinking water from a source they found, but it is too far away right now. With luck, they will come up with an idea for diverting the water for daily use. Erick believes this land is usable, but it will take a lunar cycle to get it ready if that becomes necessary.

That's all I know right now.

With love,
Sawchett

I roll up the parchment, a smile fixed to my face. "Everything well?" Alerta asks from her spot beside me.

"Yes." I hand her the scroll and watch her face light up as she reads. "That sounds promising," she says. I watch as she slips the parchment into a bag she carries. "Shall we continue?" She gestures out toward the town of Sarcheda, which we had been about to embark upon. Alerta is visiting a lot lately and in the last lunar cycle, our courtship has grown into something comfortable. Today, Stef has come along as well. The two will provide support as I conduct the school visit for Sarcheda. An outdated practice, if you ask me, but one the citizens and council claim to enjoy and see the importance in.

We continue walking, noticing many adults out along the route. Alerta slips her hand into mine a few houses away from my residence. I turn my head to smile at her and notice Stef has clasped the hand on the other side. It is a comfortable warmth that flares in my chest. I am starting to think this may not be exclusively the age marker that I feel.

When we arrive at the school, the students are gathered around the outside of the grassy lawn in a loose circle. In the center of the circle, someone has stacked nine blocks. This demonstration is not meant to take a title or break a record. It is a tradition for the school visit to begin with a strength demonstration from the royal presenting. I give Alerta's hand a single squeeze and make my way to the makeshift arena.

I do not speak. I simply take a deep, centering breath. My eyes slip closed on the second inhale and do not open again until the exhale is complete. Then I bend at the knees, squatting before the blocks and wrapping my arms around the lowest. I inhale again and on the exhale straighten my knees. The blocks lift easily. In one fluid motion, I push my arms straight above my head. The children cheer more wildly than their parents likely would at the show. I reverse my motions, setting the blocks back on the ground. This is done intentionally. When we lift blocks that are light for us we often set them back to the ground to show it was simple. If the blocks were the limit of our strength we would drop them quickly, sometimes even throwing them.

After the blocks are set, I clear my throat and begin reciting the text of the visit. I have given this speech since the war. I helped to write the new ending. But it isn't until I am starting it that I realize it may need revisions again, this part we left in about the giants suddenly feels outdated. I launch into the speech as written, only slightly ashamed I hadn't noticed the flaw earlier.

"The world we inhabit now was once a land of giants. The giants built massive cities of all materials they could find. No material was sacred. No land was spared. The giants created much and used more than they needed. During the time of the giants, our citizens lived quiet lives. Hidden among the houses of the giants, repurposing items the giants forgot, our kind survived. It was a lonely existence, never knowing if others lived on. But all that changed when the giants declared war on each other.

"For years, blasts and fighting were the sounds that filled the world. Our kind stayed holed up in the homes, hidden from the battle we didn't understand. When the silence began, we waited. After a time our scouts went out to find the giants all dead or gone. One man, Oberian, began to organize us." I slowly turn my body a quarter of the way around the circle, to face a different group of students. The teachers have arranged them from youngest to oldest, I deliver the part about the giants while facing our youngest citizens. As the speech goes on, I face older students.

"Bonded together by our mutual fear of an outcome similar to the giants we organized cities from the ruins of the giant villages. Fraun became our name, and Oberian our king. Oberian proved himself a good man and an honest ruler. He established many laws to keep us safe. We learned to use only what we needed and waste not, to rectify the wrongs of the giants who had died for this error. Under the rule of Oberian, Fraun became strong.

"But men, even great men, do not live forever. Oberian died, passing the rule of Fraun to his only son. Oberian the Second believed it was his right, and our duty, to amass his wealth and power. The citizens of Fraun were commissioned to build a palace for their king, which stands in Fraun to this day. The king took three wives in his time, having five boys born to him before his death. He was a greedy man, but he was not all bad.

"In the wake of the giants we were not the only race who rose. During the time of Second, we learned of large bugs who had survived and created the society of Roach. Second ordered scouts to travel to Roach and speak with them. No treaty could be reached. Instead, Second ordered a war. Frightened of this word, Fraunians hesitated. Second was an insistent man, and war ensued." I turn my body again, now facing those who fall into the oldest half of the school-aged children.

"We were triumphant, and the inhabitants of Roach became a part of Fraun. Many of them took jobs as servants in exchange for food and homes. They are small to the ground, many-legged, and fast. They are excellent warriors and they mind not being ridden into battle. Earning their partnership was the legacy of Second.

"After the death of this king, the sons wanted to avoid a fight over the throne. The brothers agreed upon a plan to divide the power five ways. Absolute power, they claimed, was dangerous to Fraun. Each realm would have a royal family to rule them. In the realm, your ruler would be the final word. The five realms would be numbered, the royal family of the first realm would lead the council of rulers. The council would vote on all decisions affecting Fraun as a whole. No decision would be carried forth without a majority vote of the council.

"The numbering of realms would be flexible. The council can choose to renumber at any time in favor of a strong ruler, a weak ruler, or majority blood. Rule of the realm would pass through families, descendants of the great brothers who gave their names to our realms." Finally, I turn myself until I am facing the oldest students. The ones who may have been influenced by the man I am about to speak of. I watch their faces as I finish the speech.

"After annuals of ruling in this way, without any need for change, one king took the life of a prince. He claimed responsibility for the death and declared war on Fraun. The council, blindsided by the anger and the declaration, threw together an army to stand for our Kingdom. Scouts, defects of Fraun who choose to live outside our boundaries, came to our aid. With their help, Fraun was able to rally and come back stronger than ever." I am impressed by what I see. No outward hatred, no festering anger. This is promising.

I throw my hands up and deliver the final lines in a loud triumphant voice. "Today, representatives join those rulers of royal blood at the meetings. We stand, shoulder to shoulder, to make Fraun stronger than it ever was."

A loud cheer erupts from the children seated on the lawn. After a beat, someone stands and continues the clapping. I bow a little, feeling pride swell my chest at the show of support.

I turn until I find Alerta and Stef in the crowd. They are also standing and cheering. Alerta offers me a thumbs up and wink.

Everything is going to be fine.

Chapter 47

Again, the mysterious stranger sits in the shadows at the back of a room. He is alone, waiting for one other person to join him. But this time he is not at the tavern. He is no longer welcome at the tavern. The employee there has made his choice and it will not be forgotten.

Finally, the younger man enters the dimly lit room. He crosses to the table and sits in the only other empty chair. "Thank you for inviting me to your home," he starts. "Are we here to talk about the giants?"

"No. That is a stunt," the stranger answers. "It is a story concocted by the imposter and his friends to scare everyone into following them. It's working, too, which is the worst part of the whole thing. Just look at the Fraunians who have started following the disgrace since the announcement. The bartender at the tavern is just the latest example." He curls his upper lip in disgust.

"What makes you so sure it is a stunt?"

The man gets up from his table and fetches a small bottle of fermented drink from the shelf. He pours two hearty glasses, sets them down, and waits for his guest to take a drink. "Every single person who has confirmed the story is a friend of the false king." He waves his hand dismissively. "It's not important, trust me." He takes a sip of his wine. "Tell me, who have you found for me?"

The younger man runs his hand down his face as if trying to wipe away stress lying under the skin. "Do you honestly still believe Tutor is a disgrace to the name of Sarcheda? After everything King Hector shared with us, after all the things citizens have been saying. Are you still so sure that you are right?"

The stranger leans forward, putting his entire face into the small light from his ceiling. From this angle, the younger man can see the anger written plainly on his face. "I didn't ask you to think. I asked you to find me someone who could lead Sarcheda. Do you not believe in a strong Sarcheda?"

"No, I do." The younger man rapidly shakes his head, eager to be supportive of this pillar of the community. "There just haven't been a lot of citizens willing to talk to me lately. There are some in every realm who are starting to take his side."

"That is bad news, indeed." The stranger cracks his knuckles and the sound echoes through the room.

"You know Tutor stands by the claim that he was not the one to end Tin's life. You heard that. You were there. I'm thinking he can learn—"

The mysterious stranger stands slowly, his every move calculated. He leans down until his nose is practically touching the other man's. "Stop thinking," he commands in a stern but quiet voice. "Leave that to the weak men and women of Renchenda." He wrinkles his nose when he says the name of the other realm as if the name smells of rotten food. "I no longer require your services."

The younger man never sees the blade drawn from the sheath on the old man's left hip. He draws it deftly and has it buried to the hilt in the man's chest before he can even think to move or respond. Marcus cocks his lips in a half-smile, watching the blood sputter from the younger man's lips and the life drain from his eyes. He watches until the body slumps in the chair. He watches as the weight shifts and the body drops to the floor with a sickening thud.

Then he wipes the blade along the shirt of the man and returns the cleaner knife to his sheath. He finishes both glasses of wine. He opens his front door, the smell of the bakery wafting on the air. A young man is nearby, moving bags of ingredients. "You," Marcus calls. "Come here."

He waits in his doorway for the young man to approach. When they are face to face, Marcus leans enough to the left to allow the boy to see into the dark room. "I will pay you well to remove that body for me."

The boy trembles. "What exactly would you like me to do with him?" he asks.

"I'll take care of everything. I'm not asking you to be secretive. I will take responsibility for this death the way a true king would." He lays his hand on the boys' shoulder. "When I am King of Sarcheda I will remember that you helped me. I will take care of you and your family."

"You're going to be King?" the boy asks.

Marcus smiles. "There is no one else who loves Sarcheda enough to kill for it. I am doing this for us. It is time for Sarcheda to be great again."

Chapter 48

Toby stands up and stretches his limbs. "I am going for a quick swim in the pond. Anyone care to join?" he asks. The group of sleepy scouts all shake their heads. It has been a long, hot day. Today, they needed to gather more food. They took an excursion out to the woods to find and take down an ant. This can be quite a task, owing to the large size of the creatures and their tendency to never be alone. Jordyn was able to find three ants away from the group. Toby isolated one while Kurt took the creature's life as quickly as possible. Evelyn led the group in giving thanks before the body was transported back to their camp.

Even that task alone would have exhausted the crew. But once back at the camp, the ant still needed to be taken apart, the exoskeleton removed, the meat treated and prepared. Now, as the sun just begins its path down the sky, the tasks are ending and the group is exhausted.

Toby waves dismissively at the tired faces. "Fine, I'll be back shortly." He treks off to the pond, recently developed after some rains, strips off his clothes and wades in. He is unsure how long he spends in the water, lazily swimming around in circles. The cool water feels wonderful on his skin. He can feel his temperature drop to something more acceptable.

He swims to the shore, slips his clothes on and runs his fingers through his hair. He can't bring himself to walk back to the camp right now. Instead, he flops down on the ground, leaning back and closing his eyes against the setting sun.

He doesn't think, just breaths. He can feel himself drifting off to sleep and doesn't fight it. He is confident they are safe here. They have never seen anything out here that is too large for him to handle. That thought gives him pause. The giants are that big, he supposes. But they are under watch by the visitors from Fraun. They are always under watch.

He sighs, slowing his breathing again. The sun is so warm on his face. He revels in the warmth.

Without warning the sun cuts out and Toby startles awake. His eyes fly open, thinking he may have fallen asleep and night has fallen. No, the truth is more shocking.

A huge eye, blue and wide, is looming over him. His breath catches in his throat as the eye retreats. This allows Toby to see the face of a giant come into view. He's small for a giant but still larger than Toby could've ever imagined up close. Curly brown hair frames the young face. As Toby watches, panic paralyzing him, the giant tips its head to the side. The expression that crosses its face can only be described as confused.

"What are you?" it booms.

Empowering

Sawchett

Empowering Sawchett was first published in the summer of 2021. By now you recognize the pattern and know this is Sawchett's story. It's driven by the question: what happens when everything you love is threatened and you may not be able to save it?

It's time to admit something about the titles of this series. The adjectives chosen were always about the Kingdom of Fraun more than they were about the characters who live there. We broke it in book 1, we redeemed its ideals in book 2. In book 3 we had to train it up again, without the issues and secrets. Then, in book 4 we had to empower the people of Fraun to have the courage to do what needed to be done in the face of trouble and danger. I considered the adjectives of evaluating or saving for the title, but at the end of the day empowering was the right choice. I'm happy with it.

Did I always know the series was going to end this way? No. I actually considered a lot of possibilities. But at the end of the day, this one was the most realistic and the most true to the characters.

I had to consider all of the major and minor characters we'd grown to love and give them an ending they deserved. For this reason, a lot of people make a comeback in this one. Look for your favorites, they're probably on the page somewhere.

Ready for those fun facts?

1. I mentioned not always knowing how this one was going to end, which is true, but I always knew Toby would do the drastic thing he does in this one. It's been in my handwritten notes since I started writing notes for the series.
2. My favorite character in this one is probably Toby. I put that poor guy through a lot and he came out stronger. Sorry, dude. Truly.
3. My favorite scene to write in this one was probably the epilogue. If you're the kind of person who skips Epilogues, maybe don't skip this one. It's the bow on the series that we really needed.

I've always said I wrote the finale of this series to be what everyone needed it to be. Healing, empowering, and freeing. Enjoy it.

Tabatha

Prologue

"The new building is being erected right in the heart of Fraun. They know to expect you there and to give you time and space needed. We want you to give this living history a voice."

"I will paint it. I will give those one hundred seventy-four individuals the recognition they deserve. Then you will sit under it to meet and remember the thousands who aren't being put up there. The ones being tracked only in the medicine tents. You will remember that those citizens are as important to what you do day in and day out as the names I will paint. You remember that and maybe Fraun has a chance."

"Actually, those citizens are more important."

Chapter 1

I will never get used to people calling me "Majesty". So when the poor girl standing on her front lawn along the path to the town square hollers it and waves, the smile I give her is probably more like a wince. I don't mean to be rude but I hate that word. I'm barely thirteen annuals. By Fraun standards, I'm not even an adult yet. I can speak, that happened at five annuals. My full height, two marks and three clicks, was reached at ten annuals. I am also fully developed, if you know what I mean. But in the Kingdom of Fraun, we are not considered adults until fifteen annuals when our hair ceases to grow. Mine is currently longer than I'd like it to be. The straight yellow hair already brushes my waist. I can't imagine what it will be like after almost two more annuals of growth. My arms already ache when I reach to the ends to brush it out. All that is a constant reminder of how ridiculous it is to have people in Enchenda refer to me as "Majesty". I'm not considered an adult, my hair isn't done growing, and I actually hate my long hair. How regal is all that? Answer, it's not. Of course, it's also not the fault of Enchenda's citizens that they have the youngest Queen in the history of

Fraun. So, I return the child's wave and keep moving.

It really is a beautiful day today. I have plenty of things I should be doing inside the royal home. I have letters to answer, I have a patrol to check in on, and I have cooking I should probably get to. Today just felt like one of those days when I couldn't remain indoors any longer. It's as if the sunshine and air were calling to me. I knew I had a meeting in the town square so I took that excuse as an opportunity to get out of the house. If I head straight there, I will be early.

As I walk, my attention is pulled to a group of citizens sitting on the ground along the side of the road. I think I notice them simply because they're not doing anything. They're just sitting in a circle on a lawn. Citizens in Enchenda are not normally static for long, we find things to do. We will usually occupy ourselves with tasks for the greater good. What could be the reason for this relaxed mood from this group?

I approach the group as casually as I can; hands in the pockets of my skirt, smile affixed to my face, and slow steps. If I come at them like some crazy royal who wishes to judge them for their inaction I will only incite anger and resentment. "Good morning," I call. "Is there anything I can assist with today?"

The circle holds five citizens of various ages and heights. Most, if not all, appear to be adults. I recognize a few faces but cannot think of a single name. I refuse to let myself acknowledge the fact that this may mean I am spending too much time outside of this town at council meetings or in other realms. The man farthest from the road, and my position, bobs his chin in my general direction. I don't recognize him with his skin the color of the sky at twilight. "Queen Sawchett, good morning."

It turns out "Queen" is just as irritating as "Majesty".

"We are not getting into any trouble, Majesty," the woman beside him says. She has dark hair that bunches in tight curls close to her head. Her skin is the color of warm sand on the shores of River Fraun.

"I accused you of nothing, I assure you. I merely wondered if there was something you needed help with this morning." I tilt my head a little to the right. "What are the tasks we must accomplish today?"

The man directly in front of me looks the most familiar to me. His pale skin looks somehow warm. He reminds me a little of my brother, King Tutor. He turns to look at me now and I read irritation in the deep green eyes. "Are you implying we cannot have a moment of levity or relaxation?"

The truth of that stings. When did I become a Queen who would force such behavior? What was my intended purpose this morning? Could I not turn the question on myself? "Not at all. You are entitled to such pleasantries." Now my smile is real. "I'm sorry, I am out of sorts this morning. In fact, perhaps I can join you?"

They must sense a change in my tone of voice. The man with twilight skin nods again, this time with a smile. "That's more like it." He moves himself a little to the right, leaving a gap on his left. "My name is Drew. Please, have a seat."

I take my time walking around the assembled group. When my eyes return to the pale stranger who called out my arrogance, they linger. "You look familiar to me. Have we met?" I ask.

"I once helped you move a few pieces of furniture from your residence to a couple in Farcheda," he answers.

The memory comes back instantly. Tutor and I had been cleaning out an old room because I had noticed a crib for a baby buried deep within the abandoned furniture. We'd had everything that may be useful for the infant sent to Sieven and Abney, dear friends of mine. I also recall this man drawing my brother's attention. At the time I didn't notice what Tutor was implying. Now I realize he must have thought the boy was flirting with me. "I do remember you now. Did I catch your name then?"

He meets my eyes directly and the sparkling green reminds me so much of Eselda that, for a heartbeat, my breath catches in my throat. "I don't believe so, Milady. I am Bin."

"Actually, you know his Pa. At least I think you do," the woman with the dark hair speaks up. I turn my attention to her.

"Do I?"

"His Pa fought with us for Fraun. Gave his life for your cause." She lays her hand on her chest, her face a perfect mask of sadness. "You knew Lance, of Enchenda? This here is Lance's youngest boy." Her attention turns to Bin and the frown is replaced by a motherly smile. "But I suppose we can't call you young much longer, can we? Passed his tenth annual, he did."

I drop myself comfortably into the empty spot on the grass and look around the man named Drew to the woman who is speaking. "I did know Lance. He was a fine man and someone I trusted with my life." I turn to Bin. "I am sorry for your loss." Bin's eyes drop as if the sadness itself weighs them down. I return my attention to the woman. "What is your name, maiden?" Technically, Maiden may be an incorrect title for this woman. She appears to be older than the rest in the crowd. This close I can see wrinkles in her face that my mother didn't develop until she was over thirty annuals.

"We've met, actually. My sister, Annabeth, is your Ambassador."

"Oh, of course. Yes, I'm sorry for my lapse in memory." I roll through the facts and names that are stored in my head, trying to come up with a name. My ambassador is someone I meet with regularly and consider a friend. She is a medicine woman, or was before being my ambassador took up most of her time. I do recall her mentioning a sister before. I remember the name was unique. It comes to me quickly, "Shell, right?" I hope I'm right.

Her entire face lights up. "Yes. You have a good memory, Majesty."

"Please, call me Sawchett. I hate formal titles." I glance around the group again. "Okay, so I have Drew, Shell, and Bin." I point to each as I name them. "Who are you two, if you don't mind my asking?" I look to my right at the remaining two members of the circle who are holding hands between them. I realize with a start that I do recognize one of the women, the one with cinnamon skin and straight brown hair. I remember her coming to my home once with her brother to deliver a letter. "Actually, I remember you. You're Tanya, aren't you?" I ask, pointing in her direction.

"I am. This is Enya." She brushes Enya's shoulder lightly with her free hand.

"It's a pleasure to meet all of you. What were you discussing this fine morning before I rudely interrupted?" I ask.

A little chuckle comes leaking out of Bin. "Actually Tanya was updating us on the health of a roach she's become attached to, if you can believe that."

Tanya throws up her free hand. "Okay, you don't have to say it like that."

"Like what?"

"Like you're judging me. Like you think making friends with another species is ridiculous. He was sick when I met him and he needed help. We've bonded as he's been healing. It's not unusual."

"Wait," I say, breaking her tirade. I reach toward her. "Is this the roach who delivered the letter for me?"

"Yes," she says.

"He's healing?" I'm pleased to hear this. I throw my hand across my chest and give a relieved sigh. "Thank Fraun."

Bin laughs again. "You make friends with animals as well?"

"You could say that," I say. I tip my head back and whistle one long continuous note for a count of three. The group is now staring at me like I may have lost my mind. I hold up one finger, the universal sign for "wait for it".

The sound is repeated from somewhere nearby.

I don't look around to catch the surprise passing between the faces of the group. Instead, I repeat the signal.

This time I see their shock as a bird dips low overhead, repeating the call.

The group erupts in applause. "That's impressive," Bin notes. "How do you do that?"

I shrug. "They're incredibly smart creatures. I cannot take the credit for that."

"But how do you teach them to respond to you without getting attacked?" Tanya asks. Birds are significantly larger than us, as are most things around here. Most Fraunians are afraid of them simply because of this.

"One day, when I was out with the Scouts, one approached me while I was sleeping. I didn't even think to be afraid, I just shared my food with it. Since then, I've been able to get them to respond to me by offering them food. It's all in how you treat them, I think," I explain. "They are scared of us, we have to show them there is nothing to fear."

Shell shakes her head. "I'm not sure I'd have the guts to try something like that," she says in a low voice. "Do they answer any call you make?"

I scrunch up my nose, thinking. "I've tried a different signal with many different birds." Instead of trying to explain, I whistle another tune. This one is three short bursts. The group waits, their eyes on the sky.

"How long does it take?" Drew asks.

"Depends on how far away they are," I answer. I repeat the same tune.

This time, it is answered. The call is obviously far away, to our North.

Again, the group claps as my laughter shakes out of me. "I really shouldn't call them again. I try to save it for a time when I can reward them with something for answering."

"What do you reward them with?" Enya asks.

I shrug. "Grain or seeds work."

"I love animals," Tanya says. "This is completely fascinating. Do they talk, like roaches?"

"Birds aren't really able to talk with words," I explain. "At least not that I can understand." This is actually a mystery I've been trying to crack myself. My whole point of teaching birds to speak with me is to use it as a sort of code. I think I've taught the ones who respond to me a signal for danger. I have used it a few times and they appear to understand. I can't make them replicate the signal, however, no matter how many times I try. It almost seems like nothing in Fraun makes them worried enough to use the danger signal back to me. I decide to keep this little tidbit to myself.

Bin shakes his head. "I'd heard you were an impressive lady," he says, "but this is not what I had in mind."

I blush at the praise. "It's the birds, I promise. I don't do much."

He smiles. "If you say so," he says.

"Well, I think it's official," Drew says. "We take all intriguing people into our little circle here. I'd say you belong to us now."

I laugh as though it's a joke because telling a Queen they belong anywhere in their own realm should be a joke. But, secretly, I'm soaring inside like one of my bird friends. I can't even explain why it matters so much to me. I belong to the council of rulers. I belonged to a group of Scouts once. I have a brother. But a group of friends suddenly feels like something that has been missing in my life and I realize I want it more than I knew.

Chapter 2

I throw my head back and laugh at something Tanya says to the group. That simple motion brings the sun into my field of vision and squashes the pleasant bubble I've found myself in. Just that quickly I am no longer a young Fraunian laughing with a group of people in Enchenda. I'm a royal again, and one who is quickly running out of time to get myself to the town square to accept a delivery. "Look at the position of the sun," I say. "It's been a pleasure talking to all of you, but I really must meet someone in the town square." I don't want to let this little semblance of normal go, I realize. I want to repeat this easy manner of talking and telling stories. I act quickly, before I can talk myself out of it. "We should have dinner soon. I enjoy cooking and feel I could handle a meal for all of you." I stand up and point in the direction of my house. "Will you all agree to let me cook for you soon? Perhaps in a few suns?"

"Eat at the royal home?" Tanya asks. She grips Enya's forearm. "Can you believe that?"

"I'm more shocked we'd be having the Queen herself prepare us dinner," Bin says. "Are you sure you're up for that, Sawchett?"

I chuckle. "It would be my pleasure."

"Then you will see this entire crew for dinner the day after tomorrow," Drew states.

"Excellent. Until then, be well." I walk with more of a purpose after the delay. I have no regrets about stopping. The group was truly pleasant and refreshing. I enjoyed the laughter. I do, however, have someone I am supposed to be meeting in the square. I will feel terrible if the delivery has already arrived and citizens are wasting their days waiting on me to arrive.

I hustle past the house that I grew up in on the edge of the square. Never knowing I was a royal, or that my Mother was the secret daughter of a King, I played right here on the lawn at the center of the town square like everyone else. Now the couple who inherited the house I vacated when I moved into the royal home sits outside on the ground pulling green peas from inside large pods. I offer a smile and a wave, which the woman gladly returns.

Relief floods me when I do not see the cart which I was meant to greet. Apparently my detour did not keep me from being on time. I decide to take a leisurely walk around the square while I await the cart's arrival. I stop to talk with a store owner sweeping his front stoop. "Good morning."

"Morning, Majesty. How are you enjoying this fine day?" he asks. He stops and leans on his broom.

"I am well. How are things in the Realm? Anything I should be aware of?" The store keeper here is always friendly. Many from Enchenda will come speak with him and trade things in his store. He stocks all sorts of belongings including clothing and house wares. He also has a tendency to pick up on gossip.

"Nothing new to my ears. Another shop has closed." He points a little further around the square to a shop that used to specialize in clothing. I notice there are no displays in front today.

"That makes two," I note.

He nods. "People are scared of the giants. They're leaving in the dark of night."

We knew this was a possibility. We have discussed it at council. "Fraunians have always left to join Scouts or be Wilds before. Surely this is no different," I offer.

"Well I don't know much about that, I must admit. I've lived in Enchenda for my entire life. My parents owned this shop before me. I can't say that I've ever known someone who leaves to become a Scout. But I suppose you're right, people must have done just that."

I don't point out that his own Queen left to be a Scout back before the war. That's not the point the man was trying to make. His point is Fraunians are noticing. That means they're leaving in larger numbers now. I can't confirm or deny that for sure, so I say nothing. Instead, I smile. "We will find someone who's heart is set on taking that space and get it filled. I'm sure of it." I lay my hand on his shoulder. "Thank you for your loyalty to Enchenda."

I'm saved from having to say anything else by the arrival of the cart I've been waiting for. Two roaches are pulling a large wooden cart with wooden wheels creaking under the weight of the vegetables from the garden in Marchenda. "Oh, excuse me. This is the delivery I was waiting for."

We grow vegetables in Enchenda. There are many homes along the main road that I walked this morning where you can find zucchini, tomato, or cucumber. They are simple to grow and our soil supports them. But some vegetables require more space, which we do not have here. Marchenda, with their border gardens, can grow some of those. I approach the cart, already smelling the pungent onions. The roaches come to a halt.

"Good morning," I greet. Although I do not recognize these particular roaches, I am known among them. Being a Queen earns you respect and recognition only among Fraunians. These roaches value my former status as a Scout. It means I am equipped to hold my own in the wild. To them, I'm trustworthy for that alone.

"We bring you a delivery. Where are we taking it?" The voice is soft but speaks our language. Not every roach speaks Fraunian, hearing it always makes me wonder how many other species speak Fraunian, if we could only hear them or get close enough to try.

"There is a grocery for the people there on your left." I point to the large building with a few empty containers out front in anticipation of this delivery. "The men inside are waiting to empty this cart." I walk to the side, looking in at the mound of beautiful produce. "Is that raspberries I see?" Raspberries are my favorite. They are delicious with their sour tang. I reach in a grab one with two hands, taking a bite of it before returning to the front of the cart where I split the remaining fruit in half and offer it to each roach. "You must be exhausted from your journey. Let us get this cart delivered and get you a drink. Thank you so much for agreeing to transport these crops."

The two take the offered fruit. By the time we reach the grocery the men are already outside. I allow them to handle the transfer of the product from the cart to the containers while I walk with my new many legged companions to a watering tray. While they drink their fill, I have a seat on the grass nearby.

"How are things outside of Fraun?" I ask.

"The same as always," one answers. I have yet to learn whether their voices are male or female. To me, they often sound the same. Both of these two are large, which makes sense since they volunteered to transport the cart.

They finish drinking and lie on the grass beside me. "Sometimes I miss the open space outside of Fraun," I admit.

"Yes, there is certainly more of that out there."

"But there is also danger," the other one adds.

"Do you speak of animals or giants?" I inquire. I do not know which part of the larger world these roaches come from.

"We have not encountered the giants. We have only heard tales. My sister is speaking of other animals. We had an encounter with a bird the other day that was quite scary. We were lucky to escape with our lives by hiding under a tree root."

"That is truly scary. I am sorry you had to go through that. There is a safe house at the edge of Enchenda where many roaches who are employed by my Realm live. There are bedrooms, food, and water." I try to speak with a respectful tone. To indicate that these two require a job or my help can be considered rude. "You're welcome to check it out if you'd like."

"We may do that. Thank you for your hospitality." The speaker nudges the other with its head and they both rise. "Have a nice day," he offers as they walk off. I notice they walk toward the direction I was speaking of.

Strange, I muse, how Fraunians and roaches are alike in their fear of larger things and yet so different in their approaches. Fraunians crave consistency and leadership where roaches crave freedom and independence.

What does it say about me that I crave both?

Chapter 3

Jordyn's long legs are stretched out in front of him, parallel to the blade he carries when it is his turn to be on watch. The blade is long for a Fraunian. But Jordyn, the former King of wisdom, knows even something this long would be surprisingly ineffective against the giants he is watching today. So far this morning nothing out of the ordinary has occurred in the giant camp. The giants have come and gone in exactly the same way that Jordyn's own scouts do in their camp. The count is holding strong at twenty-eight giants in varying ages and sizes. Many of the older ones and a few of the younger ones often disappear when the sun is up, something he has taken notice of. It is nothing concerning. At least, not yet.

A noise behind the former King causes him to turn his head to the side. His hand closes around the handle of the blade, but he doesn't draw it. His own camp lies in the direction of the noise and it is not enough noise to be a giant or an animal. He will wait. If someone from his troop is approaching they will identify themselves shortly.

"It's just me." At the unmistakable sound of his love's voice, Jordyn releases the handle and smiles. At twenty-six annuals he is within the age marker that is known as the age of the flesh. The mere sound of her voice gives him pleasure. "I'm bringing you something to eat," Eselda says.

"Whatever it is, it smells delicious."

She sits directly next to him, opposite the sword. "Any new developments today?" she asks as she hands him a bowl of stew.

Jordyn lets his nose soak up the smell of ant and vegetables before answering. "Nothing. The small one went off again." Jordyn points to the east where the young giant boy has been disappearing every morning for about seven suns. "He hasn't returned yet." He takes a big bite of the stew, feeling the tension in his shoulders leave him. "I was hungry," he remarks. That was obvious as he digs in for more of the food, shoveling in bite after bite until the bowl is empty.

While he eats, Eselda watches the camp. In the time they've been asked to watch the movement of the giants, nothing has changed. Nothing, that is, except the Scouts themselves. That first moment they discovered the giants was pure panic. These were the creatures they'd been warned about. The creatures that destroyed each other with war. The creatures that blew up houses and left smoldering remains. The stories are legends meant to scare young Fraunians.

These giants are different. In fact, the Scouts have noticed that these giants seem similar to Fraunians. They are farmers and merchants. They have families. They live in small huts made of animal skins. They hunt and they cook. Really, there is nothing to suggest they pose any danger to Fraunians or Scouts. The longer Eselda sits here and watches them, the more she becomes convinced the stories of her youth were incorrect.

Jordyn finishes his stew and sets the bowl down on his right-hand side. He slips his left arm around Eselda's waist, pulling her a little closer. "How was your morning?" he asks.

"Uneventful. Evelyn and Nina went out looking for Toby again today and turned up nothing new. Kurt suggested asking a roach to be on the lookout. Many of the roaches are familiar with Toby, they may have seen him outside of our area. Mario thinks it's possible Toby decided to strike off on his own." She casts her eyes downward, knowing Jordyn does not believe this possibility. "He could've gone off to look for Marshawn's troop."

Jordyn shakes his head. "No, he wouldn't do that."

"You also think he wouldn't leave without telling someone, yet he's been missing for more than six suns." She keeps her voice calm and gentle. Jordyn is fiercely loyal to his Scouts and it bothers him to imagine that someone in his troop may not feel the same.

"I'm not giving up on him."

Eselda lays her hand on his thigh. "I didn't ask you to." She rubs her thumb back and forth across the fabric of his loose brown pants. "We'll keep looking until something turns up."

Jordyn lets the silent scene play out, avoiding what he knows they need to talk about. He sighs. "We can't stay here forever. This wasn't supposed to be permanent. We're Scouts. We travel." He pulls his legs up and turns his body toward her. "We have been stuck in this place, watching the giants, for lunar cycles. The giants are not a threat. They're not going anywhere." His words pick up speed with his classic enthusiasm. "It's time for our Scouts to be moving on. Don't you think?"

Eselda can't help but smile. "This is the Jordyn I was missing." She leans in and kisses him. "I love when you get excited about something."

"Does that mean you agree with me?" he asks. His eyes are a shade darker than their normally bright blue. More like the sky before a storm. His age marker always reveals itself in his darkened eyes. Since he has passed his twenty-fifth annual this now symbolizes his love for Eselda, where the same darkening in her eyes would signify anger.

"I do agree. It's time for us to move on. We should pack the troop up and move to the East. We will leave word with a roach who lives nearby in case Toby returns." She turns her eyes toward the giant camp. "They're no threat to us."

Chapter 4

I'm a part of the ruling council in Fraun. It comes with the job, Queen of Enchenda. In the beginning of Fraun, way before I was born, there was a single King who made all the decisions himself. Rumor has it he had some advisors and stuff, but basically he was the only voice that mattered.

He had five sons. Those guys created the Fraun we basically have now. They came together once a lunar cycle, at least, to talk about policy and make decisions. Then they'd split off back to their respective Realms and run things. Our Realms are named after them.

Almost three annuals ago we had to fight against a King named Tin for control. The basic gist is that Tin wanted to return to the original system, with him being the guy in charge. The rest of us wanted to keep it how it is now, balanced. Of course, in reality, I have to agree with former Queen Eselda on a few of the points she used to make. I'm not entirely sure I'm convinced that trusting people to rule solely because they're descendants of the original King and his family is the best idea. We have age markers no one else does, it makes us a little crazy sometimes.

Either way, we're back to five rulers who all come together to make decisions. We've agreed to also bring in Ambassadors, people who are not royal blood to serve as a kind of advisor. King Hector and his wife, Saren, are the rulers of Farcheda. Farcheda is known for Speed and is serving as First Realm for the first time in our history. They were given the title after the war and no one has seen any real reason to take it away from them. Today, they're looking incredibly beautiful in a deep blue color sitting together and holding hands before the flickering fire in the new council room. Their ambassador, Sieven, is standing behind them. He looks like standing is the only thing keeping his eyes open. The poor guy is exhausted.

Queen Alerta, from Marchenda, is sporting a yellow that positively radiates off of her dark skin. She is joined today by her daughter, Stef, and her ambassador, Olivia. I adore these women. I think, if it weren't for the fact that I'm expected to rule Enchenda, I'd want to live in Marchenda. They're known for their mirth and they house the most amazing garden for the Kingdom. Plus, they have no problem with age or the fact that their power seats are all held by women. Ambassador Olivia is actually younger than me, which is quite a feat.

Renchenda, the realm of wisdom, is represented today by King Thometh and his wife, Queen Lucinda. Sitting with them is Ambassador Garven. They are often quiet during the meetings unless we ask them a direct question. Apparently that is the way of the Renchenda people. Listen more and speak less. I suppose that is also true of former King Jordyn, one of my all-time favorite people.

Next along the circle is my brother, King Tutor. He represents Sarcheda today, which is weird because neither of us has any blood of Sarcheda. Actually, our explorations have shown that no one does. So, the council decided to allow Tutor, who has the blood of two former Kings, to rule Sarcheda in order to keep us at five realms. He is joined today by Ambassador Marcus, who I actually don't like at all.

Then there's me, Queen of Humility. My ambassador is Annabeth. She's a healer. One of the few Ambassadors who refused to quit their day job to take over the role. She's hard-core amazing and currently the only person we're all sitting here waiting for. "We can start without her, I'm sure she'll be along shortly," I offer. It's not the first time I've offered. We usually start these meetings when the sun is directly overhead. That time has come and gone. King Hector is actually tapping his foot, which is a sign he's annoyed. I suppose I can understand that, since he is the King of Speed.

"No, it's fine," King Thometh says. He offers me a kindly smile that crinkles his light green eyes. "We'll wait."

"Actually, I had something I wanted to talk about," Marcus starts. "It's related to the rules related to ruling a realm. If someone were to step down from a position and no relation could be found to take the spot, what happens with that realm?"

"I'm not stepping down," Tutor answers. Marcus opens his mouth to say something but Tutor waves his hand to stop him before a word has even been uttered. "But in the event you are describing, the realm would either be absorbed by the others or the council could put someone else—"

He is cut off by the opening of the main door. Annabeth bustles into the room. "Sorry I'm late, I was saving a life." She drops into the empty chair beside me and waves her hand at King Tutor, as though giving her permission for him to continue. With a smile, he does.

"As I was saying, the council could put someone else on the throne." He turns to his Ambassador. If I didn't know Tutor better I probably wouldn't catch the scorn in his eyes. He's trying to be nice but he can't stand this guy either.

Marcus stands and clears his throat. "Thank you, Majesty." The last word drips with hatred that reminds me so much of Tin it makes my heart skip a beat.

King Hector clears his throat. "Alright, now that everyone is here let's get started. Sawchett, is there an update on our patrol who went South?"

I decide against standing. "Erick tells me, through letters, that they have managed to divert the water by digging some canals. The result is a little river winding through the land and a small pond in a good location."

"That's wonderful news," Queen Alerta says.

"It is. Water is essential, obviously, but can also add some enjoyment. If it becomes necessary to abandon our Kingdom here, that water will make all the difference," I say. The purpose of the patrol I keep contact with was to determine if any other area could house our entire Kingdom. Since the giants have been found, Fraunians are concerned. At the time the group left, we didn't plan on running. It was a "just in case" sort of move. Now I have to wonder if more Fraunians would be interested, since it seems many are leaving in the middle of the night.

Annabeth runs her hand along her short grey hair. It's usually a sign she has a question. "Are the people planning to stay there indefinitely, regardless of what we decide?" she asks.

"Erick, as many of you know, is a self proclaimed Wild," I explain. "He assisted us with updating our lineage charts." I point to the large one now occupying three of the four walls of the new building. This represents the first time all five Realms have been painted on one wall to show our unity. "But he is the first to admit that he has no love for Fraun beyond that. He will stay in the new location no matter what happens."

"And the rest?" Queen Lucinda asks.

"The rest have not yet decided," I answer. "No one seems to be in a hurry to return."

"Thank you for the update," King Hector says. "Alerta, do we have a garden update?"

Alerta stands, smoothing the skirt of her yellow dress in the process. "We have cultivated—"

She is interrupted by the door opening again. This time the person popping into the room is wearing black and brown and is a face that instantly makes me smile. "Danyel of Sarcheda, we weren't expecting you today," King Hector says. "Forgive us for not waiting. Is there some emergency?"

"No, Majesty." Danyel runs his fingers back through his light hair with shaking fingers. "I was asked to come give you a few updates from the Scouts."

"You have been with the Scouts?" Olivia asks the question many in the room may have had. I cover a smile with my hand. Always trust the young to ask what everyone is thinking without fear of consequences.

"Yes. I have been going there sometimes." He shuffles his feet, nervous.

"Is there a pressing matter with the giants?" Queen Lucinda asks.

"No, nothing like that."

"Then, if you don't mind, we'll let Queen Alerta finish speaking of the gardens." The sentence does not change pitch. King Hector isn't asking.

Danyel nods. "Of course, please continue. I'm sorry for interrupting." He gestures to the Queen.

"We've cultivated all the cold weather crops that will not last through the shifting temperature and planted the seeds for the ones that can. No concerns or major issues to report." She drops back into her chair and focuses on Danyel as though ready to hear what he has to say.

"We also sent some seeds to those people Queen Sawchett was talking about," Olivia says. "Remember, Majesty?" She touches Alerta on the arm.

"Oh, that's right. We did. We sent a few different types so Erick and his crew can see what grows in that soil."

"That's good. Thank you for taking the initiative to do that," Hector says. "Alright, young Danyel. You're up. What do you have to update us on?"

"Right, so the first thing you should know is that there are seven people who travel with the group of Scouts," he begins.

Tutor locks eyes with me across the circle. We are careful not to speak Jordyn's name in mixed company. But there's no one here today who should have a problem with Jordyn, except Marcus. Jordyn killed the former King of Marcus' realm, Tin. Everyone in this room would tell you Tin deserved what he got, except Marcus. I tip my head toward the Ambassador, a signal to not use the name. Tutor nods. "This is the group of my friend, yes?" he asks.

"Yeah. Should I say who travels with them?" Danyel asks.

"No, we're good," Sieven says. He seems to have suddenly come to life back there. Like Tutor and I, Sieven used to travel with this group of Scouts. They are as much family to him as they are to me. Danyel has our attention.

"Right, well, another group approached them recently and brought along a surprise. Um," Danyel wrings his hands, "I don't really know how to explain this but it was Eselda's mother."

"Queen Rubina? We were under the impression she was dead. Are you sure it was her?" King Thometh asks.

I don't know this woman. Actually, I know next to nothing about her at all. The name is familiar, but likely only because of how much time I have spent studying lineage in my Realm lately.

"Apparently." Danyel shrugs. "I suppose we have no way to corroborate her story." He shrugs. "The scouts believed her. But she is dead now, either way. I was merely asked to tell you. But this is not all I was supposed to bring to you." He shuffles uncomfortably. "Um, I'm supposed to tell you that Toby is missing."

"Who is Toby?" Olivia asks.

"Missing how?" Tutor asks at the same time.

Danyel addresses the younger Fraunian first. "He's a Scout. He fought for us in the war. Nice guy." Then he turns to Tutor. "He went for a swim five or six suns back and never returned. They've found a shirt that he was wearing at the time near the place the water builds up when it rains. But there are no other signs of him."

"That is concerning," Queen Saren says. "This is the group that has been watching the giants for us, yes? Was this man near the giant's camp?"

"No, Majesty. He was not." Danyel makes a sound that may be a cough. "I'd like permission from the council to allow me to bring a few Fraunians out to help with the search."

"Do they believe something has happened to him, then?" Thometh asks. "He wouldn't have simply left on his own?"

Danyel shakes his head. "They aren't sure and I'm not either. But something doesn't feel quite right to me."

Since Danyel is a citizen of Sarcheda, this is a decision for Tutor to make. He must realize the same thing because he nods. "I see no reason to prevent you from helping the Scouts," he says.

Queen Saren lays her hand on her husband's arm. "If Danyel is going, we should vote on whether to allow him to bring a team with him."

"We'll vote," Hector agrees. "One thing before we do. This will be a second group of Fraunians we are sending off away from the safety of the kingdom. We have the group down South looking for places we can run to and this will be another group. We cannot protect our people if we keep sending them away." He waves his hands in front of him. "But that is just one opinion for you to keep in mind when you vote. All in favor of Danyel here assembling a group of Fraunians to take to the scout camp to help with the search for the missing Scout, say 'Aye'."

All around the room hands raise. "Aye," we call.

"No need to ask for opposing. Motion carries with all in favor and I think that's quite enough business for today." Hector holds up one finger toward the ceiling as he rises. "One Kingdom," he calls out.

"One goal," we all answer.

Chapter 5

Toby thinks his eyes are open. It's hard to tell because the darkness remains absolute whether they feel open or closed. He is not going blind, he tries to reassure himself. If he was going blind there would've been signs before this. It must merely be nighttime.

He closes his eyes and focuses with his ears, training them into every little sound. The first sound he registers is water dripping somewhere, far off. That sound has been constant while he has been inside the cave. Next, a sound that may be the wind blowing, also far off. These two sounds are in opposite directions. The water must be coming from deeper within the cave, away from the entrance. The wind, of course, will be coming from outside the cave. More important to Toby is the sounds he does not hear; no scrapping of feet along rock, no breathing, no noises to indicate someone else is in the cave.

He reaches out with his left hand until he can feel the strange metal. His fist closes around the rod, his fingers not meeting on the far side. With a grunt, he pulls himself upright. He knows the top of the small cage is just over his head even though he cannot see it. There have been plenty of minutes where it was bright enough for him to see what an awful predicament he is in. Toby is small, at two marks and two clicks on the medicine tent, but even he cannot fit through the metal that cross hatches over him. Whatever contraption contains him is a metal, glinting silver whenever the light does hit it, shaped in an arc. Like a bowl turned over him, but mesh so he can see and breathe freely. He has tried bending it, moving it, and overturning it. Nothing has worked.

By his count it happened five suns ago. He was out for a swim after a day of hunting ant with the Scouts. He was swimming in a watering hole, one that popped up after the rains. He was close to the Scout camp, he is sure of that. He came out of the water and lay on the ground, enjoying the fading sun warming his body. He may have fallen asleep. Then, without warning, the sun had been blocked. A giant had found him. One large blue eye, brown hair, young, and small by giant standards. Toby had immediately recognized him as one of the almost thirty giants from the camp they were watching. The boy had asked him a question, "what are you?" Toby had refused to answer then he was taken here and put in this cage.

Toby tries out his voice in the silent cave. "Hello," he calls. His voice cracks a little, both from fear and lack of use. He hasn't been talking during the days. The giant speaks in a tongue Toby can understand. Mostly the words are the same. For some reason, this knowledge feels valuable. It's something he'd like to keep to himself. He doesn't want the giant boy to know he and the small beings speak the same language. So he doesn't talk when the child is present.

Each sun, the boy brings Toby food. He shoves it under the lip of the bowl and watches as he eats. There are vegetables which he recognizes and meat he does not. Sometimes there are grains. Usually, there is too much food for someone as small as him. Toby will often save some of the pile for later in the day because the boy only brings food once.

He tries again to move the bowl, pushing on it with his entire upper body as he pushes with planted toes against the floor. Nothing happens. No scraping of metal on rock. No give on the surface. No shifting. He doesn't weigh enough to move it.

He drops to the floor again, drawing his knees up to his chest and wrapping his arms around them. He will not give up. This is not hopeless.

He reminds himself again of the plan he's hatched in the face of this adversity.

Listen to the boy, find out what you can about the giants.

Escape.

Get to Jordyn.

Tell him what you've learned.

Four steps. Four things to do. He repeats them.

Find out what you can. Escape. Get to Jordyn. Share information.

They all seem so simple, on the surface. It's just the second one that's proving difficult.

Chapter 6

I've really perfected the timing of cooking dinner in the annuals since I decided to start playing around in the kitchen. I'm actually in my bedroom, tying a sash around my waist, when I hear the knock on the front door. Downstairs, in the kitchen, dinner is already done. I've made cucumber and tomato salad, roast ant, and potato.

I enter the front hall and open the door, smiling at my guests. They've all arrived together; Drew, Bin, Shell, Tanya, and Enya enter the room and shed their coats. I point to a rack. "You can hang your coats there." I push the door shut before more of the cold air can come in. This room has no fireplace and absolutely does not hold the heat. "Follow me." I lead the group into the dining room. The combination of the fireplace in front of us, which is currently roaring with flames, and the heat from the kitchen, which is through a small door, has this room comfortably warm. My guests stretch their cold fingers in the new temperature.

"Have a seat, please. I'll get our dinner."

I push open the door to the kitchen, which doesn't latch, with my hip. The table has already been set with six place settings. I grab up the platter of ant and potato, balancing it on my left arm. Then I grab the bowl of cucumber and tomato salad with my free hand. I push the door again and sweep into the room.

I'll never get tired of watching the faces of the people who are about to eat my food. It's why I cook, I think. Tanya slips her eyes closed as she fills her nose with the scents. "This smells lovely," she says as her eyes pop open.

Bin rubs his hands together. "I'm starved," he says. "Who cooked this for you?" There's a hint of teasing in his eyes, maybe.

"I cooked it myself. Dig in." I take the only empty chair, the one next to Bin, and smile as they all do just that. They orchestrate the sharing perfectly. Each person takes a scoop of a dish and passes it along to their right. The last person to take each dish returns it to the center of the table. Before long, we all have one scoop of everything loaded onto our small plates.

The food disappears quickly and in silence. It's a sign that it was well cooked and well received.

As the last piece of silverware clatters to the table and the last chair is pushed back a little to allow room for our full tummies, talking begins again. Mostly it is chatter about the town, which I only half listen to. Then, a word catches my ear.

"Do you think the rumor about the giants is true?" Enya asks quietly.

"I'm not saying they're not back. I'm only saying it's odd that they've waited all this time to make themselves known," Shell says. "Seems strange, dunnit?"

"They didn't exactly wander into the open and blow a horn," I say. "They've likely been around all this time, but we didn't know. Danyel of Sarcheda says it appears as though they're a small society with very different goals than they had before. Perhaps they're learning from the err of their ways."

The room falls silent. In this moment, I suppose, they've all remembered my position. A Queen, a member of the Council of Rulers, would have this information. We do our best to get the information to the people, where it belongs, but not everything filters down to everyone. With this one statement I have shattered the image of friends grouped together to share a meal and revealed it as a cheap facade.

I roll my shoulders back and smile. “The threat seems to have faded. I feel we have nothing to fear,” I say. It’s the line I know I’m supposed to say. The people need not worry.

Worrying is my job.

Chapter 7

Eselda was asleep on the ground, curled into Jordyn's body. That's the last thing she remembers. So it's not pleasant to open her eyes and be standing in the middle of the woods in full sunlight, alone.

It takes her only a few breaths before she realizes she's inside a dream. She wants to sigh. She wants to pinch herself and wake up. But she also knows that none of that is possible. She's tried it all before in other dreams.

The dreams are not frequent. They predate deaths, usually important ones. They're vague, often unhelpful, and come in pieces. If she's having one now she'll need to force herself to watch the dream all the way through and pay attention to details.

Eselda drops herself onto the ground and sits with her back against a tree. She has just drawn her legs up and hugged them to her chest when a man she doesn't recognize saunters into the frame. She takes note of everything about his appearance. He is not a tall man. In fact, Eselda thinks if she stood up and compared he'd actually be shorter than she is. He has white hair, meaning he is over forty annuals. But he walks with the confidence of a young man. Likely, this means he has barely crossed that age marker. He is stocky and strong. Combine this with his red shirt and Eselda would guess the man in the dream is from Sarcheda.

She watches him stop and plant his feet under his shoulders. He pulls a bow around to the front and kneels down onto his left knee. He pulls an arrow from a sheath at his side and notches it, lining up with something Eselda cannot see. She stands and walks around to the direction he is aiming. She is hoping, more than knowing, that she cannot be harmed in this dream state.

She walks a few steps off into the trees, hoping to find the target. She still hasn't found it when the arrow whizzes by her. But she hears the sound of the arrow finding something. A short cry echoes off the trees.

She wakes up, curled beside Jordyn and takes shallow breaths. There's only one thing she knows about the target. Judging only by the pitch of the cry issued, the target was male.

She knows she needs to share this information with Jordyn. But it's also an important day for them and she doesn't want to start with dreams of death. She shakes him awake, promising herself she will tell him what little she knows from this dream as soon as she can. "Jordyn, it's time to wake up," she says.

His eyes pop open immediately and she can see him cataloging the surroundings as if checking their safety. "It's finally our day," she says. She kisses him on the cheek. "You said you wanted to be married when the sun was rising."

"I did say that." He sits up, stretching. "Are you sure you're ready for this? There's no going back once I can call you my wife, you know."

Eselda had promised herself to two other people in her lifetime. First, there was Prince Carsen. That was an engagement of convenience, meant to help both of their realms. There was never any love there and Prince Carsen was murdered before they were wed. In fact, he was murdered before they could even formally announce the engagement. Then there was Tin, the monster. Eselda had agreed to marry him because she thought she could love him. He had revealed his true nature before they ever married. Which, truthfully, is probably the one good thing he ever did for Eselda.

For these reasons, she hesitated to take this step. But now she smiles. "I can think of nothing that would bring me greater joy than being your wife," she says.

The ceremony is smaller than it ever would have been in Fraun. They exchange simple vows and promise to love one another until the breath is gone from their lungs. Kurt presides over the entire ceremony and the Scouts all bear witness. When they kiss as husband and wife, they are wrapped in the warm rays of the rising sun and Eselda knows it will forever be her favorite memory.

Chapter 8

Tutor is standing in front of the fireplace in an empty room of his home in Sarcheda. The large stone room is not normally empty. In fact, it normally houses a rather large wooden table and chairs. Today all the furniture has been removed because King Tutor is doing something that has never before been done in Sarcheda, inviting any citizens who wish to speak with him into his home.

He's calling it an "advisory session". Ever since the War for Fraun the royals across the kingdom have had meetings with their advisors each fortnight. Marcus, the Sarcheda advisor, is a difficult and argumentative man, at best. At worst, he is poisoning the realm's opinion of their king without outright lies. So Tutor is taking drastic measures. He is, instead, inviting all those who wish to attend to come to an "advisory session" to get their information directly from their king.

Rightfully so, he is nervous.

Alerta, the beautiful Queen of Marchenda and the woman Tutor is courting, offered to attend the meeting with him. She offered to stand by his side and field questions or simply show silent support. But this is something he must do himself. He keeps reminding himself there is nothing to fear from the people of Sarcheda and it is his job to lead them.

This is what he's thinking about as he wrings his hands nervously at the front of the room. This gesture does not project strength, which is the character trait Sarcheda is known for. For this reason, when Marcus enters the room, Tutor drops his hands quickly to his side as if caught breaking some law. He straightens to his full height, throwing his shoulders back. "Good evening, Marcus."

"Majesty," Marcus answers in a booming voice. He drops his chin to his chest briefly. It is not a bow. It is not supposed to be a bow. It is Marcus' way of showing that he doesn't believe Tutor is worthy of a bow. It's also not a fight Tutor feels like having.

"Is there anything we need to discuss alone before the rest of the population fills the house?" Marcus asks the question quickly like the words themselves are poison and he doesn't want them lingering in his mouth.

"Not that I know of." Tutor crosses his arms behind his back, linking his fingers. With his feet shoulder length apart and his chest held high, he looks like a soldier holding the front lines of a battle. This is not an accident. He was exactly that on the steps of Castle Fraun before he fought Tin's army to save it. It is an intentional reminder to Marcus and anyone else who comes tonight how Tutor earned the title King of Strength.

The two men wait in silence. They don't have to wait long. People trickle into the hall in pairs and trios, standing around in the room awkwardly. There is reverence on many faces. Most of the citizens of Sarcheda have never been inside this home. There are some who have come before the King with an issue or a request, but that is a small percentage. The people filling this room now are seeing the clean brick, the scrubbed floors, the lamps burning along the walls, and the fireplace lighting the entire room with its glow for the first time.

There are whispered conversations among people as they greet newcomers or discuss what to expect from the meeting. Tutor silently takes it all in from his post at the front of the room. If he were in Enchenda, where he once worked, he would mingle and be polite. In Enchenda they value humility so it would be in his best interest to show it is not about him. In Farcheda, where he lived as a boy, he would simply start the meeting.

Farcheda citizens value speed and wouldn't look kindly on anyone wasting their time. In Renchenda, where he attended school, it would be a meeting of the minds and he would've carefully chosen his words before calling a meeting. There, they value and honor wisdom. But here, in Sarcheda, he will be the image of stoic strength up there until it is time to begin. That, he has learned, is the best way to appeal to their appreciation of strength.

Finally, when it appears that the room cannot hold another living soul, Tutor clears his throat and begins. "Sarcheda, thank you for attending the first of what I hope will be many advisory meetings. I have asked you here today to hear your concerns or questions that relate to policy and address or answer them if I can. This will be similar to the meetings I normally have with my advisor." Tutor gestures toward Marcus, who has stationed himself to his immediate left in the front of the crowd. "He then passes anything we have discussed along to you. This new format, I hope, will eliminate that unnecessary step." He refrains from pointing out that it also keeps the information from being changed before it gets to the people. "If you have any questions or concerns, the floor is yours. Raise your hand only so I know where the voice comes from before speaking, please." He stops talking then, letting his hands fall back to his sides. He waits, making eye contact with many in the silent crowd.

A hand toward the back of the room rises above the crowd. The person is so far to the back that Tutor cannot see whom it is connected to. "Is there a food shortage, as we were led to believe under King Tin?" the voice asks.

"That is a good question." *The same issues seem to be repeated again and again*, Tutor notes. He has lost count of the number of times he has answered this exact question. He is sure citizens share the information but it seems as though everyone needs to hear it for themselves. "There was never a food shortage and there still is not. I have seen the massive gardens around Marchenda myself. There is enough food there to feed the entire Kingdom for lunar cycles and more is growing all the time. In addition to that source, each Realm has their own smaller garden. Our garden here can hold out for at least a fortnight even if we stopped planting new items now."

"We can also," Marcus interrupts, "continue to hunt ants and other assorted creatures along our borders. It's not as if vegetables are all we eat."

Tutor decides not to chastise the interruption because the

information was valid. Besides, that almost made it seem as though he and Marcus were on the same side, which they certainly should be. "That is true," he agrees. "I hope it eases your fears to hear that information. What other concerns do you have?"

Two hands go up at once, near the middle of the crowd. They notice each other. The taller of the two citizens nods to the shorter, who speaks. "Do we have any information from the group that went North after the announcement of the giants?" she asks.

"We do. The group has found an area they believe is large enough to house all the citizens of Fraun, if the need arises. They assured the council there is a decent water supply and good soil for crops. They were instructed to stay in the area, attempt to grow some things, and scout around for animal habitats."

The taller citizen now speaks. "And what about the giants themselves? Have we heard anything new on that front?"

"Nothing new, I'm afraid. Although in this case the lack of news is certainly good news. It means the giants remain unaware of our presence and have stayed away from our boundaries," Tutor answers. He is pleased with the questions and the general feeling of this meeting. In recent lunar cycles the tone in Sarcheda was often one of malice toward their King. Tutor has no blood of Sarcheda in his veins, although he does have the blood of two other Realms. This has led some citizens, including Marcus, to doubt his ability to lead them.

Another hand shoots up. "What happens to Sarcheda if something happens to you? Who is to lead us next?"

It's as if the speaker had a direct line to Tutor's brain. For a beat the strange coincidence causes him to freeze, merely capable of blinking rapidly. Finally, he recovers from the surprise. "I don't suppose I know the answer to that. I have no other living relatives, besides Queen Sawchett who is ruling in Enchenda. I suppose a royal with majority blood could be found to take the throne, as I did. But I do not anticipate myself going anywhere at this time." He tries for a smile but most of the crowd does not return it.

He suppresses a sigh. He knows the time has come to address the citizen's major concern head-on. "There are no descendants of Sarcheda himself living today. We have a lineage updater looking, but it appears that there will be none found. I'm sorry."

"Majesty, I have a question," Marcus says. He steps toward Tutor and turns to face the crowd. "Many of the our children are now learning about age markers that affect only royals. This is something that was never included in our own school curriculum. Can you tell us more about this?"

"Sure," Tutor says. While he would never prevent citizens from learning this important topic, Tutor has to wonder why it's being raised now. Nothing about his interactions with Marcus is ever simple. He wonders what his ambassador stands to gain from this line of questioning. He takes time to choose his words carefully. "At twenty annuals, a royal with the blood of Oberian goes through a malicious age. This is a time when the individual will be consumed by a dark, dangerous, angry need for power. At twenty-five, they will go through the age of the flesh. They will be consumed by their desire to further their bloodline by bringing children into the world.

"As far as we are aware, these are the only additional age markers for those born of the royal bloodline."

"And you went through these?" Marcus asks, still facing the crowd.

"I did and I still do. I am twenty-eight annuals."

A hand raises in the crowd. "Did you kill King Tin when you were twenty? Is that what happened?"

Tutor shakes his head vigorously. "No, milady. As I have said before, I did not kill Tin at all. At the time of the final battle Tin was past his malicious age marker and so was I. Any fighting either of us did during the war was not a result of that monster."

Another hand. "If you didn't kill King Tin, who did?"

"I am confident I have answered this before." The smile on Tutor's face seems to speak of infinite patience. But his sentence is clipped as if that patience wears thin. "It is not my place to speak of who did what during that battle. King Tin stood against Fraun and lied to you. Fraun fought back. I will not apologize for his death."

It surprises Tutor to see so many in the crowd nod at his statement. Perhaps the people of Sarcheda are finally listening.

Chapter 9

I know Tutor had his advisory meeting last night. He didn't want anyone else from the council of rulers present, which I respect. But it worries me to think about him handling this alone. Marcus obviously doesn't like him and the question he asked at the council meeting tells me there's something going on there that we aren't aware of. So when I woke up this morning, I asked a roach from the stable near my house to take me to Sarcheda.

Tutor flings the door open and smiles when he sees it is me. "Good morning, sister," he says. "I should have advisory meetings all the time, apparently it makes me popular." He steps back out of the way and I see Danyel sitting behind him.

I laugh and walk into the home. "Good morning, Danyel."

"Sawchett, what are you doing here?"

I shrug. "Probably the same as you. I was checking on how the meeting went yesterday."

"Really, that means neither one of you thought I could handle this meeting on my own." Tutor shakes his head. "It went fine. They asked a lot of questions, but none of them were new questions. I answered them all and Marcus seemed to behave himself. End of story." He reaches for a kettle of water and pours himself a cup of tea. Then he holds the kettle out as if offering it to us. Danyel nods and Tutor pours him a cup and hands it over.

"Have you been out with the Scouts?" I ask Danyel.

He takes a sip of the tea before answering. "Yes. They're not far from here. They're just on the other side of the ravine, really. I took a roach here this morning. Actually, I have some good news." He smiles. "Eselda and Jordyn were married at sunrise yesterday."

I'm glad I turned down the cup of tea, I'm sure I would've just dropped it with my surprise. "What?"

"It was beautiful. Simple, by Fraun standards. But, honestly, so great." He smiles. "You could really feel the love, you know?"

I don't know what to say. I think of a few things, but none of them seem right for the situation. I'm happy for them, of course. But I'm also hurt, I realize. If they were still rulers in Fraun, this would've been a big party with everyone invited. I would've been there. This, I suppose, is just one more thing to remind me how much we are separate now.

"You'll have to pass on our congratulations to the happy couple," Tutor says. I know him well enough to know that is not all he wants to say. In his voice, my hurt is mirrored.

"The scouts are going to relocate," Danyel says. "They wanted to have the ceremony performed before they did that."

Relocating is common for Scouts. They pride themselves on not taking more from the land than they need. They rarely stay in one place for a long time. They have temporary lodgings and move whenever they are ready. Honestly, it's only because we needed them that they have remained in one spot for as long as they have. "Where will they go?" I ask.

"I'm not sure." Danyel shrugs. "But I'm going to stay there, at the old camp. I'll keep an eye on the giants, just in case. Plus, if Toby happens to come back, I'll be able to tell him what's been going on."

Tutor nods. "Keep the crew we approved with you for at least the first fortnight. We'll vote on it again at the next council meeting. I don't think we need an emergency session for this."

Danyel picks up his cup, drains it, and hands the empty cup back to Tutor. "I should head back. I'm glad your meeting went well."

"Thanks. Also, thanks for bringing us the news," Tutor answers.

I hug Danyel and then he's gone. I turn my attention to Tutor. "Can you believe they got married?"

Tutor laughs. "Yes, I kind of knew they would."

"True. I guess I just always thought I'd get to see it," I admit. "They're really not a part of us anymore, are they?"

Tutor sighs. "They haven't been for a long time." He shakes his head. "I haven't even seen Jordyn in, what, two annuals? I'm starting to forget what he looks like."

I laugh to keep myself from crying, which is what I suddenly feel like doing. "You'd recognize him, he's the tallest person you've ever met. That's hard to forget."

Tutor laughs and rolls his eyes. "They've got their own thing going over there, kid. They have a Scout troop to watch out for and they don't need to keep fighting Fraun's battles. Now, with Toby missing, I'm sure Jordyn is worried. He wants to put this whole thing behind him and get on with his life." He smiles. "I'm not sure I can blame him."

I guess that's the thing about Tutor and I. We didn't grow up together, we don't live in the same realm now, and we're nothing alike. But when it comes to running away from our problems, Tutor and I always come back to them. At the end of the day, we can't bear to leave the problems unattended and unsolved.

Chapter 10

It's Jordyn's turn out looking for clues to where Toby may have gone. He's planning to be the last one to take a turn before they leave this camp. They've already packed up everything. Danyel and a group of young guys from Sarcheda are taking over the watch of the giants. The Scouts are sleeping under the stars tonight and leaving at sunrise. If they have any chance of finding Toby, this is it.

Right now, Jordyn is meandering through the woods hoping that something will change. He knows Toby likely went off on his own. But he would at least like to find evidence that his friend is safe. If they find nothing, Jordyn knows the possibility something more sinister happened will linger. That "what if" will always be with him.

Really, he shouldn't find anything. He's way off location here. The last known whereabouts for Toby, near where the water builds up when it rains, is on the other side of the camp. Jordyn is closer to the lookout for the giant camp than he is to that location. But, he reasons with himself, Kurt and Evelyn have looked all over the area near the water and found nothing.

Like a true last-ditch effort, it was time for something different.

Jordyn swipes his blond hair back off his forehead again. There's a cool breeze today and just the right amount of chill in the air but he's still sweating. He took off his long sleeves, tying them around his waist, and is walking now in the shorter ones. He picks up his water container and shakes it. Half full. He really should turn and head back to camp soon. That's the rule they live by. Travel until your water is half empty and then turn around. You'll be back at camp by the time your water is gone.

He promises himself he'll drink less on the way back and carries on, further out into the trees. The spot on the side of the mountain where Kurt would be on duty today watching the giants is on Jordyn's right. The Scout camp they've been living in is behind him. Ahead of him looms large rocks. Too large for Jordyn, at three marks, to even consider climbing. He decides he'll walk to the rocks and turn around if there is no sign of anything.

Three steps later he notices it.

Something he probably should've noticed before. He stops, literally freezing in his tracks. He can feel his blood pumping harder, his temperature rising, his breathing quickening. How long have these been here? The indentions in the dirt, pushing down on the soil. The ones he has never noticed before. The ones that seem to lead from the observation spot to the rocks in front of him.

They're footprints.

Big ones.

Chapter 11

When I arrive at the house in Farcheda, where I've been hastily summoned, I see Tutor already standing on the lawn. "How did you get here before me?" I ask, jumping out of the carriage before it has come to a full stop. "I came as quickly as I could and I live closer than you."

He laughs. "I was in Marchenda with Alerta. Come on, get in here."

I follow him through the front door of a cute little box of a home. The entire house appears to be one very large room. The windows are all open, letting the breeze blow through. In the back corner, Abney sits propped up on a pillow holding a baby in her arms.

I race right by everyone else and drop to my knees beside her. "How are you feeling?"

Abney smiles at me. "We're both good. Thank you for coming. I knew you'd want to meet the baby." She pulls the blanket back and reveals a tiny baby with wide eyes, blinking up at us. "This is Lili." Abney smiles at Sieven, who is sitting on her other side.

I turn to look at him as well. "You named her after your mother," I say. "That's beautiful."

"It was Abney's idea," he offers. "Kind of a tribute since Mom never got to meet her." Lili, Sieven's mother, was a Scout. During the war for Fraun she helped us make arrows. She fought by my side from the Castle. She was injured in the war and died within a fortnight of the final battle. Annabeth told me it was some kind of infection, there was nothing anyone could do. She was just one of many who died that day.

I lean down toward the baby, brushing my lips across her forehead. "If you are half the woman your namesake was, we are all going to be lucky to know you," I whisper.

"I agree," Abney says.

I push myself up so that I'm standing, instead of being in Abney's space. "Is there anything you need?" I offer. "Can I get you a cup of water or something?"

"We're good right now," Abney answers. "I'm just glad you're all here."

I step back and look around the room. Besides Tutor and I, Alerta and Stef are also here. "Are your parents going to get the chance to meet this little bundle?" I ask Abney. Her parents are also Scouts, and they currently travel with Jordyn and Eselda.

"I hope so," Sieven answers. "We sent word by roach that the baby was coming. I would expect they'll be here as soon as they're able." He bends down near Abney's cheek to whisper something in her ear. It's such a beautiful moment. I look away, so I'm not intruding. I remember when I first learned about Sieven and Abney. I couldn't sleep, probably because I wasn't used to the quiet of the woods, so I went out for a walk late at night. I came across Sieven and Abney, using the cover of darkness to kiss. At the time, it was incredibly embarrassing. But it was also a reminder of what kinds of things are really important.

My brother makes his way over to me, meeting me by the exit to the room. He bumps me with his shoulder. "You should come have dinner with me sometime soon."

"I'll do better than that, I'll cook for you." It was, of course, what he meant. He would never come right out and say that and if I hadn't offered he would certainly have had something prepared. But Tutor is no cook and he knows I love the kitchen. "Why don't we have dinner in five suns at your house. I'll bring everything I need for the meal."

"Do you mind terribly if I make Stef a cup of tea?" Alerta asks.

"Of course not," Abney points to an obvious kitchen area on the other side of the room. "Help yourself."

Alerta and Stef walk by, hand-in-hand. The small Princess is full of youthful energy, practically skipping along beside her mother. Alerta reaches toward Tutor's hand on the way by. I love the easy way he reaches for her, catching her hand and squeezing it with a smile. She never really slows down and before you can say "love" she and Stef have moved along.

"You should invite them as well," I say.

"Who?" he asks.

I shake my head and roll my eyes. "You're being difficult. You know who I meant." I tip my head in the direction Alerta and Stef have moved to. "Will you wed soon?" I ask him.

The question catches him off guard. His eyes, which must have been briefly closed against the sun or some unseen thought of stress, pop back open and land on my face. "It's complicated," he answers. Little circles of red pop up on his cheeks.

"Now I've embarrassed you." I laugh lightly. "It's not complicated. Tutor, do you love her?"

He takes a deep breath in through his nose and sighs it out. "Yes."

I smile and brush his arm. "Does she love you?" I ask. My voice is a little quieter.

"Yes."

"Oh, Tutor. That's wonderful. This is the easiest thing in Fraun." Suddenly my brother looks relaxed and at ease. Something like happiness dances across his features. I realize, just like I did when I caught Abney and Sieven, that love is the ultimate goal.

Chapter 12

Tutor arrives back in Sarcheda as the sun is starting to drop below the horizon. There's a beautiful yellow glow over the entire realm, which he watches from the back of the roach who agreed to bring him home. As they turn the corner and his house comes into view, he cannot suppress a groan. There is a group of people standing on his front lawn.

He takes his time disembarking from the back of the roach. He turns to thank the creature for the transportation. Only then does he turn his attention to the fifteen or so Fraunians. "Is there something I can help you all with today?"

The tallest of the group, a man whom Tutor recognizes as being a local business owner, points to the only seated person. Something in Tutor's gut tells him he already knows who this is. He looks for confirmation and sees Marcus.

"He says he killed the owner of the bar in town. He says he did it for Sarcheda. We thought you should know," the business owner says.

Tutor blinks rapidly in shock. He looks more carefully at Marcus.

The older Fraunian is holding his head up with pride, but he is uncharacteristically silent. Tutor wonders why he is sitting. He steps closer, trying to see around Marcus' form. "Do you have nothing to say for yourself, Marcus? This is a pretty serious accusation."

"Are you asking if I killed the bar owner?" Marcus says. His voice is lower than normal, somehow more dangerous.

"Did you?" Tutor asks.

Marcus meets his eyes. "I did." There's a collective gasp from the assembled crowd. "Would you like to know why?"

Tutor leans to the right, which allows him to see behind Marcus. He can clearly see that the ambassador's hands have been tied behind his back with what looks like rope. He rights himself and crosses his arms. "Was your life being threatened?" Tutor asks, knowing that there are very few things that would justify a murder in the eyes of the council.

"Sarcheda's way of life was threatened," Marcus answers. "In my eyes, that is more important than any single life."

"Marcus, you have been accused of murdering a citizen of Sarcheda. You have openly confessed to the crime in view of your king and witnesses—"

"You are not my king," Marcus interrupts.

Tutor closes his eyes and tries to gather calm from the wind. He opens his eyes and restarts. "You have openly confessed to this murder in view of the chosen king of your realm and witnesses who live here. You have also made treasonous statements against the king of your realm in view of witnesses. You will be contained for your safety and the safety of Sarcheda until such a time as the council can make a ruling on these crimes and any necessary punishments."

The man standing to Marcus' left, who Tutor also recognizes from town, steps up. "Where should I take him?" He tugs on Marcus' left arm, pulling him to a standing position.

The policy is always to handle these sorts of things as a full council. Tutor knows he has made the right call, publicly stating the accusations and the need for the council to make the decision. But housing Marcus until that moment isn't something they normally do. He doesn't exactly have a location in mind.

Then he remembers the story. Eselda was once held prisoner right here in this house. He points toward his front door. "Take him inside. I'll follow you and show you a place he can stay." Tutor turns and addresses the crowd. "I appreciate you all bringing him here. You did the right thing for Sarcheda safety. I will need someone to help me make sure Marcus stays locked in the room but stays healthy and fed. Are any of you willing or able to help with that task?"

A small woman raises her hand. "I live next door to you with my sister. We could certainly handle bringing food by and checking on Marcus."

Tutor nods at her. "That's wonderful, thank you." He sighs, the sound communicating his frustration. "This is a difficult situation for our realm, but we will handle it together. In light of this, I will recommend suspending our ambassador position to the council. In its place, I propose we continue with our open meetings, letting everyone represent Sarcheda when they are able. Will that work until we get this solved?" he asks.

"So we can all be ambassadors if we wish?" the tall shopkeeper asks.

"I suppose that is what I'm proposing."

"I rather like that idea," the neighbor states.

"Alright, well I have a lot of letters to send to the council," Tutor says. "Thank you, again, for bringing Marcus to me. Have a good night." Tutor lets himself into the front door and shows the Sarcheda citizen the room he's not using that they can repurpose for Marcus. There's a bed, a table, and a chair in this room. He looks around, making sure there is nothing Marcus can hurt himself with. The only window is rather high up on the wall. It should let in light but not let Marcus out. There's even a water closet attached to this room, meaning no one will have to worry about emptying a restroom pot. Plus, and this is the most important aspect, the door to the room locks from the outside.

Tutor lets the citizen leave, unties Marcus' hands, and leaves the room. He makes sure to lock it from outside and pocket the key. Then, although he would like nothing more than to get some food from the kitchen, he heads to his office to write out notes for the council members. Apparently, there's another Sarcheda citizen who has decided to murder. At least this time, it wasn't the king.

Chapter 13

Toby continues to stay huddled along the edge of the bowl closest to the wall until the sound of the giant's footsteps have been gone for a full count of two hundred. Only then can he convince himself the child, because that's what it turns out this small giant is, will not come back for the day. He has never returned after being gone for a count of two hundred.

He stands and crosses to what he considers to be the front of the bowl. In the fading sunlight, he examines it again. He methodically checks every bit of the mesh looking for places where he can get through. He can fit his arm through all of the holes. He can fit his legs through some. There are none where he can fit his head.

It's hopeless.

The sound of scratching from outside draws Toby's attention. He freezes and turns his eyes toward the sunlight. He cannot see the entrance to the cave from this angle. He doesn't need to see the entrance if his fears are truth.

That sound usually precedes animals that have smelled Toby.

The scratching intensifies. He moves himself to the middle of the bowl and drops to the floor. His eyes remain glued to the shaft of sunlight, waiting.

The sunlight is broken by the scurrying animal. Large, four-legged, nose twitching and whiskers wiggling. "Not again," he whispers. This is the second of these animals to find him. He curls into a ball and tries to remain as still as possible.

The first one pushed the bowl around the cave and eventually, when Toby didn't move, gave up. So long as he stays in the center the creature, which appears to have rather short paws, cannot reach him. It is the only thing this mesh has proven useful for.

He practically holds his breath as the animal approaches. It is not in a hurry. It doesn't run. It saunters over like it has all day, taking it's time to sniff around the bowl. But this one quickly becomes more aggressive than the last. Perhaps it can hear the breathing and isn't fooled by the lack of movement. Perhaps it's hungrier. Either way, Toby's heart pounds as the animal begins attacking the bowl.

He has to open his eyes to keep himself in the center of the bowl as it is pushed around the cave. Claws and teeth are gnashing at the mesh. The breath of the beast is foul. Toby gives up trying to remain still, jumping to his feet and holding his arm over his face. The square teeth look sharp and some are practically as large as Toby himself. The bowl shifts more, slamming up against the wall of the cave with tremendous force. He repositions himself in the center again.

He turns at a sudden noise and notices the metal is bending against the wall opposite of the creature who is still attacking the cage. "Oh no," he whispers. If this keeps up the space between himself and the beast will be too small. A swipe of the paw can get to him. What will happen then? Will it be quick and painless?

The cage sides creak closer again. Toby closes his eyes. He cannot watch.

A boom sounds from outside the cave. Both the creature and Toby turn their eyes to the noise. The whiskers twitch as the creature considers which to pursue. Another boom seals the decision and the creature scurries off toward the entrance to the cave.

Gasping for breath, Toby drops to his knees. He drops his head into his hands. "That was too close," he says. "Too, too close." He isn't concerned about the noise, not yet. Right now, he's thankful to still be breathing.

The beam of sunlight breaks again. Toby's eyes snap back to it. He's not sure his heart can handle another surprise. But then his eyes land on the figure. The familiar brown shirt and pants. The soft soled shoes of someone who is on a long walk. That sun-beaten face and the blond hair plastered to the forehead. He wants to cry, the relief he feels is so strong. "Finally," he says instead. "I thought you'd never figure it out."

Jordyn smiles. "Sorry it took me so long. Let's get you out of here."

He approaches the bowl and walks around the edges with a careful eye, taking in every detail. "That creature may have done you a favor," he says. He gestures with his foot to an opening that was not there before. Toby slowly stands, too afraid to believe it. He has waited so long for this opportunity. Surely the hole is still too small.

He locks eyes with his friend through the mesh. "I won't fit."

"You have to try." Jordyn shoots a nervous glance toward the shaft of sunlight. "I don't know how long he'll be gone."

That thought brings Toby back to reality. The creature was here when the noises occurred. It is not trapped, just distracted. They have to hurry.

He slowly bends at the waist and pushes his head toward the opening. It fits. He pauses for the moment, savoring it. The air couldn't possibly feel different on this side of the mesh, and yet somehow it does. He takes a deep breath and continues to push himself. At each click he's expecting to snag clothing or skin. He's expecting to have to force his way through. Perhaps even for Jordyn to have to pull on the sides of the mesh and widen the opening.

But he fits.

He pushes down the emotions that rage at him as he stands up on the outside of the bowl and faces Jordyn. "Thank you," he chokes out.

Chapter 14

Once Toby is settled down for the night, the scout troop surrounding him, Jordyn allows himself to settle beside the fire. Eselda joins him. He can tell the moment his eye stand on her face that she has something important weighing on her mind. He smiles at her, hoping she will tell him whatever it is. He doesn't have to wait long.

"I had a dream," Eselda says. She has waited until Jordyn is alone, the rest of the troop off in bed. The fire is crackling warmly between them. She offers him a comforting smile. "I don't know what it means yet. A man I don't recognize is in the woods with a bow and arrow. He is short, maybe only two marks. He has white hair but he's a young forty. He notches his arrow like a pro and takes a long shot. I haven't seen what he is shooting at. When the dream comes again I will try and get to the target. I think it's a male. When he is shot he cries out. It doesn't sound like a feminine voice."

Jordyn listens quietly, his face unresponsive. He watches her eyes for signs of anger, but sees none. "Was the man's face clear?" he asks. When Eselda dreamed of the epic battle between Jordyn and his nemesis, Tin,

Jordyn's face was unclear. Tin's was always clear to her, but the winner of the battle never was.

"It was but I didn't recognize him. He may be of Sarcheda. He was strong and wore a red shirt."

"Those dreams are unreliable," Jordyn says. He turns his attention to the fire, stirring up the logs. He doesn't like talking about the battle between himself and Tin. He doesn't like remembering what it felt like to take a life.

"I know." She lovingly lays her hand on his arm. "But they show something that could be coming. Shouldn't I know who this person is and who they're shooting at?"

"I don't know, Eselda. We don't know what this has to do with anything. You said this wasn't a giant. Those feel like our biggest threat right now, don't they?"

She smiles. "Yes, I suppose." She looks down at her pants and brushes some dirt off of them. She cannot find the words to explain to him why this feels important. Before the war, if she had been able to get word to him, would she have been able to change the future? Would she have been able to keep Jordyn from having to take a life?

Would she have wanted to prevent the death of Tin?

She was able to change the dream she had about her mother's death. That means knowing about them is important. It gives them time to analyze the situation and decide if this is the ending they want. The future is not set in stone, it's malleable.

Having no way to explain it, she simply lets the conversation die in the embers of the fire. But she knows, deep down, that she will pay attention to the dream when it comes again. Just like she knows it will come again.

Chapter 15

Sometimes when I'm alone in my kitchen and my mind is wandering I get this strange feeling that something bad is going to happen. It starts as a small feeling in my stomach, almost like I ate bad fruit. Sometimes it gets so bad that I will make myself a cup of tea to calm my stomach. I'm pouring the hot water over the tea leaves when I realize that's happening today. While the leaves steep, I decide to leave the kitchen and step outside. Maybe some fresh air will calm whatever this feeling is.

I push open my front door and walk into the yard. The royal house here in Enchenda is surrounded by a low rock wall. Usually that wall sort of frames the picture of the town as I stand here and look out. Today, there are two people sitting on the wall. Their feet are dangling into the yard, hovering just over the green grass. Tanya waves. "Good afternoon," she bellows. "Are you coming to sit with us?"

As I walk across the lawn, part of me worries that they may be bringing me bad news. Perhaps my bad feeling was grounded in this little exchange, like a premonition of sorts. Then I realize, neither of them looks upset. In fact, Tanya seems like she's on the verge of laughing. "I was only coming out for fresh air," I tell them when I arrive at the wall. "I didn't know either of you were out here."

"We were just taking a break for a bit," Bin says. "We just hauled a large crop of beans to my mother's house. Tanya figured you wouldn't mind if we rest here."

"I don't mind at all." Actually, the idea of them stopping to talk to me has the opposite effect. It makes me happier, more like I can conquer anything. "If you'd like to come inside, I have some tea steeping and some fruit tarts cooling. We could have a snack."

Tanya is off the wall practically before I can finish the sentence. Her exuberance makes me laugh. "You said my favorite word," she says. She steps forward and wraps her arm around my shoulder. "Snacks." She wiggles her eyebrows at me.

"The way to her heart is definitely through her stomach," Bin says. He rolls his eyes, but there's laughter behind it. The entire exchange, fun and lighthearted, reminds me of my time with the scouts. It's like a comforting hug, something familiar that you didn't even realize you were missing. I lead them around back, through the garden, and into the kitchen.

We've eaten a tart each when there's a tapping at my front door. We can scarcely hear it from back here in the kitchen, especially with the laughter echoing through the large room. It's Bin who registers the noise first. "Did you hear that?" he asks.

I sigh. "I think it's the door."

"You expecting company?" Tanya queries.

I shake my head. "I'm hardly ever expecting company." I gesture between the two of them, "Yet it often finds me."

I push the door of the kitchen open with my hip and head out toward the front of the house. I notice Bin follows me. "You think the door may be for you?" I tease.

He smiles, but it's fake. He looks worried. "I just have a strange feeling you may need someone to lean on," he says.

That stops me, right in the hallway of my house. I stare at him. "What does that mean?" I ask. That feeling, the one that I associate with bad things, the one I had been ignoring while I ate tarts with my friends, comes back full force. "What are you trying to say?"

Bin tips his head back and groans. "I didn't mean anything by it. Sometimes I just get these strange feelings, like bad feelings. I dunno…" he trails off. But I don't need him to finish. I understand.

I lay my hand on his arm. "Thanks," I say. This brings his face away from the ceiling and back to me. He nods just as whomever is at the door knocks again. "We should get that," I say.

I open the door and a man I do not recognize is standing there. He jumps as if startled to see someone. "Oh, I was starting to think no one was home," he says. "This is from King Tutor." He holds out a scroll, which I take.

"Thank you," I say. "Would you like to come inside for a drink?"

He gestures behind him to a waiting roach. "We have another delivery. But thank you kindly." He bows and scurries off.

I close the door. "Apparently my bad feeling was unwarranted," Bin says turning a dark shade of red. "Sorry if I scared you."

"No problem." I unroll the scroll as we start to walk back to the kitchen.

Dear Council,

When I arrived home tonight there was a group of citizens on my lawn. Evidently, the story is that Marcus has confessed to murdering a local man in cold blood. The citizens saw fit to tie his hands and bring him immediately before me.

At that time, I gave Marcus the opportunity to tell me his side of the story. He confirmed that he did, in fact, kill a Sarcheda citizen. I made sure to tell him that he was being accused of a crime and would be entitled to have his case heard before the full council. He is currently being held in a locked room of my home with assistance from my nearest neighbor until that can be arranged.

In my opinion, we do not need an emergency session of the council to deal with this. We have enough to deal with right now and, honestly, he and Sarcheda are both safe with him locked in my home. Send word if you disagree.

Respectfully,
King Tutor

We reach the kitchen as I reach the end of the scroll and let it roll back up. "Who was it?" Tanya asks, another tart halfway to her mouth.

"Her brother sent some kind of messenger," Bin answers.

Tanya, who I remember has a brother, nods. "Got it," she says. She takes a big bite of the tart in her hand.

"Someone in Sarcheda has killed another citizen," I blurt. I hadn't actually intended to tell them this news. It seems like it should be something handled by the council. But before I can make the decision to share the burden, it's out of my mouth. I watch their faces, waiting to see if they have some kind of reaction. Both of their eyes widen and Tanya swallows the bite in her mouth in one large gulp. I shrug. "I'm as surprised as you. But that's what Tutor's letter says. That's not even the worst part," I sigh. "The man was the Sarcheda ambassador."

Tanya's hand flies to her mouth. "Seriously?" she asks.

"Why would he kill someone? Who did he kill?" Bin asks.

Both very good questions. Both things I absolutely do not have the answer to. I shrug. "I guess we'll have to ask him when we get him in front of the full council."

Bin covers his mouth with his hand. It's less like the shock that Tanya displayed a beat ago and more like he's considering something. "What will happen to him?" he asks. "If the council decides he was in the wrong to kill, which we can assume he was, what will they do to punish him?"

Another good question. "We don't really have clear rules for that kind of thing," I answer. "I don't know if we have ever had to deal with that before." Just as I say it, I realize we have had to deal with it, but we have chosen not to. Historically the council decides not to look too closely at the problem or to make the problem disappear. It's as if the original council believed not having rules for something was the same as not needing rules for it. "We will have to come up with something," I answer. "If that's something you have ideas about I'll have to invite you to the council meeting when it is scheduled."

"You can't kill him, you know," Bin says.

"I didn't say—"

"That would be the same thing you're accusing him of," Bin interrupts. "Right?"

I have no idea what the solution to this problem is. I know, on some level, it would be easier to ignore the problem like the previous councils may have done. But we have to do something. "I guess we will need to consider justice and what that means for the safety of the rest of the kingdom," I answer. "But I promise you, those discussions will happen in front of a full council."

Bin nods, clearly satisfied with that answer for now. "Invite me when it's happening," he says. "I have opinions."

Chapter 16

Tutor is alone this morning in the exercise yard. It's early, the sun is barely up in the sky, and the air has a chill. He is wearing a long sleeve shirt, instead of the customary bare chest, in response to the cold. He is repeatedly picking up a block and tossing it as far as he can. Sarcheda, the Realm known for their strength, has regular strength competitions. Last annual, King Tutor participated for the first time. This year he will be expected to do so again. He will be expected to make a better showing so he now practices twice a day.

The block is over his head, his eyes closed, when he hears someone call his name. He falters under the block, sure that he heard the voice wrong. It's been a long time since this voice was heard in Fraun. He throws the block and turns. A real smile lights up his entire face.

"Jordyn, what are you doing in Fraun?" he closes the gap to his tall friend and wraps him in a hug that is eagerly returned. Tutor pulls back and looks up into the eyes of the man who taught him how to lead. The man who accepted him when he learned things about his past that he couldn't wrap his mind around. Truly one of the best friends and advisors he has ever known. Something he sees there in the blue eyes worries him. The happiness he felt at seeing Jordyn fades, replaced by a sudden fear. "This is not a friendly visit, is it?" he asks.

Jordyn shakes his head, a grimace taking residence on his face. "Is there someplace we can sit?"

Tutor turns and walks to the blocks he'd been using for practice and sits upon one. They are at the edge of Sarcheda here, approaching Renchenda. Tutor's own home is on the other side of the vast realm. Most of Sarcheda is skirted by a deep ravine. In order for Jordyn to be here he must have come wrapping around the edge of the ravine through Renchenda territory. He has passed directly through his former realm, and his uncle, to come to Tutor. Tutor has to wonder why. Is this a show of faith in Tutor's leadership or something else?

Jordyn drops onto a block beside his friend. "I will get right to the point. We have found Toby and it is worse than we feared."

"He is dead?" Tutor interrupts.

"No. He is alive and well. He was taken by a giant and held captive."

Tutor pulls back, practically tumbling from the block he's perched on. He has to throw his arms out to the sides to keep himself upright. "What?" He heard Jordyn, but the statement requires further explanation.

Jordyn nods. "Toby believes, based on size, that this was a child. He tells me that the giant seized him at the watering hole. He was taken back to a cave and placed in a sort of metal bowl, which was tipped upside down to contain him. The metal crisscrossed, forming a barrier Toby could not cross."

Tutor's eyes widen as he listens.

"He was fed regularly once a day. The child would come in the morning with a handful of food, most of which Toby did not recognize. The child would talk in a language Toby could understand."

"They speak our language?" Tutor's voice is a whisper, more like a gasp than a question.

"Evidently, yes. Toby tells me he never tried to speak to the giant, merely listened. He heard a few facts about their hunting and the names of some things they hunt, but nothing to indicate the giant child knew about

Fraun before this."

The realization hits Tutor like a bucket of snow over his head. "They know about us now," he says aloud.

"The one child knows small creatures exist now, yes. Toby had no reason to believe the other giants knew. Then again, the child may tell someone now that I have freed his pet." Jordyn rubs his hands along his arms as though trying to warm them. "A creature attacked Toby in the cave. It was not the first time he had been attacked. I was able to scare it off by making rocks tumble but not before the creature gnawed a hole through the mesh. We pulled him out of the hole. He is safely back at our camp for now."

"What are our next steps?" Tutor asks. Partially, he asks because he cannot think of the answer. Partially, he asks because Jordyn has had more time to get used to the information. But really, he asks because Jordyn, despite giving up his title to travel with the Scouts, was once the King of Wisdom. He remains one of the wisest people Tutor knows.

"I will speak to your full council tonight. There, I will lay out the plan as I see it." Jordyn stands. "You will arrange this."

It is not a question. This, Tutor realizes, is the reason Jordyn came to him and not to Thometh. Jordyn wants to speak to the full council as an equal and he thinks Tutor will get him that. Tutor stands. "I will do my best, Jordyn, but you are not King anymore." He shakes his head, sadly. "We value you, but this is no longer your Fraun."

Jordyn takes a step back in the direction he had appeared from. "That's not a problem, my friend. This is no longer about Fraun."

Chapter 17

"The new building is done?" Jordyn asks. It's a question that doesn't really need to be asked as they are not walking in the direction of the old building. But Tutor nods anyway. "I thought building new was against the rules," he adds. There's no malice in his voice, just curiosity.

Tutor smiles. "Always interested in the facts," he chuckles. He throws a smile over his shoulder so Jordyn will not think him rude. "It's repurposed from the wood in the old one and some other buildings that were falling into disrepair. We are trying to focus more on fixing buildings so they stand against the elements. The new building is large enough for what we need and strong enough to withstand annuals."

"Ironic," Jordyn whispers. "You finally have something strong enough for what you've been through and the future threatens it."

Tutor chooses to pretend he doesn't hear him. Somehow that seems easier than talking about what they're currently facing.

The council building shows between the trees and looms larger than the one Jordyn attended meetings in. It has been painted a pleasing color that somehow blends in with the nature around it. At the steps, Jordyn hesitates long enough for Tutor to pause and turn around in the doorway. Tutor watches his friend take deep breaths as though preparing for battle. "Everything alright?" he asks.

Jordyn nods. "Let's get this over with." He follows Tutor up the steps and into the large room.

Tutor bustles around, lighting a fire in the center pit and setting out chairs. Jordyn stands in front of the tree painted on the wall and takes in the names. This is the first time he has seen all of the realms represented on one wall. He walks slowly, reading the names that have been hidden for so long. His fingers caress Eselda's name. "This never got connected to mine," he says.

Tutor, who had been busy moving a few chairs, pauses. "What?" He puts the chair down and steps closer. He sees Jordyn's fingers on Eselda's name. "Oh, yeah I suppose it didn't. We can ask the council to have that done."

"Is it because our marriage was not recognized by a member of a ruling family?"

Tutor grabs the nearest chair, lifting it with little effort. "I don't think so, no. It was probably more of an oversight. Sawchett and I are probably the only Fraunians who knew you even got married and we may not have mentioned it." He drops the chair into the circle he's created, which is larger than what they would normally need.

Jordyn turns away from the wall. "You're annoyed," he states.

Tutor sighs and turns to face him. "A little, yeah. We're supposed to be friends. You ignored my letters, you refused to talk to me, and you only sent messengers when you needed something." His voice rises in frustration. "For Fraun sake, Jordyn, even your marriage was mentioned off-hand by a messenger. It was an accident that I even found out."

Tutor shakes his head and turns back to his task, straightening chairs that were already straight. "You know what? Don't worry about it. It's not important. We are facing a big problem here and you came when it mattered. Thank you for having Fraun's back." He winces. "Again," he adds.

Jordyn has a lot he'd like to add. His own anger at hearing that Eselda had been so easily banished from Fraun boils under the surface. His anger at himself for what he did to Tin, dropping down to that level, is never far either. "Maybe I shouldn't be here," he says.

Just then the door opens, admitting a dark-skinned woman and a small child. Both are smiling and laughing, completely at odds with the stress and feeling in the room. Her eyes land on Jordyn and her laughter stops. "Oh, you must be the reason for the emergency meeting," she says. She crosses the floor and kisses Tutor quickly. "You should've told me, at least."

"Alerta, meet Jordyn. Jordyn, Queen Alerta of Marchenda." Tutor swipes a hand between the two of them. She reads the stress on his face and wonders what she missed. Her smile to Jordyn is forced as she extends her hand.

"Pleasure to meet the man that goes with the legend. This is my daughter, Stef." She points to the girl who arrived with her who is currently seated before the fire with her hands warming.

"Princess Stef," the girl corrects.

Jordyn smiles. "It's a pleasure to meet you both. I've seen your gardens outside Marchenda. They're beautiful."

"Thank you." Alerta drops into the chair closest to Stef. Tutor takes a seat beside her. Jordyn turns his attention back to the wall.

This is the scene as it appears when Sawchett enters.

Chapter 18

"Jordyn?" Everyone in the room turns to look at me. Seeing that it is, in fact, the former King of wisdom, I rush across the room and wrap him in a hug. Powerful feelings flood me to the point where I can feel my eyes fill with tears. This man saved my life. If I hadn't found his Scout troop when I did…I squeeze him harder once before letting go and stepping back to look up into his face. "I'm so happy to see you."

"You look radiant, Sawchett."

"I have missed you. What are you doing here? Is it good news?" I ask. Behind me I hear the door opening and closing but I don't care. I care about the answer that I can read in those blue eyes. It's not good news. My face falls. "Eselda? Is she okay?" It's the only thing I think has ever made those eyes look so sad.

"She's as well as the rest of us," he says. "Is this the rest of your council? Can we begin?" He inclines his chin over my head at whomever has just arrived.

Turning to the room, I see King Thometh and King Hector have arrived, no wives in tow today. In addition, there are a few ambassadors present. This emergency session, which my brother called, was one Danyel promised to attend. "No, we're missing…"

I'm interrupted by the opening of the door again. This time two people who need no introduction for Jordyn enter. Both pause a few steps from the doorway, shock at the visitor evident on their faces. "Did you know he was coming?" Sieven asks Danyel.

"No," Danyel answers.

"Now we have everyone that I know of," I say. "Should we begin?"

Everyone, including Jordyn, takes a seat around the fire. Hector raises his hand for silence, although no one was talking. "I call this emergency meeting of the council of Fraun rulers to order. King Tutor, you called this meeting. You have the floor."

"Actually, I called this meeting," Jordyn says. I'm sure my surprise shows on my face. As far as I knew, Tutor called this meeting. Jordyn doesn't have the ability to call an emergency council meeting. Not anymore. I steal a glance at my brother and find him studying the floor. I turn my eyes back to Jordyn just as he continues talking.

"I'm aware that I no longer have the power to do that and I respect your policies. But I have already wasted enough time by misjudging the situation and I fear that I need to speak quickly. I was wrong about the giants."

The room collectively gasps. I see Alerta's eyes lower to check Stef, who certainly heard. The young girl's attention has snapped to the handsome face of the former king.

"One of the small giants has taken a Scout hostage. We were able to get him out but we fear this puts us all in danger. They now know we exist, which changes everything. We have to assume the child giant will tell others who will want to seek us out. I fear that they will want to study us, at best. At worst, they will want to enslave us or kill us."

I have so many questions rolling around in my head. I want time to gather them all together. I suddenly need to be reminded how many giants there are, what direction, and how far away. What makes them so sure we are in danger? Is Toby alright?

"What do you propose we do about this?" King Hector asks. I'm not surprised he was the first one to get his questions in order and speak, proving speed is a useful quality in this sort of situation.

"I don't worry myself with what Fraun will do," Jordyn says. "Not anymore. I merely needed you to be aware. My troop will leave, as planned. We will put as much distance between ourselves and the giants as we possibly can."

"Where will you go?" Alerta asks. "Maybe we should be going as well. We did already look into this possibility." Her eyes turn to me. "Perhaps it's time for us to follow Erick and the patrol you sent."

"That was just a scouting mission. They haven't been gone long and they aren't expecting us. I would have to get word to them that we were coming their way."

"You have a group who has left to find another location?" Jordyn asks. "What did they find? Is there water? Is there enough space? What about animals, are they safe from animals?"

Tutor holds up his hands. "All of that has been considered, Jordyn. But the possibility of leaving was an extreme idea. Is this really what the council wants?"

"I don't care what you do. Honestly, my Scouts are going to move." Jordyn turns his head and looks at the wall. "I only came here because the names on this wall mean something to me." He turns back to Tutor. "Even if I haven't always shown it. My blood is here. I fought for you, with you. If there is a chance that I can save Fraunians, I wanted to try."

I raise my hand, bringing the eyes of the assembled group away from Jordyn. "Are we really discussing taking all of Fraun to the lands Erick and the patrol have found? Is that what we're talking about?" I know my voice is clouded with my surprise. This is something I was in favor of trying but suddenly it seems too real. Are we really talking of leaving Fraun?

"Yes, that is a good question. What are you proposing?" Thometh asks. "Would your group come with us to the new land, if we asked you to?"

Jordyn leans his head back and stares at the ceiling as though considering it. It is a few beats before he faces us again. "I haven't been before this council in a long time. I know you all to be respectable people who mean well. But at the end of the day, family or not, the people in this room banished my wife from their grounds. Unless you plan to reverse that, we cannot help you."

"Wife?" Hector asks. "I was unaware you are married."

"Eselda and I were married in a ceremony of sorts in the woods. You can understand why I consider myself banished with her. It took something drastic, like giants threatening all of you, for me to even step foot inside your kingdom."

"Perhaps we have it backwards. Perhaps we should consider Eselda a member in good standing now that she married someone in good standing," Thometh suggests. "Of course, this is my nephew we speak of, so I may be biased." He smiles. "What says the council?"

"I was never in favor of banishing her in the first place," I say. "But I fail to see what this has to do with the giant problem."

"Love is always more important than fear, Sawchett," Tutor says. "We're going to right a wrong here, if we can."

"All in favor of reversing the questionable decision to banish the former Queen Eselda, say 'Aye'," Hector says.

Around the room everyone's hands raise, even Stef's. "Aye," we all call. Unanimous, royal blood and Fraunian alike.

Jordyn nods. "If you are asking my opinion, none of us should be here. My count stands at twenty-three giants. This child said nothing to change that count, but over twenty giants could enslave or kill all of Fraun."

"Wait, the child spoke to the Scout?" I ask, leaning forward.

"Yes," Jordyn answers. "Toby could understand what it said. He didn't try to respond."

I stand up in excitement, an idea forming in my mind. "Then we should try and respond. We should try and communicate. What if we could make them understand? What if we don't have to go?" I say.

"What if they squish you on sight?" Tutor says. He shakes his head. "That's a stupid idea, Sawchett. It's dangerous."

It's the sudden dismissal of my idea, more than anything, that makes me drop back into my chair. I am the youngest Queen on this council, but I have never felt dismissed instead of heard before this moment. It shocks me into silence.

"I have to agree with Tutor on this one, I'm afraid," Jordyn says. "This was a mere child to them and yet Toby had no defense. He was put in a cage and kept as a prisoner. If the child giant had wanted him dead, he'd be dead. I will repeat that the Scouts are moving regardless of what you decide to do with Fraun." Jordyn stands. "I cannot stay here and discuss this all day."

"If my idea has no merit, forget I mentioned it," I say, putting my hands up defensively. "If we are going to leave, we should take a vote."

"I suppose that's my cue," King Hector says. He stands. "All in favor of leaving Fraun with any citizen who is willing and able to come to follow the path of the patrol we sent South, say 'Aye'." His voice is somber as if saying the words forced him to confront the reality.

Equally somber are the voices that call, "Aye".

"I will repeat my question in light of new changes. If we were to decide to leave, would you and your Scouts come with us?" Thometh asks, his eyes on Jordyn.

Jordyn looks again at the names on the wall, a pained expression on his face. "I will. Give me one sun to speak with my troop, I cannot force them to come with us. Urgency is the most important thing right now. I will be back here by this time tomorrow. Whoever is going will need to be ready."

Chapter 19

I stand up and dash after Jordyn. "Wait, please," I call. It annoys me that he keeps walking. "Jordyn, please." I have to pick up speed even though he's keeping an even gait because his legs are so long. The air slaps my face as I step out after him. I reach him at the bottom of the steps and close my hand around his sleeve. "Jordyn, can we talk?"

The sadness of his blue eyes shocks me. I take a step back. "Please, I want to understand this. What makes you so sure that you were wrong about the giants? What makes you so sure that they are dangerous?" I ask.

"Sawchett, a child kidnapped Toby. A child." Anger darkens his face for a beat but it is gone before I can even wonder what age marker would be plaguing him now. "They're still capable of that. Of believing that they are better than us. They would seek to imprison or control us, at best. I can't see a way that this ends well for us." He turns again as if to walk away.

I keep my hand fixed to his sleeve. "Still? What do you mean, still?"

He shakes my hand off when he turns to face me. "Do you remember the large building where you and I first met?" he asks.

Of course I remember. I had fled Fraun after learning King Tin had killed Prince Carsen. I ended up with a group of Wilds who took me to a building once owned by giants. The building was easily the largest thing I have ever seen in my life. It literally blocked the sun. Inside the building I had met up with Jordyn and the crew of Scouts who had taken him in. They became my second family that day. "I will never forget it as long as I live," I answer.

"Inside that building I cleared out a house with Toby. I saw something in one of the rooms that I couldn't explain." A shudder runs through his shoulders. "There was a house inside the room. It was small. Everything inside the home was sized for us. There were beds and clothes, chairs and cabinets."

"Someone was living there?"

He narrows his eyes at me. "I don't think it was by choice. The fact that those items contained layers of dirt and grime, never taken by any Fraunian or Scout tells me that they have a dangerous history. No one wants those items, no matter how perfect they may be." He takes a step closer to me and lays a hand on my shoulder. "I always wondered if the giants took people like us as pets or slaves after I saw that house. Now we know." He lets his hand drop and turns to go. "They did and they will again, Sawchett. We can't let this happen."

I let him walk down the steps and off in the direction of Renchenda. "Surely they're not all like that," I say. I'm sure he's too far away to hear me. I don't speak loudly.

"It only takes one," he answers.

I don't want to argue with Jordyn. It means so much that he is agreeing to come back to Fraun right now. I don't want to jeopardize that and surely telling him that he is wrong would not be wise. But I'm also the Queen who talks to birds, something I was told was impossible. I have an idea, but one that will not be popular.

I plant myself outside the council building, watching for the people I need to put my plan into motion. Danyel is the first of them to arrive, walking out side-by-side with his King. "Danyel, may I borrow you for a second?" I ask. I smile at Tutor. "He'll be along in a minute." Tutor's expression is full of questions. I shrug. "It's personal," I add.

I don't know what Tutor thinks about that comment, but he winks at me and walks off in the direction of Sarcheda. I take a step closer to Danyel as Annabeth comes out the door. "Oh, Annabeth, I'll need you for just a beat if you don't mind." I turn my body away from the door, fully facing Danyel. "I'm going to need you to do something for me without questioning me. Do you think you can do that?" I ask.

"I can. I assume this is to be a secret," he says.

"It is. Can I trust you?"

He nods. "Of course. You know that."

I quickly whisper what I'll need from him, pushing a piece of parchment and a writing utensil into his hand. Then, while he sketches, I turn to Annabeth. "Good Ambassador, I have a favor. I'm going to need you to handle telling the citizens of Enchenda this new information."

"Majesty—"

"I know it's not ideal," I interrupt. "I'd prefer to do it myself, but something has come up. I am trusting you to deliver the message you heard today. Give them the option to be here tomorrow at high sun with their bags of belongings or to stay behind."

She runs her hands down her face. "This is our reality?" she says. "I cannot believe it has come to this." Her shoulders set with resolve. "I will deliver the news. Am I to tell them that you will be joining the traveling group as well?"

I smile at her. "Speak not of me. Tell them what you will choose. Annabeth, what will you do?" I realize I do not know. We have not spoken of this.

"I will go, Majesty. They will need a healer."

I reach for her, wrapping her in a hug. "Your dedication to Fraun is impressive," I say. "Thank you for being my Ambassador."

Danyel taps me on the shoulder. "Finished," he says.

Annabeth shakes her short hair and smiles at me. "I'll leave you to finish your discussion with Danyel of Sarcheda, Majesty. Thank you for your trust."

I wave to her before turning to take the parchment back from Danyel. "Will that work?" he asks.

It will. It is absolutely perfect.

Chapter 20

"It's me," Jordyn calls. The scouts will be on high alert after the return of Toby. He knows what he will see even before they come out from behind trees and rocks in the clearing. His troop armed like it is the battle for Fraun all over again. Only this time the weapons would not be enough.

"We need to talk," he says when the final member is in sight. They immediately arrange themselves on the ground in a kind of lazy circle. All eyes are on him. Kurt and Evelyn, Mario and Nina, Eselda, and Toby. "I saw the full council, which now includes one representative from each Realm who is not royal blood."

He sees this information please his wife. Her eyes light up when she smiles. He is temporarily distracted by the beauty there. He shakes his head to refocus. "I told them everything we know." His eyes travel through the group until they land back on Eselda where they stay for this next part. "They've asked me to help lead them to a safe location and I agreed."

"You are leaving us?" Kurt asks. His hair, recently gray, marks his age but his body is still lithe and strong. Again, Jordyn is tortured by the knowledge that even that build would be nothing against a giant.

"I am going to travel with Fraun. They have a location in mind. One that has been scouted by a group of Fraunians. It has water, food, and the potential for safety. We have nothing else in mind. I have decided to go with them. You are welcome to come with me as well. No one is saying you have to stay with Fraun when we arrive." Jordyn sighs. "I will not ask you to do this. You took up arms with me once on behalf of that kingdom, my kingdom. Please don't think you will offend me if you cannot travel with them now. I only want everyone to be safe."

The quiet following his statements echoes through the clearing. He waits it out, knowing that his troop is using the time to think and process. He cannot make this decision for them. It's bad enough that he is basically making it for Eselda. With that thought, he looks at her again. She is staring at the tips of her shoes as they trace lazy circles in the dirt on the ground. She looks relaxed and at ease. But he knows better. He sees the hard set of her shoulders. He knows she's avoiding meeting his eyes, which likely means hers are darkened. She still has more than two annuals left in her malicious age marker. If she is hiding her eyes, she is angry.

Evelyn rises from the ground and brushes herself off. She walks slowly across the circle until she is face-to-face with Jordyn. "Our daughter is with child and she has chosen to be Fraunian. We will travel with her. When does this group leave?"

"I didn't speak to Abney," Jordyn says. "Sieven was at the meeting but I did not have the chance to speak with him personally either. I do not know for certain that they will be there."

Kurt stands. "They will. When do we leave?"

"Tomorrow. High sun." Jordyn offers his hand to Evelyn. "Thank you for your faith."

She shakes his hand, smiling at him. "Stop assuming we do these things for you." She turns to her husband. "Let us prepare ourselves. I believe I have some arrowheads to make." He loops his arm around her shoulders as she draws even with him and the pair continue off into the tall grass.

Jordyn surveys the remaining group. He has to wait a bit longer but finally Toby pushes himself to his feet. "After what I went through, I have no strategy for facing these giants. I hate to admit it but running is all we can do." He sighs. "I can't imagine going with Fraun, I never wanted to go back there. But I also can't imagine going without all of you. I'm in." There is such a deep sadness with this statement that Jordyn has nothing to add. He merely nods.

Mario puts his head closer to Nina's. They have a quick, whispered exchange. When the whispering ceases, Mario faces Jordyn. "We will go. I don't see a reason to insist we travel alone. In this particular case, there may be safety in large numbers," he says.

Nina leans around her husband to look at Eselda. She turns her gaze up to Jordyn and widens her eyes. "We'll give you a minute," she says. When Mario and Toby have turned to go, Nina spins around to Jordyn once again. "Good luck." Her mouth makes the words obvious but there is no sound. He waves in acknowledgement.

Still standing above her, Jordyn takes a step closer. "Eselda?" he prompts.

"There's nothing wrong with how we do things here," she says. He can hear the hard edge to her voice. "We don't need anything from Fraun." She turns her face up to him and his intake of breath is sharp and jagged. Her beautiful green eyes are completely black.

He brings his hands to his mouth first, trying to get himself under control, before reaching for her shoulder. "Eselda, what can I say? Your eyes…this is the age marker. This anger you are feeling."

"Do not diminish my feelings," she barks. She takes a deep breath. Her eyes do not lighten. "That kingdom didn't want to hear reason, they didn't want to allow rulers with no royal blood. I'm not saying war was a good option. I regret that decision with my entire being. But banishing me from the only home I'd ever known was wrong."

"I agree—"

"Now you tell me," she continues as though he hadn't spoken, her voice loud. "They are allowing people to sit in those meetings who have no blood. They are using my ideas. The same ideas that they called foolish. The same ideas they refused to listen to. They are using them now." She shoves him back and stands up. They are not face-to-face, as Jordyn is much taller than Eselda, but still she glares at him as though this is his fault.

"You can follow them or lead them. Do whatever you want. But you need to remember that I am not welcome there." She shrugs. It seems her anger has dissipated a little with the screaming. Jordyn can see a little green along the very edges, like a ring. "Even if I want to, I cannot go with you."

Jordyn doesn't speak. He steps closer to Eselda, wrapping his arms around her and pulling her close. At first she resists, her body stiff. He rubs his arms along her back and feels her relax with a sigh. Her arms wind around him and squeeze tight. A warmth moves through them both.

He pulls back enough to look down into her face. Her eyes are much lighter, now a dark green all throughout. Much better than fully black. "The council believes that an error was made when you were punished. They have lifted the banishment for your safety and theirs. It was the condition of my agreeing to help them."

"You did this for me? I don't need—"

"No." He shakes his head. He brings one arm around to caress her cheek. "I didn't do it for you entirely." He steps back, letting his arms drop, and sits down on the ground. Eselda sits beside him. "There's a tree painted in the new council building they use. It has all the names of all the people in all the realms who have the blood of the brothers. Something about that wall, Eselda, it spoke to me." He reaches for her hand, squeezing it. "I'm sorry I made this decision without you. I really am. But they're going to die without us. We can't let that happen."

"They think that blood makes them better." She says the sentence slowly, letting each word have weight. "It doesn't. It doesn't make you better. It doesn't make me better. If we travel with them, we have to remember that. Every single life that travels with us is equal. Promise me."

He squeezes her hand again. "I promise. It's been a long time, but that has not changed. They need us. They all need us."

She squeezes back. "Okay. I'm in."

Chapter 21

I'm not a monster. I understand that my people will want their Queen during this difficult time. I know there will be fear. It may be chaotic for awhile. I'd like to be there for them, really. But I know, in my heart, that there's a chance Jordyn may be wrong. I may be able to prove it before they all leave.

On my back I wear a bag of seeds. It's heavy now, but as I walk it gets lighter. I whistle the long note that will bring my friends to me. I hear two answering calls, different distances away. I pull out two seeds and wait. It's not long before two birds circle overhead. I repeat the tone.

The birds land nearby. Both are taller than me, but I don't fear them. I approach, dropping the seeds which the birds happily consume.

I have taught a lot of birds from around my home to answer two distinct calls. One, the long tone, brings them to me in expectation of a treat. This call enables me to have them track me and follow me, as I can repeat it as I walk. The other call, which I will use later, sends them in large circles before coming back to me. This is useful for checking perimeters or dangers. We do not speak the same language but I am learning that does not mean we cannot communicate.

Why then would I believe that something which can speak my language is beyond my ability to reach? I have to try.

I unfold the parchment from Danyel and consult it. A simple map which should lead me to the camp of the giants. If my calculations are correct, I'm close. As soon as I step again, the birds who have been tracking me take to the sky. It's comforting to know I'm not alone, not really.

I continue with this pace, stopping occasionally to call to the birds and reward them for still being with me. Finally, the tops of the camp come into view. I stop, dropping myself onto the ground nearby, and watch.

It's different than I expected, but not in a bad way. From this far off it's easy to imagine that it is just a group of us down there. They look small nestled in a valley and standing against the backdrop of the entire skyline. Their houses, if you can call them that, look to be made of fabric. More like a temporary tent than a house.

"They're scouts," I say it out loud as it comes to me. They are even dressed in brown and some have weapons strapped to them. I remember Jordyn telling us the last count was twenty-something giants. Large for a troop, but not unheard of.

I watch for a while, confident that I have nothing to fear.

I call the birds again with the long note. The response takes longer, but they arrive to retrieve their seeds. Then I give the other signal. Three short bursts. The smaller bird cocks his head to the side, confused. When the larger bird takes off, he follows. I hope they understand.

I stay in my location and watch them as they take large circles around the giant camp. They don't pause or change speed. They don't drop or climb. The absence of these signals can mean there is no danger. I use the long signal to call them back, I can't keep this up for too long. I'm running out of seeds.

I give them no signal when they leave this time. Instead, I stretch myself onto my side along the ground. I can still watch the giants as I rest my head. I am far enough away to safely get a little sleep. I will start fresh in the morning, planning how to communicate with the giants.

Chapter 22

Eselda watches Jordyn speak in whispered tones to Kurt, returning from a quick check on the giant camp. In the days before Toby went missing the group had abandoned the idea of an around-the-clock watch. Even Jordyn had been coming around to the idea of giving up, letting them live their life without watching them. But now everything has changed, again.

The air in the camp feels stiffer, somehow. Everything feels charged and dangerous. Jordyn recognizes the fear that is palpable around the group. It is the same fear that drove them before the Great War for Fraun.

Despite wanting to be free of all that Fraun symbolizes and brings, Jordyn couldn't walk away from them. He never really could. Not when Fraunians could die.

Eselda isn't sure how to make him see what she already knows, running things the way Fraun does is simply too dangerous for citizens. They have no voice, they have no ears at the table. They are blissfully ignorant of all the things that threaten their way of life each day. The citizens around Fraun know less about what is going on in their world than a common roach out here with the Scouts. If Jordyn expects them to be a part of Fraun again when this is over, that will have to change.

"Thank you for checking on the giant camp again," Jordyn says to Kurt. "Any changes?"

"Nothing of note. Same counts. No changes in behavior or anything to indicate the child may have told them about Toby."

"Did you see the child?" Toby had described the small giant as best he could. Both Jordyn and Kurt are reasonably sure they know which one was the captor.

"I did. He was with the ones that are likely his parents. The ones who share his living accommodations. He did not leave the camp while I was there. He was playing on the ground with some sticks."

Jordyn nods. "No armor or weapons in sight?" Not that they would need them for a battle. They would need merely thick soled shoes and a desire to quickly end lives.

"Nothing unusual. There were still a few hunters preparing their bows and arrows for the day. They looked ready to head out as usual. I have no reason to believe they will come in this direction. They normally don't."

Every day since the day they started watching the giants the hunting has gone off in the same directions, out away from Fraun and the scout troop. The giants are creatures of habit, it seems. They have plenty of animals to bring down off in that area. Jordyn has never seen them return empty-handed. There is no reason to change things that are working.

"Thank you." Both men split up, heading off to their separate areas to finish packing the last of their items. Before sunset today, they will have to head to Fraun again.

Neither man is truly prepared for what lies ahead.

Chapter 23

"Here we go again," Tutor whispers. He is standing at the edge of the clearing facing a crowd that includes most of the citizens in Sarcheda. There have been entirely too many of these speeches to an entire crowd in his lifetime, things meant to motivate or inspire people. He grows weary of the task.

Tutor rolls his shoulders back, takes a deep breath, and steps forward. The crowd quiets automatically. He is careful to keep his face impassive. No smiling today. This is not a good message.

"Thank you for coming," he begins. He is careful not to call it a good afternoon. Whatever this afternoon may turn out to be, he is sure that good is not the word he would use. "New information has been presented to the council of rulers that makes it necessary for me to bring you life-changing news." The already quiet crowd gets eerily silent. Even the rustling of clothing, usually a given in a large crowd like this, seems to stop.

"The council has decided that Fraun will relocate to the area scouted by the group that left a few lunar cycles back."

Murmuring starts up. He can hear some of the questions moving through the crowd already. "Is he serious? What are we supposed to do about…" He shakes his head and holds up his hands. The murmuring grinds to a stop.

"I don't want to spend time talking about why we have to do this. We were wrong about the giants. We no longer believe they are safe. They threaten our way of life. We would be wise to move out of their path."

He doesn't call for questions, but he hears them start up again. Whispered from one citizen to another. They are panicking. He wishes he could stop the panic for them, give them a sense of peace. But he cannot give what he himself does not even have.

"It's time for me to be honest with you. The time for me to tell you what I think you need to hear is gone." He lets his shoulders fall. It's like the veneer he wears as king cracks and suddenly he's just the boy who has lived in so many of the realms. He is a citizen of Fraun as broken as any of them. "It was Jordyn, former King of Renchenda, who found the giants. It was Jordyn who assured me they were safe. It was Jordyn who came immediately to warn me the second he learned a truth that made him decide we are no longer safe.

"You once followed me in battle. You once followed Jordyn. I hate that it has come to this, that I have to ask you to follow me again. We have no real choice left, I fear. But I cannot ask you to do something you do not believe in."

He closes his eyes, runs his hand along his face. This time the crowd does not rush to fill the silence with chatter. They lean toward him, captivated by the honesty and raw emotion he is radiating. His eyes pop open again. "You may stay if you wish, under no King and no laws. I am going. Not as King. I am going because it is the safe thing to do. I am going because those who go will need help and I am healthy and strong and able to help.

"Jordyn is going as well. He will need to make peace with any Fraunians who go along the way. I'm sure he is aware of that. I am not sure what other citizens are traveling with us. I am not sure how long the journey will take."

He looks down at the ground, scuffing his shoes along the dirt. "We leave at high sun. If you are here we will travel together."

"What happens with Marcus?" someone calls.

Tutor frowns. "What would you have me do with him?" he asks.

"Give him the chance to go with you," an older Fraunian in the front says. "He could go along with his hands tied."

Tutor knows Marcus will never agree to that. He won't have any desire to follow Tutor and the council out of Fraun, not if other choices remain. "I can do that. What would you have me do with him if he refuses to travel?"

"Then he won't be your problem, will he?" someone asks.

Tutor shrugs. "Then I will offer him the chance to come safely along with me, same as I have offered you." He turns to head back to his house on the other side of Sarcheda. There's a lot to do. He must pack things to take with him. He is lost in thoughts, memories of the realms he will be leaving behind. He cannot allow himself to get lost there long. If he does, he will never be able to take those first steps out of Fraun.

"Be well," he hears from behind him. He turns to look. The crowd is standing exactly as he left them, watching him walk away. An older woman, gray hair and wrinkled face, is standing front and center. She raises her hand in a wave. "Be well, Tutor," she repeats.

"Be well, citizens," he says.

If he notices the missing title, he doesn't comment. It simply doesn't matter anymore.

Chapter 24

When I open my eyes in the morning to see the sunlight gleaming through the clouds and illuminating the camp of the giants I have a smile on my face. I loot around in my bag, finding a few seeds and a strawberry. I eat the second as I make the call to bring the birds to me. If there are any still in the area, they'll come.

I get through the entire piece of fruit, relishing in the juice that runs down my chin, before the first bird appears in my line of sight. He or she is flying low, coming in from across the giant camp. The bird stops flapping its wings, gliding across a current. The birds make flying look effortless. It is, I think, part of the reason I enjoy them so much.

While I wait for the bird to reach me I look down upon the camp. Could these giants be my enemies? Jordyn would have me believe that. He would have me believe that these creatures would crush me as soon as they meet me. Kill first, question later.

I have trouble reconciling that thought. They are moving about their camp this morning, leisurely cooking or eating. A few are cleaning the meat from bones that are certainly larger than me. But I see smaller creatures among them, crawling on the ground or flying near the food. They don't threaten those. They ignore them. Would they ignore us? Am I willing to gamble on that?

The bird swoops down and lands on the edge of the mountain where I'm sitting. He squawks, tilting his head to the side. I watch him hop from foot to foot. He's impatient for the seed. I toss it to him, giving him the call that will send him out and around. When he takes off I'm looking for signs of distress; avoiding an area, making unusual noises in an area, diving at something unseen, flying higher when approaching something. Basically, if the birds have any reason to be nervous, so do I.

His first circle is without incident.

As he starts his second loop, I turn my attention to the giants again. There is a smaller group of them returning from the woods along the opposite side of their camp. There are five of them. Four are occupied holding a device that has a very large animal draped across it. Clearly they have been hunting. The fifth drops to his knees and arms himself with his bow and arrow. He takes a practice stance, aiming at something with strong and steady arms.

I'm too busy watching him to even wonder what he's aiming at. He has impeccable form.

The arrow is loosed and I try to follow it with my eyes. I lose it against a white cloud.

But I see when it hits.

My hand flies to my mouth. "No," I call out. It's too loud. I bite my lip to keep from calling out again. There's no reason for it. My bird was not bothering them. They obviously have just been hunting, food is not an issue. There was no reason for it.

My eyes water, blurring my vision.

Jordyn was right. There was no reason for the death of the bird.

The giant stands to his feet and crosses to the body of the bird. He picks it up, pulling the arrow out and re-sheathing it. He holds the bird upside down by the feet.

He is too far away for me to clearly see his face. I wonder if there is remorse. Does he feel sorrow at the death? Shame? Does he feel like he needs to atone for it?

I have hunted with the Scouts. They only kill what they need to kill for survival or food. I can't understand the killing of this bird.

I stand up and turn my back on the giants. It's this simple act that tells me I need to abandon my idea to contact them. I will not try and reason with these giants. I will not try and convince Jordyn he was wrong. If the giants kill for reasons I cannot see then I am not safe.

I will leave Fraun with everyone else.

Chapter 25

The dream shocks her again, but Eselda recovers quickly. She doesn't wait for the man to emerge with his weapon. Instead, she immediately heads off in the direction the arrow will travel. She walks slowly, planning her steps carefully and paying attention to any landmarks. The sky is bright blue, no clouds that she can see. The trees are tall, but none stand out as being extraordinary. She doesn't recognize this area at all.

The ground is simple dirt, nothing that would indicate where she is. She reaches down and brushes her hand across it. Some dirt comes loose, leaving her hand coated in the light brown. But it's not wet, not overly. They are likely not in Enchenda where the soil stays rich and damp from the river.

She watches the sun, knowing she is traveling West. The sun is already moving down the sky in front of her, but it is not reaching the horizon yet. It is late afternoon, perhaps. The air is not cold, but it's not exactly warm either. This may be soon in the future.

Voices come to her on the air and she walks a little faster. There is more than one person nearby, that is certain. She is traveling right at their voices. Soon she may know who the target is, she just needs to hurry.

She turns and looks over her shoulder. She has to squint to see the man she knew was there, he is already lining up his shot. She turns back and searches the area in front of her. Yes, the people are just barely in her sight.

This man is a good shot, whoever he is.

The arrow whizzes by her head but she doesn't immediately wake up. Instead, she starts jogging quickly toward the people as the yell comes up again.

She draws close enough to see one man, lying on the ground, surrounded by people. She doesn't recognize any faces in the time that she is there. But she sees blood on the ground, pooling around the fallen.

This time when she wakes up she knows a few more things than she did. She knows someone who is good with a bow will shoot, and possibly kill, someone traveling in the woods with a crowd. She also knows the next time the dream comes she will have to run from the start if she wants to see more.

Chapter 26

I have to hurry. Now that I've decided to go with the group to meet Erick and the rest of our newest patrol away from Fraun, I walk with purpose. They were meeting at high sun today. I watch as the golden ball traipses further up the sky. I suppose, since I already know the direction, I could always meet up with them even if I am late.

I don't have enough in my backpack to leave right now. I'll have to stop at home. I know they're all meeting me there. I wonder, briefly, which residents of Enchenda will make the journey with us.

The fear is in the back of my head even as I hustle. The people of Fraun will not be quick to leave. They shouldn't be, should they? We are asking people to uproot annuals of businesses, growth, education, families, building, and livelihoods for what? Because we say they're in danger?

What if we're wrong?

I still can't shake the feeling that there could be more to these giants. What if, unlike what I saw with the bird, they could be given a chance? Toby said the giants spoke in Fraunian. What if, unlike the birds, I could reason with them? Don't I need to try?

I stop in the walkway and turn around.

I can't say that just watching a bird be killed was truly giving a chance to those giants. I take three steps in the direction of the camp, back where I came from. That's as far as I get before the rocks beneath me shift and I'm tumbling down the hill.

Chapter 27

The group outside the new council building is growing steadily as the sun approaches its highest point in the sky. Tutor and Alerta stand side-by-side with Stef. All three are wearing traveling clothes and have bags full of materials resting at their feet. Alerta also pulls a cart loaded up with fresh vegetables from the Marchenda gardens. Their hands are threaded between them and they look obviously nervous, shuffling with a preoccupied nature.

Jordyn and the scouts look the most comfortable in the traveling clothes they're wearing but they continue to glance around the growing crowd nervously. They're obviously not used to being in such a large group. Eselda especially looks upset. Her eyes have darkened quite a bit. Combine that sign of her age marker with the obvious discomfort she's showing and it's a sure sign that she is angry and far outside of her comfort zone.

King Hector, Queen Saren, and the new baby wrapped in her arms are accompanied by the king's sisters, Desdina and Margina. All of them are dressed warmly and wearing shoes appropriate for the journey ahead. They are somber and staring at the ground nervously. "Should we be waiting for Tell?" Margina whispers to her sister.

"No. He's not coming. He doesn't think it's right for us to abandon the realm completely."

"So, is he staying behind and trying to keep Fraun alive?" Margina asks.

"I'm not sure what he's going to do," Desdina snaps. She's not happy about this. She doesn't like the idea of being separated from her husband. But she was unable to talk him into coming along for the journey.

This is the way of Fraun at this point. Half the citizens are gathering on the lawn in travel clothes, wearing shoes and layers, carrying backpacks full of food. The other half are holed up in homes and businesses, willing to take their chances with the possibility of giants and refusing to leave what they have built.

This is a new beginning. Not everyone is ready for the journey.

Thometh and Lucinda arrive. They greet Jordyn first. "Nephew, how is everything? Are you well?" Thometh asks. He eyes Eselda nervously. "Are you both well?"

"We are." Jordyn smiles at Lucinda. "You must be my Aunt, it's a pleasure to meet you. Are you well?"

Lucinda smiles. "I am. I'm a bit worried about this journey. I have never walked long distances like what we are facing before." She turns and looks over her shoulder, back in the direction of Renchenda. "What of the citizens who stay behind? I fear for them as well."

"I have been thinking about that," Thometh says. "Once we are settled we will make it a point to come back and offer a clear path to our new area to anyone still here. Whoever we cannot convince today, we will come back for."

Jordyn smiles. "Not a bad plan. It's one you should bring up with your council."

"I think that term is going away, nephew." Thometh looks around the group gathering. All the faces show fear of equal measures. "I believe we're all on the same foot right now, regardless of the blood in our veins."

Lucinda sighs. "Well, in my case, it is a slow foot. I have a feeling I may fall behind the group before long."

"No fear, my wife. We will be sure to bring up the back. Jordyn here will tell you it is always wise to have someone at the back of the group that can be on watch from that angle," Thometh says.

Jordyn sets a hand on her shoulder. "He's not wrong. We would appreciate you keeping watch to make sure no one falls behind. Look around, there are children among this group. I'm sure you won't be the slowest among us."

Lucinda smiles up at her tall nephew. "You're too kind. Thank you."

"I'll walk with you as well," Eselda offers. "I'd hate to rush and I'd love the idea of keeping you company. We can be sure you are not doing too much and keep you healthy."

"That's kind of you, thank you."

The conversation is interrupted by the arrival of Sieven and Abney, whose arms are holding a small bundle of blankets. Jordyn waves them over. As the distance closes it becomes obvious that Abney's nose is red and tears are streaming down her face. Evelyn quickly walks to meet her daughter, wrapping her arms around her in a large hug that consumes the infant between them in a cocoon of love. "What's the matter?" she whispers.

"I've barely found Fraun and now we have to leave. We've established too much already. This is the first home Lili has ever known." Abney pulls out of the hug and looks down at the infant.

Evelyn strokes Abney's cheek and tips her chin up so her daughter's gaze returns to her mother's face. "Listen to me. Wherever you are will be home as long as you're all together."

Abney nods, a soft smile touching her face.

Sieven steps up and puts his arm around Abney's shoulders. "It'll be alright," he says. "We're all together."

Abney looks around the group, taking in the faces of all their gathered friends and the Fraunians they'll be journeying with. "Where's Sawchett?" she asks. "Isn't she coming?" She turns to Tutor, confident he'll be the one who would know. "She's coming, right?"

Tutor's eyes drop to the ground. He clears his throat once. It's obvious to everyone before he answers. "I'm not sure. I haven't seen her." He tries for a light tone, but the words fall dark and heavy.

Where is the young Queen?

Chapter 28

When I open my eyes, I'm laying among leaves on the ground somewhere. I take a minute to kind of scan over my body with my mind, searching for places that hurt. My knee is a little sore. It has kind of a burning sensation. I push myself up to a sitting position and look down. My right knee is covered in scrapes. I brush some dirt and leaves out of it and really look. It doesn't look too serious. I tentatively try bending it and find very little pain.

I push myself up off the ground. My ankle is a little sore but it holds weight.

I turn back around and glance up at the hill I slid down. There's a clear path showing where I came from like the path of a cart wheel on a dirt road. It's not a long distance but it looks too far to walk back up. I'll have to find another way back to the top.

So what else is around here?

I can still see the giant camp. In fact now that I've dropped down a level in elevation I may actually be closer to them. It's not exactly a comforting thought.

The sun is at the highest point in the sky. That is a problem. It means I'm late. It means Fraun is likely moving on without me. I was born in Enchenda. Sure, I fled the kingdom before the war and sought refuge among the scouts. It turned out to be one of the best things I ever did. But Enchenda is my home. As soon as the war was over I returned and took my place as their Queen. It pains me to think about what will be in their future. Our future.

A noise in the distance draws my attention. The rustling of leaves, the scraping of dirt. I stay silent, afraid to even move. A soft clicking reaches my ears.

"Hello," I call out tentatively. I'm certainly hoping that clicking means what I think it means. I'm hoping that is a friendly roach and not the child of a giant or some other dangerous creature drawing close to my location. "Is anyone there?"

"You are not much more than a child. What are you doing out here alone?" the roach asks as he draws into my view fully. He is a large roach with a deep booming voice. He speaks Fraunian with no trouble, meaning he's spent time around my people or scouts.

"I'm a Queen in Fraun, actually," I offer. I have the presence of mind to stand to my full height. Most roaches are friendly and have had a peace agreement with our people for a long time. I would hate to find out this gentleman was an outlier.

"You are lost?" he asks.

I look around again. Taking in the trees around us and the hill I unceremoniously slid down. "I know where I am and where I came from." I turn back to him and offer a small smile. "But as to how the two connect, I must admit I am at a loss."

"You should take the route behind you there." His antennae wiggle in the direction behind me. "It will curve to the left and take the steep incline to a better angle to traverse. You'll get yourself back to the top of that hill there. From there you'll be able to walk straight into Fraun."

I turn and look in the direction he indicated. I think I do see a path there, between the trees. "That's helpful." I turn back to him. "Thank you."

"You need to hurry. You shouldn't be here. It's not safe." His head and antenna turn toward the giant camp. His meaning is clear.

"They're dangerous?" I ask. "This is your opinion?"

He makes a sound like a growl. I have never heard such a sound from this kind of creature before. I take an involuntary step away from him. "They kill." A shudder runs through him, shaking his whole body from antenna to feet. "They put poison down on the ground disguised as food. Creatures eat it and die a few steps from the food. Worse, some creatures carry the poison back to homes and families. We have no way of knowing the food is not safe. You should not be here. Avoid this place, young Queen."

The roach's antenna twitch suddenly, like a nose that is trying to smell something. "Silence," he says.

I hadn't planned to say anything, but my blood suddenly runs cold. I tune my ears to the faint sounds. Surely his hearing must be better than mine. To me it sounds like nothing. Like voices on the wind.

Oh, voices.

My heartbeat quickens and my eyes close. Please let us be safe. Please don't be what I think it is.

We don't stand there long before the voices grow loud enough for me to hear them. "The kid said it was near here, right?" the first voice asks. It sounds feminine and yet it booms with a volume I have never heard. It must be the voice of a giant.

Despite my fear, I force myself to open my eyes and look. Sure enough, in the distance, I can see the body of a woman giant. She is far away and yet still she looms larger than life. Her head veritably blocks the sun from reaching me. I cannot see who she speaks to, but her head is turned to the right.

"Somewhere near here. Yeah. He thinks there are more of them too," a voice answers. This one is deeper, more masculine.

"What if the kid was wrong? You want me just scrambling around here all day looking for something we ain't never gonna find?" She shakes her head and bends down toward the ground. "How is we supposed to find anything that small anyway?"

"They're looking for you, little Queen," the roach whispers. "You must go. Go now."

I nod and mouth "thank you" as I turn to take the path he indicated earlier. I have to hurry.

Chapter 29

Eventually, they have no choice but to move out. It's Tutor who makes the call. "We should go. If she is coming, she'll have to catch up. We can't wait all day." The sun is already beginning its journey down the sky. Hundreds of Fraunians have gathered. If they don't leave now they won't get far enough outside of Fraun before it's time to camp out for nightfall. At that rate people may change their minds, decide to go back to their own homes for the night.

Despite fears keeping their feet heavy and their hearts leaden, the crowd begins to move. Without a word they all fall into a sort of clump, trailing after Tutor and Alerta as they travel in the direction of the forest surrounding Enchenda.

The first of the group is just approaching the river Fraun when Tutor notices the crowd of people in the distance. "What do you suppose that's about?" he points to draw Alerta's eyes to the crowd.

She shrugs. "I'm not sure. Perhaps people are joining us but didn't want to meet at the council building," she offers.

They continue to walk in silence. Tutor's eyes remain fixed on the crowd. Perhaps a hundred people await them. As they draw ever closer a few things become apparent. Firstly, this group is not prepared for a journey. They don't appear to have anything with them. Secondly, and this fact makes his heart suddenly feel even heavier than he thought possible, every single person he can see is wearing the red of Sarcheda.

"I don't have a good feeling about this," he says. He stops walking and turns to face the group following him. He smiles at a few citizens as his eyes eagerly search the crowd. He doesn't have to look long before his eyes find the head towering over the rest. "Jordyn, a word."

Jordyn nods and draws up until they are beside each other. The crowd, unsure what is happening, slows. "There is a party ahead of us," Tutor explains. "They look like they're waiting for something. I have a feeling it is Sarcheda. Things haven't been exactly perfect there. People may have doubts. I don't have a good feeling about this. I want you to take the group on without me. I'll catch up."

Jordyn listens, as Tutor knew he would. Then he signals to Alerta, standing over Tutor's shoulder. "You heard him?" he asks. She merely nods. "Good. Take the people and continue on the path. Tutor and I will deal with this group."

Alerta nods and resumes walking. The group trudges along. Jordyn steps off in the other direction, toward the gathered crowd. Tutor rushes to catch up with the taller man's steps. "Wait, why are you coming with me?"

"You're not going alone if you are worried about being unsafe, Tutor." Jordyn stops and whirls back around on him. "That's what this is, right? You are worried they will do you harm?"

"I don't know what to think. They're not happy. Jordyn, I have no blood of Sarcheda. I was never a king to them. Now I've abandoned them —"

"That's what you think you did?" Jordyn's voice slices through the air, silencing Tutor. "This isn't abandonment. This is hope." He gestures to the group traipsing together off into the woods. "This is a chance to rebuild. Do you think the giants will offer us that chance once they've gotten ahold of us?"

"I'm going with you, Jordyn. You've convinced me. You don't need to do more. Just let me handle this." Tutor begins walking again toward the group. They do not talk but he can hear the footsteps behind him. Jordyn will not leave him to do this alone.

Secretly, he is glad for it. Especially when the face of Marcus, looking positively wicked with a full smile, comes clearly into view.

Chapter 30

My feet carry me as quickly as they can over the brush. I cover a lot of ground with silent steps, my breath coming out in ragged gasps all the way. I have never been so scared in my life, and that includes the time I fought for Fraun on the steps of the castle with only a bow and arrow to defend myself.

The giants stood right there talking about looking for more creatures. They were talking about us. They were looking for us. The roaches know we're not safe. I hate myself for thinking, even for one heartbeat, that I was going to be able to fix this. It is beyond fixing. I see that now. I just have to get to Fraun before it's too late.

I can see the buildings looming in the distance, I'm close. But they're not the buildings I was expecting to draw up to. I'm closer to Sarcheda than I meant to be. The ravine will be coming soon.

I slow my steps. It wouldn't help anyone if I fell into the ravine today.

Sure enough, as the vegetation changes, I see the steep incline that borders Sarcheda. I can't help myself. I walk up to it and peer over the edge. It's exactly like I'd heard. It's the picture that haunts my nightmares. The drop off goes almost directly down. I cannot see the end. Even when I hold my breath I cannot hear sounds inside it. If there is water at the bottom, as few have suggested, I cannot hear it. I try a bird call, to see if any maybe have nests inside. There is no answer. In fact, for the first time since I've begun using bird calls to communicate with the beasts, there is only silence all around me.

I am truly alone.

I resume walking, picking my way slowly around the edge of the ravine until its end. Here there is a tree laying across a much more shallow area of the ravine. I have reached the end of Sarcheda territory. I know I can cut across here and head toward Enchenda and the river. From there I will be able to meet up with the group who left at high sun.

With any luck, I'll be able to meet up with them before nightfall.

As I walk through Sarcheda I'm equal parts comforted and shocked by the lack of citizens. Perhaps the council did a better job than I anticipated convincing people of the urgency behind this move. I had my doubts, obviously, but it seems the citizens did not. I should be glad for that. But I must admit, even if only to myself, that I am shocked. There is something about these citizens of Sarcheda that I never trusted.

I'm sure it's rooted in Tin. He scared me from the first moment I ever met him, back in Enchenda. He was courting Eselda, the then Queen. But there was something dark and dangerous about him even then. A cold whistles through my blood and I shiver. I always knew he was capable of murder. I think that's what I could tell from that first meeting. His eyes were so cold, so calculating. He treated every situation as a game he needed to win.

Enough. No more thinking of him. He is gone. We no longer have to worry about Tin. Tin represented everything dangerous about Sarcheda but there is good here as well. When we rebuild, we can find it.

Chapter 31

"Marcus," Tutor calls as they approach the group, "have you changed your mind and come to join us?"

"That's not our intention, no." He waits for the former kings to draw up to the group before continuing to speak. His hands are firmly planted on his hips, his feet shoulder width apart. Tutor recognizes the power stance. He does his best to keep his own body relaxed so as not to provoke the man further. He looks at the faces of the crowd behind the former ambassador. There is anger there but also confusion.

"We are in a hurry, but what can we do for you?" Tutor asks.

"We need answers before you leave. Honest answers," Marcus says. The crowd behind him nods.

"Marcus, we don't have time for this. Fraun is threatened. The giants are encroaching on us even now. We must move. I implore you to come with us. Please."

"You ask us to abandon everything we have built? To abandon Fraun? To start again?" Marcus' voice rings like a battle cry.

"I hate this as much as you. It must be done. I am going. Come if you'd like." Tutor turns his body in the direction he must travel, eager to show he means business. But he hesitates. His feet do not take the first step. Marcus notices and his smile widens.

"We intend to stay here and keep Fraun safe on our own. We intend to keep Sarcheda alive. Are you abdicating your throne?" he asks.

Jordyn shakes his head. "None of this matters," he mumbles.

"I am," Tutor says. "I travel as a citizen. Titles won't save you if the giants come. But if the title is what you seek, you have my permission to petition whatever citizens remain behind with you for the title, royal blood or no." Tutor looks sad, suddenly. "Marcus, none of this is important anymore. Please reconsider. Put your safety and the safety of all these people ahead of titles and come with us. We don't even need to discuss your crime. We can start over. We can clean the slate."

"We don't need you, Tutor. We needed your throne. We were prepared to fight you for it, but you've made it simple. You abdicated. That is all we needed." Marcus turns to the crowd and raises his arms triumphantly. "Sarcheda will live on," he yells. The crowd lets up a cheer.

Tutor, shaking his head, finally takes the step toward the group they've been following. They're not far behind the last people. They will catch up just outside of Fraun. It hurts both men to hear the chant "long live the king" be taken up again as they pull away from the crowd. Neither of them hoped to ever hear that again.

For Tutor, it is the final sign that he made the right choice.

Chapter 32

I'm surprised to see so many people gathered around in Sarcheda near the river. Maybe I'm not as late as I thought. I tip my head back up to the sky, checking on the position of the sun. It's already falling in the sky, confirming I'm very late. So why are this many Fraunians gathered together if not to travel to the new location?

The crowd is loud and chaotic. Is that chanting? I pick up the pace a little, eager to figure out what is going on. Most of the people appear to be from Sarcheda, they're wearing black and red. No one is in armor. Actually, I notice, no one is prepared for travel either. Where are their bags? Their walking shoes?

I cross the yard of a nearby house, drawing even closer. By now, I'm practically jogging. I have a weird feeling forming in my gut.

The weird feeling instantly becomes worse as the words of their chant become clear. It is a chant I haven't heard since the war. One I never wanted to hear again.

"Long live the King."

I stop walking, frozen in fear. Surely my brother would never insist his people chant at him like this. We are a council. We say "Long live Fraun" if we say anything at all. It is not about one person. It has never been about one person. Something is wrong.

Slowly, sure that I must get answers to this riddle, I resume walking toward the crowd. At the back of the group there is a pair of young women. They look like they might be my age. They're not chanting. They look like they're there to take attendance, maybe to judge and whisper. They don't look like participants. They don't look dangerous.

"Excuse me," I say. "What's going on? Where is King Tutor?"

"King Tutor?" The girl closest to me asks. She props her hand on her thin hip and widens her eyes. "He was never blood of Sarcheda, you know."

"I know." I don't like where this is going. "But no one is."

"King Marcus says it doesn't matter. King Marcus says in the absence of the blood someone loyal to Sarcheda should take the throne." She steps closer to me, poking me in the shoulder. "Sarcheda will get the representation they deserve now that everyone is running scared."

"King Marcus?" I take a step back from the girl. Her hand falls back to her side. Her head tips to the right and her eyes narrow.

"Where are you from?" she asks. She smacks the other girl on the arm, drawing her attention. Together they take in my appearance. The bag on my back, the dirt on my clothing and face, my shoes. It's unlikely the outfit will give a royal impression. But is it enough to disguise myself? I have a feeling they don't want council representatives here right now.

I take another step back and look for an escape route. The only way I'm getting around these people, unless I want to wade through the river, is to go right through. I mumble something that may be a sort of apology and start elbowing my way to the front. I keep my eyes trained on the ground. I'm watching for a stray foot, careful not to step on anyone or trip.

The crowd gets thick for a while. I am careful not to listen to what they're talking about. I'm sure I don't want to hear it. Part of me feels guilty for passing through like this. Shouldn't I be trying to convince them to come with us? Shouldn't I be expressing the danger I've learned about to them?

I can't bring myself to do it.

If they come with us, we'll be repeating the big war. This is too much like Tin, too much like what we already went through. I can't bring myself to do it again.

When the feet start to thin out, I look up. There he is. Marcus. The ambassador to Sarcheda. The man who has given my brother trouble at every turn. The man who rallied Sarcheda against Tutor from the beginning. The man who murdered another for his cause. He is standing in front of the group, arms raised as though he is ready to speak.

I try to hustle past, but his words stop me. He's one here who would know exactly who I am. Better to stay with the crowd until I can slip past unseen. I hide behind a tall woman and listen silently.

"Alright, my people, it is official. Those royals, they run in fear. They are our past. Our ancestors, those who lived and loved in Sarcheda, they would never have run from something. Not even from giants." The crowd explodes in applause. Marcus calms the riot with his hands before continuing. "We will remain here in Fraun. We will keep Fraun running while they turn tail. We will build Fraun in strength. Someday, when they return to check on us, they will find Sarcheda alive and well!"

This time, when the crowd begins applauding, he lets them continue. I see a path open up on the right and take it, quickly moving through to the trees surrounding Enchenda. I just reach the trees as "long live the King" starts up again.

I have to reach Tutor.

Chapter 33

By the time I make a quick stop at my home to throw things in a bag and head out, it is already darkening. I don't let myself go slow. I run into the woods, following the path I know the group should have travelled.

Ahead of me, I spot something. For a heartbeat, I'm scared. Then I realize. The two shadows, dark shapes against darkening backdrop, are Tutor and Jordyn. I'm as sure of it as I am sure that my heart is still pounding. We're outside the boundaries of Enchenda. Far enough away that the river is quiet and the voices of the gathered group at the edge of the border have silenced. I can hear animals, birds, but nothing concrete. Nothing close enough to concern me.

Jordyn is obvious enough with his height. The only other Fraunian I've ever met or heard of that clocks in at almost three marks was Mick, former King of Farcheda. He is dead and gone now. So this man, towering over the shorter companion, must be Jordyn.

As for how I know Tutor, that's harder to explain. The walk, eternally favoring that right leg just a little with long stretches, is part of it.

The hair, dirty blonde and falling against his jacket, is another. But the comfort in the woods, the ease that he moves through the brush, the general calm with what is happening outside Fraun, that is the clincher.

My brother may have played royalty for the last few annuals in Fraun, but he belongs out here. Maybe that's something else we have in common deep down inside.

"Tutor, Jordyn," I call when I'm sure to be close enough to garner their attention. Both of them turn, shock registering briefly before large smiles occupy both faces.

"Sawchett, you decided to join us," Tutor says. "I was afraid you weren't coming."

"I always intended to come, I had to check something out first."

"The giants," Jordyn says. "I knew you weren't going to be able to let that go. The fact that you are here means you agree with us, I assume."

They've both stopped to wait for me. I catch up with them easily and hug them both before answering Jordyn's insightful question. "I had to see. I hope you're not upset. I wanted to know if there was any way we could reason with them. Maybe talk to them. Start up a relationship like the society of roach has with us," I explain. I shrug my shoulders a little, a sad excuse for an apology.

Jordyn shakes his head. "Sawchett, in that relationship we would be the servants who are allowed to only hold jobs working for them in their society. Think about it, the roaches are not the same when they are outside of our society. The ones who choose to remain inside Fraun are always considered lower class. They have a relationship we wouldn't want."

"That's deep," Tutor says. He throws up his hands. "Look, I'm not happy about any of this and I'm sure we're not done talking about it. But we need to get moving. I'd like to catch up with Alerta and the group before nightfall." He turns his head up to the sun. "We don't have much time before that thing sets."

He's not wrong and I have no way to correct someone who's right, so I let them lead the way and follow them further West.

There's a lot of steps in silence. Enough for me to hear a few birds rattle trees nearby. They won't approach unless I call them or unless we are quiet enough when we're walking. Today it's the latter. I'm not calling for anyone.

I notice it's getting harder to keep up with my companions. Compared to the two of them, I'm out of shape. Jordyn lives with the scouts now, he probably walks daily and keeps himself healthy. In fact, he's even more developed with muscles than he was when I last saw him. He's also a shade darker from the sun.

Tutor, while he was living up to the title of King of Strength, has been strenuously working out for annuals. I am definitely the weak link, in more ways than one.

"Um, I saw something odd on my way out of Fraun," I finally say. I've been working up the courage to mention this to the pair of them since I found them. It feels important, as though I should mention it right away. But it also feels dangerous somehow. As if speaking the words aloud will bring our past crashing into our future. "Marcus, he…" I trail off. I'm not sure how to give it words.

"We know," Tutor says. "We saw him." He turns and looks at me. I'm not surprised to see sadness filling his eyes. I am surprised to see that he is smiling a little. "I wish them luck. I'm only sorry we couldn't convince more citizens to come with us. I really don't think they're safe."

"Have we decided what will happen when we reach the new land?" Jordyn asks. "I appreciate that everyone here has moved quickly in response to my call to action. But I know that your council does things differently than my scouts. They've probably had you in meetings for the last sun when they should've been packing."

"No," Tutor answers. His voice is a whisper on the wind. "No one wanted to think about this happening. There haven't been plans. There was packing and now this." He turns his eyes on Jordyn. "We'll have to decide together."

We walk a few more steps in silence. Then, Tutor whispers one more line. "Stop calling them a council. There is no more council. There is no more Fraun."

Chapter 34

We catch up to the group just after sunset. It's actually the fire the group has set to cook by that draws our eye after the sun slips below the horizon. Without it we may have had to stop alone for the night. That would have been disastrous as none of us was carrying anything to make fire with. I watch Alerta and Tutor embrace. He bends down to whisper the story about the meeting with Marcus in her ear. I watch her eyes darken a little. I realize I don't know her age. Are they darkening in lust for my brother or anger at the tale? If I'm to spend more time with her I suppose I should find that out.

I watch Jordyn reunite with Eselda, who nods once in acknowledgement of my arrival as well. She looks haggard and like a shell of the great woman I once knew. It deepens my sadness. Eselda is the embodiment of Fraun to me.

Of course, when I think about it like that it makes sense she's so haggard. In a way, both of those things that I always considered regal and perfect have completely crumbled. They are both unrecognizable shells of what I once loved.

I sit by myself before the fire and warm my hands. I'm not hungry so I don't search for food. I feel an emptiness inside that I know food wouldn't fill. There are people all around. More than I've ever been surrounded by in one place at one time. There is a small sense of chaos, and yet it's controlled in a way I didn't expect. People are setting up tents, people are talking. I actually hear laughter from off in the distance.

The terror I feel at the future seems removed from this setting tonight.

I consider it a small victory.

"Sawchett?" I turn my head to look at the source of the small voice. "I thought that was you. I'm glad you came along. Hungry?" Tanya tips a bowl of something in my direction. I shake my head. "Suit yourself." She tips the bowl back toward her own mouth and takes a big sip.

"Where's…" I trail off, unsure exactly which person I was going to ask her about. The girlfriend? Her brother? "Everyone?" I decide.

"Most of them are around." She reaches out and lays a hand on my thigh. "Are you alright? You look upset about something."

I shake my head. "I'll be alright. It's just the whole idea of having to run like this really gets to me. The people of Fraun, they're supposed to be safe. We were supposed to be able to keep them safe. What kind of rulers are we…were we?" I correct.

Tanya takes another sip of her soup. "You aren't a ruler anymore?" she asks. "You used the past tense."

"Everyone has to start over now," I answer.

"Hey, this isn't on you. In fact, if it wasn't for all of you we would never have known what was coming." She shakes her head. "Can you imagine how much worse it would've been to wake up and find giants had crushed our homes?" A tremor passes through her arms. She holds both her palms out to the fire as if that can warm the cold running through her at the thought.

"I know that's true. I know that's why we did it." I put my head back and look up at the dark sky with the stars twinkling. The same sky I used to look at from the lawn in Enchenda. The same sky I looked at from under the trees in the woods surrounding Renchenda. The same stars that fill the sky over the abandoned home of the giants and around the new giant camp. "Tanya, is it going to be okay? Tell me the truth."

She sighs out a long breath. "I have no idea," she says. "But we're all together and that's something." I look back at her when I feel her hand on my shoulder. She's smiling at me but it's almost sad. "When you gathered on that lawn of Castle Fraun and stood your ground, did you know everything was going to be okay?" she asks.

I almost laugh. "No, I definitely didn't. I knew there was a chance I could die or that we would lose."

"But you did it anyway because it had to be done."

"It did," I agree.

"Do you regret it?"

Do I? I regret that we had to fight. I regret that I ran from Fraun before the war broke out. I regret that I wasn't able to warn Eselda before all of it happened. But do I regret fighting for Fraun? "Never."

Tanya stands up and waves to someone across the fire. "There you go. These decisions may be hard but that doesn't mean they're wrong. We may fail but that doesn't mean we shouldn't try. Stop stressing, Majesty." She leans down and kisses me on the forehead. I'm shocked when I feel zings of pleasure across my hairline and down my face. "We are starting over."

Chapter 35

Eselda remembers what she promised herself and takes off at a run the second she recognizes the dream. With the air moving as she runs it feels colder. This is getting close, this future date. Whatever she is dreaming about will happen soon.

This time she reaches the people before the arrow flies by. She sends up a silent wish that the faces will not be blurred. She's afraid the time to figure this out is dwindling. The people are gathered in a little clearing, spread out and moving around. From the looks of it they are gathering firewood. Eselda counts six people. They are all bending down, chatting and filling their arms.

"There's no time to search you all, who are you?" she says. Her voice is breathless from the run but it doesn't matter. They wouldn't hear her anyway.

The arrow whizzes by and, as she expected, lands in the back of a man standing on the opposite side of the clearing from Eselda. He makes the noise she's been hearing and falls, face first, into the dirt. The people nearby rush to him.

Eselda sees the face of the girl nearest her as she stands and rushes to the fallen man.

The breath catches in her throat and tears sting her eyes. The scene clears and she is sitting up in bed. Her cheeks are wet with cold tears. She shakes Jordyn, sleeping beside her. She barely waits for him to open his eyes before she starts talking. "I still don't know who it is," she says. "But Sawchett is there. Sawchett is with him. It must be one of us."

Chapter 36

Well, this is familiar, I suppose. Our entire group is gathered around the campfire this morning. There are people sitting on logs or on the ground, there are people scattered out behind them standing and watching. It reminds me of our old days with the scouts but on a larger scale. Upon closer inspection I notice whether you're sitting or standing has nothing to do with royal blood. It has to do with if you got to the seat first. Or, in the case of a few people with white hair, age.

Jordyn and Tutor emerge from behind a group of trees and stop when they are standing just behind a couple of seated people off to my left. "Good morning everyone," Jordyn greets. "We wanted to do a quick check in and lay out the plan for today."

"Make sure everyone is on the same page, basically," Tutor adds.

People stop what they are doing and turn to the pair of former rulers. A silence that feels heavy under the anticipation falls on the crowd. If anyone around the group takes offense to these men taking charge, they don't show it. Everyone appears to be listening.

"The plan today is to pack up whatever camp you laid out last night as quickly as possible and begin heading out. We will travel until a good lunch time, eat quickly and keep going." Jordyn has a naturally loud voice and people stay silent. His voice carries through the crowds. "We need to cover as much ground as possible today. The group we are following in the footsteps of traveled long days and it still took them…" he trails off and looks directly at me, waiting for me to fill in the missing detail.

"Five suns," I fill in. That reminds me, I should scribble a note to Erick to warn him we are coming. I'm sure he won't be surprised but it seems appropriate.

"Alright, so if everyone is ready let's start putting back the camps." Jordyn claps his hands together. Most of the people gathered around the fire stand up and start to walk off toward the areas they slept in. It's not a fully unpacked camp, but there are various tools for cooking, clothes, and some sleeping maps laid out around the area. All of this will need to be picked up. Also, we'll need to—

"Excuse me, I'm sorry," Eselda is still standing beside the fire. She speaks in a voice that carries loud across the clearing. She shoots a warning glance at Jordyn, who immediately drops his gaze to the dirt. I'm guessing he was supposed to say something about whatever she's about to say. I'm not the only one who freezes and gives her my attention.

"Does anyone here have any reason to believe they may have an enemy, of sorts? What I mean is, I'm looking for a young man or a young adult who may have an enemy from Fraun searching for them. Someone meaning to do them harm." She runs her hands back through her hair. "I know I'm being a little vague and I'm sorry." She points off to her right. "I'll be over there, packing up some things. If this sounds like any of you, please come see me."

She turns and walks off before anyone can comment.

"What was that about?" Tanya asks, suddenly at my elbow. She points toward the direction Eselda disappeared.

I shake my head. "No idea."

"My blankets are already folded and my bag is full." She pulls the bag around to her front as if to show me. "What else needs to get done?"

I look around the clearing. Most of the people are still busy with their own belongings but there are still things for the group to do. I gesture with my chin at the fire area. "The fire needs to be put out and the ring broken up."

"Do we pour water on it or something?" she asks.

"No." I point to a bucket beside the fire pit. "We actually use dirt. It helps put out the logs and it doesn't make a muddy mess."

"Sounds good. I'll fill the pail." She doesn't wait for me to agree or argue. She drops her bag on the ground at my feet, grabs the pail, and heads toward a mound of dirt just outside the fire clearing. I watch her walk away for a few steps, wondering where her friends and brother from Enchenda may be. Then I force myself to get to work. I use the nearby pail of water, likely the one that gave Tanya the impression we were going to drown the flames, and wash a few dishes that have been dropped onto the ground.

I don't have to give my full attention to the dishes, so I let my eyes wander through the crowd. Although none of us have bothered to wear clothing that is the color of our realm in Fraun, for many citizens that is what they already owned. The result is a rainbow of colors and garments that please my eye. It's a reminder, albeit a small one, that we are a new mix out here. We are like wildflowers, growing together and learning to be one field.

When Tanya returns I pause what I'm doing to show her exactly how to break down the campfire. We have to douse the already dying flame with dirt. Then we use the bucket of water to cool the little piece of wood that is left before finding a spot to bury it. I show her how to stir up the ashes with fresh dirt. Tell her to make sure she tests the heat of the mix before she dumps a final layer of dirt over it, and make myself busy removing the rocks.

It's something I've done before, a method I used with the scouts. But it feels so strange to be using it now, in these woods. I've also never had to teach anyone else, since I was the newest scout in the troop I traveled with. I find that I enjoy this feeling of passing on something I know how to do to someone else. I've led school visits and I've made big decisions that affected all of these people. Why does teaching Tanya how to properly douse a fire pit feel like the most important thing I have ever done in my life?

I turn around to grab the last two rocks and see Tanya, resting back on her heels, smiling up at me. There's a big streak of ash across her forehead and the biggest most genuine smile across her face that I have ever seen. "I did it," she says. "It's all cold and it just looks like dirt again." She lays her palm down on the smooth dirt in front of us. "Feel it."

I drop to my knees across from her and reach out. The dirt is smooth and soft. "Not at all warm," I agree. "Nicely done."

"Thanks."

"Alright, everyone, the first group is moving out now. Grab your belongings and partner up," Tutor yells. I stand and look around. I'm surprised to see that in the time we took to break down the fire pit the rest of the camp has been completely cleaned up. I tie the handle of the water pail to my bag.

"Partner?" Tanya asks. I notice she has tied the dirt bucket to her own equipment.

"Sounds perfect." We fall into step beside each other and head off with the rest of the group. There's not much room for talking because we're keeping a pretty solid pace up.

"Thanks for showing me how to do that," Tanya says. She uses her thumb to point back behind us, as if I may need a reminder.

"It was fun," I say. "It felt important."

She smiles. "That is because you just gave me a life skill."

I squint at her. "What?"

"Taking care of that fire pit is a life skill. I didn't have that before this morning and now I do. You taught me that." She lays her hand on my shoulder. "My brother says you can do things for someone and please them for that moment but if you teach them the skill you'll please them for the rest of their lives."

I like that idea, I decide. Perhaps this will be my life's mission. To teach people skills that they need to survive. "Life skills," I repeat. "I like that."

Chapter 37

Jordyn looks over his shoulder, checking on the progress of the group from the front. Eselda is a few people back. He can tell her brain is somewhere else. She's not focused on where she's walking. She's not talking to anyone near her. He knows these dreams bother her, even if he doesn't always understand why. He slows his pace to effectively drop back near her. "Did anyone come find you to talk about enemies they may have?"

She jumps a little with surprise as she pulls herself from her thoughts. "No. But it has to be someone important to me, right? That's how this works. The first time it was you I kept dreaming about. The second time it was my mother. So this must be someone important to me."

"But you said it's someone in this group. Who in this group is important to you?"

She scrunches up her nose as she thinks. "Sawchett, but it's obviously not her. You, Tutor, Danyel, Sieven, Abney..." Her shoulders fall. "There are too many to count, obviously. There may even be Fraunians from my past traveling with us who are important to me in some way."

Jordyn rubs her upper back for a few steps. "Look, every time you've had one of these dreams it's been some big important event or revelation. Maybe we need to be thinking about that. Maybe we need to try and figure out what the big change could be. Work backwards to figure out the who."

"The first time it was tied to the war but what was the important event in the second one?" She turns her big green eyes to Jordyn and he's surprised to see she looks serious.

"Eselda, your mother died. Your mother who you thought was already dead. That was pretty drastic."

She waves her hand between them before turning back to watch where she's walking. "But that was only big and significant to me. I thought we were thinking larger. Do you think this could be showing me that where we are traveling to isn't safe?"

The women walking in front of them stop talking and start looking over their shoulders. Jordyn shakes his head a little too vehemently. "No, the place is safe." He says it loudly to reassure the women. Then he pointedly drops his voice. "Be careful what you say, we don't want to make everyone unnecessarily nervous."

This time when Eselda turns to look at him her eyes are a darker shade of green. With her being past the twenty-fifth annual this sign means her anger is getting the best of her right now. "Someone is going to die, Jordyn. Maybe they should be nervous."

He puts his hands up like a shield. "Not necessarily." Her eyes darken a little more, Jordyn knows this is not a good sign. He shakes his head. "I'm just saying, you thought the first dream was showing you my death at first. But here I stand."

"Yes, but Tin is dead."

That name, spoken from her mouth, silences Jordyn. He turns to face the direction they're walking and she can see his jaw is clenched.

Eselda regrets the words when she sees the pain her husband feels. She reaches for him. "I don't mean that I regret Tin's death. I'm not sorry he's gone." She sighs. "I just meant I had a dream and someone died. It may have been someone who deserved it, but it was a death none-the-less."

Jordyn's head shakes just a little and his jaw works like he's grinding his teeth.

"Jordyn, I'm sorry," she continues. "I didn't mean it like it sounded. I'm just worried that someone is going to die."

He shakes his head harder this time. "I don't want to talk about this right now." He picks up speed, moving back to the front of the crowd.

Eselda doesn't try to stop him.

Chapter 38

When we stop for the night my feet are screaming for some rest. Instead of giving into the desire, I join up with the group collecting wood for the fire. It's important that we keep the fire going all night, the temperatures are still dropping low enough at night to be a concern. Plus, animals will often flock to our body heat if we sleep without it. The fire keeps them at bay so it must take priority over my tired body.

There are nine of us who venture out to gather wood, including Tutor and Tanya. We work separately but in the same location, not really talking or interacting. Basically we walk to an area that has a lot of smaller logs and split out to get as much as we can carry. You keep the rest of the crew in sight so there is no danger of being ambushed by an animal. This way we can work quickly and still have enough to keep the fire going all night.

The sun is approaching the horizon meaning we have to hurry because we won't have light for long. We move into a clearing that has a fallen tree. "This is a good spot," Tutor says. "Grab what you can and meet back in the center here. We'll go back once all nine of us are here."

We all spread out. I move to the left and bend down to the ground to clear away a little of the brush. Many of the people we travel with bring hatchets. It helps to be able to take down trees that are still alive or break up fallen ones that are too large. I don't have one which means I have to resort to moving aside vegetation and looking for fallen or dead trees.

I snatch up some medium-sized logs. I have no way to carry the large ones and the small ones are useless. I have four in my arms when I hear an odd noise. It almost sounds like an arrow whizzing by my head but that doesn't make sense. The hunters shouldn't be—

The scream cuts through my thoughts. I drop the wood and run in the direction of the yell along with everyone else. I'm farthest away from that edge of the circle, so I'm the last to arrive. "What happened?" I ask.

In response, people step out of the way so I can see him. He's lying on the ground, the arrow is buried in his left shoulder. His eyes are closed from the pain, at least I hope that's why they're closed. His right hand is crossed over his chest so his fingers are near the tip of the arrow.

I kneel beside him. "It's in your shoulder, Tutor. I'm going to have to pull it out." I turn my attention to the people standing around. They look lost, scared. I need to engage them, give them some way they can be useful. I point to them in turn as I ramble off directions. "You, go get Jordyn. You, go with him and find anyone with medicine experience. You, get me leaves. As many as you can grab. You three with weapons, head off in the direction the arrow came from. We need to know if this was a hunting accident or something else." I point to the last girl. "You carry a load of firewood back to the camp and gather a new group who can help you get this back there."

I clap my hands. "Now," I finish. Everyone snaps to attention and runs off to carry out their jobs. I turn my attention to my brother. "Tutor, how bad does it hurt?"

He groans in response but his eyes open. "Hurts."

"We have to get the arrow out. It's going to hurt worse for a beat before it starts to hurt less." I'm really not sure if it will ever hurt less, but I don't say that. Lance once told me, when I was training with a bow and arrow, that the arrows must always come out of the injury. The danger, he explained, was that if they hit something vital it could make the bleeding worse. But the risk of infection is too great to leave it in, he explained. These arrows aren't exactly clean when we shoot them.

"What kind of arrow is that?" Tutor asks.

I know what he means. Is it one of ours? He wants to know if I really think this was a hunting accident. I bend closer to see the arrow in the fading light. "Wooden shaft, feather fletching, crudely carved notch. Made by someone who knows what they're doing."

"Smooth?" he asks. The arrows we are making for hunting are not smooth. We are using a lot of them in a day, we aren't taking the time to smooth them down. We're shooting short distances to hunt for a large group. They don't need to be smooth and they don't need to be pretty.

This arrow, on the other hand, is smooth. It has been sanded down and polished to look nice. It's straight. The fletching is even and trimmed. This came from stock somewhere. Someone has a lot of them. "No, it's not ours."

He sighs. "Color?"

"It's getting dark. I can't tell." I'm lying. I see the color. It's not an accident that the fletching on this arrow is red. I'll tell him, I will, but right now Tutor doesn't need to know everything.

We're spared from further conversation by the arrival of some people from the camp. Jordyn, a short woman who I don't recognize, and a few of the people who were collecting firewood with us. Jordyn drops to his knees beside Tutor's legs and the woman kneels near his right shoulder. Immediately, she presses her hands to the wound on the left shoulder. "This arrow needs to come out," she says.

I nod. "I told him that." I assume, based on her actions, that this must be the medicine woman. "I sent someone to get leaves so we can clean the wound," I say.

Right on cue, the young girl who I sent for leaves returns. I use my water to rinse them as best I can, running my fingers along them to shake off any loose dirt. The medicine woman seizes the shaft of the arrow. "On my count," she bobs her head toward the leaves, "I'll remove this arrow and you will push the leaves down on the wound. Apply steady pressure." I nod that I understand. "One, two, three," she pulls up on the arrow. It leaves Tutor's body slowly, hesitantly. His groan is loud, echoing off the trees.

The blood bubbles up from the wound before I have a chance to get the leaves down. I try not to think about each drop of that blood being vital to his life. I try not to think about how losing too much of that will mean Tutor doesn't get a tomorrow. Those are not helpful thoughts. I have to focus on the tasks at hand, the things I can accomplish.

I smash the leaves down and push hard. Tutor tries to pull away from me. The medicine woman holds him in place. "She has to push down," she explains. "Give her a bit to absorb some of the blood."

She holds up the arrow to the torch Jordyn is carrying, inspecting it. With her hands she measures the length of the shaft covered in blood. Then she holds her hand at Tutor's side. "I don't think it went all the way through your body, but we should check." She looks at Jordyn. "You're going to need to pull him up off the ground for me."

I keep my hands between the two of them as best as I can. Jordyn reaches forward and wraps his arms around Tutor. He whispers something in his ear and then pulls. Tutor comes up off the ground with a grunt and a groan. Jordyn's eyes close like it causes him physical pain to hear the noises from my brother. "Sorry," Jordyn says.

"Alright, you can put him down." The woman grabs Tutor's chin and turns it toward her. "It didn't come out the other side, which is a good thing. That means I only have one wound to close. Open your eyes, look at me." She shines the light near his face. "Thank you. You're going to be alright." She turns her attention to me.

"I'm going to clean this wound and he's going to be fine. The arrow didn't go all the way through and his eyes look good. I'm hopeful. You should be too."

"Thank you," I tell her. I don't really know what else to say.

She pushes my hands away from the wound, taking over. I sit down on my bottom, intending to watch her clean the wound. The entire process is interrupted by the arrival of some people making a lot of noise. "What now?" I groan. Of course, I'm asking the question rhetorically. No one will have the answer. I stand up merely because this seems like the kind of thing a former queen should investigate.

I'm standing with my arms crossed in the center of the little clearing, my feet buried in the fallen leaves, when the people making all the noise come into view. I recognize the people who were collecting firewood with us. The ones who I sent off chasing the shooter.

The man being dragged between them I don't recognize, not right away. I take a step toward them, only mildly aware that I'm unarmed and this could be dangerous. I remember the fletching on the arrow was red. I bend down where the face of the man is pointing toward the dirt as the two men drag him by his arms.

When I'm close enough to see his face, panic wells up in my chest. I wave my hand toward Jordyn, trying to get his attention. My fingers brush his shoulder. "We have a problem," I say simply. "Get over here. Now."

Chapter 39

Alerting Jordyn is the one thing I have time for before my anger takes over. Then I'm in his face, demanding answers. "What are you doing here?" Everyone else backs away from my anger, including the two people holding his arms. He falls to the ground and pushes himself up to his knees. I stand over him, feeling my anger surge through my body and out toward my fingertips. I know I'm overreacting. I feel it. But I don't care. I reach out and slap him, feeling the satisfying sting across my fingers. Then I lean down and put my face closer to his. Close enough that I can see the marks of my fingers staining his cheeks. "Don't make me ask again," I say. My voice is low and dangerous.

"You know why I'm here," Marcus says.

"You shot Tutor." It's not a question. I suspected it the moment I saw those red fletchings. I knew it as soon as I saw his face. What I don't know is why.

He meets my eyes. "I did."

"Why? I know you have taken the throne in the threatened lands."

His eyes register shock at my knowledge but it fades quickly. "Why did you need to come here, even though you obviously don't intend to join us. Did you come just to cause problems? Do we not have enough troubles with the giants? You thought we needed a war with Fraun at the same time?"

I'm sure the people around me will further run from the mention of war. I hate to scare them. But that's what he's trying to stir up. Why else would he shoot my brother?

Marcus raises his chin in a show of strength that makes me want to slap him again. "Tutor abandoned his people. I wanted to make him pay."

I feel a pressure on my shoulder, which pulls my attention away from Marcus. Jordyn is there. I feel his warm hand heavy through my shirt. "What's going on?" he asks.

I stand up and force myself to focus on the people in the gathering with us. I notice the medicine woman continues to attend to Tutor wound, but no one else is there with them. They are all watching me. I need to calm down and set a better example. I take a deep breath. "This man's name is Marcus. He was the ambassador to the royal council for Sarcheda. Recently, when our group left Fraun for safety, Marcus here decided to take the throne for himself. He claimed to be keeping Sarcheda alive."

"What is he doing here?" Jordyn asks.

"Apparently," I turn to face Jordyn. "He decided his first act as King in Fraun would be to shoot Tutor in the shoulder and start a war."

"Why do you keep saying that?" Marcus asks. "I cannot start a war with a non-government. You people are no one." He picks his head up so he is also addressing the group. "You are all merely wanderers. You mean nothing to Sarcheda."

I step to the side so my body is directly in front of his face, forcing him to look at me. "We meant enough for you to chase us down and shoot an arrow through Tutor's shoulder," I say. My hand raises almost of its own accord, flying toward his face again. I'm satisfied when he flinches.

When Marcus realizes I stopped myself from slapping him, he stands up and glares at me. "You are nothing," he repeats. "Shooting Tutor is the same as hunting an animal in the wild."

The pressure from Jordyn's hand increases. I'm not sure if he's trying to hold me back or if he's using me as a shield to keep him back. I turn to look at him again. "Let's take him to the group," he says. "We will decide what to do with him together."

"You have no right to hold me," Marcus says. "They're holding the King of Sarcheda against his will," he yells. "They are trying to start a war."

Jordyn wheels around, surprising Marcus who is barely able to stop before he crashes into the much taller man. "Stop talking," Jordyn commands. He pulls a black cord from around his waist and uses it to tie Marcus' hands behind him. "Don't say anything else until we are back in front of the campfire. We will all hear your argument together."

Marcus, for the first time tonight, makes the smart choice and listens. I'd like to think it's because part of him is afraid of Jordyn. More likely, I realize, it's because the promise of the full group means Marcus will have an audience.

Chapter 40

There are a lot of people gathered around the campfire when we trudge back in. I'm tired, mentally and physically. Jordyn and I are dragging Marcus between us. He has his hands tied behind his back and he's been silent as we walk. It's dark now, which means we stumble a few times along the way, but we are following the light from the campfire and finding our path.

The medicine woman is slightly in front of us with Tutor's arm over her shoulder. They're walking slowly, likely because the jostling of his body when his feet hit the ground causes him pain. Tutor keeps looking behind at us, as if ensuring we are keeping up. I notice he looks more alert than he did before. I guess anger will do that to you. I'd like to focus on Tutor and helping his injury heal. I should be able to focus on that. Instead, I find myself focused on Marcus. I want answers and I want them now.

The area around the fire pit goes silent when we come into the area. Jordyn lets go of Marcus first and, I can't help myself, I push him to the ground. He falls onto his butt and shoots me a dirty look. I still don't care.

Eselda crosses to us. "What—" she starts. Then she notices Tutor. She leaves us and rushes to him. "I should've known it was you. I'm so sorry. It all makes sense now, because you are the right height and, of course, you're so important to me. Tutor, I'm so sorry. I should have seen this coming." She talks quickly and then looks immediately up at the medicine woman. "Is he going to be alright?"

"I'm fine," Tutor answers. "I'm going to be fine." He sits down on a log next to the fire. "I'm going to sit right here and hear this discussion. I'd love to hear what Marcus has to say for himself." He pointedly looks at the man on the ground. "I assume I have you to thank for the hole in my shoulder?"

Eselda whirls around to face us again. "What is going on here?" she asks. "Who is this man?"

Jordyn looks at me, as if expecting me to explain to the group what is going on. I want to but suddenly I'm not sure I'm capable of explaining anything. When I look at Marcus all I want is vengeance, payment for what he has done. I'm too angry for this right now. I shake my head, just a little, hoping he will pick up the signal.

Jordyn clears his throat, which effectively draws the eyes of everyone in the crowd to him. "Tutor was shot with an arrow while he was searching for firewood. Three people went off in the direction the arrow came from and apprehended this man." He points at Marcus, who adjusts himself so he is kneeling on the ground with his weight back on his heels. "Sawchett recognizes this man and has identified him as the former ambassador and self-proclaimed current King of Sarcheda, Marcus." Jordyn looks away from the crowd, down toward Marcus. "Is that you?"

"It is," Marcus answers, throwing his chin up in a grotesque display of regal pride.

"Fine." Jordyn turns his back on Marcus, addressing the crowd again. "We brought this man before all of you so we can hear his story together. First, let us ask him if he is taking responsibility for firing the arrow that injured Tutor."

"I am," Marcus answers without hesitation.

There is an audible gasp from the crowd. Jordyn nods. "Would you like to tell us why you shot Tutor in the shoulder?"

There's silence in the clearing. I don't really know what I want him to say. I'm not sure there is anything he can say that would excuse the behavior. I already know, based on the conversation in the clearing, he isn't going to pretend it didn't happen or tell us there was a hunting accident. Really, is there a single thing he could say that would result in me forgiving him for what he did?

I decide there is not at the exact same moment that Marcus shrugs. Shrugs. That's the best he can do. Like he can't come up with anything. Like it doesn't mean anything to him. Like he isn't even sorry.

I take a step closer to him, my anger boiling under my skin. Jordyn's arm falls across my chest. He shakes his head slowly. I try and force myself to take a deep breath and calm down. We don't rule in anger.

Wait, that's not right. We don't have rules here. We aren't in Fraun. We can rule however we want.

So, do I want to rule in anger? Do I want to handle this without hearing him out? Do I want to be as bad as him?

That one does it. I can't take out the aggression with no purpose like Marcus did. The decision helps me feel calmer. I nod at Jordyn so he'll understand that I am restraining myself.

Jordyn lets his arm fall back to his side. "Answer the question aloud for the group," Jordyn instructs.

"I shot the arrow at the man who abandoned Sarcheda at the first sign of trouble," Marcus says.

The silence in the clearing is painful. There's now a group of gathered people, from all walks of life, who are silenced by their own guilt and shock. After all, we left Fraun as much as Tutor did. I'm sure they're having the same thoughts I am. Thoughts about how we didn't have a choice, because what was waiting for us there was dangerous. But the bottom line is there are people who stayed behind. People who needed us who we did, really, abandon.

It's Tutor who breaks the silence. He claps, slowly and loudly. The sound breaks the serious nature of the group. A few people even laugh. "Nicely done," Tutor says as the clapping stops. "You managed to make the entire group of people here feel sorry for your stupid decision to stay behind and grab at power." He pushes himself up to a standing position. "I couldn't say this to you when I was king, so it's been a long time coming." Tutor takes a few slow steps across the clearing, closing the gap between himself and Marcus. His eyes are fixed on the former Ambassador.

"You've been pushing rulers and trying to control the council for a long time. Now you have the control you wanted and your first act is to convince innocent people to stay behind and face giants on their own. Your second act is to abandon those citizens you claim to love so you can chase after me and shoot me in the shoulder." Tutor shakes his head, laughs, and then turns to face me. "You want to know why he's really here? He's scared to face the giants. He volunteered to come after me and deal me justice of his own making so that he isn't in Fraun when the giants arrive."

He steps closer to Marcus and points. His finger tip hovers just over the shirt Marcus wears, dangerously close to poking him in the chest. "You're a coward, a liar, and not at all worth my time." Tutor's voice is quiet, but it carries through the crowd. He leans forward, just a little, but it is enough for his finger to poke Marcus. "If you wanted to kill me you would need to bring more than a single arrow." Tutor drops his arm, turns on his heel, and walks away toward his tent shaking his head the entire way.

Chapter 41

After Tutor leaves the clearing, there's a calm from the assembled group as if my brother took all the stress and noise with him. I clear my throat like an apology before I shatter the silence. "What are our options here?" I ask the group. "What should we do with him?" I gesture to Marcus. I'm careful not to look at any one particular face. I don't want to give the impression that anyone here is more important than any other. None of us are kings or queens out here. There is no ruling line. There are no rules. We have to decide this together.

"You can kill me," Marcus offers. "But you'll be starting a war with the people I left behind. They know where I was going. They knew what I was coming to do. They'll know that you relished the chance to take the blood of yet another Sarcheda ruler."

I pointedly look anywhere but at Jordyn, who actually took the life of that first ruler Marcus is mentioning. I know it's not exactly common knowledge that Jordyn killed Tin. None of us really know the details of what happened out there in the forest. I should move the conversation away from that before it derails our entire discussion. "What other options are there?" I try to pretend Marcus didn't speak.

"We can find a place to keep him, like a prisoner," someone offers.

"We can release him. Send him back to the people he came from," someone else calls.

"Why would we do that?" Tanya asks. I didn't see her walk up but suddenly she's right at my elbow. "We send him home so he can come right back here and try again? He doesn't exactly scream remorseful to me."

"That's because I'm not," Marcus says.

I roll my eyes. I don't think anyone will be able to see it in the darkness that surrounds us and the gesture makes me feel like I'm doing something. "Keep the ideas coming, what else could we do?"

"We can injure him somehow so he has trouble finding his way back and then cut him loose," a voice calls.

"Like cut out his eyes?" Eselda asks.

"That's terribly cruel," someone calls.

"Thank you," Marcus says. "That is cruel."

Eselda narrows her eyes at him. "We have no need for your opinion right now."

"I'm only trying to be the voice of reason. You're all ready to start a war with Fraun. Are you so far gone from what you created there that you'd be willing to go to war with us." He widens his eyes. "Again?" he adds.

Eselda reaches behind her and unties the scarf that is wrapped around her waist. It is a small scrap of fabric which she has been hanging her water bottle from during our journey so far. She rolls it into a long cylinder, not unlike a snake. She steps closer to Marcus. "Open," she instructs.

Probably because he's unsure what she plans to do, he opens his mouth. Eselda puts the fabric between his jaws and wraps it around the back of his head, securing it. "That should bring us a little peace," she says.

Marcus tries to speak but it is little more than a mumble. I bite my lip to hold back a smile. "Alright, we've heard kill him, maim him and let him go, let him go, or keep him prisoner. Are there any other suggestions?" I ask.

Alerta raises her hand on the opposite side of the circle from me. "I believe we should find a place to keep him prisoner tonight and decide in the morning. That will give us all a chance to calm down. Emotions are running high here tonight. I would also like to check on Tutor and get his opinion. How do we feel about that?"

"I will tie him to a tree and take first watch if we all agree to this," Jordyn offers. "Any objections to voting in the morning?"

No one speaks up.

"If you have an opinion on the future of our prisoner tomorrow morning, meet here at sunrise. We will discuss it and vote at that time." Jordyn reaches down, drags Marcus up by the hand ties, and pulls him off away from the fire.

The crowd fans out, returning to their own camps for the evening. I sit down on the ground, warming my hands by the flames. Tanya sits beside me. "That was eventful," she says. "Are things always this exciting around your family?"

A little laugh escapes me. "Lately, yeah."

She laughs. "What exactly is the procedure now for stuff like this? Like, are you still a queen?"

"I don't think so, no. We haven't really discussed it. We're not in Fraun. I guess the fact that someone calling himself a king in Fraun tried to kill my brother sort of proves that, yeah?"

"I guess." She sighs. "I don't really know what we are. I suppose we can start over and make it whatever we want. Fix some of the problems, or whatever," she says. I nod in agreement. She tips her head back, looking up at the stars sparkling far above us. "Do you think we're safe out here?" she asks.

I tilt my head back to see the picture she's looking at. The dark trees reach far above our heads, tickling the black of the sky. The woods around us are basically quiet. The animals around here, if they are here, are staying away from the fire. "I don't know," I answer. It would be unreasonable for me to promise any protection, especially in light of what happened tonight.

"The giants, though, we're safe from them here?"

"They're the other direction. I don't know if we're truly safe but it seems like a good idea to get as far away from them as we can get. Don't you think?"

She nods. "I guess it feels strange that we ran away because we were so worried about giants and our biggest threat tonight was someone from Fraun." She stands up before I can answer, brushes dirt off her bottom, and lays a hand on my shoulder. "I'm going to try and get some sleep. I'll see you in the morning."

"Good night," I say. I'm not sure I'd be able to sleep right now. For the second time in my life, Fraun poses the biggest threat to my safety and the safety of everyone I care about. We are, again, our own worst enemies.

I'm not feeling very dreamy right now.

Chapter 42

When I first open my eyes, my heart is pounding and I can't figure out why I'm awake. The fire is crackling and burning in front of me, I'm curled up on the ground. I push myself up to a sitting position and look around. Judging by the coloring on the edge of the horizon, it's almost time for sunrise.

The camp is coming to life around me. People are cooking food, cleaning up tents, and chasing children around. I suppose that is what woke me, although I don't think it explains the pounding of my heart.

A man sits down on the ground beside me. I smile at him. "Good morning," I offer.

His small smile looks more like a grimace, like the gesture of smiling causes him pain. "Morning," he mumbles. At least I think that's what he says. He looks oddly familiar, somehow. I feel like I should know him. He's wearing brown, which would've marked him as a scout before all this started. Now? Now I'm not sure what it symbolizes. Perhaps they were simply the only clean clothing he has.

He puts a pan down on the fire in front of us and starts preparing some kind of meat with a knife. I watch him work. He expertly trims the fat off the meat, wrapping it in fabric for later. The now trimmed meat he rubs with something white, seasoning of some kind. Then he drops the entire slab of meat into the pan. Instantly the sizzle starts and it is not long before I can smell the cooking meat.

"That smells amazing. What is it?"

He barely glances at me. "Not sure. I came across it this morning. Something large. This is only one organ. The rest of the meat I've wrapped for the journey."

I look again at the large slab of meat in the pan. This is only a small portion? "Are there more of the creatures? Did it put up a fight?"

"I've seen them before. This one was small compared to a few I've seen. It didn't put up a fight but I'm sure the larger ones would." He looks at me intensely for a beat. "It would be good if we left soon, before larger ones come searching for this one."

I want to say something, but I'm interrupted by the arrival of Jordyn and Tutor. I jump to my feet. "Tutor, how are you feeling this morning?"

Jordyn sits down beside the man. "Good morning, Toby. What is that?" He takes a big sniff. "Smells amazing."

Toby? I squint at the man cooking. I suppose, if you add a few annuals of age and some stress onto the face this could be Toby, who traveled with the Scouts before the war. Is it truly possible I didn't recognize a man who fought beside me and saved my life?

"Not sure. I think it's a baby of the same kind of creature from the cave. I found it over there," he gestures off into the woods behind us with the knife in his hand. "I have the rest wrapped up for the journey. Should last a few days. I'm treating it with salt."

"Nicely done." Jordyn looks up at us. "Almost sunrise. Do you think more people will come for a say in the prisoner's future?"

"I hope so," Tutor says. He wraps his good arm around me, offering me a side hug. "I'm feeling better this morning, thank you for asking." There is something about his appearance today that speaks louder than his words ever could. Something in his eyes has changed. He looks happier, somehow, than he has looked in a long time. Actually, I can't remember a time when he has looked this happy.

The clearing slowly fills up with people just as the sun comes up above the horizon. By the time the entire ball is visible I'm even shocked at the size of the crowd. It seems as though everyone we travel with is here.

"Thank you for coming by this morning," Tutor says. "I'd like to start our discussion by saying I think it would be foolish of us to kill Marcus and start a war with Fraun. We are no longer part of the kingdom, we gave up that right when we fled. But someday, down the road, we may need their help or they may need ours. Killing Marcus is not the way to start that relationship."

He turns his attention to the prisoner, tied to a nearby tree and barely visible from here. "Shooting me in the shoulder without warning or discussion wasn't the way either but me making the same mistake isn't going to fix his mistake."

"What would you suggest we do with him then?" Toby asks. "If we drag him around with us it's another mouth to feed. What is the end goal? Are we to keep him prisoner forever?" He shakes his head. "No one deserves that."

That confirms my suspicion that this is the Toby I knew. The very same Toby who was held captive by the giants. Really, he's the reason we are here. I understand his hesitation to subject another living being to that fate.

"How old is he?" someone calls out.

"I'm not sure," Tutor answers. "He's been grey for a few annuals now, by my count."

His meaning dawns on me in a flash. Marcus likely doesn't have much time left. Our people grey and then die within five annuals. We may not have to worry about him for long. Marcus should be in his death spiral within a few annuals, at most.

Toby stands up slowly. "By the look on your face I have a feeling you're leaning toward keeping a man prisoner for a few annuals until he dies." He shakes his head. "Just think about this. You are condemning him to spending the last annuals of his life in captivity. If it were me tied to that tree, I'd be telling you to kill me and make it quick."

"Let's put it to a vote," Tutor says. He speaks over Toby's head, making it obvious he is addressing the group. "All in favor of keeping Marcus prisoner, raise your hand."

At quick glance, I'd say more than half the hands in the area go up. But it's hard to tell. "This isn't going to be as easy as counting to the votes of the council," I whisper. Tutor shoots me a dangerous gaze. His meaning is pretty clear. He wants me to be more helpful and less critical.

"Alright, I'm not sure how many of us there are. Let's compare, all those in favor of putting Marcus to death please raise your hand."

This time there are only about a dozen hands, Toby is one of them.

"Just to be thorough," I call, "is there anyone who wishes to set Marcus free to return to Fraun, perhaps with a message?" There are no hands.

Tutor clears his throat. "I think the vote is obviously more in favor of keeping him prisoner. I'll speak to him myself."

Eselda steps up next to me and sighs. "I've grown used to discussing Fraun as something outside my own group but this must all be strange for you. How are you holding up?" she asks.

"I'm alright," I answer. "I was born in Fraun but I left just like you did."

"But you returned," she says. "You were their Queen."

I squint at her. "So were you." Does she really not see the similarities between us? Two Queens of Enchenda who are, perhaps, more comfortable with the scouts. Two rulers who were forever changed by that war. Are we also two rulers who fear another one? I shake my head. "It doesn't feel the same, not anymore. Even just a few suns was enough to change everything." I gesture toward Marcus. "If he is Fraun, I never really was."

"You're giving up," she says. Her voice is almost sad.

I look around the circle, at the group of people who are readying themselves for a journey. The camp is already cleaned up, we are getting more efficient with our supplies and our roles. This is a group who no longer wait to hear the opinion and the ruling of the few. This is a group who will do what it takes to survive. To be a family. "I'm moving on," I say. "That's not the same thing."

"Still you'll be literally dragging someone who proclaimed himself King of the land you abandoned," she says.

"What's your point, Eselda?"

Sadness crosses her features but it is chased away as quickly as I notice it. In its place is her practiced smile, the one she used to use in front of her subjects. "I don't have a point. I was just making conversation." She saunters off toward Jordyn before I can call her out for whatever truth she may be hiding.

Can you ask someone you've grown out of touch with to share the truth with you? If you do ask, as she did, can you really expect them to share it?

What I want the most in life is to feel connected to other people. To feel like I have a family. There have been moments when I have felt this: with Eselda when it was just the two of us in her home, with the Scouts who took me in when I ran, and with Tutor when we first learned of our blood. But now? Now I'm just not sure if this group sees me as a member of the family. Sometimes it feels like I'm just one of the kids again. That is not a role I wanted to walk back into. It will certainly take some getting used to.

Chapter 43

The group of revelers disgusts the prisoner. This group abandoned the ideal of Fraun to follow the false kings out here to the woods. For what? He scowls at them all. A man who called himself King of a realm he had no rights to rule. A Queen who is barely old enough to stop schooling in Fraun. Worse? The Queen who had a female child out of wedlock. A woman who isn't worthy to even say Sarcheda, never mind lead a realm in the same kingdom as them.

He grinds his teeth and narrows his eyes at them. He's not surprised by how much he hates them, not really. None of them are worthy of what they have abandoned. None of them loves Fraun enough to kill for it. None of them would be willing to spill the blood of the unworthy, like he has done. He will fix Sarcheda. He will get out of this, somehow, and then his kingdom will be better because these people have left it to him. Really, in that way, didn't they do him a favor?

A short figure steps off from the rest, headed in his direction, For a breath he thinks it's that awful Jordyn come to ask him more questions. But no, this man is too short to be Jordyn. A smile breaks out on his face when the man is close enough for the prisoner to identify. "I wondered when you'd come speak to me," Marcus greets. "I remember you, you know. From when you were a boy."

"That was a long time ago," Toby says. He stands over the older man, arms crossed, looking down at him.

"A lifetime," Marcus agrees. "What can I do for you today?"

"You have no Sarcheda blood. How did you claim that throne?"

Marcus smiles. "I took it."

"On what grounds? You have no right to that throne."

The right side of Marcus' mouth turns up in a smirk. "I am Sarcheda, boy. I was Sarcheda when you lived there, I was Sarcheda when you ran, I was Sarcheda during the war, I am Sarcheda now."

"Fraunians are just following you?" Toby scoffs. "They don't question your blood? Yet they thought Tutor unworthy just because he didn't have the blood."

"I have better than my blood. I have the willingness to spill blood for Sarcheda." Marcus shakes his head. "What do you care, anyway? When you lived there you were just a servant. Didn't you clean the clothes and the floor of the young Prince, Tin? What does someone of your status care what happens to my realm?" Marcus tilts his head to the left. "Unless you want to untie me and follow me back. You can proclaim your loyalty. You can be my servant. The servant to the one true King who will unite the realms. It will be better than Oberian, mark my words."

Toby vehemently shakes his head. "Never." He sighs. "I just don't understand. The Sarcheda citizens are further gone than I thought if they'd accept this."

Marcus' grin is eerie, evil somehow. It makes Toby shudder. "Sarcheda does what I tell them to do. They always have."

Toby runs a hand down his face as if he can wipe away Marcus, Sarcheda, and his own past with that one motion. Then he stalks back to the group feeling anger and fear he hasn't felt since he was young. Because he, more than anyone else here today, knows there is truth behind those words. He has seen first-hand what Marcus can convince people to do.

They don't know what monster they try to hold prisoner.

Chapter 44

At first, when she realizes she is inside the dream again, she feels confusion. This already happened. Tutor was shot in the shoulder by a man from Sarcheda named Marcus, who they now hold prisoner. He didn't die.

That is the realization that brings hard balls of fear into her stomach. Tutor didn't die which means this isn't over. There is more to discover from this dream. Just like the first dream, this isn't over. Something in her brain is trying to tell her that someone important to Fraun will die. First it was Tin, whose death changed the council policies for the better. Then it was her mother, whose death changed Eselda in a meaningful way. Who will die this time?

She makes a decision not to follow the arrow. She already knows what happens. Tutor, whose face is blurry in this dream, takes the arrow in his shoulder and goes down. That has already happened. He is not dead. Perhaps her mind wants her to see the Fraunian on the other end of the bow.

She turns and walks in the direction the man will come from, hoping to spend more time looking for him. She finds him, walking toward the clearing she awoke in. She remembers, from the first time she had the dream, that he will take his shot from there. Now she can tell, clearly, that this man is Marcus. She gets closer to him, leaning toward his face. He is angry, she can see that. He is old, the hair on his head is white. This confirms what she heard Sawchett speculate about. Marcus may not have much time left.

He drops onto his left knee and pulls the bow around to the front. Eselda resists the urge to move. He cannot hit her in this dream state. This close to him, she hears him whisper something before he lets the arrow fly. "This should take care of the last of your supporters."

She pulls back in shock as the arrow flies. Supporters? He did this because Tutor had supporters? She backs up to a tree and leans on it, thinking. If Tutor has supporters in Sarcheda then someone should be sent to get them out. Perhaps they can be reasoned with. Perhaps more citizens can be saved.

Marcus sits on his bottom, as if he intends to wait for his capture and imprisonment. Eselda tilts her head, confused. Why wait? If you know that what you did was wrong, why wouldn't you run? It's as if Marcus wanted to be caught and dragged back to their camp.

She looks around, wondering for a beat if the scouts who drag him to Sawchett will be the ones who die. She turns back to Marcus, who looks relaxed there on the ground. He crosses his arms over his chest. Then, she wakes.

Confused, she blinks in the sudden darkness of the clearing. She and Jordyn have decided to sleep under the stars tonight and, besides those, the only light is the campfire still smoldering in the center. Marcus is tied up under a tree, she can see him there. As usual, she is no closer to an answer or a comfort from this dream. Who dies? Why is she seeing this dream? What future can she foresee here?

She stares up at the stars and ponders these questions knowing she isn't going to get another wink of sleep tonight.

Chapter 45

The group makes good progress over the next two suns, despite the fact that Tutor is taking more breaks and Marcus is refusing to cooperate. Various members of the group take their turns walking beside the prisoner and making sure he doesn't do anything stupid, like run off into the woods. They walk until they're exhausted and then break for the night in a quiet spot with a view of the sky through the trees.

A small fire is lit to keep the guard warm but most everyone immediately takes themselves to bed. Eselda takes first watch of Marcus, since she is feeling like she wouldn't sleep anyway. She's afraid to sleep. Afraid to have another dream of another event that she can't stop. Another event that hurts someone she cares about.

She forces herself to focus on something else, something happier. She checks on Marcus, he's asleep as well. That's good for her, actually. You can't get up and run off into the night if you're snoring peacefully on the ground. She returns to the fire, fills a pot with water, and sets in on the flames. She throws a few leaves and a sprig of mint into a cup, crushing them up with the handle of her knife. As she waits for her water to boil, she stretches her arms and legs. She is out of practice for walking this long. As a scout she is used to walking a lot in a single sun. But then they would camp for two to three suns. This has been multiple suns of walking with little rest. Every part of her body hurts.

Once her water bubbles, she pours it into the cup and lets her tea steep. Her first sip is warm and cozy, and instantly she feels more relaxed. After the long day, relaxation feels so nice that she doesn't recognize it as dangerous. How can something so pleasant be dangerous?

But it's not long before her eyes slip closed from the warmth of the tea and the fire.

In the darkness, he sees her head fall toward her chest and still he waits. When her head doesn't rise again and her breathing becomes more even, he draws a sword. Quietly, he slips to the man on the ground. Without waking him, pausing only long enough to mentally apologize for the choice he has to make, he slices the sword along the neck of the prisoner.

"It's better this way," Toby whispers, "they just can't bring themselves to do it."

Then, before he can be forced to stand a similar trial and outcome, he slips off into the night. He leaves his sword behind, the only clue they'll need to know exactly who took care of this prisoner.

Chapter 46

"Would you like to tell me why you're in a sour mood?" Tanya asks. We've walked about twenty steps this morning side-by-side in silence. I was hoping to keep this up longer, but evidently she's waited as long as she can. She bumps my shoulder with hers. "You haven't smiled in two suns." Two suns. Exactly the amount of time that has passed since we found Marcus' body.

I frown at her. "How can we just leave his body there and keep walking? He's a Fraunian. I'm not saying he's a good guy. I know better than most that he made stupid choices sometimes. I'm just saying, somebody somewhere loved him once. He was Fraunian. That used to mean something to us before we started wandering in the woods."

She blinks rapidly, trying to grasp what I'm saying. "Wasn't scouting out into the forest your idea? Wasn't this all your idea?" She wipes her arms around in a circle, indicating what she means by 'all'.

"I don't know. Doesn't it feel like we're abandoning everything?" I fix her with a cold stare. "Your brother and your girlfriend aren't even here.

Don't you feel like you've abandoned them?"

She reaches out and snags my elbow to keep up with the fast pace I'm setting. "First of all, she's my ex-girlfriend. Secondly, I believe we were in danger. I felt it. I am willing to start over with all of these fine people." She catches up with me and leans her head on my shoulder while I count four more steps. Then she looks back up. "Besides, didn't you leave Fraun once before?"

I sigh. "Yes, I went searching for Tutor." I was so much younger then. So much more frightened. Then, the problem wasn't giants. It was a seated King.

"That worked out," she says. "You came home safely, ended the war, saved Fraun, and became a Queen. Maybe this time it will work out the same." Her eyes shine. "Or better, even."

"Tell me the truth. How is this going to go for us? What do we do when we get there?" I ask. I don't know if I truly expect her to have the answers. I just need to hear someone tell me what I want to hear.

Tanya lets go of my elbow and I count fifteen steps of silence. She doesn't have an answer either, evidently. "How is this really different than the last time you left?" she finally asks as though I never changed the topic. "You actually have more support this time around, I would think." She gestures to the mass of people moving slightly ahead of us.

I can't find the words to explain why I feel guilty, not really. "I guess it's because we left people behind who we care about this time."

Tanya's hand brushes up against the back of mine. I look down in shock at the warmth that radiates up my arm at the touch. "You left Eselda last time," she offers.

"Yeah, that's true." My distracted brain trips over the words. I take a deep breath and focus on the path in front of us again. The real answer suddenly lights up my brain, surprising me. I stop walking and turn to Tanya. "Last time I knew we'd be back." It's so obvious, what's been bothering me, now that I've seen it.

Tanya nods like she's known the entire time. Then she smiles like she's proud of me for finding the truth. My heart hammers away in my chest. She reaches out and grabs my fingers, slowly pulling them up to brush against her lips. "It'll be alright, Sawchett, you'll see."

Still holding my hand, she tugs me along until our pace matches the crowd again. I don't know if it's the reassurance, the comfort, the wisdom, or the physical contact, but I feel better. We're going to be alright.

Chapter 47

As the camp is being set up for the night, I feel a hand on my elbow. I turn around to find Tutor standing beside me. His eyes are lit up with a kind of mischief I haven't seen in a long time. I smile at him. "What's up?" I ask.

"Can I borrow you?"

When I nod at him he pulls my by the elbow a little way off from the clearing into the trees. There are a few rocks here and he uses one as a seat. "Sit. Can we talk?" He gestures to another rock.

Something that reminds me of laughter tints his voice. I sit, looking at him strangely. "What's up?" I ask again. "What's gotten into you?"

"I'm going to get married," he says. The smile turns up on his face, full force.

I can't help it, my smile tugs at the corners of my own mouth in response. "To Alerta?"

He laughs. The sound echoes off the trees and back to us. I chuckle at my own stupidity right along with him. "Of course," he says. He reaches out and taps me on the forehead. "You are spending too much time in there in your head, you're forgetting about people." He gestures to the group of people setting up camp in the clearing. "This is always about people. It has always been about people. Remember that." He reaches down and snags my hand, squeezing. "I'm going to get married at sunset. You should be there. We'd like you to say the blessing."

A feeling of warm love and acceptance spreads out across my chest. He's right, of course. This move, although it felt like running when we left, is starting to feel like safety. Comfort. "I'd love to," I say. My eyes flit, briefly, toward the people setting up the campfire. A small smile plays across my lips.

Tutor turns to see who I'm looking at. "Who is he?" he asks, a note of teasing in his voice.

"What? Who's who?" I pull my attention back to him.

"Whoever you're looking at like that." Tutor laughs. "Alright, I see it before you do. I get it. That's ok." He wraps an arm around my shoulders and gives me a quick hug. "Seize love when you find it, little sister, that's my advice."

"Who is that?" I ask. I tip my head toward the person now coming toward us, quickly. We don't have to wait long before they're fully in sight. "It's Eselda," I say. Some of her old animation is back, she looks happy and full of life. I haven't seen her like that in a long time. "She looks good," I say.

"Happy," Tutor answers. Clearly he's recognized the same thing I have.

She pops into the area. "There you are," she says. "I've been looking all over for you two. I figured it out."

"Figured what out?" Tutor asks.

"The death. The death that is important to Fraun. It was Marcus."

"What are you talking about?" I ask.

Eselda sighs, disappointed that she has to backpedal to explain this. "Ok, how much do I explain?" she whispers.

Tutor and I exchange a confused look. "How about all of it," Tutor suggests. He drops his arm from around my shoulders, leans back, and pushes a rock toward Eselda with his toe. "Sit, explain." Then he leans forward on his knees, a picture of the attentive listener.

"Ok, I get these dreams sometimes. Jordyn calls them visions." She sits and straightens her jacket a little tighter around her. "In these dreams I'm watching something happen. There's always a face I don't get to see. The vision is the same scene, over and over again each time I have the dream. I can watch it, but I can't interact with it. Is this making any sense?"

"Sort of," I say. "When did you have it before? Maybe that will help us understand."

She nods. "The first time it was a dream about Tin battling with someone in the woods. The face of the other person was always blurred, I couldn't see them. It looked like Tin lost, which made me sad at the time." She looks pained by the memory. "Then I had it again and it looked like Tin won. I didn't understand why that made me so sad."

"Was this the fight with Jordyn?" Tutor asks.

"I think so. At the time, remember, I didn't know who this other person was. But the last time I had the dream Jordyn's face was revealed and I realized how much I love him." She smiles wistfully. "We've talked about the details a lot since the war. Jordyn says the dream was exactly how it really happened. It was a vision of a death that changed Fraun."

"That's amazing, Eselda. Why didn't you tell us about this?" I ask.

She waves her hand. "Because it didn't matter. Anyway, there was a second time."

"Tell us about that," I say.

"In that dream, it was my mother who died." She pauses, knowing that we will have questions.

"Danyel mentioned something about that once," Tutor says. "I'm sorry you had to go through that."

"It's fine. But in that dream my mother's face was a blur, so I didn't know it was her." She sighs. "That one doesn't really matter either. My point is that it's happening again."

"Tell us about this one," Tutor says.

"Right, so I actually start where Marcus will shoot the arrow from in the vision. Although I didn't know that it was him the first time. I watch him line up a shot and shoot an arrow across an impressive distance. The second time I had this dream I followed the path of the arrow and found that he was shooting at a group gathering something."

"The firewood," I whisper.

"I recognized Sawchett in that group," Eselda continues.

"That's why you tried to warn us. You wanted to find out who he was shooting," Tutor says.

"Exactly. I worried that whoever he shot was going to be the important death. I got close enough, in the vision, to see someone shot in the shoulder. Their face was blurred. At first, I thought this meant that person was going to die. But, obviously, that isn't what happened. Then I had the dream again and I finally figured it out." She's really getting animated now, gesturing wildly as she talks. "In the first dream I could see Tin clearly. He was the death that changed Fraun. It was Jordyn who was blurred. My brain was trying to tell me that Jordyn was my future, does that make sense?"

I nod. It makes about as much sense as any of this does. I want her to continue.

"The second time I could see myself clearly every time I had the dream. I think that meant I was the one who could change things. I had control of the events in the dream. But my mother's face was blurred because she was the death that changed things. I've figured out that the person who I can see is the one who is in control of the moment, they have the power to stop the death from happening. But the person who is blurry, that is the one who controls the future."

"Wait," Tutor interrupts, waving his hand. "How was your mother your future?"

"Because I saw how much she hated Fraun and everyone in it. She blamed every citizen for the problems. I could have easily become her. I was ready to shut out both of you, because of your connection to that kingdom. I was turning into her and running from love. I had to learn from her to fix my future."

"What does that all mean for this dream?" I ask, bringing her back on track.

"This time, I started with Marcus and he is the one who I see clearly. I thought that meant you were the one who died, because you're blurry. But don't you see now what it means? It means Marcus was in control of his own death. He is the one whose death changes the future somehow, I don't know how just yet. But it was his action that put it all into motion."

"I don't understand why you didn't just see Toby killing Marcus," I say. Because that is the part of this that makes no sense. If Eselda sees deaths and Marcus dying is important, wouldn't that be what she sees?

"Because it was Marcus' actions that led to his death. He was the one who could have acted on his power to stop the cycle. He could have changed the future. Instead he has set something big in motion with his death. We just don't know what it is yet." Her eyes land on Tutor and everything in her body stops moving. She's suddenly very serious. "I also know that my brain is trying to tell me that you are the future, Tutor. That's why your face was blurred."

He sits up. "What?"

"I will do whatever I can to convince everyone when we get to wherever we are going. When we start again, it's you we have to listen to."

"Because of some dream?" He looks at me. "Tell her that's crazy, Sawchett."

I smile. "It's not crazy. You don't see what we see, Tutor. You are so smart and so brave. I've followed you my whole life. I always listen to you. Everything good in me comes from what I learned from you. I think it's a brilliant idea."

"There are better people for this, surely," he says.

Eselda stands up, wiping dirt off her bottom. "I disagree." She tousles his hair. "Do you think I'm good?" she asks.

"Of course." He stands up so they are face-to-face. "You're a wonderful leader and a great role model for the women here.

She leans close to him and whispers. "I had a great tutor." She lightly brushes her lips across his forehead. "I would follow that man anywhere, do anything he told me to do. He's an expert in government and he has a good heart." She turns and starts walking away.

"Eselda, this is crazy. I'm not running things by myself when we get wherever we're going."

She laughs and calls over her shoulder, "I'm not asking you to. I just wanted you to know that I think you need to speak up." She resumes walking again. "You're the key, Tutor."

He shakes his head. "Are you believing this nonsense?" he asks.

I lay my hand on his shoulder. "How many times did you all try and convince her that she was the key when she was a Princess? You all had her convinced the future of Fraun required her to get married. How is her crazy dream any less valid than the old ideals we followed?"

"She was the key, as it turned out." He swallows and drops his voice. "I know we don't talk about this much but she did declare war on Fraun with him. He gets all the credit for being the bad guy, but she was the key. We weren't wrong."

I chuckle a little and stand up. "Maybe she's not wrong either."

"Where are you going?" he asks as I start walking away.

"My brother is getting married. I have a wedding to get ready for," I say over my shoulder.

I try to think about the things that should be in a wedding ceremony. I have to recall some days long past. Days before my most recent tutor, a man named Marshawn who hasn't been seen in Fraun since I left the first time, took over my education. Those were the days before I was declared a princess. The days when I was just another tiny Fraunian. When I lived in a small house on the square with my Mom, who everyone else just called Charlotte. The days before I knew the truth about my ancestry.

Tutor was in charge of my education then. I suppose that should've told me I was different. The other children went to the school in the center of Enchenda and got their education from the teacher. I had a tutor who came to my house and quizzed me on things. I also went to the school, but the two cannot be compared. That teacher knew lots of things, but Tutor was the expert in Fraun. At the time, no one knew he was my brother. Not even me.

The lesson comes back to me, watery from years of unused recall. "Every Fraun wedding must have three things; a brief history of Fraun, a promise of fidelity, and a look to the future."

I don't know how important those old ideals will be for Alerta and Tutor today, but I have to say something. I sigh my breath out with enough force to flutter the hair off my forehead. What do I say at the wedding ceremony of my only brother?

I decide, in the end, to keep it simple.

Chapter 48

"Good afternoon." I greet the assembled group standing before me. Tutor and Alerta are directly in front of me, holding hands and smiling. Alerta is wearing a wreath of flowers around her head. The yellow blossoms compliment her dark hair beautifully. Beside them Stef wears an almost identical wreath and large smile.

"Today we are here to celebrate love. For annuals we have lived inside the safety of one Kingdom. Stepping outside of that, as we have done, can be scary. But one thing remains the same. Love is love." My voice echoes a little through the trees. I smile at the repetition of the phrase.

"When two people fall in love, anything is possible." I see Tutor's hand clench around Alerta's in a squeeze. "Tutor, what promises do you make to Alerta today?" I ask.

He smiles as he turns his body to face hers. He takes her second hand in his free one, completing a circle. "I promise to care for you," he begins. His voice echoes out to everyone in attendance, but his eyes remain firmly locked on her. "I promise to let you decide what to eat at least sometimes." A little laugh floats through the crowd. "I promise to love you and Stef with everything I have. I promise to never speak for you unless you want me to. I promise to be your partner, always."

My eyes well up at the sweet words. I wish for a love exactly like that. Something that pure. "Alerta, what promises do you make for Tutor today?"

"I promise to do my share of the chores and hunting. I promise to consult you for all major decisions. I promise to tell you if your clothes get too stinky." She wrinkles her nose and everyone laughs, even Tutor. "I promise to love you, be your partner, and never dwell on the past when our future is so much better."

She leans in and Tutor meets her halfway, their lips touching in a tender kiss. When they pull back again, I speak. "May your future be safe and full of comfort and love." It is not the future blessing of Fraun, which would've included naming all five traits of the realms. It's risky, this vague shunning of the old traditions.

I hesitantly smile at Tutor and Alerta. They are beaming with a happiness that radiates off of them. The crows bursts into applause.

Tutor and Alerta join hands with Stef and turn to the assemblage. "May I present Tutor and Alerta, husband and wife," I bellow.

Tutor leans in and kisses her again to enormous cheers.

Chapter 49

The party lasts all night. We clap to songs sung by talented people and dance in large groups and in partners. Someone keeps feeding the fire long after we normally would stop, inviting everyone to keep it up. Singing is not something we regularly practiced in Fraun, neither is dancing. But as I consider dropping onto the ground for a break I have to smile at the way everyone has taken to it. The scouts started it. Abney, Sieven, Kurt, and Evelyn stood up and sang with all their voices. It was a beautiful song with lyrics about love and family.

After that song, Sieven and Kurt did a duet while the girls danced. It was during this, only the second song, when everyone jumped up and joined in. Now there are a few young girls from Fraun who I've never met standing by the fire and singing. Apparently this is something that used to exist in homes behind closed doors. A secret passion that many harbored.

It's just one more thing we are bringing to light.

I see my friends from Enchenda have all gathered together nearby. I head their direction, pausing at a small opening in the circle between

Tanya and Bin. "Can I join you?" I ask. Shell and Drew sit opposite them, leaning on each other in their exhaustion.

"Please do," Shell says. "We've been wondering when you'd notice we were all here."

"I'm sorry if it was rude that I haven't made time for you," I say, feeling guilt flush my cheeks.

"Don't be," Drew says. "We've all been a bit too busy for anything. This," he gestures to the dancing crowd, "is much needed."

I drop to the ground and sigh. "My feet disagree with you. After all the walking I didn't think it was possible for them to hurt more." I smile. "I was wrong."

"Dancing can be hard on the feet," Bin agrees. "But I'd gather you probably didn't do much dancing before this."

I put a hand on my chest and lean away from him. "Am I that bad?" Everyone laughs, including Bin. I wait for the beautiful sound to fade. "Honestly, no. I didn't do much dancing. I think the last time I danced before this was at the ball where…" I let my voice trail off because the end of that sentence is Prince Carsen was murdered. That doesn't seem like the kind of memory I need to be bringing up right now.

"That's the thing about the royals," Bin says. "They didn't take time to celebrate daily life. They thought the only things worth celebrating were big announcements that affected other people who happened to be royal."

I'd like to correct him, honestly I would. But I can't. Because he's not wrong. That last occasion when I danced was the announcement party for Eselda and Carsen's engagement. It was the prologue for an event that would've united Marchenda and Enchenda, at least temporarily. Obviously, it didn't happen. "We were hopelessly out of touch," I agree. "Whoever rules in the new location will have to do better."

Shell leans forward, reaching for me. I take her hand and she squeezes mine briefly. "Don't feel bad for what happened in the past," she says. "We cannot change the past." She lets go of my hand and shoots a look at Bin. "And you need to stop trying to make her feel bad. This thin we're doing now is proof we can change. This is all new."

"You don't plan to be in charge when we get where we're going?" Bin asks. He bumps his shoulder into mine. "I didn't know that."

I sigh. "I don't think any of us know what's happening when we get there."

Another song starts up and Tanya taps me on the shoulder. "I love this song. Let me show you." I get up and follow her, losing myself in copying her dance movements for something a few of the boys traveling with us are performing by making noises that have no words.

After the dance, which is exhausting in the most exciting way, I drop back onto an empty spot nearby. "This is the most fun I've had in a long time," Tanya says as she drops beside me on the ground. There is a sheen of sweat along her forehead which I'm sure is also on mine. "By the way, you did a great job on that ceremony." Her hand is whisper soft as it just barely brushes on the back of mine. "It may be a new traditional ceremony for all of us now. Love is love."

"Thank you," I whisper. The words feel tangled in my throat suddenly. I look around for some water, something to clear it. Maybe it's all the dancing.

"Do you really believe it?" she asks. When I turn to look at her there's a sadness there in her eyes that doesn't fit the moment. I feel like I missed a step. "Do you believe that love is love? No matter who it's between?" She repeats.

"Yes, of course I do. What is this about? I feel like you're asking something more serious than I'm understanding." I turn my body completely so that my knees are facing her. It's a small gesture but I hope it communicates that I'm really trying to take her seriously.

"Not everyone believes that, you know." Her shoulders rise and fall quickly. She blinks rapidly like she's trying to keep tears from falling. "Some people think you're only allowed to be in love if it's acceptable to them and their beliefs. Some people will tell you that it's not really love if something about the couple in question makes them uncomfortable."

"Who would say that?" I'm genuinely curious. Since I've never been in a serious relationship this is all news to me. I've never seen anyone questioned before.

Tanya gestures to the crowd in front of us. I don't turn my head to see the crowd and she doesn't either. Instead, I stay fixated on the interesting combination of passion and sadness that are playing in her brown eyes. "Everyone out there. Citizens you probably didn't really know, if you're lucky. If you walk into a store holding hands with someone they don't approve of you can bet they'll have something to say."

Confusion clouds my thoughts. I can't remember ever being treated so rudely by anyone, even before we knew of my birth right. "Why wouldn't they approve of someone? I don't understand, Tanya. I'm trying to."

This time she turns her head and searches for someone before she points. I unwillingly pry my eyes from hers and follow the path of her finger. Tutor and Alerta, curled together on the ground, her head resting lightly on his shoulder. They look peaceful, happy. I snap my eyes back to Tanya. "Are you saying Tutor said something to you?" I'm surprised at the instant anger. "What did he say?"

She touches my shoulder and shakes her head. "No. I'm saying I'm sure Tutor has had questions or comments before. Alerta is a mother and Tutor is not Stef's father. Some citizens would have had opinions about that, I'm sure."

Some of my anger fades, but not all. "Actually, he may have mentioned that once or twice when they first got together. But I guess I didn't really talk about it with him as much as I should have. Do you think it hurt him?"

She sniffles. The sound instantly reminds me of nights holding back tears in a camp on the run. It's the sound I associate with a deep pain but also of keeping a strong image. It's the sound of burying emotions.

"It hurts to be questioned for who you love," she whispers.

Her pain is raw and real right now. It makes me feel guilty. It makes me feel angry. I reach out and grab her hand, threading my fingers through hers. "I'm sorry it happened to you. I'm sorry your ruling council didn't know. Do you want to talk about it?"

She looks down at our hands and I feel her squeeze tighter. She keeps her gaze fixed there, her dark hair falling over her eyes and cheek. "People don't like seeing me holding hands with a girl, like this. Enya and I would get lots of dangerous glances, lots of questions. They made me feel…" Her eyes fall on my face again, briefly. In the glow of the fire I can see her cheeks flush before she hides behind her hair again. "…different," she finishes.

"That's ridiculous." I use my free hand to pull her chin up so she is looking at my face. I want her to hear this. I want her to see that I am serious. "Love is love. Always, no matter what." I let go of her chin but she keeps her gaze where I left it. "Did you know the family trees of the royal bloodline that we commissioned showed many royals were married to people of the same gender?"

"Really?" I can tell she didn't know that. She looks genuinely shocked.

"Erick, a friend of mine who was a member of the group who helped us find the new land we are traveling to, has all of it copied on a parchment. When we get there I'll show you. Almost every Realm had some."

She smiles and nods. "I'd like to see that. Thank you."

"For what?"

"For sitting here with me. For not judging me." She sighs. "For being a good friend."

"You're welcome." I squeeze her hand once more before letting it go so I can stand. "Now, let's go dance."

Chapter 50

The morning sun is warmer today than it has been for awhile. I actually take my coat off while we walk, wrapping it around my waist and tying the arms to keep it there. I turn my face up to the sun that is peeking through the treetops and smile as the warm fingers tickle my cheeks. This is my favorite time of year, when everything begins to warm up.

When I bring my eyes back down to the group I notice everyone is slower. In fact, the group comes to a complete stop within ten steps. I excuse myself and push my way through to the front. When the last of the people part to allow me entrance I see Erick, standing under a copse of trees, talking with Jordyn and Tutor.

Relief washes through me. Relief that we are going to be somewhere that resembles civilization. I am about to get my first glimpse into our future. Eager to do just that, I close the remaining distance at a run.

Erick catches my arm in a sort of side hug. "Nice to see you too, kid." He chuckles.

"So you did get my letter? Have you had to wait long? I feel as though we've been walking for fortnights."

"Some of the creatures warned him," Tutor answers. "He was just telling us about it."

"And we have been walking for fortnights," Jordyn adds.

"Your group isn't quiet, so the animals fled the noise in our direction. We had an influx of bugs. I noticed." Erick shrugs. "A roach confirmed it for me. He came and warned me you lot were almost here. I've been sitting here since the sun came up."

"I thought about sending you birds," I admit.

"That would've worked as well. But I suspect you'd have some trouble finding some. Birds are pretty scarce around these parts right now. We're disturbing some things, I suppose is part of it. But truth be told we haven't found a single nest in all our searching." He strikes his arms out and gestures to the people with us. "Enough about all that. Let's get into town and show you what we've done."

He leads us through the trees he'd been waiting under and we come to an area that has been partially cleared. Brush and small trees have been cut down, leaving only grass along the floor of the clearing. There are neat piles of debris along the edges. There is the start of three houses around the outer edge of the clearing. It seems obvious to me that many more would fit. In the center there's a huge fire pit, marked out with stones that likely once filled the area. "This is area one," Erick says. "It'll be for housing and ceremonies, we think."

"How many people are living here right now?" Jordyn asks.

"We brought a crew of twelve with us when we left Fraun." Erick's eyes trace along the very large group now filtering into the clearing. "We won't have enough housing yet for all you've brought with you this time."

"More people means we can build faster," Tutor offers. "We aren't opposed to helping."

"Are you planning to stay here with us?" I ask, remembering that Erick explained to me once that he was a Wild. He doesn't usually associate with Fraun. He did this as a personal favor to me.

He meets my eyes and smiles knowingly. "That depends on what we decide to do with the society, now doesn't it? Let's go on, there's a lot more here to see." He leads us through the clearing, down a small worn road opposite of the way we came in. After traveling the road for about fifteen steps we come to another clearing.

This one has channels carved into the dirt directing water. A large circle has been carved into the ground at the center of this clearing, making a pool of water that is the focal point of this area. "This here is the rerouted river," Erick explains. "We got the pool for swimming and bathing right here. Then over there," he gestures to the right. "That is the clothing wash area."

This is another small cutout in the dirt making a much smaller pool of water. Beside that the branches have been stripped off nearby trees. "Why are those branches stripped?" Alerta asks, coming up behind me.

"We've been hanging clothing on them to dry," Erick answers. "But someone is making something out of the trees we had to cut down instead. It'll be more permanent than that when we're done."

"This is coming along nicely," Jordyn says. "What about a garden?"

"Yeah that's through here." Again Erick leads us through a path between trees, this one on the left of the river area. The ground around us opens up into row after row of carved ditches in the dirt. Each one carries water from the flowing river toward various stages of growing vegetables.

"Oh my," I gasp. "This is amazing."

"Doesn't the river overwater the vegetables?" Alerta asks.

"Well, I'm not a gardener. But something about how high above the water they are, being that the plants are on the top of the ditch, keeps them from drowning."

"It's a start. I can't wait to see what we can grow," she agrees. "I'd love to meet the gardener."

Erick points to a man I didn't notice crouched down low near a row about five marks up from us. "That'll be him right there. Name's Carl."

Alerta heads on toward Carl and Erick gestures back the way we came. "Let's go back to the river room and I'll take you to area two."

We walk back to the river room and take a path directly across from the path that will lead to area one. "How many areas are there?" Jordyn asks as we walk.

"Right now there are four living areas, the river room, the garden, and the stables. There's room for more but the trees would have to be cleared."

"How are you clearing trees?" Tutor asks. He tilts his head up to see how tall the trees in this area are. I match the gesture. They are not as tall as the ones that surround Enchenda, but they are tall. I can see to the tops of them, but I'd have to climb a while to reach it.

"We've got a crew of three boys who are very good at it, actually. They climb up in partner pairs, saw a piece off and pass it down. Then they move lower on the tree and repeat. The third guy piles the wood they've brought down into piles. We use it for houses or building. No waste."

"But we're building new, not using things left behind," Jordyn says.

"We are. No law tells me otherwise out here," Erick meets the taller man's eye. "Is that a problem?"

Jordyn shrugs, a smile on his face. "Not in my opinion," he answers.

The conversation dies as we enter into a clearing that looks a lot like the first clearing. This one has five houses in various stages of build, including one that looks finished and has smoke coming from the chimney. "That there is the house of the man who's been doing our cooking," Erick says. "His was the first house we finished. I'm not sure he'll be able to cook for all of these people you brought without help. If I know him, he'll try."

A couple of men are standing in the center of this clearing hacking away at a few logs. "What are they building?" Tutor asks.

Erick follows Tutor's hand and smiles. "Tables, I think. We knew more would be needed to feed everyone."

"It seems you've really thought of everything," I say. "Is there more to see?"

"There's no reason to take you to the other two areas. They're about this same size and they've been cleared but nothing has been built yet. There's basically just piles of wood. We were focused on areas one and two right now."

"We can put crews in each area, split people up. We should put cultivators of usable crops, cooks, and builders in each one," Jordyn says. "If we divide up the work and explain what we want done it should help us make faster progress. We can make sure there are foreman in charge at each location. Erick here can be the overall face of the growth, I think. He seems the most familiar with the area."

"Good plan," Erick says. "Just one thing. Are you all planning to make laws, appoint Kings, and build a council chamber? I need to know what kind of government we're looking at if I'm to decide to stay here."

Jordyn's musings are cut short. He looks confused. "I don't think we need to make those decisions right now."

"Well, as I see it there's no better time. Right now people are following you so I'm sure they don't mind. But this group I've assembled here has been living free and answering to no one. I can't see them deciding to stay behind permanently if that is going to change."

"Let's all meet tonight around the large campfire," Tutor says. "The entire group will discuss government and ruling. We will also split into the four areas for growth."

"Sounds like a plan," Erick says.

Tutor and Jordyn wander off, looking up at the buildings and talking about something. I step closer to Erick. "You've done a remarkable job," I gush. "Honestly, it's better than I ever dared to dream it would be." I put my hand on my hip and try to trap him with a serious gaze. "What kind of government are you thinking you'd stay on for?" I ask. "Because I don't want to lose you here."

Erick crosses his arms over his chest and meets my gaze. He's had more practice than me, I think, because his is serious. "Equality. I told you that a long time ago."

"Every life is as important as the ones you once painted on the walls," I say. "I remember."

He nods. "Good, then we understand each other." He reaches out and taps my shoulder with a fist. "Welcome home," he says. Then he walks away, back in the direction of the river room.

I spin around, looking at everything they've built surrounded by the forest and the trees that will provide us food, shelter, and some protection. This is our fresh start. This is our second chance.

It's absolutely perfect.

Chapter 51

That night, I follow Tutor into the clearing in Area 1 and flop down on the ground. "Did you spread the word about the meeting tonight?" I ask.

Tutor nods. "I tried to. I said we were discussing the government and anyone who was able should come. Erick said he'd tell the original crew." He flops down beside me on the ground, legs stretched in front of him. "Now we wait and see who shows up."

At first, the number of bodies that flood into the clearing makes me smile. It's good that there is so much vested interest in our future. But, as the space starts to run out and we begin encroaching on the space for the houses, I get nervous. Our council meetings were always really about five people. Sure, citizens could listen, but at the end of the day the decision came down to a vote of only five. How are we ever supposed to make decisions with all of this input?

Finally, Tutor stands up. I'm relieved to see he looks about as nervous as I feel. He bounces on his feet a little before clearing his throat and raising his hands so it's obvious he's about to speak. "I'm going to do my best to speak loud enough for everyone to hear me," Tutor begins. "Please let me know if you have trouble and I will speak louder." There are a few nods of assent and one thumbs up from someone way in the back of the assembled group. The fire is rather low, allowing Tutor to stand directly next to it without getting too hot in the warm evening. The entire clearing is packed with bodies. I know there are a few people missing; adults who decided to put their children to bed, grayed people who are tired of traveling, and even a few who are not feeling well. Annabelle, the medicine woman who was traveling with us, told me she was not going to make it tonight. She is tending to our ill in a tent she set up in Area 3, since it had the most available space right now.

From where Tutor decided to position himself I'm a few rows back but I have no trouble hearing my brother. "We are here to talk about our plans for the future. We have the unique opportunity here to create our society from scratch following whatever rules we desire. We are no longer bound by the laws that existed inside Fraun." There are a few shocked gasps, people who perhaps just realized this. Mostly, I note, people are nodding in agreement.

"This meeting will be open to anyone who would like to speak. Please tell us your name when you have the floor so we know it. I don't expect we'll all remember the names of everyone here, but it's worth a try. I'm Tutor, by the way." He smiles. "Let's have everyone take a seat, this could take awhile. When you have something to say you can stand or raise your hand."

I follow the lead of the people surrounding me and take a seat on the ground. Tutor remains standing. "Beside me here we have someone who is taking notes of everything important we talk about." He gestures to Eselda, who waves from her seat on the ground. She has a roll of parchment stretching out in front of her and she's holding a quill. I cannot see a pot of ash, but I'm sure it's beside her somewhere.

"Let's begin with thinking about our experience with the government where we came from. What are the things you liked about Fraun?" After he asks the question, Tutor takes a quick seat on the floor.

The silence stretches through the group. No one seems to want to be the first person to talk. Either that or they have nothing nice to say about the way things were done.

That thought makes me sad. I was part of that ruling council. Wasn't there anything I was doing right? I raise my hand and stand. "I'm Sawchett and one thing I liked about the new direction of Fraun since the war was the representatives that don't have royal blood having a say in the process." Eselda's quill scratches across the parchment, recording my answer. I sit back down.

Across the fire and farther back a man stands. "My name is Sen. I liked how we didn't have to worry about payments when we traded. Everything was shared. We've all heard stories of how the giants had some kind of currency and it became a thing used to separate them." Again, Eselda's quill can be heard scratching as Sen takes his seat. I'm too far away to see what she's writing but I can see that she is smiling.

Two women toward my left stand at the same time. They smile sheepishly at each other. The one closer to me points at the other one, who speaks first. She points to her chest. "Francine. I liked how our schools had begun teaching all the character traits. I have a small child and I want her to learn all the things she needs to be a good person. That takes more than one trait." She drops back to her seat.

Immediately the other woman speaks. "I always felt safe in Fraun. Even before the patrol." She sits back down.

"I'm sorry, what is your name?" Tutor asks from the floor.

"Oh, sorry. Celestina," she answers. Tutor nods in acknowledgement.

I count that I take five breaths in and out before Tutor rises. "Alright, I think we have your input on that. If you think of anything else, feel free to stand and present it. Perhaps just tell us that it is a positive you are reporting. Let's move on. What are the things you wish had been different in Fraun?"

He barely finishes the question before more than five people are on their feet. I'm shocked. Apparently people have plenty of things they would change. One man raises his hand, indicating he will go first.

"Stannis here. I will go first and we can proceed around the circle." He points to the people standing in an order to his left. "I never understood why you had to have royal blood to rule a realm. What made them—or you, I suppose—better than the rest of us?"

"Angie," the next woman says as Stannis takes his seat. "I never liked our repurposed homes. My roof was always caving in and having to be fixed. I'd like to see us change that."

"I'm Franklin," the next man says. "I didn't think we did a good job of encouraging people to explore outside of Fraun. There's a whole world out here. There were giants this entire time. Giants we assumed were gone. We need to have people who explore and not just scout troops. People who explore for us."

The answers continue.

"Our children shouldn't be working."

"We never saw anyone from other Realms."

"There were too many people living in one house. I never understood why we couldn't build more."

It's staggering. We had been operating under the assumption that people were happy in Fraun. Maybe, on some level, they were. But when given the chance to list things they would change, there is no shortage. Why hadn't we asked them at the end of the war? Maybe things could've been different if we had.

Tanya stands. "Tanya here. I never understood why people weren't truly equal in Fraun. If you had royal blood you had private tutors and larger homes and people who worked for you. People were looked down on for certain careers, like trash collection, or even for who they chose to fall in love with. I'd like to see us start a society where you can marry a mother." She smiles at Tutor and Alerta. "Or even someone of the same gender as yourself without judgment. Thank you." She drops back to her spot on the floor.

The silence is extreme. You can clearly hear Eselda's quill scratching as she tries to catch up with all the things that were said. When she finishes I count three breaths in and out before the next person stands.

I blink rapidly in surprise. "I'm Jordyn. I never liked that Fraun didn't inform citizens of the age markers that affect all descendants of Oberian. I'd like to see that changed."

"We learned of them after the war, actually." A man offers. He stands. I recognize that he was the first person to speak when we were listing positives. I don't think I can remember his name among all the ones I've heard. "We had started to learn of them and I think, in my opinion, it left us all with more questions. It seems like this would be something that would prevent you all from being the best rulers possible. I'm not trying to be rude, I'm sorry if it comes out that way." He drops back to the ground.

Eselda stands next to Jordyn. "I'm Eselda. I don't have much to say as I've been outside Fraun for a while. I just wanted to add that my husband and I are royal blood by birth. We are two of the people who were asked to lead you in the past. But you are not offending anyone." She takes a deep breath. "Quite the opposite, actually. I'm sure I speak for everyone here who once served on the council. Our blood means nothing out here. Oberian and his sons never set foot in this clearing. They've never traveled across forests in fear of giants. They were never attacked by a self-proclaimed king of Fraun just to have him killed by someone they traveled with."

I stand up beside her. "She's right," I say. "Those old rulers never joined with scouts for their own safety. Oberian's blood represented the history of Fraun. Out here, that means nothing." Eselda smiles at me and then drops back to the ground. Jordyn takes his seat beside her.

"We are on new ground here, my friends," I continue. "I understand people do not want to blindly let those with Oberian's blood lead us. Do we believe that having rulers is still necessary? If so, how do we propose those people are identified or chosen? I guess what I'm asking is, how do we do this if we don't continue to do things the way they've always been done?" Having asked the difficult question, I flop back to the ground and wait.

I look around the assembled group. I don't know what I'm looking for. I see a lot of my own feelings mirrored back at me on the faces of people I have never met. They are scared, they are worried. But there's something else there. They have hope.

"What if we elected people?" Someone calls.

"Do you mind standing, telling us your name?" Jordyn asks.

A small girl, one who I don't even think is full height, stands up. She's absolutely adorable. She has little red ponytails falling on her shoulders and freckles all over her fair face. "Kitty is my name. What if we elected people?"

A woman beside her gets up on her knees and puts her hands on the girls' shoulders. "I'm sorry, she gets a little overzealous sometimes."

"No, no. Please, let her speak," Tutor says. "Kitty that is a good idea. Do you have anything else to add?"

The woman, who must be Kitty's mother, drops her hands. "Just that people could be nominated or, like, say they wanted to run. Then we could all vote. Kind of like how everyone did with the ambassadors except it would be for a real seat." She shuffles nervously and looks down at her feet. "Does that make sense?" she quietly asks.

"That makes perfect sense," Tutor says. "Thank you."

Kitty nods and sits back down on the ground beside her mother, curling into her shoulder and burying her face.

"I actually have an odd suggestion." Sieven stands up. "My name is Sieven, by the way. I like Kitty's idea but I think it requires us to really think things through and get an honest opinion from everyone. I propose that we make no major decisions tonight. Instead, I think we should take a few suns and consider it. If you have more ideas or questions, record them on this parchment Eselda is using. We will put it in a central location somewhere. Then we'll get back together and make the decision then. What do we think?"

Tutor stands. "All in favor of thinking this through for two suns and meeting again, raise your hand."

All around me hands reach for the sky.

As the gathering breaks up, Tanya finds her way to my side. "Well, that was interesting," she says. "I've seen you speak to groups before but that was sort of intense." She bumps into me with her shoulder. "You did a good job. It gave me bumps on my arms."

I laugh and roll my eyes. "If you say so. But did we accomplish anything?" I ask.

She closes one eye and purses her lips. Then she snaps her fingers and her eye pops open. "I got it."

"You got what?"

"I know what we accomplished." She wiggles her eyebrows. "We got two more suns of anarchy."

Chapter 52

I sleep in later than I intended to the next morning. The bed I've been given is warm and cozy. Plus, after many suns of traveling through the forest and sleeping on the ground, a pile of blankets on the floor of a finished home in Area 2 is a huge improvement. When I wake up the sweet woman who allowed me to crash on her floor is gone. The house is empty and quiet.

I actually consider curling back up and sleeping for a little longer. Then I notice sunlight and noises of a society waking for the day are coming through the window opening on the wall nearby. People are awake and being productive. I need to do the same.

I stretch and grab my bag. There's nothing clean in this bag anymore, which is a problem. I guess that shows what I will be doing first. I take my entire bag full of dirty clothes back to the river area, heading for the pool used for cleaning. There are already three people there, scrubbing and working at the dirty laundry.

"Good morning," I call. "Do you mind if I join you?" I hold up the bag. "Most of my clothes are dirty."

The closest woman smiles up at me. "If you want to just drop them here, we'll take care of it for you."

"Not necessary." I open my bag and dump the clothes out into a pile next to the watering hole. I roll up the sleeves on the shirt I'm wearing so I don't get it too wet. Looking around, I notice a few pieces of pumice laying nearby. Perfect. I grab one and submerge my first article of clothing in the water. "Oh, it's warmer than I was expecting."

"We heat rocks in the fire and drop them into the bottom of the pool before we start," the woman explains. "Honestly, if you'd like to take a bath yourself we don't mind washing these for you." She looks over the pile. "What do you have there, three outfits? That's nothing." She tips her chin to the pile on the other side of her, which is almost as tall as she is. "We're already washing for quite a few of the weary travelers. What is your passion?"

"My what?" I ask.

"Your passion," she repeats. "What do you like to do? The three of us like working with clothes and we like water. We sew, we wash, and we change the color of clothing. Is that something you like to do as well?"

"Not really. I like cooking," I offer.

Her hands freeze. "Seriously?"

"Um, yes." Is that a bad thing or a good thing?

"Well then you need to leave these clothes with us, take a bath, and get yourself to the kitchen. The cook needs more help since all the new people arrived. He doesn't have enough hands to get it all done." She takes the article of clothing I'm rubbing the pumice on right out of my hand. "Go," she says.

"Are you sure?"

"I'm sure. Go." She waves her wet hand toward the bigger pool. Reluctantly I get up and head that way. I suppose I should take a quick bath. Water sounds so inviting. It's been too long.

I move to the farthest side of the pool, furthest from the women. I'm not exactly shy, but I'm not eager to strut around the entire clearing without clothes. I strip off my clothing and drop my body into the water. This pool hasn't been warmed up with heated rocks. It's cold enough to take my breath away at first. I stand still, the water reaching almost to my shoulders, and try to get used to it.

Eventually, I do. My body goes numb enough that I can use the piece of pumice I'm still holding to scrub my skin red. I put the pumice on the shore and dip my head below the water level. I run my fingers through my hair. Then I look around, wondering if I can find any oil nearby.

"Looking for this?" the woman offers. She's suddenly right there on the shore. I swear she wasn't there before. It's the same woman from the clothing pool. She's holding out a glass vial of yellow liquid. "I need that pumice stone. Trade?"

"Yes, thank you." I reach out and take the vial from her. She takes the pumice and disappears again. Uncapping the vial, I take a sniff. I close my eyes at the sweet scent. Olive and lemon. Perfect. I let a few drops flow into my hands and then recap the bottle and put it down before rubbing the oil along my hair. It feels so nice and the smell is wonderful. I missed being clean.

After the oil is rubbed in I step out of the river. There are a few large blankets along the bank, folded up for this exact purpose. This place is amazingly efficient. I dry myself off and get dressed.

Then, feeling like a new person, I head to the kitchen we were shown yesterday. I'm ready to do my part.

Chapter 53

From the outside the kitchen appears like every other house they've constructed here. Sturdy, wooden, and with one large window looking into the center of the clearing. Inside, it's amazing. This house, unlike some of the others, appears to be mostly one large room. There are two fires, one on each side of the room. They both have large grates above the flames. There is a large man bustling about near the fire on my left. There are three pans on the grate. He is standing before them, holding a spoon. He turns to me. "Can I help you with something?" he asks. His voice is kind.

"I would like to offer my services." I remember the phrasing the girl in the river area used. "Cooking is my passion."

"Excellent. Get over here." He turns his attention back to his pans.

I cross the room. The first pan holds something thick and red. It smells like garlic and tomato. "What is this?" I ask, gesturing toward it. "Sauce?"

"You bet. It's tomato sauce. Great covering for almost any food. Gives it a little more flavor." He pulls his spoon out of the second pot, tapping it along the edge of the pan. "I could use your help with the meat."

The meat. Where is the meat?

I look around the counters, which appear to be built into the outer walls of the cabin all the way around. The one to the left of the fire has what looks like two entire ants stacked up. I don't think I've ever worked with such a large quantity of meat before. Beside it there is a wooden slab I do recognize. A cutting board.

"Where would I find a knife?" I ask, rolling up my sleeves and heading for the counter.

"Top drawer right underneath you." He points with his spoon.

I slide open the drawer, which rolls smoothly and will require more inspection for my curious mind when I have more time, and find a perfectly sharpened chef knife. I waste no time. I snap the legs off the ant and get to work slicing each one open and stripping the meat out of the center. We work in comfortable silence until I have a pretty sizable stack of raw meat.

"What should I do with this?" I ask.

"Let me get the pan ready for it."

I keep working, moving on to the thorax of the ant which is much easier to work with because of its size. Once I crack open the exoskeleton it's pretty simple to free the meat and chop into smaller sections. This means I can watch what the chef is doing with his pan.

I watch him drop some oil into the big black frying pan. Then he drops in a handful of garlic and two hands full of onion. The smell is wonderful. "As soon as these cook down we'll throw the meat in there." He says.

"Perfect. I'm Sawchett, by the way," I offer.

"Oh, right. Sorry about that. Mornings are always a little crazy in here. I'm Nib."

"Do you cook for everyone all alone?"

"Well, so far I do. But it was only a few of us in the beginning. I'm real glad you showed up today."

"This smells like lunch." I move on to the thorax of the second ant. "I knew I overslept today. Did I sleep through breakfast or do people fend for themselves in the morning?"

"I prep some fresh berries at night and leave them on the counter near the door. That means I can sleep in and people can sort of fend for themselves. How am I doing on time? Can you see the sun through that window?"

I duck down a little so I'm at the right angle. "I can't really see it. Do you want me to go outside?"

"No, no. I'm sure I'm good. When you came, was it drawing near the top of the sky?"

I try to remember. It was warming up outside, I remember that. Oh, the shadows. "It wasn't directly overhead yet, but it was getting close," I confirm. My shadow was falling at a sharp angle when I headed toward the kitchen house.

"Perfect. Alright, this pan is ready."

"We have good timing," I say as I make the last cut. "I'm done unless you wanted me to cut into the head or the abdomen, which I admit I've never used."

"No, leave those. The brains aren't bad, but they're not worth the hassle and the abdomen is too crowded with organs to be much use to us today. We can salt and save it for use another time."

I carry the cutting board over to the pan, noticing the onions are translucent and shiny. I use the knife to scrape the meat into it, loving that instant sizzle that means it's already cooking.

"What's in the last pan?" I ask, using my knife tip to point to the largest pan which looks like it contains mostly water. "Is that some kind of soup?"

"Nope, noodles. I made a huge batch in anticipation of the arrival of your big group. I cut them into small sections this morning. I'm just boiling them now." He stirs the ant with his spoon. "This is about done, actually. Would you mind grabbing the bowls from the back of the room. Get them all, we're gonna need them."

I head to the row of counters directly across from the door. Shelves line the wall above the counter. Plates are stacked on the shelves. I grab stacks and start transporting them to the counters just to the right of the doorway. I don't count them but it takes me quite a few passes across the kitchen room before I have them all stacked there.

Next, I slide open the drawer below the same counter and start moving spoons over to the same area. This time, since I'm able to carry more of them, it doesn't take me as many trips.

By the time I'm finished, Nib has moved the pans off the fire to the counter on the left of the door. "Alright, little lady, go ahead and call out the lunch warning."

I step out the door into the sunlight. There are a few people around, but no one is paying me any attention. I cup my hands around my mouth. "Lunch time," I bellow. The men nearest me turn and wave in acknowledgement.

Hoping they'll help spread the word, I turn back and enter the room. "How can I help serve?" I ask.

"Each person through the door will grab a plate and spoon. Then they'll come to me. I'll spoon some of these noodles into their bowl. You can help by putting a spoonful of the sauce on top of that and then putting a spoonful of the ant on top of that." As he speaks he holds up the spoons which he's rested in the respective pots. The spoon for the sauce is deep, round, and made from some sort of metal. The spoon for the ant is smaller, wooden. Clearly he's proportioning this for me. The message is clear. One of each of these spoon sizes for each person should last us the entire group.

I take my position in front of the two pots just as the first person enters the kitchen.

Nip and I eat last. I'm not at all surprised to find there's exactly enough in each of our pans for two more servings. After watching him cook effortlessly, watching him administer directions while continuing to cook, and seeing how he proportions I am truly impressed with this man's skills. I have so many questions for him, so many things I know I can learn. But right now, we eat.

Chapter 54

I'm alone in the spot known as Area 1 when a roach enters, antennae moving as though the creature is feeling out the area. "Who is in charge here?" he asks in a deep voice.

"I'm not sure that anyone is really in charge. What can I help you with?"

"Someone approaches this area. I was asked to warn you if that occurred. I was told I would be fed and treated well for my honesty."

"Yes, of course." I give him quick directions through Area 2 to the stables that have been created for this exact purpose. It has food, water, and ground covering the roaches like to use for bedding. There are people in that area, like Tanya, whose passion is caring for creatures.

Then I head to the house I've been staying in and grab my bow and arrow. On my way back to the entrance to our little community, I pass a man I recognize. "A roach warns me that someone is coming. I am headed that way to wait for them."

"Do you require assistance?" he asks.

"No, I should be fine. Can you please bring this basket of berries to the kitchen and give them to Nip?"

He takes the basket from me. "Be safe," he says.

I nod. That's exactly what I intend to do.

I stop in the group of trees where Erick waited for our group to arrive. I hear nothing. No leaves crunching, no voices. I suppose I should've had the presence of mind to ask the roach how far away the arriving individuals were. In fact, I'm not even sure how many people are arriving. I sigh at my own mistakes.

I watch the sun trek down the sky for what feels like a very long time. I know the meeting to discuss the government is supposed to be tonight. It is our second night since the first meeting. If I am not there, what will they decide?

I think about the two days I've spent helping in the kitchen and what I've already learned. It feels so different here, not being in charge. I'm allowed to just be like everyone else. If they were to ask me, I don't think I even want to lead again.

Still not hearing footsteps or voices I decide this is a good time to practice my shot. I repeatedly let loose an arrow, hitting my target tree over and over again. I have five arrows with me so every five shots I have to walk to the tree and retrieve them. I count four trips to the tree before I hear the crunching of leaves off in the distance.

I return to the copse of trees and wait.

The crunching gets louder as whatever is walking draws closer. Finally, the head of a person comes into view. I have awhile to watch as the tall lithe body comes into view. I don't recognize the person but I'm glad to see they are alone.

I step out toward them, holding my bow at the ready. "Stop there," I command. "State your business."

The man's hands fly up. "I am from Fraun. I mean no harm."

For a heartbeat, my bow drops. Then I remember what the last man from Fraun who followed us attempted to do to Tutor. I straighten my arms and notch an arrow, bringing the tip back to the appropriate location to bury it in the stranger's shoulder. I wouldn't kill him, just seriously injure him and make a point. "What is your business here?" I ask.

"I have a message for the kings of your kingdom."

I try not to roll my eyes. "Tell me the message, I will deliver it."

"Who are you?" he asks. He takes a hesitant step forward.

I apply a little pressure to the shaft, pulling back. "Stop there." The arrow speaks louder than my words and he freezes again. "Who I am is not important. Speak your message, turn, and go."

"The message is that those who remain in Fraun will start again." His voice rings with the authority of one who has practiced the words. "Kings have been chosen and our realms will stand tall. We mean no harm to you. We want peace from you."

I release the pressure on the string but I do not lower my arrow. This message is not a threat. But it is a clear line between us. They are moving on, we are moving on. "What are you doing about the giants?"

"We are taking our chances. Do we have your word that you are not a threat to us?" he asks.

I don't want to mention Marcus, although he is the reason I am not being open with this man. Fear of Marcus and what kind of Fraun he has created make me afraid of showing this man where we are located. I also know I don't really have the authority to promise this man anything, but we are in a state of anarchy behind me. I smile. "You have my word." I lower the arrow completely.

"Do you have the authority to make that promise?"

"You better hope I do." I lean my right leg up against the tree behind me and rest my weight on it. "You should turn and head home now," I say. "We have nothing here to offer you."

He nods. "Thank you for hearing me out."

I watch as the man disappears back in the direction he came. Not wishing to give away our location, I wait until the count of five hundred before I turn and finally head back to my own area. I'm in time for the second meeting.

Chapter 55

Again, the fire is low but warm in the clearing. This time I'm pretty sure every living being who has been working in this area is present, even children. In fact, I notice a few of the roaches are also gathered between the houses. Apparently, they are also interested in how things shape up in our new area. I wonder, briefly, if anyone has considered asking them their opinions.

At the center of the clearing I notice it is Jordyn standing beside the fire with Sieven at his side. Eselda has a parchment in her hands, but I don't see a quill. She's sitting close enough to the fire to utilize the light for reading or writing. Tutor and Alerta are holding hands in the back of the group, near where I come into the clearing. "Where have you been?" he whispers when he sees me.

"There was a messenger from Fraun. I should tell the entire group."

His eyes widen and he nods. Then he waves his free hand toward the fire. "Get up there. Now."

I do as I'm told, slowly walking up toward the fire. I didn't do anything wrong, so why do I feel like I'm heading to take punishment for something? My feet feel heavy. My stomach is churning. I'm aware that Sieven seems to be talking, but I'm not focused on whatever he's telling the group. I keep walking, picking my way around the people settled on the floor.

"Sawchett, is everything okay?" Sieven asks. My own name draws my attention.

"Actually, I have something to report." My voice is shaky. I clear my throat. "A roach came earlier and reported to me that someone was approaching. I headed off to meet the person, make sure there was no issue." The bow is still strung across my back so I make a decision not to mention that I went armed to the meeting. "It was a representative claiming to be from Fraun."

There's a smattering of talk springing up around me at the announcement. I let it die down, which it does after only a few breaths. "He claimed to be here to tell us that Fraun continues their kingdom in our absence. They are taking their chances with the giants. He wanted to make sure that we pose no threat to them and that we mean them no harm. I gave him the assurances he desired."

"You had no right to make that decision on your own," a voice calls.

"That's true, I didn't. But everything I heard here two suns ago and everything I've observed since led me to believe that we mean them no harm. We are merely trying to do our best to start up something ideal here. If we can continue to be a peaceful society with them, why wouldn't we?"

There is no answer from the assembled audience.

"I'm not sure how he knew where to look for us, although many roaches know where to find us. I did wait for him to leave the clearing before I headed this way so I'm confident he doesn't know our exact location."

"Did you recognize the man?" someone calls.

"Not really. He didn't identify himself by name or realm either."

"Did he seem to feel like Fraun can offer us the same promises of safety?" Sieven asks.

"He seemed to be offering that, yes. I did not bring up Marcus."

"Do you think he knew Marcus was dead?" Jordyn asks.

"Again, as I didn't mention it, I'm not sure. Should we send a messenger?" I say.

"Let's finish concluding our meeting here and perhaps we will send someone to speak with Fraun after we have made decisions. What say the group?" Sieven calls.

There are a few calls of "Aye" in response. I decide that is the end of my part in this meeting and sit down right where I was standing.

Sieven, apparently the leader of this particular meeting, starts speaking again immediately. "Back to the issue at hand, creating a strong government for our new land. Eselda will read for us the points which you have written on the parchment that was hanging for the last two suns at this time."

Eselda stands and lets the parchment unroll a little. She pushes her hair out of her face, angles herself toward the fire, and speaks loudly and clearly. "We need to choose a new name to fit our new society, we need to honor all people regardless of their blood, everyone needs to work, continue to let us build new, let us try out new technologies, and the last note here is a little hard to read but I think it says teach us reading and writing." She turns her eyes away from the parchment. "If that is incorrect, please accept my apologies and feel free to correct me."

She drops back to her cross-legged seat on the floor beside the fire, setting the parchment down on the ground in front of her. No one speaks up to correct her, meaning she was likely correct in her assessment of the note.

"Those are great suggestions," Sieven says. "In keeping with our discussion last time I'd like to ask anyone who has a nomination for leaders to please rise."

Six people stand.

"Please state the name of the person you are nominating in a loud, clear voice," Sieven says. "If you are the person being nominated please come take a spot up here where everyone can see you." He sits down on the ground, pulling Jordyn down with him.

"I nominate Jordyn on the basis of his wisdom and integrity." Jordyn hadn't even fully sat down on the ground yet. He puts his hands down and pushes himself back to his full three clicks. He doesn't look entirely happy about it.

"I nominate Sieven on the basis of his leadership skills." From where I'm sitting I can see the deep blush that takes up Sieven's face as he stands again.

"I nominate Hector on the basis of his caring nature." The former king of Farcheda stands and winds his way among people to stand beside Jordyn.

"I nominate Annabeth the healer on the basis of her intelligence." My former ambassador at the royal council stands and heads to stand beside Hector. As she passes me, she squeezes my shoulder and offers me a smile. I haven't seen her much on our journey but she is a wonderful woman. I'm pleased to see her standing there beside the other proud men who have been nominated.

"I nominate the former queen Eselda on the basis of humility." I recognize that voice as belonging to the former patrolman and scout, Danyel. Eselda stands slowly, obviously reluctant to accept the nomination.

I look at the group of nominated rulers with a sense of pride. This is a good group of people. Although three of the five have royal blood, I don't believe that was the reason for their nomination. These are people who have been working hard among this new group since the beginning of this journey. They are people who I would trust our future to. They are people—

"I nominate Sawchett on the basis of her honesty and integrity."

What? That can't be right. I'm not even an adult for at least another ten lunar cycles. I turn to see the person who was speaking. Nip, the man who is training me to be a chef, is taking his seat.

I slowly stand and make my way to be beside Eselda, not at all sure that I belong here. I look out among the faces of the crowd and see many faces who would be better leaders than I would. People who deserve recognition.

"Are there any other nominations at this time?" Sieven asks.

Silence wraps around the clearing. I count four shaking breaths in and out before he speaks again. "Alright, let's continue then. Each of the nominees will have a chance to openly and honestly speak about what they think being a ruler would mean to this group. After that we will vote. Please listen to each speaker. I guess I'll go first, since I'm already speaking." There's a few chuckles from the group. "I'm Sieven. I was raised a scout until the war. After meeting Jordyn and hearing how much he loved Fraun I fought side-by-side with him for the dream of what Fraun could be." He brushes Jordyn's arm as he speaks of him. "After the war, I made Farcheda my home and became the ambassador to king Hector.

"I'm a little stunned to be nominated to rule, honestly." He chuckles. "If you decide to elect me, I will continue to work on new construction as I've been doing. I believe I can help balance what I learned in my childhood as a scout with what I've learned in Farcheda since. There are a lot of good people up here, but I am honored you consider me one of them. Thank you." He blows out a deep breath. "Jordyn, your turn."

Jordyn bobs his head repeatedly, more like a rocking than a nod. He looks around the clearing. He takes a deep breath, letting it puff his chest out then slowly releases it. "I cannot express what it means to me to be nominated as a leader of this group." His voice cracks with emotion. "About four annuals ago I killed a corrupt king in a battle for the future of Fraun." There are a few gasps of shock from some of the people assembled.

"I am not sure I have ever forgiven myself for that. But I was not a ruler at the time. I had already stepped down from my throne before that day came. I stepped down because I was afraid of who I was becoming and of the age marker that plagued me. When it was time to choose whether I had what it took to stand up and fight for Fraun, my first instinct was to flee. It was better men than me who convinced me to turn back and fight for it."

He wipes at his eyes with the back of his hand before continuing. "I tell you these things, my moments of greatest weakness, because if you choose me those are the things I will know that you are forgiving me for. Do not vote for me to be a ruler because of my name, my blood, my legacy, or the best of me. I would not accept that nomination.

"However, if you vote for me because you have comprehended the worst parts of me and can forgive me for them, I will accept the role. Thank you."

He takes a step back, effectively putting himself in more shadow than the rest of us. On his right, Hector waves. "I'm not sure I want to follow that." He sighs. "I am surprised to see myself up here, truthfully. When I heard all of you speaking two suns ago I had an overwhelming sense that we all failed you. To listen to you talk, we were terrible rulers. I felt like I had been out of touch and I was disappointed in myself."

He winces. "I spent these two suns since our last meeting working among you in various locations trying to find my passion. All of you spent that time making me feel better. You are amazing people and you all deserve rulers who will highlight what you can do and work among you proudly. If you choose me to be that person, I can only tell you that I will do my best. I would not take this spot because of who I am. I would accept it because of who you are. Thank you for honoring me with this nomination."

He rests his hand on the shoulder of Annabeth. "Annabeth, you're up," he says.

"Thank you, Hector. Thank you, everyone. My name is Annabeth. I am not blood of Oberian but I guess that doesn't matter anymore. I am a healer. I have always been a healer. I'm strange and quirky, that's what I've been told." She smiles. "Only someone strange would cut hair that never grows, right?" She runs her hand along her short grey spikes. People laugh lightly, Annabeth joins them.

"I am the only person nominated who has grey hair. We all know what that means. As a healer I can tell you we have never seen someone survive past forty-five annuals. My hair has been grey for two. I have no more than three annuals remaining to teach someone to take my spot as a healer. I do not think I also have time to learn how to be a ruler and worry about what happens to that role when I die." She stops talking and coughs three times, punctuating her statements with a stark reality no one can argue with.

"Looking at the other five people who have been nominated I can tell you that I would be proud and excited to be a part of a community run by any one of them." She looks left and right. "I can also tell you all that I will promise to be an annoying bug in your ear with all of my ideas." She turns back to the audience and smiles wide. "But I must ask you not to vote for me. Allow me to respectfully decline in order to focus, as I should, on the health of our people until the day when I am the one who dies." Mimicking Jordyn, Annabeth also takes a step back into the shadows.

Eselda, next in line, stares at the fire. Silence stretches. I tap her on the shoulder. "You're up," I whisper.

"I can't believe I'm standing here," she says. Her voice carries in the clearing. "I never would've guessed anyone would nominate me." She picks her head up and looks around at the group. "Everyone else up here didn't surprise me at all. They are all deserving and wonderful people who are loved. But me?" She lays her hand on her chest. "I never really wanted to be queen. Did you know that?" She drops her hand and takes a step forward. "I tried to get out of it. I tried to find ways to step down. Even making an eight-year-old child who was never trained in the ways of royals a princess." She shakes her head. "Once I was Queen, you know the story." She sighs.

"I have already publicly stated that I am sorry for what I did. But I don't think I ever explained it, not really. There's no excuse for declaring war. There's no excuse for following the man I followed. But I can tell you that many of the ideas that you spoke out for during our meeting two suns ago were the reasons why I did what I did. I hated the idea of rulers being a certain heritage. I hated the excuses. I hated the closed-door policy. There is nothing you said that I hadn't already thought.

"Regardless of whether you choose me as a leader, which I don't think you should when I look at your other options here, I want you to know that I am one of you. I haven't been part of a society this large in probably four annuals. For me, it is huge to admit this. I am one of you. I am proud to be one of you. Thank you for having me."

She turns her green eyes on me. They are sparkling with happiness. "Your turn, little princess." I'm pretty sure her voice isn't loud enough for others to hear. But it makes me smile.

"She's right, I was too young to be a princess. Really the system was so strange. She was a princess the day she was born and no one questioned that. No one, except me, questioned an eight-year-old dropping into the role. I wasn't ready," I say.

"I became Queen at ten annuals. Right now, I'm not even done maturing. If my calculations are correct, which I guess I cannot guarantee, I am thirteen annuals. Can you believe that? Thirteen annuals and people called me "Your Majesty" when I walked around Enchenda. Thirteen annuals and you are nominating me to rule again." I feel tears welling up. I stop and take a deep breath to get myself under control.

"I look around this group and I see a shocking number of people, still sitting, who would be better rulers than me. Kurt, who taught Jordyn and Sieven how to use a sword. Linchanta, who was my lady-in-waiting and a friend who I could always count on. Danyel, who told us about the giants even when it would scare us. Abney, who can best anyone in this clearing with her bow. Tutor, my brother, who is easily the best man I have ever met in my life. Alerta, who can grow anything with a little time. Thometh, who stepped up to lead Renchenda when it mattered. Tanya, a farmer who opened my eyes to the ways of the world." I make a point of looking around at all the faces, slowly.

"I could go on all day, naming everyone here that I've met. You are all amazing. I have so much to learn from all of you. Thank you for nominating me, but please use your vote for those more deserving." I sweep my left hand out, indicating all the people who have spoken before me.

Sieven takes a step forward. "Alright, that's everyone. Time to vote. I'm thinking we'll call out aye or nay for each person, publicly right here, no hard feelings. If it's too close to call by ear, we can divide the group by moving bodies. Does that sound agreeable?"

There are nods all around.

"How many rulers will we have?" someone calls.

"I'd say anyone who garners more ayes than nays should be allowed to rule. That will give us flexibility. Does anyone say otherwise?"

Silence is his answer.

"All in favor of Sieven, say aye." The ayes ring out. "Those opposed?" There are a few soft "nays". He nods. "All in favor of Jordyn?" Ayes again, ring out. "Opposed?" This time there are more, but not nearly as many as approvals. "All in favor of Hector?" Ayes. "Opposed?" This time there are none. "All in favor of Annabeth?"

Although I know it is what she asked for, it pains me to hear the small number of agreeable answers. She is such a strong woman. She nods and smiles at the crowd, a silent thank you. "Opposed?" Sieven calls. The response is loud, clearly she is no longer needed. Annabeth waves as she turns and takes her seat among them again.

"All those in favor of Eselda?" The ayes are loud, but not as loud as they have been for others. "Opposed?" he asks. The nays sound equally balanced. "I'm afraid that one is too close to call. We will have to physically move our bodies, let's have the ayes—"

"Actually," Eselda calls. "I'm really ok with not accepting the nomination at this time." She smiles at the group. "Honestly, thank you for the nomination and the faith." She turns and takes her seat beside Annabeth. Annabeth reaches out and grips the former queen's hand.

"Ok, fine by me. I'm sure we'll have no objection to that decision?" Sieven waits anyway, just in case. No one speaks up. "Alright, all those in favor of Sawchett." I almost turn and take my seat with Eselda, just in case. I actually consider calling out that I quit too. Except, I'm the only woman left up here. Doesn't that matter for something? My eyes well up with tears as people call out 'Aye'.

"Opposed?" Sieven prompts.

The tears fall down my cheeks as silence answers him.

Chapter 56

Life feels almost normal for the next fortnight. In fact, it feels better than normal. I feel safe, comfortable, and accepted. Technically, I'm a leader here, but it doesn't feel like it did in Fraun. Being a leader doesn't make me better. I'm not getting anything for free. I get up and go to work every morning just like everyone else. Being Queen was my job in Fraun. Here, being a leader is just another responsibility. One we've decided I'll hold for an annual before we have another election.

I get up and head into the kitchen where people are grabbing the fruit that was laid out last night. On the way I wave at almost everyone and they wave back. I notice smiles on everyone's faces, people seem as happy as I feel. I walk through the doorway and wrap the fabric apron around my waist, tying it in the back. "What are we cooking this morning, chef?" I greet.

"Good morning," Nip answers. "We are pan frying zucchini in oil then roasting snails and potatoes over the fire. Which task would you prefer?"

The first day in the kitchen is the only day when Nip hasn't given me a choice. Ever since he allows me to pick what I'd like. I try to decide for today. Should I take the safe route and chop and sauté the zucchini, which I've done loads of times? Should I take the gamble of working with snail, which I've never done?

"I think I'd welcome the chance to roast the snail if you're willing to teach me your techniques." Piled high on the counters to the left of the door are stacks of the creatures, recognizable only by their shells. "Where did we get this many snails?"

"A few of the boys went on a hunt for food and found a whole slew of them down by the river. Most of them have cracked shells, which apparently kills them. We're not sure how the shells got cracked but one of the boys thought maybe birds. To free them from the shells we'll have to boil them. Then we can pop the meat from the shells and roast the meat on sticks over the fire."

I grab the biggest pot in the kitchen and head out to the river area to fill it. Just outside the door a young man jogs to catch up to me. "Sawchett, can I talk to you?"

"Sure, walk with me."

He falls in line beside me. "I just wanted to suggest that maybe people can be put in charge of certain sections or careers. Kind of how Nip is obviously in charge of the kitchen, maybe we need someone in charge of everything. I was just thinking that would make it easier for people to know who to talk to about getting involved. Does that make sense?" He talks fast, obviously nervous. He's younger than me, I can see that. I wonder, for a second, what career he wants to try that he doesn't know how to break into.

"That is a great idea. We'll put a sign up list somewhere so people can volunteer to take on that task."

We reach the water and, without being asked, the boy grabs the handle of the bucket and helps me fill the pan with water. We silently trek back to the kitchen, the pot balanced between us. Inside, we lower it into the flames. The boy lingers, looking around the room in fascination.

"Would you like to help in the kitchen today?" I offer.

"I've never cooked a thing in my life," he admits.

"Well, everyone should know how to prepare one dish," Nip says. "Get over here and help me cut up these potatoes.

"I'll be right back," I say. Although with the quick instructions happening on knife usage I'm not sure anyone hears me. I have a little bit to wait before this large pot comes to a boil.

I walk outside, looking for the towering blonde head of Jordyn. Spotting him across the clearing working on a house, I head over. Eselda, who I haven't spoken to much since the vote, is standing beside him. She's laughing, her head thrown back and her curls cascading down her back. She certainly doesn't look upset at how it went at the election.

She stops laughing, wiping a few tears that have squeezed out during the process from her face, just as I approach. "Good morning," she says.

"Good morning. I just wanted to tell you that a young boy made a great suggestion to me this morning. He thinks we should have someone in charge of each career. Someone willing to help new people learn that career."

"Passion," Jordyn says without turning around.

"Right, passion. What's the difference?" I ask.

"Passion is something you do because you love it," Eselda says. "Career is something you do because it's what you've been trained for. People need to remember that passions don't need to be permanent." She stands up. "I must be off. It turns out my passion is helping at the school and I'm going to be late. You two have fun."

"That's a good idea," Jordyn says.

"I'd like to hang a parchment somewhere so people can volunteer for that duty. Is that alright?"

Jordyn stops what he is doing and turns to look at me. "I have no problem with that." He smiles. "Are you happy with the election?"

"I'm happy that we are not expected to be only rulers. We are allowed to just be us." I hope he understands what I mean. It was so strange, before. I was given a house and expected to live a certain way. This is different. Better.

The smile that stretches across his face shows he knows exactly what I mean. "Jordyn, is Eselda alright with the results? I hope she doesn't feel insulted."

"She's more than alright with it." His eyes track up to the clouds as he thinks about his next response. When they fall back to my face he looks serious. "Eselda never liked being a ruler. She never liked being in charge of anyone. She is learning to forgive herself for the decisions she made in the past because of the acceptance we've found here and that is the most important gift the people could've given her."

"I don't think people are still upset with her. It was a long time ago."

His mouth twists in a sort of grimace. "It's only Eselda that still needs to forgive, I think."

"I have to get back to the kitchen but I will put that parchment up today," I say. "Thanks for chatting with me."

"No problem." Jordyn turns his attention back to the wooden frame of the house he's building. "Have a good day," he calls.

That's exactly what I intend to do.

Chapter 57

The clearing around Area 1 is quiet that night. A few people come and go, laughing or telling jokes. I love the feeling flooding me, that comforting idea that we're home. It's not a feeling I ever felt inside Fraun. The closest I can say is I felt this when I was having dinner with a small group of friends, or with Tutor. But to feel it right out in the open, in the middle of a large group, that's something extraordinary.

Abney comes through the passage from the river room, holding baby Lili and making noises like a song. I wave and she crosses to me, still softly singing. "Hi there," she says, turning her words into a tune.

"Lili doesn't want to sleep?" I ask.

Abney sighs. "If she had her way we'd stay up all night and watch the stars."

I tip my head back and look up. "They are beautiful tonight."

"Do not tell her that," she says. Then she laughs. "Mind if I sit?"

I scoot over on the log, making enough room for Abney to drop down beside me. She does just that. The blankets Lili is wrapped in pull back enough for me to see the baby's face. She is awake, but barely. Her eyes are half closed and she looks close to dreamland. Abney is moving slightly side-to-side, rocking her.

"Is she liking it here, do you think?" I ask. Then I realize how ridiculous that sounds. Lili is not even one annual right now, surely she doesn't have opinions about where we choose to live. "I'm sorry, that's probably foolish to ask."

"It's not foolish." Abney smiles at me. "I think she does. She is happy most of the day and really enjoys being outside. She loves the river room more than anything, honestly. Plus, once she's asleep, she sleeps so peacefully." She kisses the baby's exposed forehead. "It's funny to think this is the only real home she'll ever know."

The sentence sinks in. I don't find it funny. I find it shocking and intense. It's a lot of pressure to make sure we do things right. That we keep everyone safe. Lili, all the children, they deserve this. "That is something I absolutely needed to hear," I tell her. "Thank you."

There's a noise off to our left and I turn my head to see what is happening. I recognize my friend from Enchenda, Bin. He appears to be struggling with another boy, they're pulling on each other's arms. I squint a little in their direction, trying to see better. "Are they fighting?" I ask.

Bin shakes off the other boy and starts to stomp off in the direction of the entrance. The boy grabs him again. "No," the boy yells.

I stand up. "What's going on?" I call.

The boy holds firm. Bin appears to be trying to walk away from him, their hands stretched between them at almost painful angles. "Stop. What is the problem?" I ask, approaching them. I reach out and tap Bin's arm just above where the boy held. "Talk to me."

He turns and his eyes catch mine. Something there makes my breath catch. He reminds me of the birds who used to visit me. A mix of caution, fear, and anger swirl in them. "Let me go," he growls. The tension leaves his shoulders and the hands between the men fall slack.

"We're fine here," I tell the boy without taking my eyes from Bin. "You may go."

"But he is trying—"

"We're fine," I repeat, my voice a sharp slap. "But thank you for your help."

The boy drops Bin's arm and it falls to his side with an audible noise. Bin sighs and turns his attention over my head. "I'm leaving," he says.

The statement is so final, so shocking, that I gasp. "Where would you go?"

He catches my eye again. "Back to Fraun." He holds my gaze, daring me to say something against this idea. His chin is hard and unwavering, his brow pulled tight between his eyes. I can tell, just by this expression, that his mind is not looking to be changed.

I reach out slowly, like I would for the birds. I don't want to spook him. My hand brushes his shoulder softly. I hope I'm communicating all the care I feel for him with this gentle touch. "Be safe," I whisper. "I'm sorry we weren't what you were looking for."

He doesn't move his eyes but I think I see a softening in them, just for a beat. Then the hard edge is back. "You're not going to try and stop me?"

I grimace, feeling my eyes fill a little with unshed tears. "You don't want me to stop you, do you?"

He shakes his head. "No. My mind is set."

I take a step closer to him, noticing that we're about the same height. I lean in close to him, close my eyes, and brush my lips on his cheek. "Then be safe," I repeat.

He nods, just once. Then he turns and walks away, back in the direction of the entrance. I don't know how long I stand there, watching him walk away, but it's long enough for Abney to cross the clearing and take her place beside me. "Is he returning to Fraun?" she asks.

I nod. "I didn't try to stop him."

"We are not a prison, Sawchett. You were right to let him go." She sighs. "But, even still, we should put a guard up at the entrance just in case."

My head turns so quickly to her face that my neck actually protests. "He is not a threat to us," I insist.

She runs her free hand through her hair, a nervous gesture. "Alright, I'm not arguing. I don't really know him…" she trails off.

I turn back to the entrance and cross my arms over my chest. "Well I do."

Chapter 58

Five lunar cycles, half an annual, have come and gone since our election. Volunteers have stepped up in every passion, to help train anyone who is interested in learning. I have been given my own kitchen in Area 4. There was some discussion about naming our areas, but people are afraid that will separate us like naming the realms once did. So they're back to being called by their numbers. It doesn't bother me one way or the other, so I stay out of that. I will honor the decision of the people who feel passionate about it.

A group of people were sent off, shortly after Bin left, in the direction of Fraun. They were to give a message to the people taking charge in Fraun now. They were then instructed to go to the site of the giants. They're looking for movement, signs that the giants may have known about us, or destruction. They're making sure we have nothing to be afraid of. I wasn't sure I supported that decision after what I faced when I went searching, but I went along with it because majority rules. They just arrived back.

I close up my kitchen and head out. Just outside, I meet up with Toby. He arrived back in the camp half a fortnight ago. He admitted to killing Marcus, which we all suspected. He will be heard by a group of citizens for his crimes and we will have to come to a consensus on the punishment. He hasn't said much on the topic other than to say he knew Marcus once upon a time and the man was more toxic than we knew. Tutor, obviously, agrees with that sentiment. It remains to be seen if Toby will be allowed to remain here. I fall in step beside him and we silently trek to the fire pit in Area 1.

"Thanks for coming," Sieven greets. "Our group of explorers is back. We all wanted to be present for their report." He indicates the small group of three men and two women standing beside him with a sweep of his arm. Then, nodding at them, he takes a seat on the ground with the rest of us.

"Right, we went to Fraun first," the tallest man says. I remember that his name is Marco, or something like that. He was originally from Sarcheda, I think. He's someone who knows Tutor. "There are not as many people in Fraun as there once were, obviously. Many of the homes we passed seem abandoned. A few have been burned to the ground. Most of the people seemed to be living in Sarcheda. We were able to find the man who is calling himself King there pretty easily. He's living in the castle. It seems everyone who is left is answering to this one king, his name is Stefan."

"Are they calling themselves Fraun?" someone calls. It is a good question. I lean closer to Marco, eager for the answer.

"He referred to them as Sarcheda, actually." A silence follows his words. Interesting twist, for sure.

The woman on Marco's right speaks next. Annie, I think her name is. She's small and wiry and I've been told she has a passion for inventing. "They mean us no harm. In fact, King Stefan sees it as an opportunity to trade and help each other prosper. He seems to be making some new laws of the land there. He did ask about Marcus and what happened there." She clears her throat, uncomfortable. "We explained that he had died as our prisoner, just as we discussed."

"Was he satisfied with that?" Jordyn asks. "Did he want details of the death?"

"He merely told us to give him a proper burial, fit for a King of

Sarcheda," she answers.

"Bit late for that," Tanya whispers from just behind me. I suppress the urge to laugh, death should not be funny.

"He wasn't really King of Sarcheda," Tutor mumbles from my other side.

I turn my upper body a little to the left so I can whisper to my brother. "By the sounds of it, they are trying to start new like we are. Perhaps he was their first new King. An Oberian, of sorts. What does it hurt us? Are we not changing things as well?"

"I wish they'd called themselves something else," he whispers back. "It makes the title seem tainted, even more than I thought it was."

"You hate that you were once called King of Sarcheda? That's your real problem, isn't it?"

I notice the small nod of his head. It makes sense, I suppose. Given the title between the king who started a war and the king who tried to kill him was my brother, also King of Sarcheda. They are filled with a history that includes murder and betrayal. Not exactly something to take pride in.

"After visiting with King Stefan of Sarcheda, we went to the camp of the giants," Marco says.

The crowd, some whispering as I had been, falls silent again. This, after all, is the reason we abandoned everything we had known. It is the reason we ran. "Jordyn told us there would be more than twenty."

"Twenty-two," Jordyn says. "How many did you see?"

"Seventeen," Marco answers.

Jordyn hangs his head. "It is unlikely five giants died in a few lunar cycles," Tutor speaks up.

"Do we even know how long the life cycle of a giant is?" I ask. There's no answer because, no, we don't have any way of knowing that. Do they live for forty-five annuals, as we do?

"We thought the disappearance was odd as well," Marco says. "So we waited for two suns, camped there on the ridge. We saw no sign of the missing ones returning."

"There was a small one who seemed to be searching the woods every night. A woman, perhaps his mother, had to come collect him every sunset. We think," the woman says, "that he was waiting for some to return."

"They're looking for something?" I ask.

"They're looking for us," Jordyn answers. His eyes are still downcast.

"Then we made the right choice," Sieven says. No one takes pride in being right on this. "The people who stayed behind could still be in danger."

"That was our conclusion as well," Marco says. "So we actually went back to King Stefan with this knowledge."

"What did he say?" Jordyn says, drawing his eyes up from the ground again.

"He thanked us for our concern and dismissed us."

"He didn't look afraid?" I ask. "He didn't want to come with you? Did you make it clear that he was welcome here?"

"He asked about our rulers. We told him that we held elections and currently have four ruling side-by-side. We told him our plan was to redo the election process every annual for all time. He laughed at that. Apparently they wish to try things their way. One ruler, one united Sarcheda, one voice to rule. That is what he told us."

"That's very different than what we are doing here," I say. I push myself to stand up. "Thank you for taking that dangerous journey for us." I know I have to return to the kitchen soon. But the mood right now feels stern, somber. I don't want people discouraged. "Their journey tells us two important things. First, it tells us that we were right to be afraid of the giants. With five of the giants out looking for something, possibly for us, being too close to their location is a gamble we couldn't afford.

"Secondly, it tells us that there was dissension on how to run the government. What we have all agreed here is directly at odds with what they're doing there in Fraun." I pause for a moment, letting my words sink in. "That being said, I'm sure you have concerns. Let's take a moment to discuss any of those before returning to our passions."

Tanya raises her hand. "There are people we left behind. If we are truly better here, which I agree with you on, I think a lot of us are really worried about them."

I remember that her brother is one of the people who refused to leave. "Fair point. What does everyone think?"

"Obviously, they'll be welcome here if they do decide to leave,"

Alerta says. I nod in agreement.

"Perhaps we should write to them," someone calls out. "Tell them what we are doing here. Make sure they know it's safe and they're welcome."

"That is a good idea," I say. "Our welcoming nature and acceptance is only good if they know it exists. I like that plan. Let us agree to send roaches to our families or loved ones who stayed behind."

"We need a new name," Toby says. "Something that breaks clean of what we were there. I know we've talked about this before, but after hearing that they are calling themselves Sarcheda I feel as though it's even more important."

Across the fire pit, Danyel stands up. "I agree with Toby. Some of us were Sarcheda before. It makes us feel unwanted, dirty. We need a name of something to belong to." He sits back down. "That's just what I think."

Tutor had just said something similar. Suddenly, I want to give them this. I want to let these people have a clean break from their past. I want them to have something to belong to, a name to say proudly. The children of this new place should always know where they are from. Like Abney told me, this is all they will know. Shouldn't it have a name?

"What about Grove?" I ask. "I heard Elsbeth from the garden use that term and I just love it. A grove is a group of trees, is it not? Trees growing together. It speaks of growth, balance, and health."

"I like that," Eselda says. "All in favor of calling ourselves Grove?"

There are hearty calls of "Aye" from around the gathered group.

Eventually, the meeting breaks up. There are no more concerns for today. More will come up, but there are elected officials you can speak with about it. We can hold a meeting, bring it to everyone.

Tanya catches up to me on my way back to the kitchen. "I'm just heading to the farm. Is there anything specific you need me to bring you?" she asks.

"I'd love some garlic," I say. She knows it's my favorite, she probably already set some aside for me. But it can't hurt to ask.

She bumps my elbow with hers. "You got it." She tips her head off toward the garden and farming area. "Talk to you later?"

"Of course." I watch her walk a few steps off, smiling after her. She stops after only a few steps and turns back to me. When she sees me watching her, she smiles and comes back. "Did you need something?" I ask.

"I could ask you the same thing." She laughs and the sound floods me with a warm feeling. "Are you alright?"

"Better than alright. I'm great," I answer.

Epilogue

Eselda

Sieven stands in Grove Area 1, before our entire group. He clears his throat. "Good afternoon," he calls in a booming voice. The area immediately falls quiet. "Thank you all for being here today. Citizens much better with keeping track of time than me tell me it is the anniversary of our very first election in the Grove." A few people laugh at his self-deprecating humor. "So we are gathered in the same location, although there are certainly a lot more of us, to hold our elections again." He's not wrong about that. I recall the first election where it seemed as though the clearing was full. Now there are more houses lining the outside of Area 1 and every available space is full. I think there are even people along the corridor to Area 2.

"As the longest running elected official in Grove, I stand before you to carry out the process. If you have a nomination, please rise and tell us the name of the person you are nominating as well as a reason for your nomination. If you are nominated, please come to the front," Sieven continues. Then he drops into a seat on the ground right where he was standing.

Sieven was the only council member reelected in the second annual.

Sawchett is the first to stand to her feet. She's in the back of the group today, by the house she has been living in. "I nominate Tanya of the garden sector owing to her strength of character, her emphasis on equality, and her ability to tell it like it is." Tanya squeezes Sawchett's hand before moving to take her place at the front of the clearing.

"I nominate Toby of the building crew," someone calls as they rise. "Owing to his dedication to growth and perfection, his ability to be fair and just, and the fact that he wasn't afraid to return to us and own up to his mistakes. I think enough time has passed for us to accept he has served his punishment and allow him a chance to accept the nomination." Toby takes his place, although I notice he is shaking his head.

Kitty stands next. She's a rather outspoken little girl I've grown quite close to. She smiles down at me. I wonder, for a heartbeat, if she is going to nominate herself. Then I realize that she's still rather young and likely not ready for that kind of responsibility. "I nominate Eselda from the school owing to her strength of character, her patience with all of us kids, and her general good nature," she says. She drops immediately back to the floor and blinks innocently at me.

I stand up, brush dirt off my bottom, and head to the front. I have been nominated by a different citizen every annual. I'm not sure why they insist on bothering, I have never been voted into a position. I take my spot beside Toby. He bumps my shoulder. "Back again," he whispers.

"I'm glad we always get a different group of nominations up here," I whisper back. "You'll have my vote."

He rolls his eyes and then steps forward. "Actually, I'd like to nominate someone," he calls. "I nominate Bin, also of the building crew, owing to his dedication to projects, his attention to detail, and his willingness to return to us with more defects of Fraun who needed our safety." Bin extricates himself from a large group of young men sitting along the outside edge of the clearing and joins us.

"Seriously?" he whispers across me. "They still think of me as a Grove defect."

"What you walked away from isn't important," I whisper. "It's more important that you came back."

Someone at the front of the crowd stands. "I nominate Tae from the nursery owing to her delicate nature, caring heart, and general wish for every citizen to be safe." A woman I don't recognize comes to the front of the clearing and takes her position beside Bin.

It's quiet in the clearing for about seven breath cycles. Then Sieven stands. "Is that everyone?" he asks.

"Oh," someone toward the middle of the crowd hops to their feet. "Sieven, I nominate you. Owing to the fact that you've been a ruler since we started Grove, I feel as though you should be up there."

Sieven's shoulders sag and he takes his place beside Tae. "Is that everyone?" he asks again, sounding more tired than he did a heartbeat ago.

Directly in my line of sight, as if my eyes know exactly who they're searching for, my husband stands. He winks at me. We discussed this nomination last night, although we both hoped it wouldn't need to come from him. There is someone who, for whatever reason, has not been nominated in any of Grove's elections so far. I explained to Jordyn that I felt like this was a massive oversight. I still feel as though my dreams, which I haven't had since the day we arrived in Grove, were telling me this person was our future. "I nominate Tutor of the guard owing to his passion, leadership, and caring nature," Jordyn says.

Tutor comes out of the shadows on my right and takes his place beside Sieven. He catches Jordyn's eye and shakes his head a little. He probably thinks this nomination was a friend doing him a favor and not someone pointing out that he belongs up here.

Again about five breath cycles pass. "Is that everyone?" Sieven asks. This time, there's no answer. "Alright, cue the speeches. Tanya, you're up."

Tanya takes a deep breath and then steps forward. "Right, I'm only seventeen annuals so I'm not sure I should be up here." She shakes her head. "Although I suppose Sawchett was younger than me when you put her up here and she did a great job." She smiles wide and I get the impression she just locked eyes with our blond friend back there.

Sawchett has passed her fifteenth annual, which is when our age markers make us adults for all intents and purposes. In honor of that occasion, she started dating. Her first date was actually with Tanya. As far as I know, she hasn't been out with anyone else since.

"Anyway, if you decide to vote me up here there's a few things I can promise," Tanya continues. "I'll keep being loud and I'll keep making sure everyone gets accepted." A few people clap and she nods. "Thank you." She gives Toby a little push with her hand, making sure he knows she's ready for him to take over the talking.

"I'm Toby," he starts. "I was born in Sarcheda and I used to work for the royal family there." He sighs. "I've never told the story of why I left, but I think I'd like to." I reach over and rub his back showing he has my support. "I was in the royal carriage the day Tin pushed his parents to their deaths."

There's a lot of shocked gasps from the crowd, myself included. This is a rumor I have heard before, but not one everyone believed. I, of course, knew Tin was capable of such an act. But to know that someone could have confirmed the story all this time is shocking, to say the least. My hand pulls away from Toby instinctually as if suddenly burned by the memory of the man we both knew was capable of murder. I feel guilty for judging Toby. After all, is keeping this secret any worse than the things I have done? I let my hand return to his back, hoping he understands the message.

"I was young, not even ten annuals. Instead of doing anything about it, I ran. I took up as a scout and didn't even consider returning to Fraun until the war," Toby continues. "I fought side-by-side with Jordyn for that castle with a lot of you." He hangs his head for a breath, gathering his strength. When he picks his head up again I feel the muscles in his back tense. "Many of you have asked me why I killed Marcus. The best answer I can give you is this: Marcus was manipulative and dangerous. I watched him spread his lies to young Tin. I was afraid he would keep pulling strings and endangering everyone. I was wrong and I am sorry. Thank you for nominating me today. It shows someone has forgiven me." He sighs. "Perhaps, in time, I will be able to forgive myself." He nods at me and I pull my hand back, letting it fall in front of me where it grasps my other hand.

I swallow. "Hi again," I say, trying to lighten the mood. A few people laugh. "Every annual someone nominates me and every annual I sit back down as half of you vote to not have me lead. Do you want to know a secret?" A few people nod. "Every annual I'm grateful you don't vote me in. I have never trusted myself to lead Grove after my previous actions. Thank you for showing me that a few people believe in me. You've put a good group up here and I'm honored to be listed among them." I tap Bin on the shoulder. "You're up," I tell him.

He nods. "A lot of you don't know me," he starts. "Except to know that I left you when we first started. But the reason I left wasn't simple. There were people who I loved back in Fraun. I had to go see if they could be talked into joining us. I was glad when I found them and I was glad when you welcomed me back. Standing here in front of you today is insane. It's something I never thought I'd be doing. So thanks for giving me that chance." He nods at Tae.

"I'm Tae. I work with the newborns during the day. I'm not sure what I could bring to the council, but I love Grove and I'm honored you think I have something to offer." She taps Sieven on the shoulder. "You're turn. I don't know what else to say."

Sieven crosses his arms over his chest. "Grove was never supposed to be about lineage and heritage. It was never about one person taking control or following rules that worked once. We said we wanted flexibility. I respectfully ask you not to vote for me," he says. "Two annuals is enough. Thank you."

Tutor pauses beside our friend for a beat. Then he takes a step forward, toward the lit fire. His face, handsome with the darker tan he's developed and the faint lines now showing, falls into the light. "When we were traveling here from Fraun Eselda told me she thought I was the future. I thought she was crazy. I was content to sit in the back all these annuals and be a voice, just like the rest of you. I had no desire to prove her right and step up here."

He runs a hand through his long hair, then lets it fall back to his side. "Last night, Alerta and I were having a conversation about these elections. I mentioned to her that I thought it was funny how wrong Eselda was about me being the future. But Alerta pointed out that it was actually me who was wrong. The future of the Grove was never about one person." He throws his arms out. "We are all the future." He lets the words resonate then drops his arms again.

"I have never been elected to lead the Grove but I have been just as much a part of it as all of you. I work here at my passion day after day. I listen and I talk about our decisions. I help us decide our punishments and our retributions for crimes. I settle discrepancies. You nominating me today is a way to show me, and you, that we have officially moved on. What we look for in a ruler is not the characteristics they used to be. We are looking for Grove. If you decide to vote for me, that's exactly what I'll give you." He turns around, marches back to stand beside Sieven, and nods at the crowd. "Thank you."

Sieven takes a step forward. "The rules are simple. We will call each name and ask for an Aye and then a Nay vote. Your voice is your vote. If we cannot tell from the raised voices which way the vote has fallen, we will ask you to move your bodies around the clearing to be counted. Anyone nominated earning more than Aye than Nay will be allowed to join the council for one annual until the next election. Let's begin with Tanya. All in favor?"

Most of the assembled group calls out "Aye". Sieven nods. "All opposed?" There are no answering calls.

"All in favor of Toby?" There are calls of assent from the group, but I notice it is not as strong as Tanya's. Toby must notice as well, he shrugs.

"All opposed?" The call is too close to count.

"If you'd vote in favor of Toby, please move your body to this side of the clearing," Sieven gestures to his left. "Opposed the other way. There are no hard feelings for this vote and Toby will have his back turned. Someone will be by to count you quickly."

Although this wasn't necessary in our first vote, it did happen the following annual. Sawchett, who was nominated again, was too close to call. The clearing was split while her back was turned. I stood beside her, holding her hand. She whispered to me that she almost hoped it was unbalanced and let her stop ruling. Her passion, she assured me, lay in cooking and not in ruling.

She got her wish that day.

I lean in toward Toby, who is facing away from the group. "What are you hoping for today?" I whisper.

"Acceptance," he answers. "Which is lucky since that's what I already have."

I understand his sentiment well.

It's during this moment that I feel something shift inside me. It's not painful or scary. It's almost as if I took off a layer of clothing, something that was heavy. Of course, I didn't do that. I barely even moved.

I spend a few heartbeats blinking rapidly, trying to figure out why I feel differently. My eyes, wide in panic, fall on Jordyn. My vision darkens, just a little. I recognize the symptom, of course. My age marker.

But I'm not angry. I don't feel angry at all. I feel…I pause and catalogue everything. Calm, driven, focused. I feel as if the cloud that has been on my mind has finally passed. I think, if I had to guess, I've passed my twenty-fifth annual. I smile and wink at Jordyn who returns a confused sort of squint from where he's standing on the left side of the clearing.

"Alright, you may return to a seated position," Sieven finally calls. The sides have been counted and a ruling has been whispered in his ear. "Toby, you may turn." Beside me, he does just that. "Welcome to the council," Sieven announces. There's a small smattering of applause.

"All in favor of Eselda," Sieven prompts.

I smile as the Grove heartily calls out in favor of my ruling. It sounds like more than previous annuals, which is interesting. "All opposed?"

I stand there, in front of the group that has accepted me more than any other. In the first place I've felt truly at home anywhere other than wandering the woods with Jordyn. I hold back tears of emotion because this group who I love and admire just accepted me completely. There are no calls of dissent.

The rest of the proceedings sort of rush by me. Tutor and Tae are also accepted into the council. Sieven and Bin are not. Sieven seems pleased, Bin seems unfazed and returns to his group of friends almost immediately.

I wander over to my husband and smile up at him. "Congratulations," he says. He leans down and kisses me. When he pulls back I see him falter when he looks at my face. "What's wrong? Did you not want the position?"

I assume he's reacting to my eyes. I smile at him. "I think I just crossed into the new age marker," I tell him.

I watch his face register the surprise. Then his smile takes over his entire face. "So the darkening is not in anger," he says.

"I do believe it is love for you," I reply.

He laughs. "Can I be honest with you?"

"Always."

"There was a part of me that feared your eyes would not darken for me."

I roll my eyes at his foolishness. "I love you, you know that."

"True, but mine never darken for those I love in other ways. I don't see mine darkening for Sawchett or Tutor. They only ever respond to you. What if we only get one true love?" he asks. "What if they only truly darken for one other being?"

I smile. "Even then, I would never have doubted." But he did. That's what he's telling me. He's not saying he doubted himself. He wondered if everything I've said and done has been less than whatever I did or said to Tin. I lean my head on his chest and sigh. "I hate that you wondered that and didn't share it with me." I look up at him. "But I'm glad it gives you peace of mind now."

"I'm sorry I doubted," he says.

"I'm sorry you did too." Then he bends down at the same moment I rise up on my toes, as if we are executing a dance routine whose timing we have perfected. Our lips connect and I am sure, more than I have ever been, that everything is exactly right with the world.

The End

Did you enjoy the book? I'd love for you to leave a review or tell a like-minded friend who enjoys fantasy.

Need more Fraun? Keep reading for a sneak peek at Tin's Tale and Other Stories of Fraun, a collection of six short stories coming in May of 2023.

Tin's Tale

Chapter 1

My parents never had any other children. The way my mother tells the story, I was perfect. There was no need to keep trying. This, of course, is only partially true. It's true in my mother's mind, she's made it true after annuals of telling it to herself over and over again. But, in the beginning, it wasn't true.

There were only two truths that mattered on the day that I was born. The first is that I was the legitimate son of King Todd, a direct descendant whose lineage can be traced back to the first King of Fraun, Oberian, through his strongest son, Sarcheda. The second truth is equally important. I was a boy.

In my family history, males were adored. My family is royal blood in a realm known for strength. Women were considered the weaker sex. For this reason, female babies born to my family had a way of disappearing. I grew up being quizzed on the family tree painted on the wall of my family home. I knew that I was the ninth male born from my direct line since Sarcheda himself. My mother had hinted to me that she was born to an influential family in Sarcheda, but she would not talk about this when the King was around. Her history was not important. Her family didn't give me my royal blood. Her family didn't make me a prince.

"Prince Tin," a voice interrupts my thinking. I turn away from the wall and find my tutor standing in the dark hall, his arms behind his back. Everything about Marcus would normally be measured against me and found lacking. He is eight clicks shorter than me in a society that values height. He is rounder in the gut than I am. Although my hair has not even ceased to grow, I can also lift more than he can. But Marcus has been my tutor for as long as I can remember and something about him commands my respect. It always has.

"Yes," I answer.

"I need you to come with me, Majesty," he says. "The new servant has been hired. He will be in charge of areas of the family home in which you are regularly in. He is expected to accompany you whenever you leave the home."

I puff my chest out. "I don't need protection," I say. The reaction is instinctual. It's foolish, I know. I have not reached adulthood yet in our society. Couple that with the fact that I am the only prince of the realm and you may reach the conclusion that I am in danger. My father has certainly reached that conclusion and I cannot argue with the King. I can, however, make the show of strength that is required to argue with a tutor.

"It is not for safety. I cannot tell you what it is for. I know only that your father wills it, Majesty." Marcus bows his head. "I am sorry it displeases you. The boy has already been hired. I did my best to make sure it was someone I felt you could connect with." Marcus raises his head and I notice a glint of something in his brown eyes. Mischief, perhaps? "I do believe you'll find this young Sarcheda citizen someone who you can manipulate, Prince Tin."

This thought is pleasing, indeed. It brings a smile to my face to imagine having another young boy who wants my life. Convincing this common citizen that I am the perfect prince with the coveted life could be fun. "Take me to him, then I will decide," I answer.

"As you wish." This time, when Marcus bows, it is not only his head that folds. This is a full bow. A respectful bow for the ruler I will be.

I follow Marcus out of the room and down the dark hallway. The torches he guides me past have been lit, meaning he walked this route to get to me today. Our footsteps echo on the stones, but there are no other sounds in the home.

He opens a door and stands to the side to allow me to enter the room first, as is a custom treatment for those of royal blood. There is a young boy in the center of the room. He has black hair but his skin is lighter than my family's. He is young, perhaps not even full height. I take notice of his outfit, red shirt and black pants. They look as though they are too large for him, meaning he likely comes from a family who cannot afford to have the clothing altered properly. He is not wearing shoes, although that is common for Sarcheda citizens in this warmer weather. "How old are you?" I ask, my voice bouncing off the walls of the small room and echoing around us. Before he can answer I hit him with another question, "Are you even old enough to be capable of speech?"

In Fraun, citizens who have reached five annuals are capable of speech. This boy is small and young. Again, I have to wonder about the purpose of his being hired to work around me and accompany me to town. If my father wished me to have safety, wouldn't he have hired a larger boy?

"Nine annuals, Majesty," the boy answers. He bows deep, his nose practically reaching the clean stones of the floor.

I step closer to him, my feet falling heavy and slow. I squint my eyes as I consider him, now standing fully again before me. He waits as I walk around him as I would a roach for consideration, as if he were property of mine. When I am again facing him, I cross my arms. "You are much younger than me. I am fourteen annuals, perhaps you already knew that. You obviously aren't for my protection. Tell me what your new job is, as you see it," I command.

"I am to keep you happy, Majesty."

"How do you plan to do that?" I ask.

"I will keep your home clean, fetch you food and water if you need it, hire you a roach if you require transportation, and speak to any common citizens you wish me to speak to on your behalf."

I like the sound of all this, of course. But I still don't understand why my father wished for this. Behind me, Marcus clears his throat. "Prince Tin, a word," he says.

"Wait here," I tell the boy. Then I turn and walk to Marcus. I stand in the doorway, my back to the new hire.

Marcus leans in so he can speak to me in secret. "Your father has a man he treats in much the same way," Marcus points out. "He has a servant dedicated to his needs and happiness, surely you've noticed this."

"I have," I answer. I prefer not to think about this man too much. My father has been known to delegate everything, including the discipline of his only son, to this man. The thought, which I was trying to avoid, makes me flinch. I hate the show of weakness and I'm grateful my father wasn't here to witness it. I hope Marcus doesn't feel the need to tell his king. "Is that what this boy is to be for me?" I ask.

Marcus takes his time answering. He seems to roll the question around in his mouth, tasting it. He smiles at me like I am dinner being offered to him after a period of fasting. "He could be. Right now I believe he is a peace offering. You and I both know that your mother believed your father was wrong the other night. His punishment was too harsh."

I flinch at the memory of my father's fist, the strongest one in the realm, landing between my shoulder blades and along my side. For a breath, it feels real again. I can almost imagine I'm curled in a ball on the floor, my instinct to protect myself. I can hear my father screaming at me, his anger growing stronger the more I pull back from him. "This is what I'm talking about," he screams in my head. "Look at how weak you are. Why are you turning from this confrontation? Show me strength!"

I clench my teeth, ball my fists, and force the memory out of my head. "What is your point?" I ask.

"I think she suggested your father do something kind for you. This," Marcus gestures behind me to the boy who must still be standing there, waiting for instruction, "is your peace offering. Your father sees this as a gift, a kindness."

"He is young," I say.

"That he is. Young and impressionable."

I turn and look again at the frail, small boy. I imagine him larger, older, full height. I imagine he will have an impressive body structure if he is trained right and fed the proper diet. I approach him again. "You are from

Sarcheda, yes?"

"Yes," he answers.

"You have a family? How many of them live in your home?" I know homes in Sarcheda typically hold more than my family home. Three people in one house is unusual, but we are not ordinary. We are royal blood. Besides, we have servants who also live in our home to meet our every need.

"Four others," he answers. "All older than myself."

I nod as if this matters to me, which it doesn't. "Where is your home?" It may sound as though I care about this child. I don't, not really. What I care about is how long it will take him to get to my family home each morning.

"We're on the edge of Sarcheda, sir. Near the ravine." He gestures with his hand, off to the North.

"If there were an empty room at my family home and you were needed, is there anything to prevent you from being allowed to stay here?" I ask.

He doesn't pause, doesn't need to consider it. The answer is automatic, which earns him some of my hard-to-come-by respect. "Nothing would prevent that, Majesty."

"Alright," I nod at him. "I accept your position as my servant." I decide this is exactly what I will call him when people ask. My father has hired me a servant, I think. I can work with that.

I turn to leave the room. I'm one step from the door when I think to ask him something I probably should have asked when I met him. I turn back toward him. "What is your name?"

He smiles, glad to be asked the question that likely makes him feel as though we are to be friends. This is an important impression to give him if I desire to mold him to my whims. "My name is Toby," he answers. "It's a pleasure to meet you."

About the Author

Tabatha Shipley is an author, avid reader, and book addict from Arizona. She has an amazing husband, two remarkable children, and one really quirky dog. She can often be found on social media raving about whatever book she is most recently obsessed with. Find her to join in on the obsession and add to her TBR with your favorite titles.

tabathashipleybooks.com

www.ingramcontent.com/pod-product-compliance
Lightning Source LLC
Chambersburg PA
CBHW060637310726
48982CB00003B/812

* 9 7 9 8 9 8 8 0 1 2 9 3 1 *